"Give me a projection as you have a line of si cheerier after I've eyeballed her. He made himself lean back and wait.

The vision leaped into the screen. That lean shape rushing down the last kilometers had never been intended for peaceful use. The armament was as complete as Flandry's ship, and as smoothly integrated with the hull.

Barbarians, flashed in Flandry. *From some planet where maybe a hundred years ago they were still warring with edged iron. No wonder they haven't responded to us. Probably not one aboard knows Anglic!*

Energy stabbed blue-white out of the mercenary. Missiles followed. The barbarian had the immense advantage of high speed and high altitude relative to the planet.

Nonetheless, abrupt flame seethed around the enemy. Twisted, crumpled, blackened, half melted, the rest of the ship whirled off on a cometary path back toward outer space.

But it was not possible that the Terran escape free. Three explosions tore into the hull, bellowing, burning, shattering machines like porcelain, throwing men about and ripping them like red rag dolls.

Flandry saw the bridge crack open. Stunned, deafened, he managed to slam shut his helmet's faceplate before the last air shrieked through the hole.

Then there was a silence. Engines dead, the Terran ship reached the maximum altitude permitted by the velocity she had had, and fell back toward the planet.

—from *The Rebel Worlds*

Baen Books by Poul Anderson

The Technic Civilization Saga
The Van Rijn Method
David Falkayn: Star Trader
Rise of the Terran Empire
Young Flandry
Captain Flandry: Defender of the Terran Empire
Sir Dominic Flandry: The Last Knight of Terra
Flandry's Legacy

To Outlive Eternity and Other Stories

Time Patrol

Hokas! Pokas! (with Gordon R. Dickson)
Hoka! Hoka! Hoka! (with Gordon R. Dickson)

The High Crusade

YOUNG FLANDRY

POUL ANDERSON

YOUNG FLANDRY

"Enter a Hero, Somewhat Flawed" copyright © 2009
by Hank Davis. "A Chronology of Technic Civilization"
copyright © 2008 by Sandra Miesel.
Ensign Flandry copyright © 1966 by Poul Anderson.
A Circus of Hells copyright © 1970 by Poul Anderson.
The Rebel Worlds copyright © 1969 by Poul Anderson.

A Baen Book

Baen Publishing Enterprises
P.O. Box 1403
Riverdale, NY 10471
www.baen.com

ISBN: 978-1-4391-3465-8

Cover art by David Seeley

First Baen paperback printing, September 2011

Distributed by Simon & Schuster
1230 Avenue of the Americas
New York, NY 10020

Library of Congress Cataloging-in-Publication Data:
2009039503

Printed in the United States of America

10 9 8 7 6 5 4 3 2 1

CONTENTS

---※---

ENTER A HERO, SOMEWHAT FLAWED

❈

I'll start with a quote whose authorship is unknown but not unsuspected . . .

> Introducing . . . Dominic Flandry. Before he's through he'll have saved worlds and become the confidante of emperors. But for now he's seventeen years old, as fresh and brash a sprig of the nobility as you would care to know. The only thing as damp as the place behind his ears is the ink on his brand-new commission.
>
> Though through this and his succeeding adventures he will struggle gloriously and win (usually) mighty victories, Dominic Flandry is essentially a tragic figure: a man who knows too much, who knows that battle, scheme and even betray as he will, in the end it will mean nothing.

> For with the relentlessness of physical law the
> Long Night approaches. The Terran Empire is
> dying . . .

I didn't see how I could top that, so I hijacked it (but
please to call it research!). I can't prove it, but I think I
know who wrote that anonymous text from the back cover
of the Ace edition of the novel *Ensign Flandry* (included
in these pages). The paperback was published while Jim
Baen was in charge at that venerable sf publisher . . . and
Jim usually did his own cover copy at three different pub-
lishers, including the one he founded . . . and to me, it
reads like Jim's work. And it captures Dominic Flandry in
two well-honed paragraphs.

I'll be using somewhat more paragraphs, and less
effectively. But if you're now all revved up to read *Ensign
Flandry*, and maybe the other two novels as well without
further ado, go right ahead. I'll be here when you get
back.

I will dispute one item in the quote. Flandry arguably
isn't "a sprig of the nobility." True, his father was a minor
nobleman, but Flandry was his illegitimate offspring, born
of an affair with an opera singer. His mother's profession
makes it seem odd that Flandry repeatedly mentions he
has no interest in music, even if at one point in the following pages he is whistling an unnamed waltz tune while
piloting a ship in a scene that might be Poul Anderson's sly
nod at *2001: A Space Odyssey*. But I digress . . .

Dominic Flandry—*Captain* Dominic Flandry—made
his first appearances in 1951 in two pulp magazines,
Planet Stories and *Future*. The pulps soon died, alas, but

Flandry was just getting started. In the following years, Poul Anderson chronicled his further adventures, by which time Flandry had been knighted (Captain *Sir* Dominic Flandry, if you please), until by 1966 some back history was in order. The three novels in this set visit Flandry at the beginning of his illustrious career.

He's already obviously charming and attractive to the opposite sex, judging from their reactions. (Later, he'll pay for a biosculpt, then wonder if he's made his face *too* handsome.) And he's making an impression on his superiors. As one of them tells him in *The Rebel Worlds*, "You'll either be killed, young man, or you'll do something that will force us to step on you, or you'll go far indeed."

That's after the same superior officer refers obliquely to some of Flandry's misadventures, and says, "Don't worry . . . yet. Competent men are so heartbreakingly scarce these days, not to mention brilliant ones, that the Service keeps a blind eye handy for a broad range of escapades." That's Flandry: he's a hero, but a somewhat tarnished one; he's a rascal, but not a villain; and he's a gloomy philosopher, well aware that he's been born in the twilight of the declining Terran Empire.

As he puts it:

> . . . the night is coming—the Long Night, when the empire goes under and the howling peoples camp in its ruins. . . . Our ancestors explored further than we in these years remember. When hell cut loose and their civilization seemed about to fly into pieces, they patched it together with the Empire. And they made the

Empire function. But we . . . we've lost the will.
We've had it too easy for too long. And so the
Merseians on our Betelgeusean flank, the wild
races everywhere else, press inward . . . why do
I bother? . . . I could be more comfortable
doing almost anything else.

These glum musings are interrupted by a woman who
asks him for directions, then makes it obvious that she's
interested in more than directions, putting him in a better
mood and musing that another job might prove boring.
That's Flandry, too: aware that civilization is shot through
with irreparable cracks, but enjoying its pleasures while
he can.

Mention is made of the Polesotechnic League, long
gone, and Flandry "wistfully" thinks that he was born out
of his proper time. "He would much rather have lived in
the high and spacious days of the trader princes, when no
distance and no deed looked too vast for man, than in this
twilight of empire." Your humble scribe did wonder at
that point how Flandry and Van Rijn would have gotten
along—sparks would fly, I'd wager!

Born in the wrong century or not, he'll still charm the
ladies, enjoy the expensive creature comforts, and fiercely
oppose all enemies of the Empire, foreign and domestic.
He has no illusions about the flaws and limitations of the
Empire, but knows that it's far better than anything that
might take its place.

Poul Anderson originally conceived Flandry as a
science fictional counterpart of Leslie Charteris' celebrated
Simon Templar, better known as the Saint, but his hero

soon began to look more like a science fictional counter-part of another iconic hero with an English accent, James Bond, though the resemblance is almost certainly a case of parallel evolution, since Flandry's early adventures appeared prior to the publication of *Casino Royale* (1953), with 007's debut. Both Bond and Flandry have flamboyant adventures, have excellent taste in clothes, food and drink, and encounter far more than their share of, ah, *friendly* females (in Flandry's case, not always human). But Flandry's adventures have the additional dimension of taking place before that looming twilight of the gods back-drop. Bond is making the world safe for western civiliza-tion. Flandry is trying to keep civilization from collapsing in his lifetime, hoping that some pieces will survive the inevitable shattering of the Terran Empire.

In the first of these three novels, you'll meet Flandry, of course (or renew your acquaintance), but you'll also meet Max Abrams of the Imperial Naval Intelligence Corps, Flandry's mentor (who does his own musing on the coming Long Night, showing that it isn't Flandry's private hobgoblin). And you'll meet a character who often appears in Poul Anderson's stories in various guises: the intelligent, well-meaning, and well-connected individual who thinks that *surely, we can all just get along if we sit down and discuss this like the sane beings that we are*—and whose idealistic naiveté is a blueprint for disaster. Since there has never been a shortage of people like that, both in and out of government, in our "real" world, who think that we can reason with those who want to destroy us, this aspect of *Ensign Flandry* makes the 1966 novel very much up-to-date.

Another sort of villain, not admirable at all, appears in *The Rebel Worlds*. Bordering on the psychotic—on second thought, make that clear *over* the border—and this one also makes the story downright contemporary, when one considers the mindset of those aforementioned enemies who want to destroy us.

A villain whom you will not meet in this book is the alien Aycharaych, Flandry's most persistent nemesis, his Moriarty. But have patience, he'll have a whole novel to himself in the next volume in this series. (Flandry will not be onstage in that novel, but never fear, there'll be plenty of Flandry—Captain Flandry by then—in the rest of the next book.)

I've found that most people visualize Dominic Flandry as Errol Flynn. I've always opted for a young David Niven, probably because I first encountered Flandry in "A Handful of Stars" (later retitled "We Claim These Stars," and still later, "Hunters of the Sky Cave") in the June 1959 *Amazing Stories* shortly after seeing several vintage David Niven movies on TV (and I was startled a few years later when Algis Budrys wrote in a book review that Flandry could have only be born of a union between David Niven and Diana the Huntress). You can visualize him as you wish (but if you see him as Brad Pitt, I *don't* want to hear about it), but that's really peripheral to the fast-moving and thoughtful adventures in which you're about to join him. Bon voyage—and fasten your seat belts.

—Hank Davis, 2009

ENSIGN FLANDRY

✳

To Frank and Beverly Herbert

Excerpts (with some expansion of symbols) from *Pilot's Manual and Ephemeris, Cis-Betelgeusean Orionis Sector*, 53rd ed., Reel III, frame 28:

IGC S-52,727,061. *Saxo.* F5, mass 1.75 Sol, luminosity 5.4 Sol, photosphere diameter 1.2 Sol. . . . Estimated remaining time on main sequence, 0.9 begayear. . . .

Planetary system: Eleven major bodies. . . . V, *Starkad.* Mean orbital radius, 3.28 a.u., period 4.48 years. . . . Mass, 1.81 Terra. Equatorial diameter, 15,077 km. Mean surface gravity, 1.30 g. Rotation period, $16^h 31^m 2.75^s$. Axial inclination, 25° 50' 4.9". . . . Surface atmospheric pressure, ca. 7000 mm. Percentage composition, N_2 77.92, O_2 21.01, A 0.87, CO_2 0.03. . . .

Remarks: Though 254 light-years from Sol, the system was discovered early, in the course of the first Grand Survey. Thus the contemporary practice of bestowing literary-mythological names on humanly interesting objects was followed. Only marginally manhabitable, Starkad attracted a few xenological expeditions by its unusual autochthons. . . . These studies were not followed up, since funds went to still more rewarding projects and, later, the Polesotechnic League saw no profit potential. After the Time of Troubles, it lay outside the Imperial sphere and remained virtually unvisited until now, when a mission has been sent for political reasons.

The 54th edition had quite a different entry.

CHAPTER ONE

Evening on Terra—

His Imperial Majesty, High Emperor Georgios Manuel Krishna Murasaki, of the Wang dynasty the fourth, Supreme Guardian of the Pax, Grand Director of the Stellar Council, Commander-in-chief, Final Arbiter, acknowledged supreme on more worlds and honorary head of more organizations than any one man could remember, had a birthday. On planets so remote that the unaided eye could not see their suns among those twinkling to life above Oceania, men turned dark and leathery, or thick and weary, by strange weathers lifted glasses in salute. The light waves carrying their pledge would lap on his tomb.

Terra herself was less solemn. Except for the court, which still felt bound to follow daylight around the globe for one exhausting ceremony after another, Birthday had become simply an occasion to hold carnival. As his aircar hummed over great dusking waters, Lord Markus Hauksberg saw the east blaze with sky luminosity,

5

multi-colored moving curtains where fireworks exploded meteoric. Tonight, while the planet turned, its dark side was so radiant as to drown the very metro-centers seen from Luna. Had he tuned his vid to almost any station, he could have watched crowds filling pleasure houses and coming near riot among festively decorated towers.

His lady broke the silence between them with a murmur that made him start. "I wish it were a hundred years ago."

"Eh?" Sometimes she could still astonish him.

"Birthday meant something then."

"Well . . . yes. S'pose so." Hauksberg cast his mind back over history. She was right. Fathers had taken their sons outdoors when twilight ended parades and feasts; they had pointed to the early stars and said,—Look yonder. Those are ours. We believe that as many as four million lie within the Imperial domain. Certainly a hundred thousand know us daily, obey us, pay tribute to us, and get peace and the wealth of peace in return. Our ancestors did that. Keep the faith.

Hauksberg shrugged. You can't prevent later generations from outgrowing naïveté. In time they must realize, bone deep, that this one dustmote of a galaxy holds more than a hundred billion suns; that we have not even explored the whole of our one spiral arm, and it does not appear we ever will; that you need no telescope to see giants like Betelgeuse and Polaris which do *not* belong to us. From there, one proceeded easily to: Everybody knows the Empire was won and is maintained by naked power, the central government is corrupt and the frontier is brutal and the last organization with high morale, the

Navy, lives for war and oppression and anti-intellectualism. So get yours, have fun, ease your conscience with a bit of discreet scoffing, and never, never make a fool of yourself by taking the Empire seriously.

Could be I'll change that, Hauksberg thought.

Alicia interrupted him. "We might at least have gone to a decent party! But no, you have to drag us to the Crown Prince's. Are you hoping he'll share one of his pretty-boys?"

Hauksberg tried to ease matters with a grin. "Come, come, m'love, you do me an injustice. You know I still hunt women. Preferably beautiful women, such as you."

"Or Persis d'Io." She sagged back. "Never mind," she said tiredly. "I just don't like orgies. Especially vulgar ones."

"Nor I, much." He patted her hand. "But you'll manage. Among the many things I admire about you is your ability to carry off any situation with aplomb."

True enough, he thought. For a moment, regarding those perfect features under the diademed hair, he felt regret. So his marriage had been political; why couldn't they nonetheless have worked out a comradeship? Even love—No, he was confusing his love for ancient literature with flesh-and-blood reality. He was not Pelléas nor she Mélisande. She was clever, gracious, and reasonably honest with him; she had given him an heir; more had never been implied in the contract. For his part, he had given her position and nearly unlimited money. As for more of his time . . . how could he? Somebody had to be the repairman, when the universe was falling to pieces. Most women understood.

To entropy with it. Alicia's looks came from an

expensive biosculp job. He had seen too many slight
variations on that fashionable face.

"I've explained to you often enough," he said. "Lot
rather've gone to Mboto's or Bhatnagar's myself. But my
ship leaves in three days. Last chance to conduct a bit of
absolutely essential business."

"So you say."

He reached a decision. Tonight had not seemed to
him to represent any large sacrifice on her part. During
the months of his absence, she'd find ample consolation
with her lovers. (How else can a high-born lady who has
no special talents pass her time on Terra?) But if she did
grow embittered she could destroy him. It is vital to keep
closed that faceplate which is pretense. Never mind what
lies behind. But in front of the faceplate waits open
ridicule, as dangerous to a man in power as emptiness and
radiation to a spacefarer.

Odd, reflected the detached part of him, *for all our
millennia of recorded history, for all our socio-dynamic
theory and data, how the basis of power remains essentially magical. If I am laughed at, I may as well retire to my
estates. And Terra needs me.*

"Darlin'," he said, "I couldn't tell you anything before.
Too many ears, live and electronic, don't y' know. If the
opposition got wind of what I'm about, they'd head me
off. Not because they necessarily disagree, but because
they don't want me to bring home a jumpin' success.
That'd put me in line for the Policy Board, and everybody
hopes to sit there. By arrangin' a *fait accompli,* though—
d' you see?"

She rested a hard gaze on him. He was a tall, slender,

blond man. His features were a little too sharp; but in green tunic and decorations, gauze cloak, gold breeches and beefleather halfboots, he was more handsome than was right. "Your career," she jibed.

"Indeed," he nodded. "But also peace. Would you like to see Terra under attack? Could happen."

"Mark!" Abruptly she was changed. Her fingers, closing on his wrist beneath the lace, felt cold. "It can't be that serious?"

"Nuclear," he said. "This thing out on Starkad isn't any common frontier squabble. Been touted as such, and quite a few people honestly believe it is. But they've only seen reports filtered through a hundred offices, each one bound to gloss over facts that don't make its own job look so fiery important. I've collected raw data and had my own computations run. Conservative extrapolation gives a forty percent chance of war with Merseia inside five years. And I mean war, the kind which could get total. You don't bet those odds, do you, now?"

"No," she whispered.

"I'm s'posed to go there on a fact-findin' mission and report back to the Emperor. Then the bureaucracy may start grindin' through the preliminaries to negotiation. Or it may not; some powerful interests'd like to see the conflict go on. But at best, things'll escalate meanwhile. A settlement'll get harder and harder to reach, maybe impossible.

"What I want to do is bypass the whole wretched process. I want plenipotentiary authority to go direct from Starkad to Merseia and try negotiatin' the protocol of an agreement. I think it can be done. They're rational bein's too, y'know. S'pose many of 'em're lookin' for some way out of the quicksand. I can offer one." He straightened. "At least I can try."

She sat quiet. "I understand," she said at length. "Of course I'll cooperate."

"Good girl."

She leaned a little toward him. "Mark—"

"What?" His goal stood silhouetted against a crimson sheet.

"Oh, never mind." She sat back, smoothed her gown, and stared out at the ocean.

The Coral Palace was built on an atoll, which it engulfed even as its towers made their crooked leap skyward. Cars flittered about like fireflies. Hauksberg's set down on a flange as per GCA, let him and Alicia out, and took off for a parking raft. They walked past bowing slaves and saluting guardsmen, into an antechamber of tall waterspout columns where guests made a shifting rainbow, and so to the ballroom entrance.

"Lord Markus Hauksberg, Viscount of Ny Kalmar, Second Minister of Extra-Imperial Affairs, and Lady Hauksberg!" cried the stentor.

The ballroom was open to the sky, beneath a clear dome. Its sole interior lighting was ultraviolet. Floor, furnishings, orchestral instruments, tableware, food shone with the deep pure colors of fluorescence. So did the clothing of the guests, their protective skin paint and eyelenses. The spectacle was intense, rippling ruby, topaz, emerald, sapphire, surmounted by glowing masks and tresses, against night. Music lilted through the air with the scent of roses.

Crown Prince Josip was receiving. He had chosen to come in dead black. His hands and the sagging face floated green, weirdly disembodied; his lenses smoldered red. Hauksberg bowed and Alicia bent her knee. "Your Highness."

"Ah. Pleased to see you. Don't see you often."

"Press of business, Your Highness. The loss is ours."

"Yes. Understand you're going away."

"The Starkad affair, Your Highness."

"What? . . . Oh, yes. That. How dreadfully serious and constructive. I do hope you can relax with us here."

"We look forward to doin' so, Your Highness, though I'm 'fraid we'll have to leave early."

"Hmph." Josip half turned.

He mustn't be offended. "Goes without sayin' we both regret it the worst," Hauksberg purred. "Might I beg for another invitation on my return?"

"Well, really!"

"I'll be even more bold. My nephew's comin' to Terra. Frontier lad, y'know, but as far as I can tell from stereos and letters, quite a delightful boy. If he could actually meet the heir apparent of the Empire—why, better'n a private audience with God."

"Well. Well, you don't say. Of course. Of course." Josip beamed as he greeted the next arrival.

"Isn't that risky?" Alicia asked when they were out of earshot.

"Not for my nephew," Hauksberg chuckled. "Haven't got one. And dear Josip's memory is rather notoriously short."

He often wondered what would become of the

Empire when that creature mounted the throne. But at least Josip was weak. If, by then, the Policy Board was headed by a man who understood the galactic situation. . . . He bent and kissed his lady's hand. "Got to drift off, m'dear. Enjoy yourself. With luck, things'll still be fairly decorous when we dare scoot off."

A new dance was called and Alicia was swept away by an admiral. He was not so old, and his decorations showed that he had seen outplanet service. Hauksberg wondered if she would return home tonight.

He maneuvered to the wall, where the crowd was thinner, and worked his way along. There was scant time to admire the view above the dome's rim, though it was fantastic. The sea marched ashimmer beneath a low moon. Long waves broke intricately, virginally white on the outer ramparts; he thought he could hear them growl. The darkness enclosed by the Lunar crescent was pinpointed with city lights. The sky illumination had now formed a gigantic banner overhead, the Sunburst alive in a field of royal blue as if stratospheric winds bugled salute. Not many stars shone through so much radiance.

But Hauksberg identified Regulus, beyond which his mission lay, and Rigel, which burned in the heart of the Merseian dominions. He shivered. When he reached the champagne table, a glass was very welcome.

"Good evening," said a voice.

Hauksberg exchanged bows with a portly man wearing a particolored face. Lord Advisor Petroff was not exactly in his element at a festival like this. He jerked his head slightly. Hauksberg nodded. They gossiped a little and drifted apart. Hauksberg was detained by a couple of bores and so didn't manage to slip out the rear and catch a gravshaft downward for some while.

The others sat in a small, sealed office. They were seven, the critical ones on the Policy Board: gray men who bore the consciousness of power like added flesh. Hauksberg made the humility salute. "My sincere apologies for keepin' my lords waitin'," he said.

"No matter," Petroff said. "I've been explaining the situation."

"We haven't seen any data or computations, though," da Fonseca said. "Did you bring them, Lord Hauksberg?"

"No, sir. How could I? Every microreader in the palace is probably bugged." Hauksberg drew a breath. "My lords, you can examine the summation at leisure, once I'm gone. The question is, will you take my word and Lord Petroff's for the moment? If matters are as potentially serious as I believe, then you must agree a secret negotiator should be dispatched. If, on t'other hand, Starkad has no special significance, what have we lost by settlin' the dispute on reasonable terms?"

"Prestige," Chardon said. "Morale. Credibility, the next time we have to counter a Merseian move. I might even be so archaic as to mention honor."

"I don't propose to compromise any vital interest," Hauksberg pleaded, "and in all events, whatever concord I may reach'll have to be ratified here. My lords, we can't be gone long without someone noticin'. But if you'll listen—"

He launched his speech. It had been carefully prepared. It had better be. These six men, with Petroff, controlled enough votes to swing a decision his way. Were they prevailed on to call a privy meeting tomorrow, with a loaded quorum, Hauksberg would depart with the authority he needed.

Otherwise. . . . No, he mustn't take himself too seriously. Not at the present stage of his career. But men were dying on Starkad.

In the end, he won. Shaking, sweat running down his ribs, he leaned on the table and scarcely heard Petroff say, "Congratulations. Also, good luck. You'll need plenty of that."

CHAPTER TWO

Night on Starkad—

Tallest in the central spine of Kursoviki Island was Mount Narpa, peaking at almost twelve kilometers. So far above sea level, atmospheric pressure was near Terran standard; a man could safely breathe and men had erected Highport. It was a raw sprawl of spacefield and a few score prefabs, housing no more than five thousand; but it was growing. Through the walls of his office, Commander Max Abrams, Imperial Naval Intelligence Corps, heard metal clang and construction machines rumble.

His cigar had gone out again. He mouthed the stub until he finished reading the report on his desk, then leaned back and touched a lighter to it. Smoke puffed up toward a blue cloud which already hung under the ceiling of the bleak little room. The whole place stank. He didn't notice.

"Damn!" he said. And deliberately, for he was a religious man in his fashion, "God damn!"

Seeking calmness, he looked at the picture of his wife

and children. But they were home, on Dayan, in the Vega region of the Empire, more parsecs distant than he liked to think. And remote in time as well. He hadn't been with them for over a year. Little Miriam was changing so he'd never recognize her, Marta wrote, and David become a lanky hobbledehoy and Yael seeing such a lot of Abba Perlmutter, though of course he was a nice boy. . . . There was only the picture, separated from him by a clutter of papers and a barricade of desk machines. He didn't dare animate it.

Nor feel sorry for yourself, you clotbrain. The chair creaked beneath his shifted weight. He was a stocky man, hair grizzled, face big and hooknosed. His uniform was rumpled, tunic collar open, twin planets of his rank tarnished on the wide shoulders, blaster at belt. He hauled his mind back to work.

Wasn't just that a flitter was missing, nor even that the pilot was probably dead. Vehicles got shot down and men got killed more and more often. Too bad about this kid, who was he, yes, Ensign Dominic Flandry. *Glad I never met him. Glad I don't have to write his parents.* But the area where he vanished, that was troubling. His assignment had been a routine reconnaissance over the Zletovar Sea, not a thousand kilometers hence. If the Merseians were getting that aggressive. . . .

Were they responsible, though? Nobody knew, which was why the report had been bucked on to the Terran mission's Chief of Intelligence. A burst of static had been picked up at Highport from that general direction. A search flight had revealed nothing except the usual Tigery merchant ships and fishing boats. Well, engines did conk out occasionally; materiel was in such short supply that the ground crews couldn't detect every sign of mechanical overwork. (When in hell's flaming name was GHQ going to get off its numb butt and realize this was no "assistance operation to a friendly people" but a war?) And given a brilliant sun like Saxo, currently at a peak of its energy cycle, no tricks of modulation could invariably get a message through from high altitudes. On the other hand, a scout flitter was supposed to be fail safe and contain several backup systems.

And the Merseians were expanding their effort. *We don't do a mucking thing but expand ours in response. How about making them respond to us for a change?* The territory they commanded grew steadily bigger. It was still distant from Kursoviki by a quarter of the planet's circumference. But might it be reaching a tentacle this way?

Let's ask. Can't lose much.

Abrams thumbed a button on his vidiphone. An operator looked out of the screen. "Get me the greenskin cinc," Abrams ordered.

"Yes, sir. If possible."

"Better be possible. What're you paid for? Tell his cohorts all gleaming in purple and gold to tell him I'm about to make my next move."

"What, sir?" The operator was new here.

"You heard me, son. Snarch!"

Time must pass while the word seeped through channels. Abrams opened a drawer, got out his magnetic chessboard, and pondered. He hadn't actually been ready to play. However, Runei the Wanderer was too fascinated

by their match to refuse an offer if he had a spare moment
lying around; and damn if any Merseian son of a mother
was going to win at a Terran game.

Hm . . . promising development here, with the white
bishop . . . no, wait, then the queen might come under
attack . . . tempting to sic a computer onto the problem
. . . betcha the opposition did . . . maybe not . . . ah, so.

"Commandant Runei, sir."

An image jumped to view. Abrams could spot individual
differences between nonhumans as easily as with his own
species. That was part of his business. An untrained eye
saw merely the alienness. Not that the Merseians were so
odd, compared to some. Runei was a true mammal from a
terrestroid planet. He showed reptile ancestry a little
more than Homo Sapiens does, in hairless pale-green
skin, faintly scaled, and short triangular spines running
from the top of his head, down his back to the end of a
long heavy tail. That tail counterbalanced a forward-
leaning posture, and he sat on the tripod which it made
with his legs. But otherwise he rather resembled a tall,
broad man. Except for complex bony convolutions in
place of external ears, and brow ridges overhanging the jet
eyes, his head and face might almost have been Terran.
He wore the form-fitting black and silver uniform of his
service. Behind him could be seen on the wall a bell-
mouthed gun, a ship model, a curious statuette: souvenirs
of far stars.

"Greeting, Commander." He spoke fluent Anglic,
with a musical accent. "You work late."

"And you've dragged yourself off the rack early,"
Abrams grunted. "Must be about sunrise where you are."

Runei's glance flickered toward a chrono. "Yes, I believe so. But we pay scant attention here."

"You can ignore the sun easier'n us, all right, squatted down in the ooze. But your native friends still live by this cheap two-thirds day they got. Don't you keep office hours for them?"

Abrams' mind ranged across the planet, to the enemy base. Starkad was a big world, whose gravity and atmosphere gnawed land masses away between tectonic epochs. Thus, a world of shallow ocean, made turbulent by wind and the moons; a world of many islands large and small, but no real continents. The Merseians had established themselves in the region they called the Kimraig Sea. They had spread their domes widely across the surface, their bubblehouses over the bottom. And their aircraft ruled those skies. Not often did a recon flight, robot or piloted, come back to Highport with word of what was going on. Nor did instruments peering from spaceships as they came and went show much.

One of these years, Abrams thought, *somebody will break the tacit agreement and put up a few spy satellites. Why not us?*—'*Course, then the other side'll bring space warships, instead of just transports, and go potshooting. And then the first side will bring bigger warships.*

"I am glad you called," Runei said. "I have thanked Admiral Enriques for the conversion unit, but pleasure is to express obligation to a friend."

"Huh?"

"You did not know? One of our main desalinators broke down. Your commandant was good enough to furnish us with a replacement part we lacked."

"Oh, yeh. That." Abrams rolled his cigar between his teeth.

The matter was ridiculous, he thought. Terrans and Merseians were at war on Starkad. They killed each other's people. But nonetheless, Runei had sent a message of congratulations when Birthday rolled around. (Twice ridiculous! Even if a spaceship in hyperdrive has no theoretical limit to her pseudovelocity, the concept of simultaneity remains meaningless over interstellar distances.) And Enriques had now saved Runei from depleting his beer supplies.

Because this wasn't a war. Not officially. Not even among the two native races. Tigeries and Seatrolls had fought since they evolved to intelligence, probably. But that was like men and wolves in ancient days, nothing systematic, plain natural enemies. Until the Merseians began giving the Seatrolls equipment and advice and the landfolk were driven back. When Terra heard about that, it was sheer reflex to do likewise for the Tigeries, preserve the balance lest Starkad be unified as a Merseian puppet. As a result, the Merseians upped their help a bit, and Terrans replied in kind, and—

And the two empires remained at peace. These were simple missions of assistance, weren't they? Terra had Mount Narpa by treaty with the Tigeries of Ujanka, Merseia sat in Kimraig by treaty with whoever lived there. (Time out for laughter and applause. No Starkadian culture appeared to have anything like an idea of compacts between sovereign powers.) The Roidhunate of Merseia didn't shoot down Terran scouts. Heavens, no! Only Merseian militechnicians did, helping the Seatrolls of

Kimraig maintain inviolate their air space. The Terran Empire hadn't bushwhacked a Merseian landing party on Cape Thunder: merely Terrans pledged to guard the frontier of their ally.

The Covenant of Alfzar held. You were bound to assist civilized outworlders on request. Abrams toyed with the notion of inventing some requests from his side. In fact, that wasn't a bad gambit right now.

"Maybe you can return the favor," he said. "We've lost a flitter in the Zletovar. I'm not so rude as to hint that one of your lads was cruising along and eyeballed ours and got a wee bit overexcited. But supposing the crash was accidental, how about a joint investigation?"

Abrams liked seeing startlement on that hard green face. "You joke, Commander!"

"Oh, naturally my boss'd have to approach you officially, but I'll suggest it to him. You've got better facilities than us for finding a sunken wreck."

"But why?"

Abrams shrugged. "Mutual interest in preventing accidents. Cultivation of friendship between peoples and individual beings. I think that's what the catchword is back home."

Runei scowled. "Quite impossible. I advise you not to make any such proposal on the record."

"Nu? Wouldn't look so good if you turn us down?"

"Tension would only be increased. Must I repeat my government's position to you? The oceans of Starkad belong to the seafolk. They evolved there, it is their environment, it is not essential to the landfolk. Nevertheless the landfolk have consistently encroached. Their fisheries, their seabeast hunts, their weed harvests, their drag nets, everything disturbs an ecology vital to the other race. I will not speak of those they have killed, the underwater cities they have bombed with stones, the bays and straits they have barred. I will say that when Merseia offered her good offices to negotiate a modus vivendi, no land culture showed the slightest interest. My task is to help the seafolk resist aggression until the various landfolk societies agree to establish a just and stable peace."

"Come off that parrot act," Abrams snorted. "You haven't got the beak for it. Why are you really here?"

"I have told you—"

"No. Think. You've got your orders and you obey 'em like a good little soldier. But don't you sometimes wonder what the profit is for Merseia? I sure do. What the black and red deuce is your government's reason? It's not as if Saxo sun had a decent strategic location. Here we are, spang in the middle of a hundred light-year strip of no man's land between our realms. Hardly been explored; hell, I'll bet half the stars around us aren't so much as noted in a catalogue. The nearest civilization is Betelgeuse, and the Betelgeuseans are neutrals who wish emerods on both our houses. You're too old to believe in elves, gnomes, little men, or the disinterested altruism of great empires. So *why?*"

"I may not question the decisions of the Roidhun and his Grand Council. Still less may you." Runei's stiffness dissolved in a grin. "If Starkad is so useless, why are you here?"

"Lot of people back home wonder about that too," Abrams admitted. "Policy says we contain you wherever we can. Sitting on this planet, you would have a base fifty light-years closer to our borders, for whatever that's worth." He paused. "Could give you a bit more influence over Betelgeuse."

"Let us hope your envoy manages to settle the dispute," Runei said, relaxing. "I do not precisely enjoy myself on this hellball either."

"What envoy?"

"You have not heard? Our latest courier informed us that a . . . *khraich* . . . yes, a Lord Hauksberg is hither-bound."

"I know." Abrams winced. "Another big red wheel to roll around the base."

"But he is to proceed to Merseia. The Grand Council has agreed to receive him."

"Huh?" Abrams shook his head. "Damn, I wish our mails were as good as yours. . . . Well. How about this downed flitter? Why won't you help us look for the pieces?"

"In essence, informally," Runei said, "because we hold it had no right, as a foreign naval vessel, to fly over the waters. Any consequences must be on the pilot's own head."

Ho-ho! Abrams tautened. That was something new. Implied, of course, by the Merseian position; but this was the first time he had heard the claim in plain language. So could the greenskins be preparing a major push? Very possible, especially if Terra had offered to negotiate. Military operations exert pressure at bargaining tables, too.

Runei sat like a crocodile, smiling the least amount.

Had he guessed what was in Abrams' mind? Maybe not. In spite of what the brotherhood-of-beings sentimentalists kept bleating, Merseians did not really think in human style. Abrams made an elaborate stretch and yawn. "'Bout time I knocked off," he said. "Nice talking to you, old bastard." He did not entirely lie. Runei was a pretty decent carnivore. Abrams would have loved to hear him reminisce about the planets where he had ranged.

"Your move," the Merseian reminded him.

"Why . . . yes. Clean forgot. Knight to king's bishop four."

Runei got out his own board and shifted the piece. He sat quiet a while, studying. "Curious," he murmured.

"It'll get curiouser. Call me back when you're ready." Abrams switched off.

His cigar was dead again. He dropped the stub down the disposal, lit a fresh one, and rose. Weariness dragged at him. Gravity on Starkad wasn't high enough that man needed drugs or a counterfield. But one point three gees meant twenty-five extra kilos loaded on middle-aged bones. . . . No, he was thinking in standard terms. Dayan pulled ten per cent harder than Terra. . . . Dayan, dear gaunt hills and wind-scoured plains, homes nestled in warm orange sunlight, low trees and salt marshes and the pride of a people who had bent desolation to their needs. . . . Where had young Flandry been from, and what memories did he carry to darkness?

On a sudden impulse Abrams put down his cigar, bent his head, and inwardly recited the Kaddish.

Get to bed, old man. Maybe you've stumbled on a clue, maybe not, but it'll keep. Go to your rest.

He put on cap and cloak, thrust the cigar back between his jaws, and walked out.

Cold smote him. A breeze blew thinly under strange constellations and auroral glimmer. The nearer moon, Egrima, was up, almost full, twice the apparent size of Luna seen from Terra. It flooded distant snowpeaks with icy bluish light. Buruz was a Luna-sized crescent barely above the rooftops.

Walls bulked black on either side of the unpaved street, which scrunched with frost as his boots struck. Here and there glowed a lighted window, but they and the scattered lamps did little to relieve the murk. On his left, unrestful radiance from smelters picked out the two spaceships now in port, steel cenotaphs rearing athwart the Milky Way. Thence, too, came the clangor of night-shift work. The field was being enlarged, new sheds and barracks were going up, for Terra's commitment was growing. On his right the sky was tinted by feverish glowsigns, and he caught snatches of drumbeat, trumpets, perhaps laughter. Madame Cepheid had patriotically dispatched a shipful of girls and croupiers to Starkad. And why not? They were so young and lonely, those boys.

Maria, I miss you.

Abrams was almost at his quarters when he remembered he hadn't stashed the papers on his desk. He stopped dead. Great Emperor's elegant epiglottis! He was indeed due for an overhaul.

Briefly he was tempted to say, "Urinate on regulations." The office was built of ferroconcrete, with an armorplate door and an automatic recognition lock. But no. Lieutenant Novak might report for duty before his chief, may his pink cheeks fry in hell. Wouldn't do to set a bad security example. Not that espionage was any problem here, but what a man didn't see, he couldn't tell if the Merseians caught and hypnoprobed him.

Abrams wheeled and strode back, trailing bad words. At the end, he slammed to a halt. His cigar hit the deck and he ground down a heel on it.

The door was properly closed, the windows dark. But he could see footprints in the churned, not yet congealed mud before the entrance, and they weren't his own.

And no alarm had gone off. Somebody was inside with a truckload of roboticist's gear.

Abrams' blaster snaked into his hand. Call the guard on his wristcom? No, whoever could burgle his office could surely detect a transmission and was surely prepared for escape before help could arrive. By suicide if nothing else.

Abrams adjusted his gun to needle beam. Given luck, he might disable rather than kill. Unless he bought it first. The heart slugged in his breast. Night closed thickly inward.

He catfooted to the door and touched the lock switch. Metal burned his fingers with chill. Identified, he swung the door open and leaned around the edge.

Light trickled over his shoulder and through the windows. A thing whirled from his safe. His eyes were adapted and he made out some details. It must have looked like any workman in radiation armor as it passed through the base. But now one arm had sprouted tools; and the helmet was thrown back to reveal a face with electronic eyes, set in a head of alloy.

A Merseian face.

Blue lightning spat from the tool-hand. Abrams had yanked himself back. The energy bolt sparked and sizzled on the door. He spun his own blaster to medium beam, not stopping to give himself reasons, and snapped a shot.

The other weapon went dead, ruined. The armored shape used its normal hand to snatch for a gun taken forth in advance and laid on top of the safe. Abrams charged through the doorway while he reset for needle fire. So intense a ray, at such close range, slashed legs across. In a rattle and clash, the intruder fell.

Abrams activated his transmitter. "Guard! Intelligence office—on the double!"

His blaster threatened while he waved the lights to go on. The being stirred. No blood flowed from those limb stumps; powerpacks, piezoelectric cascades, room-temperature superconductors lay revealed. Abrams realized what he had caught, and whistled. Less than half a Merseian: no tail, no breast or lower body, not much natural skull, one arm and the fragment of another. The rest was machinery. It was the best prosthetic job he'd ever heard of.

Not that he knew of many. Only among races which didn't know how to make tissues regenerate, or which didn't have that kind of tissues. Surely the Merseians— But what a lovely all-purpose plug-in they had here!

The green face writhed. Wrath and anguish spewed from the lips. The hand fumbled at the chest. To turn off the heart? Abrams kicked that wrist aside and planted a foot on it. "Easy, friend," he said.

CHAPTER THREE

Morning on Merseia—

Brechdan Ironrede, the Hand of the Vach Ynvory, walked forth on a terrace of Castle Dhangodhan. A sentry slapped boots with tail and laid blaster to breastplate. A gardener, pruning the dwarfed koir trees planted among the flagstones, folded his arms and bent in his brown smock. To both, Brechdan touched his forehead. For they were not slaves; their families had been clients of the Ynvorys from ages before the nations merged into one; how could they take pride in it if the clan chief did not accord them their own dignity?

He walked unspeaking, though, between the rows of yellow blooms, until he reached the parapet. There he stopped and looked across his homeland.

Behind him, the castle lifted gray stone turrets. Banners snapped in a cool wind, against an infinitely blue sky. Before him, the walls tumbled down toward gardens, and beyond them the forested slopes of Bedh-Ivrich went on down, and down, and down, to be lost in mists and

shadows which still cloaked the valley. Thus he could not
see the farms and villages which Dhangodhan dominated:
nothing but the peaks on the other side. Those climbed
until their green flanks gave way to crags and cliffs of
granite, to snowfields and the far blink of glaciers. The
sun Korych had now cleared the eastern heights and cast
dazzling spears over the world. Brechdan saluted it, as was
his hereditary right. High overhead wheeled a fangryf,
hunting, and the light burned gold off its feathers.

There was a buzz in the air as the castle stirred to
wakefulness, a clatter, a bugle call, a hail and a bit of song.
The wind smelled of woodsmoke. From this terrace the
River Oiss was not visible, but its cataracts rang loud.
Hard to imagine how, a bare two hundred kilometers
west, that stream began to flow through lands which had
become one huge city, from foothills to the Wilwidh
Ocean. Or, for that matter, hard to picture those towns,
mines, factories, ranches which covered the plains east of
the Hun range.

Yet they were his too—no, not his; the Vach Ynvory's,
himself no more than the Hand for a few decades before
he gave back this flesh to the soil and this mind to the
God. Dhangodhan they had preserved little changed,
because here was the country from which they sprang,
long ago. But their real work today was in Ardaig and
Tridaig, the capitals, where Brechdan presided over the
Grand Council. And beyond this planet, beyond Korych
itself, out to the stars.

—— Brechdan drew a deep breath. The sense of power
coursed in his veins. But that was a familiar wine; today he
awaited a joy more gentle.

It did not show upon him. He was too long schooled in chieftainship. Big, austere in a black robe, brow seamed with an old battle scar which he disdained to have biosculped away, he turned to the world only the face of Brechdan Ironrede, who stood second to none but the Roidhun.

A footfall sounded. Brechdan turned. Chwioch, his bailiff, approached, in red tunic and green trousers and modishly high-collared cape. He wasn't called "the Dandy" for nothing. But he was loyal and able and an Ynvory born. Brechdan exchanged kin-salutes, right hand to left shoulder.

"Word from Shwylt Shipsbane, Protector," Chwioch reported. "His business in the Gwelloch will not detain him after all and he will come here this afternoon as you desired."

"Good." Brechdan was, in fact, elated. Shwylt's counsel would be most helpful, balancing Lifrith's impatience and Priadwyr's over-reliance on computer technology. Though they were fine males, each in his own way, those three Hands of their respective Vachs. Brechdan depended on them for ideas as much as for the support they gave to help him control the Council. He would need them more and more in the next few years, as events on Starkad were maneuvered toward their climax.

A thunderclap cut the sky. Looking up, Brechdan saw a flitter descend with reckless haste. Scalloped fins identified it as Ynvory common-property. "Your son, Protector!" Chwioch cried with jubilation.

"No doubt." Brechdan must not unbend, not even when Elwych returned after three years.

"Ah . . . shall I cancel your morning audience, Protector?"

"Certainly not," Brechdan said. "Our client folk have their right to be heard. I am too much absent from them."

But we can have an hour for our own.

"I shall meet Heir Elwych and tell him where you are, Protector." Chwioch hurried off.

Brechdan waited. The sun began to warm him through his robe. He wished Elwych's mother were still alive. The wives remaining to him were good females, of course, thrifty, trustworthy, cultivated, as females should be. But Nodhia had been—well, yes, he might as well use a Terran concept—she had been fun. Elwych was Brechdan's dearest child, not because he was the oldest now when two others lay dead on remote planets, but because he was Nodhia's. May the earth lie light upon her.

The gardener's shears clattered to the flagstones. "Heir! Welcome home!" It was not ceremonial for the old fellow to kneel and embrace the newcomer's tail, but Brechdan didn't feel that any reproof was called for.

Elwych the Swift strode toward his father in the black and silver of the Navy. A captain's dragon was sewn to his sleeve, the banners of Dhangodhan flamed over his head. He stopped four paces off and gave a service salute. "Greeting, Protector."

"Greeting, swordarm." Brechdan wanted to hug that body to him. Their eyes met. The youngster winked and grinned. And that was nigh as good.

"Are the kindred well?" Elwych asked superfluously, as he had called from the inner moon the moment his ship arrived for furlough.

"Indeed," Brechdan said.

They might then have gone to the gynaeceum for family reunion. But the guard watched. Hand and Heir could set him an example by talking first of things which concerned the race. They need not be too solemn, however.

"Had you a good trip home?" Brechdan inquired.

"Not exactly," Elwych replied. "Our main fire-control computer developed some kind of bellyache. I thought best we put in at Vorida for repairs. The interimperial situation, you know; it just might have exploded, and then a Terran unit just might have chanced near us."

"Vorida? I don't recall—"

"No reason why you should. Too hooting many planets in the universe. A rogue in the Betelgeuse sector. We keep a base—What's wrong?"

Elwych alone noticed the signs of his father being taken aback. "Nothing," Brechdan said. "I assume the Terrans don't know about this orb."

Elwych laughed. "How could they?"

How, in truth? There are so many rogues, they are so little and dark, space is so vast.

Consider: To an approximation, the size of bodies which condensed out of the primordial gas is inversely proportional to the frequency of their occurrence. At one end of the scale, hydrogen atoms fill the galaxy, about one per cubic centimeter. At the other end, you can count the monstrous O-type suns by yourself. (You may extend the scale in both directions, from quanta to quasars; but no matter.) There are about ten times as many M-type red dwarfs as there are G-type stars like Korych or Sol. Your spaceship is a thousand times more likely to be struck by a one-gram pebble than by a one-kilogram rock. And so, sunless planets are more common than suns. They usually travel in clusters; nevertheless they are for most practical purposes unobservable before you are nearly on top of them. They pose no special hazard—whatever their number, the odds against one of them passing through any particular point in space are literally astronomical—and those whose paths are known can make useful harbors.

Brechdan felt he must correct an incomplete answer. "The instantaneous vibrations of a ship under hyperdrive are detectable within a light-year," he said. "A Terran or Betelgeusean could happen that close to your Vorida."

Elwych flushed. "And supposing one of our ships happened to be in the vicinity, what would detection prove except that there was another ship?"

He had been given the wristslap of being told what any cub knew; he had responded with the slap of telling what any cub should be able to reason out for himself. Brechdan could not but smile. Elwych responded. A blow can also be an act of love.

"I capitulate," Brechdan said. "Tell me somewhat of your tour of duty. We got far too few letters, especially in the last months."

"Where I was then, writing was a little difficult," Elwych said. "I can tell you now, though. Saxo V."

"Starkad?" Brechdan exclaimed. "You, a line officer?"

"Was this way. My ship was making a courtesy call on the Betelgeuseans—or showing them the flag, whichever way they chose to take it—when a courier from Fodaich Runei arrived. Somehow the Terrans had learned about a submarine base he was having built off an archipelago. The whole thing was simple, primitive, so the seafolk could operate the units themselves, but it would have served to wreck landfolk commerce in that area. Nobody knows how the Terrans got the information, but Runei says they have a fiendishly good Intelligence chief. At any rate, they gave some landfolk chemical depth bombs and told them where to sail and drop them. And by evil luck, the explosions killed several key technicians of ours who were supervising construction. Which threw everything into chaos. Our mission there is scandalously short-handed. Runei sent to Betelgeuse as well as Merseia, in the hope of finding someone like us who could substitute until proper replacements arrived. So I put my engineers in a civilian boat. And since that immobilized our ship as a fighting unit, I must go too."

Brechdan nodded. An Ynvory did not send personnel into danger and himself stay behind without higher duties.

He knew about the disaster already, of course. Best not tell Elwych that. Time was unripe for the galaxy to know how serious an interest Merseia had in Starkad. His son was discreet. But what he did not know, he could not tell if the Terrans caught and hypnoprobed him.

"You must have had an adventurous time," Brechdan said.

"Well . . . yes. Occasional sport. And an interesting planet." The anger still in Elwych flared: "I tell you, though, our people are being betrayed."

"How?"

"Not enough of them. Not enough equipment. Not

a single armed spaceship. Why don't we support them properly?"

"Then the Terrans will support *their* mission properly," Brechdan said.

Elwych gazed long at his father. The waterfall noise seemed to louden behind Dhangodhan's ramparts. "Are we going to make a real fight for Starkad?" he murmured. "Or do we scuttle away?"

The scar throbbed on Brechdan's forehead. "Who serve the Roidhun do not scuttle. But they may strike bargains, when such appears good for the race."

"So." Elwych stared past him, across the valley mists. Scorn freighted his voice. "I see. The whole operation is a bargaining counter, to win something from Terra. Runei told me they'll send a negotiator here."

"Yes, he is expected soon." Because the matter was great, touching as it did on honor, Brechdan allowed himself to grasp the shoulders of his son. Their eyes met. "Elwych," Brechdan said gently, "you are young and perhaps do not understand. But you must. Service to the race calls for more than courage, more even than intelligence. It calls for wisdom.

"Because we Merseians have such instincts that most of us actively enjoy combat, we tend to look on combat as an end in itself. And such is not true. That way lies destruction. Combat is a means to an end—the hegemony of our race. And that in turn is but a means to the highest end of all—absolute freedom for our race, to make of the galaxy what they will.

"But we cannot merely fight for our goal. We must work. We must have patience. You will not see us masters of the galaxy. It is too big. We may need a million years. On that time scale, individual pride is a small sacrifice to offer, when it happens that compromise or retreat serves us best."

Elwych swallowed. "Retreat from Terra?"

"I trust not. Terra is the immediate obstacle. The duty of your generation is to remove it."

"I don't understand," Elwych protested. "What is the Terran Empire? A clot of stars. An old, sated, corrupt people who want nothing except to keep what their fathers won for them. Why pay them any heed whatsoever? Why not expand away from them—around them—until they're engulfed?"

"Precisely because Terra's objective is the preservation of the status quo," Brechdan said. "You are forgetting the political theory that was supposed to be part of your training. Terra cannot permit us to become more powerful than she. Therefore she is bound to resist our every attempt to grow. And do not underestimate her. That race still bears the chromosomes of conquerors. There are still brave men in the Empire, devoted men, shrewd men . . . with the experience of a history longer than ours to guide them. If they see doom before them, they'll fight like demons. So, until we have sapped their strength, we move carefully. Do you comprehend?"

"Yes, my father," Elwych yielded. "I hope so."

Brechdan eased. They had been serious for as long as their roles demanded. "Come." His face cracked in another smile; he took his son's arm. "Let us go greet our kin."

They walked down corridors hung with the shields of their ancestors and the trophies of hunts on more than one planet. A gravshaft lifted them to the gynaeceum level.

The whole tribe waited, Elwych's stepmothers, sisters and their husbands and cubs, younger brothers. Everything dissolved in shouts, laughter, pounding of backs, twining of tails, music from a record player and a ring-dance over the floor.

One cry interrupted. Brechdan bent above the cradle of his newest grandcub. *I should speak about marriage to Elwych*, he thought. *High time he begot an Heir's Heir.* The small being who lay on the furs wrapped a fist around the gnarled finger that stroked him. Brechdan Ironrede melted within himself. "You shall have stars for toys," he crooned. "Wudda, wudda, wudda."

CHAPTER FOUR

Ensign Dominic Flandry, Imperial Naval Flight Corps, did not know whether he was alive through luck or management. At the age of nineteen, with the encoding molecules hardly settled down on your commission, it was natural to think the latter. But had a single one of the factors he had used to save himself been absent—He didn't care to dwell on that.

Besides, his troubles were far from over. As a merchant ship belonging to the Sisterhood of Kursoviki, the *Archer* had been given a radio by the helpful Terrans. But it was crap-out; some thimblewit had exercised some Iron Age notion of maintenance. Dragoika had agreed to put back for her home. But with a foul wind, they'd be days at sea in this damned wallowing bathtub before they were even likely to speak to a boat with a transmitter in working order. That wasn't fatal per se. Flandry could shovel local rations through the chowlock of his helmet; Starkadian biochemistry was sufficiently like Terran that most foods wouldn't poison him, and he carried vitamin supplements. The taste, though, my God, the taste!

Most ominous was the fact that he *had* been shot down, and at no large distance from here. Perhaps the Seatrolls, and Merseians, would let this Tigery craft alone. If they weren't yet ready to show their hand, they probably would. However, his misfortune indicated their preparations were more or less complete. When he chanced to pass above their latest kettle of mischief, they'd felt so confident they opened fire.

"And then the Outside Folk attacked you?" Ferok prodded. His voice came as a purr through whistle of wind, rush and smack of waves, creak of rigging, all intensified and distorted by the thick air.

"Yes," Flandry said. He groped for words. They'd given him an electronic cram in the language and customs of Kursovikian civilization while the transport bore him from Terra. But some things are hard to explain in pre-industrial terms. "A type of vessel which can both submerge and fly rose from the water. Its radio shout drowned my call and its firebeams wrecked my craft before mine could pierce its thicker armor. I barely escaped my hull as it sank, and kept submerged until the enemy went away. Then I flew off in search of help. The small engine which lifted me was nigh exhausted when I came upon your ship."

Truly his gravity impeller wouldn't lug him much further until the capacitors were recharged. He didn't plan to use it again. What power remained in the pack on his shoulders must be saved to operate the pump and reduction valve in the vitryl globe which sealed off his head. A man couldn't breathe Starkadian sea-level air and survive. Such an oxygen concentration would burn out his lungs faster than nitrogen narcosis and carbon dioxide acidosis could kill him.

He remembered how Lieutenant Danielson had gigged him for leaving off the helmet. "Ensign, I don't give a ball of fertilizer how uncomfortable the thing is, when you might be enjoying your nice Terra-conditioned cockpit. Nor do I weep at the invasion of privacy involved in taping your every action in flight. The purpose is to make sure that pups like you, who know so much more than a thousand years of astronautics could possibly teach them, obey regulations. The next offense will earn you thirty seconds of nerve-lash. Dismissed."

So you saved my life, Flandry grumbled. *You're still a snot-nosed bastard.*

Nobody was to blame for his absent blaster. It was torn from the holster in those wild seconds of scrambling clear. He had kept the regulation knife and pouchful of oddments. He had boots and gray coverall, sadly stained and in no case to be compared with the glamorous dress uniform. And that was just about the lot.

Ferok lowered the plumy thermosensor tendrils above his eyes: a frown. "If the vaz-Siravo search what's left of your flier, down below, and don't find your body, they may guess what you did and come looking for you," he said.

"Yes," Flandry agreed, "they may."

He braced himself against pitch and roll and looked outward—tall, the lankiness of adolescence still with him—brown hair, gray eyes, a rather long and regular face which Saxo had burned dark. Before him danced and shimmered a greenish ocean, sun-flecks and whitecaps on waves that marched faster, in Starkadian gravity, than on Terra. The sky was pale blue. Clouds banked gigantic on the horizon, but in a dense atmosphere they did not portend storm. A winged thing cruised, a sea animal broached and dove again. At its distance, Saxo was only a third as broad as Sol is to Terra and gave half the illumination. The adaptable human vision perceived this as normal, but the sun was merciless white, so brilliant that one dared not look anywhere near. The short day stood at late afternoon, and the temperature, never very high in these middle northern latitudes, was dropping. Flandry shivered.

Ferok made a contrast to him. The land Starkadian, Tigery, Toborko, or whatever you wanted to call him, was built not unlike a short man with disproportionately long legs. His hands were four-fingered, his feet large and clawed, he flaunted a stubby tail. The head was less anthropoid, round, with flat face tapering to a narrow chin. The eyes were big, slanted, scarlet in the iris, beneath his fronded tendrils. The nose, what there was of it, had a single slit nostril. The mouth was wide and carnivore-toothed. The ears were likewise big, outer edges elaborated till they almost resembled bat wings. Sleek fur covered his skin, black-striped orange that shaded into white at the throat.

He wore only a beaded pouch, kept from flapping by thigh straps, and a curved sword scabbarded across his back. By profession he was the boatswain, a high rank for a male on a Kursovikian ship; as such, he was no doubt among Dragoika's lovers. By nature he was impetuous, quarrelsome, and dog-loyal to his allegiances. Flandry liked him.

Ferok lifted a telescope and swept it around an arc. That was a native invention. Kursoviki was the center of the planet's most advanced land culture. "No sign of anything yet," he said. "Do you think yon Outsider flyboat may attack us?"

"I doubt that," Flandry said. "Most likely it was simply on hand because of having brought some Merseian advisors, and shot at me because I might be carrying instruments which would give me a clue as to what's going on down below. It's probably returned to Kimraig by now." He hesitated before continuing: "The Merseians, like us, seldom take a direct role in any action, and then nearly always just as individual officers, not representatives of their people. Neither of us wishes to provoke a response in kind."

"Afraid?" Lips curled back from fangs.

"On your account," Flandry said, somewhat honestly. "You have no dream of what our weapons can do to a world."

"World . . . hunh, the thought's hard to seize. Well, let the Sisterhood try. I'm happy to be a plain male."

Flandry turned and looked across the deck. The *Archer* was a big ship by Starkadian measure, perhaps five hundred tons, broad in the beam, high in the stern, a carven post at the prow as emblem of her tutelary spirit. A deckhouse stood amidships, holding galley, smithy, carpenter shop, and armory. Everything was gaudily painted. Three masts carried yellow square sails aloft, fore-and-aft beneath; at the moment she was tacking on the latter and a genoa. The crew were about their duties on deck and in the rigging. They numbered thirty male hands and half a dozen female officers. The ship had been carrying timber and spices from Ujanka port down the Chain archipelago.

"What armament have we?" he asked.

"Our Terran deck gun," Ferok told him. "Five of your rifles. We were offered more, but Dragoika said they'd be no use till we had more people skilled with them. Otherwise, swords, pikes, crossbows, knives, belaying pins, teeth, and nails." He gestured at the mesh which passed from side to side of the hull, under the keel. "If that twitches much, could mean a Siravo trying to put a hole in our bottom. Then we dive after him. You'd be best for that, with your gear."

Flandry winced. His helmet was adjustable for underwater; on Starkad, the concentration of dissolved oxygen was almost as high as in Terra's air. But he didn't fancy a scrap with a being evolved for such an environment.

"Why are you here, yourself?" Ferok asked conversationally. "Pleasure or plunder?"

"Neither. I was sent." Flandry didn't add that the Navy reckoned it might as well use Starkad to give certain promising young officers some experience. "Promising" made him sound too immature. At once he realized he'd actually sounded unaggressive and prevaricated in haste: "Of course, with the chance of getting into a fight, I would have asked to go anyway."

"They tell me your females obey males. True?"

"Well, sometimes." The second mate passed by and Flandry's gaze followed her. She had curves, a tawny mane rippling down her back, breasts standing fuller and firmer than any girl could have managed without technological assistance, and a nearly humanoid nose. Her clothing consisted of some gold bracelets. But her differences from the Terran went deeper than looks. She didn't lactate; those nipples fed blood directly to her infants. And hers was the more imaginative, more cerebral sex, not subordinated in any culture, dominant in the islands around Kursoviki. He wondered if that might trace back to something as simple as the female body holding more blood and more capacity to regenerate it.

"But who, then, keeps order in your home country?" Ferok wondered. "Why haven't you killed each other off?"

"Um-m-m, hard to explain," Flandry said. "Let me first see if I understand your ways, to compare mine. For instance, you owe nothing to the place where you live, right? I mean, no town or island or whatever is ruled, as a ship is . . . right? Instead—at any rate in this part of the world—the females are organized into associations like the Sisterhood, whose members may live anywhere, which even have their special languages. They own all important property and make all important decisions through those associations. Thus disputes among males have little effect on them. Am I right?"

"I suppose so. You might have put it more politely."

"Apology-of-courage is offered. I am a stranger. Now among my people—"

A shout fell from the crow's nest. Ferok whirled and pointed his telescope. The crew sprang to the starboard rail, clustered in the shrouds, and yelled.

Dragoika bounded from the captain's cabin under the poop. She held a four-pronged fish spear in one hand, a small painted drum beneath her arm. Up the ladder she went, to stand by the quartermistress at the wheel and look for herself. Then, coolly, she tapped her drum on one side, plucked the steel strings across the recessed head on the other. Twang and thump carried across noise like a bugle call. *All hands to arms and battle stations!*

"The vaz-Siravo!" Ferok shouted above clamor. "They're on us!" He made for the deckhouse. Restored to discipline, the crew were lining up for helmets, shields, byrnies, and weapons.

Flandry strained his eyes into the glare off the water. A score or so blue dorsal fins clove it, converging on the ship. And suddenly, a hundred meters to starboard, a submarine rose.

A little, crude thing, doubtless home-built to a Merseian design—for if you want to engineer a planet-wide war among primitives, you should teach them what they can make and do for themselves. The hull was greased leather stretched across a framework of some undersea equivalent of wood. Harness trailed downward to the four fish which pulled it; he could barely discern them as huge shadows under the surface. The deck lay awash. But an outsize catapult projected therefrom. Several dolphin-like bodies with transparent globes on their heads and powerpacks on their backs crouched alongside. They rose onto flukes and flippers; their arms reached to swing the machine around.

"Dommaneek!" Dragoika screeched. "Dommaneek Falandaree! Can you man ours?"

"Aye, aye!" The Terran ran prow-ward. Planks rolled and thudded beneath his feet.

On the forward deck, the two females whose duty it was were trying to unlimber the gun. They worked slowly, getting in each other's way, spitting curses. There hadn't yet been time to drill many competent shots, even with a weapon as simple as this, a rifle throwing 38 mm. chemical shells. Before they got the range, that catapult might—

"Gangway!" Flandry shoved the nearest aside. She snarled and swatted at him with long red nails. Dragoika's drum rippled an order. Both females fell back from him.

He opened the breech, grabbed a shell from the ammo box, and dogged it in. The enemy catapult thumped. A packet arced high, down again, made a near miss and burst into flame which spread crimson and smoky across the waves. Some version of Greek fire— undersea oil wells—Flandry put his eye to the range find-er. He was too excited to be scared. But he must lay the gun manually. A hydraulic system would have been too liable to breakdown. In spite of good balance and self-lubricating bearings, the barrel swung with nightmare slowness. The Seatrolls were rewinding their catapult . . . before Andromeda, they were fast! *They* must use hydraulics.

Dragoika spoke to the quartermistress. She put the wheel hard over. Booms swung over the deck. The jib flapped thunderous until crewmales reset the sheets. The *Archer* came about. Flandry struggled to compensate. He barely remembered to keep one foot on the brake, lest his gun travel too far. *Bet those she-cats would've forgotten.*

The enemy missile didn't make the vessel's superstructure as intended. But it struck the hull amidships. Under this oxygen pressure, fire billowed heavenward.

Flandry pulled the lanyard. His gun roared and kicked. A geyser fountained, mingled with splinters. One draught fish leaped, threshed, and died. The rest already floated bellies up. "Got him!" Flandry whooped.

Dragoika plucked a command. Most of the crew put aside their weapons and joined a firefighting party. There was a hand pump at either rail, buckets with ropes bent to them, sails to drag from the deckhouse and wet and lower.

Ferok, or someone, yelled through voices, wind, waves, brawling, and smoke of the flames. The Seatrolls were coming over the opposite rail.

They must have climbed the nets. (*Better invent a different warning gadget*, raced through Flandry's mind.) They wore the Merseian equipment which had enabled their kind to carry the war ashore elsewhere on Starkad. Waterfilled helmets covered the blunt heads, black absorbent skinsuits kept everything else moist. Pumps cycled atmospheric oxygen, running off powerpacks. The same capacitors energized their legs. Those were clumsy. The bodies must be harnessed into a supporting framework, the two flippers and the fluked tail control four mechanical limbs with prehensile feet. But they lurched across the deck, huge, powerful, their hands holding spears and axes and a couple of waterproof machine pistols. Ten of them were now aboard . . . and how many sailors could be spared from the fire?

A rifle bullet wailed. A Seatroll sprayed lead in return. Tigeries crumpled. Their blood was human color.

Flandry rammed home another shell and lobbed it into the sea some distance off. "Why?" screamed a gunner.

"May have been more coming," he said. "I hope hydrostatic shock got 'em." He didn't notice he used Anglic.

Dragoika cast her fish spear. One pistol wielder went down, the prongs in him. He scrabbled at the shaft. Rifles barked, crossbows snapped, driving his mate to shelter between the deckhouse and a lifeboat. Then combat ramped, leaping Tigeries, lumbering Seatrolls, sword against ax, pike against spear, clash, clatter, grunt, shriek, chaos run loose. Several firefighters went for their weapons. Dragoika drummed them back to work. The Seatrolls made for them, to cut them down and let the ship burn. The armed Tigeries tried to defend them. The enemy pistoleer kept the Kursovikian rifle shooters pinned down behind masts and bollards—neutralized. The battle had no more shape than that.

A bullet splintered the planks a meter from Flandry. For a moment, panic locked him where he stood. What to do, what to do? He couldn't die. He mustn't. He was Dominic, himself, with a lifetime yet to live. Outnumbered though they were, the Seatrolls need but wreak havoc till the fire got beyond control and he was done. *Mother! Help me!*

For no sound reason, he remembered Lieutenant Danielson. Rage blossomed in him. He bounded down the ladder and across the main deck. A Seatroll chopped at him. He swerved and continued.

Dragoika's door stood under the poop. He slid the panel aside and plunged into her cabin. It was appointed in barbaric luxury. Sunlight sickled through an oval port, across the bulkhead as the ship rolled, touching bronze candlesticks, woven tapestry, a primitive sextant, charts and navigation tables inscribed on parchment. He snatched what he had left here to satisfy her curiosity, his impeller, buckled the unit on his back with frantic fingers and hooked in his capacitors. Now, that sword, which she hadn't taken time to don. He re-emerged, flicked controls, and rose.

Over the deckhouse! The Seatroll with the machine pistol lay next to it, a hard target for a rifle, himself commanding stem and stern. Flandry drew his blade. The being heard the slight noise and tried awkwardly to look up. Flandry struck. He missed the hand but knocked the gun loose. It flipped over the side.

He whirred aft, smiting from above. "I've got him!" he shouted. "I've got him! Come out and do some real shooting!"

The fight was soon finished. He used a little more energy to help spread the wet sail which smothered the fire.

After dark, Egrima and Buruz again ruled heaven. They cast shivering glades across the waters. Few stars shone through, but one didn't miss them with so much other beauty. The ship plowed northward in an enormous murmurous hush.

Dragoika stood with Flandry by the totem at the prow. She had offered thanks. Kursovikian religion was a paganism more inchoate than any recorded from ancient Terra—the Tigery mind was less interested than the human in finding ultimate causes—but ritual was important. Now the crew had returned to watch or to sleep and they two were alone. Her fur was sparked with silver, her eyes pools of light.

"Our thanks belong more to you," she said softly. "I am high in the Sisterhood. They will be told, and remember."

"Oh, well." Flandry shuffled his feet and blushed.

"But have you not endangered yourself? You explained what scant strength is left in those boxes which keep you alive. And then you spent it to fly about."

"Uh, my pump can be operated manually if need be."

"I shall appoint a detail to do so."

"No need. You see, now I can use the Siravo power-packs. I have tools in my pouch for adapting them."

"Good." She looked awhile into the shadows and luminance which barred the deck. "That one whose pistol you removed—" Her tone was wistful.

"No, ma'am," Flandry said firmly. "You cannot have him. He's the only survivor of the lot. We'll keep him alive and unhurt."

"I simply thought of questioning him about their plans. I know a little of their language. We've gained it from prisoners or parleys through the ages. He wouldn't be too damaged, I think."

"My superiors can do a better job in Highport."

Dragoika sighed. "As you will." She leaned against him, "I've met vaz-Terran before, but you are the first I have really known well." Her tail wagged. "I like you."

Flandry gulped. "I . . . I like you too."

"You fight like a male and think like a female. That's

something new. Even in the far southern islands—" She laid an arm around his waist. Her fur was warm and silken where it touched his skin. Somebody had told him once that could you breathe their air undiluted, the Tigeries would smell like new-mown hay. "I'll have joy of your company."

"Um-m-m . . . uh." *What can I say?*

"Pity you must wear that helmet," Dragoika said. "I'd like to taste your lips. But otherwise we're not made so differently, our two kinds. Will you come to my cabin?"

For an instant that whirled, Flandry was tempted. He had everything he could do to answer. It wasn't based on past lectures about taking care not to offend native mores, nor on principle, nor, most certainly, on fastidiousness. If anything, her otherness made her the more piquant. But he couldn't really predict what she might do in a close relationship, and—

"I'm deeply sorry," he said. "I'd love to, but I'm under a—" what was the word?—"a geas."

She was neither offended nor much surprised. She had seen a lot of different cultures. "Pity," she said. "Well, you know where the forecastle is. Goodnight." She padded aft. En route, she stopped to collect Ferok.

—and besides, those fangs were awfully intimidating.

CHAPTER FIVE

When Lord Hauksberg arrived in Highport, Admiral Enriques and upper-echelon staff had given a formal welcoming party for their distinguished visitor and his aides as protocol required. Hauksberg was expected to reciprocate on the eve of departure. Those affairs were predictably dull. In between, however, he invited various officers to small gatherings. A host of shrewd graciousness, he thus blunted resentment which he was bound to cause by his interviewing of overworked men and his diversion of already inadequate armed forces to security duty.

"I still don't see how you rate," Jan van Zuyl complained from the bunk where he sprawled. "A lousy ensign like you."

"You're an ensign yourself, me boy," Flandry reminded him from the dresser. He gave his blue tunic a final tug, pulled on his white gloves, and buffed the jetflare insignia on his shoulders.

"Yes, but not a lousy one," said his roommate.

"I'm a hero. Remember?"

"I'm a hero too. We're all heroes." Van Zuyl's gaze prowled their dismal little chamber. The girlie animations hardly brightened it. "Give L'Etoile a kiss for me."

"You mean she'll be there?" Flandry's pulses jumped.

"She was when Carruthers got invited. Her and Sharine and—"

"Carruthers is a lieutenant j.g. Therefore he is ex officio a liar. Madame Cepheid's choicest items are not available to anyone below commander."

"He swears milord had 'em on hand, and in hand, for the occasion. So he lies. Do me a favor and elaborate the fantasy on your return. I'd like to keep that particular illusion."

"You provide the whisky and I'll provide the tales." Flandry adjusted his cap to micrometrically calculated rakishness.

"Mercenary wretch," van Zuyl groaned. "Anyone else would lie for pleasure and prestige."

"Know, O miserable one, that I possess an inward serenity which elevates me far beyond any need for your esteem. Yet not beyond need for your booze. Especially after the last poker game. And a magnificent evening to you. I shall return."

Flandry proceeded down the hall and out the main door of the junior officer's dorm. Wind struck viciously at him. Sea-level air didn't move fast, being too dense, but on this mountaintop Saxo could energize storms of more than terrestroid ferocity. Dry snow hissed through chill and clamor. Flandry wrapped his cloak about him with a sigh for lost appearances, hung onto his cap, and ran. At his age he had soon adapted to the gravity.

HQ was the largest building in Highport, which didn't say much, in order to include a level of guest suites. Flandry had remarked on that to Commander Abrams, in one of their conversations following the numerous times he'd been summoned for further questioning about his experience with the Tigeries. The Intelligence chief had a knack for putting people at their ease. "Yes, sir, quite a few of my messmates have wondered if—uh—"

"If the Imperium has sludge on the brain, taking up shipping space with luxuries for pestiferous junketeers that might've been used to send us more equipment. Hey?" Abrams prompted.

"Uh . . . nobody's committing *lèse majesté,* sir."

"The hell they aren't. But I guess you can't tell me so right out. In this case, though, you boys are mistaken." Abrams jabbed his cigar at Flandry. "Think, son. We're here for a political purpose. So we need political support. We won't get it by antagonizing courtiers who take champagne and lullaby beds for granted. Tell your friends that silly-looking hotel is an investment."

Here's where I find out. A scanner checked Flandry and opened the door. The lobby beyond was warm! It was also full of armed guards. They saluted and let him by with envious glances. But as he went up the gravshaft, his self-confidence grew thinner. Rather than making him bouncy, the graduated shift to Terran weight gave a sense of unfirmness.

"Offhand," Abrams had said when he learned about the invitation, "milord seems to want you for a novelty. You've a good yarn and you're a talented spinner. Nu, entertain him. But watch yourself. Hauksberg's no fool.

Nor any idler. In fact, I gather that every one of his little soirees has served some business purpose—off-the-record information, impressions of what we really expect will happen and expect to do and how we really feel about the whole schtick."

By that time, Flandry knew him well enough to venture a grin. "How do we really feel, sir? I'd like to know."

"What's your opinion? Your own, down inside? I haven't got any recorder turned on."

Flandry frowned and sought words. "Sir, I only work here, as they say. But . . . indoctrination said our unselfish purpose is to save the land civilizations from ruin; islanders depend on the sea almost as much as the fishfolk. And our Imperial purpose is to contain Merseian expansionism wherever it occurs. But I can't help wondering why anybody wants this planet."

"Confidentially," Abrams said, "my main task is to find the answer to that. I haven't succeeded yet."

—A liveried servant announced Flandry. He stepped into a suite of iridescent walls, comfortable loungers, an animation showing a low-gee production of *Ondine*. Behind a buffet table poised another couple of servants, and three more circulated. A dozen men stood conversing: officers of the mission in dress uniform. Hauksberg's staff in colorful mufti. Only one girl was present. Flandry was a little too nervous for disappointment. It was a relief to see Abrams' square figure.

"Ah. Our gallant ensign, eh?" A yellow-haired man set down his glass—a waiter with a tray was there before he had completed the motion—and sauntered forth. His garments were conservatively purple and gray, but they fitted like another skin and showed him to be in better physical shape than most nobles. "Welcome. Hauksberg."

Flandry saluted. "My lord."

"At ease, at ease." Hauksberg made a negligent gesture. "No rank or ceremony tonight. Hate 'em, really." He took Flandry's elbow. "C'mon and be introduced."

The boy's superiors greeted him with more interest than hitherto. They were men whom Starkad had darkened and leaned; honors sat burnished on their tunics; they could be seen to resent how patronizingly the Terran staffers addressed one of their own. "—and my concubine, the right honorable Persis d'Io."

"I am privileged to meet you, Ensign," she said as if she meant it.

Flandry decided she was an adequate substitute for L'Etoile, at least in ornamental function. She was equipped almost as sumptuously as Dragoika, and her shimmerlyn gown emphasized the fact. Otherwise she wore a fire ruby at her throat and a tiara on high-piled crow's-wing tresses. Her features were either her own or shaped by an imaginative biosculptor: big green eyes, delicately arched nose, generous mouth, uncommon vivacity. "Please get yourself a drink and a smoke," she said. "You'll need a soothed larynx. I intend to make you talk a lot."

"Uh . . . um—" Flandry barely stopped his toes from digging in the carpet. The hand he closed on a proffered wine glass was damp. "Little to talk about, Donna. Lots of men have, uh, had more exciting things happen to them."

"Hardly so romantic, though," Hauksberg said. "Sailin' with a pirate crew, et cet'ra."

"They're not pirates, my lord," Flandry blurted. "Merchants. . . . Pardon me."

Hauksberg studied him. "You like 'em, eh?"

"Yes, sir," Flandry said. "Very much." He weighed his words, but they were honest. "Before I got to know the Tigeries well, my mission here was only a duty. Now I *want* to help them."

"Commendable. Still, the sea dwellers are also sentient bein's, what? And the Merseians, for that matter. Pity everyone's at loggerheads."

Flandry's ears burned. Abrams spoke what he dared not: "My lord, those fellow beings of the ensign's did their level best to kill him."

"And in retaliation, after he reported, an attack was made on a squadron of theirs," Hauksberg said sharply. "Three Merseians were killed, plus a human. I was bein' received by Commandant Runei at the time. Embarrassin'."

"I don't doubt the Fodaich stayed courteous to the Emperor's representative," Abrams said. "He's a charming scoundrel when he cares to be. But my lord, we have an authorized, announced policy of paying back any attacks on our mission." His tone grew sardonic. "It's a peaceful, advisory mission, in a territory claimed by neither empire. So it's entitled to protection. Which means that bush-whacking its personnel has got to be made expensive."

"And if Runei ordered a return raid?" Hauksberg challenged.

"He didn't, my lord."

"Not yet. Bit of evidence for Merseia's conciliatory attitude, what? Or could be my presence influenced Runei. One day soon, though, if these skirmishes continue,

a real escalation will set in. Then everybody'll have the
devil's personal job controllin' the degree of escalation.
Might fail. The time to stop was yesterday."

"Seems to me Merseia's escalated quite a big hunk,
starting operations this near our main base."

"The seafolk have done so. They had Merseian help,
no doubt, but it's their war and the landfolk's. No one
else's."

Abrams savaged a cold cigar. "My lord," he growled,
"seafolk and landfolk alike are divided into thousands of
communities, scores of civilizations. Many never heard of
each other before. The dwellers in the Zletovar were
nothing but a nuisance to the Kursovikians, till now. So
who gave them the idea of mounting a concerted attack?
Who's gradually changing what was a stable situation into
a planet-wide war of race against race? Merseia!"

"You overreach yourself, Commander," said Captain
Abdes-Salem reluctantly. The viscount's aides looked
appalled.

"No, no." Hauksberg smiled into the angry brown
face confronting him. "I appreciate frankness. Terra's got
quite enough sycophants without exportin' 'em. How can
I find facts as I'm s'posed to without listening? Waiter—
refill Commander Abrams' glass."

"Just what are the, ah, opposition doing in local
waters?" inquired a civilian.

Abrams shrugged. "We don't know. Kursovikian ships
have naturally begun avoiding that area. We could try
sending divers, but we're holding off. You see, Ensign
Flandry did more than have an adventure. More, yet, than
win a degree of respect and good will among the Tigeries

that'll prove useful to us. He's gathered information about them we never had before, details that escaped the professional xenologists, and given me the data as tightly organized as a limerick. Above the lot, he delivered a live Seatroll prisoner."

Hauksberg lit a cheroot. "I gather that's unusual?"

"Yes, sir, for obvious environmental reasons as well as because the Tigeries normally barbecue any they take."

Persis d'Io grimaced. "Did you say you like them?" she scolded Flandry.

"Might be hard for a civilized being to understand, Donna," Abrams drawled. "We prefer nuclear weapons that can barbecue entire planets. Point is, though, our lad here thought up gadgets to keep that Seatroll in health, things a smith and carpenter could make aboard ship. I better not get too specific, but I've got hopes about the interrogation."

"Why not tell us?" Hauksberg asked. "Surely you don't think anyone here is a Merseian in disguise."

"Probably not," Abrams said. "However, you people are bound on to the enemy's home planet. Diplomatic mission or no, I can't impose the risk on you of carrying knowledge they'd like to have."

Hauksberg laughed. "I've never been called a blabbermouth more tactfully."

Persis interrupted. "No arguments, please, darling. I'm too anxious to hear Ensign Flandry."

"You're on, son," Abrams said.

They took loungers. Flandry received a goldleaf-tipped cigaret from Persis' own fingers. Wine and excitement bubbled in him. He made the tale somewhat better than true: sufficient to drive Abrams into a coughing fit.

"—and so, one day out of Ujanka, we met a ship that could put in a call for us. A flier took me and the prisoner off."

Persis sighed. "You make it sound such fun. Have you seen your friends again since?"

"Not yet, Donna. I've been too busy working with Commander Abrams." In point of fact he had done the detail chores of data correlation on a considerably lower level. "I've been temporarily assigned to this section. I do have an invitation to visit down in Ujanka, and imagine I'll be ordered to accept."

"Right," Captain Menotti said. "One of our problems has been that, while the Sisterhood accepts our equipment and some of our advice, they've remained wary of us. Understandable, when we're so foreign to them, and when their own Seatroll neighbors were never a real menace. We've achieved better liaison with less developed Starkadian cultures. Kursoviki is too proud, too jealous of its privacies, I might say too sophisticated, to take us as seriously as we'd like. Here we may have an entering wedge."

"And also in your prisoner," Hauksberg said thoughtfully. "Want to see him."

"What?" Abrams barked. "Impossible!"

"Why?"

"Why—that is—"

"Wouldn't fulfill my commission if I didn't," Hauksberg said. "I must insist." He leaned forward. "You see, could be this is a wedge toward something still more important. Peace."

"How so . . . my lord?"

"If you pump him as dry's I imagine you plan, you'll find out a lot about his culture. They won't be the faceless enemy, they'll be real bein's with real needs and desires. He can accompany an envoy of ours to his people. We can—not unthinkable, y' know—we can p'rhaps head off this latest local war. Negotiate a peace between the Kursovikians and their neighbors."

"Or between lions and lambs?" Abrams snapped. "How do you start? They'd never come near any submarine of ours."

"Go out in native ships, then."

"We haven't the men for it. Damn few humans know how to operate a windjammer these days, and sailing on Starkad is a different art anyhow. We should get Kursovikians to take us on a peace mission? Ha!"

"What if their chum here asked 'em? Don't you think that might be worth a try?"

"Oh!" Persis, who sat beside him, laid a hand over Flandry's. "If you could—"

Under those eyes, he glowed happily and said he would be delighted. Abrams gave him a bleak look. "If ordered, of course," he added in a hurry.

"I'll discuss the question with your superiors," Hauksberg said. "But gentlemen, this is s'posed to be a social evenin'. Forget business and have another drink or ten, eh?"

His gossip from Terra was scandalous and comical. "Darling," Persis said, "you mustn't cynicize our guest of honor. Let's go talk more politely, Ensign."

"W-w-with joy, Donna."

The suite was interior, but a viewscreen gave on the

scene outside. Snowfall had stopped; mountaintops lay
gaunt and white beneath the moons. Persis shivered.
"What a dreadful place. I pray we can bring you home
soon."

He was emboldened to say, "I never expected a, uh,
highborn and, uh, lovely lady to come this long, dull,
dangerous way."

She laughed. "I highborn? But thanks. You're sweet."
Her lashes fluttered. "If I can help my lord by traveling
with him . . . how could I refuse? He's working for Terra.
So are you. So should I. All of us together, wouldn't that
be best?" She laughed again. "I'm sorry to be the only girl
here. Would your officers mind if we danced a little?"

He went back to quarters with his head afloat.
Nonetheless, next day he gave Jan van Zuyl a good bottle's
worth.

At the center of a soundproofed room, whose fluoros
glared with Saxo light, the Siravo floated in a vitryl tank
surrounded by machines.

He was big, 210 centimeters in length and thick of
body. His skin was glabrous, deep blue on the back, paler
greenish blue on the stomach, opalescent on the gillcovers.
In shape he suggested a cross between dolphin, seal, and
man. But the flukes, and the two flippers near his middle,
were marvels of musculature with some prehensile
capability. A fleshy dorsal fin grew above. Not far behind
the head were two short, strong arms; except for vestigial
webs, the hands were startlingly humanlike. The head was
big and golden of eyes, blunt of snout, with quivering cilia
flanking a mouth that had lips.

Abrams, Hauksberg and Flandry entered. ("You come

too," the commander had said to the ensign. "You're in this thing ass deep.") The four marines on guard presented arms. The technicians straightened from their instruments.

"At ease," Abrams said. "Freely translated: get the hell back to work. How's she coming, Leong?"

"Encouraging, sir," the scientific chief answered. "Computation from neurological and encephalographic data shows he can definitely stand at least a half-intensity hypnoprobing without high probability of permanent lesion. We expect to have apparatus modified for under-water use in another couple of days."

Hauksberg went to the tank. The swimmer moved toward him. Look met look; those were beautiful eyes in there. Hauksberg was flushing as he turned about. "D'you mean to torture that bein'?" he demanded.

"A light hypnoprobing isn't painful, my lord," Abrams said.

"You know what I mean. Psychological torture. 'Specially when he's in the hands of utter aliens. Ever occur to you to talk with him?"

"That's easy? My lord, the Kursovikians have tried for centuries. Our only advantages over them are that we have a developed theory of linguistics, and vocalizers to reproduce his kind of sounds more accurately. From the Tigeries and xenological records we have a trifle of his language. But only a trifle. The early expeditions investigated this race more thoroughly in the Kimraig area, where the Merseians are now, no doubt for just that reason. The cultural patterns of Charlie here are completely unknown to us. And he hasn't been exactly cooperative."

"Would you be, in his place?"

"Hope not. But my lord, we're in a hurry too. His people may be planning a massive operation, like against settlements in the Chain. Or he may up and die on us. We think he has an adequate diet and such, but how can we be certain?"

Hauksberg scowled. "You'll destroy any chance of gettin' his cooperation, let alone his trust."

"For negotiation purposes? So what have we lost? But we won't necessarily alienate him forever. We don't know his psyche. He may well figure ruthlessness is in the day's work. God knows Tigeries in small boats get short shrift from any Seatrolls they meet. And—" The great blue shape glided off to the end of the tank—"he looks pretty, but he is no kin of you or me or the landfolk."

"He thinks. He feels."

"Thinks and feels what? I don't know. I do know he isn't even a fish. He's homeothermic; his females give live birth and nurse their young. Under high atmospheric pressure, there's enough oxygen dissolved in water to support an active metabolism and a good brain. That must be why intelligence evolved in the seas: biological competition like you hardly ever find in the seas of Terra-type planets. But the environment is almost as strange to us as Jupiter."

"The Merseians get along with his kind."

"Uh-huh. They took time to learn everything we haven't. We've tried to xenologize ourselves, in regions the conflict hasn't reached so far, but the Merseians have always found out and arranged trouble."

"Found out how?" Hauksberg pounced. "By spies?"

"No, surveillance. 'Bout all that either side has available. If we could somehow get access to their undersea information—" Abrams snapped his mouth shut and pulled out a cigar.

Hauksberg eased. He smiled. "Please don't take me wrong, Commander. Assure you I'm not some weepin' idealist. You can't make an omelet, et cet'ra. I merely object to breakin' every egg in sight. Rather messy, that." He paused. "Won't bother you more today. But I want a full report on this project to date, and regular bulletins. I don't forbid hypnoprobin' categorically, but I will not allow any form of torture. And I'll be back." He couldn't quite suppress a moue of distaste. "No, no, thanks awf'lly but you needn't escort me out. Good day, gentlemen."

The door closed on his elegance. Abrams went into a conference with Leong. They talked low. The hum, click, buzz of machines filled the room, which was cold. Flandry stood staring at the captive he had taken.

"A millo for 'em," Abrams said.

Flandry started. The older man had joined him on cat feet. "Sir?"

"Your thoughts. What're you turning over in your mind, besides the fair d'Io?"

Flandry blushed. "I was wondering, sir. Hau—milord was right. You are pushing ahead terribly fast, aren't you?"

"Got to."

"No," said Flandry earnestly. "Pardon, sir, but we could use divers and subs and probes to scout the Zletovar. Charlie here has more value in the long run, for study. I've read what I could find about the Seatrolls. They *are* an unknown quantity. You need a lot more information before you can be sure that any given kind of questioning will show results."

Beneath lowered bushy brows, behind a tobacco cloud, Abrams regarded him. "Telling me my business?" His tone was mild.

"No, sir. Certainly not. I—I've gotten plenty of respect for you." The idea flamed. "Sir! You do have more information than you admit! A pipeline to—"

"Shut up." The voice stayed quiet, but Flandry gulped and snapped to an automatic brace. "Keep shut up. Understand?"

"Y-yes, sir."

Abrams glanced at his team. None of them had noticed. "Son," he murmured, "you surprise me. You really do. You're wasted among those flyboys. Ever considered transferring to the spyboys?"

Flandry bit his lip. "All right," Abrams said. "Tell uncle. Why don't you like the idea?"

"It—I mean—No, sir, I'm not suited."

"You look bundled to the ears to me. Give me a break. Talk honest. I don't mind being called a son of a bitch. I've got my birth certificate."

"Well—" Flandry rallied his courage. "This is a dirty business, sir."

"Hm. You mean for instance right here? Charlie?"

"Yes, sir. I . . . well, I sort of got sent to the Academy. Everybody took for granted I'd go. So did I. I was pretty young."

Abrams' mouth twitched upward.

"I've . . . started to wonder, though," Flandry stumbled. "Things I heard at the party . . . uh, Donna d'Io said—You know, sir, I wasn't scared in that sea action, and afterward it seemed like a grand, glorious victory. But now I—I've begun remembering the dead. One Tiger took a whole day to die. And Charlie, he doesn't so much as know what's going to happen to him!"

Abrams smoked awhile. "All beings are brothers, eh?" he said.

"No, sir, not exactly, but—"

"Not exactly? You know better'n that. They aren't! Not even all men are. Never have been. Sure, war is degrading. But there are worse degradations. Sure, peace is wonderful. But you can't always have peace, except in death, and you most definitely can't have a peace that isn't founded on hard common interest, that doesn't pay off for everybody concerned. Sure, the Empire is sick. But she's ours. She's all we've got. Son, the height of irresponsibility is to spread your love and loyalty so thin that you haven't got enough left for the few beings and the few institutions which rate it from you."

Flandry stood motionless.

"I know," Abrams said. "They rammed you through your education. You were supposed to learn what civilization is about, but there wasn't really time, they get so damned few cadets with promise these days. So here you are, nineteen years old, loaded to the hatches with technical information and condemned to make for yourself every philosophical mistake recorded in history. I'd like you to read some books I pack around in micro. Ancient stuff mostly, a smidgin of Aristotle, Machiavelli, Jefferson, Clausewitz, Jouvenel, Michaelis. But that'll take awhile. You just go back to quarters today. Sit. Think over what I said."

❦ ❦ ❦

"Has the Fodaich not seen the report I filed?" asked Dwyr the Hook.

"Yes, of course," Runei answered. "But I want to inquire about certain details. Having gotten into the Terran base, even though your objective was too well guarded to burgle, why did you not wait for an opportunity?"

"The likelihood did not appear great, Fodaich. And dawn was coming. Someone might have addressed me, and my reply might have provoked suspicion. My orders were to avoid unnecessary risks. The decision to leave at once is justified in retrospect, since I did not find my vehicle in the canyon when I returned. A Terran patrol must have come upon it. Thus I had to travel overland to our hidden depot, and hence my delay in returning here."

"What about that other patrol you encountered on the way? How much did they see?"

"Very little, I believe, Fodaich. We were in thick forest, and they shot blindly when I failed to answer their challenge. They did, as you know, inflict considerable damage on me, and it is fortunate that I was then so close to my goal that I could crawl the rest of the way after escaping them."

"*Khr-r-r,*" Runei sighed. "Well, the attempt was worth making. But this seems to make you supernumerary on Starkad, doesn't it?"

"I trust I may continue to serve in honor." Dwyr gathered nerve. "Fodaich, I did observe one thing from afar while in Highport, which may or may not be significant. Abrams himself walked downstreet in close conversation with a civilian who had several attendants—I suspect the delegate from Terra."

"Who is most wonderfully officious," Runei mused, "and who is proceeding on from here. Did you catch anything of what was said?"

"The noise level was high, Fodaich. With the help of aural amplification and focussing, I could identify a few words like 'Merseia.' My impression is that Abrams may be going with him. In such case, Abrams had better be kept under special watch."

"Yes." Runei stroked his chin. "A possibility. I shall consider it. Hold yourself in readiness for a quick departure."

Dwyr saluted and left. Runei sat alone. The whirr of ventilators filled his lair. Presently he nodded to himself, got out his chessboard, and pondered his next move. A smile touched his lips.

CHAPTER SIX

Starkad rotated thrice more. Then the onslaught came.

Flandry was in Ujanka. The principal seaport of Kursoviki stood on Golden Bay, ringed by hills and slashed by the broad brown Pechaniki River. In the West Housing the Sisterhood kept headquarters. Northward and upward, the High Housing was occupied by the homes of the wealthy, each nestled into hectares of trained jungle where flowers and wings and venomous reptiles vied in coloring. But despite her position—not merely captain of the *Archer* but shareholder in a kin-corporation owning a whole fleet, and speaker for it among the Sisterhood— Dragoika lived in the ancient East Housing, on Shiv Alley itself.

"Here my mothers dwelt since the town was founded," she told her guest. "Here Chupa once feasted. Here the staircase ran with blood on the Day of the Gulch. There are too many ghosts for me to abandon." She chuckled, deep in her throat, and gestured around the stone-built room, at furs, carpets, furnishings, books, weapons, bronze vases and candelabra, goblets of glass and seashell, souvenirs and plunder from across a quarter of the planet. "Also, too much stuff to move."

Flandry glanced out the third-floor window. A cobbled way twisted between tenements that could double as fortresses. A pair of cowled males slunk by, swords drawn; a drum thuttered; the yells and stampings and metal on metal of a brawl flared brief but loud. "What about robbers?" he asked.

Ferok grinned. "They've learned better."

He sprawled on a couch whose curves suggested a ship. Likewise did his skipper and Iguraz, a portly grizzled male who had charge of Seatraders' Castle. In the gloom of the chamber, their eyes and jewelry seemed to glow. The weather outside was bright but chill. Flandry was glad he had chosen to wear a thick coverall on his visit. They wouldn't appreciate Terran dress uniform anyhow.

"I don't understand you people," Dragoika said. She leaned forward and sniffed the mild narcotic smoke from a brazier. "Good to see you again, Dommaneek, but I *don't* understand you. What's wrong with a fight now and then? And—after personally defeating the vaz-Siravo— you come here to babble about making peace with them!"

Flandry turned. The murmur of his airpump seemed to grow in his head. "I was told to broach the idea," he replied.

"But you don't like it yourself?" Iguraz wondered. "Then why beneath heaven do you speak it?"

"Would you tolerate insubordination?" Flandry said.

"Not at sea," Dragoika admitted. "But land is different."

"Well, if nothing else, we vaz-Terran here find ourselves in a situation like sailors." Flandry tried to ease his nerves by pacing. His boots felt heavy.

"Why don't you simply wipe out the vaz-Siravo for us?" Ferok asked. "Shouldn't be hard if your powers are as claimed."

Dragoika surprised Flandry by lowering her tendrils and saying, "No such talk. Would you upset the world?" To the human: "The Sisterhood bears them no vast ill will. They must be kept at their distance like any other dangerous beasts. But if they would leave us alone there would be no occasion for battle."

"Perhaps they think the same," Flandry said. "Since first your people went to sea, you have troubled them."

"The oceans are wide. Let them stay clear of our islands."

"They cannot. Sunlight breeds life, so they need the shoals for food. Also, you go far out to chase the big animals and harvest weed. They have to have those things too." Flandry stopped, tried to run a hand through his hair, and struck his helmet. "I'm not against peace in the Zletovar myself. If nothing else, because the vaz-Merseian would be annoyed. They started this arming of one folk against another, you know. And they must be preparing some action here. What harm can it do to talk with the vaz-Siravo?"

"How do so?" Iguraz countered. "Any Toborko who went below'd be slaughtered out of hand, unless you equipped her to do the slaughtering herself."

"Be still," Dragoika ordered. "I asked you here because you have the records of what ships are in, and

Ferok because he's Dommaneek's friend. But this is female talk."

The Tigeries took her reproof in good humor. Flandry explained: "The delegates would be my people. We don't want to alarm the seafolk unduly by arriving in one of our own craft. But we'll need a handy base. So we ask for ships of yours, a big enough fleet that attack on it is unlikely. Of course, the Sisterhood would have to ratify any terms we arrived at."

"That's not so easy," Dragoika said. "The Janjevar va-Radovik reaches far beyond Kursovikian waters. Which means, I suppose, that many different Siravo interests would also be involved in any general settlement." She rubbed her triangular chin. "Nonetheless . . . a local truce, if nothing else . . . hunh, needs thinking about—"

And then, from the castle, a horn blew.

Huge, brazen, bellows-driven, it howled across the city. The hills echoed. Birds stormed from trees. *Hoo-hoo! Fire, flood, or foe! To arms, to arms! Hoo, hoo-hoo, hoo-oo!*

"What the wreck?" Ferok was on his feet, snatching sword and shield from the wall, before Flandry had seen him move. Iguraz took his ponderous battleax. Dragoika crouched where she was and snarled. Bronze and crystal shivered.

"Attack?" Flandry cried among the horn-blasts. "But they can't!"

The picture unreeled for him. The mouth of Golden Bay was guarded by anchored hulks. Swimmers under-water might come fairly close, unseen by those garrisons, but never past. And supposing they did, they still had kilometers to go before they reached the docks, which with Seatraders' Castle commanded that whole face of Ujanka. They might, of course, come ashore well outside, as at Whitestrands, and march overland on their mechanical legs. The city was unwalled. But no, each outlying house was a defense post; and thousands of Tigeries would swarm from town to meet them; and—

Terra had worried about assaults on the archipelago colonies. Ujanka, though, had not seen war for hundreds of years, and that was with other Tigeries. . . . *Hoo, hoo!*

"We'll go look." Dragoika's gorgeous fur stood on end, her tail was rigid, her ears aquiver; but now she spoke as if suggesting dinner and flowed from her couch with no obvious haste. On the way, she slung a sword over her back.

Blaster in hand, Flandry followed her into a hall dominated by a contorted stone figure, three meters high, from the Ice Islands. Beyond an archway, a stair spiraled upward. His shoulders scraped the walls. Arrow slits gave some light. Ferok padded behind him, Iguraz wheezed in the rear.

They were halfway to the top when the world said *Crump!* and stones trembled. Dragoika was thrown back against Flandry. He caught her. It was like holding steel and rubber, sheathed in velvet. A rumble of collapsing masonry beat through his helmet. Screams came thin and remote.

"What's happened?" Iguraz bawled. Ferok cursed. Even then, Flandry noted some of his expressions for later use. If there was a later. Dragoika regained balance. "Thanks," she murmured, and stroked the human's arm. "Come." She bounded on.

They emerged on the house tower as a second explosion went off. That one was further away. But thunder rolled loud in Starkad's air. Flandry ran to the parapet. He stared across steeply pitched red tile roofs whose beam ends were carved with flowers and monster heads. Northward, beyond these old gray walls, the High Housing lifted emerald green, agleam with villas. He could see the Concourse pylon, where Pride's Way, the Upland Way, the Great East Road, and The Sun and Moons came together. Smoke made a pillar more tall.

"There!" Ferok yelled. He pointed to sea. Dragoika went to a telescope mounted under a canopy.

Flandry squinted. Light dazzled him off the water. He found the hulks, out past the Long Moles. They lay ablaze. Past them—Dragoika nodded grimly and pulled him to her telescope.

Where the bay broadened, between Whitestrands to west and Sorrow Cliff to east, a whale shape basked. Its hide was wet metal. A turret projected amidships; Flandry could just see that it stood open and held a few shapes not unlike men. Fore and aft were turrets more low, flat, with jutting tubes. As he looked, fire spat from one of those dragon snouts. A moment later, smoke puffed off the high square wall of Seatraders' Castle. Stones avalanched onto the wharf below. One of the ships which crowded the harbor was caught under them. Her mast reeled and broke, her hull settled. Noise rolled from waterfront to hills and back again.

"Lucifer! That's a submarine!"

And nothing like what he had fought. Yonder was a Merseian job, probably nuclear-propelled, surely Merseian crewed. She wasn't very big, some twenty meters in length, must have been assembled here on Starkad. Her guns, though of large caliber, were throwing chemical H.E. So the enemy wasn't introducing atomics into this war. (Yet. When somebody did, all hell would let out for noon.) But in this soup of an atmosphere, the shock waves were ample to knock down a city which had no defenses against them.

"We'll burn!" Ferok wailed.

On this planet, no one was ashamed to stand in terror of fire. Flandry raced through an assessment. Detested hours and years of psych drill at the Academy paid off. He knew rage and fear, his mouth was dry and his heart slammed, but emotion didn't get in the way of logic. Ujanka wouldn't go up fast. Over the centuries, stone and tile had replaced wood nearly everywhere. But if fire started among the ships, there went something like half the strength of Kursoviki. And not many shells were needed for that.

Dragoika had had the same thought. She wheeled to glare across the Pechaniki, where the Sisterhood centrum lifted a green copper dome from the West Housing. Her mane fluttered wild. "Why haven't they rung Quarters?"

"Surely none need reminding," Iguraz puffed. To Flandry: "Law is that when aught may threaten the ships, their crews are to report aboard and take them out on the bay."

A shell trundled overhead. Its impact gouted near Humpback Bridge.

"But today they may indeed forget," Dragoika said between her fangs. "They may panic. Those tallywhackers yonder must've done so, not to be hanging on the bell ropes now." She started forward. "Best I go there myself. Ferok, tell them not to await me on the *Archer*."

Flandry stopped her. She mewed anger. "Apology-of-courage," he said. "Let's try calling first."

"Call—argh, yes, you've given 'em a radio, haven't you? My brain's beaten flat."

Crash! Crash! The bombardment was increasing. As yet it seemed almost random. The idea must be to cause terror and conflagration as fast as possible.

Flandry lifted wristcom to helmet speaker and tuned the Sisters' waveband. His hope that someone would be at the other end was not great. He let out a breath when a female voice replied, insect small beneath whistle and boom: "Ey-ya, do you belong to the vaz-Terran? I could not raise any one of you."

No doubt all switchboards're flooded with yammer from our men in Ujanka, Flandry thought. He couldn't see their dome in the hills, but he could imagine the scene. Those were Navy too, of course—but engineers, technicians, hitherto concerned merely with providing a few gadgets and training Tigeries in the use of same. Nor was their staff large. Other regions, where the war was intense, claimed most of what Terra could offer. (Five thousand or so men get spread horribly thin across an entire world; and then a third of them are not technical but combat and intelligence units, lest Runei feel free to gobble the whole mission.) Like him, the Ujanka team had sidearms and weaponless flitters: nothing else.

"Why haven't Quarters been rung?" Flandry demanded as if he'd known the law his whole life.

"But no one thought—"

"So start thinking!" Dragoika put her lips close to Flandry's wrist. Her bosom crowded against him. "I see no sign of craft readying to stand out."

"When that thing waits for them?"

"They'll be safer scattered than docked," Dragoika said. "Ring the call."

"Aye. But when do the vaz-Terran come?"

"Soon," Flandry said. He switched to the team band.

"I go now," Dragoika said.

"No, wait, I beg you. I may need you to . . . to help." *I would be so lonely on this tower.* Flandry worked the signal button with an unsteady forefinger. This microunit couldn't reach Highport unless the local 'caster relayed, but he could talk to someone in the dome, if anybody noticed a signal light, if every circuit wasn't tied up— *Brrum!* A female loped down Shiv Alley. Two males followed, their young in their arms, screaming.

"Ujanka Station, Lieutenant Kaiser." Shellburst nearly drowned the Anglic words. Concussion struck like a fist. The tower seemed to sway.

"Flandry here." He remembered to overlook naming his rank, and crisped his tone. "I'm down on the east side. Have you seen what's on the bay?"

"Sure have. A sub—"

"I know. Is help on the way?"

"No."

"What? But that thing's Merseian! It'll take this town apart unless we strike."

"Citizen," said the voice raggedly, "I've just signed off

from HQ. Recon reports the greenskin air fleet at hover in the stratosphere. Right over your head. Our fliers are scrambled to cover Highport. They're not going anywhere else."

Reckon they can't at that, Flandry thought. *Let a general dogfight develop, and the result is up for grabs. A Merseian could even break through and lay an egg on our main base.*

"I understand Admiral Enriques is trying to get hold of his opposite number and enter a strenuous protest," Kaiser fleered.

"Never mind. What can you yourselves do?"

"Not a mucking thing, citizen. HQ did promise us a couple of transports equipped to spray firefighting chemicals. They'll fly low, broadcasting their identity. If the gatortails don't shoot them regardless, they should get here in half an hour or so. Now, where are you? I'll dispatch a flitter."

"I have my own," Flandry said. "Stand by for further messages."

He snapped off his unit. From across the river began a high and strident peal.

"Well?" Dragoika's ruby eyes blazed at him.

He told her.

For a moment, her shoulders sagged. She straightened again. "We'll not go down politely. If a few ships with deck guns work close—"

"Not a chance," Flandry said. "That vessel's too well armored. Besides, she could sink you at twice your own range."

"I'll try anyhow." Dragoika clasped his hands. She

smiled. "Farewell. Perhaps we'll meet in the Land of Trees Beyond."

"No!" It leaped from him. He didn't know why. His duty was to save himself for future use. His natural inclination was identical. But he wasn't about to let a bunch of smug Merseians send to the bottom these people he'd sailed with. Not if he could help it!

"Come on," he said. "To my flier."

Ferok stiffened. "I, flee?"

"Who talked about that? You've guns in this house, haven't you? Let's collect them and some assistants." Flandry clattered down the stairs.

He entered the alley with a slugthrower as well as his blaster. The three Tigeries followed, bearing several modern small arms between them. They ran into the Street Where They Fought and on toward Seatraders' Castle.

Crowds milled back and forth. No one had the civilized reflex of getting under cover when artillery spoke. But neither did many scuttle about blinded by terror. Panic would likeliest take the form of a mob rush to the waterfront, with weapons—swords and bows against pentanitro. Sailors shoved through the broil, purpose restored to them by the bells.

A shell smote close by. Flandry was hurled into a clothdealer's booth. He climbed to his feet with ears ringing, draped in multicolored tatters. Bodies were strewn between the walls. Blood oozed among the cobbles. The wounded ululated, most horribly, from beneath a heap of fallen stones.

Dragoika lurched toward him. Her black and orange fur was smeared with red. "Are you all right?" he shouted.

"Aye." She loped on. Ferok accompanied them. Iguraz lay with a smashed skull, but Ferok had gathered his guns.

By the time he reached the castle, Flandry was reeling. He entered the forecourt, sat down beside his flitter, and gasped. Dragoika called males down from the parapets and armed them. After a while, Flandry adjusted his pump. An upward shift in helmet pressure made his abused eardrums protest, but the extra oxygen restored some vitality.

They crowded into the flitter. It was a simple passenger vehicle which could hold a score or so if they filled seats and aisle and rear end. Flandry settled himself at the board and started the grav generators. Overloaded, the machine rose sluggishly. He kept low, nigh shaving the heads of the Tigeries outside, until he was across the river and past the docks and had a screen of forest between him and the bay.

"You're headed for Whitestrands," Dragoika protested.

"Of course," Flandry said. "We want the sun behind us."

She got the idea. Doubtless no one else did. They huddled together, fingered what guns they had; and muttered. He hoped their first airborne trip wouldn't demoralize them.

"When we set down," he said loudly, "everyone jump out. You will find open hatches on the deck. Try to seize them first. Otherwise the boat can submerge and drown you."

"Then their gunners will drown too," said a vindictive voice at his back.

"They'll have reserves." Flandry understood, suddenly and shatteringly, how insane his behavior was. If he didn't get shot down on approach, if he succeeded in landing, he still had one blaster and a few bullet projectors against how many Merseian firespitters? He almost turned around. But no, he couldn't, not in the presence of these beings. Moral cowardice, that's what was the matter with him.

At the beach he veered and kicked in emergency overpower. The vehicle raced barely above the water, still with grisly slowness. A gust threw spray across the windshield. The submarine lay gray, indistinct, and terrible.

"Yonder!" Dragoika screeched.

She pointed south. The sea churned with dorsal fins. Fish-drawn catapult boats had begun to rise, dotting it as far as one could eye. *Of course,* trickled through the cellars of Flandry's awareness. *This has to be largely a Seatroll operation, partly to conserve Merseian facilities, partly to conserve the fiction. That sub's only an auxiliary . . . isn't it? Those are only advisors—well, volunteers this time—at the guns . . . aren't they? But once they've reduced Ujanka's defenses, the Seatrolls will clean the place out.*

I don't give a hiss what happens to Charlie.

An energy bolt tore through the thin fuselage. No one was hit. But he'd been seen.

But he was under the cannon. He was over the deck.

He stopped dead and lowered his wheels. A seat-of-the-pants shiver told him they had touched. Dragoika flung wide the door. Yelling, she led the rush.

Flandry held his flitter poised. These were the worst seconds, the unreal ones when death, which must not be real, nibbled around him. Perhaps ten Merseians were topside, in air helmets and black uniforms: three at either gun, three or four in the opened conning tower. For the moment, that tower was a shield between him and the after crew. The rest wielded blasters and machine pistols. Lightnings raged.

Dragoika had hit the deck, rolled, and shot from her belly. Her chatterbox spewed lead. Flame raked at her. Then Ferok was out, snapping with his own pistol. And more, and more.

The officers in the tower, sheltered below its bulwark, fired. And now the after crew dashed beneath them. Bolts and slugs seethed through the flitter. Flandry drew up his knees, hunched under the pilot board, and nearly prayed.

The last Tigery was out. Flandry stood the flitter upward. His luck had held; she was damaged but not crippled. (He noticed, vaguely, a burn on his arm.) In a wobbling arc, he went above the tower, turned sideways, hung onto his seat with one hand and fired out the open door with the other. Return bursts missed him. However inadequate it was, he had some protection. He cleared the Merseians away.

An explosion rattled his teeth. Motor dead, the flitter crashed three meters down, onto the conning tower.

After a minute, Flandry was back to consciousness. He went on hands and knees across the buckled, tilted fuselage, took a quick peek, and dropped to the bridge deck. A body, still smoking, was in his path. He shoved it aside and looked over the bulwark. The dozen Tigeries who remained active had taken the forward gun and were using it for cover. They had stalled the second gang beneath Flandry. But reinforcements were boiling from the after hatch.

Flandry set his blaster to wide beam and shot.

Again. Again. The crew must be small. He'd dropped—how many?—whoops, don't forget the hatch in the tower itself, up to this place he commanded! No, his flitter blocked the way. . . .

Silence thundered upon him. Only the wind and the slap-slap of water broke it, that and a steady sobbing from one Merseian who lay with his leg blasted off, bleeding to death. Satan on Saturn, they'd done it. They'd actually done it. Flandry stared at his free hand, thinking in a remote fashion how wonderful a machine it was, look, he could flex the fingers.

Not much time to spare. He rose. A bullet whanged from the bows. "Hold off there, you tubehead! Me! Dragoika, are you alive?"

"Yes." She trod triumphant from behind the gun. "What next?"

"Some of you get astern. Shoot anybody who shows himself."

Dragoika drew her sword. "We'll go after them."

"You'll do no such idiot thing," Flandry stormed. "You'll have trouble enough keeping them bottled."

"And you . . . now," she breathed ecstatically, "you can turn these guns on the vaz-Siravo."

"Not that either," Flandry said. God, he was tired! "First, I can't man something so heavy alone and you don't know how to help. Second, we don't want any heroic bastards who may be left below to get the idea they can best serve the cause by dunking the lot of us."

He tuned his communicator. Call the Navy team to come get him and his people off. If they were too scared of violating policy to flush out this boat with anesthetic gas and take her for a prize, he'd arrange her sinking personally. But no doubt the situation would be accepted. Successes don't bring courts-martial and policy is the excuse you make up as you go along, if you have any sense. Call the Sisterhood, too. Have them peal the battle command. Once organized, the Kursovikian ships could drive off the Seatroll armada, if it didn't simply quit after its ace had been trumped.

And then—and then—Flandry didn't know what. By choice, a week abed, followed by a medal and assignment to making propaganda tapes about himself back on Terra. Wasn't going to work that way, however. Merseia had ratcheted the war another step upward. Terra had to respond or get out. He glanced down at Dragoika as she disposed her followers on guard. She saw him and flashed back a grin. He decided he didn't really want out after all.

CHAPTER SEVEN

Runei the Wanderer leaned forward until black-clad shoulders and gaunt green visage seemed to enter the office room of the suite. "My lord," he said, "you know the juridical position of my government. The sea people are sovereign over the Starkadian high seas. At most, landfolk ships may be conceded a limited right of transit—provided the sea people agree. Likewise, outworld craft fly above entirely on their sufferance. You accuse us of escalation? Frankly, I think I showed remarkable forbearance in not ordering my air fleet into action after your attack on a Merseian submarine."

Hauksberg managed a smile. "If I may speak rather frankly in return, Commandant," he said, "the fact that Terra's airborne forces would then have joined the fight may have stayed your hand. Eh?"

Runei shrugged. "In such case, who would have been escalating?"

"By usin' a purely Merseian unit against a, ah, Toborkan city, you've directly involved your planet in the war."

"Retaliation, my lord, and not by Merseia; by the Six-point of Zletovar, using foreign volunteers temporarily detached from duty with their regular units. It is Terra which has long promulgated the doctrine that limited retaliation is not a casus belli."

Hauksberg scowled. Speaking for the Empire, he could not utter his full disapproval of that principle. "Goes far back into our hist'ry, to the era of international wars. We use it these days so our people in remote parts of space'll have some freedom of action when trouble develops, 'stead of havin' to send couriers home askin' for orders. Unfortunate. P'rhaps its abolition can be arranged, at least as between your government and mine. But we'll want guarantees in exchange, y'know."

"You are the diplomat, not I," Runei said. "As of now, I chiefly want back any prisoners you hold."

"Don't know if there were any survivors," Hauksberg said. He knew quite well there were some, and that Abrams wouldn't release them till they'd been interrogated at length, probably hypnoprobed; and he suspected Runei knew he knew. Most embarrassing. "I'll inquire, if you wish, and urge—"

"Thank you," Runei said dryly. After a minute: "Not to ask for military secrets, but what will the next move be of your, *khraich*, allies?"

"Not allies. The Terran Empire is not a belligerent."

"Spare me," Runei snorted. "I warn you, as I have warned Admiral Enriques, that Merseia won't stand idle if the aggressors try to destroy what Merseia has helped create to ameliorate the lot of the sea people."

An opening! "Point o' fact," Hauksberg said, as casually

as he was able, "with the assault on Ujanka repelled, we're tryin' to restrain the Kursovikians. They're hollerin' for vengeance and all that sort o' thing, but we've persuaded 'em to attempt negotiations."

A muscle jumped in Runei's jaw, the ebony eyes widened a millimeter, and he sat motionless for half a minute. "Indeed?" he said, flat-toned.

"Indeed." Hauksberg pursued the initiative he had gained. "A fleet'll depart very soon. We couldn't keep that secret from you, nor conceal the fact of our makin' contact with the Siravoans. So you'll be told officially, and I may's well tell you today, the fleet won't fight except in self-defense. I trust none o' those Merseian volunteers participate in any violence. If so, Terran forces would natur'lly have to intervene. But we hope to send envoys underwater, to discuss a truce with the idea of makin' permanent peace."

"So." Runei drummed his desktop.

"Our xenological information is limited," Hauksberg said. "And o' course we won't exactly get childlike trust at first. Be most helpful if you'd urge the, ah, Sixpoint to receive our delegation and listen to 'em."

"A joint commission, Terran and Merseian—"

"Not yet, Commandant. Please, not yet. These'll be nothin' but informal preliminary talks."

"What you mean," Runei said, "is that Admiral Enriques won't lend men to any dealings that involve Merseians."

Correct.

"No, no. Nothin' so ungracious. Nothin' but a desire to avoid complications. No reason why the sea people shouldn't keep you posted as to what goes on, eh? But we have to know where we stand with 'em; in fact, we have to know 'em much better before we can make sensible suggestions; and you, regrettably, decline to share your data."

"I am under orders," Runei said.

"Quite. Policy'll need to be modified on both sides before we can cooperate worth mentionin', let alone think about joint commissions. That sort o' problem is why I'm goin' on to Merseia."

"Those hoofs will stamp slowly."

"Hey? Oh. Oh, yes. We'd speak of wheels. Agreed, with the best will in the universe, neither government can end this conflict overnight. But we can make a start, you and us. We restrain the Kursovikians, you restrain the Sixpoint. All military operations suspended in the Zletovar till further notice. You've that much discretionary power, I'm sure."

"I do," Runei said. "You do. The natives may not agree. If they decide to move, either faction, I am bound to support the sea people."

Or if you tell them to move, Hauksberg thought. *You may. In which case Enriques will have no choice but to fight. However, I'll assume you're honest, that you'd also like to see this affair wound up before matters get out of hand. I have to assume that. Otherwise I can only go home and help Terra prepare for interstellar war.*

"You'll be gettin' official memoranda and such," he said. "This is preliminary chit-chat. But I'll stay on, myself, till we see how our try at a parley is shapin' up. Feel free to call on me at any time."

"Thank you. Good day, my lord."

"Good day, Com—Fodaich." Though they had been using Anglic, Hauksberg was rather proud of his Eriau.

The screen blanked. He lit a cigaret. Now what? Now you sit and wait, m' boy. You continue gathering reports, conducting interviews, making tours of inspection, but this is past the point of diminishing returns, among these iron-spined militarists who consider you a meddlesome ass. You'll see many an empty hour. Not much amusement here. Good thing you had the foresight to take Persis along.

He rose and drifted from the office to the living room. She sat there watching the animation. *Ondine* again— poor kid, the local tape library didn't give a wide selection. He lowered himself to the arm of her lounger and laid a hand on her shoulder. It was bare, in a low-cut blouse; the skin felt warm and smooth, and he caught a violet hint of perfume.

"Aren't you tired o' that thing?" he asked.

"No." She didn't quite take her eyes from it. Her voice was dark and her mouth not quite steady. "Wish I were, though."

"Why?"

"It frightens me. It reminds me how far we are from home, the strangeness, the—And we're going on."

Half human, the mermaid floated beneath seas which never were.

"Merseia's p'rhaps a touch more familiar," Hauksberg said. "They were already industrialized when humans discovered 'em. They caught onto the idea of space travel fast."

"Does that make them anything like us? Does it make us like . . . like ourselves?" She twisted her fingers together. "People say 'hyperdrive' and 'light-year' so casually. They don't understand. They can't or won't. Too shallow."

"Don't tell me you've mastered the theory," he jollied her.

"Oh, no. I haven't the brain. But I tried. A series of quantum jumps which do not cross the small intervening spaces, therefore do not amount to a true velocity and are not bound by the light-speed limitation . . . sounds nice and scientific to you, doesn't it? You know what it sounds like to me? Ghosts flitting forever in darkness. And have you ever thought about a light-year, one measly light-year, how *huge* it is?"

"Well, well." He stroked her hair. "You'll have company."

"Your staff. Your servants. Little men with little minds. Routineers, yes-men, careerists who've laid out their own futures on rails. They're nothing, between me and the night. I'm sick of them, anyway."

"You've me," he said.

She smiled a trifle. "Present company excepted. You're so often busy, though."

"We'll have two or three Navy chaps with us. Might interest you. Diff'rent from courtiers and bureaucrats."

She brightened further. "Who?"

"Well, Commander Abrams and I got talkin', and next thing I knew I'd suggested he come along as our expert on the waterfolk. We could use one. Rather have that Ridenour fellow, 'course; he's the real authority, insofar as Terra's got any. But on that account, he can't be spared here."

Hauksberg drew in a long tail of smoke. "Obvious dangers involved. Abrams wouldn't leave his post either, if he didn't think this was a chance to gather more information than he can on Starkad. Which could compromise our mission. I still don't know but what I was cleverly maneuvered into co-optin' him."

"That old bear, manipulating you?" Persis actually giggled.

"A shrewd bear. And ruthless. Fanatical, almost. However, he can be useful, and I'll be sure to keep a spot on him. Daresay he'll bring an aide or two. Handsome young officers, hm?"

"You're handsome and young enough for me, Mark." Persis rubbed her head against him.

Hauksberg chucked his cigaret at the nearest disposal. "I'm not so frightfully busy, either."

The day was raw and overcast, with whitecaps on a leaden sea. Wind piped in rigging; timbers creaked; the *Archer* rocked. Astern lay the accompanying fleet, hove to. Banners snapped from mastheads. One deck was covered by a Terra-conditioned sealtent. But Dragoika's vessel bore merely a tank and a handful of humans. She and her crew watched impassive as Ridenour, the civilian head of xenological studies, went to release the Siravo.

He was a tall, sandy-haired man; within the helmet, his face was intense. His fingers moved across the console of the vocalizer attached to one wall. Sounds boomed forth which otherwise only a sea dweller's voice bladder could have made.

The long body in the tank stirred. Those curiously human lips opened. An answer could be heard. John Ridenour nodded. "Very well," he said. "Let him go."

Flandry helped remove the cover. The prisoner arched his tail. In one dizzying leap he was out and over the side. Water spouted across the deck.

Ridenour went to the rail and stood staring down. "So long, Evenfall," he said.

"That his real name?" Flandry asked.

"What the phrase means, roughly," the xenologist answered. He straightened. "I don't expect anyone'll show for some hours. But be ready from 1500. I want to study my notes."

He walked to his cabin. Flandry's gaze followed him. *How much does he know?* the ensign wondered. *More'n he possibly could learn from our Charlie, or from old records, that's for sure. Somehow Abrams has arranged—Oh, God, the shells bursting in Ujanka!*

He fled that thought and pulled his gaze back, around the team who were to go undersea. A couple of assistant xenologists; an engineer ensign and four burly ratings with some previous diving experience. They were almost more alien to him than the Tigeries.

The glory of having turned the battle of Golden Bay was blown away on this mordant wind. So, too, was the intoxicating sequel: that he, Dominic Flandry, was no longer a wet-eared youngster but appreciated as he deserved, promised a citation, as the hero of all Kursoviki, the one man who could talk the landfolk into attempting peace. What that amounted to, in unromantic fact, was that he must go along with the Terran envoys, so their mission would have his full approval in Tigery eyes. And Ridenour had told him curtly to keep out of the way.

Jan van Zuyl was luckier!

Well—Flandry put on his best nonchalance and strolled to Dragoika. She regarded him gravely. "I hate your going down," she said.

"Nonsense," he said. "Wonderful adventure. I can't wait."

"Down where the bones of our mothers lie, whom they drowned," she said. "Down where there is no sun, no moons, no stars, only blackness and cold sliding currents. Among enemies and horrors. Combat was better."

"I'll be back soon. This first dive is just to ask if they'll let us erect a dome on the bottom. Once that's done, your fleet can go home."

"How long will you be there yourself, in the dome?"

"I don't know. I hope for not more than a few days. If things look promising, I—" Flandry preened—"won't be needed so much. They'll need me more on land again."

"I will be gone by then," Dragoika said. "The *Archer* still has an undelivered cargo, and the Sisterhood wants to take advantage of the truce while it lasts."

"You'll return, won't you? Call me when you do, and I'll flit straight to Ujanka." He patted her hand.

She gripped his. "Someday you will depart forever."

"Mm . . . this isn't my world."

"I would like to see yours," she said wistfully. "The stories we hear, the pictures we see, like a dream. Like the lost island. Perhaps it is in truth?"

"I fear not." Flandry wondered why the Eden motif was universal in the land cultures of Starkad. Be interesting to know. Except for this damned war, men could come here and really study the planet. He thought he might like to join them.

But no. There was little pure research, for love, in the Empire any more. Outwardness had died from the human spirit. Could that be because the Time of Troubles had brutalized civilization? Or was it simply that when he saw he couldn't own the galaxy and consolidated what little he had, man lost interest in anything beyond himself? No doubt the ancient eagerness could be regained. But first the Empire might have to go under. And he was sworn to defend it. *I better read more in those books of Abrams'. So far they've mainly confused me.*

"You think high thoughts," Dragoika said.

He tried to laugh. "Contrariwise. I'm thinking about food, fun, and females."

"Yes. Females." She stood quiet a while, before she too laughed. "I can try to provide the fun, anyhow. What say you to a game of Yavolak?"

"I haven't yet straightened out those cursed rules," Flandry said. "But if we can get a few players together, I have some cards with me and there's a Terran game called poker."

—A head rose sleek and blue from the waves. Flandry couldn't tell if it belonged to Evenfall or someone else. The flukes slapped thrice. "That's our signal," Ridenour said. "Let's go."

He spoke by radio. The team were encased in armor which was supposed to withstand pressures to a kilometer's depth. *Wish I hadn't thought of "supposed,"* Flandry regretted. He clumped across the deck and in his turn was lowered over the side. He had a last glimpse of Dragoika, waving. Then the hull was before his faceplate, and then green water. He cast loose, switched his communicator to sonic, and started the motor on his back. Trailing bubbles, he moved to join the others. For one who'd been trained in spacesuit maneuvers, underwater was simple. . . . Damn! He'd forgotten that friction would brake him.

"Follow me in close order," Ridenour's voice sounded in his earplugs. "And for God's sake, don't get trigger happy."

The being who was not a fish glided in advance. The water darkened. Lightbeams weren't needed, though, when they reached bottom; this was a shallow sea. Flandry whirred through a crepuscule that faded into sightlessness. Above him was a circle of dim radiance, like a frosted port. Below him was a forest. Long fronds rippled upward, green and brown and yellow. Massive boles trailed a mesh of filaments from their branches. Shellfish, often immense, covered with lesser shells, gripped lacy, delicately hued coraloid. A flock of crustaceans clanked—no other word would do—across a weed meadow. A thing like an eel wriggled over their heads. Tiny finned animals in rainbow stripes flitted among the sea trees. *Why, the place is beautiful!*

Charlie—no, Evenfall had directed the fleet to a spot in midsea where ships rarely passed. How he navigated was a mystery. But Shellgleam lay near.

Flandry had gathered that the vaz-Siravo of Zletovar lived in, and between, six cities more or less regularly spaced around a circle. Tidehome and Reefcastle were at the end of the Chain. The Kursovikians had long known about them; sometimes they raided them, dropping stones, and sometimes the cities were bases for attacks on Tigery craft. But Shellgleam, Vault, Crystal, and Outlier on the verge of that stupendous downfall of sea bottom called the Deeps—those had been unsuspected. Considering how intercity traffic patterns must go, Flandry decided that the Sixpoint might as well be called the Davidstar. You couldn't make good translations anyway from a language so foreign.

A drumming noise resounded through the waters. A hundred or more swimmers came into view, in formation. They wore skull helmets and scaly leather corselets, they were armed with obsidian-headed spears, axes, and daggers. The guide exchanged words with their chief. They englobed the party and proceeded.

Now Flandry passed above agricultural lands. He saw tended fields, fish penned in wicker domes, cylindrical woven houses anchored by rocks. A wagon passed not far away, a skin-covered torpedo shape with stabilizer fins, drawn by an elephant-sized fish which a Siravo led. Belike he traveled from some cave or depth, because he carried a lantern, a bladder filled with what were no doubt phosphorescent microorganisms. As he approached town, Flandry saw a mill. It stood on an upthrust—go ahead and say "hill"—and a shaft ran vertically from an eccentric drive wheel. Aiming his laser light and adjusting his faceplate lens for telescopic vision, he made out a sphere at the other end, afloat on the surface. So, a tide motor.

Shellgleam hove in sight. The city looked frail, unstable, unreal: what a place to stage that ballet! In this weatherless world, walls and roofs need but give privacy;

they were made of many-colored fabrics, loosely draped so they could move with currents, on poles which gave shapes soaring in fantastic curves. The higher levels were more broad than the lower. Lanterns glowed perpetually at the corners, against night's advent. With little need for ground transport, streets did not exist; but whether to control silt or to enjoy the sight, the builders had covered the spaces between houses with gravel and gardens.

A crowd assembled. Flandry saw many females, holding infants to their breasts and slightly older offspring on leash. Few people wore clothes except for jewelry. They murmured, a low surf sound. But they were more quiet, better behaved, than Tigeries or humans.

In the middle of town, on another hill, stood a building of dressed stone. It was rectangular, the main part roofless and colonnaded; but at the rear a tower equally wide thrust up and up, with a thick glass top just below the surface. If, as presumably was the case, it was similarly sealed further down, it should flood the interior with light. Though the architecture was altogether different, that whiteness reminded Flandry of Terra's Parthenon. He had seen the reconstruction once. . . . He was being taken thither.

A shape darkened the overhead luminance. Looking, he saw a fish team drawing a submarine. The escort was a troop of swimmers armed with Merseian-made guns. Suddenly he remembered he was among his enemies.

CHAPTER EIGHT

Once a dome was established outside town and equipped for the long-term living of men, Flandry expected to make rapid progress in Professor Abrams' Instant Philosophy of History Course. What else would there be to do, except practice the different varieties of thumbtwiddling, until HQ decided that sufficient of his prestige had rubbed off on Ridenour and ordered him back to Highport?

Instead, he found himself having the time of his life.

The sea people were every bit as interested in the Terrans as the Terrans in them. Perhaps more so; and after the horror stories the Merseians must have fed them, it was astonishing that they could make such an effort to get at the truth for themselves. But then, while bonny fighters at need and in some ways quite devoid of pity, they seemed less ferocious by nature than humans, Tigeries, or Merseians.

Ridenour and his colleagues were held to the Temple of Sky, where talk went on endlessly with the powers that were in the Davidstar. The xenologist groaned when his unoccupied followers were invited on a set of tours. "If you were trained, my God, what you could learn!—Well, we simply haven't got any more professionals to use here, so you amateurs go ahead, and if you don't observe in detail I'll personally operate on you with a butter knife."

Thus Flandry and one or another companion were often out for hours on end. Since none of them understood the native language or Eriau, their usual guide was Isinglass, who had some command of Kursovikian and had also been taught by the Merseians to operate a portable vocalizer. (The land tongue had been gotten gradually from prisoners. Flandry admired the ingenuity of the methods by which their technologically backward captors had kept them alive for weeks, but otherwise he shuddered and hoped with all his heart that the age-old strife could indeed be ended.) Others whom he got to know included Finbright, Byway, Zoomboy, and the *weise Frau* Allhealer. They had total individuality, you could no more characterize one of them in a sentence than you could a human.

"We are glad you make this overture," Isinglass said on first acquaintance. "So glad that, despite their helpfulness to us, we told the Merseians to keep away while you are here."

"I have suspected we and the landfolk were made pieces in a larger game," added Allhealer through him. "Fortunate that you wish to resign from it."

Flandry's cheeks burned inside his helmet. He knew too well how little altruism was involved. Scuttlebutt claimed Enriques had openly protested Hauksberg's proposal, and yielded only when the viscount threatened to get him reassigned to Pluto. Abrams approved because any chance at new facts was good, but he was not sanguine.

Nor was Byway. "Peace with the Hunters is a contradiction in terms. Shall the gilltooth swim beside the tail-on-head? And as long as the green strangers offer us assistance, we must take it. Such is our duty to the cities and our dependents."

"Yet evidently, while they support us, their adversaries are bound to support the Hunters," Finbright said. "Best might be that both sets of foreigners withdrew and let the ancient balance return."

"I know not," Byway argued. "Could we win a final victory—"

"Be not so tempted by that as to overlook the risk of a final defeat," Allhealer warned.

"To the Deeps with your bone-picking!" Zoomboy exclaimed. "We'll be late for the theater." He shot off in an exuberant curve.

Flandry did not follow the drama which was enacted in a faerie coraloid grotto. He gathered it was a recently composed tragedy in the classic mode. But the eldritch grace of movement, the solemn music of voices, strings, percussion, the utter balance of every element, touched his roots. And the audience reacted with cries, surges back and forth, at last a dance in honor of author and cast.

To him, the sculptures and oil paintings he was shown were abstract; but as such they were more pleasing than anything Terra had produced for centuries. He looked at fishskin scrolls covered with writing in grease-based ink and did not comprehend. Yet they were so many that they must hold a deal of accumulated wisdom.

Then he got off into mathematics and science, and went nearly delirious. He was still so close to the days when such things had been unfolded for him like a flower that he could appreciate what had been done here.

For the people (he didn't like using the Kursovikian name "Siravo" in their own home, and could certainly never again call them Seatrolls) lived in a different conceptual universe from his. And though they were handicapped—fireless save for volcanic outlets where glass was made as a precious material, metalless, unable to develop more than a rudimentary astronomy, the laws of motion and gravity and light propagation obscured for them by the surrounding water—they had thought their way through to ideas which not only made sense but which drove directly toward insights man had not had before Planck and Einstein.

To them, vision was not the dominant sense that it was for him. No eyes could look far undersea. Hence they were nearsighted by his standards, and the optical centers of their brains appeared to have slightly lower information-processing capability. On the other hand, their perception of tactile, thermal, kinesthetic, olfactory, and less familiar nuances was unbelievably delicate. The upper air was hostile to them; like humans vis-a-vis water, they could control but not kill an instinctive dread.

So they experienced space as relation rather than extension. For them, as a fact of daily life, it was unbounded but finite. Expeditions which circumnavigated the globe had simply given more weight and subtlety to that apprehension.

Reflecting this primitive awareness, undersea mathematics rejected infinity. A philosopher with whom Flandry talked via Isinglass asserted that it was empirically meaningless to speak of a number above factorial N, where N was the total of distinguishable particles in the universe. What could a large number count? Likewise, he recognized zero as a useful notion, corresponding to the null class, but not as a number. The least possible amount must be the inverse of the greatest. You could count from there, on to N!, but if you proceeded beyond, you would get decreasing quantities. The number axis was not linear but circular.

Flandry wasn't mathematician enough to decide if the system was entirely self-consistent. As far as he could tell, it was. It even went on to curious versions of negatives, irrationals, imaginaries, approximational calculus, differential geometry, theory of equations, and much else of whose Terran equivalents he was ignorant.

Physical theory fitted in. Space was regarded as quantized. Discontinuities between kinds of space were accepted. That might only be an elaboration of the every-day—the sharp distinction between water, solid ground, and air—but the idea of layered space accounted well for experimental data and closely paralleled the relativistic concept of a metric varying from point to point, as well as the wave-mechanical basis of atomistics and the hyper-drive.

Nor could time, in the thought of the People, be infinite. Tides, seasons, the rhythm of life all suggested a universe which would eventually return to its initial state and resume a cycle which it would be semantically empty to call endless. But having no means of measuring time with any precision, the philosophers had concluded that it was essentially immeasurable. They denied simultaneity; how could you say a distant event happened simultaneously with a near one, when news of the former must be brought by a swimmer whose average speed was unpredictable? Again the likeness to relativity was startling.

Biology was well developed in every macroscopic facet, including genetic laws. Physics proper, as opposed to its conceptual framework, was still early Newtonian, and chemistry little more than an embryo. But Judas on Jupiter, Flandry thought, give these fellows some equipment tailored for underwater use and watch them lift!

"Come along," Zoomboy said impatiently. "Wiggle a flipper. We're off to Reefcastle."

En route, Flandry did his unskilled best to get an outline of social structure. The fundamental Weltanschauung eluded him. You could say the People of the Davidstar were partly Apollonian and partly Dionysian, but those were mere metaphors which anthropology had long discarded and were worse than useless in dealing with nonhumans. Politics (if *that* word was applicable) looked simpler. Being more gregarious and ceremony-minded than most humans, and less impulsive, and finding travel easier than land animals do, the sea dwellers on Starkad tended to form large nations without strong rivalries.

The Zletovar culture was organized hieratically. Governors inherited their positions, as did People in most other walks (swims?) of life. On the individual level there existed a kind of serfdom, binding not to a piece of territory but to the person of the master. And females had that status with respect to their polygamous husbands.

Yet such expressions were misleading. The decision makers did not lord it over the rest. No formalities were used between classes. Merit brought promotion; so had Allhealer won her independence and considerable authority. Failure, especially the failure to meet one's obligation to dependents, brought demotion. For the system did nothing except apportion rights and duties.

Terra had known similar things, in theory. Practice had never worked out. Men were too greedy, too lazy. But it seemed to operate among the People. At least, Isinglass claimed it had been stable for many generations, and Flandry saw no evidence of discontent.

Reefcastle was nothing like Shellgleam. Here the houses were stone and coraloid, built into the skerries off a small island. The inhabitants were more brisk, less contemplative than their bottom-dwelling cousins; Isinglass scoffed at them as a bunch of wealth-grubbing traders. "But I must admit they have bravely borne an undue share of trouble from the Hunters," he added, "and they went in the van of our late attack, which took courage, when none knew about the Merseian boat."

"None?" asked Flandry in surprise.

"I daresay the governors were told beforehand. Otherwise we knew only that when the signal was given our leg-equipped troops were to go ashore and lay waste what they could while our swimmers sank the ships."

"Oh." Flandry did not describe his role in frustrating that. He felt an enormous relief. If Abrams had learned from Evenfall about the planned bombardment, Abrams ought to have arranged countermeasures. But since the information hadn't been there to obtain—Flandry was glad to stop finding excuses for a man who was rapidly becoming an idol.

The party went among the reefs beyond town to see their tide pools. Surf roared, long wrinkled azure-and-emerald billows which spouted white under a brilliant sky. The People frolicked, leaping out of the waves, plunging recklessly through channels where cross-currents ramped. Flandry discarded the staleness of his armor for a plain helmet and knew himself fully alive.

"We shall take you next to Outlier," Isinglass said on the way home to Shellgleam. "It is something unique. Below its foundations the abyss goes down into a night where fish and forests glow. The rocks are gnawed by time and lividly hued. The water tastes of volcano. But the silence—the silence!"

"I look forward," Flandry said.

"—?—. So. You scent a future perfume."

When he cycled through the airlock and entered the Terran dome, Flandry was almost repelled. This narrow, stinking, cheerless bubble, jammed with hairy bodies whose every motion was a jerk against weight! He started peeling off his undergarment to take a shower.

"How was your trip?" Ridenour asked.

"Wonderful," Flandry glowed.

"All right, I guess," said Ensign Quarles, who had been along. "Good to get back, though. How 'bout putting on a girlie tape for us?"

Ridenour flipped the switch of the recorder on his desk. "First things first," he said. "Let's have your report."

Flandry suppressed an obscenity. Adventures got spoiled by being reduced to data. Maybe he didn't really want to be a xenologist.

At the end, Ridenour grimaced. "Wish to blazes my part of the job were doing as well."

"Trouble?" Flandry asked, alarmed.

"Impasse. Problem is, the Kursovikians are too damned efficient. Their hunting, fishing, gathering do make serious inroads on resources, which are never as plentiful in the sea. The governors refuse any terms which don't involve the landfolk stopping exploitation. And of course the landfolk won't. They can't, without undermining their own economy and suffering famine. So I'm trying to persuade the Sixpoint to reject further Merseian aid. That way we might get the Zletovar out of the total-war mess. But they point out, very rightly, that what we've given the Kursovikians has upset the balance of power. And how can we take our presents back? We'd antagonize them—which I don't imagine Runei's agents would be slow to take advantage of." Ridenour sighed. "I still have some hopes of arranging for a two-sided phaseout, but they've grown pretty dim."

"We can't start killing the People again!" Flandry protested.

"Can't we just?" Quarles said.

"After what we've seen, what they've done for us—"

"Grow up. We belong to the Empire, not some barnacle-bitten gang of xenos."

"You may be out of the matter anyhow, Flandry," Ridenour said. "Your orders came through several hours ago."

"Orders?"

"You report to Commander Abrams at Highport. An amphibian will pick you up at 0730 tomorrow, Terran clock. Special duty, I don't know what."

Abrams leaned back, put one foot on his battered desk, and drew hard on his cigar. "You'd really rather've stayed underwater?"

"For a while, sir," Flandry said from the edge of his chair. "I mean, well, besides being interesting, I felt I was accomplishing something. Information—friendship—" His voice trailed off.

"Modest young chap, aren't you? Describing yourself as 'interestin'." Abrams blew a smoke ring. "Oh, sure, I see your point. Not a bad one. Were matters different, I wouldn't've hauled you topside. You might, though, ask what I have in mind for you."

"Sir?"

"Lord Hauksberg is continuing to Merseia in another couple days. I'm going along in an advisory capacity, my orders claim. I rate an aide. Want the job?"

Flandry goggled. His heart somersaulted. After a minute he noticed that his mouth hung open.

"Plain to see," Abrams continued, "my hope is to collect some intelligence. Nothing melodramatic; I hope I'm more competent than that. I'll keep my eyes and ears open. Nose, too. But none of our diplomats, attachés, trade-talk representatives, none of our sources has ever been very helpful. Merseia's too distant from Terra. Almost the only contact has been on the level of brute, chip-on-your-shoulder power. This may be a chance to circulate under fewer restrictions.

"So I ought to bring an experienced, proven man. But we can't spare one. You've shown yourself pretty tough and resourceful for a younker. A bit of practical experience in Intelligence will give you a mighty long leg up, if I do succeed in making you transfer. From your standpoint, you get off this miserable planet, travel in a luxury ship, see exotic Merseia, maybe other spots as well, probably get taken back to Terra and then probably not reassigned to Starkad even if you remain a flyboy—and make some highly useable contacts. How about it?"

"Y-y-yes, *sir!*" Flandry stammered.

Abrams' eyes crinkled. "Don't get above yourself, son. This won't be any pleasure cruise. I'll expect you to forget about sleep and live on stimpills from now till departure, learning what an aide of mine has to know. You'll be saddled with everything from secretarial chores to keeping my uniforms neat. En route, you'll take an electrocram in the Eriau language and as much Merseiology as your brain'll hold without exploding. I need hardly warn you that's no carnival. Once we're there, if you're lucky you'll grind through a drab list of duties. If you're unlucky—if things should go nova—you won't be a plumed knight of the skies any longer, you'll be a hunted animal, and if they take you alive their style of quizzing won't leave you any personality worth having. Think about that."

Flandry didn't. His one regret was that he'd likely never see Dragoika again, and it was a passing twinge. "Sir," he declaimed, "you've got yourself an aide."

CHAPTER NINE

The *Dronning Margrete* was not of a size to land safely on a planet. Her auxiliaries were small spaceships in their own right. Officially belonging to Ny Kalmar, in practice a yacht for whoever was the current viscount, she did sometimes travel in the Imperial service: a vast improvement with respect to comfort over any Navy vessel. Now she departed her orbit around Starkad and accelerated outward on gravitics. Before long she was into clear enough space that she could switch over to hyperdrive and outpace light. Despite her mass, with her engine power and phase frequency, top pseudospeed equalled that of a Planet class warcraft. The sun she left behind was soon dwindled to another star, and then to nothing. Had the viewscreens not compensated for aberration and Doppler effect, the universe would have looked distorted beyond recognition.

Yet the constellations changed but slowly. Days and nights passed while she fled through the marches. Only once was routine broken, when alarms sounded. They were followed immediately by the All Clear. Her force screens, warding off radiation and interstellar atoms, had for a microsecond brushed a larger piece of matter, a pebble estimated at five grams. Though contact with the hull would have been damaging, given the difference in kinetic velocities, and though such meteoroids occur in the galaxy to the total of perhaps 10^{50}, the likelihood of collision was too small to worry about. Once, also, another vessel passed within a light-year and thus its "wake" was detected. The pattern indicated it was Ymirite, crewed by hydrogen breathers whose civilization was nearly irrelevant to man or Merseian. They trafficked quite heavily in these parts. Nonetheless this sign of life was the subject of excited conversation. So big is the cosmos.

There came at last the time when Hauksberg and Abrams sat talking far into the middle watch. Hitherto their relationship had been distant and correct. But with journey's end approaching they saw a mutual need to understand each other better. The viscount invited the commander to dinner *a deux* in his private suite. His chef transcended himself for the occasion and his butler spent considerable time choosing wines. Afterward, at the cognac stage of things, the butler saw he could get away with simply leaving the bottle on the table plus another in reserve, and went off to bed.

The ship whispered, powerplant, ventilators, a rare hail when two crewmen on duty passed in the corridor outside. Light glowed soft off pictures and drapes. A heathery scent in the air underlay curling smoke. After Starkad, the Terran weight maintained by the gravitors was good; Abrams still relished a sense of lightness and often in his sleep had flying dreams.

"Pioneer types, eh?" Hauksberg kindled a fresh cheroot. "Sounds int'restin'. Really must visit Dayan someday."

"You wouldn't find much there in your line," Abrams grunted. "Ordinary people."

"And what they've carved for themselves out of howlin' wilderness. I know." The blond head nodded. "Natural you should be a little chauvinistic, with such a background. But's a dangerous attitude."

"More dangerous to sit and wait for an enemy," Abrams said around his own cigar. "I got a wife and kids and a million cousins. My duty to them is to keep the Merseians at a long arm's length."

"No. Your duty is to help make that unnecess'ry."

"Great, if the Merseians'll cooperate."

"Why shouldn't they? No, wait." Hauksberg lifted a hand. "Let me finish. I'm not int'rested in who started the trouble. That's childish. Fact is, there we were, *the* great power among oxygen breathers in the known galaxy. S'pose they'd been? Wouldn't you've plumped for man acquirin' a comparable empire? Otherwise we'd've been at their mercy. As it was, they didn't want to be at our mercy. So, by the time we took real notice, Merseia'd picked up sufficient real estate to alarm us. We reacted, propaganda, alliances, diplomacy, economic maneuvers, subversion, outright armed clashes now and then. Which was bound to confirm their poor opinion of our intentions. They re-reacted, heightenin' our fears. Positive feedback. Got to be stopped."

"I've heard this before," Abrams said. "I don't believe a word of it. Maybe memories of Assyria, Rome, and Germany are built into my chromosomes, I dunno. Fact is, if Merseia wanted a real detente she could have one today. We're no longer interested in expansion. Terra is old and fat. Merseia is young and full of beans. She hankers for the universe. We stand in the way. Therefore we have to be eaten. Everything else is dessert."

"Come, come," Hauksberg said. "They're not stupid. A galactic government is impossible. It'd collapse under its own weight. We've everything we can do to control what we have, and we don't control tightly. Local self-government is so strong, most places, that I see actual feudalism evolvin' within the Imperial structure. Can't the Merseians look ahead?"

"Oh, Lord, yes. Can they ever. But I don't imagine they want to copy us. The Roidhunate is not like the Empire."

"Well, the electors of the landed clans do pick their supreme chief from the one landless one, but that's a detail."

"Yes, from the Vach Urdiolch. It's not a detail. It reflects their whole concept of society. What they have in mind for their far future is a set of autonomous Merseian-ruled regions. The race, not the nation, counts with them. Which makes them a hell of a lot more dangerous than simple imperialists like us, who only want to be top dogs and admit other species have an equal right to exist. Anyway, so I think on the basis of what information is available. While on Merseia I hope to read a lot of their philosophers."

Hauksberg smiled. "Be my guest. Be theirs. Long's you don't get zealous and upset things with any cloak-and-dagger stuff, you're welcome aboard." The smile faded. "Make trouble and I'll break you."

Abrams looked into the blue eyes. They were suddenly very cold and steady. It grew on him that Hauksberg was not at all the fop he pretended to be.

"Thanks for warning me," the officer of Intelligence said. "But damnation!" His fist smote the table. "The Merseians didn't come to Starkad because their hearts bled for the poor oppressed seafolk. Nor do I think they stumbled in by mistake and are looking for any face-saving excuse to pull out again. They figure on a real payoff there."

"F'r instance?"

"How the devil should I know? I swear none of their own personnel on Starkad do. Doubtless just a hatful of higher-ups on Merseia itself have any idea what the grand strategy is. But those boys see it in clockwork detail."

"Valuable minerals undersea, p'rhaps?"

"Now you must realize that's ridiculous. Likewise any notion that the seafolk may possess a great secret like being universal telepaths. If Starkad per se had something useful, the Merseians could have gotten it more quietly. If it's a base they're after, say for the purpose of pressuring Betelgeuse, then there are plenty of better planets in that general volume. No, they for sure want a showdown."

"I've speculated along those lines," Hauksberg said thoughtfully. "S'pose some fanatical militarists among 'em plan on a decisive clash with Terra. That'd have to be built up to. If nothin' else, lines of communication are so long that neither power could hope to mount a direct attack on the other. So if they escalate things on an intrinsically worthless Starkad—well, eventually there could be a confrontation. And out where no useful planet got damaged."

"Could be," Abrams said. "In fact, it's sort of a working hypothesis for me. But it don't smell right somehow."

"I aim to warn them," Hauksberg said. "Informally and privately, to keep pride and such from complicatin' matters. If we can discover who the reasonable elements are in their government, we can cooperate with those— most discreetly—to freeze the warhawks out."

"Trouble is," Abrams aid, "the whole bunch of them are reasonable. But they don't reason on the same basis as us."

"No, you're the unreasonable one, old chap. You've gotten paranoid on the subject." Hauksberg refilled their glasses, a clear gurgle through the stillness. "Have another drink while I explain to you the error of your ways."

The officers' lounge was deserted. Persis had commandeered from the bar a demi of port but had not turned on the fluoros. Here in the veranda, enough light came through the viewport which stretched from deck to overhead. It was soft and shadowy, caressed a cheek or a lock of hair and vanished into susurrant dark.

Stars were the source, uncountable throngs of them, white, blue, yellow, green, red, cold and unwinking against an absolute night. And the Milky Way was a shining smoke and the nebulae and the sister galaxies glimmered at vision's edge. That was a terrible beauty.

Flandry was far too conscious of her eyes and of the shape enclosed by thin, slightly phosphorescent pajamas, where she faced him in her lounger. He sat stiff on his. "Yes," he said, "yonder bright one, you're right, Donna, a nova. What . . . uh . . . what Saxo's slated to become before long."

"Really?" Her attentiveness flattered him.

"Yes. F-type, you know. Evolves faster than the less massive suns like Sol, and goes off the main sequence more spectacularly. The red giant stage like Betelgeuse is short—then bang."

"But those poor natives!"

Flandry made a forced-sounding chuckle. "Don't worry, Donna. It won't happen for almost a billion years, according to every spectroscopic indication. Plenty of time to evacuate the planet."

"A billion years." She shivered a little. "Too big a number. A billion years ago, we were still fish in the Terran seas, weren't we? All the numbers are too big out here."

"I, uh, guess I'm more used to them." His nonchalance didn't quite come off.

He could barely see how her lips curved upward. "I'm sure you are," she said. "Maybe you can help me learn to feel the same way."

His tunic collar was open but felt tight anyhow. "Betelgeuse is an interesting case," he said. "The star expanded slowly by mortal standards. The autochthons could develop an industrial culture and move out to Alfzar and the planets beyond. They didn't hit on the hyperdrive by themselves, but they had a high-powered interplanetary society when Terrans arrived. If we hadn't provided a better means, they'd have left the system altogether in sublight ships. No real rush. Betelgeuse won't be so swollen that Alfzar becomes uninhabitable for another million years or better. But they had their plans in train. A fascinating species, the Betelgeuseans."

"True." Persis took a sip of wine, then leaned forward. One leg, glimmering silky in the starlight, brushed his. "However," she said, "I didn't lock onto you after dinner in hopes of a lecture."

"Why, uh, what can I do for you, Donna? Glad to, if—" Flandry drained his own goblet with a gulp. His pulse racketed.

"Talk to me. About yourself. You're too shy."

"About me?" he squeaked. "Whatever for? I mean, I'm nobody."

"You're the first young hero I've met. The others, at home, they're old and gray and crusted with decorations. You might as well try to make conversation with Mount Narpa. Frankly, I'm lonesome on this trip. You're the single one I could relax and feel human with. And you've hardly shown your nose outside your office."

"Uh, Donna, Commander Abrams has kept me busy. I didn't want to be unsociable, but, well, this is the first time he'd told me I could go off duty except to sleep. Uh, Lord Hauksberg—"

Persis shrugged. "He doesn't understand. All right, he's been good to me and without him I'd probably be an underpaid dancer on Luna yet. But he does not understand."

Flandry opened his mouth, decided to close it again, and recharged his goblet.

"Let's get acquainted," Persis said gently. "We exist for such a short time at best. Why were you on Starkad?"

"Orders, Donna."

"That's no answer. You could simply have done the minimum and guarded your neck. Most of them seem to. You must have some belief in what you're doing."

"Well—I don't know, Donna. Never could keep out of a good scrap, I suppose."

She sighed. "I thought better of you, Dominic."

"Beg pardon?"

"Cynicism is boringly fashionable. I didn't think you would be afraid to say mankind is worth fighting for."

Flandry winced. She had touched a nerve. "Sort of thing's been said too often, Donna. The words have gone all hollow. I . . . I do like some ancient words. '. . . the best fortress is to be found in the love of the people.' From Machiavelli."

"Who? Never mind. I don't care what some dead Irishman said. I want to know what you care about. You are the future. What did Terra give you, for you to offer your life in return?"

"Well, uh, places to live. Protection. Education."

"Stingy gifts," she said. "You were poor?"

"Not really, Donna. Illegitimate son of a petty nobleman. He sent me to good schools and finally the Naval Academy."

"But you were scarcely ever at home?"

"No. Couldn't be. I mean, my mother was in opera then. She had her career to think of. My father's a scholar, an encyclopedist, and, uh, everything else is sort of incidental to him. That's the way he's made. They did their duty by me. I can't complain, Donna."

"At least you won't." She touched his hand. "My name is Persis."

Flandry swallowed.

"What a hard, harsh life you've had," she mused. "And still you'll fight for the Empire."

"Really, it wasn't bad . . . Persis."

"Good. You progress." This time her hand lingered.

"I mean, well, we had fun between classes and drills. I'm afraid I set some kind of record for demerits. And later, a couple of training cruises, the damnedest things happened."

She leaned closer. "Tell me."

He spun out the yarns as amusingly as he was able.

She cocked her head at him. "You were right fluent there," she said. "Why are you backward with me?"

He retreated into his lounger. "I—I, you see, never had a chance to, uh, learn how to, well, behave in circumstances like—"

She was so near that beneath perfume he caught the odor of herself. Her eyes were half closed, lips parted. "Now's your chance," she whispered. "You weren't afraid of anything else, were you?"

Later, in his cabin, she raised herself to one hand and regarded him for a long moment. Her hair spilled across his shoulder. "And I thought I was your first," she said.

"Why, Persis!" he grinned.

"I felt so—And every minute this evening you knew exactly what you were doing."

"I had to take action," he said. "I'm in love with you. How could I help being?"

"Do you expect me to believe that? Oh, hell, just for this voyage I will. Come here again."

CHAPTER TEN

Ardaig, the original capital, had grown to surround that bay where the River Oiss poured into the Wilwidh Ocean; and its hinterland was now a megalopolis eastward to the Hun foothills. Nonetheless it retained a flavor of antiquity. Its citizens were more tradition-minded, ceremonious, leisurely than most. It was the cultural and artistic center of Merseia. Though the Grand Council still met here annually, and Castle Afon was still the Roidhun's official primary residence, the bulk of government business was transacted in antipodal Tridaig. The co-capital was young, technology-oriented, brawling with traffic and life, seething with schemes and occasional violence. Hence there had been surprise when Brechdan Ironrede wanted the new Navy offices built in Ardaig.

He did not encounter much opposition. Not only did he preside over the Grand Council; in the space service he had attained fleet admiral's rank before succeeding to Handship of the Vach Ynvory, and the Navy remained his special love and expertise. Characteristically, he had offered little justification for his choice. This was his will, therefore let it be done.

In fact he could not even to himself have given fully logical reasons. Economics, regional balance, any such argument was rebuttable. He appreciated being within a short flit of Dhangodhan's serenity but hoped and believed that had not influenced him. In some obscure fashion he simply knew it was right that the instruments of Merseia's destiny should have roots in Merseia's eternal city.

And thus the tower arose, tier upon gleaming tier until at dawn its shadow engulfed Afon. Aircraft swarmed around the upper flanges like seabirds. After dark its windows were a constellation of goblin eyes and the beacon on top a torch that frightened stars away. But Admiralty House did not clash with the battlements, dome roofs, and craggy spires of the old quarter. Brechdan had seen to that. Rather, it was a culmination of them, their answer to the modern skyline. Its uppermost floor, decked by nothing except a level of traffic control automata, was his own eyrie.

A while after a certain sunset he was there in his secretorium. Besides himself, three living creatures were allowed entry. Passing through an unoccupied antechamber before which was posted a guard, they would put eyes and hands to scanner plates in the armored door. Under positive identification, it would open until they had stepped through. Were more than one present, all must be identified first. The rule was enforced by alarms and robotic blasters.

The vault behind was fitted with spaceship-type air recyclers and thermostats. Walls, floor, ceiling were a sable against which Brechdan's black uniform nigh vanished, the medals he wore tonight glittering doubly fierce. The furnishing was usual for an office—desk, communicators, computer, dictoscribe. But in the center a beautifully grained wooden pedestal supported an opalescent box.

He walked thither and activated a second recognition circuit. A hum and swirl of dim colors told him that power had gone on. His fingers moved above the console. Photoelectric cells fired commands to the memory unit. Electromagnetic fields interacted with distorted molecules. Information was compared, evaluated, and assembled. In a nanosecond or two, the data he wanted—ultrasecret, available to none but him and his three closest, most trusted colleagues—flashed onto a screen.

Brechdan had seen the report before, but on an interstellar scale (every planet a complete world, old and infinitely complex) an overlord was doing extraordinarily well if he could remember that a specific detail was known let alone the fact itself. A sizeable party in the Council wanted to install more decision-making machines on that account. He had resisted them. Why ape the Terrans? Look what a state their dominions had gotten into. Personal government, to the greatest extent possible, was less stable but more flexible. Unwise to bind oneself to a single approach, in this unknowable universe.

"*Khraich.*" He switched his tail. Shwylt was entirely correct, the matter must be attended to without delay. An unimaginative provincial governor was missing a radium opportunity to bring one more planetary system into the power of the race.

And yet—He sought his desk. Sensing his absence, the data file went blank. He stabbed a communicator button. On sealed and scrambled circuit, his call flew across a third of the globe.

Shwylt Shipsbane growled. "You woke me. Couldn't you pick a decent hour?"

"Which would be an indecent one for me," Brechdan laughed. "This Therayn business won't wait on our joint convenience. I have checked, and we'd best get a fleet out there as fast as may be, together with a suitable replacement for Gadrol."

"Easy to say. But Gadrol will resent that, not without justice, and he has powerful friends. Then there are the Terrans. They'll hear about our seizure, and even though it's taken place on the opposite frontier to them, they'll react. We have to get a prognostication of what they'll do and a computation of how that'll affect events on Starkad. I've alerted Lifrith and Priadwyr. The sooner the four of us can meet on this problem, the better."

"I can't, though. The Terran delegation arrived today. I must attend a welcoming festival tonight."

"What?" Shwylt's jaws snapped together. "One of *their* stupid rites? Are you serious?"

"Quite. Afterward I must remain available to them. In Terran symbology, it would be grave indeed if the, gr-r-rum, the prime minister of Merseia snubbed the special representative of his Majesty."

"But the whole thing is such a farce!"

"They don't know that. If we disillusion them

promptly we'll accelerate matters off schedule. Besides, by encouraging their hopes for a Starkadian settlement we can soften the emotional impact of our occupying Therayn. Which means I shall have to prolong these talks more than I originally intended. Finally, I want some personal acquaintance with the significant members of this group."

Shwylt rubbed the spines on his head. "You have the strangest taste in friends."

"Like you?" Brechdan jibed. "See here. The plan for Starkad is anything but a road we need merely walk at a precalculated pace. It has to be watched, nurtured, modified according to new developments, almost day by day. Something unforeseeable—a brilliant Terran move, a loss of morale among them, a change in attitude by the natives themselves—anything could throw off the timing and negate our whole strategy. The more subliminal data we possess, the better our judgments. For we do have to operate on their emotions as well as their military logic, and they are an alien race. We need empathy with them. In their phrase, we must play it by ear."

Shwylt looked harshly out of the screen. "I suspect you actually like them."

"Why, that's no secret," Brechdan said. "They were magnificent once. They could be again. I would love to see them our willing subjects." His scarred features drooped a little. "Unlikely, of course. They're not that kind of species. We may be forced to exterminate."

"What about Therayn?" Shwylt demanded.

"You three take charge," Brechdan said. "I'll advise from time to time, but you will have full authority. After the postseizure configuration has stabilized enough for evaluation, we can all meet and discuss how this will affect Starkad."

He did not add he would back them against an outraged Council, risking his own position, if they should make some ruinous error. That went without saying.

"As you wish," nodded Shwylt. "Hunt well."

"Hunt well." Brechdan broke the circuit.

For a space he sat quiet. The day had been long for him. His bones felt stiff and his tail ached from the weight on it. Yes, he thought, one grows old; at first the thing merely creeps forward, a dulling of sense and a waning of strength, nothing that enzyme therapy can't handle—then suddenly, overnight, you are borne on a current so fast that the landscape blurs, and you hear the cataract roar ahead of you.

Dearly desired he to flit home, breathe the purity which blew around Dhangodhan's towers, chat over a hot cup with Elwych and tumble to bed. But they awaited him at the Terran Embassy; and afterward he must return hither and meet with . . . who was that agent waiting down in Intelligence? . . . Dwyr the Hook, aye; and then he might as well bunk here for what remained of the night.

He squared his shoulders, swallowed a stimpill, and left the vault.

His Admiralty worked around the clock. He heard its buzz, click, foot-shuffle, mutter through the shut anteroom door. Because he really had not time for exchanging salutes according to rank and clan with every officer, technician, and guard, he seldom passed that way. Another door opened directly on his main suite of offices.

Opposite, a third door gave on a private corridor which ran black and straight to the landing flange.

When he stepped out onto that, the air was cool and damp. The roof screened the beacon from him and he saw clearly over Ardaig.

It was not a Terran city and knew nothing of hectic many-colored blaze after dark. Ground vehicles were confined to a few avenues, otherwise tubeways; the streets were for pedestrians and gwydh riders. Recreation was largely at home or in ancient theaters and sports fields. Shops—as contrasted to mercantile centers with communicator and delivery systems—were small enterprises, closed at this hour, which had been in the same house and the same family for generations. Tridaig shouted. Ardaig murmured, beneath a low salt wind. Luminous pavements wove their web over the hills, trapping lit windows; aircraft made moving lanterns above; spotlights on Afon simply heightened its austerity. Two of the four moons were aloft, Neihevin and Seith. The bay glowed and sparkled under them.

Brechdan's driver folded arms and bowed. Illogical, retaining that old gaffer when this aircar had a robopilot. But his family had always served the Ynvorys. Guards made their clashing salute and entered the vehicle too. It purred off.

The stimulant took hold. Brechdan felt renewed eagerness. What might he not uncover tonight? Relax, he told himself, *keep patience, wait for the one gem to appear from a dungheap of formalisms. . . . If we must exterminate the Terrans, we will at least have rid the universe of much empty chatter.*

His destination was another offense, a compound of residences and offices in the garish bubble style of the Imperium four hundred years ago. Then Merseia was an up-and-coming planet, worth a legation but in no position to dictate architecture or site. Qgoth Heights lay well outside Ardaig. Later the city grew around them and the legation became an embassy and Merseia could deny requests for expanded facilities.

Brechdan walked the entranceway alone, between rosebushes. He did admire that forlorn defiance. A slave took his cloak, a butler tall as himself announced him to the company. The usual pack of civilians in fancy dress, service attachés in uniform—no, yonder stood the newcomers. Lord Oliveira of Ganymede, Imperial Ambassador to his Supremacy the Roidhun, scurried forth. He was a thin and fussy man whose abilities had on a memorable occasion given Brechdan a disconcerting surprise.

"Welcome, Councillor," he said in Eriau, executing a Terran style bow. "We are delighted you could come." He escorted his guest across the parquet floor. "May I present his Majesty's envoy, Lord Markus Hauksberg, Viscount of Ny Kalmar?"

"I am honored, sir." (Languid manner belied by physical condition, eyes that watched closely from beneath the lids, good grasp of language.)

". . . Commander Max Abrams."

"The Hand of the Vach Ynvory is my shield." (Dense accent, but fluent; words and gestures precisely right, dignified greeting of one near in rank to his master who is your equal. Stout frame, gray-shot hair, big nose, military carriage. So this was the fellow reported by courier to be coming along from Starkad. Handle with care.)

Introductions proceeded. Brechdan soon judged that none but Hauksberg and Abrams were worth more than routine attention. The latter's aide, Flandry, looked alert; but he was young and very junior.

A trumpet blew the At Ease. Oliveira was being especially courteous in following local custom. But as this also meant females were excluded, most of his staff couldn't think what to do next. They stood about in dismal little groups, trying to make talk with their Merseian counterparts.

Brechdan accepted a glass of arthberry wine and declined further refreshment. He circulated for what he believed was a decent minimum time—let the Terrans know that he could observe their rituals when he chose—before he zeroed in on Lord Hauksberg.

"I trust your journey here was enjoyable," he began.

"A bit dull, sir," the viscount replied, "until your naval escort joined us. Must say they put on a grand show; and the honor guard after we landed was better yet. Hope no one minded my taping the spectacle."

"Certainly not, provided you stopped before entering Afon."

"Haw! Your, ah, foreign minister is a bit stiff, isn't he? But he was quite pleasant when I offered my credentials, and promised me an early presentation to his Supremacy."

Brechdan took Hauksberg's arm and strolled him toward a corner. Everyone got the hint; the party plodded on at a distance from where they two sat down below an abominable portrait of the Emperor.

"And how was Starkad?" Brechdan asked.

"Speaking for myself, sir, grim and fascinating," Hauksberg said. "Were you ever there?"

"No." Sometimes Brechdan was tempted to pay a visit. By the God, it was long since he had been on a planet unraped by civilization! Impossible, however, at any rate for the next few years when Starkad's importance must be underplayed. Conceivably near the end—He decided that he hoped a visit would not be called for. Easier to make use of a world which was a set of reports than one whose people had been seen in their own lives.

"Well, scarcely in your sphere of interest, eh, sir?" Hauksberg said. "We are bemused by, ah, Merseia's endeavors."

"The Roidhunate has explained over and over."

"Of course. Of course. But mean to say, sir, if you wish to practice charity, as you obviously do, well, aren't there equal needs closer to home? The Grand Council's first duty is to Merseia. I would be the last to accuse you of neglecting your duty."

Brechdan shrugged. "Another mercantile base would be useful in the Betelgeuse region. Starkad is not ideal, either in location or characteristics, but it is acceptable. If at the same time we can gain the gratitude of a talented and deserving species, that tips the balance." He sharpened his gaze. "Your government's reaction was distressing."

"Predictable, though." Hauksberg sprawled deeper into his antique chromeplated chair. "To build confidence on both sides, until a true general agreement can be reached—" mercifully, he did not say "between our great races"—"the inter-imperial buffer space must remain inviolate. I might add, sir, that the landfolk are no less deserving than the seafolk. Meaningless quibble, who was the initial aggressor. His Majesty's government feels morally bound to help the landfolk before their cultures go under."

"Now who is ignoring needs close to home?" Brechdan asked dryly.

Hauksberg grew earnest. "Sir, the conflict can be ended. You must have received reports of our efforts to negotiate peace in the Zletovar area. If Merseia would join her good offices to ours, a planet-wide arrangement could be made. And as for bases there, why should we not establish one together? A long stride toward real friendship, wouldn't you say?"

"Forgive possible rudeness," Brechdan parried, "but I am curious why your pacific mission includes the chief of Intelligence operations on Starkad."

"As an advisor, sir," Hauksberg said with less enthusiasm. "Simply an advisor who knows more about the natives than anyone else who was available. Would you like to speak with him?" He raised an arm and called in Anglic, which Brechdan understood better than was publicly admitted: "Max! I say, Max, come over here for a bit, will you?"

Commander Abrams disengaged himself from an assistant secretary (Brechdan sympathized; that fellow was the dreariest of Oliveira's entire retinue) and saluted the Councillor. "May I serve the Hand?"

"Never mind ceremony, Max," Hauksberg said in Eriau. "We're not talking business tonight. Merely sounding each other out away from protocol and recorders. Please explain your intentions here."

"Give what facts I have and my opinions for whatever they are worth, if anyone asks," Abrams drawled. "I don't expect I'll be called on very often."

"Then why did you come, Commander?" Brechdan gave him his title, which he had not bothered to do for Hauksberg.

"Well, Hand, I did hope to ask a good many questions."

"Sit down," Hauksberg invited.

Abrams said, "With the Hand's leave?"

Brechdan touched a finger to his brow, feeling sure the other would understand. He felt a higher and higher regard for this man, which meant Abrams must be watched closer than anyone else.

The officer plumped his broad bottom into a chair. "I thank the Hand." He lifted a glass of whisky-and-soda to them, sipped, and said: "We really know so little on Terra about you. I couldn't tell you how many Merseiological volumes are in the archives, but no matter; they can't possibly contain more than a fraction of the truth. Could well be we misinterpret you on any number of important points."

"You have your Embassy," Brechdan reminded him. "The staff includes xenologists."

"Not enough, Hand. Not by a cometary orbit. And in any event, most of what they do learn is irrelevant at my level. With your permission, I'd like to talk freely with a lot of different Merseians. Please keep those talks surveyed, to avoid any appearance of evil." Brechdan and

Abrams exchanged a grin. "Also, I'd like access to your libraries, journals, whatever is public information as far as you're concerned but may not have reached Terra."

"Have you any specific problems in mind? I will help if I can."

"The Hand is most gracious. I'll mention just one typical point. It puzzles me, I've ransacked our files and turned researchers loose on it myself, and still haven't found an answer. How did Merseia come upon Starkad in the first place?"

Brechdan stiffened. "Exploring the region," he said curtly. "Unclaimed space is free to all ships."

"But suddenly, Hand, there you were, active on the confounded planet. Precisely how did you happen to get interested?"

Brechdan took a moment to organize his reply. "Your people went through that region rather superficially in the old days," he said. "We are less eager for commercial profit than the Polesotechnic League was, and more eager for knowledge, so we mounted a systematic survey. The entry for Saxo, in your pilot's manual, made Starkad seem worth thorough study. After all, we too are attracted by planets with free oxygen and liquid water, be they ever so inhospitable otherwise. We found a situation which needed correction, and proceeded to send a mission. Inevitably, ships in the Betelgeuse trade noted frequent wakes near Saxo. Terran units investigated, and the present unhappy state of affairs developed."

"Hm." Abrams looked into his glass. "I thank the Hand. But it'd be nice to have more details. Maybe, buried somewhere among them, is a clue to something our side has misunderstood—semantic and cultural barrier, not so?"

"I doubt that," Brechdan said. "You are welcome to conduct inquiries, but on this subject you will waste your energy. There may not even be a record of the first several Merseian expeditions to the Saxo vicinity. We are not as concerned to put everything on tape as you."

Sensing his coldness, Hauksberg hastened to change the subject. Conversation petered out in banalities. Brechdan made his excuses and departed before midnight.

A good opponent, Abrams, he thought. *Too good for my peace of mind. He is definitely the one on whom to concentrate attention.*

Or is he? Would a genuinely competent spy look formidable? He could be a—yes, they call it a stalking horse—for someone or something else. Then again, that may be what he wants me to think.

Brechdan chuckled. This regression could go on forever. And it was not his business to play watchbeast. The supply of security officers was ample. Every move that every Terran made, outside the Embassy which they kept bugproof with annoying ingenuity, was observed as a matter of course.

Still, he was about to see in person an individual Intelligence agent, one who was important enough to have been sent especially to Starkad and especially returned when wily old Runei decided he could be more valuable at home. Dwyr the Hook might carry information worthy of the Council president's direct hearing. After which Brechdan could give him fresh orders. . . .

In the icy fluorescence of an otherwise empty office,

the thing waited. Once it had been Merseian and young. The lower face remained, as a mask rebuilt by surgery; part of the torso; left arm and right stump. The rest was machine.

Its biped frame executed a surprisingly smooth salute. At such close quarters Brechdan, who had keen ears, could barely discern the hum from within. Power coursed out of capacitors which need not be recharged for several days, even under strenuous use: out through microminiaturized assemblies that together formed a body. "Service to my overlord." A faint metal tone rang in the voice.

Brechdan responded in honor. He did not know if he would have had the courage to stay alive so amputated. "Well met, Arlech Dwyr. At ease."

"The Hand of the Vach Ynvory desired my presence?"

"Yes, yes." Brechdan waved impatiently. "Let us have no more etiquette. I'm fed to the occiput with it. Apology that I kept you waiting, but before I could talk meaningfully about those Terrans I must needs encounter them for myself. Now then, you worked on the staff of Fodaich Runei's Intelligence corps as well as in the field, did you not? So you are conversant both with collated data and with the problems of gathering information in the first place. Good. Tell me in your own words why you were ordered back."

"Hand," said the voice, "as an operative I was useful but not indispensable. The one mission which I and no other might have carried out, failed: to burgle the office of the Terran chief of Intelligence."

"You expected success?" Brechdan hadn't known Dwyr was that good.

"Yes, Hand. I can be equipped with electromagnetic sensors and transducers, to feel out a hidden circuit. In addition, I have developed an empathy with machines. I can be aware, on a level below consciousness, of what they are about to do, and adjust my behavior accordingly. It is analogous to my former perception, the normal one, of nuances in expression, tone, stance on the part of fellow Merseians whom I knew intimately. Thus I could have opened the door without triggering an alarm. Unfortunately, and unexpectedly, living guards were posted. In physical strength, speed, and agility, this body is inferior to what I formerly had. I could not have killed them unbeknownst to their mates."

"Do you think Abrams knows about you?" Brechdan asked sharply.

"No, Hand. Evidence indicates he is ultra-cautious by habit. Those Terrans who damaged me later in the jungle got no good look at me. I did glimpse Abrams in companionship with the other, Hauksberg. This led us to suspect early that he would accompany the delegation to Merseia, no doubt in the hope of conducting espionage. Because of my special capabilities, and my acquaintance with Abrams' working methods, Fodaich Runei felt I should go ahead of the Terrans and await their arrival."

"*Khraich.* Yes. Correct." Brechdan forced himself to look at Dwyr as he would at a fully alive being. "You can be put into other bodies, can you not?"

"Yes, Hand," came from the blank visage. "Vehicles, weapons, detectors, machine tools, anything designed to receive my organic component and my essential prostheses.

I do not take long to familiarize myself with their use. Under his Supremacy, I stand at your orders."

"You will have work," Brechdan said. "In truth you will. I know not what as yet. You may even be asked to burgle the envoy's ship in orbit. For a beginning, however, I think we must plan a program against our friend Abrams. He will expect the usual devices; you may give him a surprise. If you do, you shall not go unhonored."

Dwyr the Hook waited to hear further.

Brechdan could not forebear taking a minute for plain fleshly comradeship. "How were you hurt?" he asked.

"In the conquest of Janair, Hand. A nuclear blast. The field hospital kept me alive and sent me to base for regeneration. But the surgeons there found that the radiation had too much deranged my cellular chemistry. At that point I requested death. They explained that techniques newly learned from Gorrazan gave hope of an alternative, which might make my service quite precious. They were correct."

Brechdan was momentarily startled. This didn't sound right—Well, he was no biomedic.

His spirits darkened. Why pretend pity? You can't be friends with the dead. And Dwyr was dead, in bone, sinew, glands, gonads, guts, everything but a brain which had nothing left except the single-mindedness of a machine. So, use him. That was what machines were for.

Brechdan took a turn around the room, hands behind back, tail unrestful, scar throbbing. "Good," he said. "Let us discuss procedure."

CHAPTER ELEVEN

"Oh, no," Abrams had said. "I thank most humbly the government of his Supremacy for this generous offer, but would not dream of causing such needless trouble and expense. True, the Embassy cannot spare me an airboat. However, the ship we came in, *Dronning Margrete,* has a number of auxiliaries now idle. I can use one of them."

"The Commander's courtesy is appreciated," bowed the official at the other end of the vidiphone line. "Regrettably, though, law permits no one not of Merseian race to operate within the Korychan System a vessel possessing hyperdrive capabilities. The Commander will remember that a Merseian pilot and engineer boarded his Lordship's vessel for the last sublight leg of the journey here. Is my information correct that the auxiliaries of his Lordship's so impressive vessel possess hyperdrives in addition to gravitics?"

"They do, distinguished colleague. But the two largest carry an airboat apiece as their own auxiliaries. I am sure

Lord Hauksberg won't mind lending me one of those for my personal transportation. There is no reason to bother your department."

"But there is!" The Merseian threw up his hands in quite a manlike gesture of horror. "The Commander, no less than his Lordship, is a guest of his Supremacy. We cannot disgrace his Supremacy by failing to show what hospitality lies within our power. A vessel will arrive tomorrow for the Commander's personal use. The delay is merely so that it may be furnished comfortably for Terrans and the controls modified to a Terran pattern. The boat can sleep six, and we will stock its galley with whatever is desired and available here. It has full aerial capability, has been checked out for orbital use, and could no doubt reach the outermost moon at need. I beg for the Commander's acceptance."

"Distinguished colleague, I in turn beg that you, under his Supremacy, accept my sincerest thanks," Abrams beamed.

The beam turned into a guffaw as soon as he had cut the circuit. Of course the Merseians weren't going to let him travel around unescorted—not unless they could bug his transportation. And of course they would expect him to look for eavesdropping gimmicks and find any of the usual sorts. Therefore he really needn't conduct that tedious search.

Nonetheless, he did. Negligence would have been out of character. To those who delivered his beautiful new flier he explained that he set technicians swarming through her to make certain that everything was understood about her operation; different cultures, different engineering, don't y'know. The routine disclaimer was met by the routine pretense of believing it. The airboat carried no spy gadgets apart from the one he had been hoping for. He found this by the simple expedient of waiting till he was alone aboard and then asking. The method of its concealment filled him with admiration.

But thereafter he ran into a stone wall—or, rather, a pot of glue. Days came and went, the long thirty-seven-hour days of Merseia. He lost one after another by being summoned to the chamber in Castle Afon where Hauksberg and staff conferred with Brechdan's puppets. Usually the summons was at the request of a Merseian, who wanted elucidation of some utterly trivial question about Starkad. Having explained, Abrams couldn't leave. Protocol forbade. He must sit there while talk droned on, inquiries, harangues, haggles over points which a child could see were unessential—oh, yes, these greenskins had a fine art of making negotiations interminable.

Abrams said as much to Hauksberg, once when they were back at the Embassy. "I know," the viscount snapped. He was turning gaunt and hollow-eyed. "They're so suspicious of us. Well, we're partly to blame for that, eh? Got to show good faith. While we talk, we don't fight."

"They fight on Starkad," Abrams grumbled around his cigar. "Terra won't wait on Brechdan's comma-counting forever."

"I'll dispatch a courier presently, to report and explain. We are gettin' somewhere, don't forget. They're definitely int'rested in establishin' a system for continuous medium-level conference between the governments."

"Yah. A great big gorgeous idea which'll give political

leverage to our accommodationists at home for as many years as Brechdan feels like carrying on discussions about it. I thought we came here to settle the Starkad issue."

"I thought I was the head of this mission," Hauksberg retorted. "That'll do, Commander." He yawned and stretched stiffly. "One more drink and ho for bed. Lord Emp'ror, but I'm tired!"

On days when he was not immobilized, Abrams ground through his library research and his interviews. The Merseians were most courteous and helpful. They flooded him with books and periodicals. Officers and officials would talk to him for hours on end. That was the trouble. Aside from whatever feel he might be getting for the basic setup, he learned precisely nothing of value.

Which was a kind of indicator too, he admitted. The lack of hard information about early Merseian journeys to the Saxo region might be due to sloppiness about record keeping as Brechdan had said. But a check of other planets showed that they were, as a rule, better documented. Starkad appeared to have some secret importance. *So what else is new?*

At first Abrams had Flandry to help out. Then an invitation arrived. In the cause of better understanding between races, as well as hospitality, would Ensign Flandry like to tour the planet in company with some young Merseians whose rank corresponded more or less to his?

"Would you?" Abrams asked.

"Why—" Flandry straightened at his desk. "Hell, yes. Right now I feel as if every library in the universe should be bombed. But you need me here . . . I suppose."

"I do. This is a baldpated ruse to cripple me still worse. However, you can go."

"You *mean* that?" Flandry gasped.

"Sure. We're stalled here. You just might discover something."

"Thank you, sir!" Flandry rocketed out of his chair.

"Whoa there, son. Won't be any vacation for you. You've got to play the decadent Terran nogoodnik. Mustn't disappoint their expectations. Besides, it improves your chances. Keep your eyes and ears open, sure, but forget the rule about keeping your mouth shut. Babble. Ask questions. Foolish ones, mainly; and be damned sure not to get so inquisitive they suspect you of playing spy."

Flandry frowned. "Uh . . . sir, I'd look odd if I didn't grab after information. Thing to do, I should guess, is be clumsy and obvious about it."

"Good. You catch on fast. I wish you were experienced, but—Nu, everybody has to start sometime, and I'm afraid you will not run into anything too big for a pup to handle. So go get yourself some experience."

Abrams watched the boy bustle off, and a sigh gusted from him. By and large, after winking at a few things, he felt he'd have been proud to have Dominic Flandry for a son. Though not likely to hit any pay dirt, this trip would further test the ensign's competence. If he proved out well, then probably he must be thrown to the wolves by Abrams' own hand.

Because events could not be left on dead zero as long as Brechdan wished. The situation right now carried potentials which only a traitor would fail to exploit.

Nonetheless, the way matters had developed, with the mission detained on Merseia for an indefinite period, Abrams could not exploit them as he had originally schemed. The classically neat operation he had had in mind must be turned into an explosion.

And Flandry was the fuse.

Like almost every intelligent species, the Merseians had in their past evolved thousands of languages and cultures. Finally, as in the case of Terra, one came to dominate the others and slowly absorb them into itself. But the process had not gone as far on Merseia. The laws and customs of the lands bordering the Wilwidh Ocean were still a mere overlay on some parts of the planet. Eriau was the common tongue, but there were still those who were less at home in it than in the languages they had learned from their mothers.

Perhaps this was why Lannawar Belgis had never risen above yqan—CPO, Flandry translated—and was at the moment a sort of batman to the group. He couldn't even pronounce his rating correctly. The sound rendered by q, approximately kdh where $dh = th$ as in "the," gave him almost as much trouble as it did an Anglic speaker. Or perhaps he just wasn't ambitious. For certainly he was able, as his huge fund of stories from his years in space attested. He was also a likeable old chap.

He sat relaxed with the Terran and Tachwyr the Dark, whose rank of mei answered somewhat to lieutenant j.g. Flandry was getting used to the interplay of formality and ease between officers and enlisted personnel in the Merseian service. Instead of the mutual aloofness on

Terran ships, there was an intimacy which the seniors led but did not rigidly control, a sort of perpetual dance.

"Aye, foreseers," Lannawar rumbled, "yon was a strange orb and glad I was to see the last of it. Yet somehow, I know not, ours was never a lucky ship afterward. Nothing went ever wholly right, you track me? Speaking naught against captain nor crew, I was glad for transfer to the *Bedh-Ivrich*. Her skipper was Runei the Wanderer, and far did he take us on explores."

Tachwyr's tailtip jerked and he opened his mouth. Someone was always around to keep a brake on Lannawar's garrulousness. Flandry, who had sat half drowsing, surged to alertness. He beat Tachwyr by a millisecond in exclaiming: "Runei? The same who is now Fodaich on Starkad?"

"Why . . . aye, believe so, foreseer." Eyes squinched in the tattooed face across the table. A green hand scratched the paunch where the undress tunic bulged open. "Not as I know much. Heard naught of Starkad ere they told me why you Terrans is come."

Flandry's mind went into such furious action that he felt each of the several levels on which it was operating. He had to grab whatever lead chance had offered him after so many fruitless days; he must fend off Tachwyr's efforts to wrench the lead away from him, for a minute or two anyhow; at the same time, he must maintain his role. (Decadent, as Abrams had suggested, and this he had enjoyed living up to whenever his escorts took him to some place of amusement. But not fatuous; he had quickly seen that he'd get further if they respected him a little and were not bored by his company. He was naive, wide-eyed,

pathetically hoping to accomplish something for Mother
Terra, simultaneously impressed by what he saw here. In
wry moments he admitted to himself that this was hardly
a faked character.) On lower levels of consciousness,
excitement opened the sensory floodgates.

Once more he noticed the background. They sat,
with a bench for him, in a marble pergola intricately
arabesqued and onion-domed. Tankards of bitter ale
stood before them. Merseian food and drink were
nourishing to a Terran, and often tasty. They had entered
this hilltop restaurant (which was also a shrine, run by the
devotees of a very ancient faith) for the view and for a rest
after walking around in Dalgorad. That community
nestled below them, half hidden by lambent flowers and
deep-green fronds, a few small modern buildings and many
hollowed-out trees which had housed untold generations
of a civilized society. Past the airport lay a beach of red
sand. An ocean so blue it was nearly black cast breakers
ashore; their booming drifted faint to Flandry on a wind
that smelled cinnamon. Korych shone overhead with
subtropical fierceness, but the moons Wythna and Lythyr
were discernible, like ghosts.

Interior sensations: muscles drawn tight in thighs and
belly, bloodbeat in the eardrums, chill in the palms. No
feeling of excess weight; Merseian gravity was only a few
percent above Terra's. Merseian air, water, biochemistry,
animal and plant life, were close parallels to what man had
evolved among. By the standards of either world, the
other was beautiful.

Which made the two races enemies. They wanted the
same kind of real estate.

"So Runei himself was not concerned with the original missions to Starkad?" Flandry asked.

"No, foreseer. We surveyed beyond Rigel." Lannawar reached for his tankard.

"I imagine, though," Flandry prompted, "from time to time when space explorers got together, as it might be in a tavern, you'd swap yarns?"

"Aye, aye. What else? 'Cept when we was told to keep our hatches dogged about where we'd been. Not easy, foreseer, believe you me 'tis not, when you could outbrag the crew of 'em save 'tis a Naval secret."

"You must have heard a lot about the Betelgeuse region, regardless."

Lannawar raised his tankard. Thereby he missed noticing Tachwyr's frown. But he did break the thread, and the officer caught the raveled end deftly.

"Are you really interested in anecdotes, Ensign? I fear that our good Yqan has nothing else to give you."

"Well, yes, Mei, I am interested in anything about the Betelgeuse sector," Flandry said. "After all, it borders on our Empire. I've already served there, on Starkad, and I daresay I will again. So I'd be grateful for whatever you care to tell me." Lannawar came up for air. "If you yourself, Yqan, were never there, perhaps you know someone who was. I ask for no secrets, of course, only stories."

"Khr-r-r-." Lannawar wiped foam off his chin. "Not many about. Not many what have fared yonderways. They're either back in space, or they've died. Was old Ralgo Tamuar, my barracks friend in training days. He was there aplenty. How he could lie! But he retired to one of the colonies, let me see now, which one?"

"Yqan Belgis." Tachwyr spoke quietly, with no special inflection, but Lannawar stiffened. "I think best we leave this subject. The Starkadian situation is an unfortunate one. We are trying to be friends with our guest, and I hope we are succeeding, but to dwell on the dispute makes a needless obstacle." To Flandry, with sardonicism: "I trust the ensign agrees?"

"As you wish," the Terran mumbled.

Damn, damn, and damn to the power of hell! He'd been on a scent. He could swear he'd been. He felt nauseated with frustration.

Some draughts of ale soothed him. He'd never been idiot enough to imagine himself making any spectacular discoveries or pulling off any dazzling coups on this junket. (Well, certain daydreams, but you couldn't really count that.) What he had obtained now was—a hint which tended to confirm that the early Merseian expeditions to Starkad had found a big and strange thing. As a result, secrecy had come down like a candlesnuffer. Officers and crews who knew, or might suspect, the truth were snatched from sight. Murdered? No, surely not. The Merseians were not the antlike monsters which Terran propaganda depicted. They'd never have come as far as this, or be as dangerous as they were, had that been the case. To shut a spacefarer's mouth, you reassigned him or retired him to an exile which might well be comfortable and which he himself might never realize was an exile.

Even for the post of Starkadian commandant, Brechdan had been careful to pick an officer who knew nothing beforehand about his post, and could not since have been told the hidden truth. Why . . . aside from those exploratory personnel who no longer counted, perhaps only half a dozen beings in the universe knew!

Obviously Tachwyr didn't. He and his fellows had simply been ordered to keep Flandry off certain topics.

The Terran believed they were honest, most of them, in their friendliness toward him and their expressed wish that today's discord could be resolved. They were good chaps. He felt more akin to them than to many humans.

In spite of which, they served the enemy, the real enemy, Brechdan Ironrede and his Grand Council, who had put something monstrous in motion. Wind and surf-beat sounded all at once like the noise of an oncoming machine.

I haven't found anything Abrams doesn't already suspect, Flandry thought. *But I have got for him a bit more proof. God! Four days to go before I can get back and give it to him.*

His mouth still felt dry. "How about another round?" he said.

"We're going for a ride," Abrams said.

"Sir?" Flandry blinked.

"Little pleasure trip. Don't you think I deserve one too? A run to Gethwyd Forest, say, that's an unrestricted area."

Flandry looked past his boss's burly form, out the window to the compound. A garden robot whickered among the roses, struggling to maintain the microecology they required. A secretary on the diplomatic staff stood outside one of the residence bubbles, flirting boredly with the assistant naval attaché's wife. Beyond them, Ardaig's modern towers shouldered brutally skyward. The afternoon was hot and quiet.

"Uh . . . sir—" Flandry hesitated.

"When you 'sir' me in private these days, you want something," Abrams said. "Carry on."

"Well, uh, could we invite Donna d'Io?" Beneath those crow's-footed eyes, Flandry felt himself blush. He tried to control it, which made matters worse. "She, uh, must be rather lonesome when his Lordship and aides are out of town."

Abrams grinned. "What, I'm not decorative enough for you? Sorry. It wouldn't look right. Let's go."

Flandry stared at him. He knew the man by now. At least, he could spot when something unadmitted lurked under the skin. His spine tingled. Having reported on his trip, he'd expected a return to desk work, dullness occasionally relieved after dark. But action must be starting at last. However much he had grumbled, however sarcastic he had waxed about the glamorous life in romantic alien capitals, he wasn't sure he liked the change.

"Very good, sir," he said.

They left the office and crossed aboveground to the garages. The Merseian technies reported periodically to inspect the luxury boat lent Abrams, but today a lone human was on duty. Envious, he floated the long blue teardrop out into the sunlight. Abrams and Flandry boarded, sealed the door, and found chairs in the saloon. "Gethwyd Forest, main parking area," Abrams said. "Five hundred kph. Any altitude will do."

The machine communicated with other machines. Clearance was granted and lane assigned. The boat rose noiselessly. On Terra, its path could have been monitored, but the haughty chieftains of Merseia had not allowed that sort of capability to be built in for possible use against them. Traffic control outside of restricted sections was automatic and anonymous. Unless they shadowed a boat, or bugged it somehow, security officers were unable to keep it under surveillance. Abrams had remarked that he liked that, on principle as well as because his own convenience was served.

He groped in his tunic for a cigar. "We could have a drink," he suggested. "Whisky and water for me."

Flandry got it, with a stiff cognac for himself. By the time he returned from the bar, they were leveled off at about six kilometers and headed north. They would take a couple of hours, at this ambling pace, to reach the preserve which the Vach Dathyr had opened to the public. Flandry had been there before, on a holiday excursion Oliveira arranged for Hauksberg and company. He remembered great solemn trees, gold-feathered birds, the smell of humus and the wild taste of a spring. Most vividly he remembered sun-flecks patterned across Persis' thin gown. Now he saw the planet's curve through a broad viewport, the ocean gleaming westward, the megalopolitan maze giving way to fields and isolated castles.

"Sit down," Abrams said. His hand chopped at a lounger. Smoke hazed him where he sprawled.

Flandry lowered himself. He wet his lips. "You've business with me, haven't you?" he said.

"Right on the first guess! To win your Junior Spy badge and pocket decoder, tell me what an elephant is."

"Huh, sir?"

"An elephant is a mouse built to government specifications. Or else a mouse is a transistorized elephant." Abrams didn't look jovial. He was delaying.

Flandry took a nervous sip. "If it's confidential," he asked, "should we be here?"

"Safer than the Embassy. That's only probably debugged, not certainly, and old-fashioned listening at doors hasn't ever quite gone out of style."

"But a Merseian runabout—"

"We're safe. Take my word." Abrams glared at the cigar he rolled between his fingers. "Son, I need you for a job of work and I need you bad. Could be dangerous and sure to be nasty. Are you game?"

Flandry's heart bumped. "I'd better be, hadn't I?"

Abrams cocked his head at the other. "Not bad repartee for a nineteen-year-old. But do you mean it, down in your bones?"

"Yes, sir." *I think so.*

"I believe you. I have to." Abrams took a drink and a long drag. Abruptly:

"Look here, let's review the circumstances as she stands. I reckon you have the innate common sense to see what's written on your eyeballs, that Brechdan hasn't got the slightest intention of settling the squabble on Starkad. I thought for a while, maybe he figured to offer us peace there in exchange for some other thing he really wants. But if that were the case, he wouldn't have thrown a triple gee field onto the parley the way he has. He'd have come to the point with the unavoidable minimum of waste motion. Merseians don't take a human's glee in forensics. If Brechdan wanted to strike a bargain, Hauksberg would be home on Terra right now with a preliminary report.

"Instead, Brechdan's talkboys have stalled, with one quibble and irrelevancy after another. Even Hauksberg's getting a gutful. Which I think is the reason Brechdan personally invited him and aides to Dhangodhan for a week or two of shootin' and fishin'. Partly because that makes one more delay by itself; partly to smooth our viscount's feelings with a 'gesture of good will.'" The quotes were virtually audible. "I was invited too, but begged off on ground of wanting to continue my researches. If he'd thought of it, Brechdan'd likely have broken custom and asked Donna Persis, as an added inducement for staying in the mountains a while. Unless, hm, he's provided a little variety for his guests. There are humans in Merseian service, you know."

Flandry nodded. For a second he felt disappointment. Hauksberg's absence when he returned had seemed to provide a still better opportunity than Hauksberg's frequent exhaustion in Ardaig. But excitement caught him. Never mind Persis. She was splendid recreation, but that was all.

"I might be tempted to think like his Lordship, Brechdan is fundamentally sincere," he said. "The average Merseian is, I'm sure."

"Sure you're sure. And you're right. Fat lot of difference that makes."

"But anyhow, Starkad *is* too important. Haven't you told that idi—Lord Hauksberg so?"

"I finally got tired of telling him," Abrams said. "What have I got to argue from except a prejudice based on experiences he's never shared?"

"I wonder why Brechdan agreed to receive a delegation in the first place."

"Oh, easier to accept than refuse, I suppose. Or it might have suited his plans very well. He doesn't want total war yet. I do believe he originally intended to send us packing in fairly short order. What hints I've gathered suggest that another issue has arisen—that he's planning quite a different move, not really germane to Starkad—and figures to put a better face on it by acting mild toward us. God alone knows how long we'll be kept here. Could be weeks more."

Abrams leaned forward. "And meanwhile," he continued, "anything could happen. I came with some hopes of pulling off a hell of a good stunt just before we left. And it did look hopeful at first, too. Could give us the truth about Starkad. Well, things have dragged on, configurations have changed, my opportunity may vanish. We've got to act soon, or our chance of acting at all will be mighty poor."

This is it, Flandry thought, and a part of him jeered at the banality, while he waited with hardheld breath.

"I don't want to tell you more than I've got to," Abrams said. "Just this: I've learned where Brechdan's ultrasecret file is. That wasn't hard; everybody knows about it. But I think I can get an agent in there. The next and worst problem will be to get the information out, and not have the fact we're doing so be known.

"I dare not wait till we all go home. That gives too much time for too many things to go wrong. Nor can I leave beforehand by myself. I'm too damn conspicuous. It'd look too much as if I'd finished whatever I set out to do. Hauksberg himself might forbid me to go, precisely because he suspected I was going to queer his pea-ea-eace mission. Or else . . . I'd be piloted out of the system by Merseians. Brechdan's bully boys could arrange an unfortunate accident merely as a precaution. They could even spirit me off to a hynoprobe room, and what happened to me there wouldn't matter a hoot-let compared to what'd happen to our forces later. I'm not being melodramatic, son. Those are the unbuttered facts of life."

Flandry sat still. "You want me to convey the data out, if you get them," he said.

"Ah, you do know what an elephant is."

"You must have a pretty efficient pipeline to Merseian HQ."

"I've seen worse," Abrams said rather smugly.

"Couldn't have been developed in advance." Flandry spoke word by word. Realization was freezing him. "Had it been, why should you yourself come here? Must be something you got hold of on Starkad, and hadn't a chance to instruct anyone about that you trusted and who could be spared."

"Let's get down to business," Abrams said fast.

"No. I want to finish this."

"You?"

Flandry stared past Abrams like a blind man. "If the contact was that good," he said, "I think you got a warning about the submarine attack on Ujanka. And you didn't tell. There was no preparation. Except for a fluke, the city would have been destroyed." He rose. "I saw Tigeries killed in the streets."

"Sit down!"

"One mortar planted on a wharf would have gotten that boat." Flandry started to walk away. His voice lifted. "Males and females and little cubs, blown apart, buried alive under rubble, and you did nothing!"

Abrams surged to his feet and came after him. "Hold on, there," he barked.

Flandry whirled on him. "Why the obscenity should I?"

Abrams grabbed the boy's wrists. Flandry tried to break free. Abrams held him where he was. Rage rode across the dark Chaldean face. "You listen to me," Abrams said. "I did know. I knew the consequences of keeping silent. When you saved that town, I went down on my knees before God. I'd've done it before you if you could've understood. But suppose I had acted. Runei is no man's fool. He'd have guessed I had a source, and there was exactly one possibility, and after he looked into that my pipeline would've been broken like a dry stick. And I was already developing it as a line into Brechdan's own files. Into the truth about Starkad. How many lives might that save? Not only human. Tigery, Siravo, hell, Merseian! Use your brains, Dom. You must have a couple of cells clicking together between those ears. Sure, this is a filthy game. But it has one point of practicality which is also a point of honor. You don't compromise your sources. You don't!"

Flandry struggled for air. Abrams let him go. Flandry went back to his lounger, collapsed in it, and drank deep. Abrams stood waiting.

Flandry looked up. "I'm sorry, sir," he got out. "Overwrought, I guess."

"No excuses needed." Abrams clapped his shoulder. "You had to learn sometime. Might as well be now. And you know, you give me a tinge of hope. I'd begun to wonder if anybody was left on our side who played the game for anything but its own foul sake. When you get some rank—Well, we'll see."

He sat down too. Silence lay between them for a while.

"I'm all right now, sir," Flandry ventured.

"Good," Abrams grunted. "You'll need whatever all rightness you can muster. The best way I can see to get that information out soon involves a pretty dirty trick too. Also a humiliating one. I'd like to think you can hit on a better idea, but I've tried and failed."

Flandry gulped. "What is it?"

Abrams approached the core gingerly. "The problem is this," he said. "I do believe we can raid that file unbeknownst. Especially now while Brechdan is away, and the three others who I've found have access to that certain room. But even so, it'd look too funny if anyone left right after who didn't have a plausible reason. You can have one."

Flandry braced himself. "What?"

"Well . . . if Lord Hauksberg caught you *in flagrante delicto* with his toothsome traveling companion—"

That would have unbraced a far more sophisticated person. Flandry leaped from his seat. "Sir!"

"Down, boy. Don't tell me the mice haven't been playing while the cat's elsewhere. You've been so crafty that I don't think anybody else guesses, even in our gossipy little enclave. Which augurs well for your career in

Intelligence. But son, I work close to you. When you report draggle-tailed on mornings after I noticed Lord Hauksberg was dead tired and took a hypnotic; when I can't sleep and want to get some work done in the middle of the night and you aren't in your room; when you and she keep swapping glances—Must I spell every word? No matter. I don't condemn you. If I weren't an old man with some eccentric ideas about my marriage, I'd be jealous.

"But this does give us our chance. All we need do is keep Persis from knowing when her lord and master is coming back. She don't mix much with the rest of the compound—can't say I blame her—and you can provide the distraction to make sure. Then the message sent ahead—which won't be to her personally anyhow, only to alert the servants in the expectation they'll tell everyone—I'll see to it that the word doesn't reach her. For the rest, let nature take its course."

"No!" Flandry raged.

"Have no fears for her," Abrams said. "She may suffer no more than a scolding. Lord Hauksberg is pretty tolerant. Anyway, he ought to be. If she does lose her position . . . our corps has a slush fund. She can be supported in reasonable style on Terra till she hooks someone else. I really don't have the impression she'd be heartbroken at having to trade Lord Hauksberg in on a newer model."

"But—" Confound that blush! Flandry stared at the deck. His fists beat on his knees. "She trusts me. I can't."

"I said this was a dirty business. Do you flatter yourself she's in love with you?"

"Well—uh—"

"You do. I wouldn't. But supposing she is, a psych treatment for something that simple is cheap, and she's cool enough to get one. I've spent more time worrying about you."

"What about me?" asked Flandry miserably.

"Lord Hauksberg has to retaliate on you. Whatever his private feelings, he can't let something like this go by; because the whole compound, hell, eventually all Terra is going to know, if you handle the scene right. He figures on dispatching a courier home a day or two after he gets back from Dhangodhan, with a progress report. You'll go on the same boat, in disgrace, charged with some crime like disrespect for hereditary authority.

"Somewhere along the line—I'll have to work out the details as we go—my agent will nobble the information and slip it to me. I'll pass it to you. Once on Terra, you'll use a word I'll give you to get the ear of a certain man. Afterward—son, you're in. You shouldn't be fumbly-diddling this way. You should be licking my boots for such an opportunity to get noticed by men who count. My boots need polishing."

Flandry shifted, looked away, out to the clouds which drifted across the green and brown face of Merseia. The motor hum pervaded his skull.

"What about you?" he asked finally. "And the rest?"

"We'll stay here till the farce is over."

"But . . . no, wait, sir . . . so many things could go wrong. Deadly wrong."

"I know. That's the risk you take."

"You more." Flandry swung back to Abrams. "I

might get free without a hitch. But if later there's any suspicion—"

"They won't bother Persis," Abrams said. "She's not worth the trouble. Nor Hauksberg. He's an accredited diplomat, and arresting him would damn near be an act of war."

"But you, sir! You may be accredited to him, but—"

"Don't fret," Abrams said. "I aim to die of advanced senile decay. If that starts looking unlikely, I've got my blaster. I won't get taken alive and I won't go out of the cosmos alone. Now: are you game?"

It took Flandry's entire strength to nod.

CHAPTER TWELVE

Two days later, Abrams departed the Embassy again in his boat. Ahead, on the ocean's rim, smoldered a remnant of sunset. The streets of Ardaig glowed ever more visible as dusk deepened into night. Windows blinked to life, the Admiralty beacon flared like a sudden red sun. Traffic was heavy, and the flier's robopilot must keep signals constantly flickering between itself, others, and the nearest routing stations. The computers in all stations were still more tightly linked, by a web of data exchange. Its nexus was Central Control, where the total pattern was evaluated and the three-dimensional grid of air-lanes adjusted from minute to minute for optimum flow.

Into this endless pulsation, it was easy to inject a suitably heterodyned and scrambled message. None but sender and recipient would know. Nothing less than a major job of stochastic analysis could reveal to an outsider that occasional talk had passed (and even then, would not show what the talk had been about). Neither the boat nor the Terran Embassy possessed the equipment for that.

From the darkness where he lay, Dwyr the Hook willed a message forth. Not sent: willed, as one wills a normal voice to speak; for his nerve endings meshed directly with the circuits of the vessel and he felt the tides in the electronic sea which filled Ardaig like a living creature feeling the tides in its own blood.

"Prime Observer Three to Intelligence Division Thirteen." A string of code symbols followed. "Prepare to receive report."

Kilometers away, a Merseian tautened at his desk. He was among the few who knew about Dwyr; they alternated shifts around the clock. Thus far nothing of great interest had been revealed to them. But that was good. It proved the Terran agent, whom they had been warned was dangerous, had accomplished nothing. "Division Thirteen to Prime Three. Dhech on duty. Report."

"Abrams has boarded alone and instructed the 'pilot to take him to the following location." Dwyr specified. He identified the place as being in a hill suburb, but no more; Ardaig was not his town.

"Ah, yes," Dhech nodded. "Fodaich Qwynn's home. We knew already Abrams was going there tonight."

"Shall I expect anything to happen?" Dwyr asked.

"No, you'll be parked for several hours, I'm sure, and return him to the Embassy. He's been after Qwynn for some time for an invitation, so they could talk privately and at length about certain questions of mutual interest. Today he pressed so hard that Qwynn found it impossible not to invite him for tonight without open discourtesy."

"Is that significant?"

"Hardly. We judge Abrams makes haste simply

because he got word that his chief will return tomorrow with the Hand of the Vach Ynvory, great protector of us all. Thereafter he can expect once more to be enmeshed in diplomatic maneuverings. This may be his last chance to see Qwynn."

"I could leave the boat and spy upon them," Dwyr offered.

"No need. Qwynn is discreet, and will make his own report to us. If Abrams hopes to pick up a useful crumb, he will be disappointed. Quite likely, though, his interest is academic. He appears to have abandoned any plans he may have entertained for conducting espionage."

"He has certainly done nothing suspicious under my surveillance," Dwyr said, "in a boat designed to make him think it ideal for hatching plots. I will be glad when he leaves. This has been a drab assignment."

"Honor to you for taking it," Dhech said. "No one else could have endured so long." A burst of distortion made him start. "What's that?"

"Some trouble with the communicator," said Dwyr, who had willed the malfunction. "It had better be checked soon. I might lose touch with you."

"We'll think of some excuse to send a technician over in a day or so. Hunt well."

"Hunt well." Dwyr broke the connection.

Through the circuits, which included scanners, he observed both outside and inside the hull. The boat was slanting down toward its destination. Abrams had risen and donned a formal cloak. Dwyr activated a speaker. "I have contacted Division Thirteen," he said. "They are quite unsuspicious. I planted the idea that my sender may go blank, in case for some reason they try to call me while I am absent."

"Good lad." Abrams' tones were likewise calm, but he took a last nervous pull on his cigar and stubbed it out viciously. "Now remember, I'll stay put for several hours. Should give you ample time to do your job and slip back into this shell. But if anything goes wrong, I repeat, what matters is the information. Since we can't arrange a safe drop, and since mine host tonight will have plenty of retainers to arrest me, in emergency you get hold of Ensign Flandry and tell him. You recall he should be in Lord Hauksberg's suite, or else his own room; and I've mapped the Embassy for you. Now also, make damn sure the phone here is hooked to the 'pilot, so you or he can call this boat to him. I haven't told him about you, but I have told him to trust absolutely whoever has the key word. You remember?"

"Yes, of course. *Meshuggah*. What does it mean?"

"Never mind." Abrams grinned.

"What about rescuing you?"

"Don't. You'd come to grief for certain. Besides, my personal chances are better if I invoke diplomatic immunity. I hope, though, our stunt will go off without a hitch." Abrams looked about. "I can't see you, Dwyr, and I can't shake your hand, but I'd sure like to. And one day I plan to." The boat grounded. "Good luck."

Dwyr's electronic gaze followed the stocky figure out, down the ramp and across the small parking strip in the garden. A pair of clan members saluted the Terran and followed him toward the mansion. A screen of trees soon hid them. No one else was in view. Shadows lay heavy around the boat.

Let us commence, Dwyr thought. His decision was altogether unperturbed. Once he would have tasted fear, felt his heart thud, clutched to him the beloved images of wife and young and their home upon far Tanis. Courage would have followed, sense of high purpose, joy of proving his maleness by a leap between the horns of death—thus did you know yourself wholly alive! But those things had departed with his body. He could no longer recollect how they felt. The one emotion which never left him, like an unhealing wound, was the wish to know all emotions again.

He had a few. Workmanship gave a cerebral pleasure. Hate and fury could still burn . . . though cold, cold. He wondered if they were not mere habits, engraved in the synapses of his brain.

He stirred in the womblike cubicle where he lay. Circuit by circuit, his living arm disconnected his machine parts from the boat. For a moment he was totally cut off. How many hours till sensory deprivation broke down his sanity? He had been kept supplied with impressions of the world, and asleep he never dreamed. But suppose he stayed where he was, in this lightless, soundless, current-less nothing. When he began to hallucinate, would he imagine himself back on Tanis? Or would Sivilla his wife come to him?

Nonsense. The objective was that he come to her, whole. He opened a panel and glided forth. The systems that kept him functional were mounted in a tiny gravsled. His first task would be to exchange it for a more versatile body.

Emerging, he floated low, keeping to the bushes and

shadows. Stars were plainer to see here, away from the
city web and the beacon flare which lay at the foot of these
hills. He noted the sun of Tanis, where Merseians had
made their homes among mountains and forests, where
Sivilla lived yet with their children. She thought him dead,
but they told him she had not remarried and the children
were growing up well.

Was that another lie?

The problem of weaving his way unseen into the
city occupied a bare fragment of Dwyr's attention. His
artificial senses were designed for this kind of task, and he
had a decade of experience with them. Mostly he was
remembering.

"I was reluctant to leave," he had confessed to
Abrams on Starkad. "I was happy. What was the conquest
of Janair to me? They spoke of the glory of the race. I saw
nothing except that other race, crushed, burned, enslaved
as we advanced. I would have fought for my liberty as they
did for theirs. Instead, being required to do my military
service, I was fighting to rob them of their birthright. Do
not misunderstand. I stayed loyal to my Roidhun and my
people. It was they who betrayed me."

"They sure as the seventh hell did," Abrams said.

That was after the revelation which knocked Dwyr's
universe apart. "What?" Abrams had roared. "You could
not be regenerated? Impossible!"

"But radiation damage to the cells—"

"With that kind of radiation damage, you'd've been
dead. The basic gene pattern governs the organism
throughout life. If everything mutated at once, life would
have to stop. And the regeneration process uses the

chromosomes for a chemical template. No, they saw their chance to make a unique tool out of you, and lied. I suppose they must've planted an unconscious mental block too, so you'd never think to study basic biomedicine for yourself, and avoid situations where somebody might tell you. God! I've seen some vile tricks in my time, but this one takes the purple shaft, with pineapple clusters."

"You can heal me?" Dwyr screamed.

"Our chemosurgeons can. But slow down. Let's think a bit. I could order the job done on you, and would as a matter of ethics. Still, you'd be cut off from your family. What we ought to do is smuggle them out also. We could resettle you on an Imperial planet. And I haven't the authority to arrange that. Not unless you rate it. Which you could, by serving as a double agent."

"To you too, then, I am nothing but a tool."

"Easy. I didn't say that. I just said that getting back your family won't come cheap. It'll involve some risk to the crew who fetch them. You've got to earn a claim on us. Willing?"

Oh, very willing!

As he darted between towers, Dwyr was no more conspicuous than a nightbird. He could easily reach the place assigned him, on an upper level of a control station where only computers dwelt, without being noticed. That had been arranged on Brechdan Ironrede's own command. The secret of Dwyr's existence was worth taking trouble to preserve. A recognition lock opened for him and he glided into a room crowded with his bodies and attachments. There was nothing else; an amputated personality did not carry around the little treasures of a mortal.

He had already chosen what to take. After detaching from the sled, he hitched himself to the biped body which lay stretched out like a metal corpse. For those moments he was without any senses but sight, hearing, a dim touch and kinesthesia, a jab of pain through what remained of his tissues. He was glad when he had finished making the new connections.

Rising, he lumbered about and gathered what else he would need and fastened it on: special tools and sensors, a gravity impeller, a blaster. How weak and awkward he was. He much preferred being a vehicle or a gun. Metal and plastic did not substitute well for cells, nerves, muscles, the marvelous structure which was bone. But tonight an unspecialized shape was required.

Last came some disguise. He could not pass for Merseian (after what had been done to him) but he could look like a spacesuited human or Iskeled. The latter race had long ago become resigned to the domination of his, and furnished many loyal personnel. No few had been granted Merseian citizenship. It had less significance than the corresponding honor did for Terra, but it carried certain valuable privileges.

Ready. Dwyr left his room and took to the air again, openly this time. Admiralty House grew before him, a gaunt mountain where caves glared and the beacon made a volcano spout. A sound of machines mumbled through the sky he clove. He sensed their radiation as a glow, a tone, a rising wave. Soaring, he approached the forbidden zone and spoke, on a tight beam, those passwords Brechdan had given him. "Absolute security," he added. "My presence is to be kept secret."

When he landed on the flange, an officer had joined the sentries. "What is your business on this level?" the Merseian demanded. "Our protector the Hand is not in Ardaig."

"I know," Dwyr said. "I am at his direct orders, to conduct some business inside. That is as much as I am allowed to tell you. You and these males will admit me, and let me out in a while, and forget I was ever here. It is not to be mentioned to anyone in any circumstances. The matter is sealed."

"Under what code?"

"Triple Star."

The officer saluted. "Pass."

Dwyr went down the corridor. It echoed a little to his footfalls. When he reached the anteroom, he heard the buzz of work in the offices beyond; but he stood alone at the door of the vault. He had never seen this place. However, the layout was no secret and had been easy to obtain.

The door itself, though—He approached with immense care, every sensor at full amplification. The scanners saw he was not authorized to go by, and might trigger an alarm. No. Nothing. After all, people did use this route on certain errands. He removed the false glove on his robot arm and extended tendrils to the plates.

They reacted. By induction, his artificial neurones felt how signals moved into a comparison unit and were rejected. So now he must feed in pulses which would be interpreted as the right eye and hand patterns. Slowly . . . slowly, micrometric exactitude, growing into the assembly, feeling with it, calling forth the response he wanted, a seduction which stirred instincts until his machine heart and lungs moved rapidly and he was lost to the exterior world . . . *there!*

The door opened, ponderous and silent. He trod through. It closed behind him. In a black chamber, he confronted a thing which shone like opal.

Except for possessing a recognition trigger of its own, the molecular file was no different from numerous others he had seen. Still full of oneness with the flow of electrons and intermeshed fields, still half in a dream, he activated it. The operation code was unknown to him, but he detected that not much information was stored here. Stood to reason, the thought trickled at the back of his awareness. No individual could singlehandedly steer an empire. The secrets which Brechdan reserved for himself and his three comrades must be few, however tremendous. He, Dwyr the Hook, need not carry on a lengthy random search before he got the notes on Starkad.

Eidhafor: Report on another Hand who often opposed Brechdan in Council; data which could be used, at need, to break him.

Maxwell Crawford: Ha, the Terran Emperor's governor of the Arachnean System was in Merseian pay. A sleeper, kept in reserve.

Therayn: So that was what preoccupied Brechdan's friends. Abrams was evidently right; Hauksberg was being delayed so as to be present, influenceable, when the news broke.

Starkad!

Onto the screen flashed a set of numbers. 0.17847, 3° 14' 22" .591, 1818 h.3264. . . . Dwyr memorized them automatically, while he stood rigid with shock. Something had happened in the file. An impulse had passed. Its transient radiation had given his nerves a split second's wispy shiver. Might be nothing. But better finish up and get out fast!

The screen blanked. Dwyr's fingers moved with blurring speed. The numbers returned. Why—they were the whole secret. They were what Starkad was about. And he didn't know what they meant.

Let Abrams solve this riddle. Dwyr's task was done. Almost.

He went toward the door. It opened and he stepped into the antechamber. The door behind, to the main offices, was agape. A guard waited, blaster poised. Two more were hurrying toward him. Desk workers scuttled from their path.

"What is the matter?" Dwyr rapped. Because he could not feel terror or dismay, a blue flame of wrath sheeted through him.

Sweat glistened on the guard's forehead and ran down over the brow ridges. "You were in his secretorium," he whispered.

So terrible is the magic in those numbers that the machine has had one extra geas laid upon it. When they are brought forth, it calls for help.

"I am authorized," Dwyr said. "How else do you think I could enter?"

He did not really believe his burglary could long remain unknown. Too many had seen. But he might gain a few hours. His voice belled. "No one is to speak of this to anyone else whatsoever, not even among yourselves.

The business is sealed under a code which the officer of the night knows. He can explain its significance to you. Let me pass."

"No." The blaster trembled.

"Do you wish to be charged with insubordination?"

"I . . . I must take that risk, foreseer. We all must. You are under arrest until the Hand clears you in person."

Dwyr's motors snarled. He drew his own gun as he flung himself aside. Fire and thunder broke free. The Merseian collapsed in a seared heap. But he had shot first. Dwyr's living arm was blasted off.

He did not go into shock. He was not that alive. Pain flooded him, he staggered for a moment in blindness. Then the homeostats in his prostheses reacted. Chemical stimulation poured from tubes into veins. Electronic impulses at the control of a microcomputer joined the nerve currents, damped out agony, forced the flesh to stop bleeding. Dwyr whirled and ran.

The others came behind him. Guns crashed anew. He staggered from their impact. Looking down, he saw a hole drilled in him from back to breast. The energy beam must have wrecked some part of the mechanism which kept his brain alive. What part, he didn't know. Not the circulation, for he continued moving. The filtration system, the purifier, the osmotic balancer? He'd find out soon enough. *Crash!* His left leg went immobile. He fell. The clatter was loud in the corridor. Why hadn't he remembered his impeller? He willed the negagravity field to go on. Still he lay like a stone. The Merseians pounded near, shouting. He flipped the manual switch and rose.

The door to the flange stood shut. At top speed,

he tore the panels asunder. A firebolt from a guard rainbowed off his armor. Out . . . over the verge . . . down toward shadow!

And shadows were closing in on him. His machinery must indeed have been struck in a vital spot. It would be good to die. No, not yet. He must hang on a while longer. Get by secret ways to the Terran Embassy; Abrams was too far, and effectively a prisoner in any event. Get to the Embassy—don't faint!—find this Flandry—how it roared in his head—summon the airboat—the fact that his identity was unknown to his pursuers until they called Brechdan would help—try for an escape—if you must faint, hide yourself first, and do not die, do not die— perhaps Flandry can save you. If nothing else, you will have revenged yourself a little if you find him. Darkness and great rushing waters. . . . Dwyr the Hook fled alone over the night city.

CHAPTER THIRTEEN

That afternoon, Abrams had entered the office where Flandry was at work. He closed the door and said, "All right, son, you can knock off."

"Glad to," Flandry said. Preparing a series of transcribed interviews for the computer was not his idea of sport, especially when the chance of anything worthwhile being buried in them hovered near zero. He shoved the papers across his desk, leaned back, and tensed cramped muscles against each other. "How come?"

"Lord Hauksberg's valet just called the majordomo here. They're returning tomorrow morning. Figure to arrive about Period Four, which'd be fourteen or fifteen hundred Thursday, Terran Prime Meridian."

Flandry sucked in a breath, wheeled his chair about, and stared up at his chief. "Tonight—?"

"Uh-huh," Abrams nodded. "I won't be around. For reasons you don't need to know, except that I want attention focused my way, I'm going to wangle me an invite to a local Poo-Bah."

"And a partial alibi, if events go sour." Flandry spoke with only the top half of his mind engaged. The rest strove to check pulse, lungs, perspiration, tension. It had been one thing to dash impulsively against a Merseian watercraft. It would be quite another to play against incalculable risks, under rules that would change minute by minute, in cold blood, for x many hours.

He glanced at his chrono. Persis was doubtless asleep. Unlike Navy men, who were trained to adapt to nonterrestrial diurnal periods by juggling watches, the Embassy civilians split Merseia's rotation time into two short, complete "days." She followed the practice. "I suppose I'm to stand by in reserve," Flandry said. "Another reason for our separating."

"Smart boy," Abrams said. "You deserve a pat and a dog biscuit. I hope your lady fair will provide the same."

"I still hate to . . . to use her this way."

"In your position, I'd enjoy every second. Besides, don't forget your friends on Starkad. They're being shot at."

"Y-yes." Flandry rose. "What about, uh, emergency procedure?"

"Be on tap, either in her place or yours. Our agent will identify himself by a word I'll think of. He may look funny, but trust him. I can't give you specific orders. Among other reasons, I don't like saying even this much here, however unbuggable we're alleged to be. Do whatever seems best. Don't act too damned fast. Even if the gaff's been blown, you might yet manage to ride out the aftermath. But don't hesitate too long, either. If you must move, then: no heroics, no rescues, no consideration for any living soul. Plain get that information out!"

"Aye, aye, sir."

"Sounds more like 'I-yi-yi, sir!'" Abrams laughed. He seemed at ease. "Let's hope the whole operation proves dull and sordid. Good ones are, you know. Shall we review a few details?"

—Later, when twilight stole across the city, Flandry made his way to the principal guest suite. The corridor was deserted. Ideally, Lord Hauksberg should come upon his impudence as a complete surprise. That way, the viscount would be easier to provoke into rage. However, if this didn't work—if Persis learned he was expected and shooed Flandry out—the scandal must be leaked to the entire compound. He had a scheme for arranging that.

He chimed on the door. After a while, her voice came drowsy. "Who's there?" He waved at the scanner. "Oh. What is it, Ensign?"

"May I come in, Donna?"

She stopped to throw on a robe. Her hair was tumbled and she was charmingly flushed. He entered and closed the door. "We needn't be so careful," he said. "Nobody watching. My boss is gone for the night and a good part of tomorrow." He laid hands on her waist. "I couldn't pass up the chance."

"Nor I." She kissed him at great length.

"Why don't we simply hide in here?" he suggested.

"I'd adore to. But Lord Oliveira—"

"Call the butler. Explain you're indisposed and want to be alone till tomorrow. Hm?"

"Not very polite. Hell, I'll do it. We have so little time, darling."

Flandry stood in back of the vidiphone while she

talked. If the butler should mention that Hauksberg was due in, he must commence Plan B. But that didn't happen, as curt as Persis was. She ordered food and drink 'chuted here and switched off. He deactivated the instrument. "I don't want any distractions," he explained.

"What wonderful ideas you have," she smiled.

"Right now I have still better ones."

"Me too." Persis rejoined him.

Her thoughts included refreshments. The Embassy larder was lavishly stocked, and the suite had a small server to prepare meals which she knew well how to program. They began with eggs Benedict, caviar, akvavit, and champagne. Some hours later followed Perigordian duck, with trimmings, and Bordeaux. Flandry's soul expanded. "My God," he gusted, "where has this sort of thing been all my life?"

Persis chuckled. "I believe I have launched you on a new career. You have the makings of a gourmet first class."

"So, two causes why I shall never forget you."

"Only two?"

"No, I'm being foolish. Aleph-null causes at the minimum. Beauty, brains, charm—Well, why'm I just talking?"

"You have to rest sometime. And I do love to hear you talk."

"Hn? I'm not much in that line. After the people and places you've known—"

"What places?" she said with a quick, astonishing bitterness. "Before this trip, I was never further than Luna. And the people, the articulate, expensive, brittle people, their intrigues and gossip, the shadow shows that are their adventures, the words they live by—words, nothing but words, on and on and on—No, Dominic my dearest, you've made me realize what I was missing. You've pulled down a wall for me that was shutting off the universe."

Did I do you any favor? He dared not let conscience stir, he drowned it in the fullness of this moment.

They were lying side by side, savoring an ancient piece of music, when the door recognized Lord Hauksberg and admitted him.

"Persis? I say, where—Great Emperor!"

He stopped cold in the bedroom archway. Persis smothered a scream and snatched for her robe. Flandry jumped to his feet. *But it's still dark! What's happened?*

The blond man looked altogether different in green hunting clothes and belted blaster. Sun and wind had darkened his face. For an instant that visage was fluid with surprise. Then the lines congealed. The eyes flared like blue stars. He clapped hand to weapon butt. "Well, well," he said.

"Mark—" Persis reached out.

He ignored her. "So you're the indisposition she had," he said to Flandry.

Here we go. *Off schedule, but lift gravs anyway.* The boy felt blood course thickly, sweat trickle down ribs; worse than fear, he was aware how ludicrous he must look. He achieved a grin. "No, my lord. You are."

"What d'you mean?"

"You weren't being man enough." Flandry's belly grew stiff, confronting that gun. Strange to hear Mozart lilting on in the background.

The blaster stayed sheathed. Hauksberg moved only to breathe. "How long's this been between you?"

"It was my fault, Mark," Persis cried. "All mine." Tears whipped over her cheeks.

"No, my sweet, I insist," Flandry said. "My idea entirely. I must say, my lord, you weren't nice to arrive unannounced. Now what?"

"Now you're under nobleman's arrest, you whelp," Hauksberg said. "Put on some clothes. Go to your quarters and stay there."

Flandry scrambled to obey. On the surface, everything had gone smoothly, more so than expected. Too much more so. Hauksberg's tone was not furious; it was almost absentminded.

Persis groped toward him. "I tell you, Mark, I'm to blame," she wept. "Let him alone. Do what you want to me, but not him!"

Hauksberg shoved her away. "Stop blubberin'," he snapped. "D' you think I care a pip on a 'scope about your peccadillos, at a time like this?"

"What's happened?" Flandry asked sharply.

Hauksberg turned and looked at him, up and down, silent for an entire minute. "Wonder if you really don't know," he said at the end. "Wonder quite a lot."

"My lord, I don't!" Flandry's mind rocked. Something *was* wrong.

"When word came to Dhangodhan, natur'lly we flitted straight back," Hauksberg said. "They're after Abrams this minute, on my authority. But you—what was your part?"

I've got to get out. Abrams' agent has to be able to

reach me. "I don't know anything, my lord. I'll report to my room."

"Stop!"

Persis sat on the bed, face in hands, and sobbed. She wasn't loud.

"Stay right here," Hauksberg said. "Not a step, understand?" His gun came free. He edged from the chamber, keeping Flandry in sight, and went to the phone. "Hm. Turned off, eh?" He flipped the switch. "Lord Oliveira."

Silence lay thick while the phone hunted through its various scanner outlets. The screen flickered, the ambassador looked forth. "Hauksberg! What the devil?"

"Just returned," said the viscount. "We heard of an attempt to rifle Premier Brechdan's files. May have been a successful attempt, too; and the agent escaped. The premier accused me of havin' a finger in it. Obvious thought. Somebody wants to sabotage my mission."

"I—" Oliveira collected himself. "Not necessarily. Terra isn't the only rival Merseia has."

"So I pointed out. Prepare to do likewise at length when you're notified officially. But we've got to show good faith. I've deputed the Merseians to arrest Commander Abrams. He'll be fetched back here. Place him under guard."

"Lord Hauksberg! He's an Imperial officer, and accredited to the diplomatic corps."

"He'll be detained by Terrans. By virtue of my commission from his Majesty, I'm assumin' command. No back talk if you don't want to be relieved of your position."

Oliveira whitened but bowed. "Very good, my lord. I must ask for this in properly recorded form."

"You'll have it when I get the chance. Next, this

young fella Flandry, Abrams' assistant. Happens I've got him on deck. Think I'll quiz him a while myself. But have a couple of men march him to detention when I give the word. Meanwhile, alert your staff, start preparin' plans, explanations, and disclaimers, and stand by for a visit from Brechdan's foreign office."

Hauksberg cut the circuit. "Enough," he said. "C'mon out and start talkin', you."

Flandry went. Nightmare hammered at him. In the back of his head ran the thought: *Abrams was right. You don't really want drama in these things.*

What'll happen to him?

To me? To Persis? To Terra?

"Sit down." Hauksberg pointed his gun at a lounger and swung the barrel back at once. With his free hand he pulled a flat case from his tunic pocket. He appeared a little relaxed; had he begun to enjoy the tableau?

Flandry lowered himself. *Psychological disadvantage, looking upward. Yes, we underestimated his Lordship badly.* Persis stood in the archway, red-eyed, hugging herself and gulping.

Hauksberg flipped open the case—an unruly part of Flandry noticed how the chased silver shone beneath the fluoroceiling—and stuck a cheroot between his teeth. "What's your role in this performance?" he asked.

"Nothing, my lord." Flandry stammered. "I don't know—I mean, if—if I were concerned, would I have been here tonight?"

"Might." Hauksberg returned the case and extracted a lighter. His glance flickered to Persis. "What about you, m' love?"

"I don't know anything," she whispered. "And neither does he. I swear it."

"Inclined to believe you." The lighter scritted and flared. "In this case, though, you've been rather cynic'lly used."

"He wouldn't!"

"Hm." Hauksberg dropped the lighter on a table and blew smoke from his nostrils. "Could be you both were duped. We'll find that out when Abrams is probed."

"You can't!" Flandry shouted. "He's an officer!"

"They certainly can on Terra, my boy. I'd order it done this very hour, and risk the repercussions, if we had the equipment. 'Course, the Merseians do. If necess'ry, I'll risk a much bigger blowback and turn him over to them. My mission's too important for legal pettifoggin'. You might save the lot of us a deal of grief by tellin' all, Ensign. If your testimony goes to prove we Terrans are not involved—d' you see?"

Give him a story, any story, whatever gets you away. Flandry's brain was frozen. "How could we have arranged the job?" he fumbled. "You saw what kind of surveillance we've been under."

"Ever hear about agents provocateurs? I never believed Abrams came along for a ride." Hauksberg switched the phone to Record. "Begin at the beginnin', continue to the end, and stop. Why'd Abrams co-opt you in the first place?"

"Well, I—that is, he needed an aide." *What actually did happen? Everything was so gradual. Step by step. I never really did decide to go into Intelligence. But somehow, here I am.*

Persis squared her shoulders. "Dominic had proven himself on Starkad," she said wretchedly. "Fighting for the Empire."

"Fine, sonorous phrase." Hauksberg tapped the ash from his cheroot. "Are you really infatuated with this lout? No matter. P'rhaps you can see anyhow that I'm workin' for the Empire myself. Work sounds less romantic than fight, but's a bit more useful in the long haul, eh? Go on, Flandry. What'd Abrams tell you he meant to accomplish?"

"He . . . he hoped to learn things. He never denied that. But spying, no. He's not stupid, my lord." *He's simply been outwitted.* "I ask you, how could he arrange trouble?"

"Leave the questions to me. When'd you first get together with Persis, and why?"

"We—I—" Seeing the anguish upon her, Flandry knew in full what it meant to make an implement of a sentient being. "My fault. Don't listen to her. On the way—"

The door opened. There was no more warning than when Hauksberg had entered. But the thing which glided through, surely the lock was not keyed to that!

Persis shrieked. Hauksberg sprang back with an oath. The thing, seared and twisted metal, blood starting afresh from the cauterized fragment of an arm, skin drawn tight and gray across bones in what was left of a face, rattled to the floor.

"Ensign Flandry," it called. The voice had volume yet, but no control, wavering across the scale and wholly without tone. Light came and went in the scanners which were eyes.

Flandry's jaws locked. Abrams' agent? Abrams' hope, wrecked and dying at his feet?

"Go on," Hauksberg breathed. The blaster crouched in his fist. "Talk to him."

Flandry shook his head till the sweat-drenched hair flew.

"Talk, I say," Hauksberg commanded. "Or I'll kill you and most surely give Abrams to the Merseians."

The creature which lay and bled before the now shut main door did not seem to notice. "Ensign Flandry. Which one is you? Hurry. *Meshuggah.* He told me to say *meshuggah.*"

Flandry moved without thinking, from his lounger, down on his knees in the blood. "I'm here," he whispered.

"Listen." The head rolled, the eyes flickered more and more dimly, a servomotor rattled dry bearings inside the broken shell. "Memorize. In the Starkad file, these numbers."

As they coughed forth, one after the next in the duodecimals of Eriau, Flandry's training reacted. He need not understand, and did not; he asked for no repetitions; each phoneme was burned into his brain.

"Is that everything?" he asked with someone else's throat.

"Aye. The whole." A hand of metal tendrils groped until he clasped it. "Will you remember my name? I was Dwyr of Tanis, once called the Merry. They made me into this. I was planted in your airboat. Commander Abrams sent me. That is why he left this place, to release me unobserved. But an alarm order was on the Starkad reel. I was ruined in escaping. I would have come sooner to you but I kept fainting. You must phone for the boat and . . . escape, I think. Remember Dwyr."

"We will always remember."

"Good. Now let me die. If you open the main plate you can turn off my heart." The words wobbled insanely, but they were clear enough. "I cannot hold Sivilla long in my brain. It is poisoned and oxygen starved. The cells are going out, one by one. Turn off my heart."

Flandry disengaged the tendrils around his hand and reached for the hinged plate. He didn't see very well, nor could he smell the oil and scorched insulation.

"Hold off," Hauksberg said. Flandry didn't hear him. Hauksberg stepped close and kicked him. "Get away from there, I say. We want him alive."

Flandry lurched erect. "You can't."

"Can and will." Hauksberg's lips were drawn back, his chest rose and fell, the cheroot had dropped from his mouth into the spreading blood. "Great Emperor! I see the whole thing. Abrams had this double agent. He'd get the information, it'd be passed on to you, and you'd go home in disgrace when I caught you with Persis." He took a moment to give the girl a look of triumph. "You follow, my dear? You were nothin' but an object."

She strained away from them, one hand to her mouth, the other fending off the world. "Sivilla, Sivilla," came from the floor. "Oh, hurry!"

Hauksberg backed toward the phone. "We'll call a medic. I think if we're fast we can save this chap."

"But don't you understand?" Flandry implored. "Those numbers—there *is* something about Starkad—your mission never had a chance. We've got to let our people know!"

"Let me worry 'bout that," Hauksberg said. "You face a charge of treason."

"For trying to bail out the Empire?"

"For tryin' to sabotage an official delegation. Tryin' to make your own policy, you and Abrams. Think you're his Majesty? You'll learn better." Flandry took a step forward. The gun jerked. "Stand back! Soon blast you as not, y' know." Hauksberg's free hand reached for the phone.

Flandry stood over Dwyr, in a private Judgment Day. Persis ran across the floor. "Mark, no!"

"Get away." Hauksberg held his gun on the boy.

Persis flung her arms around him. Suddenly her hands closed on his right wrist. She threw herself down, dragging the blaster with her. "Nicky!" she screamed.

Flandry sprang. Hauksberg hit Persis with his fist. She took the blow on her skull and hung on. Flandry arrived. Hauksberg struck at him. Flandry batted the hand aside with one arm. His other, stiff-fingered, drove into the solar plexus. Hauksberg doubled. Flandry chopped him behind the ear. He fell in a heap.

Flandry scooped up the blaster and punched the phone controls. "Airboat to Embassy," he ordered in Eriau.

Turning he strode back to Dwyr, knelt, and opened the frontal plate. Was this the switch he wanted? He undid its safety lock. "Good-bye, my friend," he said.

"One moment," wavered from the machine. "I lost her. So much darkness. Noise. . . . Now."

Flandry pulled the switch. The lights went out in the eyes and Dwyr lay still.

Persis sprawled by Hauksberg, shaken with crying.

Flandry returned and raised her. "I'll have to make a dash," he said. "Might not finish it. Do you want to come?"

She clung to him. "Yes, yes, yes. They'd have killed you."

He embraced her one-armed, his other hand holding the blaster on Hauksberg, who stirred and choked. Wonder broke upon him like morning. "Why did you help me?" he asked low.

"I don't know. Take me away from here!"

"Well . . . you may have done something great for the human race. If that information really is important. It has to be. Go put on a dress and shoes. Comb your hair. Find me a clean pair of pants. These are all bloody. Be quick." She gripped him tighter and sobbed. He slapped her. "Quick, I said! Or I'll have to leave you behind."

She ran. He nudged Hauksberg with his foot. "Up, my lord."

Hauksberg crawled to a stance. "You're crazy," he gasped. "Do you seriously expect to escape?"

"I seriously expect to try. Give me that holster belt." Flandry clipped it on. "We'll walk to the boat. If anyone asks, you're satisfied with my story, I've given you news which can't wait, and we're off to report in person to the Merseian authorities. At the first sign of trouble, I'll start shooting my way through, and you'll get the first bolt. Clear?"

Hauksberg rubbed the bruise behind his ear and glared.

With action upon him, Flandry lost every doubt. Adrenalin sang in his veins. Never had he perceived

more sharply—this over-elegant room, the bloodshot
eyes in front of him, the lovely sway of Persis re-entering
in a fire-red gown, odors of sweat and anger, sigh of a
ventilator, heat in his skin, muscle sliding across muscle,
the angle of his elbow where he aimed the gun, by eternity,
he was alive!

Having changed pants, he said, "Out we go. You first,
my lord. Me a pace behind, as fits my rank. Persis next to
you. Watch his face, darling. He might try to signal with it.
If he blows a distress rocket from his nose, tell me and I'll
kill him."

Her lips trembled. "No. You can't do that. Not to
Mark."

"He'd've done it to me. We're committed, and not to
any very genteel game. If he behaves himself he'll live,
maybe. March."

As they left, Flandry saluted that which lay on the
floor.

But he did not forget to screen the view of it with his
body on his way out to the corridor, until the door shut
behind him. Around a corner, they met a couple of young
staffmen headed in their direction. "Is everything well, my
lord?" one asked. Flandry's fingers twitched near his
sheathed gun. He cleared his throat loudly.

Hauksberg made a nod. "Bound for Afon," he said.
"Immediately. With these people."

"Confidential material in the suite," Flandry added.
"Don't go in, and make sure nobody else does."

He was conscious of their stares, like bullets hitting
his back. Could he indeed bluff his way clear? Probably.
This is no police or military center, wasn't geared to

violence, only created violence for others to quell. His danger lay beyond the compound. Surely, by now, the place was staked out. Dwyr had wrought a miracle in entering unseen.

They were stopped again in the lobby, and again got past on words. Outside, the garden lay aflash with dew under Lythyr and a sickle Neihevin. The air was cool. It quivered with distant machine sounds. Abrams' speedster had arrived. *O God, I have to leave him behind!* It sat on the parking strip, door open. Flandry urged Hauksberg and Persis aboard. He closed the door and waved on the lights. "Sit down at the console," he ordered his prisoner. "Persis, bring a towel from the head. My lord, we're about to talk our way through their security cordon. Will they believe we're harmlessly bound for Dhangodhan?"

Hauksberg's face contorted. "When Brechdan isn't here? Don't be ridiculous. C'mon, end the comedy, surrender and make things easier for yourself."

"Well, we'll do it the hard way. When we're challenged, tell 'em we're headed back to your ship to fetch some stuff we need to show Brechdan in connection with this episode."

"D'you dream they'll swallow that?"

"I think they might. Merseians aren't as rule-bound as Terrans. To them, it's in character for a boss noble to act on his own, without filing twenty different certificates first. If they don't believe us, I'll cut out the safety locks and ram a flier of theirs; so be good." Persis gave Flandry the towel. "I'm going to tie your hands. Cooperate or I'll slug you."

He grew conscious, then, of what power meant, how it worked. You kept the initiative. The other fellow's instinct was to obey, unless he was trained in self-mastery.

But you dared not slack off the pressure for a second. Hauksberg slumped in his seat and gave no trouble.

"You won't hurt him, Nicky?" Persis begged.

"Not if I can avoid it. Haven't we troubles enough?" Flandry took the manual-pilot chair. The boat swung aloft.

A buzz came from the console. Flandry closed that circuit. A uniformed Merseian looked from the vidscreen. He could see nothing but their upper bodies. "Halt!" he ordered. "Security."

Flandry nudged Hauksberg. The viscount said, "Ah . . . we must go to my ship—" No human would have accepted a tale so lamely delivered. Nor would a Merseian educated in the subtleties of human behavior. But this was merely an officer of planetary police, assigned here because he happened to be on duty at the time of emergency. Flandry had counted on that.

"I shall check," said the green visage.

"Don't you realize?" Hauksberg snapped. "I am a diplomat. Escort us if you like. But you have no right to detain us. Move along, pilot."

Flandry gunned the gravs. The boat mounted. Ardaig fell away beneath, a glittering web, a spot of light. Turning in the after viewscreen, Flandry saw two black objects circle about and trail him. They were smaller than this vessel, but they were armed and armored.

"Nice work, there at the end, my lord," he said.

Hauksberg was rapidly regaining equilibrium. "You've done rather well yourself," he answered. "I begin to see why Abrams thinks you've potentialities."

"Thanks." Flandry concentrated on gaining speed. The counteracceleration field was not quite in tune; he felt a tug weight that, uncompensated, would have left him hardly able to breathe.

"But it won't tick, y' know," Hauksberg continued. "Messages are flyin' back and forth. Our escort'll get an order to make us turn back."

"I trust not. If I were them, I'd remember *Queen Maggy* was declared harmless by her Merseian pilot. I'd alert my forces, but otherwise watch to see what you did. After all, Brechdan must be convinced you're sincere."

Ardaig was lost. Mountains gleamed in moonlight, and high plains, and cloud cover blanketing the planet in white. The wail of air grew thin and died. Stars trod forth, wintry clear.

"More I think about it," Hauksberg said, "more I'd like to have you on the right side. Peace needs able men even worse'n war does."

"Let's establish peace first, huh?" Flandry's fingers rattled computer keys. As a matter of routine, he had memorized the six elements of the spaceship's orbit around Merseia. Perturbation wouldn't have made much difference yet.

"That's what I'm tryin' for. We can have it, I tell you. You've listened to that fanatic Abrams. Give me a turn."

"Sure." Flandry spoke with half his attention. "Start by explaining why Brechdan keeps secrets about Starkad."

"D'you imagine we've no secrets? Brechdan has to defend himself. If we let mutual fear and hate build up, of course we'll get the big war."

"If we let Terra be painted into a corner, I agree, my lord, the planet incinerators will fly."

"Ever look at it from the Merseian viewpoint?"

"I didn't say it's wise to leave them with no out but to try and destroy us." Flandry shrugged. "That's for the statesmen, though, I'm told. I only work here. Please shut up and let me figure my approach curve."

Korych flamed over the edge of the world. That sunrise was gold and amethyst, beneath a million stars.

The communicator buzzed anew. "Foreseer," said the Merseian, "you may board your ship for a limited time provided we accompany you."

"Regrets," Hauksberg said. "But quite impossible. I'm after material which is for the eyes of Protector Brechdan alone. You are welcome to board as soon as I have it in this boat, and escort me straight to Castle Afon."

"I shall convey the foreseer's word to my superiors and relay their decision." Blankoff.

"You're wonderful," Persis said.

Hauksberg barked a laugh. "Don't fancy this impetuous young hero of yours includin' me in his Divine Wind dive." Seriously: "I s'pose you figure to escape in an auxiliary. Out of the question. Space patrol'll overhaul you long before you can go hyper."

"Not if I go hyper right away," Flandry said.

"But—snakes alive, boy! You know what the concentration of matter is, this near a sun. If a microjump lands you by a pebble, even—"

"Chance we take. Odds favor us, especially if we head out normally to the ecliptic plane."

"You'll be in detection range for a light-year. A ship with more legs can run you down. And will."

"You won't be there," Flandry said. "Dog your hatch. I'm busy."

The minutes passed. He scarcely noticed when the call came, agreeing that Hauksberg's party might board alone. He did reconstruct the reasoning behind that agreement. *Dronning Margrete* was unarmed and empty. Two or three men could not start her up in less than hours. Long before then, warcraft would be on hand to blast her. Hauksberg must be honest. Let him have his way and see what he produced.

The great tapered cylinder swam into sight. Flandry contacted the machines within and made rendezvous on instruments and trained senses. A boatlock gaped wide. He slid through. The lock closed, air rushed into the turret, he killed his motor and stood up. "I'll have to secure you, my lord," he said. "They'll find you when they enter."

Hauksberg regarded him. "You'll not reconsider?" he asked. "Terra shouldn't lose one like you."

"No. Sorry."

"Warn you, you'll be outlawed. I don't aim to sit idle and let you proceed. After what's happened, the best way I can show my bona fides is to cooperate with the Merseians in headin' you off."

Flandry touched his blaster. Hauksberg nodded. "You can delay matters a trifle by killin' me," he said.

"Have no fears. Persis, another three or four towels. Lie down on the deck, my lord."

Hauksberg did as he was told. Looking at the girl, he said: "Don't involve yourself. Stay with me. I'll tell 'em you were a prisoner too. Hate to waste women."

"They are in short supply hereabouts," Flandry agreed. "You'd better do it, Persis."

She stood quiet for a little. "Do you mean you forgive me, Mark?" she asked.

"Well, yes," Hauksberg said.

She bent and kissed him lightly. "I think I believe you. But no, thanks. I've made my choice."

"After the way your boyfriend's treated you?"

"He had to. I have to believe that." Persis helped bind Hauksberg fast.

She and Flandry left the boat. The passageways glowed and echoed as they trotted. They hadn't far to go until they entered another turret. The slim hull of a main auxiliary loomed over them. Flandry knew the model: a lovely thing, tough and versatile, with fuel and supplies for a journey of several hundred parsecs. Swift, too; not that she could outpace a regular warcraft, but a stern chase is a long chase and he had some ideas about what to do if the enemy came near.

He made a quick check of systems. Back in the control room, he found Persis in the copilot's seat. "Will I bother you?" she asked timidly.

"Contrariwise," he said. "Keep silent, though, till we're in hyperdrive."

"I will," she promised. "I'm not a complete null, Nicky. You learn how to survive when you're a low-caste dancer. Different from space, of course. But this is the first time I've done anything for anyone but myself. Feels good. Scary, yes, but good."

He ran a hand across the tangled dark hair, smooth cheek and delicate profile, until his fingers tilted her chin and he bestowed his own kiss on her. "Thanks more'n I can say," he murmured. "I was doing this mainly on account of Max Abrams. It'd have been cold, riding alone with his ghost. Now I've got you to live for."

He seated himself. At his touch, the engine woke. "Here we go," he said.

CHAPTER FOURTEEN

Dawn broke over Ardaig, and from the tower on Eidh Hill kettledrums spoke their ancient prayer. Admiralty House cast its shadow across the Oiss, blue upon the mists that still hid early river traffic. Inland the shadow was black, engulfing Castle Afon.

Yet Brechdan Ironrede chose to receive the Terrans there instead of in his new eyrie. *He's shaken*, Abrams thought. *He's rallying quick, but he needs the help of his ancestors.*

Entering the audience chamber, a human was at first dazed, as if he had walked into a dream. He needed a moment to make sense of what he saw. The proportions of long, flagged floor, high walls, narrow windows arched at both top and bottom, sawtoothed vaulting overhead, were wrong by every Terran canon and nonetheless had a rightness of their own. The mask helmets on suits of armor grinned like demons. The patterns of faded tapestries and rustling battle banners held no human symbology. For this was Old Wilwidh, before the machine came to impose universal sameness. It was the wellspring of Merseia. You had to see a place like this if you would understand, in your bones, that Merseians would never be kin to you.

I wish my ancestors were around. Approaching the dais beside a silent Hauksberg, his boots resounding hollow, bitter incense in his nostrils, Abrams conjured up Dayan in his head. *I too have a place in the cosmos. Let me not forget.*

Black-robed beneath a dragon carved in black wood, the Hand of Vach Ynvory waited. The men bowed to him. He lifted a short spear and crashed it down in salute. Brusquely, he said: "This is an evil thing that has happened."

"What news, sir?" Hauksberg asked. His eyes were sunken and a tic moved one corner of his mouth.

"At latest report, a destroyer had locked detectors on Flandry's hyperwake. It can catch him, but time will be required, and meanwhile both craft have gone beyond detection range."

"The Protector is assured anew of my profoundest regrets. I am preferring charges against this malefactor. Should he be caught alive, he may be treated as a common pirate."

Yah, Abrams thought. *Dragged under a hypnoprobe and wrung dry. Well, he doesn't have any vital military secrets, and testimony about me can't get me in any deeper than I am. But please, let him be killed outright.*

"My lord," he said, "to you and the Hand I formally protest. Dominic Flandry holds an Imperial commission.

At a minimum the law entitles him to a court-martial. Nor can his diplomatic immunity be removed by fiat."

"He was not accredited by his Majesty's government, but myself," Hauksberg snapped. "The same applies to you, Abrams."

"Be still," Brechdan ordered him. Hauksberg gaped unbelieving at the massive green countenance. Brechdan's look was on Abrams. "Commander," the Merseian said, "when you were seized last night, you insisted that you had information I must personally hear. Having been told of this, I acceded. Do you wish to talk with me alone?"

Hang on, here we go. I boasted to Dom once, they wouldn't take me in any condition to blab, and they'd pay for whatever they got. Nu, here I am, whole-skinned and disarmed. If I'm to justify my brag, these poor wits will have to keep me out of the interrogation cell. "I thank the Hand," Abrams said, "but the matter concerns Lord Hauksberg also."

"Speak freely. Today is no time for circumlocutions."

Abram's heart thudded but he held his words steady. "Point of law, Hand. By the Covenant of Alfzar, Merseia confirmed her acceptance of the rules of war and diplomacy which evolved on Terra. They evolved, and you took them over, for the excellent reason that they work. Now if you wish to declare us personae non gratae and deport us, his Majesty's government will have no grounds for complaint. But taking any other action against any one of us, no matter what the source of our accreditation, is ground for breaking off relations, if not for war."

"Diplomatic personnel have no right to engage in espionage," Brechdan said.

"No, Hand. Neither is the government to which they are sent supposed to spy on them. And in fact, Dwyr the Hook was planted on me as a spy. Scarcely a friendly act, Hand, the more so when urgent negotiations are under way. It happened his sympathies were with Terra—"

Brechdan's smile was bleak. "I do not believe it merely happened, Commander. I have the distinct impression that you maneuvered to get him posted where he would be in contact with you. Compliments on your skill."

"Hand, his Majesty's government will deny any such allegation."

"How dare you speak for the Empire?" Hauksberg exploded.

"How dare you, my lord?" Abrams replied. "I am only offering a prediction. But will the Hand not agree it is probably correct?"

Brechdan rubbed his chin. "Charge and counter-charge, denial and counter-denial . . . yes, no doubt. What do you expect the Empire to maintain?"

"That rests with the Policy Board, Hand, and how it decides will depend on a number of factors, including mood. If Merseia takes a course which looks reasonable in Terran eyes, Terra is apt to respond in kind."

"I presume a reasonable course for us includes dropping charges against yourself," Brechdan said dryly.

Abrams lifted his shoulders and spread his palms. "What else? Shall we say that Dwyr and Flandry acted on impulse, without my knowledge? Isn't it wise to refrain from involving the honor of entire planets?"

"*Khraich*. Yes. The point is well taken. Though frankly, I am disappointed in you. I would stand by a subordinate."

"Hand, what happens to him is outside your control or mine. He and his pursuer have gone past communication range. It may sound pompous, but I want to save myself for further service to the Empire."

"We'll see about that," Hauksberg said venomously.

"I told you to be silent," Brechdan said. "No, Commander, on Merseia your word is not pompous at all." He inclined his head. "I salute you. Lord Hauksberg will oblige me by considering you innocent."

"Sir," the viscount protested, "surely he must be confined to the Embassy grounds for the duration of our stay. What happens to him on his return will lie with his service and his government."

"I do request the commander to remain within the compound," Brechdan said. He leaned forward. "Now, delegate, comes your turn. If you are willing to continue present discussions, so are we. But there are certain preconditions. By some accident, Flandry might yet escape, and he does carry military secrets. We must therefore dispatch a fast courier to the nearest Terran regional headquarters, with messages from us both. If Terra disowns him and cooperates with Merseia in his capture or destruction, then Terra has proven her desire for peaceful relations and the Grand Council of His Supremacy will be glad to adjust its policies accordingly. Will you lend your efforts to this end?"

"Of course, sir! Of course!"

"The Terran Empire is far away, though," Brechdan continued. "I don't imagine Flandry would make for it. Our patrols will cover the likeliest routes, as insurance. But the nearest human installation is on Starkad, and if somehow he eludes our destroyer, I think it probable he will go either there or to Betelgeuse. The region is vast and little known. Thus our scouts would have a very poor chance of intercepting him—until he is quite near his destination. Hence, if he should escape, I shall wish to guard the approaches. But as my government has no more desire than yours to escalate the conflict, your commandant on Starkad must be told that these units are no menace to him and he need not send for reinforcements. Rather, he must cooperate. Will you prepare such orders for him?"

"At once, sir," Hauksberg said. Hope was revitalizing him. He paid no attention to Abrams' stare.

"Belike this will all prove unnecessary," Brechdan said. "The destroyer estimated she would overtake Flandry in three days. She will need little longer to report back. At such time we can feel easy, and so can his Majesty's government. But for certainty's sake, we had best get straight to work. Please accompany me to the adjacent office." He rose. For a second he locked eyes with Abrams. "Commander," he said, "your young man makes me proud to be a sentient creature. What might our united races not accomplish? Hunt well."

Abrams could not speak. His throat was too thick with unshed tears. He bowed and left. At the door, Merseian guards fell in, one either side of him.

Stars crowded the viewscreens, unmercifully brilliant against infinite night. The spaceboat thrummed with her haste.

Flandry and Persis returned from their labor. She had

been giving him tools, meals, anything she could that seemed to fit his request, "Just keep feeding me and fanning me." In a shapeless coverall, hair caught under a scarf, a smear of grease on her nose, she was somehow more desirable than ever before. Or was that simply because death coursed near?

The Merseian destroyer had called the demand to stop long ago, an age ago, when she pulled within range of a hypervibration 'cast. Flandry refused. "Then prepare your minds for the God," said her captain, and cut off. Moment by moment, hour by hour, he had crept in on the boat, until instruments snouted his presence.

Persis caught Flandry's hand. Her own touch was cold. "I don't understand," she said in a thin voice. "You told me he can track us by our wake. But space is so big. Why can't we go sublight and let him hunt for us?"

"He's too close," Flandry said. "He was already too close when we first knew he was on our trail. If we cut the secondaries, he'd have a pretty good idea of our location, and need only cast about a small volume of space till he picked up the neutrino emission of our powerplant."

"Couldn't we turn that off too?"

"We'd die inside a day. Everything depends on it. Odds-on bet whether we suffocated or froze. If we had suspended-animation equipment—But we don't. This is no warcraft, not even an exploratory vessel. It's just the biggest lifeboat-cum-gig *Queen Maggy* could tote."

They moved toward the control room. "What's going to happen?" she asked.

"In theory, you mean?" He was grateful for a chance to talk. The alternative would have been that silence which pressed in on the hull. "Well, look. We travel faster than light by making a great many quantum jumps per second, which don't cross the intervening space. You might say we're not in the real universe most of the time, though we are so often that we can't notice any difference. Our friend has to phase in. That is, he has to adjust his jumps to the same frequency and the same phase angle as ours. This makes each ship a completely solid object to the other, as if they were moving sublight, under ordinary gravitic drive at a true velocity."

"But you said something about the field."

"Oh, that. Well, what makes us quantum-jump is a pulsating force-field generated by the secondary engine. The field encloses us and reaches out through a certain radius. How big a radius, and how much mass it can affect, depends on the generator's power. A big ship can lay alongside a smaller one and envelop her and literally drag her at a resultant pseudospeed. Which is how you carry out most capture and boarding operations. But a destroyer isn't that large in relation to us. She does have to come so close that our fields overlap. Otherwise her beams and artillery can't touch us."

"Why don't we change phase?"

"Standard procedure in an engagement. I'm sure our friends expect us to try it. But one party can change as fast as another, and runs a continuous computation to predict the pattern of the opposition's maneuvers. Sooner or later, the two will be back in phase long enough for a weapon to hit. We're not set up to do it nearly as well as he is. No, our solitary chance is the thing we've been working on."

She pressed against him. He felt how she trembled. "Nicky, I'm afraid."

"Think I'm not?" Both pairs of lips were dry when they touched. "Come on, let's to our posts. We'll know in a few minutes. If we go out—Persis, I couldn't ask for a better traveling companion." As they sat down, Flandry added, because he dared not stay serious: "Though we wouldn't be together long. You're ticketed for heaven, my destination's doubtless the other way."

She gripped his hand again. "Mine too. You won't escape me th-th-that easily."

Alarms blared. A shadow crossed the stars. It thickened as phasing improved. Now it was a torpedo outline, still transparent; now the gun turrets and missile launchers showed clear; now all but the brightest stars were occulted. Flandry laid an eye to the crosshairs of his improvised fire-control scope. His finger rested on a button. Wires ran aft from it.

The Merseian destroyer became wholly real to him. Starlight glimmered off metal. He knew how thin that metal was. Force screens warded off solid matter, and nothing protected against nuclear energies: nothing but speed to get out of their way, which demanded low mass. Nevertheless he felt as if a dinosaur stalked him.

The destroyer edged nearer, swelling in the screens. She moved leisurely, knowing her prey was weaponless, alert only for evasive tactics. Flandry's right hand went to the drive controls. So . . . so . . . he was zeroed a trifle forward of the section where he knew her engines must be.

A gauge flickered. Hyperfields were making their first

tenuous contact. In a second it would be sufficiently firm for a missile or a firebolt to cross from one hull to another. Persis, reading the board as he had taught her, yelled, "Go!"

Flandry snapped on a braking vector. Lacking the instruments and computers of a man-of-war, he had estimated for himself what the thrust should be. He pressed the button.

In the screen, the destroyer shot forward in relation to him. From an open hatch in his boat plunged the auxiliary's auxiliary, a craft meant for atmosphere but propellable anywhere on gravity beams. Fields joined almost at the instant it transitted them. At high relative velocity, both pseudo and kinetic, it smote.

Flandry did not see what happened. He had shifted phase immediately, and concentrated on getting the hell out of the neighborhood. If everything worked as hoped, his airboat ripped the Merseian plates, ruinously, at kilometers per second. Fragments howled in air, flesh, engine connections. The destroyer was not destroyed. Repair would be possible, after so feeble a blow. But before the ship was operational again, he would be outside detection range. If he zigzagged, he would scarcely be findable.

He hurtled among the stars. A clock counted one minute, two, three, five. He began to stop fighting for breath. Persis gave way to tears. After ten minutes he felt free to run on automatic, lean over and hold her.

"We did it," he whispered. "Satan in Sirius! One miserable gig took a navy vessel."

Then he must leap from his seat, caper and crow till the boat rang. "We won! Ta-ran-tu-la! We won! Break out the champagne! This thing must have champagne among the rations! God is too good for anything else!" He hauled Persis up and danced her over the deck. "Come on, you! We won! Swing your lady! I gloat, I gloat, I gloat!"

Eventually he calmed down. By that time Persis had command of herself. She disengaged from him so she could warn: "We've a long way to Starkad, darling, and danger at the end of the trip."

"Ah," said Ensign Dominic Flandry, "but you forget, this is the beginning of the trip."

A smile crept over her mouth. "Precisely what do you mean, sir?"

He answered with a leer. "That it *is* a long way to Starkad."

CHAPTER FIFTEEN

Saxo glittered white among the myriads. But it was still so far that others outshone it. Brightest stood Betelgeuse. Flandry's gaze fell on that crimson spark and lingered. He sat at the pilot board, chin in hand, for many minutes; and only the throb of the engine and murmur of the ventilators were heard.

Persis entered the control room. During the passage she had tried to improvise a few glamorous changes of garment from the clothes in stock, but they were too resolutely utilitarian. So mostly, as now, she settled for a pair of shorts, and those mostly for the pockets. Her hair swept loose, dark-bright as space; a lock tickled him when she bent over his shoulder, and he sensed its faint sunny odor, and her own. But this time he made no response.

"Trouble, darling?" she asked.

"'It ain't the work, it's them damn decisions,'" he quoted absently.

"You mean which way to go?"

"Yes. Here's where we settle the question. Saxo or Betelgeuse?"

He had threshed the arguments out till she knew them by heart, but he went on anyhow: "Got to be one or the other. We're not set up to lie doggo on some undiscovered planet. The Empire's too far; every day of travel piles up chances for a Merseian to spot our wake. They'll have sent couriers in all directions—every kind of ship that could outrun our skulker's course—soon's they learned we escaped. Maybe before, even. Their units must be scouring these parts.

"Saxo's the closer. Against heading there is the consideration they can keep a pretty sharp watch on it without openly using warcraft in the system. Any big, fast merchantman could gobble us, and the crew come aboard with sidearms. However, if we were in call range, I might raise Terran HQ on Starkad and pass on the information we're carrying. Then we might hope the Merseians would see no further gain in damaging us. But the whole thing is awful iffy.

"Now Betelgeuse is an unaligned power, and very jealous of her neutrality. Foreign patrols will have to keep their distance, spread so thin we might well slip through. Once on Alfzar, we could report to the Terran ambassador. *But* the Betelgeuseans won't let us enter their system secretly. They maintain their own patrols. We'd have to go through traffic procedures, starting beyond orbital radius of the outermost planet. And the Merseians can monitor those com channels. A raider could dash in quick-like and blast us."

"They wouldn't dare," Persis said.

"Sweetheart, they'd dare practically anything, and apologize later. You don't know what's at stake."

She sat down beside him. "Because you won't tell me."

"Right."

He had gnawed his way to the truth. Hour upon hour, as they fled through Merseia's dominions, he hunched with paper, penstyl, calculator, and toiled. Their flight involved nothing dramatic. It simply meandered through regions where one could assume their enemies rarely came. Why should beings with manlike biological requirements go from a dim red dwarf star to a planetless blue giant to a dying Cepheid variable? Flandry had ample time for his labors.

Persis was complaining about that when the revelation came. "You might talk to me."

"I do," he muttered, not lifting his eyes from the desk. "I make love to you as well. Both with pleasure. But not right now, please!"

She flopped into a seat. "Do you recall what we have aboard for entertainment?" she said. "Four animations: a Martian travelogue, a comedian routine, a speech by the Emperor, and a Cynthian opera on the twenty-tone scale. Two novels: *Outlaw Blastman* and *Planet of Sin*. I have them memorized. They come back to me in my dreams. Then there's a flute, which I can't play, and a set of operation manuals."

"M-hm." He tried putting Brechdan's figures in a different sequence. It had been easy to translate from Merseian to Terran arithmetic. But what the devil did the symbols refer to? Angles, times, several quantities with no dimensions specified . . . rotation? Of what? Not of Brechdan; no such luck.

A nonhuman could have been similarly puzzled by something from Terra, such as a periodic table of isotopes. He wouldn't have known which properties out of many were listed, nor the standardized order in which quantum numbers were given, nor the fact that logarithms were to the base ten unless e was explicit, nor a lot of other things he'd need to know before he could guess what the table signified.

"You don't have to solve the problem," Persis sulked. "You told me yourself, an expert can see the meaning at a glance. You're just having fun."

Flandry raised his head, irritated. "Might be hellish important for us to know. Give us some idea what to expect. How in the name of Copros can Starkad matter so much? One lonesome planet!"

And the idea came to him.

He grew so rigid, he stared so wildly out into the universe, that Persis was frightened. "Nicky, what's wrong?" He didn't hear. With a convulsive motion, he grabbed a fresh sheet of paper and started scrawling. Finished, he stared at the result. Sweat stood on his brow. He rose, went into the control room, returned with a reel which threaded into his microreader. Again he wrote, copying off numbers. His fingers danced on the desk computer. Persis held herself moveless.

Until at last he nodded. "That's it," he said in a cold small voice. "Has to be."

"What is?" she could then ask.

He twisted around in his chair. His eyes took a second to focus on her. Something had changed in his face. He was almost a stranger.

"I can't tell you," he said.

"Why not?"

"We might get captured alive. They'd probe you and find you knew. If they didn't murder you out of hand, they'd wipe your brain—which to my taste is worse."

He took a lighter from his pocket and burned every paper on the desk and swept the ashes into a disposal. Afterward he shook himself, like a dog that has come near drowning, and went to her.

"Sorry," he smiled. "Kind of a shock for me there. But I'm all right now. And I really will pay attention to you, from here on in."

She enjoyed the rest of the voyage, even after she had identified the change in him, the thing which had gone and would never quite come back. Youth.

The detector alarm buzzed. Persis drew a gasp and caught Flandry's arm. He tore her loose, reaching for the main hyperdrive switch.

But he didn't pull it, returning them to normal state and kinetic velocity. His knuckles stood white on the handle. A pulse fluttered in his throat. "I forgot what I'd already decided," he said. "We don't have an especially good detector. If she's a warship, we were spotted some time ago."

"But this time she can't be headed straight at us." Her tone was fairly level. She had grown somewhat used to being hunted. "We have a big sphere to hide in."

"Uh-huh. We'll try that if necessary. But first let's see which way yonder fellow is bound." He changed course. Stars wheeled in the viewports, otherwise there was no sensation. "If we can find a track on which the intensity stays constant, we'll be running parallel to him and he isn't trying to intercept." Saxo burned dead ahead. "S'pose he's going there—"

Minutes crawled. Flandry let himself relax. His coverall was wet. "Whew! What I hoped. Destination, Saxo. And if he's steered on a more or less direct line, as is probable, then he's come from the Empire."

He got busy, calculating, grumbling about rotten civilian instrumentation. "Yes, we can meet him. Let's go."

"But he could be Merseian," Persis objected. "He needn't have come from a Terran planet."

"Chance we take. The odds aren't bad. He's slower than us, which suggests a merchant vessel." Flandry set the new path, leaned back and stretched. A grin spread across his features. "My dilemma's been solved for me. We're off to Starkad."

"Why? How?"

"Didn't mention it before, for fear of raising false hopes in you. When I'd rather raise something else. But I came here first, instead of directly to Saxo or Betelgeuse, because this is the way Terran ships pass, carrying men and supplies to Starkad and returning home. If we can hitch a ride . . . you see?"

Eagerness blossomed in her and died again, "Why couldn't we have found one going home?"

"Be glad we found any whatsoever. Besides, this way we deliver our news a lot sooner." Flandry rechecked his figures. "We'll be in call range in an hour. If he should prove to be Merseian, chances are we can outspeed and lose him." He rose. "I decree a good stiff drink."

Persis held her hands up. They trembled. "We do need something for our nerves," she agreed, "but there are psychochemicals aboard."

"Whisky's more fun. Speaking of fun, we have an hour."

She rumpled his hair. "You're impossible."

"No," he said. "Merely improbable."

The ship was the freighter *Rieskessel*, registered on Nova Germania but operating out of the Imperial frontier world Irumclaw. She was a huge, potbellied, ungainly and unkempt thing, with a huge, potbellied, ungainly and unkempt captain. He bellowed a not quite sober welcome when Flandry and Persis came aboard.

"Oh, ho, ho, ho! Humans! So soon I did not expect seeing humans. And never this gorgeous." One hairy hand engulfed Flandry's, the other chucked Persis under the chin. "Otto Brummelmann is me."

Flandry looked past the bald, wildly bearded head, down the passageway from the airlock. Corroded metal shuddered to the drone of an ill-tuned engine. A pair of multi-limbed beings with shiny blue integuments stared back from their labor; they were actually swabbing by hand. The lights were reddish orange, the air held a metallic tang and was chilly enough for his breath to smoke. "Are you the only Terran, sir?" he asked.

"Not Terran. Not me. Germanian. But for years now on Irumclaw. My owners want Irumclagian spacehands, they come cheaper. No human language do I hear from end to end of a trip. They can't pronounce." Brummelmann kept his little eyes on Persis, who had donned her one gown, and tugged at his own soiled tunic in an effort at getting some wrinkles out. "Lonely, lonely. How nice to find you. First we secure your boat, next we go for drinks in my cabin, right?"

"We'd better have a private talk immediately, sir," Flandry said. "Our boat—no, let's wait till we're alone."

"You wait. I be alone with the little lady, right? Ho, ho, ho!" Brummelmann swept a paw across her. She shrank back in distaste.

On the way, the captain was stopped by a crew member who had some question. Flandry took the chance to hiss in Persis' ear: "Don't offend him. This is fantastic luck."

"This?" Her nose wrinkled.

"Yes. Think. No matter what happens, none of these xenos'll give us away. They can't. All we have to do is stay on the good side of the skipper, and that shouldn't be hard."

He had seen pigpens, in historical dramas, better kept up than Brummelmann's cabin. The Germanian filled three mugs, ignoring coffee stains, with a liquid that sank fangs into stomachs. His got half emptied on the first gulp. "So!" he belched. "We talk. Who sent you to deep space in a gig?"

Persis took the remotest corner. Flandry stayed near Brummelmann, studying him. The man was a failure, a bum, an alcoholic wreck. Doubtless he kept his job because the owners insisted on a human captain and couldn't get anyone else at the salary they wanted to pay. Didn't matter greatly, as long as the mate had some competence. For the most part, antiquated though her systems must be, the ship ran herself.

"You are bound for Starkad, aren't you, sir?" Flandry asked.

"Yes, yes. My company has a Naval contract. Irumclaw is a transshipment point. This trip we carry food and construction equipment. I hope we go on another run soon. Not much pleasure in Highport. But we was to talk about you."

"I can't say anything except that I'm on a special mission. It's vital for me to reach Highport secretly. If Donna d'Io and I can ride down with you, and you haven't radioed the fact ahead, you'll have done the Empire a tremendous service."

"Special mission . . . with a lady?" Brummelmann dug a blackrimmed thumb into Flandry's ribs. "I can guess what sort of mission. Ho, ho, ho!"

"I rescued her," Flandry said patiently. "That's why we were in a boat. A Merseian attack. The war's sharpening. I have urgent information for Admiral Enriques."

Brummelmann's laughter choked off. Behind the matted whiskers, that reached to his navel, he swallowed. "Attack, you said? But no, the Merseians, they have never bothered civilian ships."

"Nor should they bother this one, Captain. Not if they don't know I'm aboard."

Brummelmann wiped his pate. Probably he thought of himself as being in the high, wild tradition of early spacefaring days. But now his daydreams had orbited.

"My owners," he said weakly. "I have obligation to my owners. I am responsible for their ship."

"Your first duty is to the Empire." Flandry considered taking over at blaster point. No; not unless he must; too chancy. "And all you need do is approach Starkad in the usual fashion, make your usual landing at Highport, and let us off. The Merseians will never know, I swear."

"I—but I—"

Flandry snatched an idea from the air. "As for your owners," he said, "you can do them a good turn as well. Our boat had better be jettisoned out here. The enemy has her description. But if we take careful note of the spot, and leave her powerplant going for neutrino tracing, you pick her up on your way home and sell her there. She's worth as much as this entire ship, I'll bet." He winked. "Of course, you'll inform your owners."

Brummelmann's eyes gleamed. "Well. So. Of course." He tossed off the rest of his drink. "By God, yes! Shake!"

He insisted on shaking hands with Persis also. "Ugh," she said to Flandry when they were alone, in an emptied locker where a mattress had been laid. She had refused the captain's offer of his quarters. "How long to Starkad?"

"Couple days." Flandry busied himself checking the spacesuits he had removed from the boat before she was cast adrift.

"I don't know if I can stand it."

"Sorry, but we've burned our britches. Myself, I stick by my claims that we lucked out."

"You have the strangest idea of luck," she sighed. "Oh, well, matters can't get any worse."

They could.

Fifteen hours later, Flandry and Persis were in the saloon. Coveralled against the chill but nonetheless shivering, mucous membranes aching from the dryness, they tried to pass time with a game of rummy. They weren't succeeding very well.

Brummelmann's voice boomed hoarse from the intercom: "You! Ensign Flandry! To the bridge!"

"Huh?" He sprang up. Persis followed his dash, down halls and through a companionway. Stars glared from the viewports. Because the optical compensator was out of adjustment, they had strange colors and were packed fore and aft, as if the ship moved through another reality.

Brummelmann held a wrench. Beside him, his first mate aimed a laser torch, a crude substitute for a gun but lethal at short range. "Hands high!" the captain shrilled.

Flandry's arms lifted. Sickness caught at his gullet. "What is this?"

"Read." Brummelman thrust a printout at him. "You liar, you traitor, thought you could fool me? Look what came."

It was a standard form, transcribed from a hypercast that must have originated in one of several automatic transmitters around Saxo. *Office of Vice Admiral Juan Enriques, commanding Imperial Terrestrial Naval forces in a region*—Flandry's glance flew to the text.

> *General directive issued under martial law: By statement of his Excellency Lord Markus Hauksberg, Viscount of Ny Kalmar on Terra, special Imperial delegate to the Roidhunate of Merseia . . . Ensign Dominic*

Flandry, an officer of his Majesty's Navy attached to the delegation . . . mutinied and stole a spaceboat belonging to the realm of Ny Kalmar; description as follows . . . charged with high treason. . . . Pursuant to interstellar law and Imperial policy, Ensign Flandry is to be apprehended and returned to his superiors on Merseia. . . . All ships, including Terran, will be boarded by Merseian inspectors before proceeding to Starkad. . . . Terrans who may apprehend this criminal are to deliver him promptly, in their own persons, to the nearest Merseian authority . . . secrets of state—

Persis closed her eyes and strained fingers together. The blood had left her face.

"Well?" Brummelmann growled. "Well, what have you to say for yourself?"

Flandry leaned against the bulkhead. He didn't know if his legs would upbear him. "I . . . can say . . . that bastard Brechdan thinks of everything."

"You expected you could fool me? You thought I would do your traitor's work? No, no!"

Flandry looked from him, to the mate, to Persis. Weakness vanished in rage. But his brains stayed machine precise. He lowered the hand which held the flimsy paper. "I'd better tell you the whole truth," he husked.

"No, I don't want to hear, I want no secrets."

Flandry let his knees go. As he fell, he yanked out his blaster. The torch flame boomed blue where he had been. His own snap shot flared off that tool. The mate yowled and dropped the red-hot thing. Flandry regained his feet. "Get rid of your wrench," he said.

It clattered on the deck. Brummelmann backed off, past his mate who crouched and keened in pain. "You cannot get away," he croaked. "We are detected by now. Surely we are. You make us turn around, a warship comes after."

"I know," Flandry said. His mind leaped as if across ice floes. "Listen. This is a misunderstanding. Lord Hauksberg's been fooled. I do have information, and it does have to reach Admiral Enriques. I want nothing from you but transportation to Highport. I'll surrender to the Terrans. Not to the Merseians. The Terrans. What's wrong with that? They'll do what the Emperor really wants. If need be, they can turn me over to the enemy. But not before they've heard what I have to tell. Are you a man, Captain? Then behave like one!"

"But we will be boarded," Brummelmann wailed.

"You can hide me. A thousand possible places on a ship. If they have no reason to suspect you, the Merseians won't search everywhere. That could take days. Your crew won't blab. They're as alien to the Merseians as they are to us. No common language, gestures, interests, anything. Let the greenskins come aboard. I'll be down in the cargo or somewhere. You act natural. Doesn't matter if you show a bit of strain. I'm certain everybody they've checked has done so. Pass me on to the Terrans. A year from now you could have a knighthood."

Brummelmann's eyes darted back and forth. The breath rasped sour from his mouth.

"The alternative," Flandry said, "is that I lock you up and assume command."

"I . . . no—" Tears started forth, down into the dirty beard. "Please. Too much risk—" Abruptly, slyly, after a breath: "Why, yes. I will. I can find a good hiding spot for you."

And tell them when they arrive, Flandry thought. *I've got the upper hand and it's worthless. What am I to do?*

Persis stirred. She approached Brummelmann and took his hands in hers. "Oh, thank you," she caroled.

"Eh? Ho?" He gawped at her.

"I knew you were a real man. Like the old heroes of the League, come back to life."

"But you—lady—"

"The message doesn't include a word about me," she purred. "I don't feel like sitting in some dark hole."

"You . . . you aren't registered aboard. They will read the list. Won't they?"

"What if they do? Would I be registered?"

Hope rushed across Flandry. He felt giddy with it. "There are some immediate rewards, you see," he cackled.

"I—why, I—" Brummelmann straightened. He caught Persis to him. "So there are. Oh, ho, ho! So there are!"

She threw Flandry a look he wished he could forget.

He crept from the packing case. The hold was gut-black. The helmet light of his spacesuit cast a single beam to guide him. Slowly, awkward in armor, he wormed among crates to the hatch.

The ship was quiet. Nothing spoke but powerplant, throttled low, and ventilators. Shadows bobbed grotesque where his beam cut a path. Orbit around Starkad, awaiting clearance to descend—must be. He had survived. The Merseians had passed within meters of him, he heard them talk and curled his finger around the trigger; but they had gone again and the *Rieskessel* resumed acceleration. So Persis had kept Brummelmann under control; he didn't like to think how.

The obvious course was to carry on as he had outlined, let himself be taken planetside and turn himself in. Thus he would certainly get his message through, the word which he alone bore. (He had wondered whether to give Persis those numbers, but decided against it. A list for her made another chance of getting caught; and her untrained mind might not retain the figures exactly, even in the subconscious for narcosynthesis to bring forth.) But he didn't know how Enriques would react. The admiral was no robot; he would pass the information on to Terra, one way or another. But he might yield up Flandry. He would most likely not send an armed scout to check and confirm, without authorization from headquarters. Not in the face of Hauksberg's message, or the command laid on him that he must take no escalating action save in response to a Merseian initiative.

So at best, the obvious course entailed delay, which the enemy might put to good use. It entailed a high probability of Brechdan Ironrede learning how matters stood. Max Abrams (*Are you alive yet, my father?*) had said, "What helps the other fellow most is knowing what you know." And, finally, Dominic Flandry wasn't about to become a God damned pawn again!

He opened the hatch. The corridor stretched empty. Unhuman music squealed from the forecastle. Captain Brummelmann was in no hurry to make planetfall, and his crew was taking the chance to relax.

Flandry sought the nearest lifeboat. If anyone noticed, well, all right, he'd go to Highport. But otherwise, borrowing a boat would be the smallest crime on his docket. He entered the turret, dogged the inner valve, closed his faceplate, and worked the manual controls. Pumps roared, exhausting air. He climbed into the boat and secured her own airlock. The turret's outer valve opened automatically.

Space blazed at him. He nudged through on the last possible impetus. Starkad was a huge wheel of darkness, rimmed with red, day blue on one edge. A crescent moon glimmered among the stars. Weightlessness caught Flandry in an endless falling.

It vanished as he turned on interior gravity and applied a thrust vector. He spiraled downward. The planetary map was clear in his recollection. He could reach Ujanka without trouble—Ujanka, the city he had saved.

CHAPTER SIXTEEN

Dragoika flowed to a couch, reclined on one elbow, and gestured at Flandry. "Don't pace in that caged way, Dommaneek," she urged. "Take ease by my side. We have scant time alone together, we two friends."

Behind her throaty voice, up through the window, came the sounds of feet shuffling about, weapons rattling, a surflike growl. Flandry stared out. Shiv Alley was packed with armed Kursovikians. They spilled past sight, among gray walls, steep red roofs, carved beams: on into the Street Where They Fought, a cordon around this house. Spearheads and axes, helmets and byrnies flashed in the harsh light of Saxo; banners snapped to the wind, shields bore monsters and thunderbolts luridly colored. It was no mob. It was the fighting force of Ujanka, summoned by the Sisterhood. Warriors guarded the parapets on Seatraders' Castle and the ships lay ready in Golden Bay.

Lucifer! Flandry thought, half dismayed. *Did I start this?*

He looked back at Dragoika. Against the gloom of the

chamber, the barbaric relics which crowded it, her ruby eyes and the striped orange-and-white fur seemed to glow, so that the curves of her body grew disturbingly rich. She tossed back her blonde mane, and the half-human face broke into a smile whose warmth was not lessened by the fangs. "We were too busy since you came," she said. "Now, while we wait, we can talk. Come."

He crossed the floor, strewn with aromatic leaves in his honor, and took the couch by hers. A small table in the shape of a flower stood between, bearing a ship model and a flagon. Dragoika sipped. "Will you not share my cup, Dommaneek?"

"Well . . . thanks." He couldn't refuse, though Starkadian wine tasted grim on his palate. Besides, he'd better get used to native viands; he might be living off them for a long while. He fitted a tube to his chowlock and sucked up a bit.

It was good to wear a regular sea-level outfit again, air helmet, coverall, boots, after being penned in a spacesuit. The messenger Dragoika sent for him, to the Terran station in the High Housing, had insisted on taking back such a rig.

"How have you been?" Flandry asked lamely.

"As always. We missed you, I and Ferok and your other old comrades. How glad I am the *Archer* was in port."

"Lucky for me!"

"No, no, anyone would have helped you. The folk down there, plain sailors, artisans, merchants, ranchers, they are as furious as I am." Dragoika erected her tendrils. Her tail twitched, the winglike ears spread wide. "That those vaz-giradek would dare bite you!"

"Hoy," Flandry said. "You have the wrong idea. I haven't disowned Terra. My people are simply the victims of a lie and our task is to set matters right."

"They outlawed you, did they not?"

"I don't know what the situation is. I dare not communicate by radio. The vaz-Merseian could overhear. So I had your messenger give our men a note which they were asked to fly to Admiral Enriques. The note begged him to send a trustworthy man here."

"You told me that already. I told you I would make quite plain to the vaz-Terran, they will not capture my Dommaneek. Not unless they want war."

"But—"

"They don't. They need us worse than we need them, the more so when they failed to reach an accord with the vaz-Siravo of the Zletovar."

"They did?" Flandry's spirit drooped.

"Yes, as I always said would happen. Oh, there have been no new Merseian submarines. A Terran force blasted the Siravo base when we vaz-Kursovikian were unable to. The vaz-Merseian fought them in the air. Heaven burned that night. Since then, our ships often meet gunfire from swimmers, but most of them get through. They tell me combat between Terran and Merseian has become frequent—elsewhere in the world, however."

Another step up the ladder, Flandry thought. *More men killed, Tigeries, seafolk. By now, I suppose, daily. And in a doomed cause.*

"But you have given small word about your deeds," Dragoika continued. "Only that you bear a great secret. What?"

"I'm sorry." On an impulse, Flandry reached out and stroked her mane. She rubbed her head against his palm. "I may not tell even you."

She sighed. "As you wish." She picked up the model galley. Her fingers traced spars and rigging. "Let me fare with you a ways. Tell me of your journey."

He tried. She struggled for comprehension. "Strange, that yonder," she said. "The little stars become suns, this world of ours shrunk to a dustmote; the weirdness of other races, the terrible huge machines—" She clutched the model tight. "I did not know a story could frighten me."

"You will learn to live with a whole heart in the universe." *You must.*

"Speak on, Dommaneek."

He did, censoring a trifle. Not that Dragoika would mind his having traveled with Persis; but she might think he preferred the woman to her as a friend, and be hurt.

"—trees on Merseia grow taller than here, bearing a different kind of leaf—"

His wristcom buzzed. He stabbed the transmitter button. "Ensign Flandry." His voice sounded high in his ears. "Standing by."

"Admiral Enriques," from the speaker. "I am approaching in a Boudreau X-7 with two men. Where shall I land?"

Enriques in person? My God, have I gotten myself caught in the gears! "A-a-aye aye, sir."

"I asked where to set down, Flandry."

The ensign stammered out directions. A flitter, as his letter had suggested, could settle on the tower of

Dragoika's house. "You see, sir, the people here, they're—well, sort of up in arms. Best avoid possible trouble, sir."

"Your doing?"

"No, sir. I mean, not really. But, well, you'll see everyone gathered. In combat order. They don't want to surrender me to . . . uh . . . to anyone they think is hostile to me. They threaten, uh, attack on our station if— Honest, sir, I haven't alienated an ally. I can explain."

"You'd better," Enriques said. "Very well, you are under arrest but we won't take you into custody as yet. We'll be there in about three minutes. Out."

"What did he say?" Dragoika hissed. Her fur stood on end.

Flandry translated. She glided from her couch and took a sword off the wall. "I'll call a few warriors to make sure he keeps his promise."

"He will. I'm certain he will. Uh . . . the sight of his vehicle might cause excitement. Can we tell the city not to start fighting?"

"We can." Dragoika operated a communicator she had lately acquired and spoke with the Sisterhood centrum across the river. Bells pealed forth, the Song of Truce. An uneasy mutter ran through the Tigeries, but they stayed where they were.

Flandry headed for the door. "I'll meet them on the tower," he said.

"You will not," Dragoika answered. "They are coming to see you by your gracious permission. Lirjoz is there, he'll escort them down."

Flandry seated himself, shaking his head in a stunned fashion.

He rocketed up to salute when Enriques entered. The admiral was alone, must have left his men in the flitter. At a signal from Dragoika, Lirjoz returned to watch them. Slowly, she laid her sword on the table.

"At ease," Enriques clipped. He was gray, bladenosed, scarecrow gaunt. His uniform hung flat as armor. "Kindly present me to my hostess."

"Uh . . . Dragoika, captain-director of the Janjevar va-Radovik . . . Vice Admiral Juan Enriques of the Imperial Terrestrial Navy."

The newcomer clicked his heels, but his bow could have been made to the Empress. Dragoika studied him a moment, then touched brow and breasts, the salute of honor.

"I feel more hope," she said to Flandry.

"Translate," Enriques ordered. That narrow skull held too much to leave room for many languages.

"She . . . uh . . . likes you, sir," Flandry said.

Behind the helmet, a smile ghosted at one corner of Enriques' mouth. "I suspect she is merely prepared to trust me to a clearly defined extent."

"Won't the Admiral be seated?"

Enriques glanced at Dragoika. She eased to her couch. He took the other one, sitting straight. Flandry remained on his feet. Sweat prickled him.

"Sir," he blurted, "please, is Donna d'Io all right?"

"Yes, except for being in a bad nervous state. She landed soon after your message arrived. The *Riekessel*'s captain had been making one excuse after another to stay in orbit. When we learned from you that Donna d'Io was aboard, we said we would loft a gig for her. He came down at once. What went on there?"

"Well, sir—I mean, I can't say. I wasn't around, sir. She told you about our escape from Merseia?"

"We had a private interview at her request. Her account was sketchy. But it does tend to bear out your claims."

"Sir, I know what the Merseians are planning, and it's monstrous. I can prove—"

"You will need considerable proof, Ensign," Enriques said bleakly. "Lord Hauksberg's communication laid capital charges against you."

Flandry felt nervousness slide from him. He doubled his fists and cried, with tears of rage stinging his eyes: "Sir, I'm entitled to a court-martial. By my own people. And you'd have let the Merseians have me!"

The lean visage beneath his hardly stirred. The voice was flat. "Regulations provide that personnel under charges are to be handed over to their assigned superiors if this is demanded. The Empire is too big for any other rule to work. By virtue of being a nobleman, Lord Hauksberg holds a reserve commission, equivalent rank of captain, which was automatically activated when Commander Abrams was posted to him. Until you are detached from your assignment, he is your senior commanding officer. He declared in proper form that state secrets and his mission on behalf of the Imperium have been endangered by you. The Merseians will return you to him for examination. It is true that courts-martial must be held on an Imperial ship or planet, but the time for this may be set by him within a one-year limit."

"Will be never! Sir, they'll scrub my brain and kill me!"

"Restrain yourself, Ensign."

Flandry gulped. Dragoika bared teeth but stayed put. "May I hear the exact charges against me, sir?" Flandry asked.

"High treason," Enriques told him. "Mutiny. Desertion. Kidnapping. Threat and menace. Assault and battery. Theft. Insubordination. Shall I recite the entire bill? I thought not. You have subsequently added several items. Knowing that you were wanted, you did not surrender yourself. You created dissension between the Empire and an associated country. This, among other things, imperils his Majesty's forces on Starkad. At the moment, you are resisting arrest. Ensign, you have a great deal to answer for."

"I'll answer to you, sir, not to . . . to those damned gatortails. Nor to a Terran who's so busy toadying to them he doesn't care what happens to his fellow human beings. My God, sir, you let Merseians search Imperial ships!"

"I had my orders," Enriques replied.

"But Hauksberg, you rank him!"

"Formally and in certain procedural matters. He holds a direct Imperial mandate, though. It empowers him to negotiate temporary agreements with Merseia, which then become policy determinants."

Flandry heard the least waver in those tones. He pounced. "You protested your orders, sir. Didn't you?"

"I sent a report on my opinion to frontier HQ. No reply has yet been received. In any event, there are only six Merseian men-of-war here, none above Planet class, plus some unarmed cargo carriers told off to help them." Enriques smacked hand on knee. "Why am I arguing with you? At the very least, if you wanted to see me, you could have stayed aboard the *Rieskessel*."

"And afterward been given to the Merseians, sir?"

"Perhaps. The possibility should not have influenced you. Remember your oath."

Flandry made a circle around the room. His hands writhed behind his back. Dragoika laid fingers on sword hilt. "No," he said to her in Kursovikian. "No matter what happens."

He spun on his heel and looked straight at Enriques. "Sir, I had another reason. What I brought from Merseia is a list of numbers. You'd undoubtedly have passed them on. But they do need a direct check, to make sure I'm right about what they mean. And if I am right, whoever goes to look may run into a fight. A space battle. Escalation, which you're forbidden to practice. You couldn't order such a mission the way things have been set up to bind you. You'd have to ask for the authority. And on what basis? On my say-so, me, a baby ex-cadet, a mutineer, a traitor. You can imagine how they'd buckpass. At best, a favorable decision wouldn't come for weeks. Months, more likely. Meanwhile the war would drag on. Men would get killed. Men like my buddy, Jan van Zuyl, with his life hardly begun. With forty or fifty years of Imperial service in him."

Enriques spoke so softly that one heard the wind whittering off the sea, through the ancient streets outside. "Ensign van Zuyl was killed in action four days ago."

"Oh, no." Flandry closed his eyes.

"Conflict has gotten to the point where—we and the Merseians respect each other's base areas, but roving aircraft fight anyplace else they happen to meet."

"And *still* you let them search us." Flandry paused. "I'm sorry, sir. I know you hadn't any choice. Please let me finish. It's even possible my information would be discredited, never acted on. Hard to imagine, but . . . well, we have so many bureaucrats, so many people in high places like Lord Hauksberg who insists the enemy doesn't really mean harm . . . and Brechdan Ironrede, God, but he's clever. . . . I couldn't risk it. I had to work things so you, sir, would have a free choice."

"You?" Enriques raised his brows. "Ensign Dominic Flandry, all by himself?"

"Yes, sir. You have discretionary power, don't you? I mean, when extraordinary situations arise, you can take what measures are indicated, without asking HQ first. Can't you?"

"Of course. As witness these atmospheric combats." Enriques leaned forward, forgetting to stay sarcastic.

"Well, sir, this is an extraordinary situation. You're supposed to stay friends with the Kursovikians. But you can see I'm the Terran they care about. Their minds work that way. They're barbaric, used to personal leadership; to them, a distant government is no government; they feel a blood obligation to me—that sort of thing. So to preserve the alliance, you must deal with me. I'm a renegade, but you must."

"And so?"

"So if you don't dispatch a scout into space, I'll tell the Sisterhood to dissolve the alliance."

"What?" Enriques started. Dragoika bristled.

"I'll sabotage the whole Terran effort," Flandry said. "Terra has no business on Starkad. We've been trapped, conned, blued and tattooed. When you present physical evidence, photographs, measurements, we'll all go home. Hell, I'll give you eight to one the Merseians go home as soon as you tell old Runei what you've done. Get your courier off first, of course, to make sure he doesn't use those warships to blast us into silence. But then call him and tell him."

"There are no Terran space combat units in this system."

Flandry grinned. The blood was running high in him. "Sir, I don't believe the Imperium is that stupid. There has to be some provision against the Merseians suddenly marshaling strength. If nothing else, a few warcraft orbiting 'way outside. We can flit men to them. A round-about course, so the enemy'll think it's only another homebound ship. Right?"

"Well—" Enriques got up. Dragoika stayed where she was, but closed hand on hilt. "You haven't yet revealed your vast secret," the admiral declared.

Flandry recited the figures.

Enriques stood totem-post erect. "Is that everything?"

"Yes, sir. Everything that was needed."

"How do you interpret it?"

Flandry told him.

Enriques was still for a long moment. The Tigeries growled in Shiv Alley. He turned, went to the window, stared down and then out at the sky.

"Do you believe this?" he asked most quietly.

"Yes, sir," Flandry said. "I can't think of anything else that fits, and I had plenty of time to try. I'd bet my life on it."

Enriques faced him again. "Would you?"

"I'm doing it, sir."

"Maybe. Suppose I order a reconnaissance. As you say, it's not unlikely to run into Merseian pickets. Will you come along?"

A roar went through Flandry's head. "Yes, sir!" he yelled.

"Hm. You trust me that much, eh? And it would be advisable for you to go: a hostage for your claims, with special experience which might prove useful. Although if you didn't return here, we could look for trouble." ·

"You wouldn't need Kursoviki any longer," Flandry said. He was beginning to tremble.

"If you are truthful and correct in your assertion." Enriques was motionless a while more. The silence grew and grew.

All at once the admiral said, "Very good, Ensign Flandry. The charges against you are held in abeyance and you are hereby re-attached temporarily to my command. You will return to Highport with me and await further orders."

Flandry saluted. Joy sang in him. "Aye, aye, sir!"

Dragoika rose. "What were you saying, Dommaneek?" she asked anxiously.

"Excuse me, sir, I have to tell her." In Kursovikian: "The misunderstanding has been dissolved, for the time being anyhow. I'm leaving with my skipper."

"Hr-r-r." She looked down. "And then what?"

"Well uh, then we'll go on a flying ship, to a battle which may end this whole war."

"You have only his word," she objected.

"Did you not judge him honorable?"

"Yes. I could be wrong. Surely there are those in the Sisterhood who will suspect a ruse, not to speak of the commons. Blood binds us to you. I think it would look best if I went along. Thus there is a living pledge."

"But—but—"

"Also," Dragoika said, "this is our war too. Shall none of us take part?" Her eyes went back to him. "On behalf of the Sisterhood and myself, I claim a right. You shall not leave without me."

"Problems?" Enriques barked.

Helplessly, Flandry tried to explain.

CHAPTER SEVENTEEN

The Imperial squadron deployed and accelerated. It was no big force to cast out in so much blackness. True, at the core was the *Sabik,* a Star-class, what some called a pocket battleship; but she was old and worn, obsolete in several respects, shunted off to Saxo as the last step before the scrap orbit. No one had really expected her to see action again. Flanking her went the light cruiser *Umbriel,* equally tired, and the destroyers *Antarctica, New Brazil,* and *Murdoch's Land.* Two scoutships, *Encke* and *Ikeya-Seki,* did not count as fighting units; they carried one energy gun apiece, possibly useful against aircraft, and their sole real value lay in speed and maneuverability. Yet theirs was the ultimate mission, the rest merely their helpers. Aboard each of them reposed a document signed by Admiral Enriques.

At first the squadron moved on gravitics. It would not continue thus. The distance to be traversed was a few light-days, negligible under hyperdrive, appalling under true velocity. However, a sudden burst of wakes, outbound from a large orbit, would be detected by the Merseians. Their suspicions would be excited. And their strength in the Saxonian System, let alone what else they might have up ahead, was fully comparable to Captain Einarsen's command. He wanted to enter this water carefully. It was deep.

But when twenty-four hours had passed without incident, he ordered the *New Brazil* to proceed at superlight toward the destination. At the first sign of an enemy waiting there, she was to come back.

Flandry and Dragoika sat in a wardroom of the *Sabik* with Lieutenant (j.g.) Sergei Karamzin, who happened to be off watch. He was as frantic to see new faces and hear something new from the universe as everyone else aboard. "Almost a year on station," he said. "A year out of my life, bang, like that. Only it wasn't sudden, you understand. Felt more like a decade."

Flandry's glance traveled around the cabin. An attempt had been made to brighten it with pictures and home-sewn draperies. The attempt had not been very successful. Today the place had come alive with the thrum of power, low and bone-deep. A clean tang of oil touched air which circulated briskly again. But he hated to think what this environment had felt like after a year of absolutely eventless orbit. Dragoika saw matters otherwise, of course; the ship dazzled, puzzled, frightened, delighted, enthralled her, never had she known such wonder! She poised in her chair with fur standing straight and eyes bouncing around.

"You had your surrogates, didn't you?" Flandry asked. "Pseudosensory inputs and the rest."

"Sure," Karamzin said. "The galley's good, too. But those things are just medicine, to keep you from spinning off altogether." His young features hardened. "I hope we meet some opposition. I really do."

"Myself," Flandry said, "I've met enough opposition to last me for quite a while."

His lighter kindled a cigarette. He felt odd, back in horizon blue, jetflares on his shoulders and no blaster at his waist: back in a ship, in discipline, in tradition. He wasn't sure he liked it.

At least his position was refreshingly anomalous. Captain Einarsen had been aghast when Dragoika boarded—an Iron Age xeno on *his* vessel? But the orders from Enriques were clear. This was a VIP who insisted on riding along and could cause trouble if she wasn't humored. Thus Ensign Flandry was appointed "liaison officer," the clause being added in private that he'd keep his pet savage out of the way or be busted to midshipman. (Nothing was said on either side about his being technically a prisoner. Einarsen had received the broadcast, but judged it would be dangerous to let his men know that Merseians were stopping Terran craft. And Enriques' message had clarified his understanding.) At the age of nineteen, how could Flandry resist conveying the impression that the VIP really had some grasp of astronautics and must be kept posted on developments? So he was granted communication with the bridge.

Under all cheer and excitement, a knot of tension was in him. He figured that word from the *New Brazil* would arrive at any minute.

"Your pardon," Dragoika interrupted. "I must go

to the—what you say—the head." She thought that installation the most amusing thing aboard.

Karamzin watched her leave. Her supple gait was not impeded by the air helmet she required in a Terran atmosphere. The chief problem had been coiling her mane to fit inside. Otherwise her garments consisted of a sword and a knife.

"Way-hay," Karamzin murmured. "What a shape! How is she?"

"Be so good as not to talk about her like that," Flandry rapped.

"What? I didn't mean any harm. She's only a xeno."

"She's my friend. She's worth a hundred Imperial sheep. And what she's got to face and survive, the rest of her life—"

Karamzin leaned across the table. "How's that? What sort of cruise are we on, anyway? Supposed to check on something the gatortails might have out in space; they didn't tell us more."

"I can't, either."

"I wasn't ordered to stop thinking. And you know, I think this Starkad affair is a blind. They'll develop the war here, get our whole attention on this sinkhole, then bang, they'll hit someplace else."

Flandry blew a smoke ring. "Maybe." *I wish I could tell you. You have no military right to know, but haven't you a human right?*

"What's Starkad like, anyway? Our briefing didn't say much."

"Well—" Flandry hunted for words. They were bloodless things at best. You could describe, but you could not make real: dawn white over a running sea, slow heavy winds that roared on wooded mountainsides, an old and proud city, loveliness on a shadowy ocean floor, two brave races, billions of years since first the planet coalesced, the great globe itself. . . . He was still trying when Dragoika returned. She sat down quietly and watched him.

"—and, uh, a very interesting paleolithic culture on an island they call Rayadan—"

Alarms hooted.

Karamzin was through the door first. Feet clattered, metal clanged, voices shouted, under the shrill *woop-woop-woop* that echoed from end to end of the long hull. Dragoika snatched the sword off her shoulder. "What's happening?" she yelled.

"Battle stations." Flandry realized he had spoken in Anglic. "An enemy has been . . . sighted."

"Where is he?"

"Out there, put away that steel. Strength and courage won't help you now. Come." Flandry led her into the corridor.

They wove among men who themselves pelted toward their posts. Near the navigation bridge was a planetary chartroom equipped for full audiovisual intercom. The exec had decided this would serve the VIP and her keeper. Two spacesuits hung ready. One was modified for Starkadian use. Dragoika had gotten some drill with it en route to the squadron, but Flandry thought he'd better help her before armoring himself. "Here; this fastens so. Now hold your breath till we change helmets on you. . . . Why did you come?"

"I would not let you fare alone on my behalf," Dragoika said after her faceplate was closed.

Flandry left his own open, but heard her in his radio earplugs. The alarm penetrated them; and, presently, a voice:

"Now hear this. Now hear this. Captain to all officers and men. The *New Brazil* reports two hyperdrives activated as she approached destination. She is returning to us and the bogies are in pursuit. We shall proceed. Stand by for hyperdrive. Stand by for combat. Glory to the Emperor."

Flandry worked the com dials. Tuning in on a bridge viewscreen, he saw space on his own panel, black and starstrewn. Briefly, as the quantum field built up, the cosmos twisted. Compensators clicked in and the scene grew steady; but now *Sabik* outran light and kilometers reeled aft more swiftly than imagination could follow. The power throb was a leonine growl through every cell of his body.

"What does this mean?" Dragoika pressed close to him, seeking comfort.

Flandry switched to a view of the operations tank. Seven green dots of varying size moved against a stellar background. "See, those are our ships. The big one, that's this." Two red dots appeared. "Those are the enemy, as near as we can tell his positions. Um-m-m, look at their size. That's because we detect very powerful engines. I'd say one is roughly equal to ours, though probably newer and better armed. The other seems to be a heavy destroyer."

Her gauntlets clapped together. "But this is like magic!" she cried with glee.

"Not much use, actually, except to give a quick

overall picture. What the captain uses is figures and calculations from our machines."

Dragoika's enthusiasm died. "Always machines," she said in a troubled voice. "Glad I am not to live in your world, Dommaneek."

You'll have to, I'm afraid, he thought. *For a while, anyway. If we live.*

He scanned the communications office. Men sat before banks of meters, as if hypnotized. Occasionally someone touched a control or spoke a few words to his neighbor. Electromagnetic radio was mute beyond the hull. But with hyperdrive going, a slight modulation could be imposed on the wake to carry messages. *Sabik* could transmit instantaneously, as well as receive.

As Flandry watched, a man stiffened in his seat. His hands shook a little when he ripped off a printout and gave it to his pacing superior. That officer strode to an intercom and called the command bridge. Flandry listened and nodded.

"Tell me," Dragoika begged. "I feel so alone here."

"Shhh!"

Announcement: "Now hear this. Now hear this. Captain to all officers and men. It is known that there are six Merseian warships in Saxo orbit. They have gone hyper and are seeking junction with the two bogies in pursuit of *New Brazil.* We detect scrambled communication between these various units. It is expected they will attack us. First contact is estimated in ten minutes. Stand by to open fire upon command. The composition of the hostiles is—"

Flandry showed Dragoika the tank. Half a dozen

sparks drove outward from the luminous globelet which represented her sun. "They are one light cruiser, about like our *Umbriel,* and five destroyers. Then ahead, remember, we have a battleship and a quite heavy destroyer."

"Eight against five of us." Tendrils rose behind the faceplate, fur crackled, the lost child dropped out of her and she said low and resonant: "But we will catch those first two by themselves."

"Right. I wonder. . . ." Flandry tried a different setting. It should have been blocked off, but someone had forgotten and he looked over Captain Einarsen's shoulder.

Yes, a Merseian in the outercom screen! And a high-ranking one, too.

"—interdicted region," he said in thickly accented Anglic. "Turn back at once."

"His Majesty's government does not recognize interdictions in unclaimed space," Einarsen said. "You will interfere with us at your peril."

"Where are you bound? What is your purpose?"

"That is of no concern to you, Fodaich. My command is bound on its lawful occasions. Do we pass peacefully or must we fight?"

Flandry translated for Dragoika as he listened. The Merseian paused, and she whispered: "He will say we can go on, surely. Thus he can join the others."

Flandry wiped his brow. The room felt hot, and he stank with perspiration in his suit. "I wish you'd been born in our civilization," he said. "You have a Navy mind."

"Pass, then," the Merseian said slowly. "Under protest, I let you by."

Flandry leaned forward, gripping a table edge, struggling not to shout what Einarsen must do.

The Terran commander said, "Very good. But in view of the fact that other units are moving to link with yours, I am forced to require guarantees of good faith. You will immediately head due galactic north at full speed, without halt until I return to Saxo."

"Outrageous! You have no right—"

"I have the right of my responsibility for this squadron. If your government wishes to protest to mine, let it do so. Unless you withdraw as requested, I shall consider your intentions hostile and take appropriate measures. My compliments to you, sir. Good day." The screen was blanked.

Flandry switched away from Einarsen's expressionless countenance and stood shaking. There trickled through the turmoil in him, *I guess an old-line officer does have as much sense as a fresh-caught ensign.*

When he brought Dragoika up to date, she said coolly, "Let us see that tank again."

The Merseians ahead were not heeding the Terran order. They were, though, sheering off, one in either direction, obviously hoping to delay matters until help arrived. Einarsen didn't cooperate. Like a wolf brought to bay, *New Brazil* turned on her lesser pursuer. *Murdoch's Land* hurried to her aid. On the other side, *Umbriel* and *Sabik* herself accelerated toward the Merseian battlewagon. *Antarctica* continued as before, convoying the scoutboats.

"Here we go," Flandry said between clenched jaws. His first space battle, as terrifying, bewildering, and exalting as his first woman. He lusted to be in a gun turret. After dogging his faceplate, he sought an exterior view.

For a minute, nothing was visible but stars. Then the ship boomed and shuddered. She had fired a missile salvo: the monster missiles which nothing smaller than a battleship could carry, which had their own hyperdrives and phase-in computers. He could not see them arrive. The distance was as yet too great. But close at hand, explosions burst in space, one immense fireball after another, swelling, raging, and vanishing. Had the screen carried their real intensity, his eyeballs would have melted. Even through airlessness, he felt the buffet of expanding gases; the deck rocked and the hull belled.

"What was that?" Dragoika cried.

"The enemy shot at us. We managed to intercept and destroy his missiles with smaller ones. Look there." A lean metal thing prowled across the screen. "It seeks its own target. We have a cloud of them out."

Again and again energies ran wild. One blast almost knocked Flandry off his feet. His ears buzzed from it. He tuned in on damage control. The strike had been so near that the hull was bashed open. Bulkheads sealed off that section. A gun turret was wrecked, its crew blown to fragments. But another nearby reported itself still functional. Behind heavy material and electromagnetic shielding, its men had not gotten a lethal dose of radiation: not if they received medical help within a day. They stayed at their post.

Flandry checked the tank once more. Faster than either battleship, *Umbriel* had overhauled her giant foe. When drive fields touched, she went out of phase, just sufficient to be unhittable, not enough that her added mass did not serve as a drag. The Merseian must be trying to get in phase and wipe her out before—No, here *Sabik* came!

Generators that powerful extended their fields for a long radius. When she first intermeshed, the enemy seemed a toy, lost among so many stars. But she grew in the screen, a shark, a whale, Leviathan in steel, bristling with weapons, livid with lightnings.

The combat was not waged by living creatures. Not really. They did nothing but serve guns, tend machines, and die. When such speeds, masses, intensities met, robots took over. Missile raced at missile; computer matched wits with computer in the weird dance of phasing. Human and Merseian hands did operate blaster cannon, probing, searing, slicing through metal like a knife through flesh. But their chance of doing important harm, in the short time they had, was small.

Fire sheeted across space. Thunder brawled in hulls. Decks twisted, girders buckled, plates melted. An explosion pitched Flandry and Dragoika down. They lay in each other's arms, bruised, bleeding, deafened, while the storm prevailed.

And passed.

Slowly, incredulously, they climbed to their feet. Shouts from outside told them their eardrums were not ruptured. The door sagged and smoke curled through. Chemical extinguishers rumbled. Someone called for a medic. The voice was raw with pain.

The screen still worked. Flandry glimpsed *Umbriel* before relative speed made her unseeable. Her bows gaped open, a gun barrel was bent in a quarter circle, plates resembled seafoam where they had liquefied and congealed. But she ran yet. And so did *Sabik*.

He looked and listened awhile before he could reconstruct the picture for Dragoika. "We got them. Our two destroyers took care of the enemy's without suffering much damage. We're hulled in several places ourselves, three turrets and a missile launcher are knocked out, some lines leading from the main computer bank are cut, we're using auxiliary generators till the engineers can fix the primary one, and the casualties are pretty bad. We're operational, though, sort of."

"What became of the battleship we fought?"

"We sank a warhead in her midriff. One megaton, I believe . . . no, you don't know about that, do you? She's dust and gas."

The squadron reunited and moved onward. Two tiny green flecks in the tank detached themselves and hastened ahead. "See those? Our scoutboats. We have to screen them while they perform their task. This means we have to fight those Merseians from Saxo."

"Six of them to five of us," Dragoika counted. "Well, the odds are improving. And then, we have a bigger ship, this one, than remains to them."

Flandry watched the green lights deploy. The objective was to prevent even one of the red sparks from getting through and attacking the scouts. This invited annihilation in detail, but—Yes, evidently the Merseian commander had told off one of his destroyers to each of Einarsen's. That left him with his cruiser and two destroyers against *Sabik* and *Umbriel*, which would have been fine were the latter pair not half crippled. "I'd call the odds even, myself," Flandry said. "But that may be good enough. If we stand off the enemy for . . . a couple of hours, I'd guess . . . we've done what we were supposed."

"But what is that, Dommaneek? You spoke only of some menace out here." Dragoika took him by the shoulders and regarded him levelly. "Can you not tell me?"

He could, without violating any secrecy that mattered any longer. But he didn't want to. He tried to stall, and hoped the next stage of combat would begin before she realized what he was doing. "Well," he said, "we have news about, uh, an object. What the scouts must do is go to it, find out what it is like, and plot its path. They'll do that in an interesting way. They'll retreat from it, faster than light, so they can take pictures of it not where it is at this moment but where it was at different times in the past. Since they know where to look, their instruments can pinpoint it at more than a light year. That is, across more than a year of time. On such basis, they can easily calculate how it will move for the next several years to come."

Again dread stirred behind her eyes. "They can reach over time itself?" she whispered. "To the past and its ghosts? You dare too much, you vaz-Terran. One night the hidden powers will set free their anger on you."

He bit his lip—and winced, for it was swollen where his face had been thrown against a mouth-control radio switch. "I often wonder if that may not be so, Dragoika. But what can we do? Our course was set for us ages agone, before ever we left our home world, and there is no turning back."

"Then . . . you fare bravely." She straightened in her

armor. "I may do no less. Tell me what the thing is that you hunt through time."

"It—" The ship recoiled. A drumroll ran. "Missiles fired off! We're engaging!"

Another salvo and another. Einarsen must be shooting off every last hyperdrive weapon in his magazines. If one or two connected, they might decide the outcome. If not, then none of his present foes could reply in kind.

Flandry saw, in the tank, how the Merseian destroyers scattered. They could do little but try to outdodge those killers, or outphase them if field contact was made. As formation broke up, *Murdoch's Land* and *Antarctica* closed in together on a single enemy of their class. That would be slugfest, minor missiles and energy cannon and artillery, more slow and perhaps more brutal than the nearly abstract encounter between two capital ships, but also somehow more human.

The volleys ended. Dragoika howled. "Look, Dommaneek! A red light went out! There! First blood for us!"

"Yes . . . yes, we did get a destroyer. Whoopee!" The exec announced it on the intercom, and cheers sounded faintly from those who still had their faceplates open. The other missiles must have been avoided or parried, and by now were destroying themselves lest they become threats to navigation. Max Abrams would have called that rule a hopeful sign.

Another Merseian ship sped to assist the one on which the two Terrans were converging, while *New Brazil* and a third enemy stalked each other. *Umbriel* limped on an intercept course for the heavy cruiser and her attendant. Those drove straight for *Sabik*, which lay in wait licking her wounds.

The lights flickered and died. They came back, but feebly. So there was trouble with the spare powerplant, too. And damn, damn, damn, Flandry couldn't do a thing except watch that tank!

The cruiser's escort detached herself and ran toward *Umbriel* to harry and hinder. Flandry clenched his teeth till his jaws ached. "The greenskins can see we have problems here," he said. "They figure a cruiser can take us. And they may be right."

Red crept up on green. "Stand by for straight-phase engagement," said the intercom.

"What did that mean?" Dragoika asked.

"We can't dodge till a certain machine has been fixed." It was as near as Flandry could come to saying in Kursovikian that phase change was impossible. "We shall have to sit and shoot."

Sabik wasn't quite a wingless duck. She could revert to sublight, though that was a desperation maneuver. At superlight, the enemy must be in phase with her to inflict damage, and therefore equally vulnerable. But the cruiser did, now, possess an extra capability of eluding her opponent's fire. *Sabik* had no shield except her antimissiles. To be sure, she was better supplied with those.

It looked as if a toe-to-toe match was coming.

"Hyperfield contact made," said the intercom. "All units fire at will."

Flandry switched to exterior view. The Merseian zigzagged among the stars. Sometimes she vanished, always she reappeared. She was a strictly spacegoing

vessel, bulged at the waist like a double-ended pear.
Starlight and shadow picked out her armament. Dragoika
hissed in a breath. Again fire erupted.

A titan's fist smote. A noise so enormous that it
transcended noise bellowed through the hull. Bulkheads
split asunder. The deck crashed against Flandry. He
whirled into night.

Moments later he regained consciousness. He was
falling, falling, forever, and blind . . . no, he thought
through the ringing in his head, the lights were out, the
gravs were out, he floated free amidst the moan of
escaping air. Blood from his nose formed globules which,
weightless, threatened to strangle him. He sucked to draw
them down his throat. "Dragoika!" he rasped. "Dragoika!"

Her helmet beam sprang forth. She was a shadow
behind it, but the voice came clear and taut: "Dommaneek,
are you hale? What happened? Here, here is my hand."

"We took a direct hit." He shook himself, limb by
limb, felt pain boil in his body but marveled that nothing
appeared seriously injured. Well, space armor was designed
to take shocks. "Nothing in here is working, so I don't
know what the ship's condition is. Let's try to find out. Yes,
hang onto me. Push against things, not too hard. It's like
swimming. Do you feel sick?"

"No. I feel as in a dream, nothing else." She got the
basic technique of null-gee motion fast.

They entered the corridor. Undiffused, their lamplight
made dull puddles amidst a crowding murk. Ribs thrust out
past twisted, buckled plates. Half of a spacesuited man
drifted in a blood-cloud which Flandry must wipe off his
helmet. No radio spoke. The silence was of a tomb.

The nuclear warhead that got through could not have been very large. But where it struck, ruin was total. Elsewhere, though, forcefields, bulkheads, baffles, breakaway lines had given what protection they could. Thus Flandry and Dragoika survived. Did anyone else? He called and called, but got no answer.

A hole filled with stars yawned before him. He told her to stay put and flitted forth on impellers. Saxo, nearly the brightest of the diamond points around him, transited the specter arch of the Milky Way. It cast enough light for him to see. The fragment of ship from which he had emerged spun slowly—luck, that, or Coriolis force would have sickened him and perhaps her. An energy cannon turret looked intact. Further off tumbled larger pieces, ugly against cold serene heaven.

He tried his radio again, now when he was outside screening metal. With her secondary engines gone, the remnants of *Sabik* had reverted to normal state. "Ensign Flandry from Section Four. Come in, anyone. Come in!"

A voice trickled through. Cosmic interference seethed behind it. "Commander Ranjit Singh in Section Two. I am assuming command unless a superior officer turns out to be alive. Report your condition."

Flandry did. "Shall we join you, sir?" he finished.

"No. Check that gun. Report whether it's in working order. If so, man it."

"But sir, we're disabled. The cruiser's gone on to fight elsewhere. Nobody'll bother with us."

"That remains to be seen, Ensign. If the battle pattern should release a bogie, he may decide he'll make sure of us. Go to your gun."

"Aye, aye, sir."

Dead bodies floated in the turret. They were not mutilated; but two or three roentgens must have sleeted through all shielding. Flandry and Dragoika hauled them out and cast them adrift. As they dwindled among the stars, she sang to them the Song of Mourning. *I wouldn't mind such a sendoff,* he thought.

The gun was useable. Flandry rehearsed Dragoika in emergency manual control. They'd alternate at the hydraulic aiming system and the handwheel which recharged the batteries that drove it. She was as strong as he.

Thereafter they waited. "I never thought to die in a place like this," she said. "But my end will be in battle, and with the finest of comrades. How we shall yarn, in the Land of Trees Beyond!"

"We might survive yet," he said. Starlight flashed off the teeth in his bruised and blood-smeared face.

"Don't fool yourself. Unworthy of you."

"Unworthy my left one! I plain don't intend to quit till I'm dead."

"I see. Maybe that is what has made you vaz-Terran great."

The Merseian came.

She was a destroyer. *Umbriel,* locked in combat with the badly hurt enemy cruiser, had inflicted grave harm on her, too. *Murdoch's Land* was shattered, *Antarctica* out of action until repairs could be made, but they had accounted for two of her fellows. *New Brazil* dueled yet with the third. This fourth one suffered from a damaged hyper-drive alternator. Until her sweating engineers could repair it, which would take an hour or so, her superlight speed was a crawl; any vessel in better shape could wipe her from the universe. Her captain resolved he would go back to where the remnants of *Sabik* orbited and spend the interim cleaning them out. For the general order was that none but Merseians might enter this region and live.

She flashed into reality. Her missiles were spent, but guns licked with fire-tongues and shells. The main part of the battleship's dismembered hulk took their impact, glowed, broke, and returned the attack.

"Yow-w-w!" Dragoika's yell was pure exultation. She spun the handwheel demoniacally fast. Flandry pushed himself into the saddle. His cannon swung about. The bit of hull counter-rotated. He adjusted, got the destroyer's after section in his cross-hairs, and pulled the trigger.

Capacitors discharged. Their energy content was limited; that was why the gun must be laid by hand, to conserve every last erg for revenge. Flame spat across kilometers. Steel sublimed. A wound opened. Air gushed forth, white with condensing water vapor.

The destroyer applied backward thrust. Flandry followed, holding his beam to the same spot, driving inward and inward. From four other pieces of *Sabik,* death vomited.

"Man," Flandry chanted, "but you've got a Tigery by the tail!"

Remorselessly, spin took him out of sight. He waited fuming. When he could again aim, the destroyer was further away, and she had turned one battleship section into gas. But the rest fought on. He joined his beam to theirs. She was retreating under gravitics. Why didn't she go hyper and get the hell out of here? Maybe she couldn't. He himself had been shooting to disable her quantum-field generator. Maybe he'd succeeded.

"Kursoviki!" Dragoika shrieked at the wheel. "Archers all! Janjevar va-Radovik for aye!"

A gun swiveled toward them. He could see it, tiny at its distance, thin and deadly. He shifted aim. His fire melted the muzzle shut.

The destroyer scuttled away. And then, suddenly, there was *New Brazil*. Flandry darted from his seat, caught Dragoika to him, held her faceplate against his breast and closed his own eyes. When they looked again, the Merseian was white-hot meteorites. They hugged each other in their armor.

Umbriel, Antarctica, and *New Brazil:* torn, battered, lame, filled with the horribly wounded, haunted by their dead, but victorious, victorious—neared the planet. The scoutships had long since finished their work and departed Empire-ward. Yet Ranjit Singh would give his men a look at the prize they had won.

On the cruiser's bridge, Flandry and Dragoika stood with him. The planet filled the forward viewscreen. It was hardly larger than Luna. Like Terra's moon, it was bereft of air, water, life; such had bled away to space over billions of years. Mountains bared fangs at the stars, above ashen plains. Barren, empty, blind as a skull, the rogue rushed on to its destiny.

"One planet," the acting captain breathed. "One wretched sunless planet."

"It's enough, sir," Flandry said. Exhaustion pulsed

through him in huge soft waves. To sleep . . . to sleep, perchance to dream. . . . "On a collision course with Saxo. It'll strike inside of five years. That much mass, simply falling from infinity, carries the energy of three years' stellar radiation. Which will have to be discharged somehow, in a matter of seconds. And Saxo is an F5, short lived, due to start expanding in less than a begayear. The instabilities must already be building up. The impact— Saxo will go nova. Explode."

"And our fleet—"

"Yes, sir. What else? The thing's wildly improbable. Interstellar distances are so big. But the universe is bigger still. No matter how unlikely, anything which is possible must happen sometime. This is one occasion when it does. Merseian explorers chanced on the datum. Brechdan saw what it meant. He could develop the conflict on Starkad, step by step, guiding it, nursing it, keeping it on schedule . . . till our main strength was marshaled there, just before the blowup came. We wouldn't be likely to see the invader. It's coming in 'way off the ecliptic, and has a very low albedo, and toward the end would be lost in Saxo's glare and traveling at more than 700 kilometers per second. Nor would we be looking in that direction. Our attention would be all on Brechdan's forces. They'd be prepared, after the captains opened their sealed orders. They'd know exactly when to dash away on hyperdrive. Ours— well, the initial radiation will move at the speed of light. It would kill the crews before they knew they were dead. An hour or so later, the first wave of gases would vaporize their ships. The Empire would be crippled and the Merseians could move in. That's why there's war on Starkad."

Ranjit Singh tugged his beard. The pain seemed to strengthen him. "Can we do anything? Plant bombs to blow this object apart, maybe?"

"I don't know, sir. Offhand, I doubt it. Too many fragments would stay on essentially the same path, I believe. Of course, we can evacuate Starkad. There are other planets."

"Yes. We can do that."

"Will you tell me now?" Dragoika asked.

Flandry did. He had not known she could weep.

CHAPTER EIGHTEEN

Highport lay quiet. Men filled the ugly barracks, drifted along the dusty streets, waited for orders and longed for home. Clamor of construction work, grumble of traffic, whine of aircraft bound to battle, were ended. So likewise, after the first tumultuous celebrations, was most merry-making. The war's conclusion had left people too dazed. First, the curt announcement that Admiral Enriques and Fodaich Runei were agreed on a cease-fire while they communicated with their respective governments. Then, day after day of not knowing. Then the arrival of ships; the proclamation that, Starkad being doomed, Empire and Roidhunate joined in hoping for a termination of the interracial conflict; the quick departure of the Merseians, save for a few observers; the imminent departure of most Imperial Navy personnel; the advent of civilian experts to make preliminary studies for a massive Terran project of another sort. And always the rumors, scuttlebutt, so-and-so knew somebody who knew for a fact that—How could you carry on as if this were ordinary? Nothing would ever again be quite ordinary. At night, you saw the stars and shivered.

Dominic Flandry walked in silence. His boots made a soft, rhythmic thud. The air was cool around him. Saxo spilled radiance from an enormous blue sky. The peaks beyond Mount Narpa thrust snowfields toward the ghost of a moon. Never had the planet looked so fair.

The door was ajar to the xenological office. He entered. Desks stood vacant. John Ridenour's staff was in the field. Their chief stayed behind, replacing sleep with stimulants as he tried to coordinate their efforts around an entire world. He was in conversation with a visitor. Flandry's heart climbed into his throat. Lord Hauksberg!

Everyone knew *Dronning Margrete* had arrived yesterday, in order that his Majesty's delegate might make a final inspection tour. Flandry had planned on keeping far out of sight. He snapped to a salute.

"Well, well." The viscount did not rise from his chair. Only the blond sharp face turned. The elegantly clad body stayed relaxed, the voice was amused. "What have we here?"

"Ensign Flandry, sir. I—I beg pardon. Didn't mean to interrupt. I'll go."

"No. Sit. Been meanin' to get hold of you. I do remember your name, strange as that may seem." Hauksberg nodded at Ridenour. "Go ahead. Just what is this difficulty you mention?"

The xenologist scarcely noticed the newcomer, miserable on a chair. Weariness harshened his tone. "Perhaps I can best illustrate with a typical scene, my lord, taken last week. Here's the Sisterhood HQ in Ujanka."

A screen showed a room whose murals related ancient glories. A Terran and several Tigery females in the plumes and striped cloaks of authority sat in front of a vidiphone. Flandry recognized some. He cursed the accident which brought him here at this minute. His farewells in the city had hurt so much.

Ostrova, the mistress, glared at the piscine face projected before her. "Never," she snapped. "Our rights and needs remain with us. Better death than surrender what our mothers died to gain."

The view shifted, went underwater, where also a human team observed and recorded. Again Flandry saw the Temple of Sky, from within. Light pervaded the water, turned it into one emerald where the lords of the Seafolk floated free. They had summoned Isinglass and Evenfall for expert knowledge. *Those I never did get a chance to say good-bye to,* Flandry thought, *and now I never will.* Through the colonnade he looked down on elfin Shellgleam.

"You would steal everything, then, through the whole cycle, as always you have done," said he who spoke for them. "It shall not be. We must have those resources, when great toil is coming upon us. Do not forget, we keep our guns."

The record included the back-and-forth interpretation of Ridenour's men at either end, so Flandry followed the bitter argument in Kursovikian. Hauksberg could not, and grew restless. After a few minutes, he said, "Most int'restin', but s'pose you tell me what's goin' on."

"A summary was prepared by our station in the Chain," Ridenour said. He flicked a switch. In the screen appeared a lagoon where sunlight glittered on wavelets and trees rustled behind a wide white beach: heartbreakingly beautiful. It was seen from the cabin of a waterboat, where a man with dark-rimmed eyes sat. He gave date and topic, and stated:

"Both factions continue to assert exclusive rights to the archipelago fishing grounds. Largely by shading their translations, our teams have managed to prevent irrevocable loss of temper, but no compromise is yet in sight. We shall continue to press for an equitable arrangement. Success is anticipated, though not for a considerable time."

Ridenour switched off. "You see, my lord?" he said. "We can't simply load these people aboard spaceships. We have to determine which of several possible planets are most suitable for them; and we have to prepare them, both in organization and education. Under ideal conditions, the psychic and cultural shock will still be terrible. Groundlaying will take years. Meanwhile, both races have to maintain themselves."

"Squabblin' over somethin' that'll be a whiff of gas in half a decade? Are such idiots worth savin'?"

"They're not idiots, my lord. But our news, that their world is under a death sentence, has been shattering. Most of them will need a long while to adapt, to heal the wound, before they can think about it rationally. Many never will. And . . . my lord, no matter how logical one believes he is, no matter how sophisticated he claims to be, he stays an animal. His forebrain is nothing but the handmaiden of instinct. Let's not look down on these Starkadians. If we and the Merseians, we big flashy space-conquering races, had any better sense, there'd be no war between us."

"There isn't," Hauksberg said.

"That remains to be seen, my lord."

Hauksberg flushed. "Thank you for your show," he said coldly. "I'll mention it in my report."

Ridenour pleaded. "If your Lordship would stress the need for more trained personnel here. . . . You've seen a little bit of what needs doing in this little bit of the planet. Ahead of us is the whole sphere, millions of individuals, thousands of societies. Many aren't even known to us, not so much as names, only blank spots on the map. But those blank spots are filled with living, thinking, feeling beings. We have to reach them, save them. We won't get them all, we can't, but each that we do rescue is one more justification for mankind's existence. Which God knows, my lord, needs every justification it can find."

"Eloquent," Hauksberg said. "His Majesty's government'll have to decide how big a bureaucratic empire it wants to create for the benefit of some primitives. Out o' my department." He got up. Ridenour did too. "Good day."

"Good day, my lord," the xenologist said. "Thank you for calling. Oh. Ensign Flandry. What'd you want?"

"I came to say good-bye, sir." Flandry stood at attention. "My transport leaves in a few hours."

"Well, good-bye, then. Good luck." Ridenour went so far as to come shake hands. But even before Hauksberg, with Flandry behind, was out of the door, Ridenour was back at his desk.

"Let's take a stroll beyond town," Hauksberg said. "Want to stretch my legs. No, beside me. We've things to discuss, boy."

"Yes, sir."

Nothing further was said until they halted in a meadow of long silvery quasigrass. A breeze slid from the glaciers where mountains dreamed. A pair of wings cruised overhead. Were every last sentient Starkadian rescued, Flandry thought, they would be no more than the tiniest fraction of the life which joyed on this world.

Hauksberg's cloak flapped. He drew it about him. "Well," he said, looking steadily at the other. "We meet again, eh?"

Flandry made himself give stare for stare. "Yes, sir. I trust the remainder of my lord's stay on Merseia was pleasant."

Hauksberg uttered a laugh. "You are shameless! Will go far indeed, if no one shoots you first. Yes, I may say Councillor Brechdan and I had some rather int'restin' talks after the word came from here."

"I . . . I understand you agreed to, uh, say the space battle was only due to both commanders mistaking their orders."

"Right. Merseia was astonished as us to learn about the rogue after our forces found it by accident." Hauksberg's geniality vanished. He seized Flandry's arm with unexpected force and said sternly: "Any information to the contrary is a secret of state. Revealin' it to anyone, even so much as hintin' at it, will be high treason. Is that clear?"

"Yes, my lord. I've been briefed."

"And's to your benefit, too." Hauksberg said in a milder voice. "Keepin' the secret necessarily involves quashin' the charges against you. The very fact that they were ever brought, that anything very special happened after we reached Merseia, goes in the ultrasecret file also. You're safe, my boy."

Flandry put his hands behind his back, to hide how they doubled into fists. He'd have given ten years, off this end of his life, to smash that smiling face. Instead he must say, "Is my lord so kind as to add his personal pardon?"

"Oh, my, yes!" Hauksberg beamed and clapped his shoulder. "You did absolutely right. For absolutely the wrong reasons, to be sure, but by pure luck you accomplished my purpose for me, peace with Merseia. Why should I carry a grudge?" He winked. "Regardin' a certain lady, nothin' between friends, eh? Forgotten."

Flandry could not play along. "But we have no peace!" he exploded.

"Hey? Now, now, realize you've been under strain and so forth, but—"

"My lord, they were planning to destroy us. How can we let them go without even a scolding?"

"Ease down. I'm sure they'd no such intention. It was a weapon to use against us if we forced 'em to. Nothin' else. If we'd shown a genuine desire to cooperate, they'd've warned us in ample time."

"How can you say that?" Flandry choked. "Haven't you read any history? Haven't you listened to Merseian speeches, looked at Merseian books, seen our dead and wounded come back from meeting Merseians in space? They want us out of the universe!"

Hauksberg's nostrils dilated. "That will do, Ensign. Don't get above yourself. And spare me the spewed-back propaganda. The full story of this incident is bein' suppressed precisely because it'd be subject to your kind of misinterpretation and so embarrass future relations between the governments. Brechdan's already shown his desire for peace, by withdrawin' his forces in toto from Starkad."

"Throwing the whole expensive job of rescue onto us. Sure."

"I told you to control yourself, Ensign. You're not quite old enough to set Imperial policy."

Flandry swallowed a foul taste. "Apologies, my lord."

Hauksberg regarded him for a minute. Abruptly the viscount smiled. "No. Now I was gloatin'. Apologies to you. Really, I'm not a bad sort. And you mean well too. One day you'll be wiser. Let's shake on that."

Flandry saw no choice. Hauksberg winked again. "B'lieve I'll continue my stroll alone. If you'd like to say good-bye to Donna d'Io, she's in the guest suite."

Flandry departed with long strides.

By the time he had reached HQ and gone through the rigamarole of gaining admittance, fury had faded. In its place lay emptiness. He walked into the living room and stopped. Why go further? Why do anything?

Persis ran to him. She wore a golden gown and diamonds in her hair. "Oh, Nicky, Nicky!" She laid her head on his breast and sobbed.

He consoled her in a mechanical fashion. They hadn't had many times together since he came back from the rogue. There had been too much work for him, in Ujanka on Ridenour's behalf. And that had occupied him so greatly that he almost resented the occasions when he must return to Highport. She was brave and intelligent and fun, and twice she had stepped between him and catastrophe, but she did not face the end of her world. Nor was her own world the same as his: could never be.

They sat down on a divan. He had an arm around her waist, a cigarette in his free hand. She looked at the floor. "Will I see you on Terra?" she asked dully.

"I don't know," he said. "Not for some time anyway, I'm afraid. My orders have come through officially, I'm posted to the Intelligence academy for training, and Commander Abrams warns me they work the candidates hard."

"You couldn't transfer out again? I'm sure I could arrange an assignment—"

"A nice, cushy office job with regular hours? No, thanks, I'm not about to become anyone's kept man."

She stiffened as if he had struck her. "I'm sorry," he floundered. "Didn't mean that. It's only, well, here's a job I am fitted for, that serves a purpose. If I don't take it, what meaning has life got?"

"I could answer that," she said low, "but I guess you wouldn't understand."

He wondered what the devil to say.

Her lips brushed his cheek. "Go ahead, then," she said. "Fly."

"Uh . . . you're not in trouble, Persis?"

"No, no. Mark's a most civilized man. We might even stay together a while longer, on Terra. Not that that makes any big difference. No matter how censored, some account of my adventures is bound to circulate. I'll be quite a novelty, quite in demand. Don't worry about me. Dancers know how to land on their feet."

A slight gladness stirred in him, largely because he was relieved of any obligation to fret about her. He kissed her farewell with a good imitation of warmth.

It was so good, in fact, that his loneliness returned redoubled once he was in the street again. He fled to Max Abrams.

The commander was in his office, straightening out details before leaving on the same transport that would bear Flandry home. From Terra, though, he would go on furlough to Dayan. His stocky frame leaned back as Flandry burst through the doorway. "Well, hello, hero," he said. "What ails you?"

The ensign flung himself into a chair. "Why do we keep trying?" he cried. "What's the use?"

"Hey-hey. You need a drink." Abrams took a bottle from a drawer and poured into two glasses. "Wouldn't mind one myself. Hardly set foot on Starkad before they tell me I'm shipping out again." He lifted his tumbler. "*Shalom.*"

Flandry's hand shook. He drained his whisky at a gulp. It burned on the way down.

Abrams made a production of lighting a cigar. "All right, son," he said. "Talk."

"I've seen Hauksberg," jerked from Flandry.

"Nu? Is he that hideous?"

"He . . . he . . . the bastard gets home free. Not a stain on his bloody damned escutcheon. He'll probably pull a medal. And still he quacks about peace!"

"Whoa. He's no villain. He merely suffers from a strong will to believe. Of course, his political career is bound up with the position he's taken. He can't afford to admit he was wrong. Not even to himself, I imagine. Wouldn't be fair to destroy him, supposing we could. Not expedient. Our side needs him."

"Sir?"

"Think. Never mind what the public hears. Consider what they'll hear on the Board. How they'll regard him. How neatly he can be pressured if he should get a seat on it, which I hope he does. No blackmail, nothing so crude, especially when the truth can't be told. But an eyebrow lifted at a strategic moment. A recollection, each time he opens his mouth, of what he nearly got us into last time around. Sure, he'll be popular with the masses. He'll have influence. So, fine. Better him than somebody else, with the same views, that hasn't yet bungled. If you had any charity in you, young man—which no one does at your age—you'd feel sorry for Lord Hauksberg."

"But . . . I . . . well—"

Abrams frowned into a cloud of smoke. "Also," he said, "in the longer view, we need the pacifists as a counter-weight to the armchair missileers. We can't make peace, but we can't make real war either. All we can do is hold the line. And man is not an especially patient animal by nature."

"So the entire thing is for zero?" Flandry nigh screamed. "Only to keep what little we have?"

The grizzled head bent. "If the Lord God grants us that much," Abrams said. "He is more merciful than He is just."

"Starkad, though—Death, pain, ruin, and at last, the rotten status quo! What were we doing here?"

Abrams caught Flandry's gaze and would not let go. "I'll tell you," he said. "We had to come. The fact that we did, however futile it looked, however distant and alien and no-business-of-ours these poor people seemed, gives me a little hope for my grandchildren. We were resisting the enemy, refusing to let any aggression whatsoever go unpunished, taking the chance he presented us to wear him down. And we were proving once more to him, to ourselves, to the universe, that we will not give up to him even the least of these. Oh, yes, we belonged here."

Flandry swallowed and had no words.

"In this particular case," Abrams went on, "because we came, we can save two whole thinking races and every-thing they might mean to the future. We'd no way of knowing that beforehand; but there we were when the time arrived. Suppose we hadn't been? Suppose we'd said it didn't matter what the enemy did in these marches. Would he have rescued the natives? I doubt it. Not unless there happened to be a political profit in it. He's that kind of people."

Abrams puffed harder. "You know," he said, "ever since Akhnaton ruled in Egypt, probably since before then, a school of thought has held we ought to lay down our weapons and rely on love. That, if love doesn't work, at least we'll die guiltless. Usually even its opponents have said this a noble idea. I say it stinks. I say it's not just unrealistic, not just infantile, it's evil. It denies we have any duty to *act* in this life. Because how can we, if we let go of our capability?

"No, son, we're mortal—which is to say, we're ignorant, stupid and sinful—but those are only handicaps. Our pride is that nevertheless, now and then, we do our best. A few times we succeed. What more dare we ask for?"

Flandry remained silent.

Abrams chuckled and poured two fresh drinks. "End of lecture." he said. "Let's examine what's waiting for you. I wouldn't ordinarily say this to a fellow at your arrogant age, but since you need cheering up . . . well, I will say, once you hit your stride, Lord help the opposition!"

He talked for an hour longer. And Flandry left the office whistling.

A CIRCUS
OF HELLS

This book thanks William R. Johnson, wherever he is nowadays, for several excellent ideas about Talwin which he contributed, and will gladly stand him a drink any time it can get together with him.

CHAPTER ONE

The story is of a lost treasure guarded by curious monsters, and of captivity in a wilderness, and of a chase through reefs and shoals that could wreck a ship. There is a beautiful girl in it, a magician, a spy or two, and the rivalry of empires. So of course—Flandry was later tempted to say—it begins with a coincidence.

However, the likelihood that he would meet Tachwyr the Dark was not fantastically low. They were in the same profession, which had them moving through a number of the same places; and they also shared the adventurousness of youth. To be sure, once imperialism is practiced on an interstellar scale, navies grow in size until the odds are huge against any given pair of their members happening on each other. Nevertheless, many such encounters were taking place, as was inevitable on one of the rare occasions when a Merseian warship visited a Terran planet. A life which included *no* improbable events would be the real statistical impossibility.

The planet was Irumclaw, some 200 light-years from Sol in that march of the human realm which faced Betelgeuse. Lieutenant (j.g.) Dominic Flandry had been posted there not long before, with much wailing and gnashing of teeth until he learned that even so dismal a clod had its compensations. The Merseian vessel was the cruiser *Brythioch,* on a swing through the buffer region of unclaimed, mostly unknown suns between the spaces ruled in the names of Emperor and Roidhun. Neither government would have allowed any craft belonging to its rival, capable of spouting nuclear fire, any appreciable distance into its territory. But border authorities could, at discretion, accept a "goodwill visit." It broke the monotony and gave a slight hope of observing the kind of trivia which, fitted together, now and then revealed a fact the opposition would have preferred to keep secret.

In this case Merseia profited, at least initially.

Official hospitality was exchanged. Besides protocol, the humans were motivated, whether they knew it or not, to enjoy the delicate *frisson* that came from holding converse with those who—beneath every diplomatic phrase—were the enemy. Flandry did know it; he had seen more of life than the average twenty-one-year-old. He was sure the liberty parties down in Old Town were being offered quite a few drinks, and other amenities in certain cases.

Well, why not? They had been long in the deeps between the stars. If they went straight back from here, they must travel a good 140 light-years—about ten standard days at top hyperspeed, but still an abyss whose immensity and strangeness wore down the hardiest spirit—before they could raise the outermost of the worlds they called their own. They needed a few hours of small-scale living, be their hosts never so hostile.

Which we aren't anyway, Flandry thought. *We should be, but we aren't, most of us.* He grinned. *Including me.*

Though he would have liked to join the fun, he couldn't. The junior officers of Irumclaw Base must hold the customary reception for their opposite numbers from the ship. (Their seniors gave another in a separate building. The Merseians, variously bemused or amused by the rigid Terran concept of rank, conformed. They set more store by ceremony and tradition, even that of aliens, than latter-day humans did.) While some of the visitors spoke Anglic, it turned out that Flandry was the only man on this planet who knew Eriau. The mess hall had no connection to the linguistic computer and there was no time to jury-rig one. His translations would be needed more than his physical presence.

Not that the latter was any disgrace, he reflected rather smugly. He was tall and lithe and wore his dress uniform with panache and had become a favorite among the girls downhill. Despite this, he remained well liked by the younger men, if not always by his superiors.

He entered at the appointed evening hour. Under Commander Abdullah's fishy eye, he saluted the Emperor's portrait not with his usual vague wave but with a snap that well-nigh dislocated his shoulder. *And a heel click to boot,* he reminded himself. Several persons being in line ahead of him, he had a minute for taking stock.

Its tables removed except for one bearing refreshments—and its chairs, in deference to the guests—

the room stretched dreary. Pictures of former personnel, trophies and citations for former accomplishments, seemed to make its walls just the more depressing. An animation showed a park on Terra, trees nodding, in the background the skyward leap of a rich family's residential tower and airborne vehicles glittering like diamond dust; but it reminded him too well of how far he was from those dear comforts. He preferred the darkness in the real window. It was open and a breeze gusted through, warm, laden with unearthly odors.

The Merseians were a more welcome sight, if only as proof that a universe did exist beyond Irumclaw. Forty of them stood in a row, enduring repeated introductions with the stoicism appropriate to a warrior race.

They resembled especially large men . . . somewhat. A number of their faces might have been called good-looking in a craggy fashion; their hands each had four fingers and a thumb; the proportions and articulations of most body parts were fairly anthropoid. But the posture was forward-leaning, balanced by a heavy tail. The feet, revealed by sandals, were splayed, webbed, and clawed. The skin was hairless and looked faintly scaled; depending on subspecies, its color ranged from the pale green which was commonest through golden brown to ebony. The head had two convoluted bony orifices where man's has external ears. A ridge of serrations ran from its top, down the spine to the end of the tail.

Most of this anatomy was concealed by their uniforms: baggy tunic, snug breeches, black with silver trim and insignia. The latter showed family connections and status as well as rank and service. The Merseians had politely disarmed themselves, in that none carried a pistol at his wide belt; the Terrans, in turn, had refrained from asking them to remove their great knuckleduster-handled war knives.

It wasn't the differences between them and men that caused trouble, Flandry knew. It was the similarities—in planets of origin and thus in planets desired; in the energy of warm-blooded animals, the instincts of ancestors who hunted, the legacies of pride and war—

"*Afal* Ymen, may I present Lieutenant Flandry," Abdullah intoned. The young man bowed to the huge form, whose owner corresponded approximately to a commander, and received a nod of the ridged and shining pate. He proceeded, exchanging names and bows with every subordinate Merseian and wondering, as they doubtless did too, when the farce would end and the drinking begin.

"Lieutenant Flandry."

"*Mei* Tachwyr."

They stopped, and stared, and both mouths fell open.

Flandry recovered first, perhaps because he became aware that he was holding up the parade. "Uh, this is a, uh, pleasant surprise," he stammered in Anglic. More of his wits returned. He made a formal Eriau salutation: "Greeting and good fortune to you, Tachwyr of the Vach Rueth."

"And . . . may you be in health and strength, Dominic Flandry . . . of Terra," the Merseian replied.

For another moment their eyes clashed, black against gray, before the man continued down the line.

After a while he got over his astonishment. Albeit unexpected, the happenstance that he and Tachwyr had met again did not look especially important. Nonetheless, he went robotlike through the motions of sociability and of being an interpreter. His gaze and mind kept straying toward his former acquaintance. And Tachwyr himself was too young to mask entirely the fact that he was as anxious to get together with Flandry.

Their chance came in a couple of hours, when they managed to dodge out of their respective groups and seek the refreshment table. Flandry gestured. "May I pour for you?" he asked. "I fear that except for the telloch, we've run out of things native to your planet."

"I regret to say you have been had," Tachwyr answered. "It is a dreadful brand. But I like your—what is it called?—skoksh?"

"That makes two of us." Flandry filled glasses for them. He had already had several whiskies and would have preferred this one over ice. However, he wasn't about to look sissified in front of a Merseian.

"Ah . . . cheers," Tachwyr said, lifting his tumbler. His throat and palate gave the Anglic word an accent for which there were no Anglic words.

Flandry could form Merseian speech better if not perfectly. "*Tor ychwei.*" With both hands he extended his glass so that the other might take the first sip.

Tachwyr followed it with half of his own in a single gulp. "*Arrach!*" Relaxed a little, he cocked his head and smiled; but under the shelf of brow ridge, his glance held very steady on the human. "Well," he said, "what brings you here?"

"I was assigned. For a Terran year, worse luck. And you?"

"The same, to my present ship. I see you are now in the Intelligence Corps."

"Like yourself."

Tachwyr the Dark—his skin was a slightly deeper green than is usual around the Wilwidh Ocean—could not altogether suppress a scowl. "I started in that branch," he said. "You were a flyer when you came to Merseia." He paused. "Were you not?"

"Oh, yes," Flandry said. "I transferred later."

"At Commander Abrams' instigation?"

Flandry nodded. "Mostly. He's a captain now, by the way."

"So I have heard. We . . . take an interest in him."

After the Starkad affair, Flandry thought, *you would. Between us, Max Abrams and I wrecked a scheme concocted by none less than Brechdan Ironrede, Protector of the Roidhun's Grand Council.*

How much do you know about that, Tachwyr? You were only put to showing me around and trying to pump me, when Abrams and I were on your world as part of the Hauksberg mission. And the truth about Starkad was never made public; no one concerned could afford to let it come out.

You do remember us, though, Tachwyr. If nothing else, you must have gathered that we were instrumental in causing Merseia quite a bit of trouble. It bothers you to have found me here.

Better get off the subject. "You remain through tomorrow? I admit Irumclaw has less to offer than

Merseia, but I'd like to return part of the courtesy you gave me."

Again Tachwyr was slow to speak. "Thank you, negative. I have already arranged to tour the area with shipmates." The Eriau phrasing implied a commitment which no honorable male would break.

Flandry reflected that a male would not ordinarily bind himself so strongly to something so minor.

What the devil? the human thought. *Maybe they aim to sample our well-known Terran decadence and he doesn't want me to realize their well-known Merseian virtue can slack off that much.* "Stay in a party," he warned. "Some of those bars are almost as dangerous as the stuff they serve."

Tachwyr uttered the throaty laugh of his species, settled down on the tripod of feet and tail, and started yarning. Flandry matched him. They enjoyed themselves until the man was called away to interpret a tedious conversation between two engineer officers.

CHAPTER TWO

Such was the prologue. He had practically forgotten it when the adventure began. That was on a certain night about eight months later.

Soon after the red-orange sun had set, he left the naval compound and walked downhill. No one paid him any heed. A former commandant had tried to discourage his young men from seeking the occasionally lethal corruptions of Old Town. He had declared a large part of it off limits. Meeting considerable of the expense out of his own pocket, he had started an on-base recreation center which was to include facilities for sports, arts, and crafts, as well as honest gambling and medically certified girls. But the bosses below knew how to use money and influence. The commandant was transferred to a still more bleak and insignificant outpost. His successor dismantled what had been built, informed the men jovially that what they did off duty was their business, and was said to be drawing a nice extra income.

Flandry sauntered in elegance. The comet gleaming on either shoulder was so new that you might have looked for diffidence from him. But his bonnet was tilted more rakishly on his seal-brown hair than a strict interpretation of rules would have allowed; his frame was draped in a fantastic glittergold version of dress tunic and snowy trousers rucked into handmade beefleather halfboots; the cloak that fluttered behind him glowed with phosphorescent patterns through the chill dusk; and while he strolled, he sang a folk ballad concerning the improbable adventures of a Highland tinker.

It made a good cover for the fact that he was not out for pleasure.

Beyond the compound walls, the homes of the wealthy loomed amidst grandly downsweeping private parks. In a way, Flandry thought, they epitomized man's trajectory. Once the settlement had been sufficiently large and prosperous, and sufficiently within the Imperial sphere, to attract not only merchants but aristocrats. Old Town had bustled with culture as well as commerce— provincial, no doubt, this far from Terra; nevertheless, live and genuine, worthy of the respectful emulation of the autochthons.

Tonight Irumclaw lay like a piece of wreckage at the edge of the receding tide of empire. What mansions were not standing hollow had become the property of oafs, and showed it. (The oafs were not to be scoffed at. Several of them directed large organizations devoted to preying on the spacemen who visited and the Navy men who guarded what transshipment facilities remained in use.) Outside the treaty port boundaries, barbarism rolled forward as the natives abandoned civilization with a perhaps justifiable contempt.

Past the residential section, workshops and warehouses hulked black in the night, and Flandry moved alert with a hand near the needle gun under his tunic. Robberies and murders had happened here. Lacking the police to clean out this area, assuming he wanted to, the commandant had settled for advising men on liberty not to go through alone.

Flandry had been shocked to learn that when he first arrived. "We could do it ourselves—establish regular patrols—if he'd order it. Doesn't he care? What kind of chief is he?"

His protest had been delivered in private to another scout, Lieutenant Commander Eisenschmitt. The latter, having been around for a while, shrugged. "The kind that any place like this gets," he answered. "We don't rate attention at GHQ, so naturally we're sent the hacks, boobs, and petty crooks. Good senior officers are too badly needed elsewhere. When Irumclaw does get one it's an accident, and he doesn't stay long."

"Damn it, man, we're on the border!" Flandry pointed out the window of the room where they sat. It had been dark then, too. Betelgeuse glowed bloody-brilliant among the hosts of stars where no writ ran. "Beyond there—Merseia!"

"Yeh. And the gatortails expanding in all directions except when we bar the way. I know. But this is the far edge of nowhere . . . in the eyes of an Imperial government that can't see past its perfume-sniffing nose. You're fresh from Terra, Dom. You ought to understand better than me. I expect we'll pull out of Irumclaw entirely inside another generation."

"No! Can't be! Why, that'd leave this whole flank exposed for six parsecs inward. We'd have no way of protecting its commerce . . . of, of staying around in any force—"

"Uh-huh." Eisenschmitt nodded. "On the other hand, the local commerce isn't too profitable any more, less each year. And think of the saving to the Imperial treasury if we end operations. The Emperor should be able to build a dozen new palaces complete with harems."

Flandry had not been able to agree at the time. He was too lately out of a fighting unit and a subsequent school where competence was demanded. Over the months, though, he saw things for himself and drew his own sad conclusions.

There were times when he would have welcomed a set-to with a bandit. But it had not befallen, nor did it on this errand into Old Town.

The district grew around him, crumbling buildings left over from pioneer days, many of them simply the original beehive-shaped adobes of the natives slightly remodeled for other life forms. Streets and alleys twisted about under flimmering glowsigns. Traffic was mainly pedestrian, but noise beat on the eardrums, clatter, shuffle, clop, clangor, raucous attempts at music, a hundred different languages, once in a while a muffled scream or a bellow of rage. The smells were equally strong, body odors, garbage, smoke, incense, dope. Humans predominated, but many autochthons were present and space travelers of numerous different breeds circulated among them.

Outside a particular joyhouse, otherwise undistinguished from the rest, an Irumclagian used a vocalizer to chant in Anglic: "Come one, come all, come in, no cover, no minimum. Every type of amusement, pleasure, and thrill. No game too exotic, no stakes too high or low. Continuous sophisticated entertainment. Delicious food and drink, stimulants, narcotics, hallucinogens, emphasizers, to your order, to your taste, to your purse. Every sex and every technique of seventeen, yes, seventeen intelligent species ready to serve your desires, and this does not count racial, mutational, and biosculp variations. Come one, come all—" Flandry went in. He chanced to brush against two or three of the creature's arms. The blue integument felt cold in the winter air.

The entrance hall was hot and stuffy. An outsize human in a gaudy uniform said, "Welcome, sir. What is your wish?" while keeping eyes upon him that were like chips of obsidian.

"Are you Lem?" Flandry responded.

"Uh, yeh. And you—?"

"I am expected."

"Urh. Take the gravshaft to the top, that's the sixth floor, go left down the hall to a door numbered 666, stand in front of the scan and wait. When it opens, go up the stairs."

"Six-six-six?" murmured Flandry, who had read more than was common in his service. "Is Citizen Ammon a humorist, do you think?"

"No names!" Lem dropped a hand to the stunner at his hip. "On your way, kid."

Flandry obeyed, even to letting himself be frisked and leaving his gun at the checkstand. He was glad when Door

666 admitted him; that was the sado-maso level, and he had glimpsed things.

The office which he entered, and which sealed itself behind him, recalled Terra in its size and opulence and in the animation of a rose garden which graced a wall. Or so it seemed; then he looked closer and saw the shabbiness of the old furnishings, the garishness of the new. No other human save Leon Ammon was present. A Gorzunian mercenary stood like a shaggy statue in one corner. When Flandry turned his back, the being's musky scent continued to remind him that if he didn't behave he could be plucked into small pieces.

"G'evening," said the man behind the desk. He was grossly fat, hairless, sweating, not especially clean, although his scarlet tunic was of the finest. His voice was high and scratchy. "You know who I am, right? Sit down. Cigar? Brandy?"

Flandry accepted everything offered. It was of prime quality too. He said so.

"You'll do better than this if you stick by me," Ammon replied. His smile went no deeper than his lips. "You haven't told about the invitation my man whispered to you the other night?"

"No, sir, of course not."

"Wouldn't bother me if you did. Nothing illegal about inviting a young chap for a drink and a gab. Right? But you could be in trouble yourself. Mighty bad trouble, and not just with your commanding officer."

Flandry had his suspicions about the origin of many of the subjects on the floor below. Consenting adults . . . after brain-channeling and surgical disguise . . . He studied the tip of his cigar. "I don't imagine you'd've asked me here, sir, if you thought I needed threatening," he said.

"No. I like your looks, Dominic," Ammon said. "Have ever since you started coming to Old Town for your fun. A lot of escapades, but organized like military maneuvers, right? You're cool and tough and close-mouthed. I had a check done on your background."

Flandry expanded his suspicions. Various incidents, when he had been leaned on one way or another, began to look like engineered testing of his reactions. "Wasn't much to find out, was there?" he said. "I'm only a j.g., routinely fresh-minted after serving here for two months. Former flyboy, reassigned to Intelligence, sent back to Terra for training in it and then to Irumclaw for scouting duty."

"I can't really compute that," Ammon said. "If they aim to make you a spy, why have you spend a year flitting in and out of this system?"

"I need practice in surveillance, especially of planets that are poorly known. And the no-man's-land yonder needs watching. Our Merseian chums could build an advanced base there, for instance, or start some other kettle boiling, unbeknownst to us, if we didn't keep scoutboats sweeping around." *Maybe they have anyway.*

"Yes, I got that answer before when I asked, and it still sounds to me like a waste of talent. But it got you to Irumclaw, and I did notice you and had you studied. I learned more than stands on any public record, boy. The whole Starkad business pivoted on you."

Shocked, Flandry wondered how deeply the rot had eaten, if the agent of a medium-scale vice boss on a tenth-rate frontier planet could obtain such information.

"Well, your tour'll soon be up," Ammon said. "Precious little to show for it, right? Right. How'd you like to turn a profit before you leave? A mighty nice profit, I promise you." He rubbed his hands. "Mighty nice."

"Depends," Flandry said. If he'd been investigated as thoroughly as it appeared, there was no use in pretending he had private financial resources, or that he didn't require them if he was to advance his career as far as he hoped. "The Imperium has my oath."

"Sure. sure. I wouldn't ask you to do anything against His Majesty. I'm a citizen myself, right? No, I'll tell you exactly what I want done, if you'll keep it confidential."

"It'd doubtless not do me any good to blab, the way you'll tell me."

Ammon giggled. "Right! Right! You're a sharp one, Dominic. Handsome, too," he added exploringly.

"I'll settle for the sharpness now and buy the handsomeness later," Flandry said. As a matter of fact, while he enjoyed being gray-eyed, he considered his face unduly long and thin, and planned to get it remodeled when he could afford the best.

Ammon sighed and returned to business. "All I want is for you to survey a planet for me. You can do it on your next scouting trip. Report back, privately, of course, and it's worth a flat million, in small bills or whatever shape you prefer." He reached into his desk and extracted a packet. "If you take the job, here's a hundred thousand on account."

A million! Ye gods and demons!

Flandry fought to keep his mask. *No enormous fortune, really. But enough for that necessary nest-feathering—the special equipment, the social contacts—no more wretched budgeting of my pleasure on furlough*—A distant part of him noted with approval how cool his tone stayed. "I have to carry out my assignment."

"I know, I know. I'm not asking you to skimp it. I told you I'm a loyal citizen. But if you jogged off your track awhile—it shouldn't cost more than a couple of weeks extra—"

"Cost me my scalp if anyone found out," Flandry said.

Ammon nodded. "That's how I'll know I can trust you to keep quiet. And you'll trust me, because suborning an Imperial officer is a capital offense—anyhow, it usually is when it involves a matter like this, that's not going to get mentioned to the authorities or the tax assessors."

"Why not send your personal vessel to look?"

Ammon laid aside his mannerisms. "I haven't got one. If I hired a civilian, what hold would I have on him? Especially an Old Town type. I'd likely end up with an extra mouth in my throat, once the word got around what's to be had out there. Let's admit it, even on this miserable crudball I'm not so big."

He leaned forward. "I want to become big," he said. It smoldered in eyes and voice; he shook with the intensity of it. "Once I know, from you, that the thing's worthwhile, I'll sink everything I own and can borrow into building up a reliable outfit. We'll work secretly for the first several years, sell through complicated channels, sock away the profits. Then maybe I'll surface, doctor the story, start paying taxes, move to Terra—maybe buy my way to a patent of nobility, maybe go into politics, I don't know, but I'll be *big*. Do you understand?"

Far too well, Flandry thought.

Ammon dabbed at his glistening forehead. "It would-n't hurt you, having a big friend," he said. "Right?"

Associate, please, Flandry thought. *Perhaps that, if I must. Never friend.*

Aloud: "I suppose I could cook my log, record how trouble with the boat caused delay. She's fast but super-annuated, and inspections are lackadaisical. But you haven't yet told me, sir, what the bloody dripping hell this is all about."

"I will, I will." Ammon mastered his emotions. "It's a lost treasure, that's what it is. Listen. Five hundred years ago, the Polesotechnic League had a base here. You've heard?"

Flandry, who had similarly tamed his excitement into alertness, nodded wistfully. He would much rather have lived in the high and spacious days of the trader princes, when no distance and no deed looked too vast for man, than in this twilight of empire. "It got clobbered during the Troubles, didn't it?" he said.

"Right. However, a few underground installations survived. Not in good shape. Not safe to go into. Tunnels apt to collapse, full of nightskulks—you know. Now I thought those vaults might be useful for—Never mind. I had them explored. A microfile turned up. It gave the coordinates and galactic orbit of a planetary system out in what's now no-man's-land. Martian Minerals, Inc., was mining one of the worlds. They weren't publicizing the fact; you remember what rivalries got to be like toward the end of the League era. That's the main reason why knowledge of this system was completely lost. But it was quite a place for a while."

"Rich in heavy metals," Flandry pounced.

Ammon blinked. "How did you guess?"

"Nothing else would be worth exploiting by a minerals outfit, at such a distance from the centers of civilization. Yes." A renewed eagerness surged in Flandry. "A young, metal-rich star, corresponding planets, on one of them a robotic base . . . It was robotic, wasn't it? High-grade central computer—consciousness grade, I'll bet—directing machines that prospected, mined, refined, stored, and loaded the ships when they called. Probably manufactured spare parts for them too, and did needful work on them, besides expanding its own facilities. You see, I don't suppose a world with that concentration of violently poisonous elements in its ground would attract people to a manned base. Easier and cheaper in the long run to automate everything."

"Right. Right." Ammon's chins quivered with his nodding. "A moon, actually, of a planet bigger than Jupiter. More massive, that is—a thousand Terras—though the file does say its gravity condensed it to a smaller size. The moon itself, Wayland they named it, Wayland has about three percent the mass of Terra but half the surface pull. It's that dense."

Mean specific gravity circa eleven, Flandry calculated. *Uranium, thorium—probably still some neptunium and plutonium—and osmium, platinum, rare metals simply waiting to be scooped out—my God! My greed!*

From behind his hard-held coolness he drawled: "A million doesn't seem extravagant pay for opening that kind of opportunity to you."

"It's plenty for a look-see," Ammon said. "That's all I

want of you, a report on Wayland. I'm taking the risks, not you.

"First off, I'm risking you'll go report our talk, trying for a reward and a quick transfer elsewhere before my people can get to you. Well, I don't think that's a very big risk. You're too ambitious and too used to twisting regulations around to suit yourself. And too smart, I hope. If you think for a minute, you'll see how I could fix it to get any possible charges against me dropped. But maybe I've misjudged you.

"Then, supposing you play true, the place could turn out to be no good. I'll be short a million, for nothing. More than a million, actually. There's the hire of a partner; reliable ones don't come cheap. And supplies for him; and transporting them to a spot where you can pick them and him up after you've taken off; and—oh, no, boy, you consider yourself lucky I'm this generous."

"Wait a minute," Flandry said. "A partner?"

Ammon leered. "You don't think I'd let you travel alone, do you? Really, dear boy! What'd prevent your telling me Wayland's worthless when it isn't, coming back later as a civilian, and 'happening' on it?"

"I presume if I give you a negative report, you'll . . . request . . . I submit to a narcoquiz. And if I didn't report to you at all, you'd know I had found a prize."

"Well, what if you told them you'd gotten off course somehow and found the system by accident? You could hope for a reward. I can tell you you'd be disappointed. Why should the bureaucrats care, when there'd be nothing in it for them but extra work? I'd lay long odds they'd classify your 'discovery' an Imperial secret and forbid you under criminal penalties ever to mention it anywhere. You might guess differently, though. No insult to you, Dominic. I believe in insurance, that's all. Right?

"So my agent will ride along, and give you the navigational data after you're safely away in space, and never leave your side till you've returned and told me personally what you found. Afterward, as a witness to your behavior on active duty, a witness who'll testify under hypnoprobe if need be, why, he'll keep on being my insurance against any change of heart you might suffer."

Flandry blew a smoke ring. "As you wish," he conceded. "It'll be pretty cozy, two in a Comet, but I can rig an extra bunk and—Let's discuss this further, shall we? I think I will take the job, if certain conditions can be met."

Ammon would have bristled were he able. The Gorzunian sensed his irritation and growled. "Conditions? From you?"

Flandry waved his cigar. "Nothing unreasonable, sir," he said airily. "For the most part, precautions that I'm sure you will agree are sensible and may already have thought of for yourself. And that agent you mentioned. Not 'he,' please. It could get fatally irritating, living cheek by unwashed jowl with some goon for weeks. I know you can find a capable and at the same time amiable human female. Right? Right."

He had everything he could do to maintain that surface calm. Beneath it, his pulse racketed—and not simply because of the money, the risk, the enjoyment. He had come here on a hunch, doubtless generated by equal parts of curiosity and boredom. He had stayed with the idea that, if the project seemed too hazardous, he could indeed betray Ammon and apply for duty that would keep him beyond range of assassins. Now abruptly a vision was coming to him, hazy, uncertain, and gigantic.

CHAPTER THREE

Djana was hard to shock. But when the apartment door had closed behind her and she saw what waited, her "No!" broke free as a near scream.

"Do not be alarmed," said the squatting shape. A vocalizer converted the buzzes and whistles from its lower beak into recognizable Anglic syllables. "You have nothing to fear and much to gain."

"You—a man called me—"

"A dummy. It is not desirable that Ammon know you have met me in private, and surely he has put a monitor onto you."

Djana felt surreptitiously behind her. As expected, the door did not respond; it had been set to lock itself. She clutched her large ornamental purse. A stun pistol lay inside. Her past had seen contingencies.

Bracing herself and wetting her lips, she said, "I don't. Not with xenos—" and in haste, fearing offense might be taken, "I mean nonhuman sophonts. It isn't right."

"I suspect a large enough sum would change your

mind," the other said. "You have a reputation for avarice. However, I plan a different kind of proposition." It moved slowly closer, a lumpy gray body on four thin legs which brought the head at its middle about level with her waist. One tentacle sent the single loose garment swirling about in a sinuous gesture. Another clutched the vocalizer in boneless fingers. The instrument was being used with considerable skill; it actually achieved an ingratiating note. "You must know about me in your turn. I am only Rax, harmless old Rax, the solitary representative of my species on this world. I assure you my reproductive pattern is sufficiently unlike yours that I find your assumption comical."

Djana eased a bit. She had in fact noticed the creature during the three years she herself had been on Irumclaw. A casual inquiry and answer crossed her recollection, yes, Rax was a dealer in drugs, legal or illegal, from . . . where was it? Nobody knew or cared. The planet had some or other unpronounceable name and orbited in distant parts. Probably Rax had had to make a hurried departure for reasons of health, and had drifted about until it stranded at last on this tolerant shore. Such cases were tiresomely common.

And who could remember all the races in the Terran Empire? Nobody: not when its bounds, unclear though they were, defined a rough globe 400 light-years across. That volume contained an estimated four million suns, most with attendants. Maybe half had been visited once or more, by ships which might have picked up incidental native recruits. And the hundred thousand or so worlds which enjoyed a degree of repeated contact with men—

often sporadic—and owed a degree of allegiance to the Imperium—often purely nominal—were too many for a brain to keep track of.

Djana's eyes flickered. The apartment was furnished for a human, in abominable taste. He must be the one who had called her. Now he was gone. Though an inner door stood closed, she never doubted she was alone with Rax. Silence pressed on her, no more relieved by dull traffic sounds from outside than the gloom in the windows was by a few streetlights. She grew conscious of her own perfume. *Too damn sweet*, she thought.

"Do be seated." Rax edged closer yet, with an awkwardness that suggested weight on its original planet was significantly lower than Irumclaw's 0.96 g. Did it keep a field generator at home . . . if it had any concept akin to "home"?

She drew a long breath, tossed her head so the tresses flew back over her shoulders, and donned a cocky grin. "I've a living to make," she said.

"Yes, yes." Rax's lower left tentacle groped ropily in a pouch and stretched forth holding a bill. "Here. Twice your regular hourly recompense, I am told. You need but listen, and what you hear should point the way to earning very much more."

"We-e-ell . . ." She slipped the money into her purse, found a chair, drew forth a cigarette and inhaled it into lighting. Her visceral sensations she identified as part fear—this must be a scheme against Ammon, who played rough—and part excitement—a chance to make some *real* credit? Maybe enough to quit this wretched hustle for good?

Rax placed itself before her. She had no way of reading expressions on that face.

"I will tell you what information is possessed by those whom I represent," the vocalizer said. The spoken language, constructed with pronunciation, vocabulary, and grammar in a one-one relationship to Anglic, rose and fell eerily behind the little transponder. "A junior lieutenant, Dominic Flandry, was observed speaking several times in private with Leon Ammon."

Now why should that interest them especially? she wondered, then lost her thought in her concentration on the words.

"Investigation revealed Ammon's people had come upon something in the course of excavating in this vicinity. Its nature is known just to him and a few trusted confidants. We suspect that others who saw were paid to undergo memory erasure anent the matter, except for one presumably stubborn person whose corpse was found in Mother Chickenfoot's Lane. Subsequently you too have been closeted with Ammon and, later, with Flandry."

"Well," Djana said, "he—"

"Pure coincidence is implausible," Rax declared, "especially when he could ill afford you on a junior lieutenant's pay. It is also known that Ammon has quietly purchased certain spacecraft supplies and engaged a disreputable interplanetary ferrier to take them to the outermost member of this system and leave them there at a specific place, in a cave marked by a small radio beacon that will self-activate when a vessel passes near."

Suddenly Djana realized why Skipper Orsini had

sought her out and been lavish shortly after his return. Rax's outfit had bribed him.

"I can't imagine what you're getting at," she said. A draft of smoke swirled and bit in her lungs.

"You can," Rax retorted. "Dominic Flandry is a scoutboat pilot. He will soon depart on his next scheduled mission. Ammon must have engaged him to do something extra in the course of it. Since the cargo delivered to Planet Eight included impellers and similar gear, the job evidently involves study of a world somewhere in the wilderness. Ammon's discovery was therefore, in all probability, an old record of its existence and possible high value. You are to be his observer. Knowing Flandry's predilections, one is not surprised that he should insist on a companion like you. It follows that you two have been getting acquainted, to make certain you can endure being cooped together for weeks in a small boat.

"Orsini will flit you to Eight. Flandry will surreptitiously land there, pick up you and the supplies, and proceed into interstellar space. Returning, you two will reverse the whole process, and meet in Ammon's office to report."

Djana sat still.

"You give away nothing by affirming this," Rax stated. "My organization *knows*. Where is the lost planet? What is its nature?"

"Who are you working for?" Djana asked mutedly.

"That does not concern you." Rax's tone was mild and Djana took no umbrage. The gang lords of Irumclaw were a murderous lot.

"You owe Ammon no allegiance," Rax urged. "Rather, you owe him a disfavor. Since you prefer to operate independently, and thus compete with the houses, you must pay him for his 'protection.'"

Djana sighed. "If it weren't him, it'd be somebody else."

Rax drew forth a sheaf of bills and riffled them with a fine crisp sound. She estimated—holy saints!—ten thousand credits. "This for answering my questions," it said. "Most likely a mere beginning for you."

She thought, while she inhaled raggedly, *If the business looks too dangerous, I can go tell Leon right away and explain I was playing along—of course, this bunch might learn I'd talked and I'd have to skip—*A flick of white fury: *I shouldn't have to skip! Not ever again!*

She built her sentences with care. "Nobody's told me much. You understand they wouldn't, till the last minute. Your ideas are right, but they're about as far along as my own information goes."

"Has Flandry said nothing to you?"

She plunged, "All right. Yes. Give me that packet."

Having taken the money, she described what the pilot had been able to reveal to her after she had lowered his guard for him. (An oddly sweet pair of nights; but best not think about that.) "He doesn't know the coordinates yet, you realize," she finished. "Not even what kind of sun it is, except for the metals. It must be somewhere not too far off his assigned route. But he says that leaves thousands of possibilities."

"Or more." Rax forgot to control intonation. Was the sawing rhythm that came out of the speaker an equivalent of its equivalent of an awed whisper? "So many, many stars . . . a hundred billion in this one lost lonely dust-mote of a galaxy . . . and we on the edge, remote in a spiral arm where they thin toward emptiness . . . what do we know, what can we master?"

The voice became flat and businesslike again. "This could be a prize worth contending for. We would pay well for a report from you. Under certain circumstances, a million."

What Nicky said he was getting! And Leon's paying me a bare hundred thousand—Djana shook her head. "I'll be watched for quite a while, Rax, if Wayland turns out to be any use. What good is a fortune after you've been blasted?" She shivered. "Or they might be angry enough to brain-channel me and—" The cigarette scorched her fingers. She ground it into a disposer and reached for a new one. *A million credits*, she thought wildly. *A million packs of smokes. But no, that's not it. What you do is bank it and live off the interest. No huge income, but you'd be comfortable on it, and safe, and free, free*—

"You would require disappearance, certainly," Rax said. "That is part of the plan."

"Do you mean we . . . our boat . . . would never come back?"

"Correct. The Navy will mount a search, with no result. Ammon will not soon be able to obtain another scout, and in the interim he can be diverted from his purpose or done away with. You can be taken to a suitably distant point, to Terra itself if you wish."

Djana started her cigarette. The taste was wrong. "What about, well, him?"

"Junior Lieutenant Flandry? No great harm need come if the matter is handled efficiently. For the sums involved, one can afford to hire technicians and equipment able to remove recent memories from him without damage to the rest of his personality. He can be left where he will soon be found. The natural assumption will be that he was captured by Merseians and hypnoprobed in a random-pattern search for information."

Rax hunched forward. "Let me make the proposition quite specific," it continued. "If Wayland turns out to be worthless, you simply report to Ammon as ordered. When it is safe, you seek me and tell me the details. I want especially to know as much about Flandry as you can extract from him. For example, has he anything more in mind concerning this mission than earning his bribe? You see, my organization may well have uses of its own for a buyable Navy officer. Since this puts you to no special effort or hazard, your compensation will be one hundred thousand credits."

Plus what I've already got in my purse, she exulted, *plus Leon's payment!*

"And if the moon is valuable?" she murmured.

"Then you must capture the boat. That should not be difficult. Flandry will be unsuspicious. Furthermore, our agents will have seen to it that the crates supposed to contain impellers do not. That presents no problem; the storage cave is unguarded."

Djana frowned. "Huh? What for? How can he check out the place if he can't flit around in his spacesuit?"

"It will not be considered your fault if his judgment proves erroneous, for this or any other cause. But he should be able to do well enough; it is not as if this were a xenological expedition or the like. The reason for thus

restricting his mobility is that he—young and reckless—
will thereby be less likely to undertake things which could
expose you, our contact, to danger."

"Well!" Djana chuckled. "Nice of you."

"After Flandry is your prisoner, you will steer the boat
through a volume whose coordinates will be given you,"
Rax finished. "This will bring you within detection range
of a ship belonging to us, which will make rendezvous and
take you aboard. Your reward will go to a million credits."

"Um-m-m . . ." *Check every angle, girl. The one you
don't check is sure to be the one with a steel trap in it.*
Djana flinched, recalling when certain jaws had punished
her for disobedience to an influential person. Rallying,
she asked: "Why not just trail the scout?"

"The space vibrations created by an operating
hyperdrive are detectable, instantaneously, to a distance
of about one light-year," Rax said, patient with her
ignorance of technology. "That is what limits communications over any greater reach to physical objects such as
letters or couriers. If our vessel can detect where
Flandry's is, his can do likewise and he may be expected
to take countermeasures."

"I see." Djana sat a while longer, thinking her way
forward. At last she looked up and said: "By Jesus, you do
tempt me. But I'll be honest, I'm scared. I know damn
well I'm being watched, ever since I agreed to do this
job, and Leon might take it into his head to give me a
narcoquiz. You know?"

"This has also been provided for." Rax pointed.
"Behind yonder door is a hypnoprobe with amnesiagenic
attachments. I am expert in its use. If you agree to help us

for the compensation mentioned, you will be shown the rendezvous coordinates and memorize them. Thereafter your recollection of this night will be driven from your consciousness."

"What?" It was as if a hand closed around Djana's heart. She sagged back into her chair. The cigarette dropped from cold fingers.

"Have no fears," the goblin said. "Do not confuse this with zombie-making. There will be no implanted compulsions, unless you count a posthypnotic suggestion making you want to explore Flandry's mind and persuade him to show you how to operate the boat. You will simply awaken tomorrow in a somewhat disorganized state, which will soon pass except that you cannot remember what happened after you arrived here. The suggestion will indicate a night involving drugs, and the money in your purse will indicate the night was not wasted. I doubt you will worry long about the matter, especially since you are soon heading into space."

"I—well—I don't touch the heavy drugs, Rax—"

"Perhaps your client spiked a drink. To continue: Your latent memories will be buried past the reach of any mere narcoquiz. Two alternative situations will restimulate them. One will be an interview where Flandry has told Ammon Wayland is worthless. The other will be his telling you, on the scene, that it is valuable. In either case, full knowledge will return to your awareness and you can take appropriate action."

Djana shook her head. "I've seen . . . brain-channeled . . . brain-burned—no," she choked. Every detail in the room, a checkerboard pattern on a lounger, a moving wrinkle on Rax's face, the panels of the inner door, stood before her with nightmare sharpness. "No. I won't."

"I do not speak of slave conditioning," the other said. "That would make you too inflexible. Besides, it takes longer than the hour or so we dare spend. I speak of a voluntary bargain with us which includes your submitting to a harmless cue-recall amnesia."

Djana rose. The knees shook beneath her. "You, you, you could make a mistake. No. I'm going. Let me out." She reached into her purse.

She was too late. The slugthrower had appeared. She stared down its muzzle. "If you do not cooperate tonight," Rax told her, "you are dead. Therefore, why not give yourself a chance to win a million credits? They can buy you liberation from what you are."

CHAPTER FOUR

The next stage of the adventure came a month afterward. That was when the mortal danger began.

The sun that men had once named Mimir burned with four times the brightness of Sol; but at a distance of five astronomical units it showed tiny, a bluish-white firespot too intense for the unshielded eye. Covering its disc with a finger, you became able to see the haze around it—gas, dust, meteoroids, a nebula miniature in extent but thick as any to be found anywhere in the known universe—and the spearpoints of light created by reflection within that nebula. Elsewhere, darkness swarmed with remoter stars and the Milky Way foamed around heaven.

Somewhat more than four million kilometers from the scoutboat, Regin spread over two and a half times the sky diameter of Luna seen from Terra. The day side of the giant planet cast sunlight blindingly off clouds in its intensely compressed atmosphere. The night side had an ashen-hued glow of its own, partly from aurora, partly from luminosity rebounding off a score of moons.

They included Wayland. Though no bigger than Luna, the satellite dominated the forward viewscreen: for the boat was heading straight down out of orbit. The vision of stark peaks, glacier fields, barren plains, craters old and eroded or new and raw, was hardly softened by a thin blanket of air.

Flandry sent his hands dancing over the pilot board. Technically Comet class, his vessel was antiquated and minimally equipped. Without a proper conning computer, he must make his approach manually. It didn't bother him. Having gotten the needful data during free fall around the globe, he had only to keep observant of his instruments and direct the grav drive accordingly. For him it was a dance with the boat for partner, to the lilt of cosmic forces; and indeed he whistled a waltz tune through his teeth.

Nonetheless he was taut. The faint vibrations of power, rustle and chemical-sharp odor of ventilation, pull of the interior weightmaking field, stood uncommonly strong in his awareness. He heard the blood beat in his ears.

Harnessed beside him, Djana exclaimed: "You're not aiming for the centrum. You're way off."

He spared her a look. Even now he enjoyed the sight. "Of course," he said.

"What? Why?"

"Isn't it obvious? Something mighty damn strange is going on there. I'm not about to bull in. Far better we weasel in." He laughed. "Though I'd rather continue tomcatting."

Her features hardened. "If you try to pull any—"

"Ah-ah. No bitching." Flandry gave his attention back to the board and screens. His voice went on, abstractedly: "I'm surprised at you. I am for a fact. A hooker so tough albeit delectable, not taking for granted we'd reconnoiter first. I'm going to land us in that crater—see it? Ought to be firm ground, though we'll give it a beam test before we cut the engine. With luck, any of those flying weirdies we saw that happens to pass overhead should register us as another piece of meteorite. Not that I expect any will chance by. This may be a miniworld, but it wears a lot of real estate. I'll leave you inboard and take a ver-ree cautious lookabout. If all goes well, we'll do some encores, working our way closer. And don't think I don't wish a particularly sticky hell be constructed for whatever coprolite brain it was that succeeded in packing the impeller cases with oxygen bottles."

He had not made that discovery until he was nearing Regin and had broken out the planetside gear Ammon had assembled to his order. You didn't need personal flying units on routine surveillance. The last thing you were supposed to do was land anywhere. They weren't even included in your emergency equipment. If you ran into trouble, they couldn't help you.

I should have checked the whole lot when we loaded it aboard on Planet Eight, he thought. *I'm guilty of taking something for granted. How Max Abrams would ream me out! . . . Well, I guess Intelligence agents learn their trade through sad experience like everybody else.*

After a string of remarks that made Djana herself blush, he had seriously considered aborting the Wayland mission. But no. Too many hazards were involved in a second try, starting with the difficulty of convincing his fellows that breakdowns had delayed him twice in a row. And what harm could an utterly lifeless ball of rock do him?

Strangely, the enigmatic things he had seen from orbit increased his determination to go down. Or perhaps that wasn't so strange. He was starved for action. Besides, at his age he dared not admit to any girl that he could be scared.

His whetted senses perceived that she shivered. It was for the first time in their voyage. But then, she was a creature of cities and machinery, not of the Big Deep.

And it was a mystery toward which they descended: where a complex of robots ought to have been at work, or at least passively waiting out the centuries, an inexplicable crisscross of lines drawn over a hundred square kilometers in front of the old buildings, and a traffic of objects like nothing ever seen before except in bad dreams. Daunting, yes. On a legitimate errand, Flandry would have gone back for reinforcements. But that was impractical under present circumstances.

Briefly, he felt a touch of pity for Djana. He knew she was as gentle, loving, and compassionate as a cryogenic drill. But she was beautiful (small, fine-boned, exquisite features, great blue eyes, honey-gold hair), which he considered a moral virtue. Apart from insisting that he prepare meals—and he was undoubtedly far the superior cook—she had accepted the cramped austerity of the boat with wry good humor. During their three weeks of travel she had given him freely of her talents, which commanded top price at home. While her formal education in other fields was scanty, between bouts she had proved an entertaining talkmate. Half enemy she might be, but Flandry had allowed himself the imprudent luxury of falling slightly in love with her, and felt he was a little in her debt. No other scouting sweep had been as pleasant!

Now she faced the spacefarers' truth, that the one thing we know for certain about this universe is that it is implacable. He wanted to reach across and console her.

But the vessel was entering atmosphere. A howl began to penetrate the hull, which bucked.

"Come on, *Jake*," Flandry said. "Be a good girl."

"Why do you always call the boat *Jake*?" his companion asked, obviously trying to get her mind off the crags lancing toward her.

"*Giacobini-Zinner* is ridiculous," he answered, "and the code letters can't be fitted into anything bawdy." *I refrain from inquiring what you were called as a child*, he thought. *I prefer not to believe in, say, an Ermintrude Bugglethwaite who invested in a, ah, house name and a total-body biosculp job. . . .* "Quiet, please. This is tricky work. Thin air means high-velocity winds."

The engine growled. Interior counteracceleration force did not altogether compensate for lurching; the deck seemed to stagger. Flandry's hands flew, his feet shoved pedals, occasionally he spoke an order to the idiot-grade central computer that the boat did possess. But he'd done this sort of thing before, often under more difficult conditions. He'd make planetfall without real trouble—

The flyers came.

He had scarcely a minute's warning of them. Djana

screamed as they whipped from a veil of driving gray cloud. They were metal, bright in the light of Mimir and of Regin's horizon-scraping dayside crescent. Wide, ribbed wings upbore sticklike torsos, grotesque empennage, beaks and claws. They were much smaller than the spacecraft, but they numbered a score or worse.

They attacked. They could do no real harm directly. Their hammering and scraping resounded wild in the hull. But however frail by the standards of a real ship, a Comet was built to resist heavier buffetings.

They did, though, rock it. Wheeling and soaring, they darkened vision. More terribly, they interfered with radar, sonic beams, every probing of every instrument. Suddenly, except for glimpses when they flashed aside, Flandry was piloting blind. The wind sent his craft reeling.

He stabbed forth flame out of the single spitgun in the nose. A flyer exploded in smoke and fragments. Another, wing sheared across, spun downward to destruction. The rest were too many, too quickly reacting. "We've got to get out of here!" he heard himself yell, and crammed on power.

Shock smashed through him. Metal shrieked. The world whirled in the screens. For an instant, he saw what had happened. Without sight or sensors, in the turbulence of the air, he had descended further than he knew. His spurt of acceleration was not vertical. It had sideswiped a mountaintop.

No time for fear. He became the boat. Two thrust cones remained, not enough to escape with but maybe enough to set down on and not spatter. He ignored the flock and fought for control of the drunkenly unbalanced grav drive. If he made a straight tail-first backdown, the force would fend off the opposition; he'd have an uncluttered scan aft, which he could project onto one of the pilot board screens and use for an eyeballed landing. That was *if* he could hold her upright.

If not, well, it had been fun living.

The noise lessened to wind-whistle, engine stutter, drumbeat of beaks. Through it he was faintly astonished to hear Djana. He shot her a glance. Her eyes were closed, her hands laid palm to palm, and from her lips poured ancient words, over and over. "Hail Mary, full of grace—"

Her? And he'd thought he'd gotten to know her!

CHAPTER FIVE

They landed skull-rattlingly hard. Weakened members in the boat gave way with screeches and thumps. But they landed.

At once Flandry bent himself entirely to the spitgun. Locked onto target after target, the beam flashed blue among the attackers that wheeled overhead. A winged thing slanted downward and struck behind the rim of the crater where he had settled. A couple of others took severe damage and limped off. The remainder escorted them. In a few minutes the last was gone from sight.

No—wait—high above, out of range, a hovering spark in murky heaven? Flandry focused a viewscreen and turned up the magnification. "Uh-huh," he nodded. "One of our playmates has stayed behind to keep a beady eye on us."

"O-o-o-oh-h-h," Djana whimpered.

"Pull yourself together," he snapped. "You know how. Insert Part A in Slot B, bolt to Section C, et cetera. In case nobody's told you, we have a problem."

Mainly he was concerned with studying the indicators on the board while he unharnessed. Some air had been lost, and replenished from the reserve tanks, but there was no further leakage. Evidently the hull had cracked, not too badly for self-sealing but enough to make him doubt the feasibility of returning to space without repairs. Inboard damage must be worse, for the grav field was off—he moved under Wayland's half a terrestrial g with a bounding ease that roused no enthusiasm in him—and, oh-oh indeed, the nuclear generator was dead. Light, heat, air and water cycles, everything was running off the accumulators.

"Keep watch," he told Djana. "If you see anything peculiar, feel free to holler."

He went aft, past the chaos of galley and head, the more solidly battened-down instrument and life-support centers, to the engine room. An hour's inspection confirmed neither his rosiest hopes nor his sharpest fears. It was possible to fix *Jake,* and probably wouldn't take long: if and only if shipyard facilities were brought to bear.

"So what else is new?" he said and returned forward.

Djana had been busy. She stood in the conn with all the small arms aboard on a seat behind her—the issue blaster and needler, his private Merseian war knife—except for the stun pistol she had brought herself. That was holstered on her flank. She rested a hand on its iridivory butt.

"What the deuce?" Flandry exclaimed. "I might even ask, What the trey?"

He started toward her. She drew the gun. "Halt," she said. Her soprano had gone flat.

He obeyed. She could drop him as he attacked, in this space where there was no room to dodge, and secure him before he regained consciousness. Of course, he could perhaps work free of any knots she was able to tie, but—He swallowed his dismay and studied her. The panic was gone, unless it dwelt behind that whitened skin and drew those lips into disfiguring straight lines.

"What's wrong?" he asked slowly. "My intentions are no more shocking than usual."

"Maybe nothing's wrong, Nicky." She attempted a smile. "I've got to be careful. You understand that, don't you? You're an Imperial officer and I'm riding Leon Ammon's rocket. Maybe we can keep on working together. And maybe not. What's happened here?"

He collected his wits. "Int'resting question," he said. "If you think this is a trap for you—well, really, my sweet, you know quite well no functional trap is that elaborate. I'm every bit as baffled as you . . . and worried, if that's any consolation. I want nothing at the moment but to get back with hide entire to vintage wine, gourmet food, good conversation, good music, good books, good tobacco, a variety of charming ladies, and everything else that civilization is about."

He was ninety-nine percent honest. The remaining one percent involved pocketing the rest of his million. Though not exclusively . . .

The girl didn't relax. "Well, can we?"

He told her what the condition of the boat was.

She nodded. Wings of amber-colored hair moved softly past delicate high cheekbones. "I thought that was more or less it," she said. "What do you figure to do?"

Flandry shifted stance and scratched the back of his neck. "Another interesting question. We can't survive indefinitely, you realize. Considering the outside temperature and other factors, I'd say that if we throttle all systems down to a minimum—and if we don't have to fire the spitgun again—we have accumulator energy for three months. Food for longer, yes. But when the thermometer drops to minus a hundred, even steak sandwiches can only alleviate; they cannot cure."

She stamped a foot. "Will you stop trying to be funny!"

Why, I thought I was succeeding, Flandry wanted to say, *and incidentally, that motion of yours had fascinating effects in these snug-fitting pullovers we're wearing. Do it again?*

Djana overcame her anger. "We need help," she said.

"No point in trying to radio for it," Flandry said. "Air this thin supports too little ionosphere to send waves far past the horizon. Especially when the sun, however bright, is so distant. We might be able to bounce signals off Regin or another moon, except that that'd require aiming and monitoring gear *Jake* doesn't carry."

She stared at him in frank surprise. "Radio?"

"To the main computer at the mining centrum. It was originally a top-level machine, you know, complete with awareness—whatever it may have suffered since. And it commanded repair and maintenance equipment as well. If we could raise it and get a positive response, we should have the appropriate robots here in a few hours, and be off on the rest of my circuit in a few days."

Flandry smiled lopsidedly. "I wish now I had given it

a call from orbit," he went on. "But with the skewball things we saw—we've lost that option. We shall simply have to march there in person and see what can be done."

Djana tensed anew. "I thought that's what you'd figure on," she said, winter bleak. "Nothing doing, lover. Too chancy."

"What else—"

She had hardly begun to reply when he knew. The heart stumbled in him.

"I didn't join you blind," she said. "I studied the situation first, whatever I could learn, including the standard apparatus on these boats. They carry several couriers each. One of those can make it back to Irumclaw in a couple of weeks, with a message telling where we are and what we're sitting on."

"But," he protested. "But. Listen, the assault on us wasn't likely the last attempt. I wouldn't guarantee we can hold out. We'd better leave here, duck into the hills—"

"Maybe. We'll play that as it falls. However, I am not passing up the main chance for survival, which is to bring in a Navy ship."

Djana's laugh was a yelp. "I can tell what you're thinking," she continued. "There I'll be, along on your job. How many laws does that break? The authorities will check further. When they learn about your taking a bribe to do Ammon's work for him in an official vessel—I suppose at a minimum the sentence'll be life enslavement."

"What about you?" he countered.

Her lids drooped. Her lips closed and curved. She moved her hips from side to side. "Me? I'm a victim of circumstances. I was afraid to object, with you wicked men coercing me . . . till I got this chance to do the right thing. I'm sure I can make your commandant see it that way and give me an executive pardon. Maybe even a reward. We're good friends, really, Admiral Julius and me."

"You won't get through the wait here without my help," Flandry said. "Certainly not if we're attacked."

"I might or might not," she replied. Her expression thawed. "Nicky, darling, why must we fight? We'll have time to work out a plan for you. A story or—or maybe you can hide somewhere with supplies, and I can come back later and get you, I swear I will—" She swayed in his direction. "I swear I want to. You've been wonderful. I won't let you go."

"Regardless," he said, "you insist on sending a message."

"Yes."

"Can you launch a courier? What if I refuse?"

"Then I'll stun you, and tie you, and torture you till you agree," she said, turned altogether impersonal. "I know a lot about that."

Abruptly it blazed from her: "You'll never imagine how much I know! You'd die before I finished. Remember your boasting to me about the hardships you've met, a poor boy trying to get ahead in the service on nothing but ability? If you could've heard me laughing inside while I kissed you! *I* came up from slavery—in the Black Hole of Jihannath—what I've been through makes the worst they've thought of in Irumclaw Old Town look like a crèche game—I'm not going back to hell again—as God is my witness, I'm not!"

She drew a shaking breath and clamped the vizor once more into place. From a pocket she fetched a slip of paper. "This is the message," she said.

Flandry balanced on the balls of his feet. He might be able to take her, if he acted fast and luck fell his way . . . he just might. . . .

And swiftly as a stab, he knew the risk was needless. He gasped.

"What's the matter?" Djana's question wavered near hysteria.

He shook himself. "Nothing," he said. "All right, you win, let's ship your dispatch off."

The couriers were near the main airlock. He walked in advance, before her steady gun muzzle, though she knew the location. For that matter, the odds were she could figure out how to activate them herself. She had been quick to learn the method of putting the boat on a homeward course—feed the destination coordinates to the autopilot, lock the manual controls, et cetera—when he met her request for precautionary instruction. These gadgets, four in number, were simpler yet.

Inside each torpedo shape—120 centimeters long, but light enough for a man to lift under Terran gravity—were packed the absolute minimum of hyperdrive and gravdrive machinery; sensors and navigational computer to guide it toward a preset goal; radio to beep when it neared; accumulators for power; and a tiny space for the payload, which could be a document, a tape, or whatever else would fit.

Ostentatiously obedient, Flandry opened one compartment and stepped aside while Djana laid in her letter and closed the shell. Irumclaw's coordinates were stenciled on it for easy reference and she watched him turn the control knobs. He slid the courier forward on the launch rack. Pausing, he said: "I'd like to program this for a sixty-second delay, if you don't mind."

"Why?"

"So we can get back to the conn and watch it take off. To be sure it does, you know."

"M-m-m—that makes sense." Djana hefted the gun. "I'm keeping you covered till it's outbound, understand."

"Logical. Afterward, can we both be uncovered?"

"Be still!"

Flandry started the mechanism and returned forward with her. They stared out.

The view was of desolation. *Jake* lay close by the crater wall, which sloped steeply aloft until its rim stood fanged in heaven, three kilometers above. Its palisades reached so far that they vanished under the near horizon before their opposite side became visible. The darkling rock was streaked with white, that also covered the floor: carbon dioxide and ammonia snow. This was beginning to vaporize in Wayland's sixteen-day time of sunlight; fogs boiled and mists steamed, exposing the bluish gleam of eternal water ice.

Overhead the sky was deep violet, almost black. Stars glittered wanly across most of it, for at this early hour Mimir's fierce disc barely cleared the ringwall in that area where the latter went behind the curve of the world. Regin was half a dimness mottled with intricate cloud patterns, half a shining like burnished steel.

A whitter of wind came in through the hull.

Behind Flandry, Djana said with unexpected wistfulness: "When the courier's gone, Nicky, will you hold me? Will you be good to me?"

He made no immediate reply. His shoulder and stomach muscles ached from tension.

The torpedo left its tube. For a moment it hovered, while the idiot pseudo-brain within recognized it was on a solid body and which way was up. It rose. Once above atmosphere, it would take sights on beacons such as Betelgeuse and lay a course to Irumclaw.

Except—yes! Djana wailed. Flandry whooped.

The spark high above had struck. As one point of glitter, the joined machines staggered across the sky.

Flandry went to the viewscreen and set the magnification. The torpedo had nothing but a parchment-thin aluminum skin, soon ripped by the flyer's beak while the flyer's talons held tight. The courier had ample power to shake off its assailant, but not the acumen to do so. Besides, the stresses would have wrecked it anyway. It continued to rise, but didn't get far before some critical circuit was broken. That killed it. The claws let go and it plummeted to destruction.

"I *thought* that'd happen," Flandry murmured.

The flyer resumed its station. Presently three others joined it. "They must've sensed our messenger, or been called," Flandry said. "No use trying to loft more, eh? We need their energy packs worse for other things."

Djana, who had stood numbed, cast her gun aside and crumpled weeping into his arms. He stroked her hair and made soothing noises.

At last she pulled herself together, looked at him, and

said, still gulping and hiccoughing: "You're glad, aren't you?"

"Well, I can't say I'm sorry," he admitted.

"Y-y-you'd rather be dead than—"

"Than a slave? Yes, cliché or not, 'fraid so."

She considered him for a while that grew. "All right," she said most quietly. "That makes two of us."

CHAPTER SIX

He had topped the ringwall when the bugs found him.

His aim was to inspect the flyer which had crashed on the outer slope, while Djana packed supplies for the march. Perhaps he could get some clue as to what had gone wrong here. The possibility that those patrolling would spot him and attack seemed among the least of the hazards ahead. He could probably find a cave or crag or crevasse in time, a shelter where they couldn't get at him, on the rugged craterside. Judiciously applied at short range, the blaster in his hip sheath ought to rid him of them, in view of what the spitgun had accomplished—unless, of course, they summoned so many reinforcements that he ran out of charge.

Nothing happened. Tuning his spacesuit radio through its entire range of reception, he came upon a band where there was modulation: clicks and silences, a code reeling off with such speed that in his ears it sounded almost like an endless ululation, high-pitched and unhuman. He was tempted to transmit a few remarks on those frequencies, but decided not to draw unnecessary attention to himself. At their altitude, he might well be invisible to the flyers.

The rest of the available radio spectrum was silent, except for the seethe and crackle of cosmic static. And the world was silent, except for the moan of wind around him, the crunching of snow and rattling of stones as his boots struck, the noise of his own breath and heartbeat. The crater floor was rock, ice, drift of snow and mists, wan illumination that would nonetheless have burned him with ultraviolet rays had his faceplate let them past. Clouds drove ragged across alien constellations and the turbulent face of Regin. The crater wall lifted brutal before him.

Climbing it was not too difficult. Erosion had provided ample footing and handholds; and in this gravity, even burdened with space armor he was lighter than when nude under Terran pull. He adapted to the changed ratio of weight and inertia with an ease that would have been unconscious had he not remembered it was going to cause Djana some trouble and thereby slow the two of them down. Other than keeping a nervous eye swiveling skyward, the chief nuisance he suffered was due to imperfections of the air renewal and thermostatic units. He was soon hot, sweating, and engulfed in stench.

I'll be sure to fix that *before we start!* he thought. *And give the service crew billy hell when (if) I return.* Momentarily, the spirit sagged in him: *What's the use? They're sloppy because the higher echelons are incompetent because the Empire no longer really cares about holding this part of the marches. . . . In my grandfather's day we were still keeping what was ours, mostly. In my father's day, the slogan became "conciliation and consolidation," which means retreat. Is my day—my very own personal bit of daylight between the two infinite darknesses—is it going to turn into the Long Night?*

He clamped his teeth together and climbed more vigorously. *Not if I can help it!*

The bugs appeared.

They hopped from behind boulders and ice banks, twenty or more, soaring toward him. Some thirty centimeters long, they had ten claw-footed legs each, a tail ending in twin spikes, a head on which half a dozen antennae moved. Mimir's light shimmered purple off their intricately armored bodies.

For a second Flandry seriously wondered if he had lost his mind. The old records said Wayland was barren, always had been, always would be. He had expected nothing else. Life simply did not evolve where cold was this deep and permanent, air this tenuous, metal this dominant, background radiation this high. And supposing a strange version of it could, Mimir was a young star, that had coalesced with its planets only a few hundred megayears ago from a nebula enriched in heavy atoms by earlier stellar generations; the system hadn't yet finished condensing, as witness the haze around the sun and the rate of giant meteorite impacts; there had not been time for life to start.

Thus Flandry's thought flashed. It ended when the shapes were murderously upon him.

Two landed on his helmet. He heard the clicks, felt the astonishing impact. Looking down, he saw others at his waist, clinging to his legs, swarming around his boots.

Jaws champed, claws dug. They found the joints in his armor and went to work.

No living thing smaller than a Llynathawrian elephant wolf should have been able to make an impression on the alloys and plastics that encased Flandry. He saw shavings peel off and fall like sparks of glitter. He saw water vapor puff white from the first pinhole by his left ankle. The creature that made it gnawed industriously on.

Flandry yelled an obscenity. He shook one loose and managed to kick it. The shock of striking that mass hurt his toes. The bug didn't arc far, nor was it injured. It sprang back to the fray. Flandry was trying to pluck another off. It clung too strongly for him.

He drew his blaster, set it to needle beam and low intensity, laid the muzzle against the carapace, and pulled the trigger.

The creature did not smoke or explode or do whatever else a normal organism would. But after two or three seconds it let go, dropped to the ground and lay inert.

The rest continued their senseless, furious attack. Flandry cooked them off him and slew those that hadn't reached him with a series of energy bolts. No organism that size, that powerful, that heavily shelled, ought to have been that vulnerable to his brief, frugal beams.

The last two were on his back where he couldn't see them. He widened the blaster muzzle and fanned across the air renewal unit. They dropped off him. The heat skyrocketed the temperature in his suit and drove gas faster out of the several leaks. Flandry's eardrums popped painfully. His head roared and whirled.

Training paid off. Scarcely aware of what he did, he

slapped sealpatches on the holes and bled the reserve tank for a fresh atmosphere. Only then did he sit down, gasp, shudder, and finally wet his mummy-dry mouth from the water tube.

Afterward he was able to examine the dead bugs. Throwing a couple of them into his pack, he resumed climbing. From the top of the ringwall he discerned the wrecked flyer and slanted across talus and ice patches to reach it. The crash had pretty well fractured it to bits, which facilitated study. He collected a few specimen parts and returned to *Jake*.

The trip was made in a growingly grim silence, which he scarcely broke when he re-entered the boat. Aloneness and not knowing had ground Djana down. She sped to welcome him. He gave her a perfunctory kiss, demanded food and a large pot of coffee, and brushed past her on his way to the workshop.

CHAPTER SEVEN

They had about 200 kilometers to go. That was the distance, according to the maps Flandry had made in orbit, from the scoutboat's resting place to a peak so high that a transmission from it would be line-of-sight with some of the towering radio transceiver masts he had observed at varying separations from the old computer centrum.

"We don't want to get closer than we must," he explained to the girl. "We want plenty of room for running, if we find out that operations have been taken over by something that eats people."

She swallowed. "Where could we run to?"

"That's a good question. But I won't lie down and die gracefully. I'm far too cowardly for that."

She didn't respond to his smile. He hoped she hadn't taken his remark literally, even though it contained a fair amount of truth.

The trip could be shortened by crossing two intervening maria. Flandry refused. "I prefer to skulk," he said, laying out a circuitous path through foothills and a mountain range that offered hiding places. While it would often make the going tough, and Djana was inexperienced and not in training, and they would be burdened with Ammon's supplies and planetside gear, he hoped they could average thirty or forty kilometers per twenty-four hours. A pitiful few factors worked in their favor. There was the mild gravity and the absence of rivers to ford and brush to struggle through. There was the probably steady weather. Since Wayland always turned the same face to Regin, there was continuous daylight for the span of their journey, except at high noon when the planet would eclipse Mimir. There was an ample supply of stimulants. *And,* Flandry reflected, *it helps to travel scared.*

He decreed a final decent meal before departure, and music and lovemaking and a good sleep while the boat's sensors kept watch. The party fell rather flat; Djana was too conscious that this might be the last time. Flandry made no reproaches. He did dismiss any vague ideas he might have entertained about trying for a long-term liaison with her.

They loaded up and marched. More accurately, they scrambled, across the crater wall and into a stretch of sharp hills and wind-polished slippery glaciers. Flandry allowed ten minutes' rest per hour. He spent most of those periods with map, gyrocompass, and sextant, making sure they were still headed right. When Djana declared she could do no more, he said calculatedly, "Yes, I understand; you're no use off your back." She spat her rage and jumped to her feet.

I mustn't drive her too hard, Flandry realized.

Gradual strengthening will get us where we're going faster. In fact, without that she might not make it at all.

Does that matter?

Yes, it does. I can't abandon her.

Why not? She'd do the same for me.

Um-m-m . . . I don't know exactly why . . . let's say that in spite of everything, she's a woman. Waste not, want not.

When she did begin reeling as she walked, he agreed to pitch camp and did most of the chores alone.

First he selected a spot beneath an overhanging cliff. "So our winged chums won't see us," he explained chattily, "or drop on us their equivalent of what winged chums usually drop. You will note, however, that an easy route will take us onto the top of the cliff, if we should have groundborne callers. From there we can shoot, throw rocks, and otherwise hint to them that they're not especially welcome." Slumped in exhaustion against a boulder, she paid him no heed.

He inflated the insulating floor of the sealtent and erected its framework. The wind gave him trouble, flapping the fabric he stretched across until he got it secured. Because the temperature had risen to about minus fifty, he didn't bother with extra layers, but merely filled the cells of the one skin with air.

To save accumulator charge, he worked the pump by hand, and likewise when it evacuated the tent's interior. Extreme decompression wasn't needed, since the Waylander atmosphere was mostly noble gases and nitrogen. The portable air renewer he had placed inside, together with a glower for heat, took care of remaining poisonous vapors and excess carbon dioxide, once he had refilled the tent with oxygen at 200 millibars. (The equipment for all this was heavy. But it was indispensable, at least until Djana got into such condition that she didn't frequently need the relief of shirtsleeve environment. And she'd better! Given the limitations of what they could carry, they could make possibly fifteen stops that utilized it.) While renewer and glower did their work, Flandry chipped water ice to melt for drinking and cooking.

They entered through the plastic airlock. He showed Djana how to bleed her spacesuit down to ambient pressure. When they had taken off their armor, she lay on the floor and watched him with eyes glazed by fatigue. He fitted together his still, put it on the glower, and filled it with ice. "Why are you doing that?" she whispered.

"Might have unpleasant ingredients," he answered. "Gases like ammonia come off first and are taken up by the activated colloids in this bottle. We can't let them contaminate our air; our one renewer's busy handling the stuff we breathe out; and besides, when we strike camp I must pump as big a fraction as I can manage back into its tank. When the water starts boiling, I shut the valve to the gas-impurity flask and open the one to the water can. We can't risk heavy metal salts, especially on a world where they must be plentiful. Doesn't take but a micro quantity of plutonium, say, this far from medical help, to kill you in quite a nasty fashion. À propos, I suppose you know we daren't smoke in a pure oxy atmosphere."

She shuddered and turned her glance from the desolation in the ports.

Dinner revived her somewhat. Afterward she sat

hugging her legs, chin on knees, and watched him clean the utensils. In the cramped space, his movements were economical. "You were right," she said gravely. "I wouldn't have a prayer without you."

"A hot meal, albeit freeze-dried, does beat pushing a concentrate bar through your chowlock and calling it lunch, eh?"

"You know what I mean, Nicky. What can I do?"

"You can take your turn watching for monsters," he said immediately.

She winced, "Do you really think—"

"No. I don't think. Too few data thus far to make it worth the trouble. Unhappily, though, one datum is the presence of two or more kinds of critter whose manners are as deplorable as they are inexplicable."

"But they're machines!"

"Are they?"

She stared at him from under tangled tawny bangs. He said while he labored: "Where does 'robot' leave off and 'organism' begin? For hundreds of years there've been sensor-computer-effector systems more intricate and versatile than some kinds of organic life. They function, perceive, ingest, have means to repair damage and to be reproduced; they homeostatize, if that horrible word is the one I want; certain of them think. None of it works identically with the systems evolved by organic animals and sophonts—but it works, and toward very similar ends.

"Those bugs that attacked me have metal exoskeletons underneath that purple enamel, and electronic insides. That's why they succumbed so easily to my blaster: high heat conductivity, raising the temperature of components designed for Wayland's natural conditions. But they're machinery as elaborate as any I've ever ruined. As I told you, I hadn't the time or means to do a proper job of dissection. As near as I could tell, though, they run off accumulators. Their feelers are magnificently precise sensors—magnetic, electric, radionic, thermal, et cetera. They have optical and audio systems as well. In fact, with one exception, they're such gorgeous engineering that it's a semantic quibble whether to call them robots or artificial animals.

"Same thing, essentially, for the flyers—which, by the way, I'm tempted to call snapdragonflies. They get their lift from the wings and a VTOL turbojet; they use beak and claws to rip rather than grind metal; but they have sensors and computers akin to the bugs'. And they seem able to act more independently, as you'd expect with a larger 'brain.'"

He put away the last dish, settled back, and longed for a cigarette. "What do you mean by 'one exception'?" Djana asked.

"I can imagine a robotic ecology, based on self-reproducing solar-cell units that'd perform the equivalent of photosynthesis," Flandry said. "I seem to recall it was actually experimented with once. But these things we've met don't have anything I can identify as being for nourishment, repair, or reproduction. No doubt they have someplace to go for replacement parts and energy recharges—someplace where new ones are also manufactured—most likely the centrum area. But what about the wrecked ones? There doesn't seem to be any interest in reclaiming those marvelous parts, or even the metal. It's not an ecology, then; it's open-ended. Those machines have no purpose except destruction."

He drew breath. "In spite of which," he said, "I don't believe they're meant for guarding this world or any such job. Because who save a lunatic would build a fighting robot and omit guns?

"Somehow, Djana, Wayland's come down with a plague of monsters. Until we know how many of what kinds, I suggest we proceed on the assumption that everything we meet will want to do us in."

A few times in the course of the next several Terran days, the humans concealed themselves when shapes passed by. These might be flyers cruising far overhead, in one case stooping on some prey hidden by a ridge. Or a pair of dog-sized, huge-jawed, sensor-bristling hunters loped six-legged on a quest; or a bigger object, horned and spike-tailed, rumbled on caterpillar treads along the bottom of a ravine. Twice Flandry lay prone and watched combats: bugs swarming over a walking red globe with lobsterish claws; a constrictor shape entangled with a mobile battering ram. Both end results appeared to confirm his deductions. The vanquished were left where they fell while the victors resumed prowling. Remnants from earlier battles indicated the same aftermath.

Otherwise the journey was nothing but a struggle to make distance. There was little opportunity while afoot, little wakefulness while at rest, to think about the significance of what had been seen. Nor did Flandry worry about encountering a killer. If it happened, it happened. On the whole, he didn't expect that kind of trouble . . . yet. This was too vast and rugged a land for any likelihood of it. Given due caution, he and Djana ought to make their first objective. What occurred after that might be a different story.

He did notice that the radio traffic got steadily thicker on the nonstandard band the robots used. No surprise. He was nearing what had been the center of operations, which must still be the center of whatever the hell was going on nowadays.

Hell indeed, he thought through the dullness of the exhaustion. *Did somebody sabotage Wayland, maybe long ago, by installing a predator factory? Or was it perhaps an accident? People may have fought hereabouts, and I suppose a nearby explosion could derange the main computer.*

None of the guesses seemed reasonable. The beast machines couldn't offer effective opposition to modern weapons. They threatened the lives of two marooned humans; but a single spacecraft, well-armed, well-equipped with detectors, crew alerted to the situation, could probably annihilate them with small difficulty. That fact ruled out sabotage—didn't it? As for damage to the ultimate control engine: Imprimis, it must have had heavy shielding, plus extensive self-repair capability, the more so in view of the meteorite hazard. Secundus, assuming it did sustain permanent harm, that implied a loss of components; it would then scarcely be able to design and produce these superbly crafted gargoyles.

Flandry gave up wondering.

The time came when he and Djana halted within an hour of the mountaintop that was their goal. They found a cave, screened by tall pinnacles, wherein they erected the sealtent. "It's not going any further," the man said. "Among other reasons, you know how long it takes to raise and to knock down again; and we can't stand many more losses of unrecovered oxygen each time we break camp. So if we don't succeed in getting help, and in particular if we provoke a hunt for us, the burden won't be worth carrying. This is a nice, hard-to-find, defensible spot to sit in."

"When do we call?" the girl asked.

"When we've corked off for about twelve hours," Flandry said. "I want to be well rested."

She herself was tired enough that she dropped straight into sleep.

In the "morning" his spirits were somewhat restored. He whistled as he led the way upward, and when he stood on the peak he declaimed, "I name thee Mt. Maïdens." All the while, though, his attention ranged ahead.

Behind and on either side was the familiar jumble of rock, ice, and inky shadows. Above gloomed the sky, its scattered stars and clouds, Mimir's searing brilliance now very near the dim, bright-edged shield of Regin. The wind whimpered around. He was glad to be inside his warm if smelly armor.

Ahead, as his topographical maps had revealed, the mountain dropped with a steepness that would have been impossible under higher gravity. The horizon was flat, betokening the edge of the plain where the centrum lay, and the squares he had seen, and he knew not what else. Through binoculars he made out the cruciform tops of four radio transceiver masts. Those had risen since man abandoned Wayland; others were scattered about in the

wilds; from orbit, he had identified a few as being under
construction by robots of recognizable worker form. He
had considered making for one of those sites instead of
here, but decided against it. That kind of robot was too
specialized, also in its "brain," to understand his problem.
Besides, the nearest was dangerously far from *Jake*'s resting
place.

He unfolded a light tripod-based directional transmitter. He plugged in the ancillary apparatus, including a
jack to his own helmet radio. Squatting, he directed the
assembly in its rotation until it had locked onto one of the
masts. Djana waited. Her face showed still more gaunt
and grimy than his, her eyes hollow and fever-bright.

"Here goes," Flandry said.

"O God, have mercy, help us," breathed in his earplugs.
He wondered briefly, pityingly, if religion was what had
kept her going, ever since her nightmare childhood. But he
had to tell her to keep silence.

He called on the standard band. "Two humans, ship-
wrecked, in need of assistance. Respond." And again. And
again. Nothing answered but the fire-crackle of cosmic
energies.

He tried on the robots' band. The digital code
chattered with no alteration that he could detect.

He tried other frequencies.

After an hour or more, he unplugged and rose. His
muscles ached, his mouth was parched, his voice came
hoarse out of a roughened throat. "No go, I'm afraid."

Djana had been seated on the sanitary unit from her
pack, which doubled as a stool protecting against the
elemental cold beneath. He had watched her shrink

further and further into herself. "So we're finished," she mumbled.

He sighed. "The circumstances could be more promising. The big computer should've replied instantly to a distress call." He paused. The wind blew, the stars jeered. He straightened. "I'm going for a first-hand look."

"Out in the open?" She scrambled erect. Her gauntlets closed spastically around his. "You'll be swarmed and killed!"

"Not necessarily. We saw from the boat, things do appear to be different yonder from elsewhere. For instance, none of the accumulated wreckage you'd expect if fighting went on. Anyhow, it's our last resort." Flandry patted her in a fatherly way, which he might as well under present conditions. "You'll stay in the tent, of course, and wait for me."

She moistened her lips. "No, I'll come along," she said.

"Whoa! You could get scragged."

"Rather that than starve to death, which I will if you don't make it. I won't handicap you, Nicky. Not any more. If we aren't loaded down the way we were, I can keep up with you. And I'll be extra hands and eyes."

He pondered. "Well, if you insist." *She's more likely to be an asset than not—a survivor type like her.*

Sardonically: *Yes, just like her. I suspect she's got more than one motive for this. Exempla gratia, to make damn sure I don't gain anything she doesn't get in on.*

Not that a profit seems plausible.

CHAPTER EIGHT

As they neared the plain, Mimir went into eclipse.

The last arc of brilliance edging Regin vanished with the sun. Instead, the planet showed as a flattened black disc overlaid with faint, flickering auroral glow and ringed with sullen red where light was refracted through atmosphere.

Flandry had anticipated it. The stars, suddenly treading forth many and resplendent, and the small crescents of two companion moons, ought to give sufficient illumination for cautious travel. At need, he and Djana could use their flash-beams, though he would rather not risk drawing attention.

He had forgotten how temperature would tumble. Fog started forming within minutes, until the world was swirling shapeless murk. It gave way after a while to snow borne on a lashing, squealing wind. Carbon dioxide mostly, he guessed; maybe some ammonia. He leaned into the thrust, squinted at his gyrocompass, and slogged on.

Djana caught his arm. "Shouldn't we wait?" he barely heard through the noise.

He shook his head before he remembered that to her

he had become a shadow. "No. A chance to make progress without being spotted."

"First luck we've had. Thanks, Jesus!"

Flandry refrained from observing that when the storm ended they might be irrevocably far into a hostile unknown. What had they to lose?

For a time, as they groped, he thought the audio pickups in his helmet registered a machine rumble. Did he actually feel the ground quiver beneath some great moving mass? He changed direction a trifle, without saying anything to the girl.

In this region, eclipse lasted close to two hours. The station would have been located on farside, escaping the darknesses altogether, except for the offsetting advantage of having Regin high in the night sky. When full, the planet must flood this hemisphere with soft radiance, an impossibly beautiful sight.

Though I doubt the robots ever gave a damn about scenery, Flandry thought, peering down to guide his boots past boulders and drifts. *Unless maybe the central computer . . . yes, I suppose. Imperial technology doesn't use many fully conscious machines—little need for them when we're no longer adventuring into new parts of the galaxy—so I, at any rate, know less about them than my ancestors did. Still, I can guess that a "brain" that powerful would necessarily develop interests outside its regular work. Its function—its desire, to get anthropomorphic—was to serve the human masters. But in between prospectings, constructions, visiting ships, when routine could only have occupied a minor part of its capacity, did it turn sensors onto the night sky and admire?*

Daylight began to filter through the snowfall. The wind died to a soughing. The ground flattened rapidly. Before precipitation had quite ended, fog was back, the newly frozen gases subliming under Mimir's rays and recondensing in air.

Flandry said, low and by sonic transmission: "Radio silence. Move quiet as you can." It was hardly a needful order. Earplugs were loud with digital code and there came a metallic rattle from ahead.

Once more Wayland took Flandry by surprise. He had expected the mists to lift slowly, as they'd done near dawn, giving him and Djana time to make out something of what was around them before they were likely to be noticed. His observations in orbit had indicated as much. For minutes the whiteness did veil them. Two meters away, wet ice and rock, tumbling rivulets, steaming puddles, faded into smoky nothing.

It broke apart. Through the rifts he saw the plain and the machines. The holes widened with tearing rapidity. The fog turned into cloudlets which puffed aloft and vanished.

Djana screamed.

Knowledge struck through Flandry: *Damn me for a witling! Why didn't I think? It takes a long while to heat things up again after half a month of night. But not after two hours. And evaporation goes fast at low pressures. What I saw from space, and assumed were lingering ground hazes, were clouds higher up, like those I see steaming away above us—*

That was at the back of his brain. Most of him saw what surrounded him. The blaster sprang into his hand.

Though the mountain was not far behind, soaring
from a knife-edge boundary, he and Djana had passed by
the nearest radio mast and were down on the plain. Like
other Waylander maria, it was not perfectly level; it rolled,
reared in scattered needles and minor craters, seamed
itself with narrow cracks, was bestrewn with rocks and
overlaid in places by ice banks. The travelers had entered
the section that was marked into squares. More than a
kilometer apart, the lines ran arrow straight, east and
west, north and south, further than he could see before
curvature shut off vision. He happened to be near one and
could identify it as a wide streak of black granules driven
permanently into the stone.

What he truly saw in that moment was the robots.

A hundred meters to his right went three of the
six-legged lopers. Somewhat further off on his left rolled
a horned and treaded giant. Still further ahead, but not
too far to catch him, straggled half a dozen different
monstrosities. Bugs by the score leaped and crawled
across the ground. Flyers were slanting down the sky. He
threw a look to rear and saw retreat cut off by a set of legs
upbearing a circular saw.

Djana cast herself on her knees. Flandry crouched
above, teeth skinned, and waited in the racket of his heart
for the first assailant.

There was none.

The killers ignored them.

Nor did they pay attention to each other.

While not totally unexpected, the relief sent
Flandry's mind whirling. When he had recovered, he saw
that the machines were converging on a point. Nothing

appeared above the horizon; their goal was too distant. He knew what it was, though—the central complex of buildings.

Djana began to laugh, wilder and wilder. Flandry didn't think they could afford hysteria. He hauled her to her feet. "Turn off that braying before I shake it out of you!" When words didn't work, he took her by her ankles, held her upside down, and made his threat good.

While she sobbed and gulped and wrestled her way back to control, he held her in a more gentle embrace and studied the robots across her shoulder. Most were in poor shape, holes torn in their skins, limbs missing. No wonder he'd heard them rattle and clank in the fog. Some looked unhurt aside from minor scratches and dents. Probably their accumulators were about drained.

In the end, he could explain to her: "I always figured those which survived the battles would get recharge and repair in this area. Um-m-m . . . it can't well serve all Wayland . . . I daresay the critters never wander extremely far from it . . , and we did spot construction work, the setup's being steadily expanded, probably new centers are planned. . . . Anyhow, this place is crucial. Elsewhere, they're programed to attack anything that moves and isn't like their own particular breed. Here, they're perfect lambs. Or so goes my current guess."

"W-we're safe, then?"

"I wouldn't swear to that. What's caused this whole insanity? But I do think we can proceed."

"Where to?"

"The centrum, of course. Giving those fellows a respectful berth. They seem to be headed offside. I imagine their R & R stations lie some ways from the main computer's old location."

"Old?"

"We don't know if it exists any longer," Flandry reminded her.

Nonetheless he walked with ebullience. He was still alive. How marvelous that his arms swung, his heels smote ground, his lungs inhaled, his unwashed scalp itched! Regin had begun to wax, the thinnest of bows, drawing back from Mimir's incandescent arrowpoint. Elsewhere glittered stars. Djana walked silent, exhausted by emotion. She'd recover, and when he got her back inside the seal-tent . . .

He was actually whistling as they crossed the next line. A moment later he took her arm and pointed. "Look," he said.

A new kind of robot was approaching from within the square. It was about the size of a man. The skin gleamed golden. Iridescence was lovely over the great batlike wings that helped the springing of its two long hoofed and spurred legs. The body was a horizontal barrel, a balancing tail behind, a neck and head rearing in front. With its goggling optical and erect audio sensors, its muzzle that perhaps held the computer, its mane of erect antennae, that head looked eerily equine. From its forepart, swivel-mounted, thrust a lance.

"We could almost call it a rockinghorsefly, couldn't we?" Flandry said. "As for the bread-and-butterfly—" His classical reference was lost on the girl.

She screamed afresh when the robot wheeled and came toward them in huge leaps. The lance was aimed to kill.

CHAPTER NINE

Djana was the target. She stood paralyzed. "Run!" Flandry bawled. He sped to intercept. The gun flamed in his grasp. Sparks showered where the beam struck.

Djana bolted. The robot swerved and bounded after her. It paid no attention to Flandry. And his shooting had no effect he could see.

*Must be armored against energy beams—unlike the things we've met hitherto—*He thumbed the power stud to full intensity. Fire cascaded blinding off the metal shape. Heedless, it bore down on his unarmed companion.

"Dodge toward me!" Flandry cried.

She heard and obeyed. The lance struck her from behind. It did not penetrate the air tank, as it would have the thinner cuirass of the spacesuit. The blow knocked her sprawling. She rolled over, scrambled up and fled on. Wings beat. The machine was hopping around to get at her from the front.

It passed by Flandry. He leaped. His arms locked around the neck of the horsehead. He threw a leg over the body. The wings boomed behind him where he rode.

And still the thing did not fight him, still it chased Djana. But Flandry's mass slowed it, made it stumble. Twisting about, he fired into the right wing. Sheet metal and a rib gave way. Crippled, the robot went to the ground. It threshed and bucked. Somehow Flandry hung on. Battered, half stunned, he kept his blaster snout within centimeters of the head and the trigger held back. His faceplate darkened itself against furious radiance. Heat struck at him like teeth.

Abruptly came quiet. He had pierced through to an essential part and slain the killer.

He sprawled across it, gasping the oven-hot air into his mouth, aware of undergarments sodden with sweat and muscles athrob with bruises, dimly aware that he had better arise. Not until Djana returned to him did he feel able to.

A draught of water and a stimpill shoved through his chowlock restored a measure of strength. He looked at the machine he had destroyed and thought vaguely that it was quite handsome. Like a dreamworld knight . . . Almost of themselves his arm lifted in salute and his voice murmured, "Ahoy, ahoy, check."

"What?" Djana asked, equally faintly.

"Nothing." Flandry willed the aches out of his consciousness and the shakes out of his body. "Let's get going."

"Y-y-yes." She was suffering worse from reaction than him. Her features seemed completely drained. She started off with mechanical strides, back toward the mountain.

"Wait a tick!" Flandry grabbed her shoulder. "Where're you bound?"

"Away," she said without tone. "Before something else comes after us."

"To sit in the sealtent—or at best, the boat—and wait for death? No, thanks." Flandry turned her about. She was too numbed to resist. "Here, swallow a booster of your own."

He had lost all but a rag of hope himself. The centrum was at the far side of the pattern, some ten kilometers hence. If robots were programed actually to attack humans, this close to where the great computer had been—*We'll explore a wee bit further, regardless. Why not?*

A machine appeared. At first it was a glint on the horizon, metal reflecting Mimirlight. Traveling fast across the plain, it gained shape within minutes. *Headed straight this way. And big!* Flandry cursed. Half dragging Djana, he made for a house-sized piece of meteoritic stone. From its top, defense might be possible.

The robot went past.

Djana sobbed her thanks. After a second, Flandry recovered from the shock of his latest deliverance. He stood where he was, holding the girl against him, and watched. The machine wasn't meant for combat. It was not much more than a self-operating flatbed truck with a pair of lifting arms.

It loaded the fallen lancer aboard and returned whence it came.

"For repairs," Flandry breathed. "No wonder we don't find stray parts in this neighborhood."

Djana shuddered in his arms.

His words went slowly on, shaping the thoughts they uttered: "Two classes of killer robot, then. One is free-ranging, fights indiscriminately, comes here to get fixed if it can make the trip, and doubtless returns to the wilderness for more hunting. While it's here, it keeps the peace.

"The other kind stays here, does fight here—though it doesn't interfere with the first kind or the maintenance machines—and is carefully salvaged when it comes to grief."

He shook his head in bewilderment. "I don't know if that's encouraging or not." Gazing down at Djana: "How do you feel?"

The drug he had forced on her was taking hold. It was not magical; it couldn't marshal resources which were no longer there. But for a time he and she would be alert, cool-headed, strong, quick-reacting. *And we'd better complete our business before the metabolic bill is presented,* Flandry recalled.

Her lips twitched in a woebegone smile. "I guess I'll do," she said. "Are you certain we should continue?"

"No. However, we will."

The next two squares they crossed were empty. One to their left was occupied. The humans kept a taut watch on that robot as they went past, but it did not stir. It was a tread-mounted cylinder, taller and broader than a man, its two arms ending in giant mauls, its head—the top of it, anyway, where there were what must be sensors—crowned with merlons like the battlements of some ancient tower. The sight jogged at Flandry's memory. An idea stirred in him but vanished before he could seize it. It could wait; readiness for another assault could not.

Djana startled him: "Nicky, does each of them stay inside its own square?"

"And defend that particular bit of territory against intruders?" Flandry's mind sprang. He smacked fist into palm. "By Jumbo, I think you're right! It could be a scheme for guarding the centrum . . . against really dangerous gizmos that don't behave themselves on this plain . . . a weird scheme, but then, everything on Wayland is weird.—Yes. The types of, uh, wild robot we've seen, and the ambulance and such, they're recognized as harmless and left alone. We don't fit into that program, so we're fair game."

"Not all the squares are occupied," she said dubiously.

He shrugged. "Maybe a lot of sentries are under repair at present." Excitement waxed in him. "The important point is, we can get across. Either directly across the lines, or over to a boundary and then around the whole layout. We simply avoid sections where any machine is. Making sure none are lurking behind a rock or whatever, of course." He hugged her. "Sweetheart, I do believe we're going to make it!"

The same eagerness kindled in her. They stepped briskly forth.

A figure that came into view, two kilometers ahead, as they passed the hillock which had concealed it, drew a cry from her. "Nicky, a man!" He jolted to a stop and raised his binoculars in unsteady hands. The object was indeed creepily similar to a large spacesuited human. But there were differences of detail, and it stood as death-still as the tower thing, and it was armed with sword and shield. Rather, its arms terminated in those pieces of war gear. Flandry lowered the glasses.

"No such luck," he said. "Not that it'd be luck. Anybody who's come here and taken charge like this would probably scupper us. It's yet another brand of guard robot." He tried to joke. "That means a further detour. I'm getting more exercise than I really want, aren't you?"

"You could destroy it."

"Maybe. Maybe not. If our friend the knight was typical, as I suspect, the lot of them are fairly well armored against energy beams. Besides, I don't care to waste charge. Used too bloody much in that last encounter. Another fracas, and we could be weaponless." Flandry started off on a slant across the square. "We'll avoid him and go catercorner past the domain of that comparatively mild-looking chap there."

Djana's gaze followed his finger. Remotely gleamed other immobile forms, including a duplicate of the hippoid and three of the anthropoid. Doubtless more were hidden by irregularities of terrain or its steep fall to the horizon. The machine which Flandry had in mind was closer, just left of his intended path. It was another cylinder, more tall and slim than the robot with the hammers. The smooth bright surface was unbroken by limbs. The conical head was partly split down the middle, above an array of instruments.

"He may simply be a watcher," Flandry theorized.

They had passed by, the gaunt abstract statue was falling behind, when Djana yelled.

Flandry spun about. The thing had left its square and was entering the one they were now in.

Dust and sparkling ice crystals whirled in the meter of space between its base and the ground. *Air cushion drive,* beat through Flandry. He looked frantically around for shelter. Nothing. This square held only basalt and frozen water.

"Run!" he cried. He retreated backward himself, blaster out. The heart slugged in him, the breath rasped, still hot from his prior battle.

A pencil of white fire struck at him from the cleft head. It missed at its range, but barely. He felt heat gust where the energy splashed and steam exploded. A sharp small thunderclap followed.

This kind does pack a gun!

Reflexively, he returned a shot. Less powerful, his beam bounced off the alloy hide. The robot moved on in. He could hear the roar of its motor. A direct hit at closer quarters would pierce his suit and body. He fired again and prepared to flee.

If I can divert that tin bastard—It did not occur to Flandry that his action might get him accused of gallantry. He started off in a different direction from the girl's. Longer-legged, he had a feebly better chance than she of keeping ahead of death, reaching a natural barricade and making a stand. . . .

Tensed with the expectation of lightning, the hope that his air unit would give protection and not be ruined, he had almost reached the next line when he realized there had been no fire. He braked and turned to stare behind.

The robot must have halted right after the exchange. Its top swung back and forth, as if in search. Surely it must sense him.

It started off after Djana.

Flandry spat an oath and pounded back to help. She had a good head start, but the machine was faster, and if it had crossed one line, wouldn't it cross another? Flandry's boots slammed upon stone. Oxygen-starved, his brain cast forth giddiness and patches of black. His intercepting course brought him nearer. He shot. The bolt went wild. He bounded yet more swiftly. Again he shot. This time he hit.

The robot slowed, veered as if to meet this antagonist who could be dangerous, faced away once more and resumed its pursuit of Djana. Flandry held down his trigger and hosed it with flame. The girl crossed the boundary. The robot stopped dead.

But—but—gibbered in Flandry's skull.

The robot stirred, lifted, and swung toward him. It moved hesitantly, wobbling a trifle, not as if damaged—it couldn't have been—but as if . . . puzzled?

I shouldn't be toting a blaster, Flandry thought in the turmoil. *With my shape, I'm supposed to carry sword and shield.*

The truth crashed into him.

He took no time to examine it. He knew simply that he must get into the same square as Djana. An anthropoid with blade and scute in place of hands could not crawl very well. Flandry went on all fours. He scuttled backward. The lean tall figure rocked after him, but no faster. Its limited computer—an artificial brain moronic and monomaniacal—could reach no decision as to what he was and what to do about him.

He crossed the line. The robot settled to the ground.

Flandry rose and tottered toward Djana. She had collapsed several meters away. He joined her. Murk spun down upon him.

It lifted in minutes, after his air unit purified the atmosphere in his suit and his stimulated cells drank the oxygen. He sat up. The machine that had chased them was retreating to the middle of the adjacent square, another gleam against the dark plain, under the dark sky. He looked at his blaster's charge indicator. It stood near zero. He could reload it from the powerpack he carried, but his life-support units needed the energy worse. Maybe.

Djana was rousing too. She half raised herself, fell across his lap, and wept. "It's no use, Nicky. We can't make it. We'll be murdered. And if we do get by, what'll we find? A thing that builds killing engines. Let's go back. We can go back the way we came. Can't we? And have a little, little while alive together—"

He consoled her until the chill and hardness of the rock on which he sat got through to him. Then, stiffly, he rose and assisted her to her feet. His voice sounded remote and strange in his ears. "Ordinarily I'd agree with you, dear. But I think I see what the arrangement is. The way the bishop behaved. Didn't you notice?"

"B-b-bishop?"

"Consider. Like the knight, I'm sure, the bishop attacks when the square he's on is invaded. I daresay the result of a move on this board depends on the outcome of the battle that follows it. Now a bishop can only proceed *offensively* along a diagonal. And the pieces are only programed to fight one other piece at a time: of certain kinds, at that." Flandry stared toward his hidden destination. "I imagine the anthropoids are the pawns. I wonder why. Maybe because they're the most numerous pieces, and the computer was lonely for mankind?"

"Computer?" She huddled against him.

"Has to be. Nothing else could have made this. It used the engineering facilities it had, possibly built some additional manufacturing plant. It didn't bother coloring the squares or the pieces, knowing quite well which was which. That's why I didn't see at once we're actually on a giant chessboard." Flandry grimaced. "If I hadn't . . . we'd've quit, returned, and died. Come on." He urged her forward.

"We can't go further," she pleaded. "We'll be set on."

"Not if we study the positions of the pieces," he said, "and travel on the squares that nobody can currently enter."

After some trudging: "My guess is, the computer split its attention into a number of parts. One or more to keep track of the wild robots. Two, with no intercommunication, to be rival chessmasters. That could be why it hasn't noticed something strange is going on today. I wonder if it can notice anything new any longer, without being nudged."

He zigzagged off the board with Djana, onto the blessed safe unmarked part of the land, and walked around the boundary. En route he saw a robot that had to be a king. It loomed four meters tall in the form of a man who wore the indoor dress of centuries ago, goldplated

and crowned with clustered diamonds. It bore no
weapons. He learned later that it captured by divine right.

They reached the ancient buildings. The worker
machines that scuttled about had kept them in good
repair. Flandry stopped before the main structure. He
tuned his radio to standard frequency. "At this range," he
said to that which was within, "you've got to have some
receiver that'll pick up my transmission."

Code clicked and gibbered in his earplugs; and then,
slowly, rustily, but gathering sureness as the words
advanced, like the voice of one who has been heavily
asleep: "Is . . . it . . . you? A man . . . returned at last? . . .
No, two men, I detect—"

"More or less," Flandry said.

Across the plain, beasts and chessmen came to a halt.

"Enter. The airlock . . . Remove your spacesuits inside.
It is Earth-conditioned, with . . . furnished chambers.
Inspection reveals a supply of undeteriorated food and
drink. . . . I hope you will find things in proper order.
Some derangements are possible. The time was long and
empty."

CHAPTER TEN

Djana stumbled to bed and did not wake for thirty-odd hours. Flandry needed less rest. After breakfast he busied himself, languidly at first but with increasing energy. What he learned fascinated him so much that he regretted not daring to spend time exploring in depth the history of these past five centuries on Wayland.

He was in the main control room, holding technical discussions with the prime computer, when the speaker in its quaint-looking instrument bank said in its quaint-sounding Anglic: "As instructed, I have kept your companion under observation. Her eyelids are moving."

Flandry got up. "Thanks," he said automatically. It was hard to remember that no living mind flickered behind those meters and readout screens. An awareness did, yes, but not like that of any natural sophont, no matter how strange to man; this one was in some ways more and in some ways less than organic. "I'd better go to her. Uh, have a servitor bring hot soup and, uh, tea and buttered toast, soon's it can."

He strode down corridors silent except for the hum of machines, past apartments that held a few moldering possessions of men long dead, until he found hers.

"Nicky—" She blinked mistily and reached tremulous arms toward him. How thin and pale she'd grown! He could just bear her. Bending for a kiss, he felt her lips passive beneath his.

"Nicky . . . are we . . . all right?" The whisper-breath tickled his ear.

"Assuredly." He stroked her cheek. "Everything's on orbit."

"Outside?"

"Safe as houses. Safer than numerous houses I could name." Flandry straightened. "Relax. We'll start putting meat back on those lovely bones in a few minutes. By departure date, you ought to be completely yourself again."

She frowned, shook her head in a puzzled way, tried to sit up. "Hoy, not yet," he said, laying hands on the bare slight shoulders. "I prescribe lots of bed rest. When you're strong enough to find that boring, I'll arrange for entertainment tapes to be projected. The computer says there're a few left. Ought to be interesting, a show that old."

Still she struggled feebly. The chemical-smelling air fluttered fast, in and out of her lungs. Alarm struck him. "What's the trouble. Djana?"

"I . . . don't know. Dizzy—"

"Oh, well. After what you've been through."

Cold fingers clutched his arm. "Nicky. This moon. Is it . . . worth . . . anything?"

"Huh?"

"Money!" she shrieked like an insect. "Is it worth money?"

Why should that make that much difference, right now? flashed through him. *Her past life's made her fanatical on the subject, I suppose, and—*"Sure."

"You're certain?" she gasped.

"My dear," he said, "Leon Ammon will have to work hard at it if he does *not* want to become one of the richest men in the Empire."

Her eyes rolled back till he saw only whiteness. She sagged in his embrace.

"Fainted," he muttered, and eased her down. Rising, scratching his scalp: "Computer, what kind of medical knowledge do you keep in your data banks?"

Reviving after a while, Djana sobbed. She wouldn't tell him why. Presently she was as near hysteria as her condition permitted. The computer found a sedative which Flandry administered.

On her next awakening she was calm, at any rate on the surface, but somehow remote from him. She answered his remarks so curtly as to make it clear she didn't want to talk. She did take nourishment, though. Afterward she lay frowning upward, fists clenched at her sides. He left her alone.

She was more cheerful by the following watch, and gradually reverted to her usual self.

But they saw scant of each other until they were again in space, bound back to the assigned round that was to end on Irumclaw where it began. She had spent most of the time previous in bed, waited on by robots while she recovered. He, vigor regained sooner, was preoccupied with setting matters on the moon to rights and supervising the repair of *Jake*. The latter job was complicated by the requirement that no clue remain to what had really taken place. He didn't want his superiors disbelieving his entries in the log concerning a malfunction of the hyperdrive oscillator which it had taken him three weeks to fix by himself.

Stark Wayland fell aft, and mighty Regin, and lurid Mimir; and the boat moved alone amidst a glory of stars. Flandry sat with Djana in the conn, which was the single halfway comfortable area to sit. Rested, clean, depilated, fed, liquored, in crisp coverall, breathing ample air, feeling the tug of a steady Terran g and the faint throb of the power that drove him toward his destination, he inhaled of a cigarette, patted Djana's hand, and grinned at her fresh-born comeliness. "Mission accomplished," he said. "I shall expect you to show your gratitude in the ways you know best."

"Well-l-l," she purred. After a moment: "How could you tell, Nicky?"

"Hm?"

"I don't yet understand what went wrong. You tried to explain before, but I was too dazed, I guess."

"Most simple," he said, entirely willing to parade his cleverness anew. "Once I saw we were caught in a chess game, everything else made sense. For instance, I remembered those radio masts being erected in the wilds. An impossible job unless the construction robots were free from attack. Therefore the ferocity of the roving machines was limited to their own kind. Another game, you see, with more potentialities and less predictability than chess, even the chess-cum-combat that had been developed when the regular sort got boring. New types of killer were produced at intervals and sent forth to see how they'd do against the older models. Our boat, and later we ourselves, were naturally taken for such newcomers; the robots weren't supplied with information about humans, and line-of-sight radio often had them out of touch with the big computer."

"When we tried to call for help, though—"

"You mean from the peak of Mt. Maidens? Well, obviously none of the wild robots would recognize our signal, on the band they used. And that part of the computer's attention which 'listened in' on its children simply filtered out my voice, the way you or I can fail to hear sounds when we're busy with something else. With so much natural static around, that's not surprising.

"Those masts were constructed strictly as relays for the robots—for the high frequencies which carried the digital transmissions—so that's why they didn't buck on my calls on any other band. The computer always did keep a small part of itself on the *qui vive* for a voice call on standard frequencies. But it assumed that, if and when humans came back, they would descend straight from the zenith and land near the buildings as they used to. Hence it didn't make arrangements to detect people radio from any other direction."

Flandry puffed. Smoke curled across the viewscreen, as if to veil off the abysses beyond. "Maybe it should have done so, in theory," he said. "However, after all those centuries, the poor thing was more than a little bonkers.

Actually, what it did—first establish that chess game, then modify it, then produce fighters that obeyed no rules, then extend the range and variety of their battles further and further across the moon—that was done to save most of its sanity."

"What?" Djana said, surprised.

"Why, sure. A thinking capability like that, with nothing but routine to handle, no new input decade after decade—" Flandry shivered, "Br-rr! You must know what sensory deprivation does to organic sophonts. Our computer rescued itself by creating something complicated and unpredictable to watch." He paused before adding slyly: "I refrain from suggesting analogies to the Creator you believe in."

And regretted it when she bridled and snapped, "I want a full report on how you influenced the situation."

"Oh, for the best, for the best," he said. "Not that that was hard. The moment I woke the White King up, the world he'd been dreaming of came to an end." His metaphor went over her head so he merely continued: "The computer's pathetically impatient to convert back to the original style of operations. Brother Ammon will find a fortune in metals waiting for his first ship.

"I do think you are morally obliged to recommend me for a substantial bonus, which he is morally obliged to pay."

"Morally!" The bitterness of a life which had never allowed her a chance to consider such questions whipped forth. But it seemed to him she exaggerated it as if to provide herself an excuse for attacking. "Who are you to blat about morals, Dominic Flandry, who took an oath to serve the Empire and a bribe to serve Leon Ammon?"

Stung, he threw back: "What else could I do?"

"Refuse." Her mood softened. She shook her amber-locked head, smiled a sad smile, and squeezed his hand. "No, never mind. That would be too much to expect of anyone nowadays, wouldn't it? Let's be corrupt together, Nicky darling, and kind to each other till we have to say goodbye."

He looked long at her, and at the stars, where his gaze remained, before he said quietly, "I suppose I can tell you what I've had in mind. I'll take the pay because I can use it; also the risk, for the rest of my life, of being found out and broken. It seems a reasonable price for holding a frontier."

Her lips parted. Her eyes widened. "I don't follow you."

"Irumclaw was due to be abandoned," he said. "Everybody knows—knew—it was. Which made the prophecy self-fulfilling: The garrison turned incompetent. The able civilians withdrew, taking their capital with them. Defensibility and economic value spiraled down toward the point where it really wouldn't be worth our rational while to stay. In the end, the Empire would let Irumclaw go. And without this anchor, it'd have to pull the whole frontier parsecs back; and Merseia and the Long Night would draw closer."

He sighed. "Leon Ammon is evil and contemptible," he went on. "Under different circumstances, I'd propose we gut him with a butterknife. But he does have energy, determination, actual courage and foresight of sorts.

"I went to his office to learn his intentions. When he told me, I agreed to go along because—well—

"If the Imperial bureaucrats were offered Wayland, they wouldn't know what to do with it. Probably they'd stamp its existence Secret, to avoid making any decisions or laying out any extra effort. If nothing else, a prize like that would make 'conciliation and consolidation' a wee bit difficult, eh?

"Ammon, though, he's got a personal profit to harvest. He'll go in to stay. His enterprise will be a *human* one. He'll make it pay off so well—he'll get so much economic and thereby political leverage from it—that he can force the government to protect his interests. Which means standing fast on Irumclaw. Which means holding this border, and even extending control a ways outward.

"In short," Flandry concluded, "as the proverb phrases it, he may be a son of a bitch, but he's our son of a bitch."

He stubbed out the cigarette with a violent gesture and turned back to the girl, more in search of forgetfulness than anything else.

Strangely, in view of the fellow-feeling she had just shown him, she did not respond. Her hands fended him off. The blue glance was troubled upon his. "Please, Nicky. I want to think . . . about what you've told me."

He respected her wish and relaxed in his seat, crossing shank over knee. "I daresay I can contain myself for a bit." The sight of her mildened the harshness that had risen in him. He chuckled. "Be warned, it won't be a long bit. You're too delectable."

Her mouth twitched, but not in any smile. "I never realized such things mattered to you," she said uncertainly.

Having been raised to consider idealism gauche, he shrugged. "They'd better. I live in the Terran Empire."

"But if—" She leaned forward. "Do you seriously believe, Nicky, Wayland can make that big a difference?"

"I like to believe it. Why do you ask? I can't well imagine you giving a rusty horntoot about future generations."

"That's what I mean. Suppose . . . Nicky, suppose, oh, something happens so Leon doesn't get to exploit Wayland. So nobody does. How'd that affect us—you and me?"

"Depends on our lifespans, I'd guess, among other items. Maybe we'd see no change. Or maybe, twenty-thirty years hence, we'd see the Empire retreat the way I was talking about."

"But that wouldn't mean its end!"

"No, no. Not at once. We could doubtless finish our lives in the style to which we want to become accustomed." Flandry considered. "Or could we? Political repercussions at home . . . unrest leading to upheaval . . . well, I don't know."

"We could always find ourselves a safe place. A nice offside colony planet—not so offside it's primitive, but—"

"Yes, probably." Flandry scowled. "I don't understand what's gnawing you. We'll report to Ammon and that will finish our part. Remember, he's holding the rest of our pay."

She nodded. For a space they were both silent. The stars in the viewscreen made an aureole behind her gold head.

Then craftiness came upon her, and she smiled and murmured: "It wouldn't make any difference, would it, if somebody else on Irumclaw—somebody besides Leon—got Wayland. Would it?"

"I guess not, if you mean one of his brother entrepreneurs." Flandry's unease waxed. "What're you thinking of, wench? Trying to rake in more for yourself, by passing the secret on to a competitor? I wouldn't recommend that. Bloody dripping dangerous."

"You—"

"Emphatically not! I'll squirrel away my money, and for the rest of my Irumclaw tour, you won't believe what a good boy I'll be. No more Old Town junkets whatsoever; wholesome on-base recreation and study of naval manuals. Fortunately, my Irumclaw tour is nearly done."

Flandry captured her hands in his. "I won't even risk seeing you," he declared. "Nor should you take any avoidable chances. The universe would be too poor without you."

Her lips pinched together. "If that's how you feel—"

"It is." Flandry leered. "Fortunately, we've days and days before we arrive. Let's use them, hm-m-m?"

Her eyes dropped, and rose, and she was on his lap embracing him, warm, soft, smiling, pupils wide between the long lashes, and "Hm-m-m indeed," she crooned.

Thunder ended a dream. Nothingness.

He woke, and wished he hadn't. Someone had scooped out his skull to make room for the boat's nuclear generator.

No . . . He tried to roll over, and couldn't.

When he groaned, a hand lifted his head. Cool wetness touched his mouth. "Drink this," Djana's voice told him from far away.

He got down a couple of tablets with the water, and could look around him. She stood by the bunk, staring down. As the stimpills took hold and the pain receded, her image grew less blurred, until he could identify the hardness that sat on her face. Craning his neck, he made out that he lay on his back with wrists and ankles wired—securely—to the bunkframe.

"Feel better?" Her tone was flat.

"I assume you gave me a jolt from your stun gun after I feel asleep," he succeeded in croaking.

"I'm sorry, Nicky." Did her shell crack the tiniest bit, for that tiniest instant?

"What's the reason?"

She told him about Rax, ending: "We're already bound for the rendezvous. If I figured right, remembering what you taught me, it's about forty or fifty light-years; and I set the 'pilot for top cruising hyperspeed, the way you said I ought to."

He was too groggy for the loss of his fortune to seem more than academic. But dismay struck through him like a blunt nail. "Four or five days! With me trussed up?"

"I'm sorry," she repeated. "I don't dare give you a chance to grab me or—or anything—" She hesitated. "I'll take care of you as best I can. Nothing personal in this. You know? It's that million credits."

"What makes you think your unknown friends will honor their end of the deal?"

"If Wayland's what you say, a megacredit's going to be a microbe to them. And I can keep on being useful till I leave them." All at once, it was as if a sword spoke: "That payment will make me my own."

Flandry surrendered to his physical misery.

Which passed. But was followed by the miseries of confinement. He couldn't do most isometric exercises. The wires would have cut him. A few were possible; and he spent hours flexing what muscles he was able to; and Djana was fairly good about massaging him. Nonetheless he ached and tingled.

Djana also kept her promise to give him a nurse's attentions. Hers weren't the best, for lack of training and equipment, but they served. And she read to him by the hour, over the intercom, from the bookreels he had along. She even offered to make love to him. On the third day he accepted.

Otherwise little passed between them: the constraints were too many for conversation. They spent most of their time separately, toughing it out. Once he was over the initial shock and had disciplined himself, Flandry didn't do badly at first. While no academician, he had many experiences, ideas, and stray pieces of information to play with. Toward the end, though, environmental impoverishment got to him and each hour became a desert century. When at last the detectors buzzed, he had to struggle out of semi-delirium to recognize what the noise was. When the outercom boomed with words, he blubbered for joy.

But when hypervelocities were matched and phasing in was completed and airlocks were joined and the other crew came aboard, Djana screamed.

CHAPTER ELEVEN

The Merseians treated him correctly if coolly. He was unbound, conducted aboard their destroyer, checked by a physician experienced in dealing with foreign species, given a chance to clean and bestir himself. His effects were returned, with the natural exception of weapons. A cubbyhole was found and curtained off for him and the girl. Food was brought them, and the toilet facilities down the passage were explained for her benefit. A guard was posted, but committed no molestation. Prisoners could scarcely have been vouchsafed more on this class of warcraft; and the time in space would not be long.

Djana kept keening, "I thought they were human, I thought they were human, only an-an-another damn gang—" She clung to him. "What'll they do with us?"

"I can't say," he replied with no measurable sympathy, "except that I don't imagine they care to have us take home our story."

A story of an intelligence ring on Irumclaw, headed by

that Rax—whose planet of origin is doubtless in the Roidhunate, not the Empire—and probably staffed by members of the local syndicates. Not to mention the fact that apparently there is a Merseian base in the wilderness, this close to our borders. A crawling went along his spine. *Then too, when word gets back to their headquarters, somebody may well want a personal interview with me.*

The destroyer grappled the spaceboat alongside and started off. Flandry tried to engage his guard in conversation, but the latter had orders to refrain. The one who brought dinner did agree to convey a request for him. Flandry was surprised when it was granted: that he might observe approach and landing. *Though why not? To repeat, they won't return me to blab what I've seen.*

Obviously the destination coordinates that Rax had given Djana meant the boat would be on a course bringing her within detection range of a picket ship; and any such wouldn't go far from the base. Flandry got his summons in two or three hours. He left Djana knotted around her wretchedness—*serves her right, the stupid slut!*—and preceded his armed guide forward.

The layout resembled that of a human vessel. Details varied, to allow for variations in size, shape, language, and culture. Yet it was the same enclosing metal narrowness, the same drone and vibration, the same warm oily-smelling gusts from ventilator grilles, the same duties to perform.

But the crew were big, green-skinned, hairless, spined and tailed. Their outfits were black, of foreign cut and drape, belts holding war knives. They practiced rituals and deferences—a gesture, a word, a stepping-aside—with the smoothness of centuried tradition. The glimpses of

something personal, a picture or souvenir, showed a taste
more austere and abstract than was likely in a human
spacehand. The body odors that filled this crowded air
were sharper and, somehow, drier than man's. The dark
eyes that followed him had no whites.

Broch—approximately, Second Mate—Tryntaf the
Tall greeted him in the chartroom. "You are entitled to the
courtesies, Lieutenant. True, you are under arrest for violation of ensovereigned space; but our realms are not at
war."

"I thank the *broch*," Flandry said in his best Eriau,
complete with salute of gratitude. He refrained from
adding that, among other provisions, the Covenant of
Alfzar enjoined both powers from claiming territory in the
buffer zone. Surely here, as on Starkad and elsewhere, a
"mutual assistance pact" had been negotiated with an
amenable, or cowed, community of autochthons.

He was more interested in what he saw. Belike he
looked on his deathplace.

The viewport displayed the usual stars, so many as to
be chaos to the untrained perception. Flandry had
learned the tricks—strain out the less bright through your
lashes; find your everywhere-visible markers, like the
Magellanic Clouds; estimate by its magnitude the distance
of the nearest giant, Betelgeuse. He soon found that he
didn't need them for a guess at where he was. Early in the
game he'd gotten Djana to recite those coordinates for
him and stored them in his memory; and the sun disc he
saw was of a type uncommon enough, compared to the
red dwarf majority, that only one or two would exist in any
given neighborhood.

The star was, in fact, akin to Mimir—somewhat less massive and radiant, but of the same furious whiteness, with the same boiling spots and leaping prominences. It must be a great deal older, though, for it had no surrounding nebulosity. At its distance, it showed about a third again the angular diameter of Sol seen from Terra.

"F5," Tryntaf said, "mass 1.34, luminosity 3.06, radius 1.25." The standard to which he referred was, in reality, his home sun, Korych; but Flandry recalculated the values in Solar terms with drilled-in ease. "We call it Siekh. The planet we are bound for we call Talwin."

"Ah." The man nodded. "And what more heroes of your Civil Wars have you honored?"

Tryntaf threw him a sharp glance. *Damn, I forgot again,* he thought. *Always make the opposition underestimate you.* "I am surprised at your knowledge of our history before the Roidhunate, Lieutenant," the Merseian said. "But then, considering that our pickets were ordered to watch for a Terran scout, the pilot must be of special interest."

"Oh, well," Flandry said modestly.

"To answer your question, few bodies here are worth naming. Swarms of asteroids, yes, but just four true planets, the smallest believed to be a mere escaped satellite. Orbits are wildly skewed and eccentric. Our astronomers theorize that early in the life of this system, another star passed through, disrupting the normal configuration."

Flandry studied the world growing before him. The ship had switched from hyperdrive to sublight under gravs—so few KPS as to support the idea of many large meteoroids. (They posed no hazard to a vessel which

could detect them in plenty of time to dodge, or could
simply let them bounce off a forcefield; but they would
jeopardize the career of a skipper who thus inelegantly
wasted power.) Talwin's crescent, blinding white, blurred
along the edges, indicated that, like Venus, it was entirely
clouded over. But it was not altogether featureless; spots
and bands of red could be seen.

"Looks none too promising," he remarked. "Aren't we
almighty close to the sun?"

"The planet is," Tryntaf said. "It is late summer—
everywhere; there is hardly any axial tilt—and temperatures remain fierce. Dress lightly before you disembark,
Lieutenant! At periastron, Talwin comes within 0.87
astronomical units of Siekh; but apastron is at a full
2.62 a.u."

Flandry whistled. "That's as eccentric as I can remember ever hearing of in a planet, if not more. Uh . . . about
one-half, right?" He saw a chance to appear less than a
genius. "How can you survive? I mean, a good big axial tilt
would protect one hemisphere, at least, from the worst
effects of orbital extremes. But this ball, well, any life it
may have has got to be unlike yours or mine."

"Wrong," was Tryntaf's foreseeable reply. "Atmosphere
and hydrosphere moderate the climate to a degree; likewise
location. Those markings you see are of biological origin,
spores carried into the uppermost air. Photosynthesis
maintains a breathable oxynitrogen mixture."

"Uh-h-h . . . diseases?" *No, wait, now you're acting
too stupid. True, what's safe for a Merseian isn't necessarily
so for a man. We may have extraordinarily similar biochemistries, but still, we've fewer bugs in common that are*

*dangerous to us than we have with our respective domestic
animals. By the same token, though, a world as different
as Talwin isn't going to breed anything that'll affect us . . .
at least, nothing that'll produce any syndrome modern
medicine can't easily slap down. Tryntaf knows I know
that much.* The thought had flashed through Flandry in
part of a second. "I mean allergens and other poisons."

"Some. They cause no serious trouble. The bioform is
basically akin to ours, L-amino proteins in water solution.
Deviations are frequent, of course. But you or I could
survive awhile on native foods, if we chose them with
care. Over an extended period we would need dietary
supplements. They have been compounded for emergency
use."

Flandry decided that Tryntaf lacked any sense of
humor. Most Merseians had one, sometimes gusty, sometimes cruel, often incomprehensible to men. He had in his
turn baffled various of them when he visited their planet;
even after he put a joke into their equivalents, they did not
see why it should be funny that one diner said, "*Bon
appetit*" and the other said, "Ginsberg."

*Sure. They differ, same as us. My life could depend on
the personality of the commandant down there. Will I be
able to recognize any chance he might give me?*

He sought to probe his companion, but was soon
left alone on grounds of work to do, except for the close-
mouthed rating who tail-sat by the door.

Watching the view took his mind partly off his
troubles. He could pick up visual clues that a layman
would be blind to, identify what they represented, and
conclude what the larger pattern must be.

Talwin had no moon—maybe once, but not after the invader star had virtually wrecked this system. Flandry did see two relay satellites glint, in positions indicating they belonged to a synchronous triad. If the Merseians had installed no more than that, they had a barebones base here. It was what you'd expect at the end of this long a communications line: a watchpost, a depot, a first-stage receiving station for reports from border-planet agents like Rax.

Aside from their boss, those latter wouldn't have been told Siekh's coordinates, or of its very existence. They'd have courier torpedoes stashed away in the hinterland, target preset and clues to the target removed. Given elementary precautions, no Imperial loyalist was likely to observe the departure of one. Replenishment would be more of a problem, dependent on smuggling, but not overly difficult when the Terran service was undermanned and lax. Conveyance of fresh orders to the agents was no problem at all; who noticed what mail or what visitors drifted into Rax's dope shop?

The value of Talwin was obvious. Besides surveillance, it allowed closer contact with spies than would otherwise be possible. Flandry wondered if his own corps ran an analogous operation out Roidhunate way. Probably not. The Merseians were too vigilant, the human government too inert, its wealthier citizens too opposed to pungling up the cost of positive action.

Flandry shook himself, as if physically to cast off apprehension and melancholy, and concentrated on what he saw.

Clearances given and path computed, the destroyer

dropped in a spiral that took her around the planet. Presumably her track was designed to avoid storms. Cooler air, moving equatorward from the poles, must turn summer into a "monsoon" season. Considering input energy, atmospheric pressure (which Tryntaf had mentioned was twenty percent greater than Terran), and rotation period (a shade over eighteen hours, he had said), weather surely got more violent here than ever at Home; and a long, thin, massive object like a destroyer was more vulnerable to wind than you might think.

Water vapor rose high before condensing into clouds. Passing over dayside below those upper layers, Flandry got a broad view.

A trifle smaller (equatorial diameter 0.97) and less dense than Terra, Talwin in this era had but a single continent. Roughly wedge-shaped, it reached from the north-pole area with its narrow end almost on the equator. Otherwise the land consisted of islands. While multitudinous, in the main they were thinly scattered.

Flandry guessed that the formation and melting of huge icecaps in the course of the twice-Terran year disturbed isostatic balance. Likewise, the flooding and great rainstorms of summer, the freezing of winter, would speed erosion and hence the redistribution of mass. Tectony must proceed at a furious rate; earthquake, vulcanism, the sinking of old land and the rising of new, must be geologically common occurrences.

He made out one mountain range, running east-west along the 400-kilometer width of the continent near its middle. Those peaks dwarfed the Himalayas but were snowless, naked rock. Elsewhere, elevations were generally low, rounded, worn. North of the wall, the country seemed to be swamp. *Whew! That means in winter the icecap grows down to 45 degrees latitude! The glaciers grind everything flat.* The far southlands were a baked desolation, scoured by hurricanes. Quite probably, at midsummer lakes and rivers there didn't simply dry up, they boiled; and the equatorial ocean became a biological fence. It would be intriguing to know how evolution had diverged in the two hemispheres.

Beyond the sterile tropics, life not long ago had been outrageously abundant, jungle choking the central zone, the arctic abloom with low-growing plants. Now annual drought was taking its toll in many sections, leaves withering, stems crumbling, fires running wild, bald black patches of desiccation and decay. But other districts, especially near the coasts, got enough rain yet. Immense herds of grazers were visible on open ground; wings filled the air; shoal waters were darkened by weeds and swimmers. Most islands remained similarly fecund.

The dominant color of vegetation was blue, in a thousand shades—the photosynthetic molecule not chlorophyll, then, though likely to be a close chemical relative—but there were the expected browns, reds, yellows, the unexpected and stingingly Homelike splashes of green.

Descending, trailing a thunderclap, the ship crossed nightside. Flandry used photomultiplier and infrared step-up controls to go on with his watching. It confirmed the impressions he had gathered by day.

And the ship was back under the hidden sun, low, readying for setdown. Her latitude was about 40 degrees.

In the north, the lesser members of the giant range gave way to foothills of their own. Flandry made out one volcano in that region, staining heaven with smoke. A river flowed thence, cataracting through canyons until it became broad and placid in the wooded plains further south. The diffuse light made it shine dully, like lead, on its track through yonder azure lands. Finally it ran out in a kilometers-wide bay.

The greenish-gray sea creamed white with surf along much of the coast. The tidal pull of Siekh in summer approximated that of Luna and Sol on Terra, and ocean currents flowed strongly. For some distance inland, dried, cracked, salt-streaked mud was relieved only by a few tough plant species adapted to it.

Uh-huh, Flandry reflected. *In spring the icecaps melt. Sea level rises by many meters. Storms get really stiff, they, and increasing tides, drive the waves in, over and over, to meet the floods running down from the mountains. . . . And Djana believes in a God Who gives a damn?*

Or should I say, Who gives a blessing?

He rubbed his cheek, observing with what exquisite accuracy nerves recorded pressure, texture, warmth, location, motion. *Well*, he thought, *I must admit, if Anyone's been in charge of my existence, He's furnished it with noble pleasures.* Despite everything, fear knocked in his heart and dried his mouth. *He's not about to take them away, is He? Not now! Later, when I'm old, when I don't really care, all right; but not now!*

He remembered comrades in arms who didn't make it as far through time as he'd done. That was no consolation, but rallied him. They hadn't whined.

And maybe something would turn up.

The scene tilted. The engines growled on a deeper note. The ship was landing.

The Merseian base stood on a bluff overlooking the river, thirty or so kilometers north of its mouth, well into fertile territory. The spaceport was minute, the facilities in proportion, as Flandry had surmised; nothing fancier than a few destroyers and lesser craft could work out of here. But he noticed several buildings within the compound that didn't seem naval.

Hm. Do the Merseians have more than one interest in Talwin? . . . I imagine they do at that. Otherwise they'd find a more hospitable planet for their base—or else a better-camouflaged one, say a sunless rogue. . . . You know, their intelligence activities here begin to look almost like an afterthought.

The ship touched down. Air pressure had gradually been raised during descent to match sea-level value. When interior gravity was cut off, the planet's reasserted itself and Flandry felt lighter. He gauged weight at nine-tenths or a hair less.

Tryntaf reappeared, issued an order, and redisappeared. Flandry was escorted to the lock. Djana waited by her own guard. She seemed incredibly tiny and frail against the Merseian, a porcelain doll. "Nicky," she stammered, reaching toward him, "Nicky, please forgive me, please be good to me. I don't even know what they're saying."

"Maybe I will later," he snapped, "if they leave me in shape to do it."

She covered her eyes and shrank back. He regretted his reaction. She'd been suckered—by her cupidity;

nonetheless, suckered—and the feel of her hand in his would have eased his isolation. But pride would not let him soften.

The lock opened. The gangway extruded. The prisoners were gestured out.

Djana staggered. Flandry choked. *Judas on a griddle, I was warned to change clothes and I forgot!*

The heat enveloped him, entered him, became him and everything else which was. Temperature could not be less than 80 Celsius—might well be higher—20 degrees below the Terran-pressure boiling point of water. A furnace wind roared dully across the ferrocrete, which wavered in his seared gaze. He was instantly covered, permeated, not with honest sweat but with the sliminess that comes when humidity reaches an ultimate. Breathing was like drowning.

Noises came loud to his ears through that dense air: wind, voices, clatter of machines. Odors borne from the jungle were pungent and musky, with traces of sulfurous reek. He saw a building blocky against the clouds, and on its roof a gong to call for prayers to the God of a world two and a half light-centuries hence. The shadowless illumination made distances hard to gauge; was that air-conditioned interior as remote as he dreaded?

The crew were making for it. They weren't in formation, but discipline lived in their close ranks and careful jog-trot. What Merseians had tasks to do outside wore muffling white coveralls with equipment on the back.

"Move along, Terran," said Flandry's guard. "Or do you enjoy our weather?"

The man started off. "I've known slightly more comfortable espresso cookers," he answered; but since the guard had never heard of espresso, or coffee for that matter, his repartee fell flat again.

CHAPTER TWELVE

In the Spartan tradition of Vach lords, the office of Ydwyr the Seeker lacked any furniture save desk and cabinets. Though he and Morioch Sun-in-eye were seated, it was on feet and tails, which looked to a human as if they were crouched to spring. That, and their size, great even for Wilwidh Merseians, and faint but sharp body odors, and rumbling bass tones, and the explosive gutturals of Eriau, gave Djana a sense of anger that might break loose in slaughter. She could see that Flandry was worried and caught his hand in the cold dampness of hers. He made no response; standing rigid, he listened.

"Perhaps the *datholch* has been misinformed about this affair," Morioch said with strained courtesy. Flandry didn't know what the title signified—and Merseian grades were subtle, variable things—but it was plainly a high one, since the aristocratic-deferential form of address was used.

"I shall hearken to whatever the *qanryf* wishes to say,"

Ydwyr replied, in the same taut manner but with the merely polite verbal construction. Flandry would have understood "*qanryf*" (the first letter representing, more or less, *k* followed by *dh* = voiced *th*) from the argent saltire on Morioch's black uniform, had he not met the word often before. Morioch was the commandant of this base, or anyhow of its naval aspect; but the base was a minor one.

He—stockily built, hard of features, incongruous against the books and reelboxes whose shelves filled every available square centimeter of wall space—declared: "This is no capture of a scout who simply chanced by. The female alone should . . . unquestionably does tell the *datholch* that. But I didn't want to intrude on your work by speaking to you of mine. Besides, since it's confidential, the fewer who are told, the better. Correct?"

No guards had come in with their chief. They waited beyond the archway curtains, which were not too soundproof to pass a cry for help. Opposite, seen through a window, waited Talwin's lethal summer. Blue-black and enormous, a thunderhead was piling up over the stockade, where the banners of those Vachs and regions that had members here whipped on their staffs.

Ydwyr's mouth drew into thinner lines. "*I* could have been trusted," he said. Flandry didn't believe that mere wounded vanity spoke. Had a prerogative been infringed? What was Ydwyr?

He wore a gray robe without emblems; at its sash hung only a purse. He was taller than Morioch, but lean, wrinkled, aging. At first he had spoken softly, when the humans were brought before him from their quarters—on his demand after he learned of their arrival. As soon as the commandant had given him a slight amount of back talk, he had stiffened, and power fairly blazed from him.

Morioch confronted it stoutly. "That needs no utterance," he said. "I hope the *datholch* accepts that I saw no reason to trouble you with matters outside your own purposes here."

"Does the *qanryf* know every conceivable limit of my purposes?"

"No . . . however—" Rattled but game, Morioch re-donned formality. "May I explain everything to the *datholch*?"

Ydwyr signed permission. Morioch caught a breath and commenced:

"When the *Brythioch* stopped by, these months agone, her chief intelligence officer gave me a word that did not then seem very interesting. You recall she'd been at Irumclaw, the Terran frontier post. There a *mei*—I have his name on record but don't remember it—had come on a scoutship pilot he'd met previously. The pilot, the male before you here, was running surveillance as part of his training for their Intelligence Corps. Normally that'd have meant nothing—standard procedure of theirs—but this particular male had been on Merseia in company with a senior Terran agent. Those two got involved in something which is secret from me but, I gather, caused major trouble to the Roidhunate. Protector Brechdan Ironrede was said to have been furious."

Ydwyr started. Slowly he lifted one bony green hand and said, "You have not told me the prisoner's name."

"Let the *datholch* know this is Junior Lieutenant Dominic Flandry."

Silence fell, except for the wind whose rising skirl began to pierce the heavily insulated walls. Ydwyr's gaze probed and probed. Djana whispered frantic, repeated prayers. Flandry felt the sweat slide down his ribs. He needed all his will to hold steady.

"Yes," Ydwyr said at last, "I have heard somewhat about him."

"Then the *datholch* may appreciate this case more than I do," Morioch said, looking relieved. "To be honest, I knew nothing of Flandry till the *Brythioch*—"

"Continue your account," Ydwyr said unceremoniously.

Morioch's relief vanished, but he plowed on: "As the *datholch* wishes. Whatever the importance of Flandry himself—he appears a cub to me—he was associated with this other agent . . . *khraich*, yes, it comes back . . . Max Abrams. And Abrams was, is, definitely a troublemaker of the worst sort. Flandry appears to be a *protégé* of his. Perhaps, already, an associate? Could his assignment to Irumclaw involve more than showed on the skin?

"This much the *mei* reported to the chief intelligence officer of his ship. The officer, in turn, directed our agents in the city"—*Rax, of course, and those in Rax's pay,* Flandry thought through the loudening wind—"to keep close watch on this young male. If he did anything unusual, it should be investigated as thoroughly as might be.

"The officer asked me to stand by. As I've said, nothing happened for months, until I'd almost forgotten. We get so many leads that never lead anywhere in intelligence work.

"But lately a courier torpedo arrived. The message was that Flandry was collaborating closely but, apparently, secretly, with the leader of an underworld gang. The secrecy is understandable—ultra-illegal behavior—and our agent's first guess was that normal corruption was all that was involved." Scorn freighted Morioch's voice. "However, following orders, they infiltrated the operation. They learned what it was."

He described Wayland, to the extent of Ammon's knowledge, and Ydwyr nodded. "Yes," the old Merseian said, "I understand. The planet is too far from home to be worth our while—at present—but it is not desirable that Terrans reoccupy it."

"Our Irumclaw people are good," Morioch said. "They had to make a decision and act on their own. Their plan succeeded. Does the *datholch* agree they should get extra reward?"

"They had better," Ydwyr said dryly, "or they might decide Terrans are more generous masters. You have yet to tell them to eliminate those who know about the lost planet, correct?—Well, but what did they do?"

"The *datholch* sees this female. After Flandry had investigated the planet, she captured him and brought his boat to a section where our pickets were bound to detect it."

"Hun-n-nh . . . is she one of ours?"

"No, she thought she was working for a rival human gang. But the *datholch* may agree she shows a talent for that kind of undertaking."

Flandry couldn't help it, too much compassion welled through his despair, he bent his head down toward Djana's and muttered: "Don't be afraid. They're pleased with what you did for them. I expect they'll pay you something and let you go."

To spy on us—driven by blackmail as well as money— but you can probably vanish into the inner Empire. Or . . . maybe you'd like the work. Your species never treated you very kindly.

"And that is the whole tale, *qanryf?*" Ydwyr asked.

"Yes," Morioch said. "Now the *datholch* sees the importance. Bad enough that we had to capture a boat. That'll provoke a widespread search, which might stumble on places like Talwin. The odds are against it, true, and we really had no choice. But we cannot release Flandry."

"I did not speak of that," Ydwyr said, cold again. "I did, and do, want both these beings in my custody."

"But—"

"Do you fear they may escape?"

"No. Certainly not. But the *datholch* must know . . . the value of this prisoner as a subject for interrogation—"

"The methods your folk would use would leave him of no value for anything else," Ydwyr rapped. "And he can't have information we don't already possess; I assume the Intelligence Corps is not interested in his private life. He is here only through a coincidence."

"Can the *datholch* accept that strong a coincidence? Flandry met the *mei* by chance, yes. But that he, of every possible pilot, went off to the lost planet as a happenstance: to that I must say no."

"I say yes. He is precisely the type to whom such things occur. If one exposes oneself to life, *qanryf*, life will come to one. I have my own uses for him and will not see him ruined. I also want to learn more about this female. They go into my keeping."

Morioch flushed and well-nigh roared: "The *datholch*

forgets that Flandry worked tail-entwined with Abrams to thwart the Protector!"

Ydwyr lifted a hand, palm down, and chopped it across his breast. Flandry sucked in a breath. That gesture was seldom used, and never by those who did not have the hereditary right. Morioch swallowed, bent head above folded hands, and muttered, "I beg the *datholch's* forgiveness." Merseians didn't often beg, either.

"Granted," Ydwyr said. "Dismissed."

"Kh-h . . . the *datholch* understands I must report this to headquarters, with what recommendations my duty demands I make?"

"Certainly. I shall be sending messages of my own. No censure will be in them." Ydwyr's hauteur vanished. Though his smile was not a man's, but only pulled the upper lip back off the teeth, Flandry recognized friendliness. "Hunt well, Morioch Sun-in-eye."

"I thank . . . and wish a good hunt . . . to you." Morioch rose, saluted, and left.

Outside, the sky had gone altogether black. Lightning flamed, thunder bawled, wind yammered behind galloping sheets of rain, whose drops smoked back off the ground. Djana fell into Flandry's arms; they upheld each other.

Releasing her, he turned to Ydwyr and made the best Merseian salute of honor which a human could. "The *datholch* is thanked with my whole spirit," he said in Eriau.

Ydwyr smiled anew. The overhead fluoropanel, automatically brightening as the storm deepened, made the room into a warm little cave. (Or a cool one; that rain was not far below its boiling point.) The folds in his robe showed him relaxing. "Be seated if you desire," he invited.

The humans were quick to accept, lowering themselves to the rubbery floor and leaning back against a cabinet. Their knees were grateful. To be sure, there was a psychological drawback; now Ydwyr loomed over them like a heathen god.

But I'm not going to be drugged, brainscrubbed, or shot. Not today. Maybe . . . maybe, eventually, an exchange deal . . .

Ydwyr had returned to dignified impassivity. *I mustn't keep him waiting.* Strength seeped back into Flandry's cells. He said, "May I ask the *datholch* to tell me his standing, in order that I can try to show him his due honor?"

"We set most ritual aside—of necessity—in my group here," the Merseian answered. "But I am surprised that one who speaks Eriau fluently and has been on our home planet has not encountered the term before."

"The uh, the *datholch*—may I inform the *datholch*, his language was crammed into me in tearing haste; my stay on his delightful world was brief; and what I was taught at the Academy dealt mainly with—uh—"

"I told you the simple forms of respect will do on most occasions." Ydwyr's smile turned downward this time, betokening a degree of grimness. "And I know how you decided not to end your sentence. Your education dealt with us primarily as military opponents." He sighed. "*Khraich*, I don't fear the tactless truth. We Merseians have plenty of equivalents of you, the God knows. It's regrettable but inevitable, till your government changes its policies. I bear no personal animosity, Lieutenant Dominic Flandry. I far prefer friendship, and hope a measure of it may take root between us while we are together.

"As for your question, *datholch* is a civilian rather than a military rank." He did not speak in exact equivalents, for Merseia separated "civilian" and "military" differently from Terra, and less clearly; but Flandry got the idea. "It designates an aristocrat who heads an enterprise concerned with expanding the Race's frontier." (Frontier of knowledge, trade, influence, territory, or what? He didn't say, and quite likely it didn't occur to him that there was any distinction.) "As for my standing, I belong to the Vach Urdiolch and"—he stood up and touched his brow while he finished—"it is my high honor that a brother of my late noble father is, in the glory of the God, Almighty Roidhun of Merseia, the Race, and all holdings, dominions, and subordinates of the Race."

Flandry scrambled to his feet and yanked Djana to hers. "Salute!" he hissed in her ear, in Anglic. "Like me! This chap's a nephew of their grand panjandrum!"

Who might or might not be a figurehead, depending on the circumstances of his reign—and surely, that he was always elected from among the Urdiolchs, by the Hands of the Vachs and the heads of Merseian states organized otherwise than the anciently dominant culture—from among the Urdiolchs, the only landless Vach—surely this was in part a check on his powers—but surely, too, the harshest, most dictatorial Protector regarded his Roidhun with something of the same awe and pride that inspired the lowliest "foot" or "tail"—for the Roidhun stood for the God, the unity, and the hope of a warrior people— Flandry's mind swirled close to chaos before he brought it under control.

"Be at ease." Ydwyr reseated himself and gestured

the humans to do likewise. "I myself am nothing but a scientist." He leaned forward. "Of course, I served my time in the Navy, and continue to hold a reserve commission; but my interests are xenological. This is essentially a research station. Talwin was discovered by accident about—uh-h-h-h—fifteen Terran years ago. Astronomers had noted an unusual type of pulsar in this vicinity: extremely old, close to extinction. A team of physicists went for a look. On the way back, taking routine observations as they traveled, they detected the unique orbital scramble around Siekh and investigated it too."

Flandry thought sadly that humans might well have visited that pulsar in early days—it was undoubtedly noted in the pilot's data for these parts, rare objects being navigationally useful—but that none of his folk in the present era would venture almost to the ramparts of a hostile realm just to satisfy their curiosity.

Ydwyr was proceeding: "When I learned about Talwin's extraordinary natives, I decided they must be studied, however awkwardly near your borders this star lies."

Flandry could imagine the disputes and wire-pullings that had gone on, and the compromise which finally was reached, that Talwin should also be an advanced base for keeping an eye on the Terrans. No large cost was involved, nor any large risk . . . nor any large chance of glory and promotion, which last fact helped explain Morioch's eagerness to wring his prisoners dry.

The lieutenant wet his lips. "You, uh, you are most kind, sir," he said; the honorific appeared implicitly in the pronoun. "What do you wish of us?"

"I would like to get to know you well," Ydwyr said frankly. "I have studied your race in some detail; I have met individual members of it; I have assisted in diplomatic business; but you remain almost an abstraction, almost a complicated forcefield rather than a set of beings with minds and desires and souls. It is curious, and annoying, that I should be better acquainted with Domrath and Ruadrath than with Terrans, our one-time saviors and teachers, now our mighty rivals. I want to converse with you.

"Furthermore, since any intelligence agent must know considerable xenology, you may be able to help us in our research on the autochthons here. Of a different species and culture, you may gain insights that have escaped us.

"This is the more true, and you are the more intriguing in your own right, because of who you are. By virtue of my family connections, I obtained the story—or part of the story—behind the Starkad affair. You are either very capable, Dominic Flandry, or else very lucky, and I wonder if there may not be a destiny in you."

The term he used was obscure, probably archaic, and the man had to guess its meaning from context and cognation. Fate? Mana? Odd phrasing for a scientist.

"In return," Ydwyr finished, "I will do what I can to protect you." With the bleak honesty of his class: "I do not promise to succeed."

"Do you think, sir . . . I might ever be released?" Flandry asked.

"No. Not with the information you hold. Or not without so deep a memory wiping that no real personality would remain. But you should find life tolerable in my service."

If you find my service worthwhile, Flandry realized, *and if higher-ups don't overrule you when they learn about me.* "I have no doubt I shall, sir. Uh, maybe I can begin with a suggestion, for you to pass on to the *qanryf* if you see fit."

Ydwyr waited.

"I heard the lords speaking about, uh, ordering that the man who hired me—Leon Ammon—" *might as well give him the name, it'll be in Rax's dispatch* "—that he be eliminated, to eliminate knowledge of Wayland from the last Terrans. I'd suggest going slow and cautious there. You know how alarmed and alerted they must be, sir, even on sleepy old Irumclaw Base, when I haven't reported in. It'd be risky passing on an order to your agents, let alone having them act. Best wait awhile. Besides, I don't know myself how many others Ammon told. I should think your operatives ought to make certain they've identified everyone who may be in on the secret, before striking.

"And there's no hurry, sir. Ammon hasn't any ship of his own, nor dare he hire one of the few civilian craft around. Look how easy it was to subvert the interplanetary ferrier we used, without ever telling him what a treasure was at stake. Oh, you haven't heard that detail yet, have you, sir? It's part of how I was trapped.

"Ammon will have to try discovering what went wrong; then killing those who betrayed him, or those he can find or thinks he's found; and making sure they don't kill him first; and locating another likely-looking scoutship pilot, and sounding him out over months, and waiting for assignment rotation to put him on the route passing nearest Wayland, and—Well, don't you see, sir, nothing's going to happen that you need bother about for more than a year? If you want to be ultra-cautious, I suppose you can post a warcraft in the Mimirian System; I can tell you the coordinates, though frankly, I think you'd be wasting your effort. But mainly, sir, your side has everything to lose and nothing to gain by moving fast against Ammon."

"*Kkraich.*" Ydwyr rubbed palm across chin, a sandpapery sound—under the storm-noise—despite his lack of beard. "Your points are well taken. Yes, I believe I will recommend that course to Morioch. And, while my authority in naval affairs is theoretically beneath his, in practice—"

His glance turned keen. "I take for granted, Dominic Flandry, you speak less in the hope of ingratiating yourself with me than in the hope of keeping events on Irumclaw in abeyance until you can escape."

"Uh—uh, well, sir—"

Ydwyr chuckled. "Don't answer. I too was a young male, once. I do trust you won't be so foolish as to try a break. If you accomplished it, the planet would soon kill you. If you failed, I would have no choice but to turn you over to Morioch's Inquisitors."

CHAPTER THIRTEEN

The airbus was sturdier and more powerful than most, to withstand violent weather. But the sky simmered quiet beneath its high gray cloud deck when Flandry went to the Domrath.

That was several of Talwin's eighteen-hour days after he had arrived. Ydwyr had assigned the humans a room in the building that housed his scientific team. They shared the mess there. The Merseian civilians were cordial and interested in them. The two species ate each other's food and drank each other's ale with, usually, enjoyment as well as nutrition. Flandry spent the bulk of his time getting back into physical shape and oriented about this planet. Reasonably reconciled with Djana—who'd been caught in the fortunes of war, he thought, and who now did everything she could to mollify her solitary fellow human—he made his nights remarkably pleasant. In general, aside from being a captive whose fate was uncertain and from having run out of tobacco, he found his stay diverting.

Nor was she badly off. She had little to fear, perhaps much to gain. If she never returned to the Empire, well, that was no particular loss when other humans lived under the Roidhunate. Like a cat that has landed on its feet, she set about studying her new environment. This involved long conversations with the thirty-plus members of Ydwyr's group. She had no Merseian language except for the standard loan words, and none of her hosts had more than the sketchiest Anglic. But they kept a translating computer for use with the natives. The memory bank of such a device regularly included the major tongues of known space.

She'll make out, Flandry decided. *Her kind always does, right up to the hour of the asp.*

Then Ydwyr offered him a chance to accompany a party bound for Seething Springs. He jumped at it, both from curiosity and from pragmatism. If he was to be a quasi-slave, he might have a worse master; he must therefore see about pleasing the better one. Moreover, he had not inwardly surrendered hope of gaining his freedom, to which end anything he learned might prove useful.

Half a dozen Merseians were in the expedition. "It's fairly ordinary procedure, but should be stimulating," said Cnif hu Vanden, xenophysiologist, who had gotten friendliest with him. "The Domrath are staging their fall move to hibernating grounds—in the case of this particular group, from Seething Springs to Mt. Thunderbelow. We've never observed it among them, and they do have summer-time customs that don't occur elsewhere, so maybe their migration has special features too." He gusted a sigh. "This pouchful of us . . . to fathom an entire world!"

"I know," Flandry answered. "I've heard my own scholarly acquaintances groan about getting funds." He spread his hands. "Well, what do you expect? As you say: an entire world. It took our races till practically yesterday to begin to understand their home planets. And now, when we have I don't know how many to walk on if we know the way—"

Cnif was typical of the problem, crossed his mind. The stout, yellowish, slightly flat-faced male belonged to no Vach; his ancestors before unification had lived in the southern hemisphere of Merseia, in the Republic of Lafdigu, and to this day their descendants maintained peculiarities of dress and custom, their old language and many of their old laws. But Cnif was born in a colony; he had not seen the mother world until he came there for advanced education, and many of its ways were strange to him.

The bus glided forward. The first valve of the hangar heatlock closed behind it, the second opened, and it climbed with a purr of motor and whistle of wind. At 5000 meters it leveled off and bore north-northeast. That course by and large followed the river. Mainly the passengers sat mute, preparing their kits or thinking their thoughts. Merseians never chattered like humans. But Cnif pointed out landmarks through the windows.

"See, behind us, at the estuary, what we call Barrier Bay. In early winter it becomes choked with icebergs and floes, left by the receding waters. When they melt in spring, the turbulence and flooding is unbelievable."

The stream wound like a somnolent snake through the myriad blues of jungle. "We call it the Golden River in spite of its being silt-brown. Auriferous sands, you see, washed down from the mountains. Most of the place names are unavoidably ours. Some are crude translations from Domrath terms. The Ruadrath don't have place names in our sense, which is why we seldom borrow from them."

Cnif's words for the aborigines were artificial. They had to be. "Dom" did represent an attempt at pronouncing what one of the first communities encountered called themselves; but "-rath" was an Eriau root meaning, approximately, "folk," and "Ruadrath" had originally referred to a class of nocturnal supernatural beings in a Merseian mythology—"elves."

The forested plain gave way to ever steeper foothills. The shadowless gray light made contours hard to judge, but Flandry could see how the Golden ran here through a series of deep canyons. "Those are full to the brim when the glaciers melt," Cnif said. "But we've since had so much evaporation that the level is well down; and we'll soon stop getting rain, it'll become first fog, later snow and hail. We are at the end of summer."

Flandry reviewed what he had read and heard at the base. Talwin went about Siekh in an eccentric ellipse which, of course, had the sun at one focus. You could define summer arbitrarily as follows: Draw a line through that focus, normal to the major axis, intersecting the curve at two points. Then summer was the six-month period during which Talwin passed from one of those points, through periastron, to the other end of the line segment. Fall was the six weeks or so which it took to get from the latter point to the nearest intersection of the minor axis with the ellipse. Winter occupied the fifteen months wherein Talwin swung out to its remotest distance and back again to the opposite minor-axis intersection. Thereafter spring took another six weeks, until the point was reached again which defined the beginning of summer.

In practice, things were nowhere near that simple. There were three degrees of axial tilt; there were climatic zones; there were topographical variations; above all, there was the thermal inertia of soil, rock, air, and water. Seasons lagged planetary positions by an amount depending on where you were and on any number of other factors, not every one of which the Merseians had unraveled.

Nonetheless, once weather started to change, it changed with astonishing speed. Cnif had spoken in practical rather than theoretical terms.

Vague through haze, the awesome peaks of the Hellkettle Mountains came to view beyond their foothills. Several plumes of smoke drifted into gloomy heaven. An isolated titan stood closer, lifting scarred black flanks in cliffs and talus slopes and grotesquely congealed lava beds, up to a cone that was quiet now but only for now. "Mt. Thunderbelow." The bus banked left and descended on a long slant, above a tributary of the Golden. Vapors roiled white on those waters. "The Neverfreeze River. Almost all streams, even the biggest, go stiff in winter; but this is fed by hot springs that draw their energy from the volcanic depths. That's why the Ruadrath—of Wirrda's, I mean—have prospered so well in these parts. Aquatic life remains active and furnishes a large part of their food."

Fuming rapids dashed off a plateau. In the distance, forest gave way to sulfur beds, geysers, and steaming pools. The bus halted near the plateau edge. Flandry spied a clearing and what appeared to be a village, though seeing was poor through the tall trees. While the bus hovered, the expedition chief spoke through its outercom. "We've distributed miniature transceivers," Cnif explained to Flandry. "It's best to ask leave before landing. Not that we have anything to fear from them, but we don't want to make them shy. We lean backwards. Why . . . do you know, a few years past, a newcomer to our group blundered into a hibernation den before the males were awake. He thought they would be, but they weren't; that was an especially cold spring. Two of them were aroused. They tore him to shreds. And we refrained from punishment. They weren't really conscious; instinct was ruling them."

His tone—insofar as a human could interpret—was not unkindly but did imply: Poor animals, they aren't capable of behaving better. *You gatortails get a lot of dynamism out of taking for granted you're the natural future lords of the galaxy,* the man thought, *but your attitude has its disadvantages. Not that you deliberately antagonize any other races, provided they give you no trouble. But you don't use their talents as fully as you might. Ydwyr seems to understand this. He mentioned that I could be valuable as a non-Merseian—which suggests he'd like to have team members from among the Roidhunate's client species—but I imagine he had woes enough pushing his project through a reluctant government, without bucking attitudes so ingrained that the typical Merseian isn't even conscious of them.*

Given a radio link to the base, the expedition leader didn't bother with a vocalizer. He spoke Eriau directly to the computer back there. It rendered his phrases into the

dialect spoken here at Ktha-g-klek, to the limited extent
that the latter was "known" to its memory bank. Grunting,
clicking noises emerged from the mindsets of whatever
beings listened in the village. The reverse process operated,
via relay by the bus. An artificial Merseian voice said: "Be
welcome. We are in a torrent of toil, but can happen a
sharing of self is possible."

"The more if we can help you with your transportation,"
the leader offered.

The Dom hesitated. *A primitive's conservatism,*
Flandry recognized. *He can't be sure airlifts aren't unlucky,
or whatever.* Finally: "Come to us."

That was not quickly done. First everybody aboard
must get into his heat suit. One had been modified for
Flandry. It amounted to a white coverall bedecked
with pockets and sheaths; boots; gauntlets—everything
insulated around a web of thermoconductor strands. A
fishbowl helmet was equipped with chowlock, mechanical
wipers, two-way sonic amplification, and short-range
radio. A heat pump, hooked to the thermoconductors and
run off accumulators, was carried on a backpack frame.
Though heavy, the rig was less awkward than might have
been expected. Its weight was well distributed; the gloves
were thick and stiff, but apparatus was designed with that
in mind, and plectrum-like extensions could be slipped
over the fingers for finer work. *Anyway,* Flandry thought,
consider the alternative.

*It's not that man or Merseian can't survive a while in
this sauna. I expect we could, if the while be fairly short.
It's that we wouldn't particularly want to survive.*

Checked out, the party set down its vehicle and

stepped forth. At this altitude, relay to base continued automatically.

Flandry's first awareness was of weight, enclosure, chattering pump, cooled dried air blown at his nostrils. Being otherwise unprocessed, the atmosphere bore odors— growth, decay, flower and animal exudations, volcanic fumes—that stirred obscure memories at the back of his brain. He dismissed them and concentrated on his surroundings.

The river boomed past a broad meadow, casting spray and steam over its banks. Above and on every side loomed the jungle. Trees grew high, brush grew wide, leaf crowding serrated blue leaf until the eye soon lost itself in dripping murk. But the stems looked frail, pulpy, and the leaves were drying out; they rattled against each other, the fallen ones scrittled before a breeze, the short life of summer's forest drew near to an end.

Sturdier on open ground was that vegetable family the Merseians called *wair*: as widespread, variegated, and ecologically fundamental as grass on Terra. In spring it grew from a tough-hulled seed, rapidly building a cluster of foliage and a root that resembled a tuber without being one. The leaves of the dominant local species were ankle height and lacy. They too were withering, the wair was going dormant; but soon, in fall, it would consume its root and sprout seeds, and when frost cracked their pods, the seeds would fall to earth.

Darkling over treetops could be glimpsed Mt. Thunderbelow. A slight shudder went through Flandry's shins, he heard a rumble, the volcano had cleared its throat. Smoke puffed forth.

But the Domrath were coming. He focused on them.

Life on Talwin had followed the same general course as on most terrestroid planets. Differences existed. It would have been surprising were there none. Thus, while tissues were principally built of L-amino proteins in water solution like Flandry's or Cnif's, here they normally metabolized levo sugars. A man could live on native food, if he avoided the poisonous varieties; but he must take the dietary capsules the Merseians had prepared.

Still, the standard division into photosynthetic vegetable and oxygen-breathing animal had occurred, and the larger animals were structurally familiar with their interior skeletons, four limbs, paired eyes and ears. Set beside many sophonts, the Domrath would have looked homelike.

They were bipeds with four-fingered hands, their outline roughly anthropoid except for the proportionately longer legs and huge, clawed, thickly soled feet necessary to negotiate springtime swamps and summer hardpan. The skin was glabrous, bluish, with brown and black mottlings that were beginning to turn gaudy colors as mating season approached. The heads were faintly suggestive of elephants': round, with beady eyes, large erect ears that doubled as cooling surfaces, a short trunk that was a chemosensor and a floodtime snorkel, small down-curving tusks on the males. The people wore only loincloths, loosely woven straw cloaks to help keep off "insects," necklaces and other ornaments of bone, shell, horn, teeth, tinted clay. Some of their tools and weapons were bronze, some—incongruously—paleolithic.

That much was easily grasped. And while their size

was considerable, adult males standing over two meters and massing a hundred or more kilos, females even larger, it was not overwhelming. They were bisexual and viviparous. Granted, they were not mammals. A mother fed her infants by regurgitation. Bodies were poikilothermic, though now functioning at a higher rate than any Terran reptile. That was not unheard of either.

Nonetheless, Flandry thought, it marked the foundation of their uniqueness. For when your energy, your very intelligence was a function of temperature; when you not only slept at night, but spent two-thirds of your life among the ghostly half-dreams of hibernation—

About a score had come to meet the xenologists, with numerous young tagging after. The grownups walked in ponderous stateliness. But several had burdens strapped on their backs; and behind them Flandry saw others continue work, packing, loading bundles onto carrier poles, sweeping and garnishing soon-to-be-deserted houses.

The greeting committee stopped a few meters off. Its leader elevated his trunk while dipping his ax. Sounds that a human palate could not reproduce came from his mouth. Flandry heard the computer's voice in his radio unit. "Here is Seething Springs. I am"—no translation available, but the name sounded like "G'ung"—"who speaks this year for our tribe." An intonation noted, in effect, that "tribe" (Eriau "*maddeuth*," itself not too close an equivalent of the Anglic word by which Flandry rendered it) was a debatable interpretation of the sound G'ung made, but must serve until further studies had deepened comprehension of his society. "Why have you come?"

The question was not hostile, nor was the omission

of a spoken welcome. The Domrath were gregarious, unwarlike although valiant fighters at need, accustomed to organizing themselves in nomadic bands. And, while omnivorous, they didn't make hunting a major occupation. Their near ancestors had doubtless lived entirely off the superabundant plant life of summer. Accordingly, they had no special territorial instincts. Except for their winter dens, it did not occur to them that anyone might not have a perfect right to be anywhere.

The Seething Springs folk were unusual in returning annually to permanent buildings, instead of constructing temporary shelters wherever they chanced to be. And this custom had grown up among them only because their hibernation site was not too far from this village. No one had challenged their occupation of it.

Quite simply and amiably, G'ung wondered what had brought the Merseians.

"We explained our reasons when last we visited you . . . with gifts," their leader reminded. His colleagues bore trade goods, metal tools and the like, which had hitherto delighted all recipients. "We wish to learn about your tribe."

"Is understood." Neither G'ung nor his group acted wildly enthusiastic.

No Domrath had shown fear of the Merseians. Being formidable animals, they had never developed either timidity or undue aggressiveness; being at an early prescientific stage, they lived among too many marvels and mysteries to see anything terrifyingly strange about spaceships bearing extraplanetarians; and Ydwyr had enforced strict correctness in every dealing with them. So why did these hesitate?

The answer was manifest as G'ung continued: "But you came before in high summer. Fastbreaking Festival was past, the tribes had dispersed, food was ample and wit was keen. Now we labor to bring the season's gatherings to our hibernation place. When we are there, we shall feast and mate until we drowse off. We have no time or desire for sharing self with outsiders."

"Is understood, G'ung," the Merseian said. "We do not wish to hamper or interfere. We do wish to observe. Other tribes have we watched as fall drew nigh, but not yours, and we know your ways differ from the lowlanders' in more than one regard. For this privilege we bid gifts and, can happen, the help of our flying house to transport your stores."

The Domrath snorted among themselves. They must be tempted but unsure. Against assistance in the hard job of moving stuff up toward Mt. Thunderbelow must be balanced a change in immemorial practice, a possible angering of gods . . . yes, it was known the Domrath were a religious race. . . .

"Your words shall be shared and chewed on," G'ung decided. "We shall assemble tonight. Meanwhile is much to do while light remains." The darkness of Talwin's clouded summer was pitchy; and in this dry period, fires were restricted and torches tabooed. He issued no spoken invitation, that not being the custom of his folk, but headed back. The Merseians followed with Flandry.

The village was carefully laid out in a spiderweb pattern of streets—for defense? Buildings varied in size and function, from hut to storage shed, but were all of stone, beautifully dressed, dry-laid, and chinked. Massive

wooden beams supported steeply pitched sod roofs. Both
workmanship and dimensions—low ceilings, narrow door-
ways, slit windows with heavy shutters—showed that, while
the Domrath used this place, they had not erected it.

They boiled about, a hundred or so of every age;
doubtless more were on the trail to the dens. Voices and
footfalls surged around. In spite of obvious curiosity, no
one halted work above a minute to stare at the visitors.
Autumn was too close.

At a central plaza, where the old cooked a communal
meal over a firepit, G'ung showed the Merseians some
benches. "I will speak among the people," he said. "Come
day's end, you shall receive us here and we shall share self
on the matter you broach. Tell me first: would the
Ruadrath hold with your plan?"

"I assure you the Ruadrath have nothing against it,"
Cnif said.

From what I've studied, Flandry thought, *I'm not
quite sure that's true, once they find out.*

"I have glimpsed a Ruad—I think—when I was small
and spring came early," said an aged female. "That you see
them each year—" She wandered off, shaking her head.

With Cnif's assent, Flandry peeked into a house
fronting on the square. He saw a clay floor, a hearth and
smokehole, daises along two sides with shelves above.
Bright unhuman patterns glowed on walls and intricately
carved timbers. In one corner stood a loaded rack, ready
to go. But from the rafters, with ingenious guards against
animals, hung dried fruits and cured meat—though the
Domrath were rarely eaters of flesh. A male sat carefully
cleaning and greasing bronze utensils, knives, bowls, an

ax, a saw. His female directed her young in tidying the single room while she spread the daises with new straw mats.

Flandry greeted the family. "Is this to be left?" he asked. It seemed like quite a bit for these impoverished savages.

"In rightness, what else?" the male replied. He didn't stop his work, nor appear to notice that Flandry was not a Merseian. In his eyes, the differences were probably negligible. "The metal is of the Ruadrath, as is the house. For use we give payment, that they may be well pleased with us when they come out of the sea." He did pause then, to make a sign that might be avertive or might be reverent—or both or neither, but surely reflected the universal sense of a mortal creature confronting the unknown. "Such is the law, by which our forebears lived while others died. *Thch rar.*"

Ruadrath: elves, gods, winter ghosts.

CHAPTER FOURTEEN

More and more, as the weeks of Flandry's absence passed, her existence took on for Djana an unreality. Or was it that she began slowly to enter a higher truth, which muted the winds outside and made the walls around her shadowy?

Not that she thought about it in that way, save perhaps when the magician wove her into a spell. Otherwise she lived in everydayness. She woke in the chamber that the man had shared with her. She exercised and groomed herself out of habit, because her living had hitherto depended on her body. At mess she stood respectfully aside while the Merseians went through brief rituals religious, familial, and patriotic—oddly impressive and stirring, those big forms and deep voices, drawn steel and talking drums— and afterward joined in coarse bread, raw vegetables, *gwydh*-milk cheese, and the Terran-descended tea which they raised throughout the Roidhunate. There followed study, talk, sometimes a special interview, sometimes recreation for a while; a simple lunch; a nap in deference to

her human circadian rhythm; more study, until evening's
meat and ale. (Since Merseia rotated at about half the rate
of Talwin, a night had already gone over the land.) Later
she might have further conversation, or attend a concert
or recorded show or amateur performance of something
traditional; or she might retire alone with a tape. In any
event, she was early abed.

Talk, like perusal of a textreel or watching of a
projection, was via the linguistic computer. It had plenty
of spare channels, and could throw out a visual translation
as easily as a sonic one. However, she was methodically
being given a working knowledge of Eriau, along with an
introduction to Merseian history and culture.

She cooperated willingly. Final disposition of her case
lay with superiors who had not yet been heard from. At
worst, though, she wasn't likely to suffer harm—given a
prince of the blood on her side—and at best . . . well, who
dared predict? Anyway, her education gave her something
to do. And as it advanced, it started interesting, at last
entrancing her.

Merseia, rival, aggressor, troublemaker, menace lairing
out beyond Betelgeuse: she'd accepted the slogans like
everybody else, never stopping to think about them. Oh,
yes, the Merseians were terrible, but they lived far off and
the Navy was supposed to keep them there while the
diplomatic corps maintained an uneasy peace, and she
had troubles of her own.

Here she dwelt among beings who treated her with
gruff kindness. Once you got to know them, she thought,
they were . . . they had homes and kin the same as people,
that they missed the same as people; they had arts,

melodies, sports, games, jokes, minor vices, though of course you had to learn their conventions, their whole style of thinking, before you could appreciate it. . . . They didn't want war with Terra, they only saw the Empire as a bloated sick monstrosity which had long outlived its usefulness but with senile cunning contrived to hinder and threaten *them*. . . . No, they did not dream of conquering the galaxy, that was absurd on the face of it, they simply wanted freedom to range and rule without bound, and "rule" did not mean tyranny over others, it meant just that others should not stand in the way of the full outfolding of that spirit which lay in the Race. . . .

A spirit often hard and harsh, perhaps, but bone-honest with itself; possessed of an astringency that was like a sea breeze after the psychic stench of what Djana had known; not jaded or rootless, but reaching for infinity and for a God beyond infinity, while planted deep in the consciousness of kinship, heroic ancestral memories, symbols of courage, pride, sacrifice. . . . Djana felt it betokened much that the chief of a Vach—not quite a clan—was called not its Head but its Hand.

Were those humans who served Merseia really traitors . . . to anything worth their loyalty?

But it was not this slow wondering that made the solid world recede from her. It was Ydwyr the Seeker and his spells; and belike they had first roused the questions in her.

To start with, he too had merely talked. His interest in her background, experiences, habits, and attitudes appeared strictly scientific. As a rule they met *à deux* in his office. "Thus I need not be a nephew of the Roidhun," he explained wryly. Fear stabbed her for a second. He gave her a shrewd regard and added, "No one is monitoring our translator channel."

She gathered nerve to say, "The *qanryf*—"

"We have had our differences," Ydwyr replied, "but Morioch is a male of honor."

She thought: *How many Imperial officers in this kind of setup would dare skip precautions against snooping and blackmail?*

He had a human-type chair built for her, and poured her a glass of arthberry wine at each colloquy. Before long she was looking forward to the sessions and wishing he were less busy elsewhere, coordinating his workers in the field and the data they brought back. He didn't press her for answers, he relaxed and let conversation ramble and opened for her the hoard of his reminiscences about adventures on distant planets.

She gathered that xenology had always fascinated him and that he was seldom home. Almost absent-mindedly, in obligation to his Vach, he had married and begotten; but he took his sons with him from the time they were old enough to leave the gynaeceum until they were ready for their Navy hitches. Yet he did not lack warmth. His subordinates adored him. When he chanced to speak of the estate where he was born and raised, his parents and siblings, the staff whose fathers had served his fathers for generations, she came to recognize tenderness.

Then finally—it was dark outside, the hot still dark of summer's end, heat lightning aflicker beyond stockade and skeletal trees—he summoned her; but when she entered the office, he rose and said: "Let us go to my private quarters."

For a space she was again frightened. He bulked so big, so gaunt and impassive in his gray robe, and they were so alone together. A fluoro glowed cold, and the air that slid and whispered across her skin had likewise gone chill.

He smiled his Merseian smile, which she had learned to read as amicable. Crinkles radiated through the tiny scales of his skin, from eyes and mouth. "I want to show you something I keep from most of my fellows," he said. "You might understand where they cannot."

The little voicebox hung around his neck, like the one around hers, spoke with the computer's flat Anglic. She filled that out with his Eriau. No longer did the language sound rough and guttural; it was, in truth, rather soft, and rich in tones. She could pick out individual words by now. She heard nothing in his invitation except—

—*the father I never knew.*

Abruptly she despised herself for what she had feared. How must she look to him? Face: hag-thin, wax-white, save for the bizarrely thick and red lips; behind it, two twisted flaps of cartilage. Body: dwarfish, scrawny, bulge-breasted, pinch-waisted, fat-bottomed, tailless, feet outright deformed. Skin: no intricate pattern of delicate flexible overlap; a rubberiness relieved only by lines and coarse pores; and hair, everywhere hair in ridiculous bunches and tufts, like fungus on a corpse. Odor: what? Sour? Whatever it was, no lure for a natural taste.

Men! she thought. *God, I don't mean to condemn Your work, but You also made the dogs men keep, and don't You agree they're alike, those two breeds? Dirty, smelly, noisy, lazy, thievish, quick to attack when you aren't watching, quick to run or cringe when you are;*

they're useless, they create nothing, you have to wait on
them, listen to their boastful bayings, prop up their silly
little egos till they're ready to slobber over you again. . . .

I'm sorry. Jesus wore the shape of a man, didn't he?

But he wore it—in pity—because we needed him—
and what've we done with his gift?

Before her flashed the image of a Merseian Christ,
armed and shining, neither compassionate nor cruel but
the Messiah of a new day. . . . She hadn't heard of any
such belief among them. Maybe they had no need of
redemption; maybe they were God's chosen. . . .

Ydwyr caught her hands between his, which were
cool and dry. "Djana, are you well?"

She shook the dizziness from her head. *Too much*
being shut in. Too much soaking myself in a world that
can't be mine. Nicky's been gone too long. (I saw a grey-
hound once, well-trained, proud, clean and swift. Nicky's
a greyhound.) I can't get away from my humanness. And
I shouldn't want to, should I? "N-nothing, sir. I felt a little
faint. I'll be all right."

"Come rest." Stooping, he took her arm—a Terran
gesture she had told him about—and led her through the
inner curtain to his apartment.

The first room was what she might have expected and
what officers of the base had no doubt frequently seen:
emblem of the Vach Urdiolch, animation of a homeworld
scene where forested hills plunged toward an ocean
turbulent beneath four moons, shelves of books and
mementos, racked weapons, darkly shimmering drapes;
on the resilient floor, a carved and inlaid table of black
wood, a stone in a shallow crystal bowl of water, an alcove

shrine, and nothing else except spaciousness. One archway, half unscreened, gave on a monastic bedchamber and 'fresher cubicle.

But they passed another hanging. She stopped in the dusk beyond and exclaimed.

"Be seated if you wish." He helped her shortness to the top of a couch upholstered in reptilian hide. The locks swirled over her shoulders as she stared about.

The mounted skulls of two animals, one horned, one fanged; convoluted tubes and flasks crowding a bench in the gloom of one corner; a monolith carved with shapes her eye could not wholly follow, that must have required a gravsled to move; a long-beaked leathery-skinned thing, the span of its ragged wings equal to her height, that sat unblinking on its gnarled perch; and more and more, barely lit by flambeaux in curiously wrought sconces, whose restless blue glow made shadows move like demons, whose crackling was a thin song that almost meant something she had forgotten, whose smoke was pungent and soon tingled in her brain.

She looked up to the craggy highlights of Ydwyr's countenance, tremendously above her. "Do not be afraid," said the lion voice. "These are not instruments of the darkness, they are pathfinders to enter it."

He sat down on his tail, bringing his ridged head level with hers. Reflections moved like flames deep within the caverns under his brow ridges. But his speech stayed gentle, even wistful.

"The Vach Urdiolch are the landless ones. So is the Law, that they may have time and impartiality to serve the Race. Our homes, where we have dwelt for centuries, we keep by leasehold. Our wealth comes less from ancient dues than from what we may win offplanet. This has put us in the forefront of the Race's outwardness; but it has also brought us closest to the unknowns of worlds never ours.

"A witch was my nurse. She had served us since my grandfather was a cub. She had four arms and six legs, what was her face grew between her upper shoulders, she sang to me in tones I could not always hear, and she practiced magic from the remembered Ebon Mountains of her home. Withal, she was good and faithful; and in me she found a ready listener.

"I think that may be what turned me toward searching out the ways of alien folk. It helps Merseia, yes; we need to know them; but I have wanted their lore for its own sake. And Djana, I have not perpetually found mere primitive superstition. A herb, a practice, a story, a philosophy . . . how dare we say nothing real is in them, when we come new to a world that gave birth to those who live on it? Among folk who had no machines I saw, a few times, happenings that I do not believe any machine could bring about.

"In a sense, I became a mystic; in another sense, none, for where is the border between 'natural' and 'transcendental'? Hypnosis, hysterical strength and stigmata, sensory heightening, psychosomatics, telepathy—such things are scorned in the scientific youth of civilizations, later accepted, when understanding has grown. I am simply using techniques that may, perhaps, advance comprehension where gauges and meters cannot.

"Once I got leave to visit Chereion. That is the most

eldritch planet I have seen, a dominion of the Roidhunate but only, I think, because that serves the ends of its dwellers, whatever those ends are. For they are old, old. They had a civilization a million years ago that may have reached beyond this galaxy, where we have barely started to burrow about at the end of one spiral arm. It disappeared; they cannot or will not say why, and it suits a few of them to be too useful to Merseia for us to risk angering the rest. Yes, we haughty conquerors walk softly among them!

"I was received among the disciples of Aycharaych, in his castle at Raal. He has looked deeper into the mind—not the mind of his people, or yours, or any single one, but somehow into that quality of pandemic Mind which the scientists deny can exist—he has looked deeper into this, I believe, than any other being alive. He could not evoke in me what I did not have to be evoked; or else he did not choose to. But he taught me what he said I could use; and without that skill, that way of existing in the cosmos, I would never have done half what I have. Think: in a single decade, we are well on the way to full communication with both races on Talwin.

"I want, not to probe your soul, Djana, but to join with you in exploring it. I want to know the inwardness of being human; and you may see what it is to be Merseian."

The flames danced and whispered among moving shadows; the figures on the monolith traced a path that could almost be followed; the smoke whirled in her veins; around her and through her crooned the lullaby voice of Father.

"Do not be afraid of what you see, Djana. These things are archaic, yes, they speak of pagan cults and witchcraft, but that is because they come from primeval sources, from the beast that lived before mind was kindled in it. One day these tokens may no longer be needed. Or perhaps they will be, perhaps they go deeper even than I imagine. I do not know and I want to know. It will help to mesh awarenesses with a human, Djana . . . no terrified captive, no lickspittle turncoat, no sniveler about peace and brotherhood, no pseudomorph grown up among us apart from his own breed . . . but one who has come to me freely, out of the depths of the commonalty that bred her, one who has known alike the glory and the tragedy of being human.

"These are symbols, Djana, certain objects, certain rites, which different thinking species have found will help raise buried parts of the soul. And brought forth, those parts can be understood, controlled, strengthened. Remember what the discipline of the body can do. Remember likewise the discipline of the spirit; calm, courage, capability can be learned, if the means are known; they take nothing but determination. Now ask yourself: What more remains?

"Djana, you could become *strong.*"

"Yes," she said.

And she was gazing into the water, and the fire, and the crystal, and the shadows within. . . .

A hostel at night. Fire leaping red and gold, chuckling as it lights the comradely company, rough-hewn furniture, fiddler on a chair tuning to play a dance; at the table's far end, a woman, long-gowned, deep-bosomed, who bears a sheaf and an infant on her lap.

Wind. A black bird sudden athwart the pane. The sound of its beak rapping.

Descent down endless stairs in the dark, led by one who never looks back. The boat. The river.

On the far side they have no faces.

"I am sorry," Ydwyr said. "We do not keep a pharmacopoeia for your species. You must forgo drugs. Furthermore, the Old Way is not for you to tread to its end—nor me, I confess. We have the real world to cope with, and we will not do so by abandonment of reason.

"Tell me your dreams. If they grow too bad, call me on my private line—thus—and I will come to you, no matter the hour."

The snake that engirdles the universe lifts its starry head. It gapes. Scream. Run.

The coils hiss after. The swamp clings to feet. A million years, a step a year out of the sucking muck, and the snake draws close behind.

Lightning. Sinking. Black waters.

He held her, simply held her, at night in her room. "From my viewpoint," he said, "I am gaining matchless experience with human archetypes." The dry practicality, itself comforting, yielded to mildness. A big hand stroked her hair. "But you, Djana, are more than a thing. You are becoming like a child to me, did you know? I want to raise you up again and lead you through this valley of shadows you must pass before you can stand by your own strength."

At mornwatch he left her. She slept a short while, but

got to breakfast and subsequently continued her regular schooling. It did not keep her from dwelling within her dreams.

Outside, the first mists of autumn sneaked white over the wet earth.

The waters are peace. Dream, drowse . . . no, the snake is not dead.

The snake is not dead.

His poisonous teeth. Struggle. Scream. The warm waters are gone, drained out with a huge hollow roaring. Hollow, hollow.

The hollow sound of hoofs, shaking a bridge that nine dead kings could not make thunder. Light.

The snake burns backward from the light.

Raise hands to it. But bow down from its brilliance.

That blaze is off the spear of the Messiah.

"*Khraich.* I would be interested to know if an abortion was attempted on you. Not important, since you survived. Your need is to learn that you did survive, and that you can.

"Do you feel ready for another session this evening? I would like for you to come and concentrate on the Graven Stone. It seems to have traits in common with what I have read your Terran usage calls a . . . a mandala?"

A mirror.

The face within.

One comes from behind on soundless feet and holds a mirror to the mirror.

Endlessness dwindles toward nothingness.

At the heart of nothingness, a white spark. It flames, and nothingness recoils and flees back outward to endlessness, while trumpets triumph.

"Ur-r-rh." Ydwyr scowled at her test scores. They sat prosaically in his living room—though what was prosaic about its austere serenity? "Something developing, beyond question. A hitherto unrealized potential—not telepathy. I'd hoped—"

"The Old Way to the One," she said, and watched the wall dissolve.

He gave her a long stare before he replied, crisply: "You have gone as far down that road as I dare take you, my dear. Perhaps not far enough, but I am not able—I suspect none less than Aycharaych would be able—to guide you further; and alone, you would lose yourself in yourself."

"Hm?" she said vaguely. "Ydwyr, I know I touched your mind, I felt you."

"Delusion. Mysticism is a set of symbols. Symbols are to live by, yes—why else banners?—but they are not to be confused with the reality for which they stand. While we know less about telepathy than psychologists usually pretend, we do know it's a perfectly physical phenomenon. Extremely long waves travel at light speed, subject to inverse-square diminution and the other laws of nature; the principles of encoding apply, nothing but the radical variation of sensitivity, from time to time and individual to individual, ever made its existence doubtful. Today we can identify it when it occurs.

"Whatever happened in these last experiments of ours, you are not becoming a telepathic receiver. An influence of that general nature was present, true. The meters registered it, barely over threshold level. But analysis shows you were not calling the signs I dealt with above-random accuracy. Instead, I was not dealing them completely at random.

"Somehow, slightly, unconsciously, you were *influencing* me toward turning up the signs you guessed I would be turning up."

"I wanted to reach you," Djana mumbled.

Ydwyr said sternly: "I repeat, we have entered realms where I am not fit to conduct you. The dangers are too great—principally to you, possibly to me. At a later date, maybe, Aycharaych—for the present, we stop. You shall return to the flesh world, Djana. No more magic. Tomorrow we set you to gymnastics and flogging, exhausting, uninspiring work with Eriau. That should bring you back."

He on the throne: "For that they have sinned beyond redemption, the sin that may not be forgiven, which is to blaspheme against the Holy Spirit, no more are they My people.

"Behold, I cast them from Me; and I will raise against them a new people under a new sun; and their name shall be Strength.

"Open now the book of the seven thunders."

Talwin's short autumn was closing when the ship came from headquarters. That was not Merseia. No domain like the Roidhunate could be governed from a single planet, even had the Race been interested in trying. However, she did bear a direct word from the Protector.

She stood on the field, slim, sleek, a destroyer with guns whippet-wicked against the sky, making a pair of counterparts from Morioch's command that were likewise in port look outmoded and a little foolish. The captured Terran scoutboat hunched in a corner, pathetic.

Few trees showed above the stockade. Early frosts had split their flimsy trunks and brought them down, already to crumble back into the soil. The air was cool and moist. Mists coiled about Merseians working outdoors; but overhead heaven reached clear, deep blue, and what clouds there were shone dazzling white beneath Siekh.

Djana was not invited to the welcoming ceremonies, nor had she anticipated it. Ydwyr gave her a quick intercom call—"Have no fears, I am authorized to handle your case, as I requested in my dispatch"—and wasn't that wonderful of him? She went for a walk, a real tramp, kilometers along the bluffs above the Golden River and back through what had been enclosing jungle and was becoming open tundra, space, freedom, full lungs and taut muscles, for hour after hour until she turned home of her own desire.

I've changed, she thought. *I still don't know how much.*

The weeks under Ydwyr's—tutelage?—were vague in her recollection, often difficult or impossible to separate from the dreams of that time. Later she had gradually regained herself. But it was no longer the same self. Old Djana was scarred, frightened, greedy with the greed that tries to fill inner emptiness, lonely with the loneliness that dares not love. New Djana was . . . well, she was trying to find out. She was someone who would go for a hike and stop to savor the scarlet of a late-blooming flower. She was someone who, in honest animal wise, hoped Nicky would soon finish with his expedition, and daydreamed about something between him and her that would last, but did not feel she needed him or anybody to guard her from monsters.

Maybe none existed. Dangers, of course, but dangers can't do worse than kill you, and they said in the Vachs, "He cannot respect life who does not respect death." No, wait, she *had* met monsters, back in the Empire. Though she no longer quailed at the remembrance of them, she could see they must be crushed underfoot before they poisoned the good beings like Ydwyr and Nicky and Ulfan-gryf and Avalrik and, well, yes, all right, in his fashion, Morioch. . . .

Wind lulled, tossing her hair, caressing her skin, which wore less clothes than she would formerly have required on this kind of day. Occasionally she tried to call to her the winged creatures she saw, and twice she succeeded; a bright guest sat on her finger and seemed content, till she told it to continue toward its hibernation. To her, the use of her power felt like being a child again—she had been, briefly, once in a rare while—and wishing hard. Ydwyr guessed that it was a variety of projective telepathy and that its sporadic appearance in her species had given rise to legends about geases, curses, and allurements.

But I can't control it most of the time, and don't care that I can't. I don't want to be a superwoman. I'm happy just to be a woman—a full female, no matter what race— which is what Ydwyr made me.

How can I thank him?

The compound court was deserted when she entered it. Probably all personnel were fraternizing with the ship's crew. Dusk was falling, chill increased minute by minute, the wind grew louder and stars blinked forth. She hurried to her room.

The intercom was lit. She punched the replay. It said: "Report to the *datholch* in his office immediately on return," with the time a Merseian hour ago. That meant almost four of Terra's; they split their day decimally.

Her heart bumped. She operated the controls as she had done when the nightmares came. "Are you there, Ydwyr?"

"You hear me," said the reassuringly professorial voice he could adopt. By now she seldom needed the computer.

She sped down empty halls to him. Remotely, she heard hoarse lusty singing. When Merseians celebrated, they were apt to do so at full capacity. The curtain at his door fell behind her to cut off that sound.

She held fist to breast and breathed hard. He rose from the desk where he had been working. "Come," he said. The gray robe flapped behind him.

When they were secret among the torches and skulls, he leaned down through twilight and breathed—each word stirred the hair around her ear—

"The ship brought unequivocal orders. You are safe. They do not care about you, provided you do not bring the Terrans the information you have. But Dominic Flandry has powerful enemies. Worse, his mentor Max Abrams does; and they suspect the younger knows secrets of the older. He is to go back in the destroyer. The probing will leave mere flesh, which will probably be disposed of."

"Oh, Nicky," she said, with a breaking within her.

He laid his great hands on her shoulders, locked eyes with eyes, and went on: "My strong recommendation having been overruled, my protest would be useless. Yet I respect him, and I believe you have affection for him yourself. This thing is not right, neither for him nor for Merseia. Have you learned to honor clean death?"

She straightened. The Eriau language made it natural to say, "Yes, Ydwyr, my father."

"You know your intercom has been connected to the linguistic computer, which on a different channel is in touch with the expedition he is on," he told her. "It keeps no records unless specifically instructed. Under guise of a personal message, the kind that commonly goes from here to those in the field, you can tell him what you like. You have thus exchanged words before, have you not? None of his companions know Anglic. He could wander away— 'lost'—and cold is a merciful executioner."

She said with his firmness: "Yes, sir."

Back in her room she lay for a time crying. But the thought that flew in and out was: *He's good. He wouldn't let them gouge the mind out of my Nicky. No Imperial Terran would care. But Ydwyr is like most of the Race. He has honor. He is* good.

CHAPTER FIFTEEN

The fog of autumn's end hid Mt. Thunderbelow and all the highlands in wet gray that drowned vision within meters. Flandry shivered and ran a hand through his hair, trying to brush the water out. When he stooped and touched the stony, streaming ground, it was faintly warm; now and then he felt a shudder in it and heard the volcano grumble.

His Merseian companions walked spectral before and behind him, on their way up the narrow trail. Most of them he could not see, and the Domrath they followed were quite lost in the mists ahead.

But he had witnessed the departure of the natives from camp and could visualize them plodding toward their sleep: the hardiest males, their speaker G'ung at the rear. That was a position of some danger, when late-waking summer or early-waking winter carnivores might suddenly pounce. (It wouldn't happen this year, given a tail of outworld observers armed with blasters and slugthrowers.

However, the customs of uncounted millennia are not fast set aside.) The Domrath were at their most vulnerable, overburdened with their own weight, barely conscious in an energy-draining chill.

Flandry sympathized. To think that heatsuits were needed a month ago! Such a short time remained to the xenologists that it hadn't been worthwhile bringing along electric-grid clothes. Trying to take attention off his discomfort, he ran through what he had seen.

Migration—from Ktha-g-klek to the grounds beneath this footpath, a well-watered meadowland on the slopes of Thunderbelow, whose peak brooded enormous over it. Unloading of the food hoard gathered during summer. Weaving of rude huts.

That was the happy time of year. The weather was mild for Talwin. The demoniac energy promoted by the highest temperatures gave way to a pleasant idleness. Intelligence dropped too, but remained sufficient for routine tasks and even rituals. A certain amount of foraging went on, more or less *ad libitum.* For the main part, though, fall was one long orgy. The Domrath ate till they were practically globular and made love till well after every nubile female had been impregnated. Between times they sang, danced, japed, and loafed. They paid scant attention to their visitors.

But Talwin swung further from Siekh; the spilling rains got colder, as did the nights and then the days; cloud cover broke, revealing sun and stars before it re-formed on the ground; wair and trees withered off; grazing and browsing animals vanished into their own hibernations; at morning the puddles were sheeted over with ice, which crackled when you stepped on it; the rations dwindled away, but that made no difference, because appetite dropped as the people grew sluggish; finally they dragged themselves by groups to those dens whither the last were now bound.

And back to base for us, Flandry thought, *and Judas, but I'll be glad to warm myself with Djana again! Why hasn't she called me for this long, or answered my messages? They claim she's all right. She'd better be, or I'll explode.*

The trail debouched on a ledge beneath an overhang. Black in the dark basaltic rock gaped a cave mouth. Extinct fumaroles, blocked off at the rear by collapse during eruptions, were common hereabouts, reasonably well sheltered from possible lava flows, somewhat warmed by the mountain's molten core. Elsewhere, most Domrath moved south for the winter, to regions where the cold would get mortally intense. They could stand temperatures far below freezing—among other things, their body fluids became highly salty in fall, and transpiration during sleep increased that concentration—but in north country at high altitudes, without some protection, they died. The folk of Seething Springs took advantage of naturally heated dens.

Among the basic problems which life on Talwin must solve was: How could hibernators and estivators prevent carnivores active in the opposite part of the year from eating them? Different species solved it in different ways: by camouflage; by shells or spines or poisonous tissues; by tunneling deep, preferably under rock; by seeking areas where glaciers would cover them; by being so prolific that a percentage were bound to escape attention; and on and on. The Domrath, who were large and possessed weapons, lashed out in blind berserkergang if they were roused; winter animals tended to develop an instinct to leave them alone. They remained subject to a few predators, but against these they constructed shelters, or went troglodyte as here.

Shivering with hands in jacket pockets, breath puffing forth to join the mists, Flandry stood by while G'ung shepherded his males into the den. They moved somnambulistically. "I think we can go inside," murmured the Merseian nearest the Terran. "Best together, ready for trouble. We can't predict how they'll react, and when I asked earlier, they told me they never remember this period clearly."

"Avoid contact," advised another.

The scientists formed up with a precision learned in their military service. Flandry joined. They hadn't issued him weapons, though otherwise they had treated him pretty much as an equal; but he could duck inside their square if violence broke loose.

It didn't. The Domrath seemed wholly unaware of them.

This cave was small. Larger ones contained larger groups, each of which had entered in a body. The floor had been heaped beforehand with leaves, hay, and coarse-woven blankets. The air within was less bleak than outside— according to Wythan Scarcheek's thermometer. Slowly, grunting, rustling the damp material, the Domrath groped and burrowed into it. They lay close together, the stronger protecting the weaker.

G'ung stayed alone on his feet. Heavily he peered

through the gloom: heavily he moved to close a gate installed in the mouth. It was a timber framework covered with hides and secured by a leather loop to a post.

"*Ngugakathch*," he mumbled like one who talks in his sleep. "*Shoa t'kuhkeh*." No translation came from the computer. It didn't have those words. A magical formula, a prayer, a wish, a noise? How many years before the meaning was revealed?

"Best get out," a Merseian, shadowy in mist and murk, whispered.

"No, we can undo the catch after they're unconscious," the leader said as softly. "And reclose it from the outside; the crack'll be wide enough to reach through. Watch this. Watch well. No one has found anything quite similar."

A camera lens gleamed.

They would sleep, those bulky friendly creatures— Flandry reflected—through more than a Terran year of ice age. No, not sleep; hibernate: comatose, barely alive, nursing the body's fuel as a man in illimitable darkness would nurse the single lamp he had. A sharp stimulus could trigger wakefulness, by some chemical chain the Merseians had not traced; and the murderous rage that followed was a survival mechanism, to dispose of any threat and return to rest before too great a reserve was spent. Even undisturbed, they were not few who would never wake again.

The first who did were the pregnant females. They responded to the weak warmth of early spring, went out into the storms and floods of that season, joined forces and nourished themselves on what food could be gotten, free of competition from their tribesmates. Those were revived by higher temperatures, when the explosion of plant growth was well under way. They came forth gaunt and irritable, and did little but eat till they were fleshed out.

Then—at least in this part of the continent—tribes customarily met with tribes at appointed places. Fastbreaking Festival was held, a religious ceremony which also reinforced interpersonal relationships and gave opportunity for new ones.

Afterward the groups dispersed. Coastal dwellers sought the shorelands where rising sea level and melting ice created teeming marshes. Inlanders foraged and hunted in the jungles, whose day-by-day waxing could almost be seen. The infants were born.

Full summer brought the ripeness of wair roots and other vegetables, the fat maturity of land and water animals. And its heat called up the full strength and ingenuity of the Domrath. That was needful to them; now they must gather for fall. Females, held closer to home by their young than the males, became the primary transmitters of what culture there was.

Autumn: retirement toward the hibernation dens; rest, merrymaking, gorging, breeding. Winter and the long sleep.

G'ung fumbled with the gate. Leaned against the wall nearby was a stone-headed spear. *How long have they lived this way, locked into this cycle?* Flandry mused. *Will they ever break free of it? And if they do, what next? It's amazing how far they've come under these handicaps. Strike off the manacles of Talwin's year . . . somehow . . . and, hm, it could turn out that the new dominators of this part of the galaxy will look a bit like old god Ganesh.*

His communicator, and the Merseians', said with Cnif hu Vanden's voice: "Dominic Flandry." "Quiet!" breathed the leader.

"Uh, I'll go outside," the man proposed. He slipped by the creakily closing gate and stood alone on the ledge. Fog eddied and dripped. Darkness was moving in. The cold deepened.

"Switch over to local band, Cnif," he said, and did himself. His free hand clenched till the nails bit. "What is this?"

"A call for you from base." The xenophysiologist, who had been assigned to watch the bus while the rest accompanied the last Domrath, sounded puzzled. "From your female. I explained you were out and could call her back later, but she insisted the matter is urgent."

"What—?"

"You don't understand? I certainly don't. She lets weeks go by with never a word to you, and suddenly calls—speaking fair Eriau, too—and can't wait. That's what comes of your human sex-equality nonsense. Not that the sex of a non-Merseian concerns us. . . . Well, I said I'd try to switch you in. Shall I?"

"Yes, of course," Flandry said. "Thank you." He appreciated Cnif's thoughtfulness. They'd gotten moderately close on this often rugged trip, helping each other—on this often monotonous trip, when days of waiting for something noteworthy were beguiled by swapping yarns. You could do worse than pass your life among friends like Cnif and Djana—

A click, a faint crackling, and her utterance, unnaturally level: "Nicky?"

"Here, wishing I were there," he acknowledged, trying for lightness. But the volcano growled in stone and air.

"Don't show surprise," said the quick Anglic words. "This is terrible news."

"I'm alone," he answered. *How very alone.* Night gnawed at his vision.

"Nicky, darling, I have to say goodbye to you. Forever."

"What? You mean you—" He heard his speech at once loud and muffled in the clouds, hers tiny and as if infinitely removed.

"No. You. Listen. I may be interrupted any minute."

Even while she spoke, he wondered what had wrought the change in her. She should have been half incoherent, not giving him the bayonet-bare account she did. "You must have been told, the Merseian ship's arrived. They'll take you away for interrogation. You'll be a vegetable before they kill you. Your party's due back soon, isn't it? Escape first. Die decently, Nicky. Die free and yourself."

It was strange how detached he felt, and stranger still that he noticed it. Perhaps he hadn't yet realized the import. He had seen beings mortally wounded, gaping at their hurts without immediate comprehension that their lives were running out of them. "How do you know, Djana? How can you be sure?"

"Ydwyr—Wait. Someone coming. Ydwyr's people, no danger, but if somebody from the ship gets curious about—Hold on."

Silence, fog, night seeping over a land whose wetness

had started to freeze. A few faint noises and a wan gleam
of light slipped past the cave gate. The Domrath must be
snuggling down, the Merseians making a final inspection
by dimmed flashbeams before leaving. . . .

"It's all right, Nicky. I wished him to go past. I guess
his intention to look into my room wasn't strong, if he had
any, because he did go past."

"What?" Flandry asked in his daze.

"I've been . . . Ydwyr's been working with me. I've
learned, I've developed a . . . a talent. I can wish a person,
an animal, to do a thing, and when I'm lucky, it will. But
never mind!" The stiffness was breaking in her; she
sounded more like the girl he had known. "Ydwyr's the
one who saved you, Nicky. He warned me and said I
should warn you. Oh, hurry!"

"What'll become of you?" The man spoke automatically. His main desire was to keep her voice in the circuit,
in the night.

"Ydwyr will take care of me. He's a—he's noble. The
Merseians aren't bad, except a few. We want to save you
from them. If only—you—" Her tone grew indistinct and
uneven. "Get away, darling. Before too late. I want t-t-to
remember you . . . like you were—God keep you!" she
wailed, and snapped the connection.

He stood for a timeless time until, "What's wrong,
Dominic?" Cnif asked.

"Uh, *khraich*, a complicated story." Flandry shook
himself. Anger flared. *No! I'll not go meekly off to their
brain machines. Nor will I quietly cut my throat, or slip into
the hills and gently become an icicle.* A child underneath
moaned terror of the devouring dark; but the surface

mind had mastery. *If they want to close down me and my personal universe, by Judas but they'll pay for their fun!*

"Dominic, are you there?"

"Yes." Flandry's head had gone winter clear. He had but to call them, and ideas and pieces of information sprang forward. Not every card had been dealt. Damn near every one, agreed, and his two in this hand were a deuce and a four; but they were the same suit, which meant a straight flush remained conceivable in those spades which formerly were swords.

"Yes. I was considering what she told me, Cnif. That she's about decided to go over to the Roidhunate." *No mistaking it, and they must have noticed too, so she won't be hurt by my saying this. But I'll say no more. They mustn't learn she tried to save me the worst. Let 'em assume, under Ydwyr's guidance, that the news of her defection knocked me off my cam. Never mind gratitude or affection, lad; you'll need any hole card you can keep, and she may turn out to be one.* "You'll realize I . . . I am troubled. I'd be no more use here. They'll take off soon in any case. I'll go ahead and, well, think things over."

"Come," Cnif invited gently. "I will leave you alone."

He could not regret that his side was gaining an agent; but he could perceive, or believed he could perceive, Flandry's patriotic anguish. "Thanks," the human said, and grinned.

He started back along the trail. His boots thudded; occasionally a stone went clattering down the talus slope, or he slipped and nearly fell on a patch of ice. Lightlessness closed in, save where the solitary lance of his flashbeam bobbed and smoked through the vapors. He no longer noticed the cold, he was too busy planning his next move.

Cnif would naturally inform the rest that the Terran wasn't waiting for them. They wouldn't hasten after him on that account. Where could he go? Cnif would pour a stiffish drink for his distressed acquaintance. Curtained bunks were the most private places afforded by the bus. Flandry could be expected to seek his and sulk.

Light glowed yellow ahead from the black outline of the vehicle. It spilled on the Domrath's autumnal huts, their jerry-built frames already collapsing. Cnif's flat countenance peered anxiously from the forward section. Flandry doused his flash and went on all fours. Searching about, he found a rock that nicely fitted his hand. Rising, he approached in straightforward style and passed through the heatlock which tonight helped ward off cold.

The warmth inside struck with tropical force. Cnif waited, glass in hand as predicted, uncertain smile on mouth. "Here," he said with the blunt manners of a colonial, and thrust the booze at Flandry.

The man took it but set it on a shelf. "I thank you, courteous one," he replied in formal Eriau. "Would you drink with me? I need a companion."

"Why . . . I'm on duty . . . kh-h-h, yes. Nothing can hurt us here. I'll fetch myself one while you get out of your overclothes." Cnif turned. In the cramped entry chamber, his tail brushed Flandry's waist and he stroked it lightly across the man, Merseia's gesture of comfort.

Quick! He must outmass you by twenty kilos!

Flandry leaped. His left arm circled Cnif's throat. His

right hand brought the stone down where jaw met ear. They had taught him at the Academy that Merseians were weak there.

The blow crunched. Its impact nearly dislodged Flandry's grip on the rock. The other being choked, lurched, and swept his tail around. Flandry took that on the hip. Had it had more leverage and more room to develop its swing, it would have broken bones. As was, he lost his hold and was dashed to the floor. Breath whuffed out of him. He lay stunned and saw the enormous shape tower above.

But Cnif's counterattack had been sheer reflex. A moment the Merseian tottered, before he crumpled at knees and stomach. His fall boomed and quivered in the bus body. His weight pinned down the man's leg. When he could move again, Flandry had a short struggle to extricate himself.

He examined his victim. Though flesh bled freely— the same hemoglobin red as a man's—Cnif breathed. A horny lid, peeled back, uncovered the normal uniform jet of a Merseian eye, not the white rim that would have meant contraction. *Good.* Flandry stroked shakily the bald, serrated head. *I'd've hated to do you in, old chap. I would have if need be, but I'd've hated it.*

Hurry, you sentimental thimblewit! he scolded himself. *The others'll arrive shortly, and they tote guns.*

Still, after he had rolled Cnif out onto the soil, he found a blanket to wrap the Merseian in; and he left a portable glower going alongside.

Given that, the scientists would be in no serious trouble. They'd get chilled, wet, and hungry. Maybe a few would come down with sneezles and wheezles. But when Ydwyr didn't hear from them, he'd dispatch a flyer.

Flandry re-entered the bus. He'd watched how it was operated; besides, the basic design was copied from Technic civilization. The manual controls were awkward for human hands, the pilot seat more so for a human fundament. However, he could get by.

The engine purred. Acceleration thrust him backward. The bus lifted.

When high in the night, he stopped to ponder charts and plans. He dared not keep the stolen machine. On an otherwise electricityless and virtually metalless world, it could be detected almost as soon as a ship got aloft in search of it. He must land someplace, take out what he had in the way of stores, and send the bus off in whatever direction a wild goose would pick.

But where should he hide, and how long could he, on this winter-bound world?

Flandry reviewed what he had learned in the Merseian base and nodded to himself. Snowfall was moving south from the poles. The Ruadrath would be leaving the ocean, had probably commenced already. His hope of survival was not great, but his hope of raising hell was. He laid out a circuitous route to the coastlands west of Barrier Bay.

CHAPTER SIXTEEN

When first they woke, the People had no names. He who was Rrinn ashore was an animal at the bottom of the sea.

Its changes were what roused him. Water pressure dropped with the level; lower temperatures meant a higher equilibrium concentration of dissolved oxygen, which affected the fairly shallow depths at which the People estivated; currents shifted, altering the local content of minerals raised from the ocean bed. Rrinn was aware of none of this. He knew only, without knowing that he knew, that the Little Death was past and he had come again to the Little Birth . . . though he would not be able to grasp these ideas for a while.

During a measureless time he lay in the ooze which lightly covered his submerged plateau. Alertness came by degrees, and hunger. He stirred. His gill flaps quivered, the sphincters behind them pumping for an ever more demanding bloodstream. When his strength was enough, he caught the sea with hands, webbed feet, and tail. He surged into motion.

Other long forms flitted around him. He sensed them primarily by the turbulence and taste they gave to the water. No sunlight penetrated here. Nevertheless vision picked them out as blurs of blackness. Illumination came from the dimly blue-glowing colonies of *aoao* (as it was called when the People had language) planted at the sides of the cage: it lured those creatures which dwelt always in the sea, and helped Wirrda's find their way to freedom.

Different packs had different means of guarding themselves during the Little Death, such as boulders rolled across crevices. Zennevirr's had even trained a clutch of finsnakes to stand sentry. Wirrda's slumbered in a cage—woven mesh between timbers—that nothing dangerous could enter. It had originally been built, and was annually repaired, in the spring when the People returned, still owning a limited ability to breathe air. That gave them energy to dive and do hard work below, living off the redeveloping gills an hour or two at a stretch. (Of course, not everyone labored. The majority chased down food for all.) After their lungs went completely inactive, they became torpid—besides, the sun burned so cruelly by then, the air was like dry fire—and they were glad to rest in a cool dark.

Now Rrinn's forebrain continued largely dormant, to preserve cells that otherwise would get insufficient oxygen. Instinct, reflex, and training steered him. He found one of the gates and undid it. Leaving it open, he swam forth and joined his fellows. They were browsing among the *aoao*, expropriating what undigested catch lay in those tentacles.

The supply was soon exhausted, and Wirrda's left in a

widespread formation numbering about 200 individuals. Clues of current and flavor, perhaps subtler hints, guided them in a landward direction. Had it been clear day they would not have surfaced immediately; eyes must become reaccustomed by stages to the dazzle. But a thick sleet made broaching safe. That was fortunate, albeit common at this season. In their aquatic phase, the People fared best among the waves.

They found a school of—not exactly fish—and cooperated in a battue. Again and again Rrinn leaped, dived, drove himself by threshing tail and pistoning legs until he clapped hands on a scaly body and brought it to his fangs. He persisted after he was full, giving the extra catch to whatever infants he met. They had been born with teeth, last midwinter, able to eat any flesh their parents shredded for them; but years remained before they got the growth to join in a chase.

In fact, none of the People were ideally fitted for ocean life. Their remote ancestors, epochs ago, had occupied the continental shelf and were thus forced to contend with both floods and drought. The dual aerating system developed in response, as did the adaptation of departing the land to escape summer's heat. But being evolved more for walking than swimming—since two-thirds of their lives were spent ashore—they were only moderately efficient sea carnivores and "found" it was best to retire into estivation.

Rrinn had had that theory expounded to him by a Merseian paleontologist. He would remember it when his brain came entirely awake. At present he simply felt a wordless longing for the shallows. He associated them with food, frolic, and—and—

Snowing went on through days and nights. Wirrda's swam toward the mainland, irregularly, since they must hunt, but doggedly. Oftener and oftener they surfaced. Water felt increasingly less good in the gills, air increasingly less parching. After a while Rrinn actively noticed the sensuous fluidity along his fur, the roar and surge of great wrinkled foam-streaked gray waves, skirling winds and blown salt spindrift.

Snowing ended. Wirrda's broached to a night of hyaline clarity, where the very ocean was subdued. Overhead glittered uncountable stars. Rrinn floated on his back and gazed upward. The names of the brightest came to him. So did his own. He recalled that if he had lately passed a twin-peaked island, which he had, then he ought to swim in a direction that kept Ssarro Who Mounts Endless Guard over his right shoulder. Thus he would approach the feeding grounds with more precision than the currents granted. He headed himself accordingly, the rest followed, and he knew afresh that he was their leader.

Dawn broke lambent, but the People were no longer troubled by glare. They pressed forward eagerly in Rrinn's wake. By evening they saw the traces of land, a slight haze on the horizon, floating weeds and bits of wood, a wealth of life. That night they harried and were gluttonous among a million tiny phosphorescent bodies; radiance dripped from their jaws and swirled on every wave. Next morning they heard surf.

Rrinn identified this reef, that riptide, and swam toward the ness where Wirrda's always went ashore. At midafternoon the pack reached it.

North and south, eventually to cover half the globe,

raged blizzards. Such water as fell on land, solid, did not return to the ocean; squeezed beneath the stupendous weight of later falls, it became glacier. Around the poles, the seas themselves were freezing, more territory for snow to accumulate on. In temperate climes their level dropped day by day, and the continental shelves reappeared in open air.

Rrinn would know this later. For the moment, he rejoiced to tread on ground again. Breakers roared, tumbled, and streamed among the low rocks; here and there churned ice floes. Swimming was not too dangerous, though. Winter tides were weak. And ahead, the shelf climbed, rugged and many-colored under a sparkling sky. Snow dappled its flanks, ice glistened where pools had been. The air was a riot of odors, salt, iodine, clean decomposition and fresh growth, and was crisp and windy and cool, cool.

Day after day the pack fattened itself, until blubber sleeked out the bulges of ribs and muscles. The receding waters had left a rich stratum of dead plants and animals. In it sprouted last year's saprophyte seeds, salt and alcohol in their tissues to prevent freezing, and covered the rocks with ocherous and purple patches. Marine animals swarmed between; flying creatures shrieked and whirled above by the hundred thousand; big game wandered down from the interior to feed. Rrinn's males chipped hand axes to supplement their fangs; females prepared lariats of gut and sinew; beasts were caught and torn asunder.

Yet Wirrda's were ceasing to be only hunters. They crooned snatches of song, they trod bits of dance, they spoke haltingly. Many an individual would sit alone, hours on end, staring at sunset and stars while memory drifted up from the depths. And one day Rrinn, making his way through a whiteout, met a female who had kept close to him. They stopped in the wind-shrill blankness, the sea clashing at their feet, and looked eye into eye. She was sinuous and splendid. He exclaimed in delight, "But you are Cuwarra."

"And you are Rrinn," she cried. Male and wife, they came to each other's arms.

While ovulation was seasonal among the People, the erotic urge persisted throughout winter. Hence the young had fathers who helped care for them during their initial months of existence. That relationship was broken by the Little Death—older cubs were raised in casual communal fashion—but most couples stayed mated for life.

Working inland, Wirrda's encountered Brrao's and Hrrouf's. They did every year. The ferocious territoriality which the People had for their homes ashore did not extend to the shelf; packs simply made landfall at points convenient to their ultimate destinations. These three mingled cheerfully. Games were played, stories told, ceremonies put on, marriages arranged, joint hunts carried out. Meanwhile brains came wholly active, lungs reached full development, gills dried and stopped functioning.

Likewise did the shelflands. Theirs was a brief florescence, an aftermath of summer's furious fertility. Plants died off, animals moved away, pickings got lean. Rrinn thought about Wirrda's, high in the foothills beyond the tundra, where hot springs boiled and one river did not freeze. He mounted a rock and roared. Other males of his pack passed it on, and before long everyone was assembled beneath him. He said: "We will go home now."

Various youths and maidens complained, their courtships among Brrao's or Hrrouf's being unfinished. A few hasty weddings were celebrated and numerous dates were made. (In the ringing cold of midwinter, the People traveled widely, by foot, sled, ski, and iceboat. Though hunting grounds were defended to the death, peaceful guests were welcomed. Certain packs got together at set times for trade fairs.) On the first calm day after his announcement, Rrinn led the exodus.

He did not start north at once. With full mentality regained, Wirrda's could use proper tools and weapons. The best were stored at Wirrda's—among the People, no real distinction existed among place names, possessives, and eponyms—but some had been left last spring at the accustomed site to aid this trek.

Rrinn's line of march brought his group onto the permanent littoral. It was a barren stretch of drifts. His Merseian acquaintances had shown him moving pictures of it during hot weather: flooded in spring, pullulating swamp in early summer, later baked dry and seamed with cracks. Now that the shelf was exhausted, large flesheaters were no longer crossing these white sastrugi to see what they could scoop out of the water. Rrinn pushed his folk unmercifully.

They did not mind the cold. Indeed, to them the land still was warmer than they preferred. Fur and blubber insulated them, the latter additionally a biological reserve. Theirs was a high homeothermic metabolism, with corresponding energy demands. The People needed a large intake of food. Rrinn took them over the wastelands because it would be slower and more exhausting to climb among the ice masses that choked Barrier Bay. Supplies could not be left closer to the shelf or the pack, witless on emergence, might ruin everything.

After three days' hard travel, a shimmer in the air ahead identified those piled bergs. Rrinn consulted Cuwarra. Females were supposed to be inferior, but he had learned to rely on her sense of direction. She pointed him with such accuracy that next morning, when he topped a hill, he looked straight across to his goal.

The building stood on another height, constructed of stone, a low shape whose sod roof bore a cap of white. Beyond it, in jagged shapes and fantastic rainbows, reached the bay. Northward wound the Golden River, frozen and snowed on and frozen again until it was no more than a blue-shadowed valley among the bluffs. The air was diamond-clear beneath azure heaven.

"Go!" shouted Rrinn exuberantly. Not just equipment, but smoked meat lay ahead. He cast himself on his belly and tobogganed downslope. The pack whooped after. At the bottom they picked themselves up and ran. The snow crunched, without giving, under their feet.

But when they neared the building, its door opened. Rrinn stopped. Hissing dismay, he waved his followers back. The fur stood straight on him. An animal—

No, a Merseian. What was a Merseian doing in the cache house? They'd been shown around, it had been explained to them that the stuff kept there must never be disturbed, they'd agreed and—

Not a Merseian! Too erect. No tail. Face yellowish-brown where it was not covered with hair—

Snarling in the rage of territory violation, Rrinn gathered himself and plunged forward at the head of his warriors.

After dark the sky grew majestic with stars. But it was as if their light froze on the way down and shattered on the dimly seen ice of Talwin. A vast silence overlay the world; sound itself appeared to have died of cold. To Flandry, the breath in his nostrils felt liquid.

And this was the threshold of winter!

The Ruadrath were gathered before him in a semicircle ten or twelve deep. He saw them as a shadowy mass, occasionally a glitter when eyes caught stray luminance from the doorway where he stood. Rrinn, who confronted him directly, was clearer in his view.

Flandry was not too uncomfortable. The dryness of the air made its chill actually less hard to take than the higher temperatures of foggy autumn. From the bus he had lifted ample clothing, among divers other items, and bundled it around himself. Given a glower, the structure where he had taken refuge was cozy. Warmth radiated over his back.

(However, the glower's energy cells had gotten low in the three weeks that he waited. Likewise had his food. Not daring to tamper with the natives' stockpile, he had gone hunting—lots of guns and ammo in the bus—but, ignorant of local game, hadn't bagged much. And what he did get required supplementation from a dwindling stock of capsules. Nor could he find firewood. *If you don't convince this gentlebeing,* he told himself, *you're dead.*)

Rrinn said into a vocalizer from the cache house: "How foresaw you, new skyswimmer, that any among us would know Eriau?" The transponder turned his purring, trilling vocables into Merseian noises; but since he had never quite mastered a grammar and syntax based on a worldview unlike his own, the sentences emerged peculiar.

Flandry was used to that kind of situation. "Before leaving the Merseian base," he answered, "I studied what they had learned about these parts. They had plenty of material on you Ruadrath, among them you of Wirrda's. Mention was made of your depot and a map showed it. I knew you would arrive in due course." *I knew besides that it was unlikely the gatortails would check here for me, this close to their camp.* "Now you have been in contact with them since first they came—more than the Domrath, both because you are awake more and because they think more highly of you. Your interest in their works was often . . . depicted." (He had recalled that the winter folk used no alphabet, just mnemonic drawings and carvings.) "It was reasonable that a few would have learned Eriau, in order to discourse of matters which cannot be treated in any language of the Ruadrath. And in fact it was mentioned that this was true."

"S-s-s-s." Rrinn stroked his jaw. Fangs gleamed under stars and Milky Way. His breath did not smoke like a human's or Merseian's; to conserve interior heat, his respiratory system was protected by oils, not moisture, and water left him by excretion only. He shifted the harpoon he had taken from the weapon racks inside. Sheathed on the belt he had reacquired was a Merseian war knife. "Remains for you to tell us why you are here alone and in defiance of the word we made with the skyswimmers," he said.

Flandry considered him. Rrinn was a handsome creature. He wasn't tall, about 150 centimeters, say 65 kilos, but otter-supple. Otterlike too were the shape of body, the mahogany fur, the short arms. The head was more suggestive of a sea lion's, muzzle pointed, whiskered, and sharp-toothed, ears small and closable, brain case bulging backward from a low forehead. The eyes were big and golden, with nictitating membranes, and there was no nose; breath went under the same opercula that protected the gills.

No Terran analogy ever holds very true. Those arms terminated in four-digited hands whose nails resembled claws. The stance was akin to Merseian, forward-leaning, counterbalanced by the long strong tail. The legs were similarly long and muscular, their wide-webbed feet serving as fins for swimming, snowshoes for walking. Speech was melodious but nothing that a man could reproduce without a vocalizer.

And the consciousness behind those eyes—Flandry picked his response with care.

"I knew you would be angered at my invading your cache house," he said. "I counted on your common sense to spare me when I made no resistance." *Well, I did have a blaster for backup.* "And you have seen that I harmed or took nothing. On the contrary, I make you gifts." *Generously supplied by the airbus.* "You understand I belong to a different race from the Merseians, even as you and the Domrath differ. Therefore, should I be bound by their word? No, let us instead seek a new word between Wirrda's and mine."

He pointed at the zenith. Rrinn's gaze followed. Flandry wondered if he was giving himself false reassurance in believing he saw on the Ruad that awe which any thoughtful sophont feels who lets his soul fall upward among the stars. *I'd better be right about him.*

"You have not been told the full tale, you of Wirrda's," he said into the night and their watchfulness. "I bring you tidings of menace."

CHAPTER SEVENTEEN

It was glorious to have company and be moving again.

His time hidden had not been totally a vacuum for
Flandry. True, when he unloaded the bus—before
sending it off to crash at sea, lest his enemies get a clue to
him—he hadn't bothered with projection equipment, and
therefore not with anything micro-recorded. Every erg in
the accumulators must go to keeping him unfrozen. But
there had been some full-size reading matter. Though
the pilot's manual, the *Book of Virtues*, and a couple of
scientific journals palled with repetition, the Dayr Ynvory
epic and; especially, the volume about Talwin and how to
survive on it did not. Moreover, he had found writing
materials and a genuine human-style deck of cards.

But he dared not go far from his shelter; storms
were too frequent and rough. He'd already spent most of
his resources of contemplation while wired to the bunk
in *Jake*. Besides, he was by nature active and sociable,
traits which youth augmented. Initially, whenever he

decided that reading one more paragraph would make his vitreous humor bubble, he tried sketching; but he soon concluded that his gifts in that direction fell a little short of Michelangelo. A more durable pastime was the composition of scurrilous limericks about assorted Merseians and superior officers of his own. A few ought to become interstellar classics, he thought demurely—if he got free to pass them on—which meant that he had a positive duty to survive. . . . And he invented elaborate new forms of solitaire, after which he devised ways to cheat at them.

The principal benefit of his exile was the chance to make plans. He developed them for every combination of contingencies that he could imagine. Yet he realized this must be kept within limits; unforeseen things were bound to pop up, and he couldn't risk becoming mentally rigid.

"All that thinking did raise my hopes," he told Rrinn.

"For us too?" the chief answered. He gave the man a contemplative look. "Skyswimmer, naught have we save your saying, that we should believe you intend our good."

"My existence is proof that the Merseians have not apprised you of everything. They never mentioned races in contention with them—did they?"

"No. When Ydwyr and others declared the world goes around the sun and the stars are suns themselves with worlds aspin in the same wise . . . that took years to catch. I did ask once, were more folk than theirs upon those worlds, and he said Merseia was friend to many. Further has he not related."

"Do you seize?" Flandry crowed. (He was getting the

hang of Ruadrath idioms in Eriau. A man or Merseian would have phrased it, "Do you see?")

"S-s-s-s . . . Gifts have they given us, and in fairness have they dealt."

Why shouldn't they? Flandry gibed. *The scientists aren't about to antagonize their objects of research, and the Navy has no cause to. The reasons for being a tad less than candid about the interstellar political brew are quite simple. Imprimis, as this chap here is wise enough to understand, radically new information has to be assimilated slowly; too much at once would only confuse. Secundus, by its effect on religion and so forth, it tends to upset the cultures that Ydwyr's gang came to study.*

The fact is, friend Rrinn, the Merseians like and rather admire your people. Far more than the Domrath, you resemble them—or us, in the days of our pioneering.

But you must not be allowed to continue believing that.

"Among their folk and mine is a practice of keeping meat animals behind walls," he said. "Those beasts are treated well and fed richly . . . until time for slaughter."

Rrinn arched his back. His tail stood straight. He bared teeth and clapped hand to knife.

He had been walking with Flandry ahead of the group. It consisted chiefly of young, aged, and females. The hunters were scattered in small parties, seeking game. Some would not rejoin their families for days. When Rrinn stopped stiffened, unease could be seen on all the sleek red-brown bodies behind. The leader evidently felt he shouldn't let them come to a halt. He waved, a clawing gesture, and resumed his advance.

Flandry, who had modified a pair of Merseian snowshoes for himself, kept pace. Against the fact that he wasn't really built for this environment must be set his greater size. Furthermore, the going was currently easy.

Wirrda's were bound across the tundra that had been jungle in summer. Most years they visited the Merseian base, which wasn't far off their direct route, for sightseeing, talk, and a handout. However, the practice wasn't invariable—it depended on factors like weather— and Flandry had made them sufficiently suspicious that on this occasion they jogged out of their way to avoid coming near the compound. Meanwhile he continued feeding their distrust.

The Hellkettles would have been visible except for being wrapped in storm. That part of horizon and sky was cut off by a vast blue-black curtain. Not for weeks or months would the atmosphere settle down to the clear, ever colder calm of full winter. But elsewhere the sky stood pale blue, with a few high cirrus clouds to catch sunlight.

This had dropped to considerably less than Terra gets. (In fact, the point of equal value had been passed in what meteorologically was early fall. Likewise, the lowest temperatures would come well after Talwin had gone through apastron, where insolation was about 0.45 Terran.) Flandry must nevertheless wear self-darkening goggles against its white refulgence; and, since he couldn't look near the sun disc, its dwindling angular diameter did not impinge on his senses.

His surroundings did. He had experienced winters elsewhere, but none like this.

Even on planets akin to Terra, that period is not devoid of life. On Talwin, where it occupied most of the long year, a separate ecology had developed for it.

The divorce was not absolute. Seas were less affected than land, and many shore-based animals that ate marine species neither hibernated nor estivated. Seeds and other remnants of a season contributed to the diet of those which did. The Merseians had hardly begun to comprehend the web of interactions—structural, chemical, bacteriological, none knew what more—between hot-weather and cold-weather forms. As an elementary example: No equivalent of evergreens existed; summer's wild growth would have strangled them; on the other hand, decaying in fall, it provided humus for winter vegetation.

The tundra reached in crisp dunes and a glimpse of wind-scoured frozen lake. But it was not empty. Black among the blue shadows, leaves thrust upward in clumps that only looked low and bushy; their stems often went down through meters of snow. The sooty colors absorbed sunlight with high efficiency, aided by reflection off the surface. In some, a part of that energy worked through molecular processes to liquefy water; others substituted organic compounds, such as alcohols, with lower freezing points; for most, solidification of fluids was important to one stage or another of the life cycle.

North of the mountains, the glaciers were becoming too thick for plants. But south of them, and on the islands, vegetation flourished. Thus far it was sparse, and it would never approach the luxuriance of summer. Nonetheless it supported an animal population off which other animals lived reasonably well—including the Ruadrath.

Still, you could understand why they had such intense territorial jealousies. . . .

Flandry's breath steamed into air that lay cold on his cheeks; but within his garments he was sweating a trifle. The day was quiet enough for him to hear the *shuffle-shuffle* of his walking. He said carefully:

"Rrinn, I do not ask you to follow my counsel blind. Truth indeed is that I could be telling you untruth. What harm can it do, though, to consider ways by which you may prove or disprove my speech? Must you not as leader of Wirrda's attempt this? For think. If my folk and Merseia's are in conflict, maneuvering for position among the stars, then harbors are needed for the skyswimming craft. Not so? You have surely seen that not every Merseian is here to gather knowledge. Most come and go on errands that I tell you are scoutings and attacks on my folk.

"Now a warlike harbor needs defense. In preparation for the day the enemy discovers it, a day that will unfailingly come, it has to be made into more than a single small encampment. This whole world may have to be occupied, turned into a fortress." *What a casuist I am!* "Are you certain the Merseians have not been staring into your lives in order that they may know how easiest to overwhelm you?"

Rrinn growled back, "And am I certain your folk would leave us be?"

"You have but my speech," Flandry admitted, "wherefore you should ask of others."

"How? Shall I call Ydwyr in, show him you, and scratch for truth as to why he spoke nothing about your kindred?"

"N-n-no, I counsel otherwise. Then he need but kill me and give you any smooth saying he chooses. Best you get him to come to Wirrda's, yes, but without knowledge that I live. You can there draw him out in discourse and seize whether or not that which he tells runs together with that which you know from having traveled with me."

"S-s-s-s." Rrinn gripped his vocalizer as if it were a weapon. He was plainly troubled and unhappy; his revulsion at the idea of possibly being driven from his land gave him no peace. It lay in his chromosomes, the dread inherited from a million ancestors, to whom loss of hunting grounds had meant starvation in the barrens.

"We have the rest of the trek to think about what you should do," Flandry reassured him. *More accurately: for me to nudge you into thinking the scheme I hatched in the cache house is your own notion.*

I hope we do feel and reason enough alike that I can play tricks on you.

To himself: *Don't push too hard, Flandry. Take time to observe, to participate, to get* simpatico *with them. Why, you might even figure out a way to make amends, if you survive.*

Chance changed the subject for him. A set of moving specks rounded a distant hill. Closer, they revealed themselves as a moose-sized shovel-tusked brute pursued by several Ruadrath. The hunters' yells split the air. Rrinn uttered a joyous howl and sped to help. Flandry was left floundering behind in spite of wanting to demonstrate his prowess. He saw Rrinn head off the great beast and engage it, knife and spear against its rushes, till the others caught up.

That evening there was feasting and merriment. The grace of dancers, the lilt of song and small drums, spoke to Flandry with an eloquence that went beyond language and species. He had admired Ruadrath art: the delicate carving on every implement, the elegant shapes of objects like sledges, bowls, and blubber lamps. Now tonight, sitting—bundled up—in one of the igloos that had been raised when the old females predicted a blizzard, he heard a story. Rrinn gave him a low-voiced running translation into Eriau. Awkward though that was, Flandry could identify the elements of style, dignity, and philosophy which informed a tale of heroic adventure. Afterward, meditating on it in his sleeping bag, he felt optimistic about his chances of manipulating Wirrda's.

Whether or not he could thereby wrest anything out of the Merseians was a question to be deferred if he wanted to get to sleep.

Ydwyr said quietly, "No, I do not believe you would be a traitress to your race. Is not the highest service you can render to help strike the Imperial chain off them?"

"What chain?" Djana retorted. "Where were the Emperor and his law when I tried to escape from the Black Hole, fifteen years old, and my contractor caught me and turned me over to the Giggling Man for a lesson?"

Ydwyr reached out. His fingers passed through her locks, stroked her cheek, and rested on her shoulder for a minute. To save her garments—indoors being warm and she simply an alien there, her body neither desirable nor repulsive—she had taken to wearing just a pocketed kilt. The touch on her skin was at once firm and tender; its slight roughness emphasized the strength held in check behind. Love flowed through it, into her, and radiated back out from her until the bare small office was aglow, as golden sunsets can saturate the air of worlds like Terra.

Love? No, maybe not really. That's a typical sticky Anglic word. I remember, somebody told me, I think I remember . . . isn't it caritas *that God has for us mortals?*

Above the gray robe, above her, Ydwyr's countenance waited powerful and benign. *I mustn't call you God. But I can call you Father—to myself—can't I? In Eriau they say* rohadwann; *affection, loyalty, founded on respect and on my own honor.*

"Yes, I could better have spoken of burning out a cancer," he agreed. "The breakdown of legitimate authority into weakness or oppression—which are two aspects of the same thing, the change of Hands into Heads—is a late stage of the fatal disease." A human male would have tried to cuddle her and murmur consolations for memories that to this day could knot her guts and blur her eyesight. Then he would have gotten indignant if she didn't crawl into bed with him. Ydwyr continued challengingly: "You had the toughness to outlive your torment, at last to outwit the tormentors. Is not your duty to help those of your race to freedom who were denied your heritage?"

She dropped her gaze. Her fingers twisted together. "How? I mean, oh, you would overrun humanity . . . wouldn't you?"

"I thought you had learned the worth of propaganda," he reproached her. "Whatever the final result, you will see no enormous change; centuries of effort lie ahead. And the goal is liberation—of Merseians, yes, we make no

bleat about our primary objective being anything else—
but we welcome partners—and our endeavor is, ultimately,
to impose Will on blind Nature and Chance."

Junior partners, she added to herself. *Well, is that
necessarily bad?* She closed her eyes and saw a man who
bore Nicky Flandry's face (descendant, maybe) striding in
the van of an army which followed the Merseian Christ.
He carried no exterior burden of venal superiors and
bloodless colleagues, no interior load of nasty little guilts
and doubts and mockeries; in his hand was the gigantic
simplicity of a war knife, and he laughed as he strode.
Beside him, she herself walked. Wind tossed her hair and
roared in green boughs. They would never leave each
other.

*Nicky . . . dead . . . why? These people didn't kill him;
no, not even those back yonder who wanted to wring him
empty. They'd have been his friends if they could. The
Empire wouldn't let them.*

She looked again and found Ydwyr waiting. "Seeker,"
she said timidly, "this is too sudden for me. I mean, when
Qanryf Morioch tells me I should, should, should become
a spy for the Roidhunate—"

"You desire my advice," he finished. "You are always
welcome to it."

"But how can I—"

He smiled. "That will depend on circumstances, my
dear. After training, you would be placed where it was
deemed you could be most useful. I am sure you realize
the spectacular escapades of fiction are simply fiction. The
major part of your life would be unremarkable—though
I'm sure, with your qualifications, it would have a good

share of glamour and luxury. For example, you might get a strategically placed Terran official to make you his mistress or his actual wife. Only at widely spaced intervals would you be in contact with your organization. The risks are less than those you habitually ran before coming here; the material rewards are considerable." He grew grave. "The real reward for you, my almost-daughter, will be the service itself. And knowing that your name will be in the Secret Prayers while the Vach Urdiolch endures."

"You do think I should?" she gulped.

"Yes," he said. "Those are less than half alive who have no purpose in life beyond themselves."

The intercom fluted. Ydwyr muttered annoyance and signaled it to shut up. It fluted twice more in rapid succession. He tensed. "Urgent call," he said, and switched on.

Cnif hu Vanden's image flicked into the screen. "To the *datholch*, homage," he said hurriedly. "He would not have been interrupted save that this requires his immediate attention. We have received a messenger from Seething Springs." Djana remembered hearing how fast a Ruad could travel when he had no family or goods to encumber him.

"Khr-r-r, they must be settling down there." Ydwyr's tailtip, peeking from beneath his robe, quivered, the single sign he gave of agitation. "What is their word?"

"He waits in the courtyard. Shall I give the *datholch* a direct line?"

"Do." Djana thought that a man would have asked for a briefing first. Men had not the Merseian boldness.

She couldn't follow the conversation between Ydwyr

and the lutrine being who stood in the snow outside. The scientist used a vocalizer to speak the messenger's language. When he had blanked the screen, he sat for a long period, scowling, tailtip flogging the floor.

"Can I help?" Djana finally ventured to ask. "Or should I go?"

"*Shwai—*" He noticed her. "Khr-r-r." After pondering: "No, I can tell you now. You will soon hear in any case."

She contained herself. A Merseian aristocrat did not jitter. But her pulse thumped.

"A dispatch from the chief of that community," Ydwyr said. "Puzzling: the Ruadrath aren't in the habit of using ambiguous phrases. and the courier refuses to supplement what he has memorized. As nearly as I can discern, they have come on Dominic Flandry's frozen corpse."

Darkness crossed before her. Somehow she kept her feet.

"It has to be that," he went on, glowering at a wall. "The description fits a human, and what other human could it be?' For some reason, instead of begetting wonder, this seems to have made them wary of us—as if their finding something we haven't told them about shows we may have designs on them. The chief demands I come explain."

He shrugged. "So be it. I would want to give the matter my personal attention regardless. The trouble must be smoothed out, the effects on their society minimized; at the same time, observation of those effects may teach us something new. I'll fly there tomorrow with—" He looked at her in surprise. "Why, Djana, you weep."

"I'm sorry," she said into her hands. The tears were salt on her tongue. "I can't help it."

"You knew he must be dead, the pure death to which you sent him."

"Yes, but—but—" She raised her face. "Take me along," she begged.

"*Haadoch?* No. Impossible. The Ruadrath would see you and—"

"And what?" She knelt before him and clutched at his lap. "I want to say goodbye. And . . . and give him . . . what I can of a Christian burial. Don't you understand, lord? He'll lie here alone forever."

"Let me think." Ydwyr sat motionless and expressionless while she tried to control her sobbing. At last he smiled, stroked her hair again, and told her, "You may."

She forgot to gesture gratitude. "Thank you, thank you," she said in ragged Anglic.

"It would not be right to forbid your giving your dead their due. Besides, frankly, I see where it can be of help, showing the Ruadrath a live human. I must plan what we should tell them, and you must have your part learned before morning. Can you do that?"

"Certainly." She lifted her chin. "Afterward, yes, I will work for Merseia."

"Give no rash promises; yet I hope you will join our cause. That fugitive talent you have for making others want what you want—did you use it on me?" Ydwyr blocked her denial with a lifted palm. "Hold. I realize you'd attempt no mind-intrusion consciously. But unconsciously—*Khraich,* I don't suppose it makes any difference in this case. Go to your quarters, Djana daughter. Get some rest. I will be summoning you in a few hours."

CHAPTER EIGHTEEN

Where their ranges overlapped, Domrath and Ruadrath
normally had no particular relationship. The former tended
to regard the latter as supernatural; the latter, having had
chances to examine hibernator dens, looked more matter-
of-factly on the former. Most Domrath left Ruadrath
things strictly undisturbed—after trespassing groups had
been decimated in their sleep—whereas the Ruadrath
found no utility in the primitive Domrath artifacts. The
majority of their own societies were chalcolithic.

But around Seething Springs—Ktha-g-klek, Wirrda's—
a pattern of mutuality had developed. Its origins were lost
in myth. Ydwyr had speculated that once an unusual
sequence of weather caused the pack to arrive here while
the tribe was still awake. The Ruadrath allowed summer-
time use of their sturdy buildings, fine tools, and intricate
decorations, provided that the users were careful and left
abundant food, hides, fabrics, and similar payment. To the
Domrath, this had become the keystone of their religion.

The Ruadrath had found ceremonial objects and deduced as much. It made Wirrda's a proud band.

Flandry discovered he could play on that as readily as on territorial instinct. You may admit the skyswimmers can do tricks you can't. Nevertheless, when you are accustomed to being a god, you will resent their not having told you about the real situation in heaven.

Rrinn and his councilors were soon persuaded to carry out the human's suggestion: Send an obscurely worded message, which Flandry helped compose. Keep back the fact that he was alive. Have nearly everyone go to the hinterland during the time the Merseians were expected; they could do nothing against firearms, and a youngster might happen to give the show away.

Thus the village lay silent when the airbus appeared.

Domed with the snow that paved the spiderweb passages between them, buildings looked dwarfed. The winter sky was so huge and blue, the treeless winter horizon so remote. Steam from the springs and geysers dazzled Flandry when he glimpsed it, ungoggled; for a minute residual light-spots hid the whitened mass of Mt. Thunderbelow and the glacier gleam on the Hellkettle peaks. Fast condensing out, vapors no longer smoked above the Neverfreeze River. But its rushing rang loud in today's icy quiet.

A lookout yelled, *"Trreeann!"* Flandry had learned that call. He peered upward and southward, located the glinting speck, and sprang into the house where he was to hide.

Its door had been left open, the entrance covered by a leather curtain—an ordinary practice which should not draw any Merseian heed. Within, among the strewn furs and stacked utensils of a prosperous owner, sunbeams straggled past cracks in the shutters to pick out of dimness the arsenal Flandry had taken from the vehicle he stole. He carried two handguns, blaster and stunner, plus a war knife, extra ammunition, and energy charges. That was about the practical limit. The rest Wirrda's could inherit, maybe.

The house fronted on the central plaza. Directly opposite stood Rrinn's, where the meeting was to take place. Thus the Ruad could step out and beckon the human to make a dramatic appearance if and when needed. *(That's what Rrinn thinks.)* Through a minute hole in the curtain, Flandry saw the nine males who remained. They were armed. Ydwyr had never given them guns, which would have affected their culture too radically for his liking. But those bronze swords and tomahawks could do ample damage.

Rrinn spoke grimly into his short-range transceiver. Flandry knew the words he did not understand: "Set down at the edge of our village, next to the tannery. Enter afoot and weaponless."

Ydwyr should obey. It's either that or stop xenologizing this pack. And why should he fear? He'll leave a few lads in the bus, monitoring by radio, ready to bail him out of any trouble.

That's what Ydwyr thinks.

Some minutes later the Merseians showed up. They numbered four. Despite their muffling coldsuits, Flandry recognized the boss and three who had been on that previous trip to this country—how many years of weeks ago—

A small shape, made smaller yet by the tyrannosaurian bulks preceding, entered his field of view. He caught his breath. It was not really too surprising that Djana had also come. But after so much time, her delicate features and gold hair struck through the fishbowl helmet like a blow.

The Ruadrath gave brief greeting and took the newcomers inside. Rrinn entered last, drawing his own door curtain. The plaza lay bare.

Now.

Flandry's hands shook. Sweat sprang forth on his skin, beneath which the heart thuttered. Soon he might be dead. And how piercingly marvelous the universe was!

The sweat began freezing on his unprotected face. The beard he had grown, after his last application of inhibitor lost effect, was stiff with ice. In a few more of Talwin's short days, he would have used his final dietary capsule. Eating native food, minus practically every vitamin and two essential amino acids, was a scurvy way to die. Being shot was at least quick, whether by a Merseian or by himself if capture got imminent.

He stood a while, breathing slowly of the keen air, willing his pulse rate down, mentally reciting the formulas which drugs had conditioned him to associate with calm. The Academy could train you well if you had the foresight and persistence to cooperate. Loose and cool, he slipped outdoors. Thereafter he was too busy to be afraid.

A quick run around the house, lest somebody glance out of Rrinn's and see him . . . a wall-hugging dash down the glistening streets, snow crunching under his boots . . . a peek around the corner of the outlying tannery . . . yes, the bus sat where it was supposed to be, a long stream-lined box with sun-shimmer off the windows.

If those inside spotted him and called an alarm, that was that. *The odds say nobody'll happen to be mooning in this direction. You know what liars those odds are.* He drew his stunner, crouched, and reached the main heatlock in about two seconds.

Flattened against the side, he waited. Nothing occurred, except that his cheekbone touched the bus. Pain seared. He pulled free, leaving skin stuck fast to metal. Wiping away tears with a gloved hand, he set his teeth and reached for the outer valve.

It wasn't locked. Why should it be, particularly when the Merseians might want to pass through in a hurry? He glided into the chamber. Again he waited. No sound. He cracked the inner valve and leaned into the entry. It was deserted.

They'll have somebody in front, by the controls and communication gear. And probably someone in the main room, but let's go forward for openers. He oozed down the short passage.

A Merseian, who must have heard a noise or felt a breath of cold air—in this fantastic oily-smelling warmth—loomed into the control cabin doorway. Flandry fired. A purple light ray flashed, guiding the soundless hammer-blow of a supersonic beam. The big form had not toppled, unconscious, when Flandry was there. Another greenskin was turning from the pilot console. "*Gwy*—" He didn't say further before he thudded to the deck.

Whirling, Flandry sped toward the rear. The saloon windows gave on the remaining three sides of the world;

an observation dome showed everything else. Two more
Merseians occupied that section. One was starting off to
investigate. His gun was out, but Flandry, who entered
shooting, dropped him. His partner, handicapped by
being in the turret, was easier yet, and sagged into his seat
with no great fuss.

Not pausing, the human hurried forward. Voices
drifted from a speaker: Merseian basso, Ruadrath purr
and trill, the former using vocalizers to create the latter.
He verified that, to avoid distraction, there had been no
transmission from the bus.

Then he allowed himself to sit down, gasp, and feel
dizzy. *I carried it off. I really did.*

Well, the advantage of surprise—and he was only past
the beginning. Trickier steps remained. He rose and
searched about. When he had what he needed, he
returned to his prisoners. They wouldn't wake soon, but
why take chances? One was Cnif. Flandry grinned with
half a mouth. "Am I to make a hobby of collecting you?"

Having dragged the Merseians together, he wired
them to bunks—"Thanks, Djana"—and gagged them. On
the way back, he appropriated a vocalizer and a pair of
sound recorders. In the pilot cabin he stopped the input
from Rrinn's house.

Now for the gristly part. Though he'd rehearsed a
lot, that wasn't sufficient without proper apparatus.
Over and over he went through his lines, playing them
back, readjusting the transducer, fiddling with speed
and tone controls. (Between tests, he listened to the
conference. The plan called for Rrinn to draw palaver
out at length, pumping Ydwyr's delegation. But the old

xenologist was not naive—seemed, in fact, to be one of the wiliest characters Flandry had ever collided with—and might at any time do something unforeseeable. Words continued, however.) Finally the human had what he guessed was the best voice imitation he could produce under the circumstances.

He set his recorders near the pickup for long-range radio. Impulses flew across 300 white kilometers. A machine said: "The *datholch* Ydwyr calls Naval Operations. Priority for emergency. Respond!"

"The *datholch's* call is acknowledged by *Mei Chwioch, Vach Hallen*," answered a loudspeaker.

Flandry touched the same On button. "Record this order. Replay to your superiors at once. My impression was false. The Terran Flandry is alive. He is here at Seething Springs, at the point of death from malnutrition and exposure. The attempt must be made to save him, for he appears to have used some new and fiendishly effective technique of subversion on the Ruadrath, and we will need to interrogate him about that. Medical supplies appropriate to his species ought to be in the scoutboat that was taken. Time would be lost in ransacking it. Have it flown here immediately."

"The *datholch's* command is heard and shall be relayed. Does anyone know how to operate the vessel?"

Flandry turned on his second machine. It went "Kh-h-hr," his all-purpose response. In this context, he hoped, it would pass for a rasping of scorn. *A pilot who can't figure that out in five minutes, when we use the same basic design, should be broken down to galley swabber and set to peeling electrons.* He made his first recorder say: "Land in the open circle in the center of the village. We have him in a house adjacent. Hurry! Now I must return to the Ruadrath and repair what damage I can. Do not interrupt me until the boat is down. Signing off. Honor to the God, the Race, and the Roidhun!"

He heard the response, stopped sending, and tuned the conference back in. It sounded as if fur was about to fly.

So, better not dawdle here. Besides, *Jake* should arrive in minutes if his scheme worked.

If.

Well, they wouldn't be intimately familiar with Ydwyr's speech in the Navy section . . . aside from high-ranking officers like Morioch, who might be bypassed for the sake of speed, seeing as how Merseia encouraged initiative on the part of juniors . . . or if a senior did get a replay, he might not notice anything odd, or if he did he might put it down to a sore throat . . . or, or, or—

Flandry scrambled back into the overclothes he had shucked while working. He stuffed some cord in a pocket. A chronodial said close to an hour had fled. It stopped when he fired a blaster bolt at the main radio transmitter. On his way out, he sabotaged the engine too, by lifting a shield plate and shooting up the computer that regulated the grav projectors. He hoped not to kill anyone in his escape, but he didn't want them sharing the news before he was long gone. Of course, if he must kill he would, and lose no sleep afterward, if there was an afterward.

The air stung his injury. He loped over creaking snow to Rrinn's house. Closer, he moved cautiously, and stopped at the entrance to squeeze his eyes shut while raising his goggles. Charging indoors without dark-adapted pupils would be sheer tomfoolishness. Also dickfoolishness, harryfoolishness, and—Stunner in right hand, blaster in left, he pushed by the curtain. It rustled stiffly into place behind him.

Merseians and Ruadrath swiveled about where they tail-sat. They were at the far end of the single chamber, their parties on opposite daises. A fleeting part of Flandry noticed how vivid the murals were at their backs and regretted that he was about to lose the friendship of the artist.

Djana cried out. Rrinn hissed. Ydwyr uttered a sentence in no language the man had heard before. Several males of either species started off the platforms. Flandry brandished his blaster and shouted in Eriau: "Stay where you are! This thing's set to wide beam! I can cook the lot of you in two shots!"

Tensed and snarling, they returned to their places. Djana remained standing, reaching toward Flandry, mouth open and working but no sound coming forth. Ydwyr snapped into his vocalizer. Rrinn snapped back. The Terran could guess:

"What is this treachery?"

"Indeed we had him alive; yet I know not what he would seize."

He interrupted: "I regret I must stun you. No harm will be done, aside from possible headaches when you awaken. If anyone tries to attack me, I'll blast him. The blast will likely kill others. Rrinn, I give you a few breaths to tell your followers this."

"You wouldn't!" Djana protested wildly.

"Not to you, sweetheart," Flandry said, while Ruadrath words spat around him. "Come over here by me."

She gulped, clenched fists, straightened and regarded him squarely. "No."

"Huh?"

"I don't turn my coat like you."

"I wasn't aware I had." Flandry glared at Ydwyr. "What have you done to her?"

"I showed her truth," the Merseian answered. He had regained his calm. "What do you expect to accomplish?"

"You'll see," Flandry told him. To Rrinn: "Are you finished?"

"*Ssnaga.*" No matter the Ruad was of another species; you could not mistake unutterable hatred.

Flandry sighed. "I grieve. We traveled well together. Good hunting be yours for always."

The guide ray struck and struck. The Ruadrath scuttled for shelter, but found nothing high enough. The Merseians took their medicine with iron dignity. After a minute, none among them was conscious save Ydwyr and Djana.

"Now." Flandry tossed her the loop of cord. "Tie his wrists at his back, run his tail up there and make it fast, then pass down the end and hobble him."

"No!" she shrieked.

"Girl," said the gaunt, sun-darkened, wounded visage with the frost in its beard, "more's involved than my life, and I'm fond of living to start with. I need a hostage. I'd prefer not to drag him. If I have to, though, I'll knock you both out."

"Obey," Ydwyr told her. He considered Flandry. "Well done," he said. "What is the next stage of your plan?"

"No comment," the man replied. "I don't wish to be discourteous, but what you don't know you can't arrange to counteract."

"Correct. It becomes clear that your prior achievements were no result of luck. My compliments, Dominic Flandry."

"I thank the *datholch*—Get cracking, woman!"

Djana's gaze went bewildered between them. She struggled not to cry.

Her job of tying was less than expert; but Flandry, who supervised, felt Ydwyr couldn't work out of it fast. When she was through, he beckoned her to him. "I want our playmate beyond your reach," he said. Looking down into the blue eyes, he smiled. There was no immediate need now to aim a gun. He laid both hands on her waist. "And I want you in my reach."

"Nicky," she whispered, "you don't know what you're doing. Please, please listen."

"Later." A sonic boom made pots jump on a shelf. In spite of the dictatorship he had clamped down on himself, something leaped likewise in Flandry. "Hoy, that's my ticket home."

He peered past the curtain. Yes, *Giacobini-Zinner*, dear needle-nosed *Jake*, bulleting groundward, hovering, settling in a whirl of kicked-up snow. . . . Wait! Far off in the sky whence she'd come—

Flandry groaned. It looked like another spacecraft. Morioch or somebody had played cautious and sent an escort.

Well, he'd reckoned with that possibility. A Comet had the legs over most other types, if not all; and in an atmosphere, especially Talwin's—

The lock opened. The gangway extruded. A Merseian appeared, presumably a physician since he carried the medikit he must have ferreted out on his way here. He wasn't wearing an electric coldsuit, only Navy issue winter clothes. Suddenly it was comical beyond belief to see him stand there, glancing puzzled around, with his tail in a special stocking. Flandry had seldom worked harder than to hold back whoops and yell, in his best unaided imitation of a Merseian voice: "Come here! On the double! Your pilot too!"

"Pilot—"

"*Hurry!*"

The doctor called into the boat. Both Merseians descended and started across the ground. Flandry stood bowstring-tense, squinting out the slit between jamb and curtain, back to the captives he already had, out, in, out, in. If somebody got suspicious or somebody shouted a warning before the newcomers were in stunbeam range, he'd have to blast them dead and attempt a dash for the vessel.

They entered. He sapped them.

Recovering the medikit, he waved his gun. "Let's go, Ydwyr." He hesitated. "Djana, you can stay if you want."

"No," the girl answered, nigh too weakly to hear. "I'll come."

"Best not," Ydwyr counseled. "The danger is considerable. We deal with a desperate being."

"Maybe I can help you," Djana said.

"Your help would be to Merseia," Ydwyr reproved her.

Flandry pounced. "That's what you are to him, girl," he exclaimed in Anglic. "A tool for his damned planet." In Eriau: "Move, you!"

The girl shook her head blindly. It wasn't clear which of them she meant. Forlorn, she trudged out behind the tall nonhuman figure, in front of the man's weapon.

High and distant, little more in the naked eye than a glint, the enemy ship held her position. Magniscreens would reveal that three left the house for the boat—but not their species, Flandry hoped. Just three sent out to fetch something. . . . The gangway clattered to boots.

"Aft," Flandry directed. "Sorry," he said when they were at the bunks, and stunned Ydwyr. He used the cord to secure his captive and urged Djana forward. Her lips, her whole slight body trembled.

"What will you do?" she pleaded.

"Try to escape," Flandry said. "You mean there's a different game going?"

She sank into the seat beside his control chair. He buckled her in, more as a precaution against impulsive behavior than against a failure of interior grav, and assumed his own place. She stared blankly at him. "You don't understand," she kept repeating. "He's good, he's wise, you're making such a terrible mistake, please don't."

"You want me brainscrubbed, then?"

"I don't know, I don't know. Let me alone!"

Flandry forgot her while he checked the indicators. Everything seemed in order, no deterioration, no vandalism, no boobytraps. He brought the engine murmurous to life.

The gangway retracted, the airlock shut. *Goodbye, Talwin. Goodbye, existence? We'll see.* He tickled the console. The skill had not left his fingers. *Jake* floated aloft. The village receded, the geysers, the mountains, he was skyborne.

The outercom blinked and buzzed. Flandry ignored it till he was lined out northward. The other spacecraft swung about and swooped after him. Several kilometers off, she proved to be a corvette, no capital ship but one that could eat a scoutboat for breakfast. Flandry accepted her call.

"*Saniau* to Terran vessel. Where are you bound and why?"

"Terran vessel, and she is a Terran vessel, to *Saniau*. Listen with both ears. Dominic Flandry speaks. That's right, the very same Dominic Flandry who. I'm going home. The *datholch* Ydwyr, Vach Urdiolch, nephew to the most exalted Roidhun and so forth, is my guest. If you don't believe me, check the native town and try to find him. When he recovers from a slight indisposition, I can give you a visual. Shoot me down and he goes too."

Pause.

"If you speak truth, Dominic Flandry, do you imagine the *datholch* would trade honor for years?"

"No. I do imagine you'll save him if you possibly can."

"Correct. You will be overhauled, grappled, and boarded. If the *datholch* has been harmed, woe betide you."

"First you have to do the overhauling. Second you have to convince me that any woe you can think of betides me worse than what does already. I suggest you check with the *qanryf* before you get reckless. Meanwhile," and in Anglic, "cheerio." Flandry cut the circuit.

At his velocity, he had crossed the Hellkettle Mountains. The northlands stretched vast and drear beneath, gleaming ice, glittering snow, blots that were blizzards. He cast about with his instruments for a really huge storm. There was sure to be one somewhere, this time of year . . . yes!

A wall of murk towered from earth to high heaven. Before he had pierced it, Flandry felt the thrust and heard the scream of hurricane-force winds. When he was inside, blackness and chaos had him.

A corvette would not go into such a tempest. Nothing except a weathership had any business in one; others could flit above or around readily enough. But a small spaceboat with a first-class pilot—a pilot who had begun his career in aircraft and aerial combat—could live in the fury. And detectors, straining from outside, would lose her.

Flandry lost himself in the battle to keep alive.

Half an hour later, he broke free and shot into space.

Talwin rolled enormous in his screens. Halfway down from either pole coruscated winter's whiteness; the cloud-marbled blue of seas between icecaps looked black by contrast. Flandry waved. "Goodbye," he said anew. "Good luck."

Meters shouted to his eyes of patrol ships waiting for him. You didn't normally risk hyperdrive this near a planet or a sun. Matter density was too great, as was the chance of gravitation desynchronizing your quantum jumps. The immediate scene was scarcely normal. Flandry's hands danced.

Switchover to secondary state in so strong a field made the hull ring. Screens changed to the faster-than-light optical compensation mode. Talwin was gone and Siekh dwindling among the stars. The air droned. The deck shivered.

After minutes, a beep drew Flandry's attention to a telltale. "Well," he said, "one skipper's decided to be brave and copy us. He got away with it, too, and locked onto our 'wake.' His wouldn't register that steady a bearing otherwise. We're faster, but I'm afraid we won't shake him before he's served as a guide to others who can outpace us."

Djana stirred. She had sat mute—lost, he thought when he could spare her a thought—while they ran the polar storm. Her face turned to him beneath its heavy coif of hair. "Have you any hope?" she asked tonelessly.

He punched for navigational data. "A stern chase is a long chase," he said, "and I've heard about a pulsar not many parsecs off. It may help us shed our importunate colleagues."

She made no response, simply looked back out at space. Either she didn't know how dangerous a pulsar was, or she didn't care.

CHAPTER NINETEEN

Once a blue giant sun had burned, 50,000 times more luminous than yet-unborn Sol. It lasted for a bare few million years; then the hydrogen fuel necessary to stay on the main sequence was gone. The star collapsed. In the unimaginable violence of a supernova, momentarily blazing to equal an entire galaxy, it went out.

Such energies did not soon bleed away. For ages the blown-off upper layers formed a nebula of lacy loveliness around the core, which shone less white-hot than X-ray hot. Eventually the gases dissipated, a part of them to make new suns and planets. The globe that remained continued shrinking under its own weight until density reached tons per cubic centimeter and spin was measured in seconds. Feebler and feebler did it shine, white dwarf, black dwarf, neutron star—

Compressed down near the ultimate that nature's law permitted, the atoms (if they could still be called that) went into their final transitions. Photons spurted forth, were pumped through the weirdly distorted space-time within and around the core, at last won freedom to flee at light speed. Strangely regular were those bursts, though slowly their frequencies, amplitudes, and rate declined back toward extinction—dying gasps.

Pulsar breath.

Djana stared as if hypnotized into the forward screen. Tiny but waxing among the stars went that red blink . . . blink . . . blink. She did not recall having ever seen a sight more lonely. The cabin's warmth and glow made blacker the emptiness outside; engine throb and ventilator murmur deepened the eternal silence of those infinite spaces.

She laid a hand on Flandry's arm. "Nicky—"

"Quiet." His eyes never left the board before him; his fingers walked back and forth across computer keys.

"Nicky, we can die any minute, and you've said hardly a word to me."

"Stop bothering me or we will for sure die."

She retreated into her chair. *Be strong, be strong.*

He had bound her in place for most of the hours during which the boat flew. She didn't resent that; he couldn't trust her, and he must clean himself and snatch some sleep. Afterward he brought sandwiches to his captives— she might have slipped a drug into his—and released her. But at once he was nailed to instrument and calculations. He showed no sign of feeling the wishes she thrust at him; his will to liberty overrode them.

Now he crouched above the pilot panel. He'd not been able to cut his hair; the mane denied shaven countenance, prim coverall, machine-controlling hands, and declared him a male animal who hunted.

And was hunted. Four Merseian ships bayed on his heels. He'd told her about them before he went to rest, estimating they would close the gap in 25 light-years. From Siekh to the pulsar was 17.

Blink . . . blink . . . blink . . . once in 1.3275 seconds.

Numbers emerged on a plate set into the console. Flandry nodded. He took the robotic helm. Stars wheeled with his shift of course.

In time he said, maybe to himself: "Yes. They're decelerating. They don't dare come in this fast."

"What?" Djana whispered.

"The pursuit. They spot us aiming nearly straight on for that lighthouse. Get too close—easy to do at hyperspeed—and the gravity gradient will pluck you apart. Why share the risk we have to take? If we don't make it, Ydwyr will've been more expendable than a whole ship and crew. If we do survive, they can catch us later."

And match phase, and lay alongside, and force a way *in* to rescue Ydwyr . . . and her . . . but Nicky, Nicky they would haul off to burn his brain out.

Should it matter? I'll be sorry, we both will be sorry for you, but Merseia—

He turned his head. His grin and gray eyes broke across her like morning. "That's what they think," he said.

I only care because you're a man, the one man in all this wasteland, and do I care for any man? Only my body does, my sinful body. She struggled to raise Ydwyr's face.

Flandry leaned over and cupped her chin in his right hand. "I'm sorry to've been rude," he smiled. "Sorrier to play games with your life. I should have insisted you stay on Talwin. When you wanted to come, with everything else on my mind I sort of assumed you'd decided you preferred freedom."

"I was free," she said frantically. "I followed my master."

"Odd juxtaposition, that." A buzzer sounded. "'Scuse, I got work. We go primary in half a shake. I've programed the autopilot, but in conditions this tricky I want to ride herd on it."

"Primary?" Dismay washed through her. "They'll catch you right away!" *That's good. Isn't it?*

The engine note changed. Star images vanished till the screens readapted. At true speed, limited by light's, the boat plunged on. Power chanted abaft the cabin; she was changing her kinetic velocity at maximum thrust.

Blink . . . blink . . . blink . . . The blood-colored beacon glowed ever brighter. Yet Djana could look directly into it, and she did not find any disc. Stars frosted the night around. Which way was the Empire?

Flandry had given himself back to the machines. Twice he made a manual adjustment.

After minutes wherein Djana begged God to restore Merseian courage to her, the noise and vibration stopped. Head full of it, she didn't instantly recognize its departure. Then she bit her tongue to keep from imploring a word.

When Flandry gave her one, she started shivering.

He spoke calmly, as if these were the lost days when they two had fared after treasure. "We're in the slot, near's I can determine. Let's relax and give the universe our job for a bit."

"Wh-wh-what are we doing?"

"We're falling free, in a hyperbolic orbit around the

pulsar. The Merseians aren't. They're distributing themselves to cover the region. They can't venture as close as
us. The potential of so monstrous a mass in so small a
volume, you see; differential forces would wreck their ships.
The boat's less affected, being of smaller dimensions.
With the help of the interior field—the same that gives us
artificial gravity and counteracts acceleration pressure—
she ought to stay in one piece. The Merseians doubtless
figure to wait till we kick in our hyperdrive again, and
resume the chivvy."

"But what're we getting?" Blink . . . blink . . . blink . . .
Had his winter exile driven him crazy?

"We'll pass through the fringes of a heavily warped
chunk of space. The mass concentration deforms it. If the
core got much denser, light itself couldn't break loose. We
won't be under any such extreme condition, but I don't
expect they can track us around periastron. Our emission
will be too scattered; radar beams will curve off at silly
angles. The Merseians can compute roughly where and
when we'll return to flatter space, but until we do—"
Flandry had unharnessed himself while he talked. Rising,
he stretched prodigiously, muscle by muscle. "À propos
Merseians, let's go check on old Ydwyr."

Djana fumbled with her own buckles. "I, I, I *don't*
track you, Nicky," she stammered. "What do we . . . you
gain more than time? Why did you take us aboard?"

"As to your first question, the answer's a smidge
technical. As to the second, well, Ydwyr's the reason we've
come this far. Without him, we'd've been in a missile
barrage." Flandry walked around behind her chair. "Here,
let me assist."

"You! You're not unfastening me!"

"No, I'm not, am I?" he said dreamily. Leaning over, he nuzzled her where throat met shoulder. The kiss that followed brought a breathless giddiness which had not quite faded when he led the way aft.

Ydwyr sat patient on a bunk. Prior to sleeping, Flandry had welded a short length of light cable to the frame, the other end around an ankle, and untied the rope. It wasn't a harsh confinement. In fact, the man would have to keep wits and gun ready when negotiating this passage.

"Have you been listening to our conversation?" he asked. "I left the intercom on."

"You are thanked for your courtesy," Ydwyr replied, "but I could not follow the Anglic."

"Oh!" Djana's hand went to her mouth. "I forgot—"

"And I," Flandry admitted. "We Terrans tend to assume every educated being will know our official language—by definition—and of course it isn't so. Well, I can tell you."

"I believe I have deduced it," Ydwyr said. "You are swinging free, dangerously but concealingly near the pulsar. From the relativistic region you will launch your courier torpedoes, strapped together and hyperdrives operating simultaneously. What with distortion effects, you hope my folk will mistake the impulses for this boat's and give chase. If your decoy lures them as far as a light-year off, you will be outside their hyperwave detection range and can embark on a roundabout homeward voyage. The sheer size of space will make it unlikely that they, backtracking, will pick up your vibrations."

"Right," Flandry said admiringly. "You're a sharp rascal. I look forward to some amusing chit-chat."

"If your scheme succeeds." Ydwyr made a salute of respect. "If not, and if we are taken alive, you are under my protection."

Gladness burst in Djana. *My men can be friends!*

"You are kind," said Flandry with a bow. He turned to the girl. "How about making us a pot of tea?" he said in Anglic.

"Tea?" she asked, astonished.

"He likes it. Let's be hospitable. Put the galley intercom on—low—and you can hear us talk."

Flandry spoke lightly, but she felt an underlining of his last sentence and all at once her joy froze. *Though why, why?* "Would . . . the *datholch* . . . accept tea?" she asked in Eriau.

"You are thanked." Ydwyr spoke casually, more interested in the man. Djana went forward like an automaton. The voices trailed her:

"I am less kind, Dominic Flandry, than I am concerned to keep an audacious and resourceful entity functional."

"For a servant?"

"*Khraich,* we cannot well send you home, can we? I—"

Djana made a production of closing the galley door. It cut off the words. Fingers unsteady, she turned the intercom switch.

"—sorry. You mean well by your standards, I suppose, Ydwyr. But I have this archaic prejudice for freedom over even the nicest slavery. Like the sort you fastened on that poor girl."

"A reconditioning. It improved her both physically and mentally."

No! He might be speaking of an animal!

"She does seem more, hm, balanced. It's just a seeming, however, as long as you keep that father-image hood over her eyes."

"Hr-r-r, you have heard of Aycharaych's techniques, then?"

"Aycharaych? Who? N-n-no . . . I'll check with Captain Abrams . . . Damn! I should have played along with you, shouldn't I? All right, I fumbled that one, after you dropped it right into my paws. Getting back to Djana, the father fixation is unmistakable to any careful outside observer."

"What else would you have me do? She came, an unwitting agent who had acquired knowledge which must not get back to Terra. She showed potentialities. Instead of killing her out of hand, we could try to develop them. Death is always available. Besides, depth-psychological work on a human intrigued me. Later, when that peculiar gift for sometimes imposing her desires on other minds appeared, we saw what a prize we had. My duty became to make sure of her."

"So to win her trust, you warned her to warn me?"

"Yes. About—in honesty between us, Dominic Flandry—a fictitious danger. No orders had come for your removal; I was welcome to keep you. But the chance to clinch it with her was worth more."

Anglic: "No! I'll—be—especially—damned."

"You are not angry, I hope."

"N-n-no. That'd be unsporting, wouldn't it?" Anglic: "The more so when it caused me to break from my cell with a hell of a yell far sooner than I'd expected to."

"Believe me, I did not wish to sacrifice you. I did not

want to be involved in that wretched business at all. Honor compelled me. But I begrudged every minute away from my Talwinian research."

Djana knelt on the deck and wept.

Blink . . . blink . . . blink . . . furnace glare spearing from the screens. The hull groaned and shuddered with stresses. Fighting them, the interior field set air ashake in a wild thin singing. Often, looking down a passage, you thought you saw it ripple; and perhaps it did, sliding through some acute bend in space. From time to time hideous nauseas twisted you, and your mind grew blurred. Sunward was only the alternation of night and red. Starward were no constellations nor points of light, nothing but rainbow blotches and smears.

Djana helped Flandry put the courier torpedoes, which he had programed under normal conditions, on the launch rack. When they were outside, he must don a spacesuit and go couple them. He was gone a long while and came back white and shaken. "Done," was everything he would tell her.

They sought the conn. He sat down, she on his lap, and they held each other through the nightmare hours. "You're real," she kept babbling. "You're real."

And the strangeness faded. Quietness, solidity, stars returned one by one. A haggard Flandry pored over instruments whose readings again made sense, about which he could again think clearly.

"Receding hyperwakes," he breathed. "Our stunt worked. Soon's we stop registering them—First, though, we turn our systems off."

"Why?" she asked from her seat to which she had returned, and from her weariness.

"I can't tell how many the ships are. Space is still somewhat kinky and—well, they may have left one posted for insurance. The moment we pass a threshold value of the metric, there'll be no mistaking our radiation, infrared from the hull, neutrinos from the powerplant, that kind of junk. Unless we douse the sources."

"Whatever you want, darling."

Weightlessness was like stepping off a cliff and dropping without end. Cabin dark, the pulsar flash on one side and stars on the other crowded near in dreadful glory. Nothing remained save the faintest accumulator-powered susurrus of forced ventilation; and the cold crept inward.

"Hold me," Djana beseeched into the blindness. "Warm me."

A pencil-thin flashbeam from Flandry's hand slipped along the console. Back-scattered light limned him, a shadow. Silence lengthened and lengthened until:

"Uh-oh. They're smart as I feared. Gray waves. Somebody under primary acceleration. Has to be a ship of theirs."

Son of Man, help us.

At the boat's high kinetic velocity, the pulsar shrank and dimmed while they watched.

"Radar touch," Flandry reported tonelessly.

"Th-they've caught us?"

"M-m-m, they may assume we're a bit of cosmic debris. You can't check out every blip on your scope. . . . Oof! They're applying a new vector. Wish I dared use the computer. It looks to me as if they're maneuvering for an intercept with us, but I'd need math to make sure."

"If they are?" *The abstractness of it, that's half the horror. A reading, an equation, and me closed off from touching you, even seeing you. We're not us, we're objects. Like being already dead—no, that's not right, Jesus promised we'll live. He did.*

"They aren't necessarily. No beam's latched onto us. I suspect they've been casting about more or less at random. We registered strong enough to rate a closer look, but they lost and haven't refound us. Interplanetary space is bigger than most people imagine. So they may as well direct themselves according to the orbit this whatsit seemed to have, in hopes of checking us out at shorter range."

"Will they?"

"I don't know. If we're caught . . . well, I suppose we should eschew a last-ditch stand. How would one dig a ditch in vacuum? We can surrender, hope Ydwyr can save us and another chance'll come to worm out." His voice in the dark was not as calm as he evidently wished.

"You'd trust Ydwyr?" lashed from her.

His beam stepped across the dials. "Closing in fast," he said. "Radar sweep's bound to pick us up soon. We *may* show as an interstellar asteroid, but considering the probability of a natural passage at any given time—" She heard and felt his despair. "Sorry, sweetheart. We gave 'em a good try, didn't we?"

The image might have sprung to her physical vision, shark shape across the Milky Way, man's great foes black-clad at the guns. She reached out to the stars of heaven.

"God have mercy," she cried with her whole being. "Oh, send them back where they belong!"

Blink . . . blink . . . blink.

The light ray danced. Where it touched, meters turned into pools beneath those suns that crowded the screens. "Ho-o-old," Flandry murmured. "One minute . . . They're receding!" exploded from him. "Judas priest, they, they must've decided the blip didn't mean anything!"

"They're going?" she heard herself blurt. "They are?"

"Yes. They are. Can't've felt too strongly about that stray indication they got. . . . Whoo! They've gone hyper! Already! Aimed back toward Siekh, seems like. And the— here, we can use our circuits again, lemme activate the secondary-wave receivers first—yes, yes, four indications, our couriers, their other three ships, right on the verge of detectability, headed out—Djana, we did it! Judas priest!"

"Not Judas, dear," she said in worship. "Jesus."

"Anybody you like." Flandry turned on the fluoros. Joy torrented from him. "You yourself—your wonderful, wonderful self—" Weight. Warm hearty gusts of air. Flandry was doing a fandango around the cabin. "We can take off ourselves inside an hour. Go a long way round for safety's sake—but at the end, home!" He surged to embrace her. "And never mind Ydwyr," he warbled. "We're going to celebrate the whole way back!"

CHAPTER TWENTY

Standing in the cramped, thrumming space between bulkheads, beyond reach of him who sat chained, the Terran said: "You appreciate that the whole truth about what happened would embarrass me. I want your solemn promise you'll support my account and drop no hint concerning Wayland."

"Why should I agree?" the Merseian asked blandly.

"Because if you don't," Djana told him—venom seethed in each word—"I'll have the pleasure of killing you."

"No, no, spare the dramatics," Flandry said. "Especially since he too considers an oath under duress is worthless. Ydwyr, the pilot's data list various planets where I could let you off. You can survive. A few have intelligent natives to study. Their main drawback is that no one has found any particular reason to revisit them, so you may have a slight problem in publishing your findings. But if you don't mind, I don't."

"Is that not a threat?" the prisoner rumbled.

"No more than your threat to expose my, ah, sideline financial interests. Talwin's bound to lose its military value whatever becomes of you or me. Suppose I throw in that I'll do what I can to help keep your scientific station alive. Under the circumstances, does that bargain sound fair?"

"Done!" Ydwyr said. He swore to the terms by the formulas of honor. Afterward he extended a hand. "And for your part, let us shake on it."

Flandry did. Djana watched, gripping a stunner. "You're not figuring to turn him loose now, are you?" she demanded.

"No, I'm afraid that can't be included in the deal," Flandry said. "Unless you'll give me your parole, Ydwyr."

The girl looked hurt and puzzled, then relieved when the Merseian answered:

"I will not. You are too competent. My duty is to kill you if I can." He smiled. "With that made clear, would you like a game of chess?"

Mining continued here and there in the system to which Irumclaw belonged. Hence small human colonies persisted, with mostly floating populations that weren't given to inconvenient curiosity or to gossiping with officialdom about what they might have seen.

Jake put briefly down in a spaceport on the fourth world out. It was a spot of shabbiness set in the middle of an immense rusty desert. The atmosphere was not breathable, and barely thick enough to blow dust clouds into a purple sky. A gangtube reached forth to connect airlock with airdome. Flandry escorted Djana to the exit.

"You'll be through soon?" she asked wistfully. For a moment the small slender form in the modest gown, the fine-boned features, eyes like blue lakes, lips slightly parted and aquiver, made him forget what had passed between them and think of her as a child. He had always been a sucker for little girls.

"Soon's I can," he answered. "Probably under a week. But do lie doggo till you hear from me. It's essential we report jointly to Leon Ammon. Those credits you brought with you ought to stretch. Check the general message office daily. When my 'gram comes, go ahead and shoot him word to have somebody fetch you. I'll be standing by." He kissed her more lightly than had been his wont. "Cheers, partner."

Her response was feverish. "Partners, yes!" she said afterward, in an unsteady tone. A tear broke away. She turned and walked fast from the airlock. Flandry went back to the conn and requested immediate clearance for takeoff.

Above his gorgeous tunic, Admiral Julius wore the least memorable face that Flandry had ever seen. "Well!" he said. "Quite a story, Lieutenant. Quite a story."

"Yes, sir," Flandry responded. He stood beside Ydwyr, who tail-sat at ease—if with ill-concealed contempt for the ornate office—in a robe that had been hastily improvised for him. His winter garb being unsuitable for shipboard, he had traveled nude and debarked thus on Irumclaw; and you *don't* receive princes of the blood in their nakedness.

"Ah . . . indeed." Julius shuffled some papers on his desk. "As I understand your—your supervisor's verbal redaction of what you told him—you are writing a report in proper form, are you not?—as I understand it . . . well, why don't you tell me yourself?"

"Yes, sir. Cruising on my assigned route, I detected the wake of a larger vessel. As per standing orders, I moved closer to establish identification. She was an unmistakable Merseian warcraft. My orders gave me discretion, as the admiral knows, whether to report the sighting in person with no further ado or attempt finding out more. Rightly or wrongly, I decided on the second course. Chances were against another encounter and we might be left with no further leads. I dropped back and sent a courier, which apparently never got here. My report's going to recommend tightening inspection procedures.

"Well, I shadowed the Merseian at the limits of detectability—for me—which I thought would keep my smaller vessel outside her sensor range. But we entered the range of another ship, a picket, that spotted me, closed in, and made capture. I was brought to the planet Talwin, where the Merseians turned out to have an advanced base. After miscellaneous brouhaha, I escaped via a pulsar, taking this dignitary along for a hostage."

"Um-m-m, ah." Julius squinted at Ydwyr. "An awkward affair, yes. They were technically within their rights, building that base, weren't they? But they had no right to hold an Imperial vessel and an Imperial officer . . . in a region free by treaty. Um." It was blatant that he shrank from being caught in the middle of a diplomatic crisis.

"If it please the admiral," Flandry said, "I speak Eriau. The *datholch* and I have held some long conversations. Without attempting to make policy or anything, sir—I know I'm forbidden to—I did feel free to suggest a few

thoughts. Would the admiral care to have me interpret?"
It had turned out the base's linguistic computer was on the
fritz and nobody knew how to fix it.

"Ah . . . yes. Certainly. Tell his, ah, his highness we
consider him a guest of the Imperium. We will try to, ah,
show him every courtesy and arrange for his speedy
transportation home."

"He's physicked anxious to shoot you off and bury this
whole affair deep," Flandry informed Ydwyr. "We can do
anything we choose with him."

"You will proceed according to plan, then?" the scientist
inquired. His expression was composed, but Flandry had
learned how to recognize a sardonic twinkle in a Merseian
eye.

"*Khraich,* not exactly a plan. The fact of Talwin cannot be hidden. GHQ will see a report and assign an investigator. What we want is to save face all around. You've been
offered a ride back, as I guessed you would be. Accept it
for the earliest possible moment. When you reach Talwin,
get Morioch to evacuate his ships and personnel. The
planet will be of no further use for intelligence operations
anyway; your government's sure to order them shut down.
If our Navy team finds nothing going on but peaceful
xenological research, they'll gloss over what signs are left
of extracurricular activity, and nothing will likely be said
on either side about this contretemps that you and I were
involved in."

"I have already assented to your making these proposals
in my name. Proceed."

Flandry did, in more tactful language. Julius beamed.
If his command was instrumental in halting an undesirable

Merseian project, word would circulate among the higher-ups. It would influence promotions, rotation to more promising worlds, yes, yes, no matter how discreetly the affair was handled. *A discretion which'll result in nobody's caring to notice whatever loose ends dangle out of my story,* Flandry thought.

"Excellent, Lieutenant!" Julius said. "My precise idea! Tell his highness I'll make prompt arrangements."

Ydwyr said gravely: "I fear the research will not long endure. With no bonus of military advantage—"

"I told you I'd do my best for you," Flandry answered, "and I've been mulling a scheme. Didn't want to advance it till I was sure we could write our own playbill, but now I am. See, I'll put on an indignation act for you. Maybe your folk should not have detained me; still, you are of the Vach Urdiolch and my cavalier treatment of you was an insult to the Race. Seeing that he's avid to please, you've decided to milk old Julius. You'll let yourself be mollified if he'll strongly urge that the Imperium help support the scientific work which, officially, will have been Merseia's reason for being on Talwin in the first place."

The big green body tautened. "Is that possible?"

"I imagine so. We'll have to keep watch on Talwin from here on anyway, lest your Navy sneak back. It needn't be from scoutboats, though. A few subsidized students or the like, doing their graduate thesis work, are quite as good and a lot cheaper. And . . . with us sharing the costs, I daresay you can find money at home to carry on."

A small renaissance of Terran science? Hardly. Academic hackwork. Oh, I suppose I can indulge in the hope.

"In the name of the God." Ydwyr stared before him for a length of time that made Julius shift and harrumph. At last he gripped both of Flandry's hands and said, "From that beginning, our two people working together, what may someday come?"

Nothing much, except, I do dare hope, a slight reinforcement of the reasons for our hanging onto this frontier. Those Merseians may keep us reminded who's always ready to fill any available vacuum. "The *datholch* bears a noble dream."

"What's this?" Julius puffed. "What are you two doing?"

"Sir, I'm afraid we've hit a rock or two," Flandry said.

"Really? How long will this take? I have a dinner engagement."

"Maybe we can settle the difficulty before then, sir. May I be seated? I thank the admiral. I'll do my best, sir. Got my personal affairs to handle too."

"No doubt." Julius regarded the young man calculatingly. "I am told you've applied for furlough and reassignment."

"Yes, sir. I figure those months on Talwin more than completed my tour of duty here. No reflection on this fine command, but I am supposed to specialize along other lines. And I believe I may have an inheritance coming. Rich uncle on a colonial planet wasn't doing too well, last I heard. I'd like to go collect my share before they decide a 'missing in action' report on me authorizes them to divvy up the cash elsewhere."

"Yes. I see. I'll approve your application, Lieutenant, and recommend you for promotion." ("If you bail me fast out of this mess" was understood.) "Let's get busy. What is the problem you mentioned?"

The room above Door 666 was unchanged, a less tasteful place to be than the commandant's and a considerably more dangerous one. The Gorzunian guard stirred no muscle; but light gleamed off a scimitar thrust under his gun belt. Behind the desk, Leon Ammon sweated and squeaked and never took his needle gaze off Flandry. Djana gave him head-high defiance in return; her fists, though, kept clenching and unclenching on her lap, and she had moved her chair into direct contact with the officer's.

He himself talked merrily, ramblingly, and on the whole, discounting a few reticences, truthfully. At the end he said, "I'll accept my fee—in small bills, remember— with unparalleled grace."

"You sure kept me waiting," Ammon hedged. "Cost me extra, trying to find out what'd happened and recruit somebody else. I ought to charge the cost to your payment. Right?"

"The delay wasn't my fault. You should have given your agent better protection, or remuneration such that she had no incentive to visit persons to whom she'd not been introduced." Flandry buffed fingernails on tunic and regarded them critically. "You have what you contracted for, a report on Wayland, favorable at that."

"But you said the secret's been spilled. The Merseians—"

"My friend Ydwyr the Seeker assures me he'll keep silence. The rest of whatever personnel on Talwin have heard about the Mimirian System will shortly be dispersed. In any event, why should they mention a thing that can help Terra? Oh, rumors may float around, but you only need five or ten years' concealment and communication is poor enough to guarantee you that." Flandry reached for a cigarette. Having shed the addiction in these past months, he was enjoying its return. "Admittedly," he said, "if I release Ydwyr from his promise, he may well chance to pass this interesting item—complete with coordinates— on to the captain of whatever Imperial ship arrives to look his camp over."

Ammon barked a laugh. "I expected a response from you, Dominic. You're a sharp-edge boy." He stroked his chins. "You thought about maybe resigning your commission? I could use a sharp-edge boy. You know I pay good. Right?"

"I'll know that when I've counted the bundle," Flandry said. He inhaled the tobacco into lighting and rolled smoke around his palate.

The gross bulk wallowed forward in its chair. The bald countenance hardened. "What about the agent who got to Djana?" Ammon demanded. "And what about her?"

"Ah, yes," Flandry answered. "You owe her a tidy bit, you realize."

"What? After she—"

"After she, having been trapped because of your misguided sense of economy, obtained for you the information that you've been infiltrated, yes, dear heart, you are in her debt," Flandry smiled like a tiger. "Naturally, I didn't mention the incident in my official report. I can always put my corps on the trail of those

Merseian agents without compromising myself, as for example by sending an anonymous tip. However, I felt you might prefer to deal with them yourself. Among other inducements, they've probably also corrupted members of your esteemed competitor associations. You might well obtain facts useful in your business relationships. I'm confident your interrogators are persuasive."

"They are," Ammon said. "*Who is the spy?*"

Djana started to speak. Flandry forestalled her with a reminding gesture. "The information is the property of this young lady. She's willing to negotiate terms for its transfer. I am her agent."

Sweat studded Ammon's visage. "Pay her—when she tried to sell me out?"

"My client Djana will be leaving Irumclaw by the first available ship. Incidentally, I'm booking passage on the same one. She needs funds for her ticket, plus a reasonable stake at her destination, whatever it may be."

Ammon spat a vileness. The Gorzunian sensed rage and bunched his shaggy body for attack.

Flandry streamed smoke out his nose. "As her agent," he went mildly on, "I've taken the normal precautions to assure that any actions to her detriment will prove unprofitable. You may as well relax and enjoy this, Leon. It'll be expensive at best, and the rate goes up if you use too much of our valuable time. I repeat, you can take an adequate return out of the hide of that master spy, when you've purchased the name."

Ammon waved his goon back. Hatred thickening his voice, he settled down to dicker.

✲ ✲ ✲

No liners plied this far out. The *Cha-Rina* was a tramp freighter with a few extra accommodations modifiable for various races. She offered little in the way of luxuries. Flandry and Djana brought along what pleasant items they were able to find in Old Town's stores. No other humans were aboard, and apart from the skipper, who spent her free hours in the composition of a caterwauling sonata, the Cynthian crew spoke scant Anglic. So they had privacy.

Their first few days of travel were pure hedonism. To sleep out the nightwatch, lie abed till the clock said noon, loaf about and eat, drink, read, watch a projected show, play handball, listen to music, make love in comfort—before everything else, to have no dangers and no duties—seemed ample splendor. But the ship approached Ysabeau, itself richly endowed with cities and a transfer point for everywhere else in the bustling impersonal vastness of the Empire; and they had said nothing yet about the future.

"Captain's dinner," Flandry decreed. While he stood over the cook, and ended preparing most of the delicacies himself, Djana ornamented their cabin with what cloths and furs she could find. Thereafter she spent a long while ornamenting herself. For dress she chose the thinnest, fluffiest blue gown she owned. Flandry returned, slipped into red-and-gold mufti, and popped the cork on the first champagne bottle.

They dined, and drank, and chatted, and laughed through a couple of hours. He pretended not to see that she was forcing her mirth. The moment when he must notice came soon enough.

He poured brandy, lounged back, sniffed and sipped. "Aahh! Almost as tasty as you, my love."

She regarded him across the tiny, white-clothed table. Behind her a viewscreen gave on crystal dark and a magnificence of stars. The ship shivered and hummed ever so faintly, the air was fragrant with odors from the cleared-away dishes, and with the perfume she had chosen. Her great eyes fell to rest and he could not dip his own from them.

"You use that word a lot," she said, quiet-voiced. "Love."

"Appropriate, isn't it?" Uneasiness tugged at him.

"Is it? What do you intend to do, Nicky?"

"Why . . . make a dummy trip to 'claim my inheritance.' Not that anybody'd check on me especially, but it's an excuse to play tourist. When my leave's up, I report to Terra, no less, for the next assignment. I daresay somebody in a lofty echelon has gotten word about the Talwin affair and wants to talk to me—which won't hurt the old career a bit, eh?"

"You've told me that before. You know it's not what I meant. Why have you never said anything about us?"

He reached for a cigarette while taking a fresh swallow of brandy. "I have, I have," he countered, smiling hard. "With a substantial sum in your purse, you should do well if you make the investments I suggested. They'll buy you a peaceful life on a congenial planet; or, if you prefer to shoot for larger stakes, they'll get you entry into at least the cellars of the *haut monde*."

She bit her lip. "I've been dreading this," she said.

"Hey? Uh, you may've had a trifle more than optimum to drink, Djana. I'll ring for coffee."

"No." She clenched fingers about the stem of her

glass, raised it and tossed off the contents in a gulp. Setting it down: "Yes," she said, "I did kind of guzzle tonight. On purpose. You see, I had to form the habit of not thinking past any time when I was feeling good, because knowing a bad time was sure to come, I'd spoil the good time. A . . . an inhibition. Ydwyr taught me how to order my inhibitions out of my way, but I didn't want to use any stunt of that bastard's—"

"He's not a bad bastard. I've grown positively fond of him."

"—and besides, I wanted to pull every trick in my bag on you, and for that I needed to be happy, really happy. Well, tonight's my last chance. Oh, I suppose I could stay around a while—"

"I wouldn't advise it," Flandry said in haste. He'd been looking forward to searching for variety in the fleshpots of the Empire. "I'll be too peripatetic."

Djana shoved her glass toward him. He poured, a clear gurgle in a silence where, through the humming, he could hear her breathe.

"Uh-huh," she said. "I had to know tonight. That's why I got a touch looped, to help me ask." She lifted the glass. Her gaze stayed on his while she drank. Stars made a frosty coronet for her hair. When she had finished, she was not flushed. "I'll speak straight," she said. "I thought . . . we made a good pair, Nicky, didn't we, once things got straightened out? . . . I thought it wouldn't hurt to ask if you'd like to keep on. No, wait, I don't have any notions about me as an agent. But I could be there whenever you got back."

Well, let's get it over with. Flandry laid a hand on one

of hers. "You honor me beyond my worth, dear," he said. "It isn't possible—"

"I supposed not." Had Ydwyr taught her that instant steely calm? "You'd never forget what I've been."

"I assure you, I'm no prude. But—"

"I mean my turnings, my treasons. . . . Oh, let's forget I spoke, Nicky, darling. It was just a hope. I'll be fine. Let's enjoy our evening together; and maybe, you know, maybe sometime we'll meet again."

The thought slashed through him. He sat straight with a muttered exclamation. *Why didn't that occur to me before?*

She stared. "Is something wrong?"

He ran angles and aspects through his head, chuckled gleefully at the result, and squeezed her fingers. "Contrariwise," he said, "I've hit on a sort of answer. If you're interested."

"What? I—What *is* it?"

"Well," he said, "you brushed off the idea of yourself in my line of work as a fantasy, but weren't you too quick? You've proven you're tough and smart, not to mention beautiful and charming. On top of that, there's this practically unique wild talent of yours. And Ydwyr wouldn't be hard to convince you've zigzagged back to him. Our Navy Intelligence will jump for joy to have you, after I pass word along the channels open to me. We'd see each other often, I daresay, perhaps now and then we'd work together. . . . why, even if they get you into the Roidhunate as a double agent—"

He stopped. Horror confronted him.

"What . . . what's the matter?" he faltered.

Her lips moved several times before she could speak. Her eyes stayed dry and had gone pale, as if a flame had passed behind them. There was no hue at all in her face.

"You too," she got out.

"Huh? I don't—"

She checked him by lifting a hand. "Everybody," she said, "as far back as I can remember. Ending with Ydwyr, and now you."

"What in cosmos?"

"Using me." Her tone was flat, not loud in the least. She stared past him. "You know," she said, "the funny part is, I wanted to be used. I wanted to give, serve, help, belong to somebody. . . . But you only saw a tool. A thing. Every one of you."

"Djana, I give you my word of honor—"

"Honor?" She shook her head, slowly. "It's a strange feeling," she told her God, in a voice turned high and puzzled, like that of a child who cannot understand, "to learn, once and forever, that there's no one who cares. Not even You."

She squared her shoulders. "Well, I'll manage."

Her look focused on Flandry, who sat helpless and gaping. "As for you," she said levelly, "I guess I can't stop you from having almost any woman who comes by. But I'll wish this, that you never get the one you really want."

He thought little of her remark, then. "You're over-wrought," he said, hoping sharpness would work. "Drunk. Hysterical."

"Whatever you want," she said wearily. "Please go away."

He left, and arranged for a doss elsewhere. Next

mornwatch the ship landed on Ysabeau. Djana walked down the gangway without saying goodbye to Flandry. He watched her, shrugged, sighed—*Women! The aliens among us!*—and sauntered alone toward the shuttle into town, where he could properly celebrate his victory.

THE REBEL WORLDS

———————— ✳ ————————

---- ✦ ----

Make oneness.

I/we: Feet belonging to Guardian Of North Gate and others who can be, to Raft Farer and Woe who will no longer be, to Many Thoughts, Cave Discoverer, and Master Of Songs who can no longer be; Wings belonging to Iron Miner and Lightning Struck The House and others to be, to Many Thoughts who can no longer be; young Hands that has yet to share memories: make oneness.

(O light, wind, river! They flood too strongly, they tear me/us apart.)

Strength. This is not the first young Hands which has come here to remember the journey that was made so many years before he/she was born; nor shall this be the last. Think strength, think calm.

(Blurred, two legs, faceless . . . no, had they beaks?)

Remember. Lie down at ease where leaves whisper beneath hues of upthrusting land coral; drink light and wind and sound of the river. Let reminiscence flow freely, of deeds that were done before this my/our Hands came to birth.

(Clearer, now: so very strange they were, how can the sight of them even be seen, let alone held in me/us? . . .

Answer: The eye learns to see them, the nose to smell them, the ear to hear them, the tongue of the Feet and the limbs of the Wings and the Hands to touch their skins and feel, the tendrils to taste what they exude.)

This goes well. More quickly than usual. Perhaps i/we can become a good oneness that will often have reason to exist.

(Flicker of joy. Tide of terror at the rising memories— alienness, peril, pain, death, rebirth to torment.)

Lie still. It was long ago.

But time too is one. Now is unreal; only past-and-future has the length to be real. What happened then must be known to Us. Feel in every fiber of my/our young Hands, that i/we am/are part of Us—We of Thunderstone, Ironworkers, Fellers and Builders, Plowers, Housedwellers, and lately Traders—and that each oneness We may create must know of those who come from beyond heaven, lest their dangerous marvels turn into Our ruin.

Wherefore let Hands unite with Feet and Wings. Let the oneness once again recall and reflect on the journey of Cave Discoverer and Woe, in those days when the strangers, who had but single bodies and yet could talk, marched overmountain to an unknown battle. With every such reflection, as with every later encounter, i/we gain a little more insight, go a little further along the trail that leads to understanding them.

Though it may be that on that trail, We are traveling in a false direction. The unit who led them said on a certain night that he/she/it/? doubted if they understood themselves, or ever would.

CHAPTER ONE

The prison satellite swung in a wide and canted orbit around Llynathawr, well away from normal space traffic. Often a viewport in Hugh McCormac's cell showed him the planet in different phases. Sometimes it was a darkness, touched with red-and-gold sunrise on one edge, perhaps the city Catawrayannis flickering like a star upon its night. Sometimes it was a scimitar, the sun burning dazzlingly close. Now and then he saw it full, a round shield of brilliance, emblazoned on oceans azure with clouds argent above continents vert and tenné.

Terra looked much the same at the same distance. (Closer in, you became aware that she was haggard, as is any former beauty who has been used by too many men.) But Terra was a pair of light-centuries removed. And neither world resembled rusty, tawny Aeneas for which McCormac's eyes hungered.

The satellite had no rotation; interior weight was due entirely to gravity-field generators. However, its revolution

515

made heaven march slowly across the viewport. When Llynathawr and sun had disappeared, a man's pupils readjusted and he became able to see other stars. They crowded space, unwinking, jewel-colored, winter-sharp. Brightest shone Alpha Crucis, twin blue-white giants less than ten parsecs away; but Beta Crucis, a single of the same kind, was not much further off in its part of the sky. Elsewhere, trained vision might identify the red glimmers of Aldebaran and Arcturus. They resembled fires which, though remote, warmed and lighted the camps of men. Or vision might swing out to Deneb and Polaris, unutterably far beyond the Empire and the Empire's very enemies. That was a cold sight.

Wryness tugged at McCormac's mouth. *If Kathryn were tuned in on my mind,* he thought, *she'd say there must be something in Leviticus against mixing so many metaphors.*

He dared not let the knowledge of her dwell with him long. *I'm lucky to have an outside cell. Not uncomfortable, either. Surely this wasn't Snelund's intention.*

The assistant warden had been as embarrassed and apologetic as he dared. "We, uh, well, these are orders for us to detain you, Admiral McCormac," he said. "Direct from the governor. Till your trial or . . . transportation to Terra, maybe . . . uh . . . till further orders." He peered at the fax on his desk, conceivably hoping that the words it bore had changed since his first perusal. "Uh, solitary confinement, incommunicado—state-of-emergency powers invoked— Frankly, Admiral McCormac, I don't see why you aren't allowed, uh, books, papers, even projections to pass the time. . . . I'll send to His Excellency and ask for a change."

I know why, McCormac had thought. *Partly spite; mainly, the initial stage in the process of breaking me.* His back grew yet stiffer. *Well, let them try!*

The sergeant of the housecarl platoon that had brought the prisoner up from Catawrayannis Port said in his brassiest voice, "Don't address traitors by titles they've forfeited."

The assistant warden sat bolt upright, nailed them all with a look, and rapped: "Sergeant, I was twenty years in the Navy before retiring to my present job. I made CPO. Under His Majesty's regulations, any officer of Imperials ranks every member of any paramilitary local force. Fleet Admiral McCormac may have been relieved of command, but unless and until he's decommissioned by a proper court-martial or by direct fiat from the throne, you'll show him respect or find yourself in worse trouble than you may already be in."

Flushed, breathing hard, he seemed to want to say more. Evidently he thought better of it. After a moment, during which a couple of the burly guards shifted from foot to foot, he added merely: "Sign the prisoner over to me and get out."

"We're supposed to—" the sergeant began.

"If you have written orders to do more than deliver this gentleman into custody, let's see them." Pause. "Sign him over and get out. I don't plan to tell you again."

McCormac placed the assistant warden's name and face in his mind as carefully as he had noted each person involved in his arrest. Someday—if ever—

What had become of the man's superior? McCormac didn't know. Off Aeneas, he had never been concerned

with civilian crime or penology. The Navy looked after its
own. Sending him here was an insult tempered only by
the fact that obviously it was done to keep him away from
brother officers who'd try to help him. McCormac
guessed that Snelund had replaced a former warden with
a favorite or a bribegiver—as he'd done to many another
official since he became sector governor—and that the
new incumbent regarded the post as a sinecure.

In any case, the admiral was made to exchange his
uniform for a gray coverall; but he was allowed to do so in
a booth. He was taken to an isolation cell; but although
devoid of ornament and luxury, it had room for pacing
and facilities for rest and hygiene. The ceiling held an
audiovisual scanner; but it was conspicuously placed, and
no one objected when he rigged a sheet curtain for his
bunk. He saw no other being, heard no other voice; but
edible food and clean fabrics came in through a valve, and
he had a chute for disposal of scraps and soils. Above all
else, he had the viewport.

Without that sun, planet, constellations, frosty rush of
Milky Way and dim gleam of sister galaxies, he might soon
have crumbled—screamed for release, confessed to anything, kissed the hand of his executioner, while honest
medics reported to headquarters on Terra that they had
found no sign of torture or brainscrub upon him. It would
not have been the sensory deprivation *per se* that destroyed
his will in such short order. It would have been the loss of
every distraction from the thought of Kathryn, every way of
guessing how long a time had gone by while she also lay in
Aaron Snelund's power. McCormac admitted the weakness
to himself. That was not one he was ashamed of.

Why hadn't the governor then directed he be put in a blank cell? Oversight, probably, when more urgent business demanded attention. Or, being wholly turned inward on himself, Snelund perhaps did not realize that other men might love their wives above life.

Of course, as day succeeded standard day (with never a change in this bleak white fluorescence) he must begin wondering why nothing had happened up here. If his observers informed him of the exact situation, no doubt he would prescribe that McCormac be shifted to different quarters. But agents planted in the guard corps of a small artificial moon were lowly creatures. They would not, as a rule, report directly to a sector governor, viceroy for His Majesty throughout some 50,000 cubic light-years surrounding Alpha Crucis, and a *very* good friend of His Majesty to boot. No, they wouldn't even when the matter concerned a fleet admiral, formerly responsible for the defense of that entire part of the Imperial marches.

Petty agents would report to administrative underlings, who would send each communication on its way through channels. Was somebody seeing to it that material like this got—no, not lost—shunted off to oblivion in the files?

McCormac sighed. The noise came loud across endless whisper of ventilation, clack of his shoes on metal. How long could such protection last?

He didn't know the satellite's orbit. Nevertheless, he could gauge the angular diameter of Llynathawr pretty closely. He remembered the approximate dimensions and mass. From that he could calculate radius vector and thus period. Not easy, applying Kepler's laws in your head, but what else was there to do? The result more or less confirmed his guess that he was being fed thrice in 24 hours. He couldn't remember exactly how many meals had come before he started tallying them with knots in a thread. Ten? Fifteen? Something like that. Add this to the 37 points now confronting him. You got between 40 and 50 spaceship watches; or 13 to 16 Terran days; or 15 to 20 Aenean.

Aenean. The towers of Windhome, tall and gray, their banners awake in a whistling sky; tumble of crags and cliffs, reds, ochres, bronzes, where the Ilian Shelf plunged to a blue-gray dimness sparked and veined with water-gleams that was the Antonine Seabed; clangor of the Wildfoss as it hurled itself thitherward in cataracts; and Kathryn's laughter when they rode forth, her gaze upon him more blue than the dazzlingly high sky—

"No!" he exclaimed. Ramona's eyes had been blue. Kathryn's were green. Was he already confusing his live wife with his dead one?

If he had a wife any more. Twenty days since the housecarls burst into their bedchamber, arrested them and took them down separate corridors. She had slapped their hands off her wrists and marched among their guns with scornful pride, though tears rivered over her face.

McCormac clasped his hands and squeezed them together till fingerbones creaked. The pain was a friend. *I mustn't,* he recalled. *If I wring myself out because of what I can't make better, I'm doing Snelund's work for him.*

What else can I do?

Resist. Until the end.

Not for the first time, he summoned the image of a being he had once known, a Wodenite, huge, scaly, tailed,

THE REBEL WORLDS 521

four-legged, saurian-snouted, but comrade in arms and wiser than most. "You humans are a kittle breed," the deep voice had rumbled. "Together you can show courage that may cross the threshold of madness. Yet when no one else is near to tell your fellows afterward how you died, the spirit crumbles away and you fall down empty."

"Heritage of instinct, I suppose," McCormac said. "Our race began as an animal that hunted in packs."

"Training can tame instinct," the dragon answered. "Can the intelligent mind not train itself?"

Alone in his cell, Hugh McCormac nodded. *I've at least got that damned monitor to watch me. Maybe someday somebody—Kathryn, or the children Ramona gave me, or some boy I never knew—will see its tapes.*

He lay down on his bunk, the sole furnishing besides washbasin and sanitizer, and closed his eyes. *I'll try playing mental chess again, alternating sides, till dinner. Give me enough time and I'll master the technique. Just before eating, I'll have another round of calisthenics. That drab mess in the soft bowl won't suffer from getting cold. Perhaps later I'll be able to sleep.*

He hadn't lowered his improvised curtain. The pickup recorded a human male, tall, rangy, more vigorous than could be accounted for by routine antisenescence. Little betrayed his 50 standard years except the grizzling of black hair and the furrows in his long, lean countenance. He had never changed those features, nor protected them from the weathers of many planets. The skin remained dark and leathery. A jutting triangle of nose, a straight mouth and lantern jaw, were like counterweights to the dolichocephalic skull. When he opened the eyes beneath his heavy brows, they would show the color of glaciers. When he spoke, his voice tended to be hard; and decades of service around the Empire, before he returned to his home sector, had worn away the accent of Aeneas.

He lay there, concentrating so furiously on imagined chessmen which kept slipping about like fog-wraiths, that he did not notice the first explosion. Only when another went *crump!* and the walls reverberated did he know it was the second.

"What the chaos?" He surged to his feet.

A third detonation barked dully and toned in metal. *Heavy slugthrowers,* he knew. Sweat spurted forth. The heart slammed within him. What had happened? He threw a glance at the viewport. Llynathawr was rolling into sight, unmarked, serene, indifferent.

A rushing noise sounded at the door. A spot near its molecular catch glowed red, then white. Somebody was cutting through with a blaster. Voices reached McCormac, indistinct but excited and angry. A slug went *bee-yowww* down the corridor, gonged off a wall, and dwindled to nothing.

The door wasn't thick, just sufficient to contain a man. Its alloy gave way, streamed downward, made fantastic little formations akin to lava. The blaster flame boomed through the hole, enlarging it. McCormac squinted away from that glare. Ozone prickled his nostrils. He thought momentarily, crazily, *no reason to be so extravagant of charge.*

The gun stopped torching. The door flew wide. A dozen beings stormed through. Most were men in blue Navy outfits. A couple of them bulked robotlike in combat armor and steered a great Holbert energy gun on its grav sled. One was nonhuman, a Donarrian centauroid, bigger than the armored men themselves; he bore an assortment of weapons on his otherwise nude frame, but had left them holstered in favor of a battleax. It dripped red. His simian countenance was a single vast grin.

"Admiral! Sir!" McCormac didn't recognize the youth who dashed toward him, hands outspread. "Are you all right?"

"Yes. Yes. What—" McCormac willed out bewilderment. "What is this?"

The other snapped a salute. "Lieutenant Nasruddin Hamid, sir, commanding your rescue party by order of Captain Oliphant."

"Assaulting an Imperial installation?" It was as if somebody else used McCormac's larynx.

"Sir, they meant to kill you. Captain Oliphant's sure of it." Hamid looked frantic. "We've got to move fast, sir. We entered without loss. The man in charge knew about the operation. He pulled back most of the guards. He'll leave with us. A few disobeyed him and resisted. Snelund's men, must be. We cut through them but some escaped. They'll be waiting to send a message soon's our ships stop jamming."

The event was still unreal for McCormac. Part of him wondered if his mind had ripped across. "Governor Snelund was appointed by His Majesty," jerked from his gullet. "The proper place to settle things is a court of inquiry."

Another man trod forth. He had not lost the lilt of Aeneas. "Please, sir." He was near weeping. "We can't do without you. Local uprisings on more planets every day—on ours, now, too, in Borea and Ironland. Snelund's tryin' to get the Navy to help his filthy troops put down the trouble . . . by his methods . . . by nuclear bombardment if burnin', shootin', and enslavin' don't work."

"War on our own people," McCormac whispered, "when outside the border, the barbarians—"

His gaze drifted back to Llynathawr, aglow in the port. "What about my wife?"

"I don't . . . don't know . . . anything about her—" Hamid stammered.

McCormac swung to confront him. Rage leaped aloft. He grabbed the lieutenant's tunic. "That's a lie!" he yelled. "You can't help knowing! Oliphant wouldn't send men on a raid without briefing them on every last detail. *What about Kathryn?*"

"Sir, the jamming'll be noticed. We only have a surveillance vessel. An enemy ship on picket could—"

McCormac shook Hamid till teeth rattled in the jaws. Abruptly he let go. They saw his face become a machine's. "What touched off part of the trouble was Snelund's wanting Kathryn," he said, altogether toneless. "The Governor's court likes its gossip juicy; and what the court knows, soon all Catawrayannis does. She's still in the palace, isn't she?"

The men looked away, anywhere except at him. "I heard that," Hamid mumbled. "Before we attacked, you see, we stopped at one of the asteroids—pretended we were on a routine relief—and sounded out whoever we could. One was a merchant, come from the city the day before. He said—well, a public announcement about you, sir, and your lady being 'detained for investigation' only she and the governor—"

He stopped.

After a while, McCormac reached forth and squeezed his shoulder. "You needn't continue, son," he said, with scarcely more inflection but quite softly. "Let's board your ship."

"We aren't mutineers, sir," Hamid said pleadingly. "We need you to—to hold off that monster . . . till we can get the truth before the Emperor."

"No, it can't be called mutiny any longer," McCormac answered. "It has to be revolt." His voice whipped out. "Get moving! On the double!"

CHAPTER TWO

A metropolis in its own right, Admiralty Center lifted over that part of North America's Rocky Mountains which it occupied, as if again the Titans of dawn myth were piling Pelion on Ossa to scale Olympus. "And one of these days," Dominic Flandry had remarked to a young woman whom he was showing around, and to whom he had made that comparison in order to demonstrate his culture, "the gods are going to get as irritated as they did last time—let us hope with less deplorable results."

"What do you mean?" she asked.

Because his objective was not to enlighten but simply to seduce her, he had twirled his mustache and leered: "I mean that you are far too lovely for me to exercise my doomsmanship on. Now as for that plotting tank you wanted to see, this way, please."

He didn't tell her that its spectacular three-dimensional star projections were mainly for visitors. The smallest astronomical distance is too vast for any pictorial map to have much value. The real information was stored in the memory banks of unpretentious computers which the general public was not allowed to look on.

As his cab entered the area today, Flandry recalled the little episode. It had terminated satisfactorily. But his mind would not break free of the parallel he had not uttered.

Around him soared many-tinted walls, so high that fluoro-panels must glow perpetually on the lower levels, a liana tangle of elevated ways looping between them, the pinnacles crowned with clouds and sunlight. Air traffic swarmed and glittered in their sky, a dance too dense and complex for anything but electronic brains to control; and traffic pulsed among the towers, up and down within them, deep into the tunnels and chambers beneath their foundations. Those cars and buses, airborne or ground, made barely a whisper; likewise the slideways; and a voice or a footfall was soon lost. Nevertheless, Admiralty Center stood in a haze of sound, a night-and-day hum like a beehive's above an undergroundish growling, the noise of its work.

For here was the nexus of Imperial strength; and Terra ruled a rough sphere some 400 light-years across, containing an estimated four million suns, of which a hundred thousand were in one way or another tributary to her.

Thus far the pride. When you looked behind it, though—

Flandry emerged from his reverie. His cab was slanting toward Intelligence headquarters. He took a hasty final drag on his cigarette, pitched it in the disposer, and checked his uniform. He preferred the dashing dress version, with as much elegant variation as the rather elastic rules permitted, or a trifle more. However, when your leave has been cancelled after a mere few days home, and you are ordered to report straight to Vice Admiral Kheraskov, you had better arrive in plain white tunic and trousers, the latter not tucked into your half-boots, and belt instead of sash, and simple gray cloak, and bonnet cocked to bring its sunburst badge precisely over the middle of your forehead.

Sackcloth and ashes would be more appropriate, Flandry mourned. *Three, count 'em, three gorgeous girls, ready and eager to help me celebrate my birth week, starting tomorrow at Everest House with a menu I spent two hours planning; and we'd've continued as long as necessary to prove that a quarter century is less old than it sounds. And now this!*

A machine in the building talked across seething communications to a machine in the cab. Flandry was deposited on the fiftieth-level parking flange. The gravs cut out. He lent his card to the meter, which transferred credit and unlocked the door for him. A marine guard at the entrance verified his identity and appointment with the help of another machine and let him through. He passed down several halls on his way to the lift shaft he wanted. Restless, he walked in preference to letting a strip carry him.

Crowds moved by and overflowed the offices. Their members ranged from junior technicians to admirals on whose heads might rest the security of a thousand worlds and scientists who barely kept the Empire afloat in a universe full of lethal surprises. By no means all were human. Shapes, colors, words, odors, tactile sensations when he brushed against a sleeve or an alien skin, swirled past Flandry in endless incomprehensible patterns.

Hustle, bustle, hurry, scurry, run, run, run, said his glumness. *Work, for the night is coming—the Long Night, when the Empire goes under and the howling peoples camp in its ruins. Because how can we remain forever the masters, even of our insignificant spatter of stars, on the fringe of a galaxy so big we'll never know a decent fraction of it? Probably never more than this sliver of one spiral arm that we've already seen. Why, better than half the suns, just in the micro-bubble of space we claim, have not been visited once!*

Our ancestors explored further than we in these years remember. When hell cut loose and their civilization seemed about to fly into pieces, they patched it together with the Empire. And they made the Empire function. But we . . . we've lost the will. We've had it too easy for too long. And so the Merseians on our Betelgeusean flank, the wild races everywhere else, press inward. . . . Why do I bother? Once a career in the Navy looked glamorous to me. Lately I've seen its backside. I could be more comfortable doing almost anything else.

A woman stopped him. She must be on incidental business, because civilian employees here couldn't get away with dressing in quite such a translucent wisp of rainbow. She was constructed for it. "I beg your pardon," she said. "Could you tell me how to find Captain Yuan-Li's office? I'm afraid I'm lost."

Flandry bowed. "Indeed, my lady." He had reported in there on arrival at Terra, and now directed her. "Please tell him Lieutenant Commander Flandry said he's a lucky captain."

She fluttered her lashes. "Oh, sir." Touching the insigne on his breast, a star with an eye: "I noticed you're in Intelligence. That's why I asked you. It must be fascinating. I'd love to—"

Flandry beamed. "Well, since we both know friend Yuan-Li—"

They exchanged names and addresses. She departed, wagging her tail. Flandry continued. His mood was greatly lightened. *After all, another job might prove boring.* He reached his upbound point. *Here's where I get the shaft.* Stepping through the portal, he relaxed while the negagrav field lifted him.

Rather, he tried to relax, but did not succeed a hundred percent. Attractive women or no, a new-made lieutcom summoned for a personal interview with a subchief of operations is apt to find his tongue a little dry and his palms a little wet.

Catching a handhold, he drew himself out on the ninety-seventh level and proceeded down the corridor. Here dwelt a hush; the rare soft voices, the occasional whirr of a machine, only deepened for him the silence between these austere walls. What persons he met were of rank above his, their eyes turned elsewhere, their thoughts among distant suns. When he reached Kheraskov's suite of offices, the receptionist was nothing but a scanner and talkbox hooked to a computer too low-grade to be called a brain. More was not needed. Everybody unimportant got filtered out at an earlier stage. Flandry cooled his heels a mere five minutes before it told him to proceed through the inner door.

The room beyond was large, high-ceilinged, lushly carpeted. In one corner stood an infotriever and an outsize vidiphone, in another a small refreshment unit. Otherwise there were three or four pictures, and as many shelves for mementos of old victories. The rear wall was an animation screen; at present it held an image of Jupiter seen from an approaching ship, so vivid that newcomers gasped. He halted at an expanse of desktop and snapped a salute that nearly tore his arm off. "Lieutenant Commander Dominic Flandry, reporting as ordered, sir."

The man aft of the desk was likewise in plain uniform. He wore none of the decorations that might have blanketed his chest, save the modest jewel of knighthood that was harder to gain than a patent of nobility. But his nebula and star outglistened Flandry's ringed planet. He was short and squat, with tired pugdog features under bristly gray hair. His return salute verged on being sloppy. But Flandry's heartbeat accelerated.

"At ease," said Vice Admiral Sir Ilya Kheraskov. "Sit down. Smoke?" He shoved forward a box of cigars.

"Thank you, sir." Flandry collected his wits. He chose a cigar and made a production of starting it, while the chair fitted itself around his muscles and subtly encouraged them to relax. "The admiral is most kind. I don't believe a better brand exists than Corona Australis." In fact, he knew of several: but these weren't bad. The smoke gave his tongue a love bite and curled richly by his nostrils.

"Coffee if you like," offered the master of perhaps a million agents through the Empire and beyond. "Or tea or jaine."

"No, thanks, sir."

Kheraskov studied him, wearily and apologetically; he felt X-rayed. "I'm sorry to break your furlough like this, Lieutenant Commander," the admiral said. "You must have been anticipating considerable overdue recreation. I see you have a new face."

They had never met before. Flandry made himself smile. "Well, yes, sir. The one my parents gave me had gotten monotonous. And since I was coming to Terra, where biosculp is about as everyday as cosmetics—" He shrugged.

Still that gaze probed him. Kheraskov saw an athlete's body, 184 centimeters tall, wide in the shoulders and narrow in the hips. From the white, tapered hands you might guess how their owner detested the hours of exercise he must spend in maintaining those cat-supple thews. His countenance had become straight of nose, high of cheekbones, cleft of chin. The mobile mouth and the eyes, changeable gray beneath slightly arched brows, were original. Speaking, he affected a hint of drawl.

"No doubt you're wondering why your name should have been plucked off the roster," Kheraskov said, "and why you should have been ordered straight here instead of to your immediate superior or Captain Yuan-Li."

"Yes, sir. I didn't seem to rate your attention."

"Nor were you desirous to." Kheraskov's chuckle held no humor. "But you've got it." He leaned back, crossed stumpy legs and bridged hairy fingers. "I'll answer your questions.

"First, why you, one obscure officer among tens of similar thousands? You may as well know, Flandry, if you don't already—though I suspect your vanity has informed you—to a certain echelon of the Corps, you aren't obscure. You wouldn't hold the rank you've got, at your age, if that were the case. No, we've taken quite an interest in you since the Starkad affair. That had to be hushed up, of course, but it was not forgotten. Your subsequent assignment to surveillance had intriguing consequences." Flandry could not totally suppress a tinge of alarm. Kheraskov chuckled again; it sounded like iron chains. "We've learned things that *you* hushed up. Don't worry . . . yet. Competent men are so heartbreakingly scarce these days, not to mention brilliant ones, that the Service keeps a blind eye handy for a broad range of escapades. You'll either be killed, young man, or you'll do something that will force us to step on you, or you'll go far indeed."

He drew breath before continuing: "The present business requires a maverick. I'm not letting out any great secret when I tell you the latest Merseian crisis is worse than the government admits to the citizens. It could completely explode on us. I think we can defuse it. For once, the Empire acted fast and decisively. But it demands we keep more than the bulk of our fleets out on that border, till the Merseians understand we mean business about not letting them take over Jihannath. Intelligence operations there have reached such a scale that the Corps is sucked dry of able field operatives elsewhere.

"And meanwhile something else has arisen, on the opposite side of our suzerainty. Some'hing potentially worse than any single clash with Merseia." Kheraskov lifted a hand. "Don't imagine you're the only man we're sending to cope, or that you can contribute more than a quantum to our effort. Still, stretched as thin as we are, every quantum is to be treasured. It was your bad luck but the Empire's good luck . . . maybe . . . that you happened to check in on Terra last week. When I asked Files who might be available with the right qualifications, your reel was among a dozen that came back."

Flandry waited.

Kheraskov rocked forward. The last easiness dropped from him. A grim and bitter man spoke: "As for why you're reporting directly to me—this is one place where I know there isn't any spybug, and you are one person I think won't backstab me. I told you we need a maverick. I tell you in addition, you could suck around the court and repeat what I'm about to say. I'd be broken, possibly shot or enslaved. You'd get money, possibly a sycophant's preferment. I have to take the chance. Unless you know the entire situation, you'll be useless."

Flandry said with care, "I'm a skilled liar, sir, so you'd better take my word rather than my oath that I'm not a very experienced buglemouth."

"Ha!" Kheraskov sat quiet for several seconds. Then he jumped to his feet and started to pace back and forth, one fist hammering into the other palm. The words poured from him:

"You've been away. After Starkad, your visits to Terra were for advanced training and the like. You must have been too busy to follow events at court. Oh, scandal, ribald jokes, rumor, yes, you've heard those. Who hasn't? But the meaningful news—Let me brief you.

"Three years, now, since poor old Emperor Georgios died and Josip III succeeded. Everybody knows what

Josip is: too weak and stupid for his viciousness to be highly effective. We all assumed the Dowager Empress will keep him on a reasonably short leash while she lives. And he won't outlast her by much, the way he treats his organism. And he won't have children—not him! And the Policy Board, the General Staff, the civil service, the officers corps, the Solar and extra-Solar aristocracies . . . they hold more crooks and incompetents than they did in former days, but we have a few good ones left, a few. . . .

"I've told you nothing new, have I?" Flandry barely had time to shake his head. Kheraskov kept on prowling and talking. "I'm sure you made the same quiet evaluation as most informed citizens. The Empire is so huge that no one individual can do critical damage, no matter if he's theoretically all-powerful. Whatever harm came from Josip would almost certainly be confined to a relative handful of courtiers, politicians, plutocrats, and their sort, concentrated on and around Terra—no great loss. We've survived other bad Emperors.

"A logical judgment. Correct, no doubt, as far as it went. But it didn't go far enough. Even we who're close to the seat of power were surprised by Aaron Snelund. Ever hear of him?"

"No, sir," Flandry said.

"He kept out of the media," Kheraskov explained. "Censorship's efficient on this planet, if nothing else is. The court knew about him, and people like me did. But our data were incomplete.

"Later you'll see details. I want to give you the facts that aren't public. He was born 34 years ago on Venus, mother a prostitute, father unknown. That was in Sub-

Lucifer, where you learn ruthlessness early or go down. He was clever, talented, charming when he cared to be. By his mid-teens he was a sensie actor here on Terra. I can see by hindsight how he must have planned, investigated Josip's tastes in depth, sunk his money into just the right biosculping and his time into acquiring just the right mannerisms. Once they met, it went smooth as gravitation. By the age of 25, Aaron Snelund had gone from only another catamite to the Crown Prince's favorite. His next step was to ease out key people and obtain their offices for those who were beholden to Snelund.

"It roused opposition. More than jealousy. Honest men worried about him becoming the power behind the crown when Josip succeeded. We heard mutters about assassination. I don't know if Josip and Snelund grew alarmed or if Snelund foresaw the danger and planned against it. At any rate, they must have connived.

"Georgios died suddenly, you recall. The following week Josip made Snelund a viscount and appointed him governor of Sector Alpha Crucis. Can you see how well calculated that was? Elevation to a higher rank would have kicked up a storm, but viscounts are a millo a thousand. However, it's sufficient for a major governorship. Many sectors would be too rich, powerful, close to home, or otherwise important. The Policy Board would not tolerate a man in charge of them who couldn't be trusted. Alpha Crucis is different."

Kheraskov slapped a switch. The fluoros went off. The breathtaking view of Jupiter, huge and banded among its moons, vanished. A trikon of the principal Imperial stars jumped into its place. Perhaps Kheraskov's rage

demanded that he at least have something to point at. His
blocky form stood silhouetted against a gem-hoard.

"Betelgeuse." He stabbed one finger at a red spark
representing the giant sun which dominated the border-
lands between the Terran and Merseian empires. "Where
the war threat is. Now, Alpha Crucis."

His hand swept almost 100 degrees counterclockwise.
The other hand turned a control, swinging the projection
plane about 70 degrees south. Keenly flashed the B-type
giants at that opposite end of Terra's domain, twinned
Alpha and bachelor Beta of the Southern Cross. Little
showed beyond them except darkness. It was not that the
stars did not continue as richly strewn in those parts; it
was that they lay where Terra's writ did not run, the homes
of savages and of barbarian predators who had too soon
gotten spacecraft and nuclear weapons; it was that they
housed darkness.

Kheraskov traced the approximately cylindrical outline
of the sector. "Here," he said, "is where war could really
erupt."

Flandry dared say into the shadowed silence which
followed, "Does the admiral mean the wild races are going
to try a fresh incursion? But sir, I understood they were
well in check. After the battle of—uh—I forget its name,
but wasn't there a battle—"

"Forty-three years ago." Kheraskov sagged in the
shoulders. "Too big, this universe," he said tiredly. "No
one brain, no one species can keep track of everything. So
we let the bad seed grow unnoticed until too late.

"Well." He straightened. "It was hard to see what
harm Snelund could do yonder that was worth provoking

a constitutional crisis to forestall. The region's as distant as they come among ours. It's not highly productive, not densely populated; its loyalty and stability are no more doubtful than most. There are only two things about it that count. One's the industrial rogue planet Satan. But that's an ancient possession of the Dukes of Hermes. They can be trusted to protect their own interests. Second is the sector's position as the shield between us and various raiders. But that means defense is the business of the fleet admiral; and we have—had—a particularly fine man in that post, one Hugh McCormac. You've never heard of him, but you'll get data.

"Of course Snelund would grow fat. What of it? A cento or two per subject per year, diverted from Imperial taxes, won't hurt any individual so badly he'll make trouble. But it will build a fortune to satisfy any normal greed. He'd retire in time to a life of luxury. Meanwhile the Navy and civil service would do all the real work as usual. Everyone was happy to get Snelund that cheaply off Terra. It's the kind of solution which has been reached again and again."

"Only this time," Flandry said lazily, "they forgot to allow for a bugger factor."

Kheraskov switched the map off, the fluoros on, and gave him a hard look. Flandry's return glance was bland and deferential. Presently the admiral said, "He left three years ago. Since then, increasing complaints have been received of extortion and cruelty. But no single person saw enough of those reports to stir action. And if he had, what could he do? You don't run an interstellar realm from the center. It isn't possible. The Imperium is hardly more than a policeman, trying to keep peace internal and external. Tribes, countries, planets, provinces are autonomous in most respects. The agony of millions of sentient beings, 200 light-years away, doesn't register on several trillion other sophonts elsewhere, or whatever the figure is. It can't. And we've too much else to worry about anyway.

"Think, though, what a governor of a distant region, who chose to abuse his powers, might do."

Flandry did, and lost his lightness.

"McCormac himself finally sent protests to Terra," Kheraskov plodded on. "A two-star admiral can get through. The Policy Board began talking about appointing a commission to investigate. Almost immediately after, a dispatch came from Snelund himself. He'd had to arrest McCormac for conspiracy to commit treason. He can do that, you know, and select an interim high commander. The court-martial must be held on a Naval base or vessel, by officers of suitable rank. But with this Merseian crisis—Do you follow me?"

"Too damn well." Flandry's words fell muted.

"Provincial rebellions aren't unheard of," Kheraskov said. "We can less afford one today than we could in the past."

He had stood looking down at the younger man, across his desk. Turning, he stared into the grand vision of Jupiter that had come back. "The rest you can find in the data tapes," he said.

"What do you want me to do . . . sir?"

"As I told you, we're sending what undercover agents we can spare, plus a few inspectors. With all that territory to deal with, they'll take long to compile a true picture.

Perhaps fatally long. I want to try something in between also. A man who can nose around informally but openly, with authorizations to flash when needed. The master of a warship, posted to Llynathawr as a reinforcement, has standing. Governor Snelund, for instance, has no ready way of refusing to see him. At the same time, if she's not a capital ship, her skipper isn't too blazing conspicuous."

"But I've never had a command, sir."

"Haven't you?"

Tactfully, Kheraskov did not watch while the implications of that question sank in. He proceeded: "We've found an escort destroyer whose captain is slated for higher things. The record says she has an able executive officer. That should free your attention for your true job. You'd have gotten a ship eventually, in the normal course of grooming you and testing your capabilities. We like our field operatives to have a broad background."

Not apt to be many broads in my background for a while, passed through the back of Flandry's mind. He scarcely noticed or cared. Excitement bayed in him.

Kheraskov sat down again. "Go back to your place," he said. "Pack up and check out. Report at 1600 hours to Rear Admiral Yamaguchi. He'll provide you with quarters, tapes, hypnos, synapse transforms, stimpills, every aid you need. And you will need them. I want your information to be as complete as mine, inside 48 hours. You will then report to Mars Prime Base and receive your brevet commission as a full commander. Your ship is in Mars orbit. Departure will be immediate. I hope you can fake the knowledge of her you don't have, until you've gathered it.

"If you acquit yourself well, we'll see about making that temporary rank permanent. If you don't, God help you and maybe God help me. Good luck, Dominic Flandry."

CHAPTER THREE

The third stop *Asieneuve* made on her way to Llynathawr
was her final one. Flandry recognized the need for haste.
In straight-line, flat-out hyperdrive his vessel would have
taken slightly worse than two weeks to make destination.
Perhaps he should have relied on records and interviews
after he arrived. On the other hand, he might not be given
the chance, or Snelund might have found ways to keep the
truth off his headquarters planet. The latter looked feasible,
therefore plausible. And Flandry's orders granted him
latitude. They instructed him to report to Llynathawr and
place himself under the new high command of Sector
Alpha Crucis "with maximum expedition and to the fullest
extent consistent with your fact-finding assignment." A
sealed letter from Kheraskov authorized him to detach his
ship and operate independently; but that must not be
produced except in direst need, and he'd have to answer
for his actions.

He compromised by making spot checks in three

randomly chosen systems within Snelund's bailiwick and not too far off his course. It added an extra ten days. Two globes were human-colonized. The habitable planet of the third sun was Shalmu.

So it was called in one of the languages spoken by its most technologically advanced civilization. Those communities had been in a bronze age when men discovered them. Influenced by sporadic contacts with traders, they went on to iron and, by now, a primitive combustion-powered technology which was spreading their hegemony across the world. The process was slower than it had been on Terra; Shalmuans were less ferocious, less able to treat their fellow beings like vermin or machinery, than humankind is.

They were happy to come under the Empire. It meant protection from barbarian starfarers, who had already caused them grief. They did not see the Naval base they got. It was elsewhere in the system. Why risk a living planet, if matters came to a local fight, when a barren one served equally well? But there was a small marine garrison on Shalmu, and spacemen visited it on leave, and this attracted a scattering of Imperial civilians, who traded with the autochthons as readily as with service personnel. Shalmuans found employment among these foreigners. A few got to go outsystem. A smaller but growing number were recommended for scholarships by Terran friends, and returned with modern educations. The dream grew of entering civilization as a full-fledged member.

In return, Shalmu paid modest taxes in kind: metals, fuels, foodstuffs, saleable works of art and similar luxuries, depending on what a particular area could furnish. It accepted an Imperial resident, whose word was the ultimate law but who in practice let native cultures fairly well alone. His marines did suppress wars and banditry as far as practicable, but this was considered good by most. The young Imperials, human or nonhuman, often conducted themselves arrogantly, but whatever serious harm they might inflict on an innocent Shalmuan resulted, as a rule, in punishment.

In short, the planet was typical of the majority that had fallen under Terran sway. Backward, they had more to gain than lose; they saw mainly the bright side of the Imperial coin, which was not too badly tarnished.

Or so the case had been till a couple of years ago.

Flandry stood on a hill. Behind him were five men, bodyguards from his crew. Beside him was Ch'kessa, Prime in Council of the Clan Towns of Att. Ch'kessa's home community sprawled down the slope, a collection of neat, whitewashed, drum-shaped houses where several thousand individuals lived. Though peaked, each sod roof was a flower garden, riotous with color. The ways between houses were "paved" with a tough mossy growth, except where fruit trees grew from which anyone might help himself when they bore and no one took excessively. Pastures and cultivated fields occupied the valley beneath. On its other side, the hills were wooded.

Apart from somewhat weaker gravity, Shalmu was terrestroid. Every detail might be strange, but the overall effect spoke to ancient human instincts. Broad plains, tall mountains, spindrift across unrestful seas; rustling sun-flecked shadows in a forest, unexpected sweetness of tiny white blossoms between old roots; the pride of a

great horned beast, the lonesome cries descending from
migratory wings; and the people. Ch'kessa's features were
not so different from Flandry's. Hairless bright-green
skin, prehensile tail, 140-centimeter height, details of
face, foot, hand, interior anatomy, exoticism of his
embroidered wraparound and plumed spirit wand and
other accoutrements—did they matter?

The wind shifted. On planets like this, the air had
always seemed purer than anywhere on Terra, be it in the
middle of a nobleman's enormous private park. Away from
machines, you drew more life into your lungs. But Flandry
gagged. One of his men must suddenly vomit.

"That is why we obeyed the new resident," Ch'kessa
said. He spoke fluent Anglic.

Down the hill, lining a valleyward road, ran a hundred
wooden crosses. The bodies lashed to them had not
finished rotting. Carrion birds and insects still made black
clouds around them, under a wantonly brilliant summer
sky.

"Do you see?" Ch'kessa asked anxiously. "We did
refuse at first. Not the heavy taxes the new resident laid
on us. I am told he did that throughout the world. He said
it was to pay for meeting a terrible danger. He did not say
what the danger was. However, we paid, especially after
we heard how bombs were dropped or soldiers came
with torches where folk protested. I do not think the old
resident would have done that. Nor do I think the Emperor,
may his name echo in eternity, would let those things
happen if he knew."

Actually, Flandry did not answer, *Josip wouldn't give
a damn. Or maybe he would. Maybe he'd ask to see films*

of the action, and watch them and giggle. The wind changed again, and he blessed it for taking away part of the charnel odor.

"We paid," Ch'kessa said. "That was not easy, but we remember the barbarians too well. Then this season a fresh demand was put before us. We, who had powder rifles, were to supply males. They would be flown to lands like Yanduvar, where folk lack firearms. There they would catch natives for the slave market. I do not understand, though I have often asked. Why does the Empire, with many machines, need slaves?"

Personal service, Flandry did not answer. *For instance, the sort women supply. We use enslavement as one kind of criminal penalty. But it isn't too significant. There isn't that big a percentage of slaves in the Empire. The barbarians, though, would pay well for skilled hands. And transactions with them do not get into any Imperial records for some officious computer to come upon at a later date.*

"Continue," he said aloud.

"The Council of the Clan Towns of Att debated long," Ch'kessa said. "We were afraid. Still, the thing was not right for us to do. At length we decided to make excuses, to delay as much as might be, while messengers sped overland to Iscoyn. There the Imperial marine base is, as my lord well knows. The messengers would appeal to the commandant, that he intercede for us with the resident."

Flandry caught a mutter behind him: "Nova flash! Is he saying the marines hadn't been enforcing the decrees?"

"Yeh, sure," growled an adjacent throat. "Forget your

barroom brawls with 'em. They wouldn't commit vileness like this. Mercenaries did it. Now dog your hatch before the Old Man hears you."

Me? Flandry thought in stupid astonishment. *Me, the Old Man?*

"I suppose our messengers were caught and their story twisted from them," Ch'kessa sighed. "At least, they never returned. A legate came and told us we must obey. We refused. Troops came. They herded us together. A hundred were chosen by lot and put on the crosses. The rest of us had to watch till all were dead. It took three days and nights. One of my daughters was among them." He pointed. His arm was not steady. "Perhaps my lord can see her. That quite small body, eleventh on our left. It is black and swollen, and much of it has fallen off, but she used to come stumping and laughing to meet me when I returned from work. She cried for me to help her. The cries were many, yet I heard hers. Whenever I moved toward her, a shock beam stopped me. I had not thought there could be happiness in seeing her die. We were instructed to leave the bodies in place, on pain of bombing. An aircraft flies over from time to time to make sure."

He sat down in the whispering silvery pseudograss, put face on knees and tail across neck. His fingers plucked at the dirt. "After that," he said, "we went slaving."

Flandry stood silent for a space. He had been furious at the carnage being inflicted by the more advanced Shalmuans on the weaker ones. Swooping down on a caravan of chained prisoners, he had arrested its leader and demanded an explanation. Ch'kessa had suggested they flit to his homeland.

"Where are your villagers?" Flandry asked at length, for the houses stood empty, smokeless, silent.

"They cannot live here with those dead," Ch'kessa replied. "They camp out, coming back only to maintain. And doubtless they fled when they saw your boat, my lord, not knowing what you would do." He looked up. "You have seen. Are we deeply to blame? Will you return me to my gang? A sum is promised each of us for each slave we bring in. It is helpful in meeting the tax. I will not get mine if I am absent when the caravan reaches the airfield."

"Yes." Flandry turned. His cloak swirled behind him. "Let's go."

Another low voice at his back: "I never swallowed any brotherhood-of-beings crap, you know that, Sam'l, but when our own xenos are scared by a vessel of ours—!"

"Silence," Flandry ordered.

The gig lifted with a yell and trailed a thunderbolt across half a continent and an ocean. Nobody spoke. When she tilted her nose toward jungle, Ch'kessa ventured to say, "Perhaps you will intercede for us, my lord."

"I'll do my best," Flandry said.

"When the Emperor hears, let him not be angry with us of the Clan Towns. We went unwillingly. We sicken with fevers and die from the poisoned arrows of the Yanduvar folk."

And wreck what was a rather promising culture, Flandry thought.

"If punishment must be for what we have done, let it fall on me alone," Ch'kessa begged. "That does not matter greatly after I watched my little one die."

"Be patient," Flandry said. "The Emperor has many peoples who need his attention. Your turn will come."

Inertial navigation had pinpointed the caravan, and a mere couple of hours had passed since. Flandry's pilot soon found it, trudging down a swale where ambush was less likely than among trees. He landed the gig a kilometer off and opened the airlock.

"Farewell, my lord." The Shalmuan knelt, coiled his tail around Flandry's ankles, crawled out and was gone. His slim green form bounded toward his kin.

"Return to the ship," Flandry instructed.

"Doesn't the captain wish to pay a courtesy call on the resident?" asked the pilot sarcastically. He was not long out of the Academy. His hue remained sick.

"Get aloft, Citizen Willig," Flandry said. "You know we're on an information-gathering mission and in a hurry. We didn't notify anyone except Navy that we'd been on Starport or New Indra, did we?"

The ensign sent hands dancing across the board. The gig stood on its tail with a violence that would have thrown everybody into the stern were it not for acceleration compensators. "Excuse me, sir," he said between his teeth. "A question, if the captain pleases. Haven't we witnessed outright illegality? I mean, those other two planets were having a bad time, but nothing like this. Because the Shalmuans have no way to get a complaint off their world, I suppose. Isn't our duty, sir, to report what we've seen?"

Sweat glistened on his forehead and stained his tunic beneath the arms. Flandry caught an acrid whiff of it. Glancing about, he saw the other four men leaning close, straining to hear through the throb of power and whistle

of cloven atmosphere. *Should I answer?* he asked himself,
a touch frantically. *And if so, what can I tell him that won't
be bad for discipline? How should I know? I'm too young
to be the Old Man!*

He gained time with a cigarette. Stars trod forth in
viewscreens as the gig entered space. Willig exchanged a
signal with the ship, set the controls for homing on her,
and swiveled around to join in staring at his captain.

Flandry sucked in smoke, trickled it out, and said
cautiously: "You have been told often enough, we are first
on a fact-finding mission, second at the disposal of Alpha
Crucis Command if we can help without prejudice to the
primary assignment. Whatever we learn will be duly
reported. If any man wishes to file additional material or
comment, that's his privilege. However, you should be
warned that it isn't likely to go far. And this is not because
inconvenient facts will be swept under the carpet," *though
I daresay that does happen on occasion.* "It's due to the
overwhelming volume of data."

He gestured. "A hundred thousand planets, gentlemen,
more or less," he said. "Each with its millions or billions of
inhabitants, its complexities and mysteries, its geographies
and civilizations, their pasts and presents and conflicting
aims for the future, therefore each with its own complicated,
ever-changing, unique set of relationships to the Imperium.
We can't control that, can we? We can't even hope to
comprehend it. At most, we can try to maintain the Pax. At
most, gentlemen.

"What's right in one place may be wrong in another.
One species may be combative and anarchic by nature,
another peaceful and antlike, a third peaceful and

anarchic, a fourth a bunch of aggressive totalitarian hives. I know a planet where murder and cannibalism are necessary to race survival: high radiation background, you see, making for high mutation rate coupled with chronic food shortage. The unfit must be eaten. I know of intelligent hermaphrodites, and sophonts with more than two sexes, and a few that regularly change sex. They all tend to look on our reproductive pattern as obscene. I could go on for hours. Not to mention the variations imposed by culture. Just think about Terran history.

"And then the sheer number of individuals and interests; the sheer distance; the time needed to get a message across our territory—No, we can't direct everything. We haven't the manpower. And if we did, it'd remain physically impossible to coordinate that many data.

"We've *got* to give our proconsuls wide discretion. We've *got* to let them recruit auxiliaries, and hope those auxiliaries will know the local scene better than Imperial regulars. Above all, gentlemen, for survival if nothing else, we've *got* to preserve solidarity."

He waved a hand at the forward viewscreen. Alpha Crucis blazed lurid among the constellations; but beyond it—"If we don't stick together, we Terrans and our non-human allies," he said, "I assure you, either the Merseians or the wild races will be delighted to stick us separately."

He got no reply: not that he expected one. *Was that a sufficiently stuffy speech?* he wondered.

And was it sufficiently truthful?

I don't know about that last. Nor do I know if I have any right to inquire.

His ship swam into sight. The tiny spindle, well-nigh

lost beside the vast glowing bulk of the planet she circled, grew to a steel barracuda, guns rakish across the star clouds. She was no more than an escort destroyer, she had speed but was lightly armed, her crew numbered a bare fifty. Nevertheless, she was Flandry's first official command and his blood ran a little faster each time he saw her—even now, even now.

The gig made a ragged approach. Willig probably didn't feel well yet. Flandry refrained from commenting. The last part of the curve, under computer choreography, was better. When the boat housing had closed and repressurized, he dismissed his guards and went alone to the bridge.

Halls, companionways, and shafts were narrow. They were painted gray and white. With the interior grav generators set for full Terran weight, thin deckplates resounded under boots, thin bulkheads cast the noise back and forth, voices rung, machinery droned and thumped. The air that gusted from ventilator grilles came fresh out of the renewers, but somehow it collected a faint smell of oil on the way. The officers' cabins were cubbyholes, the forecastle could be packed tighter only if the Pauli exclusion principle were repealed, the recreation facilities were valuable chiefly as a subject for jokes, and the less said about the galley the wiser. But she was Flandry's first command.

He had spent many hours en route reading her official history and playing back tapes of former logbooks. She was a few years older than him. Her name derived from a land mass on Ardèche, which was apparently a human-settled planet though not one he had ever chanced upon mention of. (He knew the designation Asieneuve in different versions on at least four worlds; and he speculated on how many other Continent-class vessels bore it. A name was a mere flourish when computers must deal with millions of craft by their numbers.) She had gone on occasional troopship convoy when trouble broke loose on a surface somewhere. Once she had been engaged in a border incident; her captain claimed a probable hit but lacked adequate proof. Otherwise her existence had been routine patrols . . . which were essential, were they not?

You didn't salute under these conditions. Men squeezed themselves aside to make way for Flandry. He entered the bridge. His executive officer had it.

Rovian of Ferra was slightly more than human size. His fur was velvet at midnight. His ponderous tail, the claws on his feet and fingers, the saber teeth in his jaws, could deal murderous blows; he was also an expert marksman. The lower pair of his four arms could assist his legs at need. Then his silent undulant gait turned into lightning. He habitually went nude except for guns and insignia. His nature and nurture were such that he would never become a captain and did not want to be. But he was capable and well liked, and Terran citizenship had been conferred on him.

"S-s-so?" he greeted. His fangs handicapped him a little in speaking Anglic.

Alone, he and Flandry didn't bother to be formal. Mankind's rituals amused him. "Bad," the master said, and explained.

"Why bad?" Rovian asked. "Unless it provokes revolt."

"Never mind the morals of it. You wouldn't understand. Consider the implications, however."

Flandry inhaled a cigarette to lighting. His gaze sought Shalmu's disc, where it floated unutterably peaceful in its day and night. "Why should Snelund do this?" he said. "It's considerable trouble, and not without hazard. Ordinary corruption would earn him more than he could live to spend on himself. He must have a larger purpose, one that requires moonsful of money. What is it?"

Rovian erected the chemosensor antennae that flanked the bony ridge on his skull. His muzzle twitched, his eyes glowed yellow. "To finance an insurrection? He may hope to become an independent overlord."

"M-m-m . . . no . . . doesn't make sense, and I gather he's not stupid. The Empire can't conceivably tolerate breakaways. He'd have to be crushed. If necessary, Josip would be deposed to clear the track for that operation. No, something else—" Flandry brought his attention back. "Get patrol clearance for us to go in half an hour. Next rendezvous, Llynathawr."

Hyperdrive vibrations are instantaneous, though the philosophers of science have never agreed on the meaning of that adjective. Unfortunately, they damp out fast. No matter how powerful, a signal cannot be received beyond a distance of about one light-year. Thus spaceships traveling at quasivelocity are not detectable by their "wakes" at any farther remove than that. Neither are the modulations that carry messages quicker than light; and the uncertainty principle makes it impossible to relay them with any hope that they will not soon degenerate into gibberish.

Accordingly, *Asieneuve* was within two hours of her goal before she got the news. Fleet Admiral Hugh McCormac had escaped to the Virgilian System. There he had raised the standard of rebellion and proclaimed himself Emperor. An unspecified number of planets had declared for him. So had an unspecified proportion of the ships and men he formerly commanded. Armed clashes had taken place and full civil war looked inevitable.

CHAPTER FOUR

When the Empire purchased Llynathawr from its Cynthian discoverers, the aim had been to strengthen this frontier by attracting settlers. Most of the world was delightful in climate and scenery, rich in natural resources, wide in unclaimed lands. Navy sector headquarters were close enough, on Ifri, and housed enough power to give ample protection. Not all the barbarians were hostile; there existed excellent possibilities of trade with a number of races—especially those that had not acquired spacecraft—as well as with Imperial planets.

Thus far the theory. Three or four generations showed that practice was something else again. The human species appeared to have lost its outward urge. Few individuals would leave a familiar, not too uncomfortable environment to start over in a place remote from government-guaranteed security and up-to-date entertainment. Those who did usually preferred city to rural life. Nor did many arrive from the older colonies nearby, like Aeneas. Such people had struck their own roots.

Catawrayannis did become a substantial town: two million, if you counted in the floating population. It became the seat of the civil authority. It became a brisk mart, though much of the enterprise was carried on by nonhumans, and a pleasure resort, and a regional listening post. But that was the end of the process. The hinterland, latifundia, mines, factories, soon gave way to forests, mountains, trafficless oceans, empty plains, a wilderness where lights gleamed rare and lonely after dark.

Of course, this has the advantage of not turning the planet as a whole into still another cesspool, Flandry thought. After reporting, he had donned mufti and spent a few days incognito. Besides sounding out various bourgeoisie and servants, he had passed through a particularly ripe Lowtown.

And now I feel so respectable I creak, his mind went on. *Contrast? No, not when I'm about to meet Aaron Snelund.* His pulse quickened. He must make an effort to keep his face and bearing expressionless. That skill he owed less to official training than to hundreds of poker games.

As a ramp lifted him toward an impressive portico, he glanced back. The gubernatorial palace crowned a high hill. It was a big pastel-tinted structure in the dome-and-colonnade style of the last century. Beneath its gardens, utilitarian office buildings for civil servants made terraces to the flatland. Homes of the wealthy ringed the hill. Beyond these, more modest residences blended gradually into cropground on the west side, city on the east. Commercial towers, none very tall, clustered near the Luana River, past which lay the slums. A haze blurred vision today and the breeze blew cool, tasting of spring. Vehicles moved insectlike through streets and sky. Their sound came as a whisper, almost hidden in the sough of trees. It was hard to grasp that Catawrayannis brawled with preparation for war, shrilled with hysteria, tensed with fear—

—until a slow thundering went from horizon to horizon, and a spatial warcraft crossed heaven on an unknown errand.

Two marines flanked the main entrance. "Please state your name and business, sir," one demanded. He didn't aim his slug-thrower, but his knuckles stood white on butt and barrel.

"Commander Dominic Flandry, captain, HMS *Asieneuve*, here for an appointment with His Excellency."

"A moment, please." The other marine checked. He didn't merely call the secretarial office, he turned a scanner on the newcomer. "All right."

"If you'll leave your sidearm with me, sir," the first man said. "And, uh, submit to a brief search."

"Hey?" Flandry blinked.

"Governor's orders, sir. Nobody who doesn't have a special pass with full physical ID goes through armed or unchecked." The marine, who was pathetically young, wet his lips. "You understand, sir. When Navy units commit treason, we . . . who dare we trust?"

Flandry looked into the demoralized countenance, surrendered his blaster, and allowed hands to feel across his whites.

A servant appeared, bowed, and escorted him down a corridor and up a gravshaft. The decor was luxurious, its bad taste more a question of subtly too much opulence than of garish colors or ugly proportions. The same applied to the chamber where Flandry was admitted. A live-fur carpet reached gold and black underfoot; iridescences swept over the walls; dynasculps moved in every corner; incense and low music tinged the air; instead of an exterior view, an animation of an Imperial court masquerade occupied one entire side; behind the governor's chair of state hung a thrice life-size, thrice flattering portrait of Emperor Josip, fulsomely inscribed.

Four mercenaries were on guard, not human but giant shaggy Gorzunians. They stirred scarcely more than their helmets, breastplates, or weapons.

Flandry saluted and stood at attention.

Snelund did not look diabolical. He had bought himself an almost girlish beauty: flame-red wavy hair, creamy skin, slightly slanted violet eyes, retroussé nose, bee-stung lips. Though not tall, and now growing paunchy, he retained some of his dancer's gracefulness. His richly patterned tunic, flare-cut trousers, petal-shaped shoes, and gold necklace made Flandry envious.

Rings sparkled as he turned a knob on a memoscreen built into the chair arm. "Ah, yes. Good day, Commander." His voice was pleasant. "I can give you fifteen minutes." He smiled. "My apologies for such curtness, and for your having to wait this long to see me. You can guess how hectic things are. If Admiral Pickens had not informed me you came directly from Intelligence HQ, I'm afraid you'd never have gotten past my office staff." He chuckled. "Sometimes I think they're overzealous about protecting me. One does appreciate their fending off as many bores and triviators as possible—though you'd be surprised, Commander, how many I cannot escape seeing—but occasionally, no doubt, undue delay is caused a person with a valid problem."

"Yes, Your Excellency. Not to waste your time—"

"Do sit down. It's good to meet someone straight from the Mother of us all. We don't even get frequent mail out here, you know. How fares old Terra?"

"Well, Your Excellency, I was only there a few days, and quite busy most of them." Flandry seated himself and leaned forward. "About my assignment."

"Of course, of course," Snelund said. "But grant me a moment first." His geniality was replaced by an appearance of concern. His tone sharpened. "Have you fresh news of the Merseian situation? We're as worried about that as anyone in the Empire, despite our own current difficulties. Perhaps more worried than most. Transfer of units to that border has gravely weakened this. Let war break out with Merseia, and we could be depleted still further—an invitation to the barbarians. That's why McCormac's rebellion must be suppressed immediately, no matter the cost."

Flandry realized: *I'm being stalled.* "I know nothing that isn't public, sir," he said at a leisured rate. "I'm sure Ifri HQ gets regular couriers from the Betelgeusean marches. The information gap is in the other direction, if I may use a metaphor which implies that gaps aren't isotropic."

Snelund laughed. "Well spoken, Commander. One grows starved for a little wit. Frontiers are traditionally energetic but unimaginative."

"Thank you, Your Excellency," Flandry said. "I'd better state my business, though. Will the governor bear with me if I sound long-winded? Necessary background . . . especially since my assignment is indefinite, really just to prepare a report on whatever I can learn. . . ."

Snelund lounged back. "Proceed."

"As a stranger to these parts," Flandry said pompously, "I had to begin with studying references and questioning a broad spectrum of people. My application for an interview with you, sir, would have been cancelled had it turned out to be needless. For I do see how busy you are in this crisis. As matters developed, however, I found I'd have to make a request of you. A simple thing, fortunately. You need only issue an order."

"Well?" Snelund invited.

He's relaxed now, Flandry judged: *takes me for the usual self-important favorite nephew, going through a charade to furnish an excuse for my next promotion.*

"I would like to interview the Lady McCormac," he said.

Snelund jerked upright where he sat.

"My information is that she was arrested together with her husband and has been detained in Your Excellency's personal custody," Flandry said with a fatuous smile. "I'm sure she has a good many valuable data. And I've speculated about using her as a go-between. A negotiated settlement with her husband—"

"No negotiation with a traitor!" Snelund's fist smote a chair arm.

How dramatic, Flandry thought. Aloud: "Pardon me, sir. I didn't mean he should get off scot free, simply that—Well, anyhow, I was surprised to discover no one has questioned the Lady McCormac."

Snelund said indignantly, "I know what you've heard. They gossip around here like a gaggle of dirty-minded old women. I've explained the facts to Admiral Pickens' chief Intelligence officer, and I'll explain them again to you. She appears to have an unstable personality, worse even than her husband's. Their arrest threw her into a completely hysterical condition. Or 'psychotic' might not be too strong a word. As a humane gesture, I put her in a private room rather than a cell. There was less evidence against her than him. She's quartered in my residential wing because that's the sole place where I can guarantee her freedom from bumbling interruptions. My agents were preparing to quiz McCormac in depth when his fellow criminals freed him. His wife heard, and promptly attempted suicide. My medical staff has had to keep her under heavy sedation ever since."

Flandry had been told otherwise, though no one dared give him more than hearsay. "I beg the governor's pardon," he said. "The admiral's staff suggested perhaps I, with a direct assignment, might be allowed where they aren't."

"Their men have met her twice, Commander. In neither case was she able to testify."

No, it isn't hard to give a prisoner a shot or a touch of brainshock, when you have an hour or two advance notice. "I see, Your Excellency. And she hasn't improved?"

"She's worsened. On medical advice, I've banned further visits. What could the poor woman relate, anyway?"

"Probably nothing, Your Excellency. However, you'll

appreciate, sir, I'm supposed to make a full report. And as my ship will soon be leaving with the fleet," *unless I produce my authority to detach her*, "this may be my lone chance. Couldn't I have a few minutes, to satisfy them on Terra?"

Snelund bristled. "Do you doubt my word, Commander?"

"Oh, no, Your Excellency! Never! This is strictly *pro forma*. To save my, uh, reputation, sir, because they'll ask why I didn't check this detail also. I could go there straight from here, sir, and your medics could be on hand to keep me from doing any harm."

Snelund shook his head. "I happen to know you would. I forbid it."

Flandry gave him a reproachful stare.

Snelund tugged his chin. "Of course, I sympathize with your position," he said, trading a scowl for a slight smile. "Terra is so far away that our reality can only come through as words, photographs, charts. Um-m-m. . . . Give me a number where you can be contacted on short notice. I'll have my chief doctor inform you when you can go to her. Some days she's more nearly sane than others, though at best she's incoherent. Will that do?"

"Your Excellency is most kind," Flandry beamed.

"I don't promise she'll be available before you depart," Snelund cautioned. "Small time remains. If not, you can doubtless see her on your return. Though that will hardly be worth the trouble, will it, after McCormac has been put down?"

"*Pro forma*, Your Excellency," Flandry repeated. The governor recorded a memorandum, including a phone exchange which would buck a message on to *Asieneuve*, and Flandry took his leave with expressions of mutual esteem.

He got a cab outside the palace and made sure he was heard directing it to the shuttleport. It was no secret that he'd been on the ground these past several days; his job required that. But the fainéant impression he wanted to give would be reinforced if he took the first excuse to return to his vessel. Ascetical though his cabin there might be, it was a considerable improvement on the flea circus dormitory which was the best planetside quarters a late arrival like him had been able to obtain. Catawrayannis was overflowing at the hatches with spacemen and marines, as ship after ship made rendezvous.

"Why here?" he had asked Captain Leclerc, the member of Admiral Pickens' staff to whom he actually reported. "Ifri is HQ."

Leclerc shrugged. "The governor wants it this way."

"But he can't—"

"He can, Flandry. I know, the Naval and civilian provincial commands are supposed to be coordinate. But the governor is the Emperor's direct representative. As such, he can invoke Imperial authority when he wants. It may get him into the kettle on Terra afterward, but that's afterward. On the spot, the Navy had better heed him."

"Why the order, though? Ifri has the main facilities. It's our natural center and starting point."

"Well, yes, but Llynathawr doesn't have Ifri's defenses. By our presence, we guard against any revengeful raids McCormac may plan. It makes a degree of sense, even. Knocking out the sector capital—or preferably occupying it—would put him a long way toward control of the entire region. Once we get started, he'll be too busy with us to think about that, although naturally we will leave some protection." Leclerc added cynically: "While they wait, our men on liberty will enjoy a good, expensive last fling. Snelund's careful to stay popular in Catawrayannis."

"Do you really think we should charge out for an immediate full-dress battle?"

"Governor's directive again, I hear. It certainly doesn't fit Admiral Pickens' temperament. Left alone, I'm convinced he'd see what could be done first by dickering and small-scale shooting . . . rather than maybe end up bombarding Imperial worlds into radioactive rubbish. But the word is, we've got to blast the infection before it spreads." Leclerc grimaced. "You're an insidious one. I've no business talking like this. Let's take up your business!"

—When he stepped out at the terminal, Flandry received the not unexpected information that he must wait a couple of hours for a seat on a ferry to Satellite Eight, where he could summon his gig. He phoned the dormitory and had his luggage shunted to him. Since this consisted merely of one handbag, already packed, he didn't bother to check it, but carried it along into a refresher booth. From there he emerged in drab civvies, with a hooded cloak and slouching gait and bag turned inside out to show a different color. He had no real reason to think he had been followed, but he believed in buying insurance when it was cheap. He took a cab to an unpretentious hotel, thence another into Lowtown. The last few blocks he walked.

Rovian had found a rooming house whose clientele

were mostly nonhumans: unchoosy ones. He shared his kennel with a betentacled hulk from an unpronounceable planet. The hulk reeked of exuded hydrogen sulfide but was personally decent enough; among other sterling qualities, it did not know the Eriau language. It rippled on its bunk when Flandry entered, mushed an Anglic greeting, and returned to contemplation of whatever it contemplated.

Rovian stretched all six limbs and yawned alarmingly. "At last!" he said. "I thought I would rot."

Flandry sat down on the floor, which carried no chairs, and lit a cigarette more against the stench than because he wanted one. "How goes the ship?" he asked in the principal Merseian tongue.

"Satisfactorily," Rovian answered likewise. "Some were curious at the exec absenting himself before the captain returned. But I passed it off as needful to our supplying and left Valencia in charge. Nothing can really happen while we idle in orbit, so no great comment followed."

Flandry met the slit-pupilled eyes. *You seem to know more about what your human shipmates think than a xeno should,* he did not say. *I don't pretend to understand what goes on in your brain. But . . . I have to rely on somebody. Sounding you out while we traveled, as well as might be, I decided you're least improbably the one.*

"I didn't ask you to locate a den, and tell me where, and wait, for sport," he declared with the explicitness required by Eriau grammar. "My idea was that we'd need privacy for laying plans. That's been confirmed."

Rovian cocked his ears.

Flandry described his session with the governor. He finished: "No reasonable doubt remains that Snelund is lying about Lady McCormac's condition. Gossip leaks through guards and servants, out of the private apartments and into the rest of the palace. Nobody cares, aside from malicious amusement. He's packed the court, like the housecarls and the residencies, with his own creatures. Snooping around, getting sociable with people off duty, I led them to talk. Two or three of them got intoxicated till they said more than they would have normally." He didn't mention the additives he had slipped into their drinks.

"Why don't the regular Intelligence officers suspect?" Rovian inquired.

"Oh, I imagine they do. But they have so much else to deal with, so obviously vital. And they don't think she can tell anything useful. And why collide with the governor, risking your career, for the sake of the arch-rebel's wife?"

"You wish to," Rovian pounced.

"*Khraich.*" Flandry squinted into the smoke he was blowing. It curled blue-gray across what sunlight straggled through a window whose grime seemed of geologic age. The rotten-egg gas was giving him a headache, unless that was due to the general odor of decay. Faintly from outside came traffic rumble and an occasional raucous cry.

"You see," he explained, "I'm on detached service. My nose isn't committed to any of the numberless grindstones which must be turned before a Naval expedition can get under way. And I have more background on Aaron Snelund than provincial officers do, even in my own corps and in his own preserve. I've been free and able to sit and wonder. And I decided it wasn't logical he should keep Kathryn McCormac locked away simply for the purpose the court is sniggering about. The admiral's staff may think so, and not care. But I doubt if he's capable of feeling more than a passing attraction for any fellow creature. Why not turn her over for interrogation? She might know a little something after all. Or she might be handy in dealing with her husband."

"Scarcely that," Rovian said. "His life is already forfeit."

"Uh-huh. Which is why my harried colleagues didn't check further. But—oh, I can't predict—her, in exchange for various limited concessions on his part—her, persuading him to give up—Well, I suppose it takes a cold-blooded bastard like me to consider such possibilities. The point is, we can't lose by trying her out, and might gain a trifle. Therefore we ought to. But Snelund is holding her back with a yarn about her illness. Why? What's in it for him, besides herself? His sector's being torn apart. Why isn't he more cooperative in this tiny matter?"

"I couldn't say." Rovian implied indifference.

"I wonder if she may not know something he would prefer didn't get out," Flandry said. "The assumption has been that Snelund may be a bad governor, but he is loyal and McCormac's the enemy. It's only an assumption."

"Should you not then invoke the authority in your second set of orders, and demand her person?"

Flandry made a face. "Huh! Give them five minutes of stalling at the gate, and I'll be presented with a corpse. Or ten minutes under a misused hypnoprobe could produce a memoryless idiot. Wherefore I walked very softly indeed. I don't expect to be summoned before the fleet leaves, either."

"And on our return—"

"She can easily have 'passed away' during the campaign."

Rovian tautened. The bunk where he crouched made a groaning noise. "You tell me this for a purpose, Captain," he said.

Flandry nodded. "How did you guess?"

Again Rovian waited, until the man sighed and proceeded:

"I think we can spring her loose, if we time it exactly right. You'll be here in town, with some crewmen you've picked and an aircar handy. An hour or so before the armada accelerates, I'll present my sealed orders to the admiral and formally remove us from his command. It's a safe bet Snelund's attention will be on the fleet, not on the palace. You'll take your squad there, serve a warrant I'll have given you, and collect Kathryn McCormac before anybody can raise the governor and ask what to do. If need be, you can shoot; whoever tries to stop you will be in defiance of the Imperium. But I doubt the necessity will arise if you work fast. I'll have the gig waiting not too far off. You and your lads flit Lady McCormac there, haul gravs for space, rendezvous with *Asieneuve*, and we'll depart this system in a hurry."

"The scheme appears hazardous," Rovian said, "and for slight probable gain."

"It's all I can think of," Flandry answered. "I know you'll be getting the operative end of the reamer. Refuse if you think I'm a fool."

Rovian licked his saber teeth and switched his tail. "I do not refuse my captain," he said, "I, a Brother of the Oath. It does seem to me that we might discuss the problem further. I believe your tactics could be made somewhat more elegant."

CHAPTER FIVE

Ship by ship, Pickens' forces departed orbit and moved outward. When the sun of Llynathawr had shrunk to a bright point, the vessels assumed formation and went into hyperdrive. Space swirled with impalpable energies. As one, the warcraft and their ministrants aimed themselves at the star called Virgil, to find the man who would be Emperor.

They were not many. Reassignments, to help confront Merseia, had depleted the sector fleet. A shocking number of units had subsequently joined McCormac. Of those which stayed true, enough must remain behind to screen—if not solidly guard—the key planets. It was estimated that the rebels had about three-fourths the strength that Pickens would be able to bring to bear on them. Given nuclear-headed missiles and firebeams powered by hydrogen fusion, such numerical comparisons are less meaningful than the layman thinks. A single penetration of defenses can put a ship out of action, often out of existence.

On that account, Pickens traveled cautiously, inside a wide-flung net of scoutboats. His fastest vessels could have covered the distance in a day and a half, his slowest in twice that time; but he planned on a whole five days. He had not forgotten the trap his former commander sprang on the Valdotharian corsairs.

And on the bridge of *Asieneuve*, Dominic Flandry leaned forward in his control chair and said: "Twenty degrees north, four degrees clockwise, 3000 kilometers negative, then match quasi-velocities and steady as she goes."

"Aye, sir." The pilot repeated the instructions and programmed the computer that operated the hyperdrive.

Flandry kept his attention on the console before him, whose meters and readouts summarized the far more complex data with which the pilot dealt, until he dared say, "Can you hold this course, Citizen Rovian?"

In point of fact, he was asking his executive officer if the destroyer was moving as planned—tagging along after the fleet in order that her wake be drowned in many and that she thus be hidden from pursuit. They both knew, and both knew the master's ritual infallibility must be preserved. Rovian studied the board and said, "Aye, sir," with complete solemnity.

Flandry opened the general intercom. "Now hear this," he intoned. "Captain to all officers and crew. You are aware that our ship has a special mission, highly confidential and of the utmost importance. We are finally embarked on it. For success, we require absolute communications silence. No messages will be received except by Lieutenant Commander Rovian or myself, nor will any be sent without my express authorization. When treason has infected His Majesty's very Navy, the danger of subversion and of ruses must be guarded against." *How's that for casuistry?* he grinned within. "The communications officer will set his circuits accordingly. Carry on."

He switched off. His gaze lifted to the simulacrum of heaven projected on the viewscreens. No spacecraft showed. The greatest of them was lost in immensity, findable only by instruments and esoteric calculations. The stars ignored them, were not touched by the wars and pains of life, were immortal—*No, not that either. They have their own Long Night waiting for them.*

"Outercom circuits ready, sir," Rovian announced after a study of the main panel. He slipped on a headband receiver. Every incoming signal would go there, to be heard by him alone.

"Take the bridge, then." Flandry rose. "I'll interrogate the prisoner. When the time comes to change vectors, notify me immediately but don't wait for me to arrive before you do it."

What he really told Rovian was: Monitor transmissions. Snelund's bound to yell when he learns what's happened. If we're out of hyperwave range by that time, he'll probably send a boat after us. Either way, he'll demand our return, and Pickens might well give in. That could make a delicate situation. The minute it looks like coming about, we're to sheer off and get the devil away. I'd rather be able to prove by the log that I never could have received any order from Pickens, than try to make a court-martial agree I was right in disregarding it.

But those two alone knew the code. Possibly the

ratings who had gone to the palace with their exec could have guessed. No matter there. They were tough and close-mouthed and, after what they had seen en route from Terra, callously cheerful about any inconvenience they might have caused His Excellency.

"Aye, sir," said Rovian.

Flandry went down a companionway and along a throbbing passage to his cabin. The door had no chime. He knocked.

"Who is it?" The voice that came through the thin panel was a husky contralto, singingly accented—and how tired, how empty!

"Captain, my lady. May I come in?"

"I can't stop you."

Flandry stepped through and closed the door behind him. His cabin had room for little more than a bunk, a desk and chair, a closet, some shelves and drawers. His bonnet brushed the overhead. A curtain hid a washbasin, toilet, and shower stall. He'd had no chance to install many personal possessions. The sound and vibration and oily-electrical odor of the ship filled the air.

He had not even seen a picture of Kathryn McCormac. Suddenly everything else dissolved around him. He thought afterward he must have given her a courtly bow, because he found his bonnet clutched in his fingers, but he couldn't remember.

She was five standard years older than him, he knew, and in no Terran fashion of beauty. Her figure was too tall, too wide-shouldered and deep-bosomed, too firmly muscled beneath a skin that was still, after her imprisonment, too suntanned. The face was broad: across the high cheekbones, between the luminous eyes (gold-flecked green under thick black brows), in the blunt nose and generous mouth and strong chin. Her hair was banged over her forehead, bobbed below her ears, thick and wavy, amber with shadings of gold and copper. She wore the brief nacreous gown and crystaflex sandals in which she had been taken from the palace.

Mother looked sort of like her, Flandry realized.

He hauled his wits back in. "Welcome aboard, my lady." He could feel his smile was a touch unstable. "Permit me to introduce myself." He did. "Entirely at your service," he finished, and held out his hand.

She did not give him hers, either to shake or kiss, nor did she rise from his chair. He observed the darknesses around and behind her eyes, hollowing of cheeks, faint dusting of freckles. . . . "Good day, Commander." Her tone was not warm or cold or anything.

Flandry lowered his bunk and himself onto it. "What may I offer you?" he asked. "We have the regular assortment of drinks and drugs. And would you like a bite to eat?" He extended his opened cigarette case.

"Nothin'."

He regarded her. *Stop skyhooting, son. You've been celibate unrightfully long. She's handsome and—he dragged it forth—no doubt you speculated about her possible availability . . . after what's happened to her. Forget it. Save your villainies for the opposition.*

He said slowly: "You don't want to accept hospitality from the Imperium. Correct? Please be sensible, my lady. You know you'll take nourishment to stay alive, as you did in Snelund's house. Why not begin now? My cause isn't necessarily irreconcilable with yours. I had you fetched here, at some risk, intending that we'd discuss matters."

She turned her head. Their glances locked. After a while that seemed lengthy, he saw part of the tension go from her. "Thanks, Commander," she said. Did her lips flutter the ghostliest bit upward? "Coffee and a sandwich 'ud taste well, for truth."

Flandry got on the intercom to the galley. She refused a cigarette but said she didn't mind if he smoked. He inhaled several times before he said, fast:

"I'm afraid an escort destroyer leaves something to be desired in the way of accommodations. You'll have this cabin, of course. I'll move in with the mates; one of them can throw a pad on the deck. But I'll have to leave my clothes and so forth where they are. I hope the steward and I won't disturb you too badly, trotting in and out. You can take your meals here or in the wardroom, as you prefer. I'll see you get some spare coveralls or whatever to wear—sorry I didn't think to lay in a female outfit—and I'll clear a drawer to keep them in. À propos which—" he rose and opened one in his desk—"I'll leave this unlocked. It has the nonsecret items. Including a souvenir of mine." He took out a Merseian war knife. "Know how to handle this cheap and chippy chopper? I can demonstrate. It's not much use if you get in the way of a bullet, a blast, a stun beam, et cetera. But you'd be surprised what it can do at close quarters." Again he caught her gaze. "Do be careful with it, my lady," he said low. "You've nothing to fear on my ship. The situation might alter. But I'd hate to think you'd gotten reckless with my souvenir and bowed out of the universe when there was no real need."

The breath hissed between her teeth. Color and pallor chased each other across her face. The hand she reached out for the knife wavered. She let it fall, raised it back to her eyes, clenched the remaining fist, and fought not to weep.

Flandry turned his back and browsed through a full-size copy of a translated *Genji Monogatari* that he'd brought along to pass the time. The snack arrived. When he had closed the door on the messman and set the tray on his desk, Kathryn McCormac was her own captain again.

"You're a strider, sir," she told him. He cocked his brows. "Aenean word," she explained. "A strong, good man . . . let me say a gentleman."

He stroked his mustache. "A gentleman manqué, perhaps." He sat back down on the bunk. Their knees brushed. "No business discussion over food. Abominable perversion, that." She flinched. "Would you care for music?" he asked hastily. "My tastes are plebeian, but I've been careful to learn what's considered high art." He operated a selector. *Eine Kleine Nachtmusik* awoke in joy.

"That's beautiful," she said when she had finished eating. "Terran?"

"Pre-spaceflight. There's a deal of antiquarianism in the inner Empire these days, revival of everything from fencing to allemandes—uh, sport with swords and a class of dances. Wistfulness about eras more picturesque, less cruel and complicated. Not that they really were, I'm sure. It's only that their troubles are safely buried."

"And we've yet to bury ours." She drained her cup and clashed it down on the bare plate. "If they don't shovel us under first. Let's talk, Dominic Flandry."

"If you feel up to it." He started a fresh cigarette.

"I'd better. Time's none too long 'fore you must decide what to do 'bout me." The dark-blonde head lifted. "I feel 'freshed. Liefer attack my griefs than slump."

"Very well, my lady." *Wish I had a pretty regional accent.*

"Why'd you rescue me?" she asked gently. He studied the tip of his cigarette.

"Wasn't quite a rescue," he said.

Once more the blood left her countenance. "From Aaron Snelund," she whispered, "anything's a rescue."

"Bad?"

"I'd've killed myself, come the chance. Didn't get it. So I tried to keep sane by plannin' ways to kill him." She strained her fingers against each other until she noticed she was doing so. "Hugh's habit," she mumbled, pulled her hands free and made them both into fists.

"You may win a little revenge." Flandry sat straight. "Listen, my lady. I'm a field agent in Intelligence. I was dispatched to investigate Sector Alpha Crucis. It occurred to me you could tell things that nobody else would. That's why you're here. Now I can't officially take your unsupported word, and I won't use methods like hypno-probing to squeeze the facts out against your will. But if you lie to me, it's worse than if you keep silence. Worse for us both, seeing that I want to help you."

Steadiness had returned to her. She came of a hardy breed. "I'll not lie," she promised. "As to whether I'll speak at all . . . depends. Is it truth what I heard, my man's in revolt?"

"Yes. We're trailing a fleet whose mission is to defeat

the rebels, seize and occupy the planets that support them—which includes your home, my lady."

"And you're with the Imperialists?"

"I'm an officer of the Terran Empire, yes."

"So's Hugh. He . . . he never wanted . . . anything but the good of the race—every race everywhere. If you'd think the matter through, I 'spect you yourself 'ud—"

"Don't count on that, my lady. But I'll listen to whatever you care to tell me."

She nodded. "I'll speak what I know. Afterward, when I'm stronger, you can give me a light probe and be sure I'm not swittlin'. I believe I can trust you'll use the machine just for confirmation, not for pryin' deeper."

"You can."

In spite of her sorrow, Flandry felt excitement sharpen each sense and riot in his blood. *By Pluto's single icy ball, I* am *on a live trail!*

She chose words and uttered them, in a flat tone but with no further hesitation. As she spoke, her face congealed into a mask.

"Hugh never planned any treason. I'd've known. He got me cleared for top security so we could also talk together 'bout his work. Sometimes I'd give him an idea. We were both murderin' mad over what Snelund's goons were doin'. Civilized worlds like Aeneas didn't suffer worse'n upratcheted taxes at first. Later, bit by bit, we saw fines, confiscations, political arrests—more and more—and when a secret police was officially installed—But that was mild compared to some of the backward planets. We had connections, we could eventu'ly raise a zoosny on

Terra, even if Snelund was a pet of the Emperor's. Those poor primitives, though—

"Hugh wrote back. To start with, he got reprimands for interferin' with civilian affairs. But gradu'ly the seriousness of his charges must've percolated through the bureaucracy. He started gettin' replies from the High Admiralty, askin' for more exact information. That was by Naval courier. We couldn't trust the mails any longer. He and I spent this year collectin' facts—depositions, photographs, audits, everything needed to make a case nobody could overlook. We were goin' to Terra in person and deliver the microfile.

"Snelund got wind. We'd taken care, but we were amateurs at sneakery, and you can't dream how poisonous horrible 'tis, havin' secret police 'round, never knowin' when you dare talk free. . . . He wrote offici'ly askin' Hugh to come discuss plans for defendin' the outermost border systems. Well, they had been havin' trouble, and Hugh's not a man who could leave without doin' something for them. I was more scared than him of a bounceplay, but I went along. We always stayed close together, those last days. I did tip the hand to Hugh's chief aide, one of my family's oldest friends, Captain Oliphant. He should stand alert in case of treachery.

"We stayed at the palace. Normal for high-rankin' visitors. Second night, as we were 'bout to turn in, a detachment of militia arrested us.

"I was taken to Snelund's personal suite. Never mind what came next. After a while, though, I noticed he could be gotten to boast. No need for pretendin' I'd changed my mind 'bout him. Contrary: he liked to see me hurtin'. But that was the way to play, then. Show hurt at the right times. I didn't really think I'd ever pass on what he told me. He said I'd leave with my mind scrubbed out of my brain. But hope—How glad I am now for grabbin' that one percent of hope!"

She stopped. Her eyes were reptile dry and did not appear to see Flandry.

"I never imagined he intended his gubernatorial antics for a full-time career," the man said, most softly. "What's his plan?"

"Return. Back to the throne. And become the puppeteer behind the Emperor."

"Hm. Does His Majesty know this?"

"Snelund claimed the two've them plotted it before he left, and've kept in touch since."

Flandry felt a sting. His cigarette had burned down to his fingers. He chucked it into the disposer and started a new one. "I hardly believe our lord Josip has three brain cells to click together," he murmured. "He might have a pair, that occasionally impact soggily. But of course, brother Snelund will have made our lord feel like a monstrous clever fellow. That's part of the manipulation."

She noticed him then. "You said that?"

"If you report me, I could get broken for *lèse majesté*," Flandry admitted. "Somehow I doubt you will."

"Surely not! 'Cause you—" She checked herself.

He thought: *I didn't mean to lead her up any garden paths. But it seems I did, if she thinks maybe I'll join her man's pathetic revolt. Well, it'll make her more cooperative, which serves the Cause, and happier for a few days, if that's doing her any favor.* He said:

"I can see part of the machinery. The Emperor wants dear Aaron back. Dear Aaron points out that this requires extracting large sums from Sector Alpha Crucis. With those, he can bribe, buy elections, propagandize, arrange events, maybe purchase certain assassinations . . . till he has a Policy Board majority on his side.

"*Ergo,* word gets passed from the throne to various powerful, handpicked men. The facts about Snelund's governorship are to be suppressed as much as possible, the investigation of them delayed as long as possible and hampered by every available trick when finally it does roll. Yes. I'd begun to suspect it on my own hook."

He frowned. "But a scandal of these dimensions can't be concealed forever," he said. "Enough people will resign themselves to having Snelund for a gray eminence that his scheme will work—*unless* they understand what he's done out here. Then they might well take measures, if only because they fear what he could do to them.

"Snelund isn't stupid, worse luck. Maybe no big, spectacular warriors or statesmen can topple him. But a swarm of drab little accountants and welfare investigators isn't that easily fended off. He must have a plan for dealing with them too. What is it?"

"Civil war," she answered.

"Huh?" Flandry dropped his cigarette.

"Goad till he's got a rebellion," she said bleakly. "Suppress it in such a way that no firm evidence of anything remains.

"He'd soonest not have this fleet win a clear victory. A prolonged campaign, with planets comin' under attack, would give him his chaos free. But s'posin', which I doubt, your admiral can beat Hugh at a stroke, there'll still be 'pacification' left for his mercenaries, and they'll have their instructions how to go 'bout it.

"Afterward he'll disband them, 'long with his overlord corps. He recruited from the scum of everywhere else in the Empire, and they'll scatter back through it and vanish automatic'ly. He'll blame the revolt on subversion, and claim to be the heroic leader who saved this frontier."

She sighed. "Oh, yes," she finished, "he knows there'll be loose ends. But he doesn't 'spect they'll be important: 'speci'ly as he reckons to supply a lot of them himself."

"A considerable risk," Flandry mused. "But Krishna, what stakes!"

"The Merseian crisis was a grand chance," Kathryn McCormac said. "Attention bent yonder and most of the local fleet gone. He wanted Hugh out of the way 'cause Hugh was dangerous to him, but also 'cause he hoped this'd clear the path for tormentin' Aeneas till Aeneas rose and touched off the fission. Hugh was more'n chief admiral for the sector. He's Firstman of Dion, which puts him as high on the planet as anybody 'cept the resident. Our Cabinet could only name him an 'expert advisor' under the law, but toward the end he was Speaker in everything save title and led its resistance to Snelund's tools. And Aeneas has tradition'ly set the tone for all human colonies out here, and a good many nonhumans besides."

Life flowed back. Her nostrils flared. "Snelund never looked, though, for havin' Hugh to fight!"

Flandry ground the dropped butt under his heel. Presently he told her, "I'm afraid the Imperium cannot allow a rebellion to succeed, regardless of how well-intentioned."

"But they'll know the truth," she protested.

"At best, they'll get your testimony," he said. "You had a bad time. Frequent drugging and brain-muddling, among other things, right?" He saw her teeth catch her lip. "I'm sorry to remind you, my lady, but I'd be sorrier to leave you in a dream that's due to vaporize. The mere fact that you believe you heard Snelund tell you these schemes does not prove one entropic thing. Confusion—paranoia—deliberate planting of false memories by agents who meant to discredit the governor—any smart advocate, any suborned psychiatrist, could rip your story to ions. You wouldn't carry it past the first investigator screening witnesses for a court of inquiry."

She stared at him as if he had struck her. "Don't you believe me?"

"I want to," Flandry said. "Among other reasons, because your account indicates where and how to look for evidence that can't be tiddlywinked away. Yes, I'll be shooting message capsules with coded dispatches off to various strategic destinations."

"Not goin' home yourself?"

"Why should I, when my written word has better odds of being taken seriously than your spoken one? Not that the odds are much to wager on." Flandry marshalled his thoughts. They were reluctant to stand and be identified. "You see," he said slowly, "bare assertions are cheap. Solid proofs are needed. A mountain of them, if you're to get anywhere against an Imperial favorite and the big men who stand to grow bigger by supporting him. And . . .

Snelund is quite right . . . a planet that's been fought over with modern weapons isn't apt to have a worthwhile amount of evidence left on it. No, I think this ship's best next move is to Aeneas."

"What?"

"We'll try a parley with your husband, my lady. I hope you can talk him into quitting. Then afterward they may turn up what's required for the legal frying of Aaron Snelund."

CHAPTER SIX

The star Virgil is type F7, slightly more massive than Sol, half again as luminous, with a higher proportion of ultraviolet in its emission. Aeneas is the fourth of its planets, completing an orbit in 1.73 standard years at an average distance of 1.50 astronomical units and thus receiving two-thirds the irradiation that Terra gets. Its mean diameter is 10,700 kilometers, its mass 0.45 Terra, hence gravity on the surface equals 0.635 g. This suffices to retain a humanly breathable atmosphere, comparable on the lowest levels to Denver Complex and on the highest to the Peruvian altiplano. (You must bear in mind that a weak pull means a correspondingly small density gradient, plus orogenic forces insufficient to raise very tall mountains.) Through ages, water molecules have ascended in the thin air and been cracked by energetic quanta; the hydrogen has escaped to space, the oxygen that has not has tended to unite with minerals. Thus little remains of the former oceans, and deserts have become extensive.

The chief original inducement to colonize was scientific: the unique races on the neighbor planet Dido, which itself was no world whereon a man would want to keep his family. Of course, various other kinds of people settled too; but the explorer-intellectuals dominated. Then the Troubles came, and the Aeneans had to survive as best they could, cut off, for generations. They adapted.

The result was a stock more virile and gifted, a society more patriotic and respectful of learning, than most. After civilization returned to the Alpha Crucis region, Aeneas inevitably became its local leader. To the present day, the University of Virgil in Nova Roma drew students and scholars from greater distances than you might expect.

Eventually the Imperium decided that proper organization of this critical sector demanded an end to Aenean independence. Intrigue and judicious force accomplished it. A hundred years later, some resentment lingered, though the ordinary dweller agreed that incorporation had been desirable on the whole and the planet supplied many outstanding men to the Terran armed services.

Its military-intellectual tradition continued. Every Aenean trained in arms—including women, who took advantage of reduced weight. The old baronial families still led. Their titles might not be recognized by the Imperial peerage, but were by their own folk; they kept their strongholds and broad lands; they furnished more than their share of officers and professors. In part this was due to their tendency to choose able spouses, regardless of rank. On its upper levels, Aenean society was rather formal and austere, though it had its sports and holidays and other depressurizing institutions. On its lower levels there was more jollity, but also better manners than you could find on Terra.

Thus a description, cataloguing several facts and omitting the really significant one: that to four hundred million human beings, Aeneas was home.

The sun was almost down. Rays ran gold across the Antonine Seabed, making its groves and plantations a patchwork of bluish-green and shadows, burning on its canals, molten in the mists that curled off a salt marsh. Eastward, the light smote crags and cliffs where the ancient continental shelf of Ilion lifted a many-tiered, wind-worn intricacy of purple, rose, ocher, tawny, black up to a royal blue sky. The outer moon, Lavinia, was a cold small horn on top of that mass.

The wind was cold too. Its whittering blent with the soft roar of a waterfall, the clop of hoofs and creak and jingle of harness as horses wound along a steep upward trail. Those were Aenean horses, shaggy, rangy, their low-gravity gait looking less rapid than it was. Hugh McCormac rode one. His three sons by his first wife accompanied him. Ostensibly they had been hunting spider wolves, but they hadn't found any and didn't care. The unspoken real reason had been to fare forth together across this land that was theirs. They might not have another chance.

A vulch wheeled into view, wings across heaven. John McCormac lifted his rifle. His father glanced behind. "No, don't," he said. "Let it live."

"Save death for the Terries, hey?" asked Bob. At nine

years of age—16 standard—he was a bit loud about his discovery that the universe wasn't quite as simple as they pretended in school.

He'll outgrow that, McCormac thought. *He's a good boy. They all are, like their sisters. How could they help being, with Ramona for a mother?* "I don't hold with killing anything unnecessarily," he said. "That isn't what war is about."

"Well, I don't know," Colin put in. He was the oldest. Since he would therefore be the next Firstman, family custom had kept him from joining the service. (Hugh McCormac had only succeeded when his elder brother was caught in a sand hell and died childless.) Perhaps his planetographic researches in the Virgilian System had not satisfied every inborn impulse. "You weren't here, Father, when the revolution reached Nova Roma. But I saw crowds—plain, kindly citizens—hound Snelund's political police down the streets, catch them, string them up, and beat them to death. And it felt right. It still does, when you think what they'd done earlier."

"Snelund himself'll be a while dyin', if I catch him," John said hotly.

"No!" McCormac snapped. "You'll not sink yourself to his ways. He'll be killed as cleanly as we kill any other mad dog. His associates will have fair trials. There *are* degrees of guilt."

"If we can find the lice," Bob said.

McCormac thought of the wilderness of suns and worlds where his life had passed, and said, "Probably most will succeed in disappearing. What of it? We'll have more urgent work than revenge."

They rode silent for a while. The trail debouched on one of the steplike plateaus and joined a paved road to Windhome. Soil lay deep, washed down from the heights, and vegetation flourished, in contrast to a few dwarf bushes on the eroded slopes. Trava decked the ground almost as luxuriantly as it did the seabed. Mainly it was fire trava here, the serrated leaves edged with scarlet; but the sword kind bristled and the plume kind nodded. Each type was curling up for the night as temperature dropped, to form a springy heat-conserving mat. Trees grew about, not only the low iron-hard native sorts but imported oak, cedar, and rasmin. The wind carried their fragrances. Some ways to the right, smoke blew from a farmer's stone cottage. Robotized latifundia weren't practical on Aeneas, and McCormac was glad of that; he felt in his bones that a healthy society needed yeomen.

Colin clucked to his horse and drew alongside. His sharp young face looked unhappy. "Father—" He stopped.

"Go ahead," McCormac invited.

"Father . . . do you think . . . do you really think we can pull it off?"

"I don't know," McCormac said. "We'll try like men, that's all."

"But—makin' you Emperor—"

McCormac felt anew how pitifully little chance he'd had to speak with his nearest, since his rescuers brought him home: too much to do, and each scant hour when something wasn't clamoring for attention, the body toppled into sleep. He had actually stolen this one day.

"Please don't imagine I want the job," he said. "You

haven't been on Terra. I have. I don't like it. I was never
happier than when they reassigned me back where I
belong."

Imperial routine, passed over his mind. *Rotate
careerists through a series of regions; but in the end,
whenever feasible, return them to the sectors they came
from. Theory: they'll defend their birthhomes more fiercely
than some clutch of planets foreign to them. Practice:
when revolt erupted, many Navy personnel, like civilians,
discovered that those homes meant more to them than a
Terra most of them had never seen. Problem: if I win,
should I discontinue the practice, as Josip doubtless will if
his admirals win?*

"But why, then?" Colin asked.

"What else could I do?" McCormac replied.

"Well . . . freedom—"

"No. The Empire is not so far decayed that it'll allow
itself to be broken apart. And even if it were, I wouldn't.
Don't you see, it's the single thing that stands between
civilization—our civilization—and the Long Night?

"As for armed protest, it might stimulate policy changes,
but the Imperium could not pardon the ringleaders.
That'd invite everybody with a grudge to start shooting,
and spell the end as clearly as partition would. And
besides—" McCormac's knuckles stood white where he
grasped the reins—"it wouldn't get Kathryn back, if any
hope remains of that."

"So you aim to preserve the Empire, but take it over,"
Colin said quickly. His desire to guide his father's thoughts
off his stepmother's captivity was so obvious that
McCormac's heart writhed. "I'm with you. You know that.

I honestly think you'd give it new life—the best Emperor we've had since Isamu the Great, maybe since Manuel I himself—and I'm layin' not just me, but my wife and son on the board for you—but can it be done?" He waved at the sky. "The Empire's that huge!"

As if at a signal, Virgil went down. The Aenean atmosphere held no twilight worth mentioning. Alpha and Beta Crucis blazed forth, then almost instantly thousands more and the frosty bridge of the Milky Way. The land mass on the right became utterly black, but Lavinia silvered the sea bottom under the left-hand cliffs. A tadmouse piped into the mordant wind.

McCormac said: "The revolution has to have a leader, and I'm its choice. Let's have no false modesty. I control the Cabinet on the principal world of this sector. I can prove by the record I'm the top Naval strategist the Empire has. My men know I'm strict about things that matter, compassionate about the rest, and always try to be fair. So do a hundred planets, human and nonhuman. It'd be no service to anyone if I claimed different."

"But how—" Colin's voice trailed off. Moonlight glimmered along his leather jacket and off his silver-mounted saddle.

"We'll take control of this sector," McCormac told him. "That's largely a matter of defeating the Josipist forces. Once we've done it, every significant community in a ten-parsec radius will come over to us. Afterward . . . I don't like the idea myself, but I know where and how to get barbarian allies. Not the few Darthan ships I've already engaged; no, really wild warriors from well outside the border. Don't worry, I won't let them plunder and I won't let them settle, even if they'll swear allegiance. They'll be hirelings paid from tax monies.

"The whole Imperial fleet can't ever come against us. It has too many other duties. If we work fast and hard, we'll be in shape to throw back whatever does attack.

"Beyond that—I can't predict. I'm hoping we'll have a well-governed region to show. I'm hoping that will underline our message: an end to corruption and tyranny, a fresh start under a fresh dynasty, long-overdue reforms. . . . What we need is momentum, the momentum of a snowball. Then all the guns in the Empire can't stop us: because most of them will be on our side."

Why a snowball? jeered his mind. *Who knows snow on Aeneas, except a thin drift in polar winter?*

They rounded a cluster of trees and spied the castle. Windhome stood on what had once been a cape and now thrust out into air, with a dizzying drop beneath. Lights glowed yellow from its bulk, outlining dark old walls and battlements. The Wildfoss River brawled past in cataracts.

But McCormac did not see this immediately. His eyes had gone to the flat Antonine horizon, far below and far away. Above a last greenish trace of sunset, beneath a wan flicker of aurora, burned pure white Dido, the evening star.

Where Kathryn worked, xenologist in its jungles, till that time I met her, five years ago (no, three Aenean years; have I really been so long in the Empire that I've forgotten the years of our planet?) and we loved and were married.

And you always wished for children of your own, Kathryn, dyuba, and we were going to have them, but there were always public troubles that ought to be settled first; and tonight—He thanked his iron God that the sun of Llynathawr was not visible in these latitudes. His throat was thick with the need to weep. Instead, he spurred his horse to a gallop.

The road crossed cultivated fields before it reached Windhome's portal. A caravan of tinerans had established itself on the meadow in front. Their trucks were parked aside, lost in gloom; light from the castle fell only on gaily striped tents, fluttering flags, half-erected booths. Men, women, children, packed around campfires, stopped their plangent music and stamping dances to give the lord of the manor a hail as he rode by. Tomorrow these tatterdemalion wanderers would open their carnival . . . and it would draw merrymakers from a hundred kilometers around . . . though the fist of the Imperium was already slamming forward. *I don't understand,* McCormac thought.

Horseshoes rang in the courtyard. A groom caught his reins. He jumped to the ground. Guards were about, the new-come Navy personnel and the liveried family retainers strutting with jealous glances at each other. Edgar Oliphant hurried from the keep. Though McCormac, as Emperor, had raised him to admiral, he hadn't yet bothered to change the captain's star on either shoulder. He had merely added a brassard in the Ilian colors to the tunic that snugged around his stocky form.

"Welcome back, sir!" he exclaimed. "I was 'bout to dispatch a search party."

McCormac achieved a laugh. "Good cosmos, do you think my boys and I can get lost on our ancestral lands?"

"N-no. No, sir. But 'tis, well, if you'll 'scuse me, sir, 'tis foolish for you to run loose with not a single security escort."

McCormac shrugged. "I'll have to endure that later, on Terra. Leave me my privacy a while." Peering closer: "You've something to tell me."

"Yes, sir. Word came in two hours ago. If the admiral, uh, the Emperor will come with me?"

McCormac tried to give his sons a rueful look. He was secretly not sorry to have his awareness taken from the orbit into which it had fallen—again.

The ancient dignity of the Firstman's office had vanished of recent weeks in a clutter of new gear: communication, computation, electronic files and scanners. McCormac sank into a chair behind his battered desk; that at least was familiar. "Well?" he said.

Oliphant closed the door. "The initial report's been confirmed by two more scouts," he said. "The Imperial armada is movin'. 'Twill be here inside three days." It made no difference whether he meant the standard period or the 20-hour rotation of Aeneas.

McCormac nodded. "I didn't doubt the first crew," he said. "Our plans still stand. Tomorrow, 0600 Nova Roma time, I board my flagship. Two hours later, our forces depart."

"But are you certain, sir, the enemy won't occupy Aeneas?"

"No. I would be surprised, though, if he did. What gain? My kinfolk and I won't be around to seize. I've arranged for the enemy to learn that when he arrives. What else can he make a prize of on Aeneas, till the fighting's past? Whoever wins in space can mop up the planets soon enough. Until then, why commit strength badly needed elsewhere, to grip a spearwasp's nest like this world? If he does occupy, then he does. But I expect he'll leave the Virgilian System the instant he discovers we aren't trying to defend it, we're off to grab the real trophy—Satan."

"Your screenin' forces, however—" Oliphant said dubiously.

"Do you mean protection for offplanet bases like Port Frederiksen? A light vessel each, mostly to guard against possible casual destructiveness."

"No, sir. I'm thinkin' of your interplanetary patrols. What effect 'ull they have?"

"They're just Darthan mercenaries. They have no other purpose than to mislead the enemy, gaining time for our fleet," McCormac said. *Have I really not made it clear to him before now? What else have I overlooked since the avalanche hit me?—No, it's all right, he's simply been too engaged with administrative details on the ground.* "A few vessels posted in local space, with orders to attack any Josipist craft they may spot. Those'll be scouts, of course, weakly armed, easily defeated. The survivors among them will carry the news back. I know Pickens' style of thinking. He'll be convinced we intend to make a fight of it at Virgil, and proceed ultra-cautiously, and therefore not detect us on our way off to Beta Crucis." *Oh, good old Dave Pickens, who always brought flowers for Kathryn when we invited you to dinner, must I indeed use against you the things I learned when we were friends?*

"Well, you're the Emperor, sir." Oliphant gestured at the machines hemming them in. "Plenty of business today. We handled it how we could in Staff, but some items seem to require your attention."

"I'll give them a look-over right away, before eating," McCormac said. "Stay available afterward, in case I need to consult."

"Aye, sir." Oliphant saluted and left.

McCormac didn't retrieve the communications at once. Instead, he went out on a balcony. It opened on the cliff and the rich eastern bottomlands. Creusa, the inner moon, was about due to rise. He filled his lungs with dry chill and waited.

Nearly full, the satellite exploded over the horizon. The shadows it cast moved noticeably; and as it hurtled, he could watch the phase change. Drowned in that living white light, the Antonine appeared to get back its vanished waters. It was as if phantom waves ran across those reaches and surf beat once more on the foot of Windhome ness.

You used to say that, Kathryn. You loved these moments best, in the whole year of our world. Dyuba, dyuba, will you ever see them again?

CHAPTER SEVEN

When Virgil showed a perceptible disc without magnification, *Asieneuve* went out of hyperdrive and accelerated inward on gravs. Every sensor strained at maximum receptivity; and nothing came through save an endless seething of cosmic energies.

"Not so much as a radio broadcast?" Flandry asked.

"Not yet, sir," Rovian's voice replied.

Flandry turned off the intercom. "I should be on the bridge myself," he muttered. "What am I doing in my—your cabin?"

"Gatherin' intelligence," the woman said with a faint smile.

"If only I were! Why total silence? Has the whole system been evacuated?"

"Hardly. But they must know the enemy'll arrive in a couple days. Hugh's a genius at deployin' scouts. He is at most things."

Flandry's gaze sharpened on her. Too restless to sit,

too cramped to pace, he stood by the door and drummed fingers on it. Kathryn McCormac occupied the chair. She appeared almost calm.

But then, she had done little except sleep, between his first talk with her and this one. It had gone far toward healing her in body and, he hoped, at least a small distance toward knitting the wounds that had been torn in her mind. The time had, however, given him a bad case of the crawlies. It had been no easy decision to race ahead of the fleet, the whole way at top quasispeed, bearing his prisoner to the rebel chieftain. He had no hint of authority to negotiate. His action could only be defended on the freest imaginable interpretation of his orders; wouldn't it be valuable to sound out the great insurrectionist, and didn't the wife's presence offer a windfall opportunity to do so?

Why does it bother me to hear love in her voice? Flandry wondered.

He said, "My own genius is in glibness. But that won't get my stern out of the sling if this maneuver doesn't show some kind of profit."

The chrysocolla eyes beneath the amber bangs focused on him. "You'll not make Hugh yield," she warned. "I'd never ask him to, no matter what. They'd shoot him, wouldn't they?"

Flandry shifted his stance. Sweat prickled under his arms. "Well—a plea for leniency—"

He had seldom heard as grim a laugh. "Of your courtesy, Commander, spare us both. I may be a colonial, and I may've spent my adult life 'fore marriage doin' scientific studies on a breed of bein's that're scarcely more concerned with mankind than Ymirites are . . . but I did

study history and politics, and bein' the Fleet Admiral's
lady did give me a lot to observe. 'Tis not possible for the
Imperium to grant Hugh a pardon." Briefly, her tone
faltered. "And I . . . 'ud rather see him dead . . . than a
brain-channeled slave or a lifelong prisoner . . . a crag bull
like him."

Flandry took out a cigarette, though his palate was
scorched leather. "The idea, my lady," he said, "is that
you'll tell him what you've learned. If nothing else, he may
then avoid playing Snelund's game. He can refuse to give
battle on or around those planets that Snelund would like
to see bombarded."

"But without bases, sources of supply—" She drew a
shaken breath. It bulged out the coverall she wore in a
way to trouble Flandry. "Well, we can talk, of course," she
said in misery. The regained strength fell from her. She
half reached toward him. "Commander . . . if you could let
me go—"

Flandry looked away and shook his head. "I'm sorry,
my lady. You've a capital charge against you, and you've
been neither acquitted nor pardoned. The single excuse I
could give for releasing you would be that it bought your
husband's surrender, and you tell me that's unthinkable."
He dragged smoke into his lungs and remembered vaguely
that he ought soon to get an anticancer booster.
"Understand, you won't be turned back to Snelund. I'd
join the rebellion too before permitting that. You'll come
with me to Terra. What you can relate of your treatment
at Snelund's hands, and his brags to you . . . well, it may
cause him difficulty. At a minimum, it ought to gain you the
sympathy of men who're powerful enough to protect you."

Glancing her way again, he was shocked to see how the blood had left her face. Her eyes stared blank, and beads of perspiration glittered forth. "My lady!" He flung the cigarette aside, made two steps, and stooped above her. "What's wrong?" he laid a palm on her brow. It was cold. So were her hands, when his slipped as if of themselves down her shoulders and arms. He hunkered in front and chafed them. "My lady—"

Kathryn McCormac stirred. "A stimpill?" she whispered.

Flandry debated calling the ship's medic, decided not to, and gave her the tablet and a tumbler of water. She gulped. When he saw the corpse color going and the breath becoming steady, it rejoiced in him.

"I'm sorry," she said, scarcely audible above the murmur of the ship. "The memory bounced out at me too quick."

"I said the wrong thing," he stammered, contrite.

"Not your fault." She stared at the deck. He couldn't help noticing how long the lashes were against her bronze skin. "Terran mores are different from ours. To you, what happened to me was . . . unfortunate, nasty, yes, but not a befoulin' I'll never quite cleanse me of, not a thing makes me wonder if I really should want to see Hugh ever again. . . . Maybe, though, you'll understand some if I tell you how often he used drugs and brainscramblers. Time and again, I was trapped in a nightmare where I couldn't think, wasn't me, had no will, wasn't anything but an animal doin' what he told me, to 'scape pain—"

I oughtn't to hear this, Flandry thought. *She wouldn't*

speak of it if her self-command had entirely returned. How can I leave?

"My lady," he attempted, "you said a fact, that it wasn't you. You shouldn't let it count. If your husband's half the man you claim, he won't."

She sat motionless a while. The stimulol acted faster than normal on her; evidently she wasn't in the habit of using chemical crutches. At length she raised her head. The countenance was deeply flushed, but the big body seemed in repose. And she smiled.

"You *are* a strider," she said.

"Uh . . . feeling well now?"

"Better, anyways. Could we talk straight business?"

Flandry gusted a secret sigh of relief. A touch weak in his own knees, he sat down on the bunk and began another cigarette. "Yes, I rather urgently want to," he said. "For the proverbial nonce, we have common interests, and your information might be what lets us carry on instead of scuttling off for home and mother."

"What d'you need to know? I may not be able to answer some questions, and may refuse to answer others."

"Agreed. But let's try on a few. We've caught no trace of astronautical activity in this system. A fleet the size of Hugh McCormac's should register one way or another. If nothing else, by neutrino emission from powerplants. What's he done? He might be fairly close to the sun, keeping behind it with respect to us; or might be lying doggo a goodly distance out, like half a light-year; or might have hauled mass for some different territory altogether; or—Have you any ideas?"

"No."

"Certain you don't?"

She bridled. "If I did, would I tell?"

"Sizzle it, one destroyer doesn't make a task force! Put it this way: How can we contact him before battle commences?"

She yielded. "I don't know, and that's honest," she said, meeting his stare without wavering. "I can tell you this, whatever Hugh's plannin' 'ull be something bold and unexpected."

"Marvelous," Flandry groaned. "Well, how about the radio silence?"

"Oh, that's easier to 'splain, I think. We don't have many stations broadcastin' with enough power, at the right wavelengths, to be detectable far out. Virgil's too apt to hash them up with solar storms. Mainly we send tight beams via relay satellites. Radiophones're common— isolated villages and steadin's need them—but they natur'ly use frequencies that the ionosphere 'ull contain. Virgil gives Aeneas a mighty deep ionosphere. In short, 'tisn't hard to get 'long without the big stations, and I s'pose they're doin' it so enemy navigators 'ull have extra trouble obtainin' in-system positions."

You understand that principle too—never giving the opposition a free ride, never missing a chance to complicate his life? Flandry thought with respect. *I've known a lot of civilians, including officers' spouses, who didn't.*

"What about interplanetary communications?" he asked. "I assume you do mining and research on the sister worlds. You mentioned having been involved yourself. Think those bases were evacuated?"

"N-no. Not the main one on Dido, at least. It's

self-supportin', kind of, and there's too big an investment in apparatus, records, relationships with natives." Pride rang: "I know my old colleagues. They won't abandon simply 'cause of an invasion."

"But your people may have suspended interplanetary talk during the emergency?"

"Yes, belike. 'Speci'ly since the Josipists prob'ly won't carry data on where everything is in our system. And what they can't find, they can't wreck."

"They wouldn't," Flandry protested. "Not in mere spite."

She retorted with an acrid: "How do you know what His Ex'lency may've told their admiral?"

The intercom's buzz saved him from devising a reply. He flipped the switch. "Bridge to captain," came Rovian's thick, hissing tones. "A ship has been identified at extreme range. It appears to have started on a high-thrust intercept course to ours."

"I'll be right there." Flandry stood. "You heard, my lady?"

She nodded. He thought he could see how she strained to hold exterior calm.

"Report to Emergency Station Three," he said. "Have the yeoman on duty fit you with a spacesuit and outline combat procedure. When we close with that chap, everyone goes into armor and harness. Three will be your post. It's near the middle of the hull, safest place, not that that's a very glowing encomium. Tell the yeoman that I'll want your helmet transceiver on a direct audiovisual link to the bridge and the comshack. Meanwhile, stay in this cabin, out of the way."

"Do you 'spect danger?" she asked quietly.

"I'd better not expect anything else." He departed.

The bridge viewscreens showed Virgil astonishingly grown. *Asieneuve* had entered the system with a high relative true velocity, and her subsequent acceleration would have squashed her crew were it not for the counteraction of the interior gee-field. Its radiance stopped down in simulacrum, the sun burned amidst a glory of corona and zodiacal light.

Flandry assumed the command chair. Rovian said: "I suppose the vessel was orbiting, generators at minimum, until it detected us. If we wish to rendezvous with it near Aeneas"—a claw pointed at a ruddy spark off the starboard quarter—"we must commence deceleration."

"M-m-m, I think not." Flandry rubbed his chin. "If I were that skipper, I'd be unhappy about a hostile warship close to my home planet, whether or not she's a little one and says she wants to parley. For all he knows, our messages are off tapes and there's nobody here but us machines, boss." He didn't need to spell out what devastation could be wrought, first by any nuclear missiles that didn't get intercepted, finally by a suicide plunge of the ship's multiple tons at perhaps a hundred kilometers a second. "When they've got only one important city, a kamikaze is worth fretting about. He could get a wee bit impulsive."

"What does the captain mean to do, then?"

Flandry activated an astronomical display. The planet-dots, orbit-circles, and vector-arrows merely gave him a rough idea of conditions, but refinements were the navigation department's job. "Let's see. The next planet inward, Dido they call it, past quadrature but far enough from conjunction that there'd be no ambiguity about our aiming for it. And a scientific base . . . cool heads . . . yes, I think it'd be an earnest of pious intentions if we took station around Dido. Set course for the third planet, Citizen Rovian."

"Aye, sir." The directives barked forth, the calculations were made, the engine sang on a deeper note as its power began to throttle down speed.

Flandry prepared a tape announcing his purposes. "If discussion is desired prior to our reaching terminus, please inform. We will keep a receiver tuned on the standard band," he finished, and ordered continuous broadcast.

Time crept by. "What if we are not allowed to leave this system afterward?" Rovian said once in Eriau.

"Chance we take," Flandry replied. "Not too big a risk, I judge, considering the hostage we hold. Besides, in spite of our not releasing her to him, I trust friend McCormac will be duly appreciative of our having gotten her away from that swine Snelund. . . . No, I shouldn't insult the race of swine, should I? His parents were brothers."

"What do you really expect to accomplish?"

"God knows, and He hasn't seen fit to declassify the information. Maybe nothing. Maybe opening some small channel, some way of moderating the war if not halting it. Keep the bridge for ten minutes, will you? If I can't sneak off and get a smoke, I'll implode."

"Can you not indulge here?"

"The captain on a human ship isn't supposed to have human failings, they hammered into me when I was a cay-det. I'll have too many explanations to invent for my superiors as is."

Rovian emitted a noise that possibly corresponded to a chuckle.

The hours trickled past. Virgil swelled in the screens. Rovian reported: "Latest data on the other ship indicate it has decided we are bound for Dido, and plans to get there approximately simultaneously. No communication with it thus far, though it must now be picking up our broadcast."

"Odd. Anything on the vessel herself?" Flandry asked.

"Judging from its radiations and our radar, it has about the same tonnage and power as us but is not any Naval model."

"No doubt the Aeneans have pressed everything into service that'll fly, from broomsticks to washtubs. Well, that's a relief. They can't contemplate fighting a regular unit like ours."

"Unless the companion—" Rovian referred to a second craft, detected a while ago after she swung past the sun.

"You told me that one can't make Dido till hours after we do, except by going hyper; and I doubt her captain is so hot for Dido that he'll do that, this deep in a gravitational well. No, she must be another picket, brought in on a just-in-case basis."

Nevertheless, he called for armor and battle stations when *Asieneuve* neared the third planet.

It loomed gibbous before him, a vast, roiling ball of snowy cloud. No moon accompanied it. The regional *Pilot's Manual and Ephemeris* described a moderately eccentric orbit whose radius vector averaged about one astronomical unit; a mass, diameter, and hence surface gravity very slightly less than Terra's; a rotation once in eight hours and 47 minutes around an axis tilted at a crazy 38 degrees; an oxynitrogen atmosphere hotter and denser than was good for men, but breathable by them; a d-amino biochemistry, neither poisonous nor nourishing to humankind—That was virtually the whole entry. The worlds were too numerous; not even the molecules of the reel could encode much information on any but the most important.

When he had donned his own space gear, aside from gauntlets and closing the faceplate, Flandry put Kathryn McCormac on circuit. Her visage in the screen, looking out of the helmet, made him think of warrior maidens in archaic books he had read. "Well?" she asked.

"I'd like to get in touch with your research base," he said, "but how the deuce can I find it under that pea soup?"

"They may not answer your call."

"On the other hand, they may; the more likely if I beamcast so they can tell I've got them spotted. That ship closing with us is maintaining her surly silence, and— Well, if they're old chums of yours on the ground, they ought to respond to *you*."

She considered. "All right, I trust you, Dominic Flandry. The base, Port Frederiksen"—a brief white smile—"one of my ancestors founded it—'s on the western end of Barca, as we've named the biggest continent. Latitude 34° 5'18" north. I 'spect you can take it from there with radar."

"And thermal and magnetic and suchlike gizmos. Thanks. Stand by to talk in, oh, maybe half an hour or an hour."

Her look was grave. "I'll speak them truth."

"That'll do till we can think of something better and cheaper." Flandry switched off, but it was as if her countenance still occupied the screen. He turned to Rovian. "We'll assume an approximate hundred-minute orbit till we've identified the base, then move out to a synchronous orbit above it."

The exec switched his space-armored tail. "Sir, that means the rebel ship will find us barely outside atmosphere."

"And it's useful to be higher in a planet's field. Well, didn't you last inform me she's coming in too fast to manage less than a hyperbolic orbit?"

"Yes, sir, unless it can brake much quicker than we can."

"Her master's suspicious. He must intend to whip by in a hurry, lest we throw things at him. That's not unnatural. I'd be nervous of any enemy destroyer myself, if I were in a converted freighter or whatever she is. When he sees we're amiable, he'll take station—by which time, with luck, we'll be another ten or fifteen thousand kilometers out and talking to the scientific lads."

"Aye, sir. Have I the captain's permission to order screen fields extended at full strength?"

"Not till we've located Port Frederiksen. They'd bedbug the instruments. But otherwise, except for the detector team, absolute combat readiness, of course."

*Am I right? If I'm wrong—*The loneliness of command engulfed Flandry. He tried to fend it off by concentrating on approach maneuvers.

Eventually *Asieneuve* was falling free around Dido. The cessation of noise and quiver was like sudden deafness. The planet filled the starboard screens, dazzling on the dayside, dark when the ship swung around into night, save where aurora glimmered and lightning wove webs. That stormy atmosphere hindered investigation. Flandry found himself gripping his chair arms till he drove the blood from his fingernails.

"We could observe the other ship optically now, sir," Rovian said, "were this disc not in between."

"It would be," Flandry said. The exec's uneasiness had begun to gnaw in him.

An intercom voice said: "I think we've found it, sir. Latitude's right, infrared pattern fits a continent to east and an ocean to west, radar suggests buildings, we may actually have gotten a neutrino blip from a nuclear installation. Large uncertainty factor in everything, though, what with the damned interference. Shall we repeat, next orbit?"

"No," Flandry said, and realized he spoke needlessly loud. He forced levelness into his tone. "Lock on radar. Pilot, keep inside that horizon while we ascend. We'll go synchronous and take any further readings from there." *I want to be under thrust when that actor arrives in his deaf-mute role. And, oh, yes,* "Maximum screen fields, Citizen Rovian."

The officer's relief was obvious as he issued commands. The ship stirred back to life. A shifting complex of gravitic forces lifted her in a curve that was nearer a straight line than a spiral. The planet's stormy crescent shrank a little.

"Give me a projection of the rendezvousing craft, soon as you have a line of sight," Flandry said. *I'll feel a lot cheerier after I've eyeballed her.* He made himself lean back and wait.

The vision leaped into the screen. A man yelled. Rovian hissed.

That lean shape rushing down the last kilometers had never been for peaceful use. She was simply, deceptively not of Imperial manufacture. The armament was as complete as *Asieneuve*'s, and as smoothly integrated with the hull. Needle nose and rakish fins declared she was meant to traverse atmosphere more often than a corresponding Terran warship . . . as for example on her way to loot a town—

Barbarians, flashed in Flandry. *From some wild country on some wild planet, where maybe a hundred years ago they were still warring with edged iron, only somebody found advantage—military, commercial—in teaching them about spaceflight, providing them with machines and a skeleton education. . . . No wonder they haven't responded to us. Probably not one aboard knows Anglic!*

"White flare," he snapped. "'Pax' broadcast." They must recognize the signals of peace. Hugh McCormac couldn't have engaged them, as he doubtless had, unless they'd been in some contact with his civilization. The order was obeyed at once.

Energy stabbed blue-white out of the mercenary. Missiles followed.

Flandry heard a roar of abused metal. He struck the combat button. *Asieneuve*'s response was instant. And it was the ship's own. At quarters this close, living flesh could not perceive what went on, let alone react fact enough. Her blaster cannon discharged. Her countermissiles soared to meet what had been sent against her. A second later, tubes opened to release her big birds.

Nuclear detonations raged. Electromagnetic screens could ward off the sleet of ions, but not the heat radiation and X-rays, nor the thrust of energy lances and the assault of material torpedoes. Negagrav forces could slow the latter, but not stop them. Interceptors must do that, if they could.

The barbarian had the immense advantage of high speed and high altitude relative to the planet. She was the harder target to come near, her defenses the harder to penetrate if you did.

Nonetheless, Rovian's work of years bore fruit. Abrupt flame seethed around the enemy. White-hot shrapnel fled from a place where armor plate had been. Twisted, crumpled, blackened, half melted, the rest of the ship whirled off on a cometary path around the world and back toward outer space.

But it was not possible that the Terran escape free. Tactical experts reckoned the life of a destroyer in this kind of fight as less than three minutes. Firebeams had seared and gouged through *Asieneuve*'s vitals. No warhead had made the direct hit that would have killed her absolutely; but three explosions were so close that the blast from their shaped charges tore into the hull, bellowing, burning, shattering machines like porcelain, throwing men about and ripping them like red rag dolls.

Flandry saw the bridge crack open. A shard of steel went through Rovian as a circular saw cuts a tree in twain. Blood sheeted, broke into a fog of droplets in the sudden weightlessness, volatilized in the dwindling pressure, and was gone except for spattered stains. Stunned, deafened, his own blood filling nose and mouth, Flandry managed to slam shut the faceplate and draw on the gloves he had forgotten about, before the last air shrieked through the hole.

Then there was a silence. Engines dead, the destroyer reached the maximum altitude permitted by the velocity she had had, and fell back toward the planet.

CHAPTER EIGHT

No boat remained spaceworthy. Where destruction was not total, crucial systems had been knocked out. Time was lacking to make repairs or cannibalize. One of the four craft offered a weak hope. Though its fusion generator was inoperative, its accumulators could energize the two drive cones that seemed usable; and the instruments and controls were undamaged. An aerodynamic landing might be possible. Every rated pilot was killed or wounded—but Flandry had flown combat aircraft before he transferred to the Intelligence Corps.

The engineers had barely finished ascertaining this much when it became urgent to abandon ship. They would soon strike atmosphere. That would complete the ruin of the hull. Struggling through airlessness, weightlessness, lightlessness, hale survivors dragged hurt to the boat housing. There wasn't room for all those bodies if they stayed space armored. Flandry pressurized from tanks and, as each man cycled through the airlock, had his bulky gear stripped off and sent out the disposal valve. He managed to find stowage for three suits, including his—which he suddenly remembered he must not wear when everyone else would be unprotected. That was more for the sake of the impellers secured to them than for anything else.

Those worst injured were placed in the safety-webbed chairs. The rest, jammed together down the aisle, would depend for their lives on the gee-field. Flandry saw Kathryn take her stand among them. He wanted wildly to give her the copilot's chair; the field circuits might well be disrupted by the stresses they were about to encounter. But Ensign Havelock had some training in this kind of emergency procedure. His help could be the critical quantum that saved her.

A shudder went through boat and bones, the first impact on Dido's stratosphere. Flandry shot free.

The rest was indescribable: riding a meteorite through incandescence, shock, thunderblast, stormwind, night, mountains and caverns of cloud, rain like bullets, crazy tilting and whirling of horribly onrushing horizon, while the noise roared and battered and vibrations shook brains in skulls and devils danced on the instrument panel.

Somehow Flandry and Havelock kept a measure of control. They braked the worst of their velocity before they got down to altitudes where it would be fatal. They did not skip helplessly off the tropopause nor flip and tumble when they crossed high winds in the lower atmosphere. They avoided peaks that raked up to catch them and a monstrous hurricane, violent beyond anything Terra had ever known, that would have sundered their boat and cast it into the sea. Amidst the straining over meters and displays, the frantic leap of hands over pilot board and feet on pedals, the incessant brutality of sound, heat, throbbing, they clung to awareness of their location.

Their desire was wholly to reach Port Frederiksen. Their descent took them around the northern hemisphere. Identifying what had to be the largest continent, they fought their way to the approximately correct latitude and slanted down westward above it.

They could have made their goal, or come near, had their initial velocity been in the right direction. But the instrumental survey had been expedited by throwing *Asieneuve* into a retrograde orbit. Now the planet's rotation worked against them, forcing extra energy expenditure in the early stages of deceleration. By the time the boat was approaching a safe speed, its accumulators were drained. Overloaded, it had no possibility of a long ballistic glide. There was nothing to do but use the last stored joules for setting down.

Nor could the tail jacks be employed. Unharnessed, men would be crushed beneath their fellows if the gee-field gave way. Flandry picked out an open area surrounded by forest. Water gleamed between hummocks and sedgy clumps. Better marsh than treetops. The keel skids hissed beneath a last rumble of engine; the boat rocked, bucked, slewed around, and came to rest at a steep angle; flying creatures fled upward in clamorous thousands; and stillness was.

A moment's dark descended on Flandry. He pulled out of it to the sound of feeble cheers. "E-e-everybody all right?" he stuttered. His fingers trembled likewise, fumbling with his harness.

"No further injuries, sir," said one voice.

"Maybe not," another responded. "But O'Brien died on the way down."

Flandry closed his eyes. *My man,* pierced him. *My men. My ship. How many are left? I counted. . . . Twenty-three with only small hurts, plus Kathryn and me. Seventeen— sixteen—seriously wounded. The rest—Those lives were in* my *hands!*

Havelock said diffidently, "Our radio's out, sir. We can't call for help. What does the captain wish?"

Rovian, I should have collected that chunk, not you. The lives that are left are still in my murderous-clumsy hands.

Flandry forced his lids back up. His ears were ringing almost too loudly for him to hear his own words, but he thought they sounded mechanical. "We can't maintain our interior field long. The final ergs are about to go. Let's get our casualties outside before we have to contend with local pull on a slanted deck." He rose and faced his men. Never had he done anything harder. "Lady McCormac," he said. "You know this planet. Have you any recommendations?"

She was hidden from him by those packed around her. The husky tones were unshaken. "Equalize pressures slowly. If we're anywhere near sea level, that air is half again as thick as Terran. Do you know where we are?"

"We were aiming for the Aenean base."

"If I remember rightly, this hemisphere's in its early summer. S'posin' we're not far below the arctic circle, we'll have more day than night, but not very much more. Bear in mind the short spin period. Don't count on a lot of light."

"Thanks." Flandry issued the obvious commands.

Saavedra, the communications officer, found some tools, took the panel off the radio transceiver, and studied it. "I might be able to cobble something together for signalling the base," he said.

"How long'll that take you?" Flandry asked. A little potency was returning to his muscles, a little clarity to his brain.

"Several hours, sir. I'll have to haywire, and jigger around till I'm on a standard band."

"And maybe nobody'll happen to be listening. And when they do hear us, they'll have to triangulate and— Uh-uh." Flandry shook his head. "We can't wait. Another ship's on her way here. When she finds the derelict we shot up, she'll hunt for us. An excellent chance of finding us, too: a sweep with metal detectors over a planet as primitive as this. I don't want us anywhere near. She's likely to throw a missile."

"What shall we do, then, sir?" Havelock asked.

"Does my lady think we've a chance of marching overland to the base?" Flandry called.

"Depends on just where we are," Kathryn replied. "Topography, native cultures, everything's as variable on Dido as 'tis on most worlds. Can we pack plenty of food?"

"Yes, I imagine so. Boats like this are stocked with ample freeze-dried rations. I assume there's plenty of safe water."

"Is. Might be stinkin' and scummy, but no Didonian bug has yet made a human sick. Biochemistry's that different."

When the lock was opened full, the air turned into a steam bath. Odors blew strange, a hundred pungencies, fragrant, sharp, rotten, spicy, nameless. Men gasped and tried to sweat. One rating started to pull off his shirt. Kathryn laid a hand on his arm. "Don't," she warned. "No matter clouds, enough UV gets past to burn you."

Flandry went first down the accommodation ladder. Weight was hardly changed. He identified a tinge of ozone in the swamp reeks and thought that an increased partial pressure of oxygen might prove valuable. His boots squelched into ankle-deep muck. The sounds of life were coming back: chatter, caw, whistle, wingbeats. They were loud in the dense air, now that his hearing had recovered. Small animals flitted among leaves in the jungle.

It was not like a rain forest on a really terrestroid world. The variety of trees was incredible, from gnarly and thorny dwarfs to soaring slim giants. Vines and fungoids covered many dark trunks. Foliage was equally diverse in its shapes. Nowhere was it green; browns and deep reds predominated, though purples and golds blent in; the same held for the spongy, springy mat on the land. The overall effect was one of somber richness. There were no real shadows, but Flandry's gaze soon lost itself in the gloom under the trees. He saw more brush than he liked to think about pushing his way through.

Overhead the sky was pearl gray. Lower cloud strata drifted across its featurelessness. A vaguely luminous area marked Virgil. Recalling where the terminator was, he knew this district was still at morning. They'd leave before sundown if they worked.

He gave himself to helping. The labor was hard. For that he was grateful. It rescued him from dead men and a wrecked ship.

First the wounded must be borne to higher, drier ground. Their injuries were chiefly broken bones and concussions. If your armor was ripped open in space, that was generally the end of you. Two men did have nasty abdominal gashes from bits of metal whose entry holes had been sufficiently small for them or friends to slap on patches before their air could flee them. One man was unconscious, skin chill, breath shallow, pulse thready. And O'Brien had died.

Luckily, the medical officer was on his feet. He got busy. Arriving with an armful of equipment, Flandry saw Kathryn giving him skilled assistance. He remembered in dull surprise that she'd disappeared for a while. It didn't seem like her not to plunge straight into a task.

By the time the last item had been unloaded, she had finished her nurse's job and supervised a burial party. He glimpsed her doing some of the digging herself. When he slogged to her, O'Brien was laid out in the grave. Water oozed upward around him. He had no coffin. She had covered him with the Imperial flag.

"Will the captain read the service?" she asked.

He looked at her. She was as muddy and exhausted as he, but stood straight. Her hair clung wet to head and cheeks, but was the sole brightness upon this world. Sheathed on a belt around her coverall, he recognized the great blade and knuckleduster half of his Merseian war knife.

Stupid from weariness, he blurted, "Do *you* want me to?"

"He wasn't the enemy," she said. "He was of Hugh's people. Give him his honor."

She handed him the prayerbook. *Me?* he thought. *But I never believed*—She was watching. They all were. His fingers stained the pages as he read aloud the majestic words. A fine drizzle began.

While trenching tools clinked, Kathryn plucked Flandry's sleeve. "A minute, of your courtesy," she said. They walked aside. "I spent a while scoutin' 'round," she told him. "Studied the vegetation, climbed a tree and saw mountains to west—and you wouldn't spy many pteropods at this season if we were east of the Stonewall, so the range ahead of us must be the Maurusian—well, I know roughly where we are."

His heart skipped a beat. "And something about the territory?"

"Less'n I'd wish. My work was mainly in Gaetulia. However, I did have my first season in this general area, more for trainin' than research. Point is, we've got a fair chance of findin' Didonians that've met humans; and the local culture is reasonably high; and if we do come on an entity that knows one of our pidgins, it'll be a version I can talk, and I should be able to understand their lingo after a little practice." The black brows knitted. "I'll not hide from you, better if we'd come down west of the Maurusians, and not just 'cause that'd shorten our march. They have some wild and mean dwellers. However, maybe I can bargain for an escort to the other side."

"Good. You didn't perchance find a trail for us?"

"Why, yes. That's what I was mainly searchin' for. We wouldn't make a kilometer 'fore sundown through muscoid and arrowbush, not if we exhausted our blasters burnin' them. I've found one just a few meters from the swamp edge, aimed more or less our way."

"Sizzle it," Flandry said, "but I wish we were on the same side, you and I!"

"We are," she smiled. "What can you do but surrender at Port Frederiksen?"

His failure rose in him, tasting of vomit. "Doubtless nothing. Let's get loaded and start." He turned on his heel and left her, but could not escape the look that followed him. It burned between his shoulderblades.

The stuff from the boat weighed heavily on men who must also take turns carrying the wounded on improvised stretchers. Besides food, changes of clothing, utensils, handguns, ammunition, ripped-off plastic sheeting for shelters, and other necessities, Flandry insisted on taking the three spacesuits. Havelock ventured to protest: "If the captain please, should we lug them? The impellers could be handy for sending scouts aloft, but they aren't good for many kilometers in planet gravity, nor will their radios reach far. And I don't imagine we'll meet any critters that we have to wear armor to fight."

"We may have to discard things," Flandry admitted, "but I'm hoping for native porters. We'll tote the suits a ways, at least."

"Sir, the men are dead on their feet as is!"

Flandry stared into the blond young face. "Would you rather be dead on your back?" he snapped. His eyes traversed the weary, dirty, stoop-shouldered creatures for whom he was responsible. "Saddle up," he said. "Lend me a hand, Citizen Havelock. I don't intend to carry less than anybody else."

A sighing went among them through the thin sad rain, but they obeyed.

The trail proved a blessing. Twigs and gravel mixed into its dirt—by Didonians, Kathryn said—gave a hard broad surface winding gradually through inwalling forest toward higher country.

Dusk fell, layer by layer. Flandry made the group continue, with flashbeams to show the way. He pretended not to hear the *sotto voce* remarks behind his back, though they hurt. Night fell, scarcely cooler than day, tomb black, full of creakings and distant cries, while the men lurched on.

After another nightmare hour, Flandry called a halt. A brook ran across the trail. High trees surrounded and roofed a tiny meadow. His light flew about, bringing leaves and eyes briefly out of murk. "Water and camouflage," he said. "What do you think, my lady?"

"Good," she said.

"You see," he tried to explain, "we have to rest, and daybreak will be soon. I don't want us observed from the air."

She didn't reply. *I rate no answer, who lost my ship,* he thought.

Men eased off their burdens. A few munched food bars before collapsing into sleep with their fellows. The medical officer, Felipe Kapunan, said to Flandry, "No doubt the captain feels he should take first watch. But I'll be busy the next hour or two, seeing to my patients. Dressings need change, they could use fresh enzymes, anti-radiation shots, pain killers—the standard stuff, no help necessary. You may as well rest, sir. I'll call you when I finish."

His last sentence was scarcely heard. Flandry went down and down into miraculous nothingness. His last knowledge was that the ground cover—carpet weed, Kathryn named it, despite its being more suggestive of miniature red-brown sponges—made a damp but otherwise gentle mattress.

The doctor shook him awake as promised and offered him a stimpill. Flandry gulped it. Coffee would have been welcome, but he dared not yet allow a campfire. He circled the meadow, found a seat between two enormous roots, and relaxed with his back against the bole. The rain had paused.

Dawn was stealthy on Dido. Light seemed to condense in the hot rank air, drop by drop, like the mists whose tendrils crawled across the sleepers. Except for the clucking brook and drip of water off leaves, a great silence had fallen.

A footstep broke it. Flandry started to rise, his blaster half out of the sheath. When he saw her, he holstered the weapon and bowed around his shivering heart. "My lady. What . . . what has you awake this early?"

"Couldn't sleep. Too much to think 'bout. Mind if I join you?"

"How could I?"

They sat down together. He contrived his position so that it was natural to watch her. She looked into the jungle for a space. Exhaustion smudged her eyes and paled her lips.

Abruptly she faced back to him. "Talk with me, Dominic Flandry," she pleaded. "I think 'bout Hugh . . . now I can hope to meet him again. . . . Can I stay with him? Wouldn't there always be that between us?"

"I said," *a cosmic cycle ago,* "that if he'd, well, let a girl like you get away from him, for any cause, he's an idiot."

"Thanks." She reached across and squeezed his hand. He felt the touch for a long while afterward. "Shall we be friends? First-name friends?"

"I'd love that."

"We should make a little ceremony of it, in the Aenean way." Her smile was wistful. "Drink a toast and— But later, Dominic, later." She hesitated. "The war's over for you, after all. You'll be interned. No prison; a room in Nova Roma ought to do. I'll come visit when I can, bring Hugh when he's free. Maybe we'll talk you into joinin' us. I do wish so."

"First we'd better reach Port Frederiksen," he said, not daring anything less banal.

"Yes." She leaned forward. "Let's discuss that. I told you I need conversation. Poor Dominic, you save me from captivity, then from death, now 'tis got to be from my personal horrors. Please talk practical."

He met the green eyes in the wide strong face. "Well," he said, "this is quite a freakish planet, isn't it?"

She nodded. "They think it started out to be Venus type, but a giant asteroid collided with it. Shock waves blew most of the atmosphere off, leavin' the rest thin enough that chemical evolution could go on, not too unlike the Terran—photosynthesis and so forth, though the amino acids that developed happened to be mainly dextro- 'stead of levorotatory. Same collision must've produced the extreme axial tilt, and maybe the high rotation. 'Cause of those factors, the oceans aren't as inert as you might 'spect on a moonless world, and storms are fierce. Lot of tectonic activity: no s'prise, is it? That's believed to be the reason we don't find traces of past ice ages, but do find eras of abnormal heat and drought. Nobody knows for sure, though. In thousands of man-lifetimes, we've barely won a glimpse into the mysteries. This is a whole *world*, Dominic."

"I understand that," he said. "Uh, any humanly comfortable areas?"

"Not many. Too hot and wet. Some high and polar regions aren't as bad as this, and Port Frederiksen enjoys winds off a cold current. The tropics kill you in a few days if you're not protected. No, we don't want this planet for ourselves, only for knowledge. It belongs to the autochthons anyway." Her mood turned suddenly defiant: "When Hugh's Emperor, he'll see that all autochthons get a fair break."

"If he ever is." It was as if someone else sat down at a control console in Flandry's brain and made him say, "Why did he bring in barbarians?"

"He must've gone elsewhere himself and needed them to guard Virgil." She looked aside. "I asked a couple of your men who'd watched on viewscreens, what that ship was like. 'Twas Darthan, from their descriptions. Not truly hostile folk."

"As long as they aren't given the chance to be! We'd offered Pax, and nevertheless they fired."

"They . . . well, Darthans often act like that. Their

culture makes it hard for them to believe a call for truce is honest. Hugh had to take what he could get in a hurry. After everything that'd happened, what reason had he to tell them someone might come for parley? He's mortal! He can't think of everything!"

Flandry slumped. "I suppose not, my lady."

A fluting went through the forest. Kathryn waited a minute before she said gently, "You know, you haven't yet spoken my right name."

He replied in his emptiness: "How can I? Men are gone because of what I did."

"Oh, Dominic!" The tears broke forth out of her. He fought to hold back his own.

They found themselves kneeling together, his face hidden against her breasts, his arms around her waist and her left around his neck, her right hand smoothing his hair while he shuddered.

"Dominic, Dominic," she whispered to him, "I know. How well I know. My man's a captain too. More ships, more lives than you could count. How often I've seen him readin' casualty reports! I'll tell you, he's come to me and closed the door so he could weep. He's made his errors that killed men. What commander hasn't? But somebody's got to command. It's your duty. You weigh the facts best's you're able, and decide, and act, and long's you did do your best, you never look back. You needn't. You mustn't.

"Dominic, we didn't make this carnivore universe. We only live here, and have to try and cope.

"Who said you were in error? Your estimate was completely reasonable. I don't believe any board of inquiry 'ud blame you. If Hugh couldn't foresee you'd come with me, how could you foresee—? Dominic, look up, be glad again."

A moment's hell-colored light struck through the eastern leaves. Seconds after, the air roared and a queasy vibration moved the ground.

Men stumbled to their feet. Flandry and Kathryn bounded apart. "What's that?" cried Saavedra.

"That," Flandry yelled into the wind that had arisen, "was the second barbarian ship making sure of our boat."

A minute later they heard the ongoing thunderclap of a large body traveling at supersonic speed. It faded into a terrible whistle and was gone. The gust died out and startled flying creatures circled noisily back toward their trees.

"High-yield warhead," Flandry judged. "They meant to kill within several kilometers' radius." He held a wet finger to the normal dawn breeze. "The fallout's bound east; we needn't worry. I'm stonkerish glad we hiked this far yesterday!"

Kathryn took both his hands. "Your doin' alone, Dominic," she said. "Will that stop your grief?"

It didn't, really. But she had given him the courage to think: *Very well. Nothing's accomplished by these idealistic broodings. Dead's dead. My job is to salvage the living . . . and afterward, if there is an afterward, use whatever tricks I can to prevent my superiors from blaming me too severely.*

No doubt my conscience will. But maybe I can learn how to jettison it. An officer of the Empire is much more efficient without one.

"At ease, men," he said. "We'll spend the next rotation period here, recuperating, before we push on."

CHAPTER NINE

The forest opened abruptly on cleared land. Stepping out, Flandry saw ordered rows of bushes. On three sides the farm was hemmed in by jungle, on the fourth it dropped into a valley full of vapors. The trend of his six Didonian days of travel had been upward.

He didn't notice the agriculture at once. "Hold!" he barked. The blaster jumped into his grasp. *A rhinoceros herd?*

No . . . not really . . . of course not. Lord Advisor Mulele's African preserve lay 200 light-years remote. The half-dozen animals before him had the size and general build of rhinos, though their nearly hairless slate-blue skins were smooth rather than wrinkled and tails were lacking. But the shoulders of each protruded sidewise to make a virtual platform. The ears were big and fanlike. The skull bulged high above a pair of beady eyes, supported a horn on the nose, then tapered to a muzzle whose mouth was oddly soft and flexible. The horn offset that effect by being a great ebony blade with a sawtoothed ridge behind it.

"Wait, Dominic!" Kathryn sped to join him. "Don't shoot. Those're nogas."

"Hm?" He lowered the gun.

"Our word. Humans can't pronounce any Didonian language."

"You mean they are the—" Flandry had encountered curious forms of sophont, but none without some equivalent of hands. What value would an intelligence have that could not actively reshape its environment?

Peering closer, he saw that the beasts were not at graze. Two knelt in a corner of the field, grubbing stumps, while a third rolled a trimmed log toward a building whose roof was visible over a hillcrest. The fourth dragged a crude wooden plow across the newly acquired ground. The fifth came behind, its harness enabling it to steer. A pair of smaller animals rode on its shoulders. That area was some distance off, details hard to make out through the hazy air. The sixth, nearer to Flandry, was not feeding so much as removing weeds from among the bushes.

"C'mon!" Kathryn dashed ahead, lightfoot under her pack.

The trip had been day-and-night trudgery. In camp, he and she had been too occupied—the only ones with wilderness experience—for any meaningful talk before they must sleep. But they were rewarded; unable to mourn, they began to mend. Now eagerness made her suddenly so vivid that Flandry lost consciousness of his surroundings. She became everything he could know, like a nearby sun.

"Halloo!" She stopped and waved her arms.

The nogas halted too and squinted nearsightedly. Their ears and noses twitched, straining into the rank dank heat. Flandry was jolted back to the world. They could attack her. "Deploy," he rapped at those of his men who carried weapons. "Half circle behind me. The rest of you stand at the trailhead." He ran to Kathryn's side.

Wings beat. A creature that had been hovering, barely visible amidst low clouds, dropped straight toward the sixth noga. "A krippo." Kathryn seized Flandry's hand. "I wish I could've told you in advance. But watch. 'Tis wonderful."

The nogas were presumably more or less mammalian, also in their reproductive pattern: the sexes were obvious, the females had udders. The krippo resembled a bird . . . did it? The body was comparable to that of a large goose, with feathers gray-brown above, pale gray below, tipped with blue around the throat, on the pinions, at the end of a long triangular tail. The claws were strong, meant to grab and hang on. The neck was fairly long itself, supporting a head that swelled grotesquely backward. The face seemed to consist mainly of two great topaz eyes. And there was no beak, only a red cartilaginous tube.

The krippo landed on the noga's right shoulder. It thrust a ropy tongue (?) from the tube. Flandry noticed a knot on either side of the noga, just below the platform. The right one uncoiled, revealing itself to be a member suggestive of a tentacle, more than two meters in length if fully outstretched. The krippo's extended equivalent, the "tongue," plunged into a sphincter at the end of this. Linked, the two organisms trotted toward the humans.

"We're still lackin' a ruka," Kathryn said. "No, wait."

The noga behind the plow had bellowed. "That entity's callin' for one. Heesh's own ruka has to unharness heesh 'fore heesh can come to us."

"But the rest—" Flandry pointed. Four nogas merely stood where they were.

"Sure," Kathryn said. "Without partners, they're dumb brutes. They won't act, 'cept for the kind of rote job they were doin', till they get a signal from a complete entity. . . . Ah. Here we go."

A new animal dropped from a tree and scampered over the furrows. It was less analogous to an ape than the noga was to a rhinoceros or the krippo to a bird. However, a Terran was bound to think of it in such terms. About a meter tall if it stood erect, it must use its short, bowed legs arboreally by choice, for it ran on all fours and either foot terminated in three well-developed grasping digits. The tail was prehensile. The chest, shoulders, and arms were enormous in proportion, greater than a man's; and besides three fingers, each hand possessed a true thumb. The head was similarly massive, round, with bowl-shaped ears and luminous brown eyes. Like the krippo, this creature had no nose or mouth, simply a nostrilled tube. Black hair covered it, except where ears, extremities, and a throat pouch showed blue skin. It—he—was male. He wore a belt supporting a purse and an iron dagger.

"Is that a Didonian?" Flandry asked.

"A ruka," Kathryn said. "One-third of a Didonian."

The animal reached the noga closest to the humans. He bounded onto the left shoulder, settled down by the krippo, and thrust out a "tongue" of his own to join the remaining "tentacle."

"You see," Kathryn said hurriedly, "we had to name them somehow. In most Didonian languages, the species are called things answerin' roughly to 'feet,' 'wings,' and 'hands.' But that'd get confusin' in Anglic. So, long's Aenean dialects contain some Russko anyhow, we settled on 'noga,' 'krippo,' 'ruka.'" The tripartite being stopped a few meters off. "Rest your gun. Heesh won't hurt us."

She went to meet it. Flandry followed, a bit dazed. Symbiotic relationships were not unknown to him. The most spectacular case he'd met hitherto was among the Togru-Kon-Tanakh of Vanrijn. A gorilloid supplied hands and strength; a small, carapaced partner had brains and keen eyes; the detachable organs that linked them contained cells for joining the two nervous systems into one. Apparently evolution on Dido had gone the same way.

But off the deep end! Flandry thought. *To the point where the two little types no longer even eat, but draw blood off the big one. Lord, how horrible. Never to revel in a tournedos or a pêche flambée—*

He and Kathryn stopped before the autochthon. A horsey aroma, not unpleasant, wafted down a light, barely cooling breeze. Flandry wondered which pair of eyes to meet.

The noga grunted. The krippo trilled through its nostrils, which must have some kind of strings and resonating chamber. The ruka inflated his throat pouch and produced a surprising variety of sounds.

Kathryn listened intently. "I'm no expert in this language," she said, "but they do speak a related one 'round Port Frederiksen, so I can follow 'long fairly well. Heesh's name is Master Of Songs, though 'name' has the wrong connotations. . . ." She uttered vocables. Flandry caught a few Anglic words, but couldn't really understand her.

I suppose all Didonians are too alien to learn a human tongue, he thought. *The xenologists must have worked out different pidgins for the different linguistic families: noises that a Terran epiglottis can wrap itself around, on a semantic pattern that a Didonian can comprehend.* He regarded Kathryn with renewed marveling. *What brains that must have taken!*

Three voices answered her. *The impossibility of a human talking a Didonian language can't just be a matter of larynx and mouth,* Flandry realized. *A vocalizer would deal with that. No, the structure's doubtless contrapuntal.*

"Heesh doesn't know pidgin," Kathryn told him. "But Cave Discoverer does. They'll assemble heesh for us."

"Heesh?"

She chuckled. "What pronoun's right, in a situation like this? A few cultures insist on some particular sex distribution in the units of an entity. But for most, sex isn't what matters, 'tis the species and individual capabilities of the units, and they form entities in whatever combinations seem best at a given time. So we call a partnership, whether complete or two-way, 'heesh.' And we don't fool 'round inflectin' the word."

The krippo took off in a racket of wings. The ruka stayed aboard the noga. But it was as if a light had dimmed. The two stared at the humans a while, then the ruka scratched himself and the noga began cropping weeds.

"You need all three for full intelligence," Flandry deduced.

Kathryn nodded. "M-hm. The rukas have the most forebrain. Alone, one of them is 'bout equal to a chimpanzee. Is that right, the smartest Terran subhuman? And the noga alone is pretty stupid. A three-way, though, can think as well as you or I. Maybe better, if comparison's possible. We're still tryin' to find tests and measurements that make sense." She frowned. "Do have the boys put away their guns. We're 'mong good people."

Flandry acceded, but left his followers posted where they were. If anything went agley, he wanted that trail held. The hurt men lay there on their stretchers.

The other partnership finished disengaging itself— no, heeshself—from the plow. The earth thudded to the gallop of heesh's noga; krippo and ruka must be hanging on tight! Kathryn addressed this Didonian when heesh arrived, also without result though she did get a response. This she translated as: "Meet Skilled With Soil, who knows of our race even if none of heesh's units have learned pidgin."

Flandry rubbed his chin. His last application of antibeard enzyme was still keeping it smooth, but he lamented the scraggly walrus effect that his mustache was sprouting. "I take it," he said, "that invidi—uh, units swap around to form, uh, entities whose natural endowment is optimum for whatever is to be done?"

"Yes. In most cultures we've studied. Skilled With Soil is evidently just what the phrase implies, a gifted farmer. In other combinations, heesh's units might be part of an outstandin' hunter or artisan or musician or whatever. That's why there's no requirement for a large population in order to have a variety of specialists within a communion."

"Did you say 'communion'?"

"Seems more accurate than 'community,' true?"

"But why doesn't everybody know what anybody does?"

"Well, learnin' does seem to go easier'n for our race, but 'tis not instantaneous. Memory traces have to be reinforced if they're not to fade out; skills have to be developed through practice. And, natur'ly, a brain holds the *kind* of memories and skills 'tis equipped to hold. For instance, nogas keep the botanical knowledge, 'cause they do the eatin'; rukas, havin' hands, remember the manual trades; krippos store meteorological and geographical data. 'Tis not quite that simple, really. All species store some information of every sort—we think—'speci'ly language. But you get the idea, I'm sure."

"Nonetheless—"

"Let me continue, Dominic." Enthusiasm sparkled from Kathryn as Flandry had never seen it from a woman before. "Question of culture. Didonian societies vary as much as ever Terran ones did. Certain cultures let entities form promiscuously. The result is, units learn less from others than they might, for lack of concentrated attention; emotional and intellectual life is shallow; the group stays at a low level of savagery. Certain other cultures are 'stremely restrictive 'bout relationships. For 'sample, the units of an entity are often s'posed to belong to each other 'sclusively till death do them part, 'cept for a grudgin' temporary linkage with immature ones as a necessity of education. Those societies tend to be further along technologically, but nowhere beyond the stone age and everywhere aesthetically impoverished. In neither case are the Didonians realizin' their full potential."

"I see," Flandry drawled. "Playboys versus puritans."

She blinked, then grinned. "As you will. Anyhow, most cultures—like this one, clearly—do it right. Every unit belongs to a few stable entities, dividin' time roughly equally 'mong them. That way, these entities develop true personalities, broadly backgrounded but each with a maximum talent in heesh's specialty. In addition, less developed partnerships are assembled temporarily at need."

She glanced skyward. "I think Cave Discoverer's 'bout to be created for us," she said.

Two krippos circled down. One presumably belonged to Master Of Songs, the other to Cave Discoverer, though Flandry couldn't tell them apart. Master Of Songs and Cave Discoverer apparently had a noga and ruka in common.

The bird shape in the lead took stance on the platform. The companion flew off to find a noga for itself. More krippos were appearing over the trees, more rukas scampering from the woods or the house. *We'll have a regular town meeting here in a minute,* Flandry anticipated.

He directed his awareness back to Kathryn and Cave Discoverer. A dialogue had commenced between them. It went haltingly at first, neither party having encountered pidgin for some years and the language of this neighborhood not being precisely identical with that which was spoken around Port Frederiksen. After a while, discourse gained momentum.

The rest of the communion arrived to watch, listen, and have the talk interpreted for them—aside from those who were out hunting or gathering, as Flandry learned later. An entity moved close to him. The ruka sprang off and approached, trailing the noga's thick "umbilicus" across a shoulder. Blue fingers plucked at Flandry's clothes and tried to unsheath his blaster for examination. The man didn't want to allow that, even if he put the weapon on safety, but Kathryn might disapprove of outright refusal. Removing his homemade packsack, he spread its contents on the ground. That served to keep the rukas of several curious entities occupied. After he saw they were not stealing or damaging, Flandry sat down and let his mind wander until it got to Kathryn. There it stayed.

An hour or so had passed, the brief day was drawing to a close, when she summoned him with a wave. "They're glad to meet us, willin' to offer hospitality," she said, "but dubious 'bout helpin' us across the mountains. The dwellers yonder are dangerous. Also, this is a busy season in the forest as well as the plowland. At the same time, the communion 'ud surely like the payment I promise, things like firearms and proper steel tools. They'll create one they call Many Thoughts and let heesh ponder the question. Meanwhile we're invited to stay."

Lieutenant Kapunan was especially pleased with that. Such medicines as he had were keeping his patients from getting worse, but the stress of travel hadn't let them improve much. If he could remain here with them while the rest went after help—Flandry agreed. The march might produce casualties of its own, but if so, they ought to be fewer.

Everyone took off for the house. The humans felt dwarfed by the lumbering bulks around them: all but Kathryn. She laughed and chattered the whole way. "Kind of a home-coming for me, this," she told her companions.

"I'd 'most forgotten how 'scitin' 'tis, field work on Dido, and how I, well, yes, love them."

You have a lot of capacity to love, Flandry thought. He recognized it as a pleasing remark that he would have used on any other girl; but he felt shy about flattering this one.

When they topped the ridge, they had a view of the farther slope. It dropped a way, then rose again, forming a shelter for the dwelling place. Artificial channels, feeding into a stream, must prevent flooding. In the distance, above trees, a bare crag loomed athwart the clouds. Thence came the rumble of a major waterfall. Kathryn pointed. "They call this region Thunderstone," she said, "'mong other things. Places come closer to havin' true names than entities do."

The homestead consisted of turf-roofed log buildings and a rude corral, enclosing a yard cobbled against the frequent mudmaking rains. Most of the structures were sheds and cribs. The biggest was the longhouse, impressive in workmanship and carved ornamentation as well as sheer size. Flandry paid more heed at first to the corral. Juveniles of all three species occupied it, together with four adults of each kind. The grownups formed pairs in different combinations, with immature third units. Other young wandered about, dozed, or took nourishment. The cows nursed the noga calves—two adults were lactating females, one was dry, one was male—and were in turn tapped by fuzzy little rukas and fledgling krippos.

"School?" Flandry asked.

"You might say so," Kathryn answered. "Primary stages of learnin' and development. Too important to interrupt for us; not that a partial entity 'ud care anyway. While they grow, the young'll partner 'mong themselves also. But in the end, as a rule, they'll replace units that've died out of established entities."

"Heh! 'If youth knew, if age could.' The Didonians appear to have solved that problem."

"And conquered death, in a way. 'Course, over several generations, a given personality 'ull fade into an altogether new one, and most of the earlier memories 'ull be lost. Still, the continuity—D' you see why they fascinate us?"

"Indeed. I haven't the temperament for being a scientist, but you make me wish I did."

She regarded him seriously. "In your fashion, Dominic, you're as much a filosof as anybody I've known."

My men are a gallant crew, he thought, *and they're entitled to my loyalty as well as my leadership, but at the moment I'd prefer them and their big flapping ears ten parsecs hence.*

The doors and window shutters of the lodge stood open, making its interior more bright and cool than he had awaited. The floor was fire-hardened clay strewn with fresh boughs. Fantastically carved pillars and rafters upheld the roof. The walls were hung with skins, crudely woven tapestries, tools, weapons, and objects that Kathryn guessed were sacred. Built in along them were stalls for nogas, perches for krippos, benches for rukas. Above were sconced torches for night illumination. Fires burned in pits; hoods, of leather stretched on wooden frames, helped draw smoke out through ventholes. Cubs, calves, and chicks, too small for education, bumbled about like the pet animals they were. Units that must be too aged or ill for daily toil waited quietly near the middle of the house. It was all one enormous room. Privacy was surely an idea which Didonians were literally incapable of entertaining. But what ideas did they have that were forever beyond human reach?

Flandry gestured at a pelt. "If they're herbivorous, the big chaps, I mean, why do they hunt?" he wondered.

"Animal products," Kathryn said. "Leather, bone, sinew, grease . . . sh!"

The procession drew up before a perch whereon sat an old krippo. Gaunt, lame in one wing, he nevertheless reminded Flandry of eagles. Every noga lowered the horn to him. The flyer belonging to Cave Discoverer let go and flapped off to a place of his (?) own. That noga offered his vacated tentacle. The ancient made union. His eyes turned on the humans and fairly blazed.

"Many Thoughts," Kathryn whispered to Flandry. "Their wisest. Heesh'll take a minute to absorb what the units can convey."

"Do that fowl's partners belong to every prominent citizen?"

"Sh, not so loud. I don't know local customs, but they seem to have special respect for Many Thoughts. . . . Well, you'd 'spect the units with the best genetic heritage to be in the best entities, wouldn't you? I gather Cave Discoverer's an explorer and adventurer. Heesh first met humans by seekin' out a xenological camp 200 kilometers from here. Many Thoughts gets the vigor and boldness of the same noga and ruka, but heesh's own journeys are of the spirit. . . . Ah, I think heesh's ready now. I'll have to repeat whatever information went away with the former krippo."

That conversation lasted beyond nightfall. The torches were lit, the fires stoked, cooking begun in stone pots. While the nogas could live on raw vegetation, they preferred more concentrated and tasty food when they could get it. A few more Didonians came home from the woods, lighting their way with luminous fungoids. They carried basketsful of edible roots. No doubt hunters and foragers remained out for a good many days at a stretch. The lodge filled with droning, fluting, coughing talk. Flandry and his men had trouble fending curiosity seekers off their injured without acting unfriendly.

At last Kathryn made the best imitation she could of the gesture of deference, and sought out her fellow humans. In the leaping red light, her eyes and locks stood brilliant among shadows. "'Twasn't easy," she said in exuberance, "but I argued heesh into it. We'll have an escort—mighty small, but an escort, guides and porters. I reckon we can start in another forty-fifty hours . . . for home!"

"Your home," growled a man.

"Dog your hatch," Flandry ordered him.

CHAPTER TEN

Centuries before, a rogue planet had passed near Beta
Crucis. Sunless worlds are not uncommon, but in astronomical immensity it is rare for one to encounter a star.
This globe swung by and receded on a hyperbolic orbit.
Approximately Terra-size, it had outgassed vapors in the
ardor of its youth. Then, as internal heat radiated away,
atmosphere froze. The great blue sun melted the oceans
and boiled the air back into fluidity. For some years,
appalling violence reigned.

Eventually interstellar cold would have reclaimed its
dominion, and the incident would have had no significance.
But chance ordained that the passage occur in the old
bold days of the Polesotechnic League, and that it be
noticed by those who saw an incalculable fortune to be
won. Isotope synthesis on the scale demanded by a
starfaring civilization had been industry's worst bottleneck.
Seas and skies were needed for coolants, continents for
dumping of radioactive wastes. Every lifeless body known
had been too frigid or too hot or otherwise unsuitable. But

here came Satan, warmed to an ideal temperature which the heat of nuclear manufacture could maintain. As soon as the storms and quakes had abated, the planet was swarmed by entrepreneurs.

During the Troubles, ownership, legal status, input and output, every aspect of relationship to the living fraction of the universe, varied as wildly for Satan as for most worlds. For a while it was abandoned. But no one had ever actually dwelt there. No being could survive that poisonous air and murderous radiation background, unless for the briefest of visits with the heaviest of protection. Robots, computers, and automatons were the inhabitants. They continued operating while civilization fragmented, fought, and somewhat reconstructed itself. When at last an Imperial aristocrat sent down a self-piloting freighter, they loaded it from a dragon's hoard.

The defense of Satan became a major reason to garrison and colonize Sector Alpha Crucis.

Its disc hung darkling among the stars in a viewscreen of Hugh McCormac's command room. Beta had long since dwindled to merely the brightest of them, and the machines had scant need for visible light. You saw the sphere blurred by gas, a vague shimmer of clouds and oceans, blacknesses that were land. It was a desolate scene, the more so when you called up an image of the surface—raw mountains, gashed valleys, naked stone plains, chill and stagnant seas, all cloaked in a night relieved only by a rare lamp or an evil blue glow of fluorescence, no sound but a dreary wind-skirl or a rushing of forever sterile waters, no happening throughout its eons but the inanimate, unaware toil of the machines.

For Hugh McCormac, though, Satan meant victory.

He took his gaze from the planet and let it stray in the opposite direction, toward open space. Men were dying where those constellations glittered. "I should be yonder," he said. "I should have insisted."

"You couldn't do anything, sir," Edgar Oliphant told him. "Once the tactical dispositions are made, the game plays itself. And you might be killed."

"That's what's wrong." McCormac twisted his fingers together. "Here we are, snug and safe in orbit, while a battle goes on to make *me* Emperor!"

"You're the High Admiral too, sir." A cigar in Oliphant's mouth wagged and fumed as he talked. "You've got to be available where the data flow in, to make decisions in case anything unpredicted happens."

"I know, I know." McCormac strode back and forth, from end to end of the balcony on which they stood. Below them stretched a murmurous complex of computers, men at desks and plotting consoles, messengers going soft-footed in and out. Nobody, from himself on down, bothered with spit-and-polish today. They had too much work on hand, coordinating the battle against Pickens' fleet. It had learned where they were from the ducal guards they chased off and had sought them out. Simply understanding that interaction of ships and energies was beyond mortal capacity.

He hated to tie up *Persei* when every gun spelled life to his outnumbered forces. She was half of the Nova-class dreadnaughts he had. But nothing less would hold the necessary equipment.

"We could do some fighting in addition," he said. "I've operated thus in the past."

"But that was before you were the Emperor," Oliphant replied.

McCormac halted and glowered at him. The stout man chewed his cigar and plodded on: "Sir, we've few enough active supporters as is. Most bein's are just prayin' they won't get involved on either side. Why should anybody put everything at stake for the revolution, if he doesn't hope you'll bring him a better day? We could risk our control center, no doubt. But we can't risk you. Without you, the revolution 'ud fall apart 'fore Terran reinforcements could get here to suppress it."

McCormac clenched his fists and looked back at Satan. "Sorry," he mumbled. "I'm being childish."

"'Tis forgivable," Oliphant said. "Two of your boys in combat—"

"And how many other people's boys? Human or xeno, they die, they're maimed. . . . Well." McCormac leaned over the balcony rail and studied the big display tank on the deck beneath him. Its colored lights gave only a hint of the information—itself partial and often unreliable—that flowed through the computers. But such three-dimensional pictures occasionally stimulated the spark of genius which no known civilization has succeeded in evoking from an electronic brain.

According to the pattern, his tactics were proving out. He had postulated that destruction of the factories on Satan would be too great an economic disaster for cautious Dave Pickens to hazard. Therefore the Josipists would be strictly enjoined not to come near the planet. Therefore McCormac's forces would have a privileged sanctuary. That would make actions possible to them which otherwise were madness. Of course, Pickens might charge straight in anyway; that contingency must be provided against. But if so, McCormac need have no compunctions about using Satan for shield and backstop. Whether it was destroyed or only held by his fleet, its products were denied the enemy. In time, that was sure to bring disaffection and weakness.

But it looked as if Pickens was playing safe—and getting mauled in consequence.

"S'pose we win," Oliphant said. "What next?"

It had been discussed for hours on end, but McCormac seized the chance to think past this battle. "Depends on what power the opposition has left. We want to take over as large a volume of space as possible without overextending ourselves. Supply and logistics are worse problems for us than combat, actually. We aren't yet organized to replace losses or even normal consumption."

"Should we attack Ifri?"

"No. Too formidable. If we can cut it off, the same purpose is better served. Besides, eventually we'll need it ourselves."

"Llynathawr, though? I mean . . . well, we do have information that your lady was removed by some government agent—" Oliphant stopped, seeing what his well-meant speech had done.

McCormac stood alone, as if naked on Satan, for a while. Finally he could say: "No. They're bound to defend it with everything they have. Catawrayannis would be wiped out. Never mind Kathryn. There're too many other Kathryns around."

Can an Emperor afford such thoughts?

A visiscreen chimed and lit. A jubilant countenance looked forth. "Sir—Your Majesty—we've won!"

"What?" McCormac needed a second to understand.

"Positive, Your Majesty. Reports are pouring in, all at once. Still being evaluated, but, well, we haven't any doubt. It's almost like reading their codes."

A piece of McCormac's splintering consciousness visualized that possibility. The reference was not to sophont-sophont but machine-machine communication. A code was more than changed; the key computers were instructed to devise a whole new language, which others were then instructed to learn and use. Because random factors determined basic elements of the language, decipherment was, if not totally impossible, too laborious a process to overtake any prudent frequency of innovation. Hence the talk across space between robots, which wove their ships into a fleet, was a virtually unbreakable riddle to foes, a nearly infallible recognition signal to friends. The chance of interpreting it had justified numerous attempts throughout history at boarding or hijacking a vessel, however rarely they succeeded and however promptly their success caused codes to be revised. If you could learn a language the hostile machines were still using—

No. A daydream. McCormac forced his attention back to the screen. "Loss of *Zeta Orionis* probably decided him. They're disengaging everywhere." *I must get busy. We should harry them while they retreat, though not too far. Tactical improvisations needed.* "Uh, we've confirmed that *Vixen* is untouched." *John's ship.* "No report from *New Phobos,* but no positive reason to fear for her."

Colin's ship. Bob's with me. "A moment, please. Important datum. . . . Sir, it's confirmed, *Aquilae* suffered heavy damage. She's almost certainly their flagship, you know. They won't be meshing any too well. We can eat them one at a time!" *Dave, are you alive?*

"Very good, Captain," McCormac said. "I'll join you right away on the command deck."

Aaron Snelund let the admiral stand, miserable in blue and gold, while he chose a cigarette from a jeweled case, rolled it in his fingers, sniffed the fragrance of genuine Terra-grown Crown grade marijuana, inhaled it into lighting, sat most gracefully down on his chair of state, and drank the smoke. No one else was in the room, save his motionless Gorzunians. The dynasculps were turned off. The animation was not, but its music was, so that masked lords and ladies danced without sound through a ballroom 200 light-years and half a century distant.

"Superb," Snelund murmured when he had finished. He nodded at the big gray-haired man who waited. "At ease."

Pickens did not relax noticeably. "Sir—" His voice was higher than before. Overnight he had become old.

Snelund interrupted him with a wave. "Don't trouble, Admiral. I have studied the reports. I know the situation consequent on your defeat. One is not necessarily illiterate, even with respect to the Navy's abominable prose, just because one is a governor. Is one?"

"No, Your Excellency."

Snelund lounged back, cross-legged, eyelids drooping. "I did not call you here for a repetition *viva voce* of what

I have read," he continued mildly. "No, I wished for a chat that would be candid because private. Tell me, Admiral, what is your advice to me?"

"That's . . . in my personal report . . . sir."

Snelund arched his brows.

Sweat trickled down Pickens' cheeks. "Well, sir," he groped, "our total remaining power must be not greatly inferior to the, the enemy's. If we count what did not go to Satan. We can consolidate a small volume of space, hold it, let him have the rest. The Merseian confrontation can't go on forever. When we have heavy reinforcements, we can go out for a showdown battle."

"Your last showdown was rather disappointing, Admiral."

A tic vibrated one corner of Pickens' mouth. "The governor has my resignation."

"And has not accepted it. Nor will."

"Sir!" Pickens' mouth fell open.

"Be calm." Snelund shifted his tone from delicate sarcasm to kindliness, his manner from idle humor to vigilance. "You didn't disgrace yourself, Admiral. You just had the misfortune to clash with a better man. Were you less able, little would have been salvaged from your defeat. As matters went, you rescued half your force. You lack imagination, but you have competence: a jewel of high price in these degenerate times. No, I don't want your resignation. I want you to continue in charge."

Pickens trembled. Tears stood in his eyes. "Sit down," Snelund invited. Pickens caved into a chair. Snelund kindled another cigarette, tobacco, and let him recover some equilibrium before saying:

"Competence, professionalism, sound organization and direction—you can supply those. I will supply the imagination. In other words, from here on I dictate policies for you to execute. Is that clear?"

His question lashed. Pickens gulped and croaked, "Yes, sir." It had been a precision job for Snelund, these past days, making the officer malleable without destroying his usefulness—an exacting but enjoyable task.

"Good. Good. Oh, by the way, smoke if you wish," the governor said. "Let me make clear what I plan.

"Originally I counted on applying various pressures through Lady McCormac. Then that dolt Flandry disappeared with her." A rage that boiled like liquid helium: "Have you any inkling what became of them?"

"No, sir," Pickens said. "Our Intelligence section hasn't yet succeeded in infiltrating the enemy. That takes time. . . . Er, from what we can piece together, she doesn't seem to have rejoined her husband. But we've had no word about her arrival anywhere else, like maybe on Terra."

"Well," Snelund said, "I don't envy Citizen Flandry once *I* get back." He rolled smoke around in his lungs until coolness returned. "No matter, really. The picture has changed. I've been rethinking this whole affair.

"What you propose, letting McCormac take most of the sector without resistance while we wait for help, is apparently the conservative course. Therefore it's in fact the most deadly dangerous. He must be counting on precisely that. Let him be proclaimed Emperor on scores of worlds, let him marshal their resources and arrange their defenses with that damnable skill he owns—and quite probably, when the Terran task force comes, it won't be able to dislodge him. Consider his short interior lines of communication. Consider popular enthusiasm roused by his demagogues and xenagogues. Consider the likelihood of more and more defections to his side as long as his affairs run smoothly. Consider the virus spreading beyond this sector, out through the Empire, until it may indeed happen that one day he rides in triumph through Archopolis!"

Pickens stuttered, "I, I, I had thought of those things, Your Excellency."

Snelund laughed. "Furthermore, assuming the Imperium can put him down, what do you expect will become of you and, somewhat more significantly from this point of view, me? It will not earn us any medals that we allowed an insurrection and then could not quench it ourselves. Tongues will click. Heads will wag. Rivals will seize the opportunity to discredit. Whereas, if we can break Hugh McCormac unaided in space, clearing the way for my militia to clean out treason on the planets—well, kudos is the universal currency. It can buy us a great deal if we spend it wisely. Knighthood and promotion for you; return in glory to His Majesty's court for me. Am I right?"

Pickens moistened his lips. "Individuals like us shouldn't count. Not when millions and millions of lives—"

"But they belong to individuals too, correct? And if we serve ourselves, we serve the Imperium simultaneously, which we swore to do. Let us have no bleeding-heart unrealism. Let us get on with our business, the scotching of this rebellion."

"What does the governor propose?"

Snelund shook a finger. "Not propose, Admiral. Decree. We will thresh out details later. But in general, your mission will be to keep the war fires burning. True, our critical systems must be heavily guarded. But that will leave you with considerable forces free to act. Avoid another large battle. Instead raid, harass, hit and run, never attack a rebel group unless it's unmistakably weaker, make a special point of preying on commerce and industry."

"Sir? Those are our people!"

"McCormac claims they're his. And, from what I know of him, the fact that he'll be the cause of their suffering distress at our hands will plague him, will hopefully make him less efficient. Mind you, I don't speak of indiscriminate destruction. On the contrary, we shall have to have justifiable reasons for hitting every civilian target we do. Leave these decisions to me. The idea is, essentially, to undermine the rebel strength."

Snelund sat erect. One fist clenched on a chair arm. His hair blazed like a conqueror's brand. "Supply and replacement," he said ringingly. "Those are going to be McCormac's nemesis. He may be able to whip us in a stand-up battle. But he can't whip attrition. Food, clothing, medical supplies, weapons, tools, spare parts, whole new ships, a navy must have them in steady flow or it's doomed. Your task will be to plug their sources and choke their channels."

"Can that be done, sir, well enough and fast enough?" Pickens asked. "He'll fix defenses, arrange convoys, make counterattacks."

"Yes, yes, I know. Yours is a single part of the effort,

albeit a valuable one. The rest is to deny McCormac an effective civil service."

"I don't, uh, don't understand, sir."

"Not many do," Snelund said. "But think what an army of bureaucrats and functionaries compose the foundation of any government. It's no difference whether they are paid by the state or by some nominally private organization. They still do the day-to-day work. They operate the space-ports and traffic lanes, they deliver the mail, they keep the electronic communication channels unsnarled, they collect and supply essential data, they oversee public health, they hold crime in check, they arbitrate disputes, they allocate scarce resources. . . . Need I go on?"

He smiled wider. "Confidentially," he said, "the lesson was taught me by experience out here. As you know, I had various changes in policy and administrative procedure that I wished to put into effect. I was only successful to a degree, chiefly on backward planets with no real indigenous civil services. Otherwise, the bureaucrats dragged their feet too much. It's not like the Navy, Admiral. I would press an intercom button, issue a top priority order—and nothing would happen. Memos took weeks or months to go from desk to desk. Technical objections were argued comma by comma. Interminable requests for clarification made their slow ways back to me. Reports were filed and forgotten. It was like dueling a fog. And I couldn't dismiss the lot of them. Quite apart from legalities, I had to have them. There were no replacements for them.

"I intend to give Hugh McCormac a taste of that medicine."

Pickens shifted uneasily. "How, sir?"

"That's a matter I want to discuss this afternoon. We must get word to those planets. The little functionaries must be persuaded that it isn't in their own best interest to serve the rebellion with any zeal. Their natural timidity and stodginess work in our favor. If, in addition, we bribe some, threaten others, perhaps carry out an occasional assassination or bombing—Do you follow? We must plant our agents throughout McCormac's potential kingdom before he can take possession of it and post his guards. Then we must keep up the pressure—agents smuggled in, for example; propaganda; disruption of interstellar transportation by your raiders—Yes, I do believe we can bring McCormac's civil service machinery to a crawling, creaking slowdown. And without it, his navy starves. Are you with me, Admiral?"

Pickens swallowed. "Yes, sir. Of course."

"Good." Snelund rose. "Come along to the conference room. My staff's waiting. We'll thresh out specific plans. Would you like a stimpill? The session will probably continue till all hours."

They had learned of him, first on Venus, then on Terra, then in Sector Alpha Crucis: voluptuary he was, but when he saw a chance or a threat that concerned himself, twenty demons could not outwork him.

CHAPTER ELEVEN

Kathryn estimated the distance from Thunderstone to Port Frederiksen as about 2000 kilometers. But that was map distance, the kind that an aircar traversed in a couple of hours, a spacecraft in minutes or seconds. Aground and afoot, it would take weeks.

Not only was the terrain difficult, most of it was unknown to the Didonians. Like the majority of primitives, they seldom ventured far beyond their home territory. Articles of trade normally went from communion to communion rather than cross-country in a single caravan. Hence the three who accompanied the humans must feel their own way. In the mountains especially, this was bound to be a slow process with many false choices.

Furthermore, the short rotation period made for inefficient travel. The autochthons refused to move after dark, and Flandry was forced to agree it would be unwise in strange areas. The days were lengthening as the season advanced; at midsummer they would fill better than seven hours out of the eight and three-quarters. But the Didonians could not take advantage of more than four or five hours. The reason was, again, practical. En route, away from the richer diet provided by their farms, a noga must eat—for three—whatever it could find. Vegetable food is less caloric than meat. The natives had to allow ample time for fueling their bodies.

"Twenty-four of us humans," Flandry counted. "And the sixteen we're leaving behind, plus the good doctor, also have appetites. I don't know if our rations will stretch."

"We can supplement some with native food," Kathryn reassured him. "There're levo compounds in certain plants and animals, same as terrestroid biochemistries involve occasional dextros. I can show you and the boys what they look like."

"Well, I suppose we may as well scratch around for them, since we'll be oysting so much in camp."

"Oystin'?"

"What oysters do. Mainly sit." Flandry ruffled his mustache. "Damn, but this is turning into a loathsome fungus! The two items I did not think to rescue would have to be scissors and a mirror."

Kathryn laughed. "Why didn't you speak before? They have scissors here. Clumsy, none too sharp, but you can cut hair with them. Let me be your barber."

Her hands across his head made him dizzy. He was glad that she let the men take care of themselves.

They were all quite under her spell. He didn't think it was merely because she was the sole woman around. They vied to do her favors and show her courtesies. He wished they would stop, but couldn't well order it. Relationships were strained already.

He was no longer the captain to them, but the commander: his brevet rank, as opposed to his lost status of shipmaster. They cooperated efficiently, but it was inevitable that discipline relaxed, even between enlisted men and other officers. He felt he must preserve its basic forms around himself. This led to a degree of—not hostility, but cool, correct aloofness as regarded him, in distinction to the camaraderie that developed among the rest.

One night, happening to wake without showing it, he overheard a muted conversation among several. Two were declaring their intention not just to accept internment, but to join McCormac's side if its chances looked reasonable when they got to the base. They were trying to convince their friends to do likewise. The friends declined, for the time being at any rate, but good-naturedly. That was what disturbed Flandry: that no one else was disturbed. He began regular eavesdropping. He didn't mean to report anyone, but he did want to know where every man stood. Not that he felt any great need for moralistic justification. The snooping was fun.

That started well after the party had left Thunderstone. The three Didonians were named by Kathryn as Cave Discoverer, Harvest Fetcher, and, to human amusement, Smith. It was more than dubious if the entities thought of themselves by name. The terms were convenient designations, based on personal qualities or events of past life. The unit animals had nothing but individual signals.

Often they swapped around, to form such combinations as Iron Miner, Guardian Of North Gate, or Lightning

Struck The House. Kathryn explained that this was partly
for a change, partly to keep fresh the habits and memories
which constituted each entity, and partly a quasi-religious
rite.

"Oneness is the ideal in this culture, I'm learnin', as 'tis
in a lot of others," she told Flandry. "They consider the
whole world to be potenti'ly a single entity. By ceremonies,
mystic contemplation, hallucinogenic foods, or whatever,
they try to merge with it. An everyday method is to make
frequent new interconnections. The matin' season, 'round
the autumnal equinox, is their high point of the year,
mainly 'cause of the ecstatic, transcendental 'speriences
that then become possible."

"Yes, I imagine a race like this has some interesting
sexual variations," Flandry said. She flushed and looked
away. He didn't know why she should react so, who had
observed life as a scientist. Associations with her captivity?
He thought not. She was too vital to let that cripple her
long; the scars would always remain, but by now she had
her merriment back. Why, then, this shyness with him?

They were following a ridge. The country belonged to
another communion which, being akin to Thunderstone,
had freely allowed transit. Already they had climbed
above the jungle zone. Here the air was tropical by Terran
standards, but wonderfully less wet, with a breeze to lave
the skin and caress the hair and carry scents not unlike
ginger. The ground was decked with spongy brown carpet
weed, iridescent blossoms, occasional stands of arrowbrush,
grenade, and lantern tree. A mass of land coral rose to the
left, its red and blue the more vivid against the sky's
eternal silver-gray.

None of the Didonians were complete. One maintained heesh's noga-ruka linkage, the other two rukas were off gathering berries, the three krippos were aloft as scouts. Separated, the animals could carry out routine tasks and recognize a need for reunion when it arose.

Besides their own ruka-wielded equipment—including spears, bows, and battleaxes—the nogas easily carried the stuff from the spaceboat. Thus liberated, the men could outpace the ambling quadrupeds. With no danger and no way to get lost hereabouts, Flandry had told them to expedite matters by helping the rukas. They were scattered across the hill.

Leaving him alone with Kathryn.

He was acutely conscious of her: curve of breast and hip beneath her coverall, free-swinging stride, locks blowing free and bright next to the sun-darkened skin, strong face, great green-gold eyes, scent of warm flesh. . . . He changed the subject at once. "Isn't the, well, pantheistic concept natural to Didonians?"

"No more than monotheism's natural, inevitable, in man," Kathryn said with equal haste. "It depends on culture. Some exalt the communion itself, as an entity distinct from the rest of the world, includin' other communions. Their rites remind me of human mobs cheerin' an almighty State and its director. They tend to be warlike and predatory." She pointed ahead, where mountain peaks were vaguely visible. "I'm 'fraid we've got to get past a society of that kind. 'Tis one reason why they weren't keen on this trip in Thunderstone. Word travels, whether or not entities do. I had to remind Many Thoughts 'bout our guns."

"People who don't fear death make wicked opponents," Flandry said. "However, I wouldn't suppose a Didonian exactly enjoys losing a unit; and heesh must have the usual desire to avoid pain."

Kathryn smiled, at ease once more. "You learn fast. Ought to be a xenologist yourself."

He shrugged. "My business has put me in contact with various breeds. I remain convinced we humans are the weirdest of the lot; but your Didonians come close. Have you any idea how they evolved?"

"Yes, some paleontology's been done. Nowhere near enough. Why is it we can always find money for a war and're always pinched for everything else? Does the first cause the second?"

"I doubt that. I think people naturally prefer war."

"Someday they'll learn."

"You have insufficient faith in man's magnificent ability to ignore what history keeps yelling at him," Flandry said. Immediately, lest her thoughts turn to Hugh McCormac who wanted to reform the Empire: "But fossils are a less depressing subject. What about evolution on Dido?"

"Well, near's can be told, a prolonged hot spell occurred—like millions of years long. The ancestors of the nogas fed on soft plants which drought made scarce. 'Tis thought they took to hangin' 'round what trees were left, to catch leaves that ancestral rukas tore loose in the course of gatherin' fruit. Belike they had a tickbird relationship with the proto-krippos. But trees were dyin' off too. The krippos could spy forage a far ways off and guide the nogas there. Taggin' 'long, the rukas got protection to boot, and repaid by strippin' the trees.

"At last some of the animals drifted to the far eastern end of the Barcan continent. 'Twas afflicted, as 'tis yet, with a nasty kind of giant bug that not only sucks blood, but injects a microbe whose action keeps the wound open for days or weeks. The ancestral nogas were smaller and thinner-skinned than today's. They suffered. Prob'ly rukas and krippos helped them, swattin' and eatin' the heaviest swarms. But then they must've started sippin' the blood themselves, to supplement their meager diet."

"I can take it from there," Flandry said. "Including hormone exchange, mutually beneficial and cementing the alliance. It's lucky that no single-organism species happened to develop intelligence. It'd have mopped the deck with those awkward early three-ways. But the symbiosis appears to be in business now. Fascinating possibilities for civilization."

"We haven't exposed them to a lot of ours," Kathryn said. "Not just 'cause we want to study them as they are. We don't know what might be good for them, and what catastrophic."

"I'm afraid that's learned by trial and error," Flandry answered. "I'd be intrigued to see the result of raising some entities from birth"—the krippos were viviparous too—"in Technic society."

"Why not raise some humans 'mong Didonians?" she flared.

"I'm sorry." *You make indignation beautiful.* "I was only snakkering. Wouldn't do it in practice, not for anything. I've seen too many pathetic cases. I did forget they're your close friends."

Inspiration! "I'd like to become friends with them

myself," Flandry said. "We have a two or three months' trip and buckets of idle time in camp ahead of us. Why don't you teach me the language?"

She regarded him with surprise. "You're serious, Dominic?"

"Indeed. I don't promise to retain the knowledge all my life. My head's overly cluttered with cobwebby information as is. But for the present, yes, I do want to converse with them directly. It'd be insurance for us. And who knows, I might come up with a new scientific hypothesis about them, too skewball to have occurred to any Aenean."

She laid a hand on his shoulder. That was her way; she liked to touch people she cared about. "You're no Imperial, Dominic," she said. "You belong with us."

"Be that as it may—" he said, confused.

"Why do you stand with Josip? You know what he is. You've seen his cronies, like Snelund, who could end by replacin' him in all but name. Why don't you join us, your kind?"

He knew why not, starting with the fact that he didn't believe the revolution could succeed and going on to more fundamental issues. But he could not tell her that, on this suddenly magical day. "Maybe you'll convert me," he said. "Meanwhile, what about language lessons?"

"Why, 'course."

—Flandry could not forbid his men to sit in, and a number of them did. By straining his considerable talent, he soon disheartened them and they quit. After that, he had Kathryn's whole notice for many hours per week. He ignored the jealous stares, and no longer felt jealous himself when she fell into cheerful conversation with one of the troop or joined a campfire circle for singing.

Nor did it perturb him when Chief Petty Officer Robbins returned from an excursion with her in search of man-edible plants, wearing a black eye and a sheepish look. Unruffled, she came in later and treated Robbins exactly as before. Word must have spread, for there were no further incidents.

Flandry's progress in his lessons amazed her. Besides having suitable genes, he had been through the Intelligence Corps' unmercifully rigorous courses in linguistics and metalinguistics, semantics and metasemantics, every known trick of concentration and memorization; he had learned how to learn. Few civilian scientists received that good a training; they didn't need it as urgently as any field agent always did. Inside a week, he had apprehended the structures of Thunderstone's language and man's pidgin— no easy feat, when the Didonian mind was so absolutely alien.

Or was it? Given the basic grammar and vocabulary, Flandry supplemented Kathryn's instruction by talking, mainly with Cave Discoverer. It went ridiculously at first, but after weeks he got to the point of holding real conversations. The Didonian was as interested in him and Kathryn as she was in heesh. She took to joining their colloquies, which didn't bother him in the least.

Cave Discoverer was more adventurous than average. Heesh's personality seemed more clearly defined than the rest, including any others in the party which incorporated heesh's members. At home heesh hunted, logged, and went on rambling explorations when not too busy.

Annually heesh traveled to the lake called Golden, where less advanced communions held a fair and Cave Discoverer traded metal implements for their furs and dried fruits. There heesh's noga had the custom of joining with a particular ruka from one place and krippo from another to make the entity Raft Farer. In Thunderstone, besides Many Thoughts, Cave Discoverer's noga and ruka belonged to Master Of Songs; heesh's krippo (female) to Leader Of Dance; heesh's ruka to Brewmaster; and all to various temporary groups.

Aside from educational duties, none of them linked indiscriminately. Why waste the time of a unit that could make part of an outstanding entity, in junction with units less gifted? The distinction was somewhat blurred but nonetheless real in Thunderstone, between "first families" and "proles." No snobbery or envy appeared to be involved. The attitude was pragmatic. Altruism within the communion was so taken for granted that the concept did not exist.

Or thus went Flandry's and Kathryn's impressions. She admitted they might be wrong. How do you probe the psyche of a creature with three brains, each of which remembers its share in other creatures and, indirectly, remembers things that occurred generations before it was born?

Separately, the nogas were placid, though Kathryn said they became furious if aroused. The krippos were excitable and musical; they produced lovely clear notes in intricate patterns. The rukas were restless, curious, and playful. But these were generalizations. Individual variety was as great as for all animals with well-developed nervous systems.

Cave Discoverer was in love with heesh's universe. Heesh looked forward with excitement to seeing Port Frederiksen and wondered about the chance of going somewhere in a spaceship. After heesh got straight the basic facts of astronomy, xenology, and galactic politics, heesh's questions sharpened until Flandry wondered if Didonians might not be inherently more intelligent than men. Could their technological backwardness be due to accidental circumstances that would no longer count when they saw the possibility of making systematic progress?

The future could be theirs, not ours, Flandry thought. *Kathryn would reply, "Why can't it be everybody's?"*

Meanwhile the expedition continued—through rain, gale, fog, heat, strange though not hostile communions, finally highlands where the men rejoiced in coolness. There, however, the Didonians shivered, and went hungry in a land of sparse growth, and, despite their krippos making aerial surveys, often blundered upon impassable stretches that forced them to retrace their steps and try again.

It was here, in High Maurusia, that battle smote them.

CHAPTER TWELVE

The easiest way to reach one pass was through a canyon. During megayears, a river swollen by winter rains had carved it, then shrunken in summer. Its walls gave protection from winds and reflected some heat; this encouraged plant life to spring up every dry season along the streambed, where accumulated soil was kinder to feet than the naked rock elsewhere. Accordingly, however twisted and boulder-strewn, it appeared to offer the route of choice.

The scenery was impressive in a gaunt fashion. The river rolled on the party's left, broad, brown, noisy and dangerous despite being at its low point. A mat of annual plants made a border whose sober hues were relieved by white and scarlet blossoms. Here and there grew crooked trees, deep-rooted, adapted to inundation. Beyond, the canyon floor reached barren: tumbled dark rocks, fantastically eroded pinnacles and mesas, on to the talus slopes and palisades. Gray sky, diffuse and shadowless light, did not bring out color or detail very well; that was a bewildering view. But human lungs found the air mild, dry, exhilarating.

Two krippos wheeled on watch overhead. Harvest Fetcher stayed complete, and every ruka rode a noga. The outworlders walked behind, except for Kathryn, Flandry, and Havelock. She was off to the right, wrapped in her private thoughts. This landscape must have made her homesick for Aeneas. The commander and the ensign kept out of their companions' earshot.

"Damn it, sir, why do we take for granted we'll turn ourselves in at Port Frederiksen without a fight?" Havelock was protesting. "This notion our case is hopeless, it's encouraging treasonable thoughts."

Flandry refrained from saying he was aware of that. Havelock had been less standoffish than the rest; but a subtle barrier persisted, and Flandry had cultivated him for weeks before getting this much confidence. He knew Havelock had a girl on Terra.

"Well, Ensign," he said, "I can't make promises, for the reason that I'm not about to lead us to certain death. As you imply, though, the death may not necessarily be certain. Why don't you feel out the men? I don't want anyone denounced to me," *having a pretty fair idea myself,* "but you might quietly find who's . . . let's not say trustworthy, we'll assume everybody is, let's say enthusiastic. You might, still more quietly, alert them to stand by in case I do decide on making a break. We'll talk like this, you and I, off and on. More off than on, so as not to provoke suspicion. We'll get Kathryn to describe the port's layout, piecemeal, and that'll be an important element in what I elect to do."

You, Kathryn, will be more important.

"Very good, sir," Havelock said. "I hope—"

Assault burst forth.

The party had drawn even with a nearby rock mass whose bottom was screened by a row of crags. From behind these plunged a score of Didonians. Flandry had an instant to think, *Ye devils, they must've hid in a cave!* Then the air was full of arrows. "Deploy!" he yelled. "Fire! Kathryn, get down!"

A shaft went *whoot* by his ear. A noga bugled, a ruka screamed. Bellyflopping, Flandry glared over the sights of his blaster at the charging foe. They were barbarically decorated with pelts, feather blankets, necklaces of teeth, body paint. Their weapons were neolithic, flint axes, bone-tipped arrows and lances. But they were not less deadly for that, and the ambush had been arranged with skill.

He cast a look to right and left. Periodically while traveling, he had drilled his men in ground combat techniques. Today it paid off. They had formed an arc on either side of him. Each who carried a gun—there weren't many small arms aboard a warship—was backed by two or three comrades with spears or daggers, ready at need to assist or to take over the trigger.

Energy beams flared and crashed. Slugthrowers hissed, stunners buzzed. A roar of voices and hoofs echoed above the river's clangor. A krippo turned into flame and smoke, a ruka toppled to earth, a noga ran off bellowing its anguish. Peripherally, Flandry saw more savages hit.

But whether in contempt for death or sheer physical

momentum, the charge continued. The distance to cover was short; and Flandry had not imagined a noga could gallop that fast. The survivors went by his line and fell on the Thunderstone trio before he comprehended it. One man barely rolled clear of a huge gray-blue body. The airborne flyers barely had time to reunite with their chief partners.

"Kathryn!" Flandry shouted into the din. He leaped erect and whirled around. The melee surged between him and her. For a second he saw how Didonians fought. Nogas, nearly invulnerable to edged weapons, pushed at each other and tried to gore. Rukas stabbed and hacked; krippos took what shelter they could, while grimly maintaining linkage, and buffeted with their wings. The objective was to put an opponent out of action by eliminating heesh's rider units.

Some mountaineer nogas, thus crippled by gunfire, blundered around in the offing. A few two-member entities held themselves in reserve, for use when a ruka or krippo went down in combat. Eight or nine complete groups surrounded the triangular formation adopted by the three from Thunderstone.

No, two and a half. By now Flandry could tell them apart. Harvest Felcher's krippo must have been killed in the arrow barrage. The body lay transfixed, pathetically small, tailfeathers ruffled by a slight breeze, until a noga chanced to trample it into a smear. Its partners continued fighting, automatically and with lessened skill.

"Get those bastards!" somebody called. Men edged warily toward the milling, grunting, yelling, hammering interlocked mass. It was hard to understand why the savages were ignoring the humans, who had inflicted all the damage on them. Was the sight so strange as not to be readily comprehensible?

Flandry ran around the struggle to see what had become of Kathryn. *I never gave her a gun!* he knew in agony.

Her tall form broke upon his vision. She had retreated a distance, to stand beneath a tree she could climb if attacked. His Merseian blade gleamed in her grasp, expertly held. Her mouth was drawn taut but her eyes were watchful and steady.

He choked with relief. Turning, he made his way to the contest.

A stone ax spattered the brains of Smith's ruka. Cave Discoverer's ruka avenged the death in two swift blows— but, surrounded, could not defend his back. A lance entered him. He fell onto the horn of a savage noga, which tossed him high and smashed him underfoot when he landed.

The humans opened fire.

It was butchery.

The mountaineer remnants stampeded down the canyon. Not an entity among them remained whole. A young Terran stood over a noga, which was half cooked but still alive, and gave it the *coup de grace;* then tears and vomit erupted from him. The Thunderstoners could assemble one full person at a time. Of the possible combinations, they chose Guardian Of North Gate, who went about methodically releasing the wounded from life.

The entire battle, from start to finish, had lasted under ten minutes.

Kathryn came running. She too wept. "So much

death, so much hurt—can't we help them?" A ruka
stirred. He didn't seem wounded; yes, he'd probably taken
a stun beam, and the supersonic jolt had affected him as
it did a man. Guardian Of North Gate approached.
Kathryn crouched over the ruka. "No! I forbid you."

The Didonian did not understand her pidgin, for only
heesh's noga had been in Cave Discoverer. But her attitude
was unmistakable. After a moment, with an almost physical
shrug, heesh had heesh's ruka tie up the animal.

Thereafter, with what assistance the humans could
give, heesh proceeded to care for the surviving
Thunderstone units. They submitted patiently. A krippo
had a broken leg, others showed gashes and bruises, but
apparently every member could travel after a rest.

No one spoke aloud a wish to move from the battle-
ground. No one spoke at all. Silent, they fared another two
or three kilometers before halting.

In the high latitudes of Dido, nights around midsummer
were not only short, they were light. Flandry walked
beneath a sky blue-black, faintly tinged with silver, faintly
adance with aurora where some of Virgil's ionizing radiation
penetrated the upper clouds. There was just sufficient
luminance for him not to stumble. Further off, crags and
cliffs made blacknesses which faded unclearly into the
dusk. Mounting a bluff that overlooked his camp, he saw
its fire as a red wavering spark, like a dying dwarf star. The
sound of the river belled subdued but clear through cool
air. His boots scrunched on gravel; occasionally they
kicked a larger rock. An unknown animal trilled somewhere close by.

Kathryn's form grew out of the shadows. He had seen her depart in this direction after the meal she refused, and guessed she was bound here. When he drew close, her face was a pale blur.

"Oh . . . Dominic," she said. The outdoor years had trained her to use more senses than vision.

"You shouldn't have gone off alone." He stopped in front of her.

"I had to."

"At a minimum, carry a gun. You can handle one, I'm sure."

"Yes. 'Course. But I won't, after today."

"You must have seen violent deaths before."

"A few times. None that I helped cause."

"The attack was unprovoked. To be frank, I don't regret anything but our own losses, and we can't afford to lament them long."

"We were crossin' the natives' country," she said. "Maybe they resented that. Didonians have territorial instincts, same as man. Or maybe our gear tempted them. No slaughter, no wounds, if 'tweren't for our travelin'."

"You've lived with the consequences of war," his inner pain said harshly. "And this particular fracas was an incident in your precious revolution."

He heard breath rush between her lips. Remorse stabbed him. "I, I'm sorry, Kathryn," he said. "Spoke out of turn. I'll leave you alone. But please come back to camp."

"No." At first her voice was almost too faint to hear. "I mean . . . let me stay out a while." She seized his hand. "But of your courtesy, don't you skite either. I'm glad you came, Dominic. You understand things."

Do I? Rainbows exploded within him.

They stood a minute, holding hands, before she laughed uncertainly and said: "Again, Dominic. Be practical with me."

You're brave enough to live with your sorrows, he thought, *but strong and wise enough to turn your back on them the first chance that comes, and cope with our enemy the universe.*

He wanted, he needed one of his few remaining cigarettes; but he couldn't reach the case without disturbing her clasp, and she might let go. "Well," he said in his awkwardness, "I imagine we can push on, day after tomorrow. They put Lightning Struck The House together for me after you left." All heesh's units had at various times combined with those that had been in Cave Discoverer: among other reasons, for heesh to gain some command of pidgin.

"We discussed things. It'd take longer to return, now, than finish our journey, and the incompletes can handle routine. The boys have gotten good at trailsmanship themselves. We'll bear today's lesson in mind and avoid places where bushwhackers can't be spotted from above. So I feel we can make it all right."

"I doubt if we'll be bothered any more," Kathryn said with a return of energy in her tone. "News'll get 'round."

"About that ruka we took prisoner."

"Yes? Why not set the poor beast free?"

"Because . . . well, Lightning isn't glad we have the potential for just one full entity. There're jobs like getting heavy loads down steep mountainsides which're a deal easier and safer with at least two, especially seeing that rukas are their hands. Furthermore, most of the time we can only have a single krippo aloft. The other will have to stay in a three-way, guiding the incompletes and making decisions, while we're in this tricky mountainland. One set of airborne eyes is damn little."

"True." He thought he heard the rustle of her hair, which she had let grow longer, as she nodded. "I didn't think 'bout that 'fore, too shocked, but you're right." Her fingers tensed on his. "Dominic! You're not plannin' to use the prisoner?"

"Why not? Lightning seems to like the idea. Been done on occasion, heesh said."

"In emergencies. But . . . the conflict, the—the cruelty—"

"Listen, I've given these matters thought," he told her. "Check my facts and logic. We'll force the ruka into linkage with the noga and krippo that were Cave Discoverer's—the strongest, most sophisticated entity we had. He'll obey at gun point. Besides, he has to drink blood or he'll starve, right? A single armed man alongside will prevent possible contretemps. However, two units against one ought to prevail by themselves. We'll make the union permanent, or nearly so, for the duration of our trip. That way, the Thunderstone patterns should go fast and deep into the ruka. I daresay the new personality will be confused and hostile at first; but heesh ought to cooperate with us, however grudgingly."

"Well—"

"We need heesh, Kathryn! I don't propose slavery. The ruka won't be absorbed. He'll give—and get—will learn something to take home to his communion—maybe an actual message of friendship, an offer to establish regular relations—and gifts, when we release him here on our way back to Thunderstone."

She was silent, until: "Audacious but decent, yes, that's you. You're more a knight than anybody who puts 'Sir' in front of his name, Dominic."

"Oh, Kathryn!"

And he found he had embraced her and was kissing her, and she was kissing him, and the night was fireworks and trumpets and carousels and sacredness.

"I love you, Kathryn, my God, I love you."

She broke free of him and moved back. "No. . . ." When he groped toward her, she fended him off. "No, please, please, don't. Please stop. I don't know what possessed me. . . ."

"But I love you," he cried.

"Dominic, no, we've been too long on this crazy trek. I care for you more'n I knew. But I'm Hugh's woman."

He dropped his arms and stood where he was, letting the spirit bleed out of him. "Kathryn," he said, "for you I'd join your side."

"For my sake?" She came close again, close enough to lay hands on his shoulders. Half sobbing, half laughing: "You can't dream how glad I am."

He stood in the fragrance of her, fists knotted, and replied, "Not for your sake. For you."

"What?" she whispered, and let him go.

"You called me a knight. Wrong. I won't play wistful friend-of-the-family rejected suitor. Not my style. I want to be your man myself, in every way that a man is able."

The wind lulled, the river boomed.

"All right," Flandry said to the shadow of her. "Till we reach Port Frederiksen. No longer. He needn't know. I'll serve his cause and live on the memory."

She sat down and wept. When he tried to comfort her, she thrust him away, not hard but not as a coy gesture either. He moved off a few meters and chainsmoked three cigarettes.

Finally she said, "I understand what you're thinkin', Dominic. If Snelund, why not you? But don't you see the difference? Startin' with the fact I do like you so much?"

He said through the tension in his throat, "I see you're loyal to an arbitrary ideal that originated under conditions that don't hold good any more."

She started to cry afresh, but it sounded dry, as if she had spent her tears.

"Forgive me," Flandry said. "I never meant to hurt you. Would've cut my larynx out first. We won't speak about this, unless you want to. If you change your mind, tomorrow or a hundred years from tomorrow, while I'm alive I'll be waiting."

Which is perfectly true, gibed a shard of him, *though I am not unaware of its being a well-composed line, and nourish a faint hope that my noble attitude will yet draw her away from that bucketheaded mass murderer Hugh McCormac.*

He drew his blaster and pushed it into her cold unsteady clasp. "If you must stay here," he said, "keep this. Give it back to me when you come down to camp. Goodnight."

He turned and left. There went through him: *Very well, if I have no reason to forswear His Majesty Josip III, let me carry on with the plan I'm developing for the discomfiture of his unruly subjects.*

CHAPTER THIRTEEN

The group spent most of the next day and night sleeping. Then Flandry declared it was needful to push harder forward than hitherto. The remaining Didonian(s?) formed several successive entities, as was the custom when important decisions were to be reached, and agreed. For them, these uplands were bleak and poor in forage. Worse lay ahead, especially in view of the hurts and losses they had suffered. Best get fast over the mountains and down to the coastal plain.

That was a Herculean undertaking. The humans spent most of their time gathering food along the way for the nogas. When exhaustion forced a stop, it likewise forced sleep. Kathryn was athletic, but she remained a woman of thirty, trying to match the pace and toil of men in their teens and twenties. She had small chance to talk, with Flandry or anyone, on trail or off.

He alone managed that. His company looked mutinous when he announced that he must be exempted from most

of the labor in order to establish communication with the
new entity. Havelock jollied them out of their mood.

"Look, you've seen the Old Man in action. You may
not like him, but he's no shirker and no fool. Somebody
has to get that xeno cooperating. If nothing else, think
how we need a guide through this damned arse-over-tip
country. . . . Why not Kathryn? Well, she *is* the wife of the
man who got us dumped where we are. It wouldn't
improve our records, that we trusted her with something
this critical. . . . Sure, you'd better think about your
records, those of you who plan on returning home."

Flandry had given him a confidential briefing.

At the outset, talk between man and Didonian was
impossible. The personality fought itself, captive ruka
pouring hate and fear of the whole troop into a noga
and krippo which detested his communion. And the
languages, habits, attitudes, thought patterns, the whole
Weltanschauungen were at odds, scarcely comprehensible
mutually. Linked under duress, the entity slogged along,
sometimes sullen, sometimes dazed, always apt to lash out
on a half insane impulse. Twice Flandry had to scramble; the
noga's horn missed him by centimeters.

He persevered. So did the two animals which had been
in Cave Discoverer. And the noga had had experience
with alien partners, the two which had annually joined
him to make Raft Farer. Flandry tried to imagine what the
present situation felt like, and couldn't. Schizophrenia? A
racking conflict of opposed desires, akin to his own as
regarded Kathryn McCormac versus the Terran Empire?
He doubted it. The being he confronted was too foreign.

He sought to guide its coalescence, initially by his

behavior, later by his words. Once the ruka nervous system was freed from expecting imminent torture or death, meshing was natural. Language followed. Part of the Thunderstone vocabulary had died with Cave Discoverer's ruka. But some was retained, and more was acquired when, for a time, the krippo was replaced by the other ruka. The savage unit objected violently—it turned out that his culture regarded a two-species three-way as perverted— but got no choice in the matter. The hookup of neurones as well as blood vessels was automatic when tendrils joined. Flandry exerted his linguistic skills to lead the combinations through speech exercises. Given scientific direction, the inborn Didonian adaptability showed quick results.

By the time the party had struggled across the passes and were on the western slope of the mountains, Flandry could talk to the mind he had called into being.

The entity did not seem especially fond of heeshself. The designation heesh adopted, more by repeated usage than by deliberate selection, was a grunt which Kathryn said might translate as "Woe." She had little to do with heesh, as much because the obvious emotional trouble distressed her as because of weariness. That suited Flandry. Conversing with Woe, alone except for a sentry who did not understand what they uttered, he could build on the partial amnesia and the stifled anger, to make what he would of the Didonian.

"You must serve me," he said and repeated. "We may have fighting to do, and you are needed in place of heesh who is no more. Trust and obey none save me. I alone can release you in the end—with rich reward for both your communions. And I have enemies among my very followers."

He would have told as elaborate, even as truthful a story as required. But he soon found it was neither necessary nor desirable. Woe was considerably less intelligent as well as less knowledgeable than Cave Discoverer. To heesh, the humans were supernatural figures. Flandry, who was clearly their chieftain and who furthermore had been midwife and teacher to heesh's consciousness, was a vortex of *mana*. Distorted recollections of what he and Kathryn had related to Cave Discoverer reinforced what he now said about conflict among the Powers. The ruka brain, most highly developed of the three, contributed its mental set to the personality of Woe, whose resulting suspicion of heesh's fellow units in the group was carefully *not* allayed by Flandry.

When they had reached the foothills, Woe was his tool. Under the influence of noga and krippo, the Didonian had actually begun looking forward to adventuring in his service.

How he would use that tool, if at all, he could not predict. It would depend on the situation at journey's terminus.

Kathryn took him aside one evening. Steamy heat and jungle abatis enclosed them. But the topography was easier and the ribs of the Didonians were disappearing behind regained flesh. He and she stood in a canebrake, screened from the world, and regarded each other.

"Why haven't we talked alone, Dominic?" she asked him. Her gaze was grave, and she had taken both his hands in hers.

He shrugged. "Too busy."

"More'n that. We didn't dare. Whenever I see you, I

think of—You're the last person after Hugh that I'd want
to hurt."

"After Hugh."

"You're givin' him back to me. No god could do anything more splendid."

"I take it, then," he said jaggedly, "that you haven't
reconsidered about us."

"No. You make me wish I could wish to. But—Oh,
I'm so grieved. I hope so hard you'll soon find your right
woman."

"I've done that," he said. She winced. He realized he
was crushing her hands, and eased the pressure. "Kathryn,
my darling, we're in the homestretch, but my offer stays
the šame. Us—from here to Port Frederiksen—and I'll
join the revolution."

"That's not worthy of you," she said, whitening.

"I know it isn't," he snarled. "Absolute treason. For
you, I'd sell my soul. You have it anyway."

"How can you say treason?" she exclaimed as if he had
struck her.

"Easy. Treason, treason, treason. You hear? The
revolt's worse than evil, it's stupid. You—"

She tore loose and fled. He stood alone till night
entirely surrounded him. *Nu, Flandry,* he thought once,
*what ever made you suppose the cosmos was designed for
your personal convenience?*

Thereafter Kathryn did not precisely avoid him. That
would have been impossible under present circumstances.
Nor was it her desire. On the contrary, she often smiled
at him, with a shyness that seared, and her tone was
warm when they had occasion to speak. He answered

somewhat in kind. Yet they no longer left the sight of their companions.

The men were wholly content with that. They swarmed about her at every chance, and this flat lowland gave them plenty of chances. No doubt she sincerely regretted injuring Flandry; but she could not help it that joy rose in her with every westward kilometer and poured from her as laughter and graciousness and eager response. Havelock had no problem in getting her to tell him, in complete innocence, everything she knew about the Aenean base.

"Damn, I hate to use her like that!" he said, reporting to his commander in privacy.

"You're doing it for her long-range good," Flandry replied.

"An excuse for a lot of cruelty and treachery in the past."

"And in the future. Yeh. However . . . Tom, we're merely collecting information. Whether we do anything more turns entirely on how things look when we arrive. I've told you before, I won't attempt valorous impossibilities. We may very well go meekly into internment.'"

"If we don't, though—"

"Then we'll be helping strike down a piece of fore-doomed foolishness a little quicker, thereby saving quite a few lives. We can see to it that those lives include Kathryn's." Flandry clapped the ensign's back. "Slack off, son. Figure of speech, that; I'd have had to be more precocious than I was to mean it literally. Nevertheless, slack off, son. Remember the girl who's waiting for you."

Havelock grinned and walked away with his shoulders

squared. Flandry stayed behind a while. *No particular girl for me, ever,* he reflected, *unless Hugh McCormac has the kindness to get himself killed. Maybe then—*

Could I arrange that somehow—if she'd never know I had—could I? A daydream, of course. But supposing the opportunity came my way . . . could I?

I honestly can't say.

Like the American Pacific coast (on Terra, Mother Terra), the western end of Barca wrinkled in hills which fell abruptly down to the sea. When she glimpsed the sheen of great waters, Kathryn scrambled up the tallest tree she could find. Her shout descended leaf by leaf, as sunshine does: "Byrsa Head! Can't be anything else! We're less'n 50 kilometers south of Port Frederiksen!"

She came down in glory. And Dominic Flandry was unable to say more than: "I'll proceed from here by myself."

"What?"

"A flit, in one of the spacesuits. First we'll make camp in some pleasant identifiable spot. Then I'll inquire if they can spare us an aircraft. Quicker than walking."

"Let me go 'long," she requested, ashiver with impatience.

You can go 'long till the last stars burn out, if you choose. Only you don't choose. "Sorry, no. Don't try to radio, either. Listen, but don't transmit. How can we tell what the situation is? Maybe bad; for instance, barbarians might have taken advantage of our family squabble and be in occupation. I'll check. If I'm not back in . . . oh . . . two of these small inexpensive days"—*You always have to clown, don't you?*—"Lieutenant Valencia will assume command and use his own judgment." *I'd prefer Havelock. Valencia's too sympathetic to the revolt. Still, I have to maintain the senior officer convention if I'm to lie to you, my dearest, if I'm to have any chance of harming your cause, my love until I die.*

His reminder dampened hilarity. The troop settled in by a creek, under screening trees, without fire. Flandry suited up. He didn't give any special alert to Woe or to his several solid allies among the men. They had arranged a system of signals many marches before.

"Be careful, Dominic," Kathryn said. Her concern was a knife in him. "Don't risk yourself. For all our sakes."

"I won't," he promised. "I enjoy living." *Oh, yes, I expect to keep on enjoying it, whether or not you will give it any real point.* "Cheers." He activated the impeller. In a second or two, he could no longer see her waving goodbye.

He flew slowly, helmet open, savoring the wind and salt smells as he followed the coastline north. The ocean of moonless Dido had no real surf, it stretched gray under the gray sky, but in any large body of water there is always motion and mystery; he saw intricate patterns of waves and foam, immense patches of weed and shoals of swimming animals, a rainstorm walking on the horizon. To his right the land lifted from wide beaches, itself a quilt of woods and meadows, crossed by great herds of grazers and flocks of flyers. *By and large,* he thought, *planets do well if man lets them be.*

Despite everything, his pulse accelerated when Port Frederiksen appeared. Here was his destiny.

The base occupied a small, readily defensible penin-sula. It was sufficiently old to have become a genuine community. The prefab sheds, shelters, and laboratories were weathered, vine-begrown, almost a part of the land-scape; and among them stood houses built from native wood and stone, in a breeze-inviting style evolved for this place, and gardens and a park. Kathryn had said the population was normally a thousand but doubtless far less during the present emergency. Flandry saw few people about.

His attention focused on the spacefield. If it held a mere interplanetary vessel, his optimum bet was to surrender. But no. Hugh McCormac had left this prized outpost a hyperdrive warship. She wasn't big—a Conqueror-class subdestroyer, her principal armament a blaster cannon, her principal armor speed and maneuverability, her normal complement twenty-five—but she stood rakish on guard, and Flandry's heart jumped.

That's my baby! He passed close. She didn't appear to have more than the regulation minimum of two on duty, to judge from the surrounding desertion. And why should she? Given her controls, instruments, and computers, a single man could take her anywhere. Port Frederiksen would know of approaching danger in time for her personnel to go aboard. Otherwise they doubtless helped the civilians.

Emblazoned above her serial number was the name *Erwin Rommel.* Who the deuce had that been? Some Germanian? No, more likely a Terran, resurrected from the historical files by a data finder programmed to christen several score thousand of Conquerors.

People emerged from buildings. Flandry had been noticed. He landed in the park. "Hello," he said. "I've had a bit of a shipwreck."

During the next hour, he inquired about Port Frederiksen. In return, he was reasonably truthful. He told of a chance encounter with an enemy vessel, a crash landing, a cross-country hike. The main detail he omitted was that he had not been on McCormac's side.

If his scheme didn't work, the Aeneans would be irritated when they learned the whole truth; but they didn't strike him as the kind who would punish a ruse of war.

Essentially they were caretakers: besides the *Rommel*'s crew, a few scientists and service personnel. Their job was to maintain the fruitful relationship with neighboring Didonians and the fabric of the base. Being what they were, they attempted in addition to continue making studies.

Physically, they were isolated. Interplanetary radio silence persisted, for Josipist ships had raided the Virgilian System more than once. Every month or so, a boat from Aeneas brought supplies, mail, and news. The last arrival had been only a few days before. Thus Flandry got an up-to-date account of events.

From the Aenean viewpoint, they were dismal. Manufacture, logistics, and communications were falling apart beneath Hugh McCormac. He had given up trying to govern any substantial volume of space. Instead, he had assigned forces to defend individually the worlds which had declared for him. They were minimal, those forces. They hampered but could not prevent badgering attacks by Snelund's squadrons. Any proper flotilla could annihilate them in detail.

Against that development, McCormac kept the bulk of his fleet around Satan. If the Josipists gathered in full strength, he would learn of it from his scouts, go meet the armada, and rely on his tactical abilities to scatter it.

"But they know that," Director Jowett said. He stroked his white beard with a hand that trembled. "They won't give our Emperor the decisive battle he needs. I wonder if Snelund 'ull even call for reinforcements when Terra can spare them. He may simply wear us down. I'm sure he'd enjoy our havin' a long agony."

"Do you think we should yield?" Flandry asked.

The old head lifted. "Not while our Emperor lives!"

Folk being starved for visitors, Flandry had no trouble in learning more than he needed to know. They fell in readily with a suggestion he made. Rather than dispatch aircars to fetch his companions, why not use the *Rommel*? No instrumental readings or flashed communication from Aeneas indicated any immediate reason to hold her in condition red. Jowett and her captain agreed. Of course, there wouldn't be room for the whole gang unless most of the crew stayed behind. The few who did ride along could use the practice.

Flandry had sketched alternative plans. However, this simplified his task.

He guided the ship aloft and southward. En route, he called the camp. Somebody was sure to be listening on a helmet radio. "All's fine," he said. "We'll land on the beach exactly west of your location and wait for you. Let me speak with Ensign Havelock. . . . Tom? It's Q. Better have Yuan and Christopher lead off."

That meant that they were to don their armor.

The ship set down. Those who manned her stepped trustfully out onto the sand. When they saw the travelers emerge from the woods, they shouted their welcomes across the wind.

Two gleaming metal shapes hurtled into view above the treetops. A second afterward, they were at hover above the ship, with blasters aimed.

"Hands up, if you please," Flandry said.

"What?" the captain yelled. A man snatched at his sidearm. A beam sizzled from overhead, barely missing him. Sparks showered and steam puffed where it struck.

"Hands up, I repeat," Flandry snapped. "You'd be dead before any shot of yours could penetrate."

Sick-featured, they obeyed. "You're being hijacked," he told them. "You might as well start home at once. It'll take you some hours on shank's mare."

"You Judas." The captain spat.

Flandry wiped his face and answered, "Matter of definition, that. Get moving." Yuan accompanied the group for some distance.

Beforehand, suddenly drawn guns had made prisoners of men whose loyalty was in question. More puzzled than angry, Lightning Struck The House guided the uncoupled units aboard. Woe marched Kathryn up the ramp. When he saw her, Flandry found business to do on the other side of the ship.

With his crew embarked and stations assigned, he hauled gravs. Hovering above the settlement, he disabled the interplanetary transmitter with a shot to its mast. Next he broadcast a warning and allowed the people time to evacuate. Finally he demolished other selected installations.

The Aeneans would have food, shelter, medicine, ground defenses. But they wouldn't be going anywhere or talking to anybody until a boat arrived from Aeneas, and none was due for a month.

"Take her east, Citizen Havelock," Flandry directed. "We'll fetch our chums at Thunderstone and let off the surplus livestock. And, yes, we'll lay in some food for the new Didonian. I think I may have use for heesh."

"Where at, sir?"

"Llynathawr. We'll leave this system cautiously, not to be spotted. When well into space, we'll run at maximum hyperspeed to Llynathawr."

"Sir?" Havelock's mien changed from adoration to puzzlement. "I beg the captain's pardon, but I don't understand. I mean, you've turned a catastrophe into a triumph, we've got the enemy's current code and he doesn't know we do, but shouldn't we make for Ifri? Especially when Kathryn—"

"I have my reasons," Flandry said. "Never fear, she will not go back to Snelund." His own expression was so forbidding that no one dared inquire further.

CHAPTER FOURTEEN

Again the metal narrowness, chemical-tainted air, incessant beat of driving energies, but also the wintry wonder of stars, the steady brightening of a particular golden point among them. From Virgil to Llynathawr, in this ship, the flit was less than two standard days.

Flandry held captain's mast. The wardroom was too cramped for everybody, but audiovisual intercoms were tuned. The crew saw him seated, in whites that did not fit well but were nonetheless the full uniform of his rank. Like theirs, his body was gaunt, the bones standing sharply forth in his countenance, the eyes unnaturally luminous by contrast with a skin burned almost black. Unlike most of them, he showed no pleasure in his victory.

"Listen carefully," he said. "In an irregular situation such as ours, it is necessary to go through various formalities." He took the depositions which, entered in the log, would retroactively legalize his seizure of *Rommel* and his status as her master.

"Some among you were put under arrest," he went
on. "That was a precautionary measure. In a civil war, one
dares not trust a man without positive confirmation, and
obviously I couldn't plan a surprise move with our entire
group. The arrest is hereby terminated and the subjects
ordered released. I will specifically record and report that
their detention was in no way meant to reflect on their
loyalty or competence, and that I recommend every man
aboard for promotion and a medal."

He did not smile when they cheered. His hard
monotone went on: "By virtue of the authority vested in
me, and in conformance with Naval regulations on
extraordinary recruitment, I am swearing the sophont
from the planet Dido, known to us by the name Woe, into
His Majesty's armed service on a temporary basis with
the rating of common spaceman. In view of the special
character of this being, the enrollment shall be entered as
that of three new crewpeople."

Laughter replied. They thought his imp had spoken.
They were wrong.

"All detection systems will be kept wide open," he
continued after the brief ceremony. "Instantly upon contact
with any Imperial ship, the communications officer will
signal surrender and ask for an escort. I daresay we'll all
be arrested when they board us, till our bona fides can be
established. However, I trust that by the time we assume
Llynathawr orbit, we'll be cleared.

"A final item. We have an important prisoner aboard.
I told Ensign Havelock, who must have told the rest of
you, that Lady McCormac will not be returned to the
custody of Sector Governor Snelund. Now I want to put

the reason on official though secret record, since otherwise our action would be grounds for court-martial.

"It is not in the province of Naval officers to make political decisions. Because of the circumstances about Lady McCormac, including the questionable legality of her original detention, my judgment is that handing her over to His Excellency would *be* a political decision, fraught with possibly ominous consequences. My duty is to deliver her to Naval authorities who can dispose of her case as they find appropriate. At the same time, we cannot in law refuse a demand for her person by His Excellency.

"Therefore, as master of this vessel, and as an officer of the Imperial Naval Intelligence Corps, charged with an informational mission and hence possessed of discretionary powers with respect to confidentiality of data, et cetera, I classify Lady McCormac's presence among us as a state secret. She will be concealed before we are boarded. No one will mention that she has been along, then or at any future date, until such time as the fact may be granted public release by a qualified governmental agency. To do so will constitute a violation of the laws and rules on security, and subject you to criminal penalties. If asked, you may say that she escaped just before we left Dido. Is that understood?"

Reverberating shouts answered him.

He sat back. "Very well," he said tiredly. "Resume your stations. Have Lady McCormac brought here for interview."

He switched off the com. His men departed. *I've got them in my pocket,* he thought. *They'd ship out for hell if I were the skipper.* He felt no exaltation. *I don't really want another command.*

He opened a fresh pack of the cigarettes he had found among stocked rations. The room enclosed him in drabness. Under the machine noises and the footfalls outside, silence grew.

But his heart knocked when Kathryn entered. He rose.

She shut the door and stood tall in front of it. Her eyes, alone in the spacecraft, looked on him in scorn. His knife had stayed on her hip.

When she didn't speak and didn't speak, he faltered, "I—I hope the captain's cabin—isn't too uncomfortable."

"How do you aim to hide me?" she asked. The voice had its wonted huskiness, and nothing else.

"Mitsui and Petrović will take the works out of a message capsule. We can pad the casing and tap airholes that won't be noticed. You can have food and drink and, uh, what else you'll need. It'll get boring, lying there in the dark, but shouldn't be longer than twenty or thirty hours."

"Then what?"

"If everything goes as I expect, we'll be ordered into parking orbit around Llynathawr," he said. "The code teams won't take much time getting their readouts from our computers. Meanwhile we'll be interrogated and the men assigned temporarily to Catawrayannis Base till extended leave can be given them. Procedure cut and dried and quick; the Navy's interested in what we bring, not our adventures while we obtained it. Those can wait for the board of inquiry on *Asieneuve*'s loss. The immediate thing will be to hit the rebels before they change their code.

"I'll assert myself as captain of the *Rommel*, on

detached service. My status could be disputed; but in the scramble to organize that attack, I doubt if any bureaucrat will check the exact wording of regs. They'll be happy to let me have the responsibility for this boat, the more so when my roving commission implies that I need the means to rove.

"As master, I'm required to keep at least two hands on watch. In parking orbit, that's a technicality, no more. And I've seen to it that technically, Woe is three crewmen. I'm reasonably confident I can fast-talk my way out of any objections to heesh. It's such a minor-looking matter, a method of not tying up two skilled spacers who could be useful elsewhere.

"When you're alone, heesh will let you out."

Flandry ran down. He had lectured her in the same way as he might have battered his fists on a steel wall.

"Why?" she said.

"Why what?" He stubbed out his cigarette and reached for another.

"I can understand . . . maybe . . . why you did what you've done . . . to Hugh. I wouldn't've thought it of you, I saw you as brave and good enough to stand for what's right, but I can imagine that down underneath, your spirit is small.

"But what I can't understand, can't grasp," Kathryn sighed, "is that you—after everything—are bringin' me back to enslavement. If you hadn't told Woe to seize me, there's not a man of your men who wouldn't've turned away while I ran into the forest."

He could not watch her any longer. "You're needed," he mumbled.

"For what? To be wrung dry of what little I know? To be dangled 'fore Hugh in the hope 'twill madden him? To be made an example of? And it doesn't matter whether 'tis an example of Imperial justice or Imperial mercy, whatever was me will die when they kill Hugh." She was not crying, not reproaching. Peripherally, he saw her shake her head in a slow, bewildered fashion. "I *can't* understand."

"I don't believe I'd better tell you yet," he pleaded. "Too many variables in the equation. Too much improvising to do. But—"

She interrupted. "I'll play your game, since 'tis the one way I can at least 'scape from Snelund. But I'd rather not be with you." Her tone continued quiet. "'Twould be a favor if you weren't by when they put me in that coffin."

He nodded. She left. Woe's heavy tread boomed behind her.

Whatever his shortcomings, the governor of Sector Alpha Crucis set a magnificent table. Furthermore, he was a charming host, with a rare gift for listening as well as making shrewd and witty comments. Though most of Flandry crouched like a panther behind his smile, a part reveled in this first truly civilized meal in months.

He finished his narrative of events on Dido as noise-less live servants cleared away the last golden dishes, set forth brandy and cigars, and disappeared. "Tremendous!" applauded Snelund. "Utterly fascinating, that race. Did you say you brought one back? I'd like to meet the being."

"That's easily arranged, Your Excellency," Flandry said. "More easily than you perhaps suspect."

Snelund's brows moved very slightly upward, his fingers

tensed the tiniest bit on the stem of his snifter. Flandry
relaxed, inhaled the bouquet of his own drink, twirled it
to enjoy the play of color within the liquid, and sipped
in conscious counterpoint to the background lilt of
music.

They sat on an upper floor of the palace. The chamber
was not large, but graciously proportioned and subtly
tinted. A wall had been opened to the summer evening.
Air wandered in from the gardens bearing scents of rose,
jasmine, and less familiar blossoms. Downhill glistened
the city, lights in constellations and fountains, upward
radiance of towers, firefly dance of aircars. Traffic sounds
were a barely perceptible murmur. You had trouble
believing that all around and spilling to the stars, it roared
with preparations for war.

Nor was Snelund laying on any pressure. Flandry might
have removed Kathryn McCormac hence for "special
interrogation deemed essential to the maximization of
success probability on a surveillance mission" in sheer
impudence. He might have lost first his ship and last his
prisoner in sheer carelessness. But after he came back
with a booty that should allow Admiral Pickens to give the
rebellion a single spectacular deathblow, without help
from Terra and with no subsequent tedious inspection of
militia operations, the governor could not well be aught
but courteous to the man who saved his political bacon.

Nevertheless, when Flandry requested a secret talk, it
had not been with the expectation of dinner *tête-à-tête*.

"Indeed?" Snelund breathed.

Flandry glanced across the table at him: wavy, fiery
hair, muliebrile countenance, gorgeous purple and gold

robe, twinkle and shimmer of jewelry. Behind that, Flandry thought, were a bowel and a skull.

"The thing is, sir," he said, "I had a delicate decision to make."

Snelund nodded, smiling but with a gaze gone flat and hard as two stones. "I suspected that, Commander. Certain aspects of your report and behavior, certain orders you issued with a normally needless haste and authoritative ring, were not lost on me. You have me to thank for passing the word that I felt you should not be argued with. I was, ah, curious as to what you meant."

"I do thank Your Excellency." Flandry started his cigar. "This matter's critical to you too, sir. Let me remind you of my dilemma on Dido. Lady McCormac became extremely popular with my men."

"Doubtless." Snelund laughed. "I taught her some unusual tricks."

I have no weapons under this blue and white dress uniform, Aaron Snelund. I have nothing but my hands and feet. And a black belt in karate, plus training in other techniques. Except for unfinished business, I'd merrily let myself be executed, in fair trade for the joy of dismantling you.

Because the creature must recall what her soul had been like when he flayed it open, and might be probing veracity now, Flandry gave him a sour grin. "No such luck, sir. She even refused *my* proposition, which fact I pray you to declare a top secret. But—well, there she was, the only woman, handsome, able, bright. Toward the end, most were a touch in love with her. She'd spread the impression that her stay here had been unpleasant. To be frank, sir, I feared a mutiny if the men expected she'd be remanded to you. Bringing in the code was too crucial to risk."

"So you connived at her escape." Snelund sipped. "That's tacitly realized by everyone, Commander. A sound judgment, whether or not we dare put it in the record. She can be tracked down later."

"But sir, I didn't."

"What!" Snelund sat bolt erect.

Flandry said fast: "Let's drop the euphemisms, sir. She made some extremely serious accusations against you. Some people might use them to buttress a claim that your actions were what caused this rebellion. I didn't want that. If you've read much history, you'll agree nothing works like a Boadicea—no?—a martyr, especially an attractive female martyr, to create trouble. The Empire would suffer. I felt it was my duty to keep her. To get the men's agreement, I had to convince them she would not be returned here. She'd go to a Naval section, where rules protect prisoners and testimony isn't likely to be suppressed."

Snelund had turned deadpan. "Continue," he said.

Flandry sketched his means of smuggling her in. "The fleet should be assembled and ready to depart for Satan in about three days," he finished, "now that scouts have verified the enemy is still using the code I brought. I'm not expected to accompany it. I am expected, though, by my men, to obtain orders for myself that will send the *Rommel* to Ifri, Terra, or some other place where she'll be safe. They'll have ways of finding out whether I do. You know how word circulates in any set of offices. If I don't—I'm not sure that secrecy will bind every one of those lads. And disclosure would inconvenience you, sir, at this highly critical time."

Snelund drained his brandy glass and refilled it. The little *glug-glug* sounded loud across the music. "Why do you tell me?"

"Because of what I've said. As a patriot, I can't allow anything that might prolong the rebellion."

Snelund studied him. "And she refused you?" he said at length.

Spite etched Flandry's tones. "I don't appreciate that, from third-hand goods like her." With quick smoothness: "But this is beside the point. My obligation . . . to you, Your Excellency, as well as to the Imperium—"

"Ah, yes." Snelund eased. "It does no harm to have a man in your debt who is on his way up, does it?"

Flandry looked smug.

"Yes-s-s, I think we resonate, you and I," Snelund said. "What is your suggestion?"

"Well," Flandry replied, "as far as officialdom knows, *Rommel* contains no life other than my multiple Didonian. And heesh will never talk. If my orders were cut tonight—not specifically to anywhere, let's say, only for 'reconnaissance and report at discretion, employing minimal crew'—a phone call by Your Excellency to someone on Admiral Pickens' staff would take care of that—I could go aboard and depart. My men would relax about Lady McCormac. When they haven't heard news of her in a year or two—well, reassignment will have scattered them and feelings will have cooled. Oblivion is a most valuable servant, Your Excellency."

"Like yourself," Snelund beamed. "I do believe

our careers are going to be linked, Commander. If I can trust you—"

"Come see for yourself," Flandry proposed.

"Eh?"

"You said you'd be interested in meeting my Didonian anyway. It can be discreet. I'll give you the *Rommel*'s orbital elements and you go up alone in your flitter, not telling anybody where you're bound." Flandry blew a smoke ring. "You might like to take personal charge of the execution. To make sure it's done in a manner suitable to the crime. We could have hours."

Then he waited.

Until sweat made beads on Snelund's skin and an avid voice said, "Yes!"

Flandry hadn't dared hope to catch the prize for which he angled. Had he failed, he would have made it his mission in life to accomplish the same result by other methods. The fact left him feeling so weak and lightheaded that he wondered vaguely if he could walk out of there.

He did, after a period of conference and arrangement-making. A gubernatorial car delivered him at Catawrayannis Base, where he changed into working garb, accepted his orders, and got a flitter to the *Rommel*.

Time must be allowed for that craft to descend again, lest the pilot notice another and ornate one lay alongside. Flandry sat on the bridge, alone with his thoughts. The viewscreen showed him planet and stars, a huge calm beauty.

Vibration sounded in the metal, as airlocks joined and magnetronic grapples made fast. Flandry went down to admit his guest.

Snelund came through the airlock breathing hard. He carried a surgical kit. "Where is she?" he demanded.

"This way, sir." Flandry let him go ahead. He did not appear to have noticed Flandry's gun, packed in case of bodyguards. There weren't any. They might have gossiped.

Woe stood outside the captain's cabin. Xenological interest or no, Snelund barely glanced at heesh and jittered while Flandry said in pidgin: "Whatever you hear, stay where you are until I command you otherwise."

The noga's horn dipped in acknowledgment. The ruka touched the ax at his side. The krippo sat like a bird of prey.

Flandry opened the door. "I brought you a visitor, Kathryn," he said.

She uttered a noise that would long run through his nightmares. His Merseian war knife flew into her hand.

He wrenched the bag from Snelund and pinioned the man in a grip that was not to be shaken. Kicking the door shut behind him, he said, "Any way you choose, Kathryn. Any way at all."

Snelund began screaming.

CHAPTER FIFTEEN

Seated at the pilot board of the gig, Flandry pushed controls to slide aside the housing and activate the viewscreens. Space leaped at him. The gloom of Satan and the glitter of stars drifted slowly past as *Rommel* swung around the planet and tumbled along her invariable plane. Twice he identified slivers of blackness crossing the constellations and the Milky Way: nearby warcraft. But unaided senses could not really prove to him that he was at the heart of the rebel fleet.

Instruments had done that as he drove inward, and several curt conversations once he came in range. Even when Kathryn spoke directly with Hugh McCormac, reserve stood between them. Warned by his communications officer what to expect, the admiral had had time to don a mask. How could he know it wasn't a trick? If he spoke to his wife at all, and not to an electronic shadow show, she might be under brain-scrub, speaking the words that her operator projected into her middle ear. Her own mostly impersonal sentences, uttered from a visage nearly blank, yet the whole of her unsteady, might lend credence to that fear. Flandry had been astonished. He had taken for granted she would cry forth in joy.

Was it perhaps a simple but strong wish for privacy, or was it that at this ultimate moment and ultimate stress she must fight too hard to keep from flying apart? There had been no chance to ask her. She obeyed Flandry's directive, revealing no secret of his, insisting that the two men hold a closed-door parley before anything else was done; and McCormac agreed, his voice rough and not altogether firm; and then things went too fast—the giving of directions, the study of meters, the maneuvers of approach and orbit matching—for Flandry to learn what she felt.

But while he prepared to go, she came from the cabin to which she had retreated. She seized his hands and looked into his eyes and whispered, "Dominic, I'm prayin' for both of you." Her lips brushed across his. They were cold, like her fingers, and tasted of salt. Before he could respond, she walked quickly away again.

Theirs had been a curious intimacy while they traveled hither. The red gift he had given her; the plan he laid out, and that she helped him perfect after she saw he was not to be moved from it; between times, dreamy talk of old days and far places, much reminiscence about little events on Dido—Flandry wondered if man and woman could grow closer in a wedded lifetime. In one aspect, yes, obviously they could; but that one they both shied off from speaking of.

And here came *Persei* into view and with her, one way or another, an end to everything which had been. The flagship loomed like a moon, mottled with thermostatic paint patterns, hilled with boat nacelles and gun turrets, thrusting out cannon and sensors like crystal forests. Satellite craft glinted around her. Indicator lights glowed on Flandry's board and his receiver said, "We have a lock on you. Go ahead."

He started the gravs. The gig left *Rommel* and surrendered to control from *Persei*. It was a short trip, but tense on both sides of the gap. How could McCormac be positive this was not a way to get a nuclear weapon inside his command vessel and detonate it? *He can't,* Flandry thought. *Especially when I wouldn't allow anyone to come fetch me. Of course that might well have been for fear of being captured by a boarding party, which indeed was partly the case, but just the same—He's courageous, McCormac. I detest him to his inmost cell, but he's courageous.*

A portal gaped and swallowed him. He sat for a minute hearing air gush back into the housing. Its personnel valves opened. He left the gig and went to meet the half dozen men who waited. They watched him somberly, neither hailing nor saluting.

He returned the stares. The insurrectionists were as marked by hunger and strain as he, but theirs was a less healthy, a sallowing, faintly grubby condition. "Relax," he said. "Inspect my vessel if you wish. No boobytraps, I assure you. Let's not dawdle, though."

"This way . . . please." The lieutenant who led the squad started off with rapid, stiff strides. Part of the group stayed behind, to check the boat. Those who walked at Flandry's back were armed. It didn't bother him. He had worse dangers to overcome before he could sleep.

They went through metal tunnels and caverns, past hundreds of eyes, in silence hardly broken save for the ship's pulse and breath. At the end, four marines guarded a door. The lieutenant addressed them and passed through. Saluting in the entrance, he said, "Commander Flandry, sir."

"Send him in," replied a deep toneless voice. "Leave us alone but stay on call."

"Aye, sir." The lieutenant stood aside. Flandry went by. The door closed with a soft hiss that betokened sound-proofing.

Quiet lay heavy in the admiral's suite. This main room was puritanically furnished: chairs, a table, a couch, a plain rug, the bulkheads and overhead an undraped light gray. A few pictures and animations gave it some personality: family portraits, views from home, scenes of wilderness. So did a chess set and a bookshelf which held both codices and spools, both classics and scientific works. One of the inner doors was ajar, showing an office where McCormac must often toil after his watches. No doubt the bedroom was downright monastic, Flandry thought, the galley and bar seldom used, the—

"Greeting," McCormac said. He stood large, straight, gaunt as his men but immaculate, the nebula and stars frosty on his shoulders. He had aged, Flandry saw: more gray in the dark hair than pictures recorded, still less flesh in the bony countenance and more wrinkles, the eyes sunken while the nose and chin had become promontories.

"Good day." Flandry felt a moment's awe and inade-quacy wash over him. He dismissed it with a measure of cold enjoyment.

"You might have saluted, Commander," McCormac said quietly.

"Against regulations," Flandry replied. "You've forfeited your commission."

"Have I? Well—" McCormac gestured. "Shall we sit down? Would you care for refreshment?"

"No, thanks," Flandry said. "We haven't time to go through the diplomatic niceties. Pickens' fleet will be on you in less than 70 hours."

McCormac lowered himself. "I am aware of that, Commander. We keep our scouts busy, you know. The mustering of that much strength could not be concealed. We're prepared for a showdown; we welcome it." He glanced up at the younger man and added: "You observe that I give you your proper rank. I am the Emperor of all Terran subjects. After the war, I plan on amnesty for nearly everyone who misguidedly opposed me. Even you, perhaps."

Flandry sat down too, opposite him, crossed ankle over knee, and grinned. "Confident, aren't you?"

"It's a measure of your side's desperation that it sent you in advance to try negotiating, with what you claim is my wife for a hostage." McCormac's mouth tightened. Momentarily, the wrath in him struck forth, though he spoke no louder. "I despise any man who'd lend himself to such a thing. Did you imagine I'd abandon everyone else who's trusted me to save any individual, however dear? Go tell Snelund and his criminals, there will be no peace or pardon for them, though they run to the ends of the universe; but there are ways and ways to die, and if they harm my Kathryn further, men will remember their fate for a million years."

"I can't very well convey that message," Flandry replied, "seeing that Snelund's dead." McCormac half rose. "What Kathryn and I came to let you know is that if you accept battle, you and your followers will be equally dead."

McCormac leaned over and seized Flandry by the upper arms, bruisingly hard. "What is this?" he yelled.

Flandry snapped that grip with a judo break. "Don't paw me, McCormac," he said.

They got back on their feet, two big men, and stood toe to toe. McCormac's fists were doubled. The breath whistled in and out of him. Flandry kept hands open, knees tense and a trifle bent, ready to move out of the way and chop downward. The impasse lasted thirty mortal seconds.

McCormac mastered himself, turned, stalked a few paces off, and faced around again. "All right," he said as if being strangled. "I let you in so I could listen to you. Carry on."

"That's better." Flandry resumed his chair and took out a cigarette. Inwardly he shook and felt now frozen, now on fire. "The thing is," he said, "Pickens has your code."

McCormac rocked where he stood.

"Given that," Flandry said redundantly, "if you fight, he'll take you apart; if you retreat, he'll chivvy you to pieces; if you disperse, he'll snatch you and your bases in detail before you can rally. You haven't time to recode and you'll never be allowed the chance. Your cause is done, McCormac."

He waved the cigarette. "Kathryn will confirm it," he

added. "She witnessed the whole show. Alone with her, you'll soon be able to satisfy yourself that she's telling the truth, under no chemical compulsions. You won't need any psych tests for that, I hope. Not if you two are the loving couple she claims.

"Besides, after talking to her, you're welcome to send a team over who'll remove my central computer. They'll find your code in its tapes. That'll disable my hyperdrive, of course, but I don't mind waiting for Pickens."

McCormac stared at the deck. "Why didn't she come aboard with you?" he asked.

"She's my insurance," Flandry said. "She won't be harmed unless your side does something ridiculous like shooting at my vessel. But if I don't leave this one freely, my crew will take the appropriate measures."

Which I trust, dear Hugh, you will interpret as meaning that I have trained spacehands along, who'll speed away if you demonstrate bad faith. It's the natural assumption, which I've been careful to do nothing to prevent you from making. The datum that my crew is Woe, who couldn't navigate a flatboat across a swimming pool, and that heesh's orders are to do nothing no matter what happens . . . you're better off not receiving that datum right at once. Among other things, first I want to tell you some home truths.

McCormac lifted his head and peered closely. With the shock ridden out, his spirit and intelligence were reviving fast. "*Your* hostage?" he said from the bottom of his throat.

Flandry nodded while kindling his cigarette. The smoke soothed him the least bit. "Uh-huh. A long story.

Kathryn will tell you most of it. But the upshot is, though I serve the Imperium, I'm here in an irregular capacity and without its knowledge."

"Why?"

Flandry spoke with the same chill steadiness as he regarded the other: "For a number of reasons, including that I'm Kathryn's friend. I'm the one who got her away from Snelund. I took her with me when I went to see what the chance was of talking you out of your lunacy. You'd left the Virgilian System, but one of your lovely barbarian auxiliaries attacked and wrecked us. We made it down to Dido and marched overland to Port Frederiksen. There I seized the warship from which the code was gotten, the same I now command. When I brought it to Llynathawr, my men and I kept Kathryn's presence secret. They think the cosmos of her too, you see. I lured Governor Snelund on board, and held him over a drain while she cut his throat. I'd have done worse, so'd you, but she has more decency in a single DNA strand than you or I will ever have in our whole organisms. She helped me get rid of the evidence because I want to return home. We tossed it on a meteorite trajectory into the atmosphere of an outer planet. Then we headed for Satan."

McCormac shuddered. "Do you mean she's gone over to your side—to you? Did you two—"

Flandry's cigarette dropped from lips yanked into a gorgon's lines. He surged up and across the deck, laid hold of McCormac's tunic, batted defending hands aside with the edge of his other palm and numbing force, shook the admiral and grated:

"Curb your tongue! You sanctimonious son of a bitch!

If I had my wish, your pig-bled body would've been the one to burn through that sky. But there's Kathryn. There's the people who've followed you. There's the Empire. Down on your knees, McCormac, and thank whatever smug God you've taken on as your junior partner, that I have to find some way of saving your life because otherwise the harm you've done would be ten times what it is!"

He hurled the man from him. McCormac staggered against a bulkhead, which thudded. Half stunned, he looked upon the rage which stood before him, and his answering anger faded.

After a while, Flandry turned away. "I'm sorry," he said in a dull voice. "Not apologetic, understand. Only sorry I lost my temper. Unprofessional of me, especially when our time is scant."

McCormac shook himself. "I said I'd listen. Shall we sit down and begin over?" Flandry had to admire him a trifle for that.

They descended stiffly to the edges of their chairs. Flandry got out a new cigarette. "Nothing untoward ever happened between Kathryn and me," he said, keeping his eyes on the tiny cylinder. "I won't deny I'd have liked for it to, but it didn't. Her entire loyalty was, is, and forever will be to you. I think I've persuaded her that your present course is mistaken, but not altogether. And in no case does she want to go anyplace but where you go, help in anything but what you do. Isn't that an awesome lot to try to deserve?"

McCormac swallowed. After a moment: "You're a remarkable fellow, Commander. How old are you?"

"Half your age. And yet I have to tell you the facts of life."

"Why should I heed you," McCormac asked, but subduedly, "when you serve that abominable government? When you claim to have ruined my cause?"

"It was ruined anyway. I know how well your opposition's Fabian strategy was working. What we hope to do— Kathryn and I—we hope to prevent you from dragging more lives, more treasure, more Imperial strength down with you."

"Our prospects weren't that bad. I was evolving a plan—"

"The worst outcome would have been your victory."

"What? Flandry, I . . . I'm human, I'm fallible, but *anyone* would be better on the throne than that Josip who appointed that Snelund."

With the specter of a smile, because his own fury was dying out and a measure of pity was filling the vacuum, Flandry replied: "Kathryn still accords with you there. She still feels you're the best imaginable man for the job. I can't persuade her otherwise, and haven't tried very hard. You see, it doesn't matter whether she's right or wrong. The point is, you might have given us the most brilliant administration in history, and nevertheless your accession would have been catastrophic."

"Why?"

"You'd have destroyed the principle of legitimacy. The Empire will outlive Josip. Its powerful vested interests, its cautious bureaucrats, its size and inertia, will keep him from doing enormous harm. But if you took the throne by force, why shouldn't another discontented admiral do the same in another generation? And another and another, till civil wars rip the Empire to shreds. Till the Merseians come in, and the barbarians. You yourself hired barbarians to fight Terrans, McCormac. No odds whether or not you took precautions, the truth remains that you brought them in, and sooner or later we'll get a rebel who doesn't mind conceding them territory. And the Long Night falls."

"I could not disagree more," the admiral retorted with vehemence. "Restructuring a decadent polity—"

Flandry cut him off. "I'm not trying to convert you either. I'm simply explaining why I did what I did." *We need not tell you that I'd have abandoned my duty for Kathryn. That makes no difference any more*—interior laughter jangled—*except that it would blunt the edge of my sermon.* "You can't restructure something that's been irreparably undermined. All your revolution has managed to do is get sophonts killed, badly needed ships wrecked, trouble brewed that'll be years in settling—on this critical frontier."

"What should I have done instead?" McCormac disputed. "Leave my wife and myself out of it. Think only what Snelund had already done to this sector. What he would do if and when he won back to Terra. Was there another solution but to strike at the root of our griefs and dangers?"

"'Root'—*radix*—you radicals are all alike," Flandry said. "You think everything springs from one or two unique causes, and if only you can get at them, everything will automatically become paradisical. History doesn't go that way. Read some and see what the result of every resort to violence by reformists has been."

"Your theory!" McCormac said, flushing. "I . . . we were faced with a fact."

Flandry shrugged. "Many moves were possible," he said. "A number had been started: complaints to Terra, pressure to get Snelund removed from office or at least contained in his scope. Failing that, you might have considered assassinating him. I don't deny he was a threat to the Empire. Suppose, specifically, after your friends liberated you, you'd gotten together a small though efficient force and mounted a raid on the palace for the limited purposes of freeing Kathryn and killing Snelund. Wouldn't that have served?"

"But what could we have done afterward?"

"You'd have put yourselves outside the law." Flandry nodded. "Same as I've done, though I hope to hide the guilt I don't feel. Quite aside from my personal well-being, the fact would set a bad precedent if it became public. Among your ignorances, McCormac, is that you don't appreciate how essential a social lubricant hypocrisy is."

"We couldn't have . . . skulked."

"No, you'd have had to do immediately what you and many others now have to do regardless—get out of the Empire."

"Are you crazy? Where to?"

Flandry rose once more and looked down upon him. "You're the crazy man," he said. "I suppose we are decadent these days, in that we never seem to think of emigration. Better stay home, we feel, and cling to what we have, what we know, our comforts, our assurances, our associations . . . rather than vanish forever into that big strange universe . . . even when everything we cling to is breaking apart in our hands. But the pioneers worked otherwise. There's room yet, a whole galaxy beyond these few stars we think we control, out on the far end of one spiral arm.

"You can escape if you start within the next several hours. With that much lead, and dispersal in addition, your ships ought to be able to pick up families, and leave off the men who don't want to go. Those'll have to take their chances with the government, though I imagine necessity will force it to be lenient. Set a rendezvous at some extremely distant star. None of your craft will likely be pursued much past the border if they happen to be detected.

"Go a long way, McCormac, as far as you possibly can. Find a new planet. Found a new society. Never come back."

The admiral raised himself too. "I can't abandon my responsibilities," he groaned.

"You did that when you rebelled," Flandry said. "Your duty is to save what you can, and live the rest of your life knowing what you wrought here. Maybe the act of leading people to a fresh beginning, maybe that'll console you." *I'm sure it will in time. You have a royal share of self-righteousness.* "And Kathryn. She wants to go. She wants it very badly." He caught McCormac's gaze. "If ever a human being had a right to be taken from this civilization, she does."

McCormac blinked hard.

"Never come back," Flandry repeated. "Don't think of recruiting a barbarian host and returning. You'd be the enemy then, the real enemy. I want your word of honor on that. If you don't give it to me, and to Kathryn, she won't be allowed to rejoin you, whatever you may do to me." *I lie like a wet rag.* "If you do give it, and break it, she will not pardon you."

"In spite of your behavior, you are an able leader. You're the one man who can hope to carry the emigration off, in as short a while as you have to inform, persuade, organize, act. Give me your word, and Kathryn will ride back in my gig to you."

McCormac covered his face. "Too sudden. I can't—"

"Well, let's thresh out a few practical questions first, if you like. I've pondered various details beforehand."

"But—I couldn't—"

"Kathryn is your woman, all right," Flandry said bitterly. "Prove to me that you're her man."

She was waiting at the airlock. The hours had circled her like wolves. He wished that his last sight of her could be without that anguish and exhaustion.

"Dominic?" she whispered.

"He agreed," Flandry told her. "You can go to him."

She swayed. He caught her and held her. "Now, now," he said clumsily, nigh to tears. He stroked the bright tousled hair. "Now, now, it's ended, we've won, you and I—" She slumped. He barely kept her from falling.

With the dear weight in his arms, he went to sickbay, laid her down and administered a stimulol injection. Color appeared in seconds, her lashes fluttered, the green eyes found him. She sat erect. "Dominic!" she cried. Weeping had harshened her voice. "'Tis true?"

"See for yourself," he smiled. "Uh, take care, though.

I gave you a minimum shot. You'll have a stiff metabolic price to pay as is."

She came to him, still weary and shaken. Their arms closed. They kissed for a long time.

"I wish," she said brokenly, "I almost wish—"

"Don't." He drew her head into the curve of his shoulder.

She stepped back. "Well, I wish you everything good there'll ever be, startin' with the girl who's really right for you."

"Thanks," he said. "Have no worries on my score. It's been worth any trouble I may have had," *and ever will have.* "Don't delay, Kathryn. Go to him."

She did. He sought the conn, where he could see the boat carry her off and await McCormac's technicians.

CHAPTER SIXTEEN

Strange suns enclouded *Persei*. A darkness aft hid the last glimpse of Imperial stars.

McCormac closed the suite door behind him. Kathryn rose. Rest, first under sedation, later under tranquilization, and medicine and nourishment had made her beautiful. She wore a gray shimmerlyn robe somebody had given her, open at throat and calf, sashed at the waist, smooth over the strong deep curves.

He stopped short. "I didn't expect you here yet!" he blurted.

"The medics released me," she answered, "seein' as how I'd come to happy news." Her smile was tremulous.

"Well . . . yes," he said woodenly. "We've verified that we shook those scouts dogging us, by our maneuvers inside that nebula. They'll never find us in uncharted interstellar space. Not that they'd want to, I'm sure. It'd be too risky, sending the power needed to deal with us as far as we're going. No, we're done with them, unless we return."

Shocked, she exclaimed: "You won't! You promised!"

"I know. Not that I mightn't—if—no, don't fear. I won't. Flandry was right, damn him, I'd have to raise allies, and those allies would have to be offered what it would split the Empire to give. Let's hope the threat that I *may* try again will force them to govern better . . . back there."

Her strickenness told him how much remained for her before the old calm strength was regained: "Dyuba, you'd think 'bout politics and fightin' in this hour?"

"I apologize," he said. "Nobody warned me you were coming. And I have been preoccupied."

She reached him, but they did not embrace. "That preoccupied?" she asked.

"Why, why, what do you mean? See here, you shouldn't be standing more than necessary. Let's get you seated. And, er, we'll have to arrange for the sleeping quarters to be remodeled—"

She closed her eyes briefly. When she opened them, she had command of herself. "Poor Hugh," she said. "You're scarred right badly too. I should've thought how you must've hurt."

"Nonsense." He urged her toward the couch.

She resisted in such a manner that his arms went around her. Laying hers about his neck and her cheek against his breast, she said, "Wait. You were tryin' to 'scape thinkin' 'bout us. 'Bout what I can be to you, after everything that was done. 'Bout whether the things I'm leavin' untold concernin' what passed 'tween Dominic and me, if they didn't include—But I've sworn they didn't."

"I cannot doubt you," rumbled through her.

"No, you're too honorable not to try hard to believe me, not to try hard to rebuild what we had. Poor Hugh, you're scared you might not be able."

"Well—associations, of course—" His clasp stiffened.

"I'll help you if you'll help me. I need it bad's you do."

"I understand," he said, gentler.

"No, you don't, Hugh," she replied gravely. "I realized the truth while I was alone, recuperatin', nothin' to do but think in a weird clear way till I'd fall asleep and the dreams came. I'm 'bout as well over what happened to me in the palace as I'll ever be. I'm the one to cure *you* of that. But you'll have to cure me of Dominic, Hugh."

"Oh, Kathryn!" he said into her hair.

"We'll try," she murmured. "We'll succeed, anyhow in part, anyhow enough to live. We must."

Vice Admiral Sir Ilya Kheraskov riffled the papers on his desk. The noise went from end to end of his office. Behind him, the projection screen today held an image of Saturn.

"Well," he said, "I've perused your account, and other relevant data, quite intensely since you arrived home. You were a busy young man, Lieutenant Commander."

"Yes, sir," said Flandry. He had taken a chair, but thought best to give the impression of sitting at attention.

"I regret leave was denied you and you've been made to spend the whole two weeks in Luna Prime. Must have been frustrating, the fleshpots of Terra glowing right overhead. But any number of irregularities had to be checked out."

"Yes, sir."

Kheraskov chuckled. "Stop worrying. We'll put you through assorted rituals, but I can tell you in confidence, you're off the hook and your brevet rank of commander will be made permanent. Till your next escapade gets you either broken or promoted, that is. I'd call the odds fifty-fifty."

Flandry leaned back. "Thank you, sir."

"You seem a touch disappointed," Kheraskov remarked. "Did you anticipate more?"

"Well, sir—"

Kheraskov cocked his head and grinned wider. "You ought to be effusive at me. I'm responsible for your getting this much. And I had to work for it!"

He drew breath. "True," he said, "your obtaining the code was an exploit which justifies overlooking a great deal else. But the else is such a very great deal. Besides losing *Asieneuve* on a trip most kindly described as reckless, you staged other performances which were high-handed at best, in gross excess of your authority at worst. Like removing the sector governor's prisoner on your own warrant; and conveying her with you; and concealing her presence on your return; and heading back out with her; and losing her to the enemy. . . . I'm afraid, Flandry, regardless of what rank you may gain, you'll never have another command."

That's no punishment. "Sir," Flandry said, "my report justifies whatever I did as according to regulations. So will the testimony of the men who served under me."

"Taking the most liberal interpretation of your discretionary rights that man, xeno, or computer can conceive of . . . yes, perhaps. But mainly, you rascal, I argued and politicked on your behalf because the Intelligence Corps needs you."

"Again I thank the admiral."

Kheraskov shoved the cigar box forward. "Take one," he said, "and show your gratitude by telling me what really happened."

Flandry accepted. "It's in my report, sir."

"Yes, and I know a weasel when one slinks by me. For instance—I read from the abstract of this wonderful document you wrote—ahem. 'Soon after leaving with Lady McCormac for Terra, with minimal crew for the sake of speed and secrecy as per orders, I was unfortunately noted and overhauled by an enemy cruiser which captured me. Brought to the flagship at Satan, I was surprised to find the rebels so discouraged that, upon learning Admiral Pickens had their code, they decided to flee the Empire. Lady McCormac prevailed upon them to spare me and my Didonian hand, leaving us behind with a disabled vessel. After the loyalists arrived, I discharged and returned home the said Didonian with the promised reward, then set course for Terra—' Well, no matter that." Kheraskov peered over the page. "Now what's the mathematical probability of a prowling cruiser just happening to come in detection range of you?"

"Well, sir," Flandry said, "the improbable has to happen sometimes. It's too bad the rebels wiped the computer's log in the course of removing my ship's hyperdrive. I'd have proof. But my account by itself ought to carry conviction."

"Yes, you build a very solid, interlocking pile of reasons, most of them unverifiable, why you had to do what you did and nothing else. You could spend your whole voyage back from Sector Alpha Crucis developing them. Be honest. You deliberately sought out Hugh McCormac and warned him about the code, didn't you?"

"Sir, that would have been high treason."

"Like doing away with a governor you didn't approve of? It's curious that he was last seen a short while before you cleared for departure."

"Much was going on, sir," Flandry said. "The city was in turmoil. His Excellency had personal enemies. Any one of them could have seen a chance to pay off scores. If the admiral suspects me of wrongdoing, he can institute proceedings to have me hypnoprobed."

Kheraskov sighed. "Never mind. You know I won't. For that matter, nobody's going to search after possible witnesses, rebels who may have elected to stay behind. Too big a job for too small a gain. As long as they keep their noses clean, we'll let them fade back into the general population. You're home free, Flandry. I'd simply hoped— But maybe it's best that I myself don't inquire too deeply. Do light your cigar. And we might send for a real potation. Do you like Scotch?"

"Love it, sir!" Flandry got the tobacco going and inhaled its perfume.

Kheraskov spoke an order on his intercom, leaned forward with elbows on desk, and blew clouds of his own. "Tell me one thing, though, prodigal son," he begged, "in exchange for my wholesale slaughter of fatted calves wearing stars and nebulas. Plain avuncular curiosity on my part. You have extended leave coming as soon as we can tie up the red tape. Where and how does your twisted ingenuity suggest you spend it?"

"Among those fleshpots the admiral mentioned," Flandry replied promptly. "Wine, women, and song. Especially women. It's been a long time."

Aside from such fun and forgetting, he thought while he grinned, *it will be the rest of my life.*

But she's happy. That's enough.

I/we remember.

The Feet is old now, slow to travel, aching in flesh when the mists creep around a longhouse that stands at the bottom of a winter night. The Wings that was of Many Thoughts is blind, and sits alone in his head save when a young one comes to learn. The Wings that was of Cave Discoverer and Woe is today in another of Thunderstone. The Hands of Many Thoughts and Cave Discoverer has long left his bones in the western mountains, whereto the Hands that was of Woe has long returned. Yet the memory lives. Learn, young Hands, of those who made oneness before i/we came to being.

It is more than the stuff of song, dance, and rite. No longer may We of this communion feel that Our narrow lands are the whole of the world. Beyond jungle and mountains is the sea; beyond heaven are those stars that Cave Discoverer dreamed of and Woe beheld. And there are the strangers with single bodies, they who visit Us rarely for trade and talk, but of whom We hear ever oftener as We in Our new search for enlightenment explore further among foreign communions. Their goods and their doings will touch Us more and more as the years pass, and will also make changes elsewhere than in Thunderstone, which changes will cause time to stream back across Us in different currents from that steadiness which i/we hitherto found easiest to imagine.

Beyond this and greater: How shall We achieve oneness with the whole world unless We understand it?

Therefore lie down at ease, young Hands, old Feet and Wings. Let wind, river, light, and time flow through. Be at rest, whole, in my/yourself, so gaining the strength that comes from peace, the strength to remember and to seek wisdom.

Be not afraid of the strangers with single bodies. Terrible are their powers, but those We can someday learn to wield like them if we choose. Rather pity that race, who are not beasts but can think, and thus know that they will never know oneness.

CHRONOLOGY OF TECHNIC CIVILIZATION

☀ COMPILED BY SANDRA MIESEL ☀

The Technic Civilization series sweeps across five millennia and hundreds of light-years of space to chronicle three cycles of history shaping both human and non-human life in our corner of the universe. It begins in the twenty-first century, with recovery from a violent period of global unrest known as the Chaos. New space technologies ease Earth's demand for resources and energy permitting exploration of the Solar system.

ca. 2055   "The Saturn Game" (*Analog Science Fiction*, hereafter *ASF*, February, 1981)

22nd C   The discovery of hyperdrive makes interstellar travel feasible early in the twenty-second century. The Breakup sends humans off to colonize the stars, often to preserve cultural identity or to try a social experiment. A loose

government called the Solar Commonwealth is
established. Hermes is colonized.

2150   "Wings of Victory" (*ASF*, April, 1972) The
Grand Survey from Earth discovers alien races
on Yithri, Merseia, and many other planets.

23rd C   The Polesetechnic League is founded as a
mutual protection association of space-faring
merchants.Colonization of Aeneas and Altai.

24th C   "The Problem of Pain" (*Fantasy and Science
Fiction*, February, 1973)

2376   Nicholas van Rijn born poor on Earth.
Colonization of Vixen.

2400   Council of Hiawatha, a futile attempt to
reform the League Colonization of Dennitza.

2406   David Falkayn born noble on Hermes, a
breakaway human grand duchy.

2416   "Margin of Profit" (*ASF*, September, 1956)
[van Rijn]"How to Be Ethnic in One Easy
Lesson" (in *Future Quest*, ed. Roger Elwood,
Avon Books, 1974)

❊ ❊ ❊

2423   "The Three-Cornered Wheel" (*ASF*, April,
1963) [Falkayn]

❊ ❊ ❊

stories overlap

2420s   "A Sun Invisible" (*ASF*, April, 1966) [Falkayn]
"The Season of Forgiveness" (*Boy's Life*,
December, 1973) [set on same planet as
"The Three-Cornered Wheel"]

The Man Who Counts (Ace Books, 1978 as
War of the Wing-Men, Ace Books, 1958 from
"The Man Who Counts,"
ASF, February-April,1958) [van Rijn]

"Esau" (as "Birthright," *ASF* February, 1970)
[van Rijn]

"Hiding Place" (*ASF*, March, 1961) [van Rijn]

❊ ❊ ❊

stories overlap

2430s   "Territory" (*ASF*, June, 1963) [van Rijn]
"The Trouble Twisters" (as "Trader Team,"*ASF*,
July-August, 1965) [Falkayn]

"Day of Burning" (as "Supernova," *ASF*
January, 1967) [Falkayn]
Falkayn saves civilization on Merseia,
mankind's future foe.
"The Master Key" (*ASF* August, 1971)
[van Rijn]

Satan's World (Doubleday, 1969 from *ASF*, May-August, 1968) [van Rijn and Falkayn]

"A Little Knowledge" (*ASF*, August, 1971)

The League has become a set of ruthless cartels.

✤ ✤ ✤

2446   "Lodestar" (in *Astounding: The John W. Campbell Memorial Anthology.* ed. Harry Harrison. Random House, 1973) [van Rijn and Falkayn]Rivalries and greed are tearing the League apart. Falkayn marries van Rijn's favorite granddaughter.

2456   *Mirkheim* (Putnam Books, 1977) [van Rijn and Falkayn]
The Babur War involving Hermes gravely wounds the League. Dark days loom.

late 25th C   Falkayn founds a joint human-Ythrian colony on Avalon ruled by the Domain of Ythri. [same planet—renamed—as "The Problem of Pain"]

26th C   "Wingless" (as "Wingless on Avalon," *Boy's Life*, July, 1973) [Falkayn's grandson]
"Rescue on Avalon" (in *Children of Infinity*, ed. Roger Elwood. Franklin Watts, 1973)
Colonization of Nyanza.

2550   Dissolution of the Polesotechnic League.

27ᵗʰ C   The Time of Troubles brings down the
               Commonwealth. Earth is sacked twice and
               left prey to barbarian slave raiders.

ca. 2700   "The Star Plunderer" (*Planet Stories*,
               hereafter *PS*, September, 1952)
               Manuel Argos proclaims the Terran Empire
               with citizenship open to all intelligent species.
               The Principate phase of the Imperium
               ultimately brings peace to 100,000 inhabited
               worlds within a sphere of stars 400 light-years
               in diameter.

28ᵗʰ C   Colonization of Unan Besar.
               "Sargasso of Lost Starships" (*PS*, January, 1952)
               The Empire annexes old colony on
               Ansa by force.

29ᵗʰ C   *The People of the Wind* (New American Library
               from *ASF*, February-April, 1973)
               The Empire's war on another civilized imperium
               starts its slide towards decadence.
               A descendant of Falkayn and an ancestor of
               Flandry cross paths.

30ᵗʰ C   The Covenant of Alfzar, an attempt at
               détente between Terra and Merseia, fails to
               achieve peace.

3000   Dominic Flandry born on Earth, illegitimate
son of a an opera diva and an aristocratic
space captain.

3019   *Ensign Flandry* (Chilton, 1966 from shorter
version in *Amazing*, hereafter *AMZ*,
October, 1966)
Flandry's first collision with the Merseians.

3021   *A Circus of Hells* (New American Library, 1970,
incorporates "The White King's War," *Galaxy*,
hereafter *Gal*, October, 1969,
Flandry is a Lieutenant (j.g.).

3022   Degenerate Emperor Josip succeeds weak old
Emperor Georgios.

3025   *The Rebel Worlds* (New American Library, 1969)
A military revolt on the frontier world of
Aeneas almost starts an age of Barracks
Emperors. Flandry is a Lt. Commander, then
promoted to Commander.

3027   "Outpost of Empire" (*Gal*, December, 1967)
[not Flandry]
The misgoverned Empire continues
fraying at its borders.

3028   *The Day of Their Return* (New American
Library, 1973) [Aycharaych but not Flandry]
Aftermath of the rebellion on Aeneas.

3032   "Tiger by the Tail" (*PS*, January, 1951) [Flandry]
Flandry is a Captain and averts
a barbarian invasion.

3033   "Honorable Enemies" (*Future Combined
with Science Fiction Stories*,
May, 1951) [Flandry]
Captain Flandry's first brush with
enemy agent Aycharaych.

3035   "The Game of Glory"
(*Venture*, March, 1958) [Flandry]
Set on Nyanza, Flandry has been knighted.

3037   "A Message in Secret" (as *Mayday Orbit*,
Ace Books, 1961 from shorter version,
"A Message in Secret," *Fantastic*,
December, 1959) [Flandry]
Set on Altai.

3038   "A Plague of Masters" (as *Earthman,
Go Home!*,
Ace Books, 1961 from "A Plague of Masters,"
Fantastic, December, 1960- January, 1961.)
[Flandry]
Set on Unan Besar.

3040   "Hunters of the Sky Cave"
(as *We Claim These Stars!*,
Ace Books, 1959 from shorter version,
"A Handful of Stars", *Amz,* June, 1959)

[Flandry and Aycharaych]
Set on Vixen.

3041   Interregnum: Josip dies.
         After three years of civil war,
         Hans Molitor will rule as sole emperor.

3042   "The Warriors from Nowhere"
         (as "The Ambassadors of Flesh,"
         PS, Summer, 1954.)
         Snapshot of disorders in the war-torn Empire.

3047   *A Knight of Ghosts and Shadows*
         (New American
         Library, 1975 from *If* September/October-
         November/December, 1974) [Flandry]
         Set on Dennitza, Flandry meets his
         illegitimate son and has a final tragic
         confrontation with Aycharaych.

3054   Emperor Hans dies and is succeeded by his sons,
         first Dietrich, then Gerhart.

3061   *A Stone in Heaven* (Ace Books, 1979) [Flandry]
         Vice Admiral Flandry pairs off with the daughter
         of his first mentor from *Ensign Flandry*.

3064   *The Game of Empire* (Baen Books, 1985)
         [Flandry]
         Flandry is a Fleet Admiral,
         meets his illegitimate daughter Diana.

early 4th

millennium   The Terran Empire becomes more rigid and
tyrannical in its Dominate phase. The Empire
and Merseia wear each other out.

mid 4th

millennium   The Long Night follows the Fall of the Terran
Empire. War, piracy, economic collapse, and
isolation devastate countless worlds.

3600   "A Tragedy of Errors" (*Gal*, February, 1968)
Further fragmentation among surviving
human worlds.

3900   "The Night Face" (Ace Books, 1978. as
Let the Spacemen Beware!, Ace Books, 1963
from shorter version
"A Twelvemonth and a Day,"
Fantastic Universe, January, 1960)
Biological and psychological divergence among
surviving humans.

4000   "The Sharing of Flesh" (*Gal*, December, 1968)
Human explorers heal genetic defects and
uplift savagery.

7100   "Starfog" (*ASF*, August. 1967)
Revived civilization is expanding. A New
Vixen man from the libertarian Commonalty
meets descendants of the rebels from Aeneas.

Although Technic Civilization is extinct, another—and perhaps better—turn on the Wheel of Time has begun for our galaxy. The Commonalty must inevitably decline just as the League and Empire did before it. But the Wheel will go on turning as long as there are thinking minds to wonder at the stars.

✻ ✻ ✻

Poul Anderson was consulted about this chart
but any errors are my own.